CHANTAL

YVONE LENARD was born in France and educated there and in the United States. She is currently a Professor of French at the California State University, and lives with her photographer husband in Los Angeles, though they spend as much time as they can in the mediaeval house they have restored in Provence, in the South of France.

'Yvone Lenard's _Chantal_ distills the essence of France. A beautifully written saga that sweeps you into history with all the right touches.' _Los Angeles Times_

'A passionate and gripping love story.'
Gloucester Citizen

'Extremely enjoyable . . . A strong novel with a well drawn plot and well defined characters, written with a compelling quality of realism. To call it simply a love story saga does it an injustice.'
South Wales Argus

YVONE LENARD

Chantal

This edition published 1993 by
Diamond Books
77-85 Fulham Palace Road
Hammersmith, London W6 8JB

Printed and bound in Great Britain by
BPCC Paperbacks Ltd
Member of BPCC Ltd

To Wayne,
who makes life a love affair

ACKNOWLEDGMENTS

The author remembers here with gratitude all those who have generously helped, and in particular:

Walter Wells, for his early and active encouragement; Michèle Cossack, for her critical reading; Kenneth Bennett and Joanna Dunklee, for their assistance in library research; Dr Robert Amonic and the late Dr Howard L. Bachrach, for the information they provided concerning medical terms and procedures; Dr Fred Allen, of Beverly Hills, formerly of Düsseldorf, for sharing his Düsseldorf memories and carefully critiquing the corresponding part of the manuscript; and Celia Morris Lovin, who tirelessly typed and retyped and still cried at the sad pages . . .

Elizabeth Pomada and Michael Larsen, literary agents, were the first to believe in the book, and it is the author's good fortune that they brought it to the attention of *the* Patricia Soliman, whose unerring editorial judgment, allied to boundless patience and unfailing enthusiasm, contributed immensely to the final text, as did Carole Baron's enlightened reading. To these, *Chantal* owes its present form.

Writing was never lonely, thanks to the four-legged support team of Truffles Chien and Jackie Lapinette, who faithfully sat on and under the desk, and knew a great deal more than they ever told.

CONTENTS

Prologue

HER BRAND-NEW Emmy statuette crashed from its shelf to the bedroom floor. This was the worst wave to hit the house, still shuddering on its frail pilings from the resounding shock of the last one.

This late winter of 1970 brought the most devastating storm Malibu had experienced in decades. For three days, the furious onslaught of the ocean had been pounding the house. Now, huddled on her bed in the dark, with only the spotlights of the deck playing on the surging water, Channing held her breath and waited. How hard would the next wave hit? How far would it reach?

Then, it was as if the entire Pacific Ocean had gathered its strength, and she watched in horror as a translucent green wall rose above the deck, rose and rose past her window. It carried in its surge an entire catamaran, twin red-and-white hulls, mast wobbling, sails billowing like shrouds, hurled aloft by the immense anger of the tempest. She held her breath in anguished anticipation as it disappeared over her head.

A terrifying thud . . . Would the roof hold?

Walls fissured. Rivulets streamed down the silk-covered walls. Her eyes widening, she saw a crack appear and grow, zigzagging down the plate-glass window, her only protection from the boiling abyss outside.

The phone rang. On and on it rang. Channing didn't move. But the ringing wouldn't stop, and when she finally held the receiver to her ear, she heard an indistinct voice.

Was it the voice that had the power to still all storms?

PART ONE

Angoulême, 1940

1

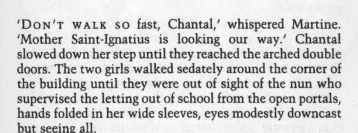

'DON'T WALK SO fast, Chantal,' whispered Martine. 'Mother Saint-Ignatius is looking our way.' Chantal slowed down her step until they reached the arched double doors. The two girls walked sedately around the corner of the building until they were out of sight of the nun who supervised the letting out of school from the open portals, hands folded in her wide sleeves, eyes modestly downcast but seeing all.

Then they stopped, and looked at each other with shining eyes.

'I wonder if the boys will be there today,' said Martine, plump and dark-haired. 'Oh, I hope so. Volodia promised.'

'How could they not be there? Where could they go? They're prisoners, you know that. They'll be waiting for us, as they said, unless, of course, the guards force them back into the barracks. We'd better hurry, though,' murmured Chantal, pushing back her flyaway blond hair.

Quickly, they rolled down their knee socks into the fashionable but strictly forbidden bobby socks, pulled up the waist of their pleated skirts so that from longish and dowdy the skirts became, they hoped, knee-skimming and flirty. The blouses were tightly knotted around the waist. That was just how Deanna Durbin, whom they had adored in *Three Smart Girls*, had dressed. With a great deal of tugging and tucking in, Chantal even managed an inch or so of scandalously bare midriff.

They unsnapped the emblem of the school from their navy blazers and stuffed it in the pocket. The emblem bore the X-shaped cross of Saint Andrew, surrounded by an embroidered scroll with the name of the school: Ecole Catholique de Jeunes Filles Saint-André. They despised that emblem, the whole uniform, in fact, an unbearable stigma they'd worn throughout their school years, but even more embarrassing now that they had reached the mature age of seventeen. Now, dressed as any teenagers in the spring of 1940, they could pretend to be not school-girls but Deanna Durbin and friend, out for a carefree stroll on the town.

In that lovely month of June, France was at war and heading to the most humiliating defeat it had endured, perhaps, since the distant days of the Hundred Years War, but no Joan of Arc had appeared to save the country this time. The French army was in headlong flight, and the Germans had already overrun the eastern and northern provinces. Where they were now, the people of Angoulême didn't exactly know, since communications were disrupted and they could only speculate. It was known, though, that the government had left Paris and sought the safety of Bordeaux.

In this green, river-laced southwest, sixty miles north of Bordeaux, panic had not yet set in. Only the schools had been required to close ahead of schedule, so they could be turned into hospitals if the need arose. Authorities remembered it had happened in the last war, and no doubt it would be the case again, when French troops made their successful stand on the Loire River.

So, the Ecole Saint-André, the best in town, was closing this afternoon, and all the usual ceremonies of distribution of prizes and commencement exercises had been dispensed with. Now, as far as the girls were concerned, finding entertainment for the long summer days ahead was going to be the only challenge.

The dreaded *baccalauréat* had been moved up a few weeks and Chantal had passed it successfully. Martine had failed and couldn't care less. Martine had one interest, single-minded and overwhelming: boys.

'Volodia! What a strange name . . . but so beautiful! . . . Do you think he likes me?' she asked her friend, then rushed on, 'Isn't it terrible that he should be a prisoner?

6

Especially since he did nothing that wasn't good. Oh, well, when he gets out, I'm sure we'll fall in love and then we can get married.'

Martine's intentions were pure and uncomplicated. Indeed, she could not meet a boy she liked without immediately thinking of marriage. But Chantal's mind wasn't on marriage. The whole situation thrilled her, puzzled her, too, so far removed from anything encompassed by her limited experience.

'We'd better hurry,' Martine chatted on. 'Remember, they said they may not be there much longer. Their guards are getting nervous because the Germans are approaching, and they're afraid the boys might want to escape to join them. It certainly would make sense! After all, they *are* Germans, even if Volodia's parents were born in Russia, as they told us. But they say they're more afraid of the arrival of the Germans than of being kept prisoners by the French gendarmes. I don't understand why they should be so scared of being caught by their own people. Wouldn't that be like going home for them?'

Chantal was almost as naive and uninformed of the military and political turmoils as her friend. But she had listened a little more attentively than Martine to what the young men had said.

'It has something to do with politics. They're German citizens, but they were political refugees in France when the war began. They left Germany because they didn't agree with Hitler's politics.'

That was about the extent of what the young men behind the barred gate had told them. Of course, the girls knew that France had been at war for almost ten months now, since the previous September, when Germany had invaded Poland. They knew that England, allied to Poland, had declared war on Germany two days later, and that within a few hours, France, allied with England, had followed suit. Complicated, and not terribly interesting to sixteen-year-old girls. Then, Poland had quickly fallen and been occupied. After that, all fall and winter, the situation had been stagnant. The excitement of being at war died down. French soldiers remained entrenched on their own side of the Rhine. Cartoons in newspapers depicted them with mushrooms growing on their shoes and cobwebs lacing their helmets. The radio played the latest hit to a dancing accordion background:

> Nous irons pend' not' linge sur la Ligne Siegfried . . .
> We'll go hang our wash along the Siegfried
> Line . . .

Each side of the combatants was protected, it was widely reported, by the impregnable defenses of its line of fortifications built after World War I. The Maginot Line protected the French from the German invasion, and the Siegfried Line right on the opposite side of the Rhine did the same, stopping any would-be French advance. The stalemate had lasted all winter.

Then, just over a month ago, the Germans had started their May offensive, scorning to attack the Maginot Line but invading Holland instead, sweeping through Belgium. Now they were marching through France, an unthinkable action in the eyes of the French High Command, who had prepared for any, except this, eventuality. Holland was neutral and therefore should have been respected. Furthermore, violating this neutrality and invading France through the vast, flat plains of Flanders was exactly what the Kaiser's army had done in 1914. How déjà vu. How could one break rules not once but *twice* in exactly the same way, showing no imagination and no sense of panache? That was not the way the great French strategists, schooled in the study of the historic campaigns, would have run the war. The only way they knew to fight a war was to follow its rules, to display *honneur* and *bravoure*, the eventual outcome, be it defeat or victory, only secondary to the honorable manner in which the campaign had been conducted.

Little of this news filtered into the school, where Chantal was a boarding student, since her parents lived on their country estate thirty miles away from town. The nuns had always forbidden papers and radios – at least where the girls could have access to them – and only informed their charges that people were suffering and dying because this is a sinful world. Lately, special rosaries were recited, asking for the mercy of God upon those who needed it in their hour of trial. Wisely preparing for any outcome, the good nuns were taking no sides.

As the Nazi advance became more threatening, an earlier closing date for classes was announced and the dining hall and dormitories were prepared for the arrival of wounded soldiers. Chantal moved into the house of her friend Martine Moreau for the final few weeks of school.

The Moreaus lived on the outskirts of town, near the River Charente, among poplars and willows, in a large complex of buildings that included the house, the offices, and the working buildings of the Moreau Paper Mills. Monsieur Moreau was proud to say that the fine, filigreed paper used for the banknotes of several European countries was made in his mill, whose wheels diverted for a moment, through a system of channels and sluices, some of the placid green waters of the Charente.

Although the two girls were good friends, Chantal tended to look down on Martine's plump figure, her total uninterest in book learning, and her devouring absorption in boys. Martine's hopes were simple: She wanted to fall in love, be married, the sooner the better, and become the mistress of a large household, just like her mother, whom she resembled. Chantal's hopes were less clear. Mostly, she knew what she did *not* want out of life. She did not want to resemble her own mother, who, like Madame Moreau, ran a large household, but unlike the gentle Madame Moreau, exerted an iron discipline on all who depended on her. Chantal's experience was too limited even to offer much of a field to her imagination, but, although she would have been surprised at the term, she was a romantic. 'You never behave like the others' had been the nuns' frequent complaint. 'Try to be more like the others.' Chantal was always unconsciously seeking some way to distinguish herself, and she had tried, at times, excessive devotion to her patron saint, Sainte Jeanne de Chantal – which had soon bored her; passionate bouts of study – ditto; but mostly flights of daydreaming in which she saw herself a princess in some distant kingdom, surrounded by hazy splendor and undefined magic.

At the moment, though, the two girls had a common interest.

A mile or so before the Moreau mill complex along a narrow, long-unused towpath, stood a dilapidated foundry. It had been built in the eighteenth century to produce cannon for the navy; but advances in technology had long since rendered it obsolete, and it had been closed down as long as anyone could remember. It was surrounded on all sides by a high stone wall, topped with broken glass embedded in mortar to discourage trespassers. Beyond the heavy, permanently locked gate lay a large yard overgrown with weeds and brambles, with smaller buildings grouped around the main one in the center. All were locked, gazing out of broken and dusty panes, in total dereliction.

The girls had started taking the detour earlier that week, just because the weather was so beautiful. They longed to stay out a little later, slowly walking the narrow path with the tall grasses brushing against their bare legs, pulling down hazelnut branches to pluck the nuts, still unripe, milky in their tender shells. There were giant stems of Queen Anne's lace arching over the path to slip under, insects at work to watch, and hundreds of invisible green frogs sitting among the rushes to be scattered and sent splashing into the water by stamping a foot. Dragonflies in shimmering colors buzzed and landed on floating poplar leaves. Stillness breathed in the afternoon sun, the gates of the old foundry chained and padlocked as usual, no signs of life among the weeds in the dusty yard.

But the following day, to their surprise, all had changed. Gendarmes were guarding the opened gates, there were trucks pulled up and being unloaded, men in civilian clothes milling around the courtyard. What was happening?

To be sure, recruits were pouring into the caserns in the upper town in a last effort at mobilization of troops, but this wasn't one of the caserns. These men were civilians, not soldiers. Who could they be? Prisoners, with all those gendarmes guarding them? Criminals? But this wasn't the prison either. That, too, stood in the upper town. The girls were puzzled, curious, but, under the presence of the gendarmes supervising the unloading of the trucks, they felt obliged to continue walking.

Around the corner of the wall, though, they came to a small back gate. There, after a quick side-glance at each other, they stopped and peered through the bars. The men were carrying bundles into buildings. A group of young men was standing nearby, talking in a foreign language. Not English, thought Chantal, who had studied it for years, and had spent several summers in English schools. This wasn't English.

The girls were about to walk away, when the young men saw them. They came over to the gate.

'*Mesdemoiselles!*' said one of them, with thick, unruly curly hair. '*Bonjour*, or should I say *Bonsoir* at this time of day?'

His French was hesitant, heavily accented. But he seemed determined to engage the girls in conversation, to hold them there a moment.

'*Bonsoir, monsieur,*' said Martine, always ready to chat. 'It is after four o'clock. We say *Bonsoir*.'

'I would like to tell you that you live in a beautiful city, but we haven't seen much of it. They brought us here in the middle of the night, after rolling for hours in closed trucks. So, not only haven't we seen the town, but we don't even know its name. The guards won't tell us where we are . . .'

'Oh,' cried Martine, always delighted to convey information. 'This is Angoulême! The Flowered Balcony of the Southwest, they call it, because it stands on its plateau high above the river you see here . . . How funny that you should not know the name of the town you're in.'

'Southwest?' repeated the young man. He turned to the others, who had been listening intently, and translated for those who did not seem to understand French. One of them broke from the group and approached the gate. He spoke French well:

'Southwest? Where in the southwest?' he asked.

'Well, it's on the main road from Paris to Spain, a little north of Bordeaux.'

'Is it far from Spain?'

'Not very, we go there sometimes for the holidays. The train gets there in a few hours, and it's even less by car . . .'

By now the whole group of five young men had come to the gate and the rest were straining to follow the conversation.

'How would you get from here to Spain most easily?' asked the young man who spoke fluent French.

Chantal noticed that where the others looked unkempt and unshaven, he alone was neat, in a self-contained, catlike way, as if dirt took no hold on his smooth olive skin and wrinkles would shed from the short-sleeved dark blue polo shirt. An arresting streak of pure white, sharply contrasting with the youthful features, and as though painted into his jet-black hair, divided it a little over to the side. When he looked directly at Chantal, she was struck by his large pale gray eyes. He followed her glance, smiled.

'Unusual, I know. It's a genetic trait. Both my father and grandfather had the same white strand.'

Chantal would have liked to trace that line with her fingertips.

Just then, however, a whistle blew sharply, an order was barked, the young men scattered, but the dark one with gray eyes called out over his shoulder. '*A demain!*'

So, the next day, the girls had taken the same path. They stopped at the small gate, and found the group waiting for them. Chantal had brought candy, and Martine had smuggled a pack of cigarettes from her father's supply. The boys accepted the gifts eagerly. They started to take long pulls on their cigarettes and thanked the girls with formal courtesy. The three who could not speak French much managed an awkward '*Merci beaucoup!*' and bowed stiffly from the waist.

'My name is Fred,' said the one with the pale eyes; extending his hand through the bars, exposing a deep jagged scar that ran along his forearm, almost from wrist to elbow. 'Fred May. And these are my friends: Volodia, with all the hair, and Mischa, with not much hair, and Herschel, and Isaac. No, we are not criminals. We are German citizens, although Mischa's parents and Volodia's too were born in Russia. And we are not Nazis. As a matter of fact, we are anti-Nazis, you understand? That is why we had to leave Germany, and why we were living in France when the war began, because we do not agree with Hitler's policies. That scar? It's nothing. Just a run in with some barbed wire.'

Martine and Chantal understood only vaguely, but they were satisfied with the sound of the words, excited by the scent of adventure. This was a far world from Mother Saint-Ignatius's classroom and the recreation yard of Saint-André. It never occurred to them to wonder what kind of disagreement these attractive men, in their early twenties, could have had with Hitler. But they knew Hitler was the Antichrist, an ogre, and that it was terrible to be a Nazi. Disagreeing with him, and fleeing from him, was clearly the reasonable thing to do. They had heard of the existence of Jews in the Bible, but not in their town, where everybody was Catholic except for a few socially isolated Protestant families. They nodded excitedly.

'The day the war between France and Germany began, all German citizens residing in Paris were asked to report to a big sports arena just outside the city. You don't understand why? Because the moment the war began, we were no longer political refugees to the French authorities but Germans. We became enemy aliens, so the French rounded us all up and put us in camps.'

'Why didn't they just send you home?' interrupted Martine, who could listen a little but could not think at all, thought Chantal scornfully.

'They were afraid that, once back home, we might take up arms against them. Also, there would always be the possibility of us having learned things, while living in France, that might help German intelligence. We might have been conducting espionage activities. It's a common practice of war to intern enemy aliens for the duration.'

'What was it like in those camps?' asked Chantal, entranced with the story.

'Oh, it wasn't too bad in a way. Surely better than Hitler's camps in the East . . .'

A blank. The girls hadn't heard of those camps. He continued, 'They put us in some unused factory, like here. They gave us army food, blankets, we slept in bunks we had to build. I don't think it was much worse than the army, except that we were under armed guard. Senegalese soldiers kept watch over us, and they were rough at times. They had us busy all winter digging ditches along the roads. There were several such camps throughout France. Ours was in Nevers, southeast of Paris. It was a long winter, though . . .'

'What did you do before the war began?' asked Chantal. She was fascinated by Fred May, who did not look like anyone she had seen before, with his neatly boned, small regular features, white-streaked black hair, olive skin, and above all those extraordinary eyes. He had a way of locking his gaze on you, as though shutting out the rest of his field of vision. Chantal wanted to keep those gray eyes on her.

'I was a student in Paris,' he said. 'A law student. My father is a buyer for a large firm doing business in Australia.'

A law student! Paris! Australia! Now, that was another world. The absolute elsewhere, as far as Chantal was concerned. Not some dull farming estate like La Prade, her home.

'Are your parents still in Paris?'

'Of course not. They were able to leave just before the war broke out. They're in Port Augusta, South Australia.'

Meanwhile, Martine was giggling with Volodia, who was reaching through the bars to examine the gold chain with the baptismal medal, engraved with her birthday, that she wore around her neck. He showed her a chain around his own neck, with a strange pendant in the shape of an n.

'Why did the gendarmes bring you here?'

'They took over from the Senegalese soldiers, who were sent to the front, and it's funny, but they are not nearly as hard on us. You see, the camp had to be moved south because the Germans are advancing so fast, they certainly have overrun Nevers by now. We hear the guards talking, and they're scared the Nazis will sneak up on them and take them prisoner.'

'What will happen to you when they arrive?' Martine asked. 'Will they take *you* prisoner too? Will they harm you? Couldn't you make them forget that you don't agree with Hitler, and go home?'

That much naiveté stopped Fred dead in his tracks. He called out to the others and repeated Martine's question. All turned to her. Volodia stopped giggling and said slowly and carefully, 'If the Germans catch us . . .' He ran his index finger across his throat.

Fred said intently, with all the others watching and listening, 'They will kill us if they catch us, you understand? They will kill us.' He added, as in an afterthought, 'Unless you can help us.'

Help them? Martine stood openmouthed. Chantal caught her breath.

'How could we possibly help you?'

'You can get us out of here. The gendarmes don't keep a very close watch. At night, most of them even go home, and there are sentries only at the main gate. We've looked the place over. It's not too difficult to climb the wall there, under the trees. It's dark, and we can throw our blankets over to cover the broken glass on top. But we need help to get to Spain.'

'To Spain!' said Martine excitedly. 'It's not that far . . . There must still be trains running, though most of them are for the troops now. If you catch the evening train, you can be in Fuenterrabia, that's the border, a few hours later. We take it sometimes, now that the Spanish Civil War is over, and we go to San Sebastián. There's a lovely beach . . .'

'You don't understand,' said Fred patiently. 'We cannot take a train because we can't risk being arrested. There are security checks everywhere along the roads, and there must be some in railroad stations as well. We'd never make it to the border, and this time, once caught, we wouldn't stand a chance of escape. We'd be sitting ducks for the Nazis when they arrive.'

'I don't see what we can do,' mused Chantal, who wished with all her heart that there was something, some way to take part in this adventure. She perversely wished, too, that somehow Mother Saint-Ignatius would know what these boys were asking her to do. That would show her!

'Can you drive?'

'Chantal knows how to drive,' teased Martine, who was lounging tantalizingly against the gate, where Volodia's fingers could just reach her shoulder and play with her hair. 'Yes, you can too,' she repeated as her friend shook her head. 'But we don't have a car.'

'Besides,' said Chantal, 'I can't drive that well. I have just been practicing a little during the holidays on my father's Citroën, but I haven't taken my driver's test yet. I have to wait for my eighteenth birthday. And we could never get a car . . . Wait a minute! Martine, there are several trucks parked in front of your father's mills at night . . .'

'A truck!' Fred exclaimed, while the others nodded enthusiastically. 'That's even better than a car! We could

16

hide in the back, and all five of us could go. Don't say no, please,' he begged Chantal, gray eyes now imperious. 'I'm *sure* you can do it. Get the truck, and bring it here at eleven tonight. Make as little noise as possible, and pull up right there, you see, under the trees. We'll be waiting for you. Make sure there's plenty of gas. You do know the way to Spain?'

'Oh, I know it well,' said Martine. 'It's the road to Bordeaux, and then it's all straight and flat through the Landes, and then on to Fuenterrabia, where the bridge is, with the border guards. I even know the detour to take, just before Bordeaux, so you don't have to drive through the town and waste a lot of time.' She added, regretfully, as the thought struck her, 'Oh, but we won't be able to make it. There are too many refugees on the road. My father said the traffic is all stopped up and there are road-blocks in many places. They stop his trucks all the time. The gendarmes are looking for German spies among the refugees.'

Fred cut in. 'Some of the traffic will have stopped for the night. As for the gendarmes, they aren't that smart, and they won't see us if we're hidden in the back of the truck. Be sure there's something we can hide under. Now hurry home, and don't make any mistakes. Chantal, you are going to save our lives, and you, too, Martine. You will be true heroines, just like in the movies.'

Chantal laughed, scared and strangely exhilarated. This is exactly what Deanna Durbin would do, she thought. Deanna would drive that truck, there would be a hair-raising chase, but they could never catch her. Well, they would not catch her, either.

'And,' Fred continued, 'try to bring some money, too, if you can. Anything you can lay your hands on. It's a loan, of course, we'll repay every cent. But we're going to need it to get where we are going. We're going to America. Aren't we?'

He turned to his friends, who nodded enthusiastically: 'Amerika!'

America, the Moon, or the Nebulous Andromeda, were comparable entities to the two provincial girls. But excitement had entered their placid lives. That distant, featureless war had touched them, they had been given a role to play in it. They dashed home, slowing to a more composed walk only as they approached the mills.

Trucks were coming in from their day's runs, and the drivers were parking them in their usual places in front of the loading dock. The girls watched the men hang the keys on a board in the dispatcher's shack in the courtyard. Then they went in, walked upstairs to their room, and sat on their twin beds, breathless and with shining eyes.

Dinner at the Moreau family table seemed endless to them, from the obligatory *potage*, creamy vegetable soup, to the salad, cheese, and fruit courses. The crystal chandelier over the table had been draped in the dark blue cloth required by the wartime blackout regulations, its dim light grayed all colors in the room and cast an ashy tint onto faces. Martine's teenage brothers, Denis and Georges, were quiet for once. Monsieur Moreau kept getting up to fiddle with the radio, trying to get some news broadcast, but all he could find was either grinding static or military music. Finally an announcer's voice came through, speaking with a German accent:

'*Achtung*, this is Paris, I repeat, this is Paris. You are listening to the voice of the Wehrmacht in Paris. The glorious troops of the Third Reich have occupied your capital without a shot fired. But if we encounter any kind of resistance, we warn you that we will show no mercy. Tell your soldiers to drop their weapons, to turn south, and to run as fast as they can. You are defeated, you have lost the war. Your government has fled. Your foolish leaders and you can now see what the price is for attacking the Thousand Year Reich and its glorious Führer. *Heil Hitler!*'

For a week, now, this chilling broadcast had been on the air. Did it mean the Germans were actually in Paris? Some thought it did, others that they were only broadcasting on the Radio-France frequency in order to frighten the population and create more havoc.

Monsieur Moreau turned off the set and sat down again.

'All right, maybe they've taken Paris. But they could not have crossed the Loire,' he assured his wife and children. 'If you boys were older, or if *I* was younger, that's where we'd be, right now, on the south bank of the Loire waiting for them. That's where our reserve army is going to make its stand. Just like in '14! Things happened the same way then. It took the Germans only a couple of weeks to reach the Marne River, almost within sight of Paris, but our army was there, waiting for them. Oh, it was bloody, but we stopped them, and eventually they were pushed back and defeated. Mark my words, that's what's going to happen this time too. We're in for a long fight, but we'll win in the end, just like in the last war.'

Chantal and Martine kept looking at the grandfather clock on the wall. It had just struck nine.

'I am sorry this is your last evening with us, Chantal,' said Madame Moreau amiably, to distract everybody's attention from the war, 'since your parents are picking you up tomorrow. We'll miss you, my child, but La Prade is not far. You and Martine can visit often during the summer. Martine, where are you going? If you're running upstairs, go to my room and bring down my sweater, please, it is getting cool.'

Darkness came late, on those long days close to the summer solstice, but finally Monsieur Moreau had finished his nightly rounds, Madame Moreau had seen the kitchen closed and the maids sent to their quarters. Martine's thirteen- and fourteen-year-old brothers were chased up to bed from their Ping-Pong game, and Madame was going upstairs to join her husband, obediently followed by the two girls, holding their breath. It was ten-thirty.

As soon as the door to their room had been pulled behind them, Chantal and Martine fell against each other, gasping. Just in time! They waited one breathless minute. Then Martine opened the door a crack, listened for sounds in the quiet house. They took off their shoes and tiptoed down the hall to the back stairs. They could hear the maids talking and laughing in their room.

It was easy to open the back door and to slip noiselessly outside. Thousands of frogs croaked in the reeds by the riverbank. Crickets trilled in the still summer night. But the loudest of all sounds, thought Chantal, is my heart, pounding in my chest. Surely, *that* will wake everybody . . .

The five trucks were still there, dark shapes looming. The one parked first in line and easiest to maneuver out was number 3. Martine took the keys hanging from the nail labeled 3 on the wall in the shack. Chantal tried the cab door, found it unlocked, climbed in, and was surprised to discover the seat so high. Martine jumped in on the other side, and was putting on her shoes, while Chantal examined the gearshift with the flashlight they had brought. She muttered under her breath, 'This is reverse, and here is first, second, and third . . . All right, I see. Now, the key. Oh!'

She jumped when the ignition sputtered and caught. So loud! Surely everybody would have heard that. No time to waste.

'Pass into first. Oops, no, that was not first, that was reverse. No harm done, and now I know. Now, this is second. See? We are going.'

Can't they hear that thunderous motor, the people in the house over there? And don't tell me they can't hear my heart pounding too . . .

Martine squirmed into a more comfortable position, giggling nervously and reaching into her pocket.

'Look, Chantal, I got caps from my brothers' room. Just like the ones the drivers wear. And while everybody was listening to the radio I went to my mother's dresser and took a little money. Not enough so she'll notice, I hope.'

They jammed the caps over their heads, and tucked their hair up under. The drive to the old foundry was short, but it took time driving without lights and at a snail's pace, with much grinding of gears. Finally, Chantal turned the truck onto the riverside towpath, and pulled up under the trees. Five shadows jumped from under the low branches and climbed onto the bed of the truck, under the high, arched tarpaulin cover. The girls had forgotten all about bringing camouflage material, but fortunately, piles of empty sacks had been left all over the floor of the truck. The young men had already disappeared underneath.

Chantal backed up and turned on the headlights. Their glass had been painted the regulation opaque blue-black, with just a narrow slit left clear near the bottom. They cast a narrow beam that lit the road just ahead, but was supposedly invisible from the sky in case planes were lurking above.

She picked up a little speed. The main road to Bordeaux was on the left, and she knew it well. It would be about an hour to the outskirts, then came the detour to avoid crossing the city. After that, they'd continue straight down south, along the flat road that bisects the piney woods of the Landes, as Martine had said. Three or four hours, maybe, and they would reach the Spanish border.

The stream of refugees that had been going down the road all day had thinned by now, and most of the cars had pulled off the main road, letting their exhausted occupants rest, now that they had hopefully put enough space between themselves and their pursuers.

A roadblock barred the highway. The low, narrow beam of light picked it up just in time to stop. Martine stifled a cry with her palm, and Chantal's heart started to pound again. Two gendarmes stood by the roadside. They had no lights, not even a flashlight. This was real wartime blackout. One of them approached. In the rising moonlight, he could make out the white lettering on the side door of the truck: MOREAU PAPER MILLS, and underneath, in a half circle, ANGOULÊME, CHARENTE. Nothing to worry about, he thought. This truck is local. He peered inside, but he could not see the driver clearly.

'You one of the Moreau drivers?' he asked.

'No,' improvised Chantal, inspired by urgency. 'This is Monsieur Moreau's daughter, and I am the wife of one of the drivers. We are going down the road, to Barbezieux, to pick up my husband who's stranded with his load, because his truck broke down. All the drivers were gone at this hour, and you know, with the war, there's already a shortage of help at the mills. Women have to pitch in these days.'

The gendarme was satisfied. With the Germans advancing fast, and probably faster than anyone was telling, he and his colleague were in mortal terror of being surprised at their post by an advance enemy unit and taken prisoner or even shot on sight. They waved the truck on nervously.

After that, it was easy. Other roadblocks farther on were dealt with in the same way, with adjustments to the story as each new location required. Chantal's assurance was growing, she was now shifting gears and lying with equal mastery. Not a sound was heard from the back of the truck.

The moon had risen, full and bright, and was shining almost like daylight when the truck reached the little bridge that marks the border between France and Spain at Fuenterrabia. Chantal stopped a short distance from the bridge. Barriers were lowered across the way, indicating that the border was closed to motor traffic. But the little footpath along the railing was open. Refugees were milling near their cars, parked helter-skelter. On the French side, the guardhouses seemed empty. Perhaps the French did not care who left their territory or else the border guards were needed elsewhere.

But at the other end of the bridge, Spanish soldiers of the Guardia Civil, in their square boiled-leather hats, stood guard on either side. Surely they would demand papers. How were the young men going to pass? Had they thought of that problem? Chantal parked the truck by the roadside, in the darkness of a large clump of trees. She turned to the back. 'We are at the border. I don't see any French sentries, but there are Spanish guards at the other end of the bridge. They are certain to stop you.'

Fred poked his head out, pushing the folds of the tarpaulin cover aside. Uncharacteristically silent, Martine handed him a thin wad of bills.

'I don't know how we can ever repay you for this, but I know that someday we will,' murmured Fred.

The five young men jumped from the truck and helped the girls down. There was much handshaking, but all were too shy to embrace, even in those highly charged moments, except Volodia, who drew Martine aside, held her tight, and as he released her, took the chain from around his neck.

'Here,' he said in his halting French, 'this is from my mother. She gave it to me when we parted for the last time. She is probably dead now. Wear it always, Martine, and remember me. I will make my way to Amerika, and I will send for you and we will go to Hollywood and we will be famous.'

Martine, in answer to his gesture, pulled her baptismal medal chain over her head and placed it around Volodia's neck. She was sobbing now, overwhelmed by an emotion deeper than she had ever known before.

Fred hesitated a moment. Then he drew a small pouch from his pocket. He fished for something inside it.

'Chantal, I don't have any other souvenir to give you, so take this, but please don't show it to anyone, and don't lose it.'

Chantal in turn removed the thin chain with the gold cross she had received on her first communion. Fred bent his smooth dark head, and she slipped it around his neck. He caught both her hands in his, and kissed them long, holding them to his lips while looking at her with those pale gray eyes, paler than his face in the moonlight. Chantal's heart rose in her throat. Does one die from ecstasy?

'The war is not ending,' Fred whispered, his eyes fixed on hers. 'It is just beginning, you will see, and by the time it's over, everything will have turned around. We are going to attempt to make our way through Spain, to Portugal, then we'll try to catch a ship to America. As soon as possible, I will write you.'

He touched the golden cross gleaming against his dark skin, voltage of pale eyes on her face.

'You are beautiful. I love you, and I will love you always,' he whispered in a voice so low only she could hear. Then he turned to join the others.

'*Adieu*,' said Chantal in a strangled voice. She added, as the nuns would have, and because she had no vocabulary for moments like this, 'God be with you.'

Through her tears, just like in the church responses, Martine added, 'And with your spirit.'

But neither girl giggled. Shining tears were streaming down Martine's round cheeks and welling from Chantal's blue eyes.

As the girls watched, the men made their way along the bridge. When they reached the Spanish Guardia Civil, they produced passports.

The guards looked at the covers, and to the stupefaction of the girls, stepped back and saluted smartly. The five men passed, and disappeared at the other end of the bridge.

The girls could not know it, but the dark green documents the men had shown the Guardia Civil were no ordinary German passports.

Stamped with a yellow *J* for *Jude*, each identified the bearer as a Jew. His middle name, whatever it might have been before, was now compulsorily *Israel*. The line for nationality read *stateless*, and the space for race bore the chilling *nonperson*. These passports were equal to a death warrant in Hitler-dominated countries.

But to the eyes of the Guardia Civil, who could not read German and even less the Gothic script favored by Hitler, they were nothing but German passports, emblazoned with the swastika and eagle of the Reich. Just a little over a year earlier, Generalissimo Franco had won a long and bloody civil war against the Spanish Liberals and replaced their republic with his own totalitarian government. The

24

Liberals, on the opposing side, had been aided by the Soviets. Franco couldn't have defeated them without the powerful help of Hitler and his Luftwaffe. Franco's party owed its victory to that swastika, which etched the wings of the bombers that had screamed over Guernica and so many other defenseless Spanish towns. Now Franco's army recognized Germany as a friend and strong ally and saluted the bearers of that passport.

Fred, Volodia, and the others were now in Spain, and off to an unknown fate.

Chantal and Martine climbed back into the truck. Chantal put it into reverse, made a turn, and drove north along the same road they had come.

Martine was wiping her eyes and blowing her nose.

'Try to go fast,' she implored, 'so we can be back before anybody misses us! Thank God it's Sunday, so nobody will be up early and the drivers won't be looking for their trucks!'

Hours later, Chantal pulled the truck back to the mill's loading dock in the bright morning sunlight. Nobody would ever suspect anything, except that when he arrived at work on Monday, the driver might not understand what had happened to the tankful of gas he'd put in on Saturday and would probably complain loudly to the others about their stupid practical jokes.

The girls tiptoed up the back stairs, met nobody except a maid, who said, 'Back from high mass, are you?'

In their room, propped on their elbows on the twin beds, they were too keyed up to rest.

'Look, Chantal,' said Martine, showing the chain Volodia had given her. 'What do you suppose this is? A letter *n*? Maybe his mother was called Nathalie . . .'

'I don't think it's an *n*,' said Chantal. 'Volodia comes from Russia, perhaps it's a letter from the Russian alphabet . . . or Greek. It looks like the Greek letter *pi*, you know, the one in the formula for finding the circumference of the circle.'

But Martine admitted happily that she never paid much

attention in math class, and besides the pendant was beautiful. She was sure it was gold, she would wear it hidden so no one ever saw it, until Volodia came back to claim her, and then they would be married. Chantal remembered the present Fred had given her. She got up, went to the chair where she had laid her clothes, and fished in her jacket pockets. She found it, lost among the crumbs of her last croissant. She brought out a shiny crystal and showed it to Martine.

'Oh, how pretty it is,' exclaimed Martine, who did not want to hurt her friend's feelings. Just a piece of glass, she thought. 'What do you think it's for?'

'It looks like one of the crystals in the chandelier downstairs. It's the size of the small ones that make the chain that swags around. I'll keep it, too, as a souvenir of Fred.'

'There should be a hole in it, so you could hang it on the chandelier,' Martine suggested, stifling yawns. Soon, she was asleep, her hand on the smooth gold of the pendant.

Only a few hours later, Chantal's parents, Monsieur and Madame Arondel, arrived to take their daughter home.

'How close can the Germans be?' asked Monsieur Moreau. 'The radio is silent now, just military music all the time, and that same blasted German broadcast. No newspapers anymore. Last time anyone heard, the Germans were approaching the Loire. I hope our troops are holding out there.'

'We don't hear any more than you do,' replied Monsieur Arondel. 'All I know is that the columns of refugees we saw on the road coming here are unbelievable. It looks like all Belgium, Holland, and northern France is going south. We wouldn't have made it to Angoulême except that I know all the small back roads. According to the refugees, the Germans have passed the Loire, even the Vienne, which is much closer to us, and they have bombers everywhere. I'll grant the refugees are panicked, but to tell you the truth, I believe the Germans have come much closer than we think.'

Chantal, still exhilarated by the excitement of the night ride and bearing in her heart the delicious weight of a secret, said good-bye to Martine and the Moreaus, and went with her mother to Saint-André school to pick up her things and say her farewell to the nuns who had housed and schooled her for the last five years. While nobody was looking she squashed her summer uniform hat, a straw sailor with ÉCOLE SAINT-ANDRÉ printed in gold letters on its navy ribbon, and crammed it into a wastebasket. She would never, never again be a schoolgirl. *Life* was now beginning. *Whatever Life was.* Unfortunately, the passive education she had received, and hated, had not prepared her for anything except obedience, and obedience would always come very hard to Chantal.

Later the Arondels met at the terrasse of the Café de la Paix on the main square opposite City Hall. The Angoulême City Hall had been, in medieval centuries, the stronghold of the counts of Angoulême, and still retained traces of its military past in the high crenelated towers, now embedded into mock Gothic wings, the whole massive building embracing a cobbled courtyard. As always, the tricolor flag flew high on the main tower, waving lazily in the soft summer breeze.

At the Café de la Paix, every table was occupied. It was a lovely, quiet afternoon. No sign of war, except that few young men were around. Only boys and old men. Veterans of the last war, still called the World War but soon to become World War I, were discussing strategy, and the best way to victory. The sure bet to win *this* time was to take lessons from the last. Historians have often remarked with some accuracy that the French always go into a war ready to fight the previous one.

'It was a mistake not to hole up in trenches like we did in '14,' declared a decorated monsieur while a waiter refilled his bock. 'Wear out the Boches, I say, and they'll give up, eventually. But today's boys are not like the *poilus* of the last . . .'

'I happen to have a close relative in High Command,' announced another gentleman, sipping his *pastis*. 'So, I have it on qualified authority that it was on purpose we let the Boches come so far. They're well removed from their bases by now and it's easy to cut through their lines of supply. They're going to run out of ammunition, food, and gas. Our reserves are waiting for them on the Loire, just like they did on the Marne in '14. They'll massacre them there.'

Chantal was sitting demurely with her parents, lost in her own dreams. Her mother wore one of her dark summer prints. She was a heavyset woman, with a handsome but stern face and a severe hairdo. Monsieur Arondel wore the leggings and riding jacket of a prosperous landowner, more often astride his horse than driving his Citroën. Dull people, thought Chantal. Pale gray eyes and a fine dark face danced in her memory. Had it really happened? Was it all a dream? She was almost dozing off, lulled by the buzz of voices. Her mother's scolding voice startled her awake.

'Where is your cross, Chantal? You haven't lost it, have you?'

'No, Mother,' answered Chantal, who was ready for the question. 'No, I didn't lose it. I took it off the other day for gym. It's in my things.'

At that moment, a motorcycle with an attached sidecar roared up the corner of the rue des Halles bearing two soldiers in unfamiliar gray uniforms with strange, awkward-looking helmets like the ones the Germans wore in the newsreels.

The war expert at the next table momentarily dropped his plans to annihilate the German army on the Loire River.

'See? Our army even has new, secret uniforms. When the time came, they were issued to our troops. It will serve to confuse the Germans. I tell you, we are better prepared than anyone may think . . .'

The motorcycle made a sharp turn, banking on its side, onto the Place de l'Hôtel de Ville, the City Hall Square, then steered into the majestic cobbled courtyard and disappeared out of sight under the Gothic arch.

Chantal was watching idly, her eyes now clouded with sleep. Such a warm, uneventful afternoon. Nothing moved, except the limp folds of the flag on top of the tower. She had passed her *bac*, she had finished with school forever, vacation was starting, and . . . Had she dreamed Fred and his gray eyes?

Somebody cried out, and all heads turned. Over the crenelated battlements of the counts of Angoulême, the flag was slowly coming down. A few seconds passed, breathless. Now, just as slowly, another was being raised. It reached the top of the mast, hung for a moment in motionless folds.

Then a gust of wind unfurled it, snapping in the cloudless sky. The flag was red, with a large white circle in the center. Over the white field, the black swastika stood out, spreading its malevolent hooked arms over the tile roofs of the city.

The *Blitzkrieg*, the lightning war, was no longer just a word. The Germans had arrived, and Angoulême was being occupied. Within minutes, a convoy of dusty trucks, also stamped with the swastika, had followed and was now parking in front of the City Hall. Soldiers in the same field-gray uniform swarmed out, shouting guttural orders. They paid no attention to the dazed population but went about their business, which apparently was to invade the City Hall.

2

THE ARMISTICE WAS signed a few days later, putting a finis to the five-week-long debacle. And the troops who had left the previous September shouting 'To Berlin!' but wondering where that Danzig they were going to fight for could possibly be, had come straggling home, exhausted and dirty, telling tales of the invincible power of the Germans, their secret weapons, and the treason of their own generals.

Like other people in the region, the Arondels had seen little of the war except for the endless passage of refugees. Streams of cars, mattresses lashed to the top as protection against strafing, had filed past for days, eventually seeping even into the remote, unpaved country lanes. Several carloads stopped at the Arondels' estate, La Prade. Shelter was found for them. Soon there were people camping in the courtyard, sleeping in the barns, washing at the courtyard well. Since Monsieur Arondel was a former mayor of the village, room was found in the house for the mayor of a small Flemish town and his family when they stopped one night asking for refuge. For several weeks Chantal shared her bedroom with the mayor's two daughters, flaxen-haired, buxom girls who spoke with a rocky, guttural accent.

Lying on makeshift beds, windows open to the warm June night, Gertrud and Dorothea told Chantal incredible stories of flight, adventure, terror, German planes overhead, people heading south on bicycles or pushing wheelbarrows, others with possessions piled high on handcarts. Cars soon ran out of gas and were abandoned by the roadside, helping to clog the traffic further. The girls had slept in ditches, with army trucks rumbling above their heads.

North of Paris, their mother had traded her rings for a few potatoes, which they had roasted at an open fire in a field and shared with fleeing soldiers. Near Orléans, their father had exchanged his gold watch and chain for a few gallons of gas, so they could push on, among the disabled cars left everywhere.

The worst moments had been when military convoys, bound for the front, had come from the opposite direction and had tried to scatter the motley civilian traffic blocking the road into the field and meadows. This was usually the time the German planes hovering overhead chose to dive-bomb and strafe. The girls remembered a woman and her child killed by the road, just as they tried to jump to the safety of a ditch; a horse, struck in the head, fallen, kicking and screaming in agony, still in the traces.

But all this, to the three teenagers, spelled excitement and novelty, a break from the deadening school routine, rather than just terror. A young soldier had hitched a ride with them, the Belgian girls giggled. He was cute, and he told them that no matter what the radio said, the war was as good as over.

'He gave us his address at home, and he said we should write him as soon as we can,' said Dorothea, the older one.

'I think he liked me,' mused Gertrud, 'he kept rubbing his leg against mine.'

'Were you afraid when the planes came?'

'Yes, but you should have seen my mother! Oh, she was crying all the time, carrying on about what we had abandoned, our house lost forever, and when the planes started diving, she got hysterical. She was afraid our father would be killed and we would be left behind there, with no place to go, since only Papa knows how to drive. So, she said, we would have to stay, try to bury his body, and then wait for the Germans to come and murder us all. She hoped they would only murder us, and do it right away, but that they could do much worse first! She told us that in the last war, the Germans raped all the women before killing them, and cut off the right hand of little boys so they could never bear arms against them.'

'Perhaps those stories aren't true,' said Chantal thoughtfully. 'Perhaps they were made up by the Germans themselves, to scare people. It would be a clever thing to do.'

A few weeks later, the radio announced it was all safe now, and the refugees headed home to their German-occupied towns. Little damage had been done, since the cities did not undergo any artillery siege or air attacks. Psychological warfare, in the form of radio addresses, had immeasurably helped the Nazi advance. As soon as the Germans occupied a town, they seized the local broadcasting station and sent messages of terror:

'Leave your home in the city, your farm, leave everything. Run for your life. For we are coming, the hordes of Attila, and we will rape, torture, and murder. Run, take to the road, run as fast and as far south as you can. We will show no mercy.'

Murdering useful civilian populations wasn't at all the intention of the German High Command. But the message had the immediate effect of sending thousands upon thousands in panicked flight. Their throngs filled the roads and impeded the movement of French troops to the front. In most towns, in fact, no fighting took place. The French retreated or, receiving no reinforcement, quickly surrendered, and the Germans easily occupied empty cities, villages, and isolated farms. After that, it was only a matter of bringing back the inhabitants once occupation had been organized.

'We found our house intact,' wrote Dorothea in her round, careful hand. 'Nothing had been taken. The Germans are very strict, and looters are severely punished. It's not true the Germans are so bad. The ones who are staying in our town are very nice, and they smile at us in the street. My father says this war was all the fault of England,

and that the French were dupes. You must come and visit us as soon as travel is allowed again.'

The summer days wore on at La Prade and life returned to its boring routine, with acres of afternoon stretching endlessly. Chantal wondered when *Life* was going to begin at last. Any vague thought of registering at the university in Bordeaux was ruled out by the new *ligne de démarcation*, the boundary line that separated the so-called Free Zone from the Occupied Zone. Bordeaux was now in the Occupied Zone, the wide strip of land along the Atlantic. Angoulême was also occupied, as was the entire northern half of the country. La Prade was in the Free Zone, about ten miles east of the line. Crossing the line was next to impossible. It required permission from German authorities obtained after endless applications to the Kommandantur, good for one time only and not renewable.

What was going to happen next? The war had been lost, and lost miserably, in spite of the messages of the Vichy government broadcasts, speaking of family, work, and motherland, of France taking her place in the just new order of nations 'liberated' from evil left-wing forces by the powerful and righteous Nazis.

'No matter,' said Monsieur Arondel – who had fought four long years in the trenches in the 'other' war, the real one, the one France had won – 'no matter, honor is lost.'

All right, thought Chantal impatiently. So Honor is Lost. But how are we to find out what the consequences of that loss are? How will we *really* know, other than by being told, that we have lost the war?

The answer came soon enough. No food, no gas. Supplies of gas were the first to be stopped, and for five years, that would be the end of free driving. There were rumors that all private cars would be requisitioned for the use of the occupation forces and soon, many were. So, the Arondels' black Citroën was driven into an unused barn, polished, and its wheels removed. It was hoisted onto wooden blocks, covered with tarpaulins, and hay was mounded over it until it was completely hidden from sight.

The last trip to Montbron, the neighboring market town, had revealed that all grocery stores were empty, no food could be bought. No soap, no coffee, no salt, no sugar. Whatever stocks there were had been taken off the shelves by farsighted, greedy shopkeepers and hidden for future sale at black-market prices. A black market, indeed, soon developed for these rare commodities, with prices shooting up ten-, twenty-, a hundredfold. No meat in the butcher shop, no bread in the bakery. Nothing. All supplies were cut off at the source. Until that happened, perhaps three weeks after the armistice had been signed, everyone had been secretly relieved to see the war had been so swiftly and painlessly over. But now, for the first time, gut terror made its way into the population. So this was what losing the war meant. The cities began slowly to starve.

The war may have been over for the French, but a much larger conflict, soon to become global, was in the making. Germany was about to take on the world, Hitler needed to feed his armies and his population, absorbed in the war effort. To that end, all supplies, agricultural and industrial, were diverted.

An armistice commission, set in the Free as well as the Occupied zones, gave notice to landowners like Monsieur Arondel that a production quota had been imposed on them. From the smallest to the largest production unit, no one escaped notice. Harsh punishment for noncompliance up to and including the death penalty was spelled out in the order.

During the following months, with great thoroughness, the German authorities set up a system of food tickets in the form of sheets of muddy-colored stamps. Long lines formed in each city hall on the first of the month to receive the precious stamps. The population was divided into groups, according to nutritional requirements. The basic allotment consisted of a few daily ounces of black bread, a few potatoes, a little gray macaroni once a month, an ice-cube-size square of margarine or equivalent amount of cooking oil (bring your own bottle) when available, which was seldom, meat the size of a matchbox once a week, again if and when available, and a pound of a strange cereal, made of some rolled oats mixed with a much larger amount of what looked like ground straw. The full official ration for the A tickets, supposing it was available at the markets, which it never was, would average around six hundred calories a day. Babies and children received a pint of skim milk daily.

No coffee for anybody, but food stamps for a small packet of ersatz, or replacement, coffee, officially named 'national' coffee, made of roasted acorns and sawdust. Soap was rationed, too, and the twice-a-year bar scratched the skin and left a residue of sand, gravel, and clay at the bottom of basins. There was no salt or sugar at all. On the free market there were a few rutabagas, turnip leaves, and Brussels sprouts. Jerusalem artichokes, usually reserved for cattle feed, were sometimes available.

Clearly, other means of survival had to be devised. People in the cities had recourse to the black market, which flourished throughout the Occupation. A sack of potatoes became the real currency unit. Needless to say, punishment for both seller and purchaser was severe if they were caught.

But for country people like the Arondels, the food restrictions represented a challenge to organize available resources – good organizers would survive. Thorough as the enemy was, he couldn't count every potato, every quart of milk, every chicken, every pig. He could not prevent Madame Arondel from having gardens planted where grass had been. Soon she learned to make a sugarless jam, by simmering fruit down for hours until moisture had evaporated and the natural sugars concentrated into a thick, almost caramelized marmalade. By the end of summer, hundreds of jam pots lined her scrubbed shelves: peach, pear, apricot, and apple with grape, which was the best.

Rows of root vegetables were half buried in dry sand in the cellars. She saw that fresh apples and pears lined open shelves, while on the lower level, easy to reach for refilling, she placed bottles holding grapevine branches, each with its clusters of golden grapes. Water replenished regularly, the grapes would stay fresh for months. Though they shriveled a little, they only became sweeter and would last until Easter.

Pigs were butchered, hams were hung to dry from the ceiling in the Arondels' winter kitchen. Tureens of pâté were put away, skeins of sausage and boudins stretched to smoke in the fireplace. Vegetables and fruit were canned in large quantities, by the Arondels' well-supervised maids. Milk, in shallow earthenware basins, was placed on the cool cellar steps. Soon, the cream would rise, thick and yellow. Butter was churned, stored in crocks. Fresh cheese in pottery strainers hung in the warm kitchen, and whatever cheeses were not consumed fresh were piled – Madame Arondel remembered the method from her own grandmother's time – in vats filled with home-pressed walnut oil made fragrant with a sprig of rosemary. 'They'll keep all winter,' she told the maids.

The Germans did receive their demanded quota, but at La Prade under the energetic management of Madame Arondel, ingenious means were devised every week. Extra eggs were painted with a thin coat of plaster to seal the porous shell, insuring preservation. Monsieur Arondel found a long-unused mill, its grinding wheels activated by a rusty crankshaft. It was cleaned and oiled, and soon a plentiful fragrant blond flour filled the bins.

Chantal's mother discovered substitutes for almost, but not quite, everything. Chocolate and coffee were the most daunting, and even the clever Madame Arondel had to give up on chocolate. But coffee soon had a substitute: Chicory was grown in the garden, its leaves providing a spicy, bitter-tasting salad green. Its roots dried, ground and roasted made a very acceptable replacement for coffee. Soap? Suet mixed with lye in earthen vats gave soap, rough to the skin but sudsy and effective.

Beehives had always been there, but now they were multiplied, escaping swarms captured and quickly housed in newly built hives like miniature thatched houses, and great jars of honey were harvested. Gathering and storing provisions had become Madame Arondel's obsession. It was too bad if the cities were starving to death, she repeated, she could not undertake to feed them all but she *would* see to those who depended on her. Meanwhile, she polished her system to perfection: Breakfast was fragrant café au lait made with chicory, sweetened with honey, and freshly baked bread spread with butter and the caramelized jam. For those who worked hard, there was also cheese, and eggs cooked in butter, with slices of smoked ham. She saw to it that all the tenant farmers on the estate followed similar systems, and that everyone under her rule was well fed.

This plentiful household was run with iron-handed discipline. Chantal was expected, as she had been ever since she was a little girl, to follow a routine that did not differ much from that of the nuns.

According to the rules, she got up at six-thirty in the morning, summer and winter alike, washed, dressed, made her bed, tidied her room, and went downstairs for breakfast, leaving the window open and closing the door behind her. She was not expected to return to her room during the day, unless she was verifiably ill. At night, and when Madame Arondel had given the order, she went to her room, undressed, washed, got into bed and turned off the light. No lounging in bed, no reading in bed. The days were dull, dull, dull . . . There was no question of visiting her school friends: most of them, like Martine Moreau, lived closer to or in Angoulême, and were therefore on the other side of the Demarcation Line between Free and Occupied zones. Writing Martine wasn't even possible: correspondence for private use between the two zones had been suspended. Special postcards were available at the post office, of the fill-in type, which might (but would not necessarily) be allowed across. They left little room for teenage confidences:

37

```
        Dear_____

We are_____

Our address is_____

Please tell us_____

            Signed_____
```

These postcards were stopped by German censors if information they contained was of a suspicious nature.

Afternoons stretched into acres of nothingness, just silence, heavy with the buzzing of bees. Chantal wanted to go swimming in the pond near the house, but that was discouraged: It was harvest season, and the farm workers must not be treated to the sight of Chantal lounging in her bathing suit. Go for rides on her bicycle? Yes, but where? Every time Chantal tried to help in the kitchen or in the barnyard or in the garden, she was rebuffed. After the expensive education that had been bestowed upon her, it would be unseemly to see her occupied at menial tasks. Needlework would be suitable, but Chantal had studied Latin and English at school and not learned how to do any needlework. Hers was a 'modern' education. Her attempts at sewing and embroidery gave such dismal results that she quickly abandoned them.

'Your father mentioned,' her mother said casually one afternoon, 'that he met Monsieur Verbois, the cattle dealer from La Rochefoucauld. He ran into him the other day, at the produce collection point of the Kommandantur, as he was supervising the delivery of grain, and Monsieur Verbois accompanied his men who had brought in some cattle.'

Chantal sneered. 'I remember Monsieur Verbois. That fat man with the red face and the loud voice. Is he still just as fat?'

'I wouldn't know,' continued her mother, ignoring the interruption, 'and be that as it may, he has made a fortune, you hear me, a very sizable pile, in his business. He was telling your father that his son has come back from the war, and that they will work in association from now on. He's so proud, he already had signs painted on the sides of his trucks: "Paul Verbois et Fils."'

Watchful silence from Chantal.

'He mentioned to your father that he will need more grazing land for the cattle in transit, and that perhaps La Prade could lease him a few acres.'

Chantal's only reactions were hostile vibrations directed at her mother and a fleeting thought of pity for the poor cows en route to the slaughterhouse.

'Monsieur Verbois asked your father about you and what you were doing these days,' Madame Arondel continued, elaborately ignoring her daughter's feelings. 'His son has seen you somewhere and thinks you are attractive. So, we have decided that Monsieur and Madame Verbois and their son should come to visit us someday soon and stay for dinner. The men can look over the pastureland, you'll meet young Henri. By the way, it seems he's already just as big and solid as his father. Who knows? It would be hard to think of a better match for you . . . Chantal! Where are you going? I am still speaking to you.'

But Chantal had run away, run back upstairs to the forbidden shelter of her bedroom, and slammed the door. Marry the fat son of a fat cattle dealer? She would die first. Her anger was so palpable that her mother refrained from following her upstairs and knocking on her door to remind her that one did not go lie on one's bed in the middle of the afternoon. For the next week, Chantal went about with a set face, speaking to no one, answering only in monosyllables after the second or third repetition of a question.

'I don't know where that girl got her stubborn streak,' complained her mother, unaware that Chantal's defiance was nothing more than a version of her own willfulness.

'Let's wait a little before asking the Verbois over. She'll get used to the idea. Such a good match!'

Then, one day, Renaud de Blazonac came to visit, on a casual walk through the woods that separated his château, Blazonac, from La Prade.

As far back as Chantal could remember, the Blazonacs had been the sole element of glamor and excitement in her life. They owned a massive castle overlooking a lake, surrounded by immense woods. The Countess de Blazonac, Renaud's mother, had died two years earlier of a mysterious and swift illness, leaving the château and the farms that constituted the estate to her two sons, Renaud, the oldest and heir to the title, and Anthenor, three years younger, born from a second marriage. She lived in Paris in the fashionable sixteenth arrondissement and only came to Blazonac with her sons for the summers. Chantal had always looked forward to their visits: She would listen in the still summer air for the sputtering engine of the Countess's little sports car as it pulled into the courtyard of La Prade. The Countess wore cloche hats, short, low-waisted dresses, and smoked with a long cigarette holder. She spoke fast, moved fast, drove fast, and, it was rumored, lived fast. Monsieur Arondel supervised the occasional sale of a stand of trees to be cut down for lumber or for barrel staves, and knew enough of her affairs to shake his head and agree with the general opinion that she was burning the candle at both ends.

Sometimes the Countess's sons had come with her, awkward in plus fours, or wearing the first alligator shirts Chantal had ever seen. *Chemises Lacoste* they were called, after the all-time great French tennis champion. School was discussed for lack of other common topics; Chantal was so much more successful in her studies than the boys. Why, Renaud had failed his *bac* again, just didn't seem to care, and Anthenor wasn't gifted for school – always so silent and withdrawn. But the Countess said it all with such lightheartedness that it was clear school did not really matter. How could it matter, when you were a Blazonac? Or almost a Blazonac, in the case of Anthenor.

There were days when the boys came to La Prade without their mother, in a group with friends who were staying at the château, walking through the lovely woods in the narrow, moss-edged shortcuts from Blazonac to La Prade. In spite of Madame Arondel's entreaties that they stay for *goûter*, there were just-baked peach tarts and bowls of pigeon-heart cherries, they said no, they only had come to see if Chantal would go for a walk or a ride with them. Where were they going? Oh, they might go to Montbron for a lemonade, or visit friends at the Château de Hubertye. They refused to gossip about the Hubertyes' poor retarded son ('Ah? He is retarded? Never knew it,' said Renaud haughtily) and got away as fast as they could, taking Chantal, laughing, excited and a little intimidated by the worldly big-city boys. Anthenor was two years older than Chantal, always silent and aloof; Renaud, five years older.

There were wonderful occasions when they invited her to Blazonac, and lunch was served in the big dining room with matching striped blue-and-white silk covering the walls and the high-backed chairs. Four French doors opened onto the lawn strewn with croquet wickets, mallets leaning against garden loungers. There were guests, older gentlemen who treated Chantal with fatherly courtesy but brushed against her breast when they pulled out her chair; there was laughter, there were off-color jokes that she did not understand but laughed at just the same; there was Ping-Pong in what had been the guard room, swimming in the lake, boating in the rowboat. Maids served tea in the garden, and the boys sat on the grass at their mother's feet. There were hide-and-seek games throughout the house, running wildly up and down the curving stairs, in and out of bedrooms, hiding in beds, under beds, in closets, in the attics, in the unused stables.

One day during such a game, Renaud took Chantal by

the hand, and led her to the *cave*, the cellars, a succession of vaulted rooms reached by wide, steeply stepped stairs that spiraled around a stone pillar. Down below, one passed from one vaulted room to another, smelling of dampness, dust, and mildew.

There, they waited in the darkness, but heard no sound of pursuit. Renaud drew her to him and kissed her on the lips, lightly at first, then more firmly, opening her lips with his and slipping his tongue into her mouth to caress the inside of her lips. This was Chantal's very first kiss. In her protected life at the nuns' school, she had long dreamed of that moment. It turned out to be as excruciatingly exquisite as she had hoped. Renaud released her, caressed her lips briefly with his fingers. They heard shouts and people running down the stairs. The moment was over. Chantal wondered with pounding heart how Renaud would behave toward her after this. Was he going to announce his love for her in public? Or keep it private between the two of them? What was going to be changed?

Nothing at all was changed. There was never a wink, a squeezing of the hand from Renaud after that. Perhaps the kiss had been an illusion? A few weeks later, back in school, Mother Saint-Ignatius handed Chantal a postcard, mailed in Paris, showing the entry to the Catacombs. The back-sloping handwriting, which Chantal was seeing for the first time, was certainly Renaud's, she decided, and it was signed *Jeanne Lacave*. Her heart pounded, the monotony of her life was relieved for days whenever she looked at the card, which she had slipped between the pages of her missal. Later, Renaud swore he had never sent such a card, but with Renaud, that meant nothing.

Then, the Countess died. Monsieur and Madame Arondel went to the funeral and spoke afterward of the two young men conducting mourning, suddenly looking older, wearing black suits and black overcoats, an extravagance Madame Arondel condemned. 'A needless expense,' she scolded, 'they are going to need every cent their mother left. Wouldn't it have been enough to wear a black armband on whatever suit they owned? When will they get any wear again out of those expensive black clothes?'

Then there was the summer of the war. Anthenor came to stay at Blazonac, but not Renaud, and Chantal saw Anthenor only once, when he came to discuss business with Monsieur Arondel. He barely acknowledged her. In early September, she heard Renaud had been drafted. Monsieur Arondel went to Blazonac, came back shaking his head.

'That boy Anthenor is living there alone, he has dismissed all the servants, no money to pay wages. He's only kept old Maria, who will stay there, paid or not. And I talked to the agent who was doing the accounts for the Countess. There is no way, he says, no way at all those boys can keep their land. The debts are enormous. Paying the interest alone would take more than the income they're getting from those mismanaged farms. And yet, Anthenor says he is going to try, and becomes angry at any suggestion that he might sell another farm. I wish him well, but I doubt he can make it.'

And now, a year later, in the middle of this war-deadened summer, Renaud had suddenly reappeared.

He came into the house as though he had left only a few days ago, greeted Madame Arondel with excessive formality, kissed her hand, and asked about everyone's health, with that bored, supercilious tone of his that made one embarrassed even to have a state of health.

Renaud was slender, narrow-faced, with the aristocratic aquiline profile of an Italian condottiere. He smoked too much, for cigarettes were still unrationed. He accepted the invitation to dinner and sat down to one of Madame Arondel's feasts, ate little, drank a lot of wine, spoke about the heroic deeds of his battalion, naming, Monsieur Arondel said later, impossible places and dates.

'Last time we heard, Count Renaud,' said Monsieur Arondel, 'you were with a battalion of engineers . . .'

'There you have it,' said Renaud, 'putting *me* in an engineers outfit tells you a lot about the efficiency of the

French army! Well, it was one disaster after another, and finally here we are pinned in Dunkirk, and the British are taking all the available boats, shooting the French soldiers who try to climb aboard, and leaving us there to be bombed into oblivion on the beach.'

Chantal was barely listening, because magic had again touched her with its fluttering wings. There he was, slender and romantic, speaking with his inimitable Paris accent, and she was sure he had come to see *her* . . .

'Well, a few fellows and I decided we weren't going to take it anymore, so we made a break and we hitched rides, and jumped on trucks, and stole a car once while the driver was answering a call of nature in the fields. That wasn't good for long, though, we soon ran out of gas. I threw away my pack, my gun, my jacket, I even lost my wallet with all my papers, and I arrived at Blazonac one night, to find the place full of Belgian refugees Anthenor had taken in. I started shouting in German, just for the hell of it, and you should have seen the panic! Like kicking an anthill. But now the refugees have all gone back to wherever they came from, and I've been there alone with Anthenor for the last six weeks, just relaxing. I needed it.'

'What are you going to do now, Count Renaud?' Monsieur Arondel asked. He had known the Blazonacs forever and affected a respectful familiarity with them. 'You cannot go back to Paris.'

'No, I can't. I think I'll just stay in Blazonac and weather the war. It cannot last long. It's only a matter of days until Hitler invades England. Then it will be all over. The British are totally unprepared. I watched them in the war. Only anxious to go back to playing tennis on the white cliffs of Dover. I saw them there when the ships took us to England.'

So, now Renaud had not after all broken through the German lines at Dunkirk? He had been to England and back? Never mind.

'What about your brother? Will he stay too?'

'Yes, he'll probably stay at Blazonac. He likes it here.

You know, he sees himself as some sort of a gentleman farmer. He thinks he can run the estate. He's welcome to try. Personally, I am not interested. Life in the country bores me.'

The estate? Their mother had sold some of the richest farmland and lumber forests. That left only a dozen hard-scrabble farms, cultivated by sharecroppers who all had the reputation of being the most incompetent, shiftless, and prolific families around. Much of the remaining valu-able timber had been sold to lumber dealers, who had hacked great barren scars among the stands of trees.

'I was walking in the woods, the other day, near the Belmont farm,' said Monsieur Arondel, 'and I saw a whole section of timber of yours being cut down and another marked for cutting. It's a crime to harvest those immature oaks. They should be allowed to grow for another ten, fifteen years. Your grandfather had them planted forty years ago, and it takes at least fifty years for oaks to mature.'

'We needed the money,' said Renaud, stifling a yawn. 'I don't go walking in the woods much myself, so I wouldn't know what my brother's up to. Who cares what happens ten years from now.'

'Are you going to replant?'

'I don't know. You'll have to ask Anthenor what his plans are, that is, supposing he has any. As soon as the situation allows, I'll sell my share to Anthenor and go back to Paris and automobile racing. That's where my life is, everything else bores me.'

Automobile racing? Paris? That's what *Life* is after all! Now I know. Summers in Blazonac, and then the races. Chantal had seen them in the newsreels, Le Mans, Rheims, Montlhéry, with the cars zooming around the track, the drivers jumping out after the race, the winner, grimy and so masculine, kissing the girl who brings him a sheaf of gladiola . . .

'What about the château?' asked Madame Arondel, for-ever obsessed with housekeeping. 'I haven't been there since the funeral of the Countess. How are you managing?'

'Old Maria takes care of things after a fashion. I stay in my room, mostly, and I read. I'm reading all of Balzac. All humanity is there. It's fascinating. Have you read him?'

'I've read some, I am sure,' said Madame Arondel vaguely. 'Do your farmers bring provisions to the château?'

'I don't think so. They probably don't have enough for themselves. I am not sure how Maria manages . . . Poorly, I should say. She serves potatoes, mostly, but then she never was much of a cook.'

Chantal was entranced by this detachment, this aristocratic indifference. In her world, food had become the subject of overwhelming interest, and she was sick of such gross preoccupation. Food was harped about, stored, checked, discussed endlessly. Her parents were so unfashionable, so thoroughly set in their dull life-style. She despised them at times, felt she did not belong in their nest, and hungered to break free. And now the dream world that had flickered that day, for an instant, in the darkness of the cellars at Blazonac opened on the aquiline profile of Renaud, his mocking eyes, his casual slouching gait in well-cut, if threadbare, clothes.

Renaud came back a few days later and found Chantal alone at home. He asked her for a walk in the woods. Chantal would always remember what they talked about. What *he* talked about, rather, because she would not have dared interrupt the glamorous stories he told while walking under the heavy canopy of the chestnut trees. Ferns were thick underfoot, their little violin necks long unfurled, now beginning to show a narrow edge of brown at the tip of their lacy leaves. The Gordini stable always did best at the circuit of Montlhéry, mused Renaud. Now, *that* was one track he enjoyed running, with a well-tuned eight-cylinder Fiat Gordini. Last time he won the twenty-four-hours . . .

'You run for the twenty-four-hours?'

'Yes, I do, with a relief driver, of course. As I was saying, that day, Rosemeyer came to me and said, "*Ach . . . du bist fabelhaft!*" That was before Rosemeyer had that terrible accident, you know, when he was winning the Rheims circuit every year with his Auto Union.'

(Never heard of the Great Rosemeyer before, thought Chantal. He must have been a German racer. Well, now I know. Tell me more, please, Renaud. A wider world was opening with his every word.)

'Montlhéry is good,' continued Renaud. 'But the only real circuit in the world, I can tell you, is in Germany. Have you ever been to the Nürburgring?'

(Well, no, come to think of it, I don't think I have. I would remember if I had. But continue, please!)

'I am not speaking of the South Loop, you understand, even though it's tough. No. I am talking of the North Loop. First, there's a downhill, maximum-speed chute culminating in a dip at the bottom. The trick, as you guessed, is to find the gentlest slope during the descent to ease the multiple g's at the nadir.'

(The multiple g's. Of course. What else?)

'And then, there was the Wehrseifen part: a series of blind, off-camber curves. They're baffling because they all look alike but they are not. And when you come to what looks like the inside of the left turn, where the track almost doubles back upon itself, and you prepare to skim, well, it suddenly becomes the corner of the bridge – the Green Hell, we call it, because of the tall hedges that obscure the track ahead. Now, *that* is racing. That's where Rosemeyer won in '36, just ahead of Caracciola in a Mercedes-Benz 36–220 . . .'

(Ah? I wasn't aware of the exact model. Now, I know.)

'There were giants, there! Fangio, Nuvolari. But the Germans were the best. They were gods! Hermann Lang, Karl Kling, Von Trips, and the greatest of all, Rosemeyer, that is, of course, until he had that terrible accident . . . Why, he would never let anyone touch the wheel of his car but me.'

In a desperate effort to contribute something other than knowing nods, she tried to tell Renaud how she and Martine had borrowed a truck from the Moreau Mills and driven a group of political refugees to the Spanish border. But he looked so evidently bored, she stopped before the end.

'And' – he yawned – 'what else is going on in the countryside?'

It was as if Fred's gray eyes were being wiped out of her memory. How silly of me to think I can bore him with schoolgirls' adventures – him who knew the Great Rose-meyer, even before the Terrible Accident.

They met several more times, always it seemed by coincidence, although Chantal helped chance the best she could. One day, pretending to herself she had been taking a shortcut to the village, she came upon him as she was walking through the woods. A fine rain started to fall, so Renaud led her through green thickets, saying he knew a barrel-stave maker's hut in a clearing nearby. They did not find the hut, but when they sat down in the shelter of a tree, on the cushiony moss, Renaud kissed her, long and hard, and Chantal thought she had recaptured the ecstasy of that day three years ago. Then he spread his jacket on the damp moss and, leaning over her, half convinced and half forced her to give in. She felt very little in the quick embrace except a sharp, brief pain, and then a mildly pleasurable sensation that her imagination translated into incipient rapture.

It was over in an instant. No words of passion, not even of love.

'See?' said Renaud, lighting a cigarette. 'See? It was all right, wasn't it?'

After that, they met several times again, and Renaud on one occasion was sufficiently carried away to whisper 'Ma *chatte*' in her ear, 'Kitten.' Now, that was tenderness, love, wasn't it? And do not forget that there can be no comparison between you, poor little Chantal, with your country ways, in your insipid dresses made by the village dressmaker, and those girls, the ones Renaud is used to, who come to the track in their low-slung sports cars, wearing their couture dresses to watch the drivers and celebrate with them after victory. One of those girls, Renaud mentioned, always carried in her purse a solid gold *mosser* to whip the bubbles out of her champagne! (Carried a what? Oh, yes, of course . . .)

And one day, as summer was close to its end, as the brown edges of the lacy ferns were growing wider and curling brittle, Renaud asked Chantal to marry him.

Her heart stopped. *Life* was spreading its wings and she felt their flutter in her throat.

It wasn't, heaven knows, that Renaud's proposal was couched in overly romantic terms.

'I am so dreadfully bored in Blazonac, it would be better if you'd come to stay there . . . Would you?'

'Stay with you? Renaud, you cannot be serious! You can imagine what my parents would say.'

'I know, I know. We'd have to be married first, of course.'

Chantal did not answer. She slipped her hand into Renaud's and whispered, 'I love you. Do you love me too?'

He looked at her skeptically. 'I don't know if I love you or not, or if I ever loved anybody. My Bugatti, yes, I did love that car.'

Chantal understood that the chic thing to do was to avoid all sentiment and act cool and collected. But inside, she was a maelstrom of churning emotions.

That night, she brought up the subject at the dinner table. Her parents stopped eating, taken aback.

'You *can't* marry Renaud,' gasped her mother. 'Don't you see what he's like? He'll never amount to anything. No energy, no stamina, the end of a race . . . Tired blood; he comes from too long a line.'

'If you marry him,' warned her father, 'you'll be poor as a church mouse.'

And yet, they did not protest that much. Had they wished to, they could easily have forbidden the marriage: Chantal was not even eighteen, and girls needed their parents' consent for marriage until they were twenty-one. But no doubt the title had something to do with the

Arondels' halfhearted arguments. Their daughter would be the Countess de Blazonac, after all, and what an alliance! The estate was in bad shape, heavy debts, poor management. But it still constituted a sizable holding: a fine forest, three lakes, the farms that could be made profitable with good management, the historic castle. This was a step up from the solid bourgeois niche into which they fit so firmly.

So they tried to dissuade Chantal, but they did it without conviction, and with typical parental insurance.

'Well, so long as it is what *you* want,' her mother insisted. 'Remember, we didn't force you, and we even warned you. Remember that well. If you ever complain, you will hear plenty of "I told you so's."'

Madame Arondel was famous for her 'I told you so's.'

3

THEY WERE MARRIED six weeks later, just as a rainy fall was giving way to a damp winter.

Chantal could not even hope to invite her friend Martine, a prisoner behind the impassable line. All she could do was send her one of those miserable yellow postcards:

Dear **Martine** _____

We are **(Count Renaud de Blazonac and I) getting married.** _____

Our address is **Château de Blazonac.** _____

Please tell us **what is new with you and if you still wear**
your pendant. _____

Signed **Chantal** _____

Martine replied, cramming as much as she could in the frustratingly inadequate space allotted:

Dear **est soon-to-be Countess Chantal,** _____

We are **so happy with you and for you. I wish with all my**
heart I would attend your wedding. When do I meet
your fairy tale count?

Our address is **the same. I'm afraid it will never change.**
No château for me on the horizon. Instead
I work in my father's office.

Please tell us **if you think those people we know (V. and F.)**
made it to America.

Your friend forever.
Lonely Martine

Signed _____

In spite of the cryptic last lines, the German censors let the card pass. When she read it, Chantal sighed and thought impatiently, How can she still be thinking of those boys? They are gone forever, she'll never see Volodia again, and I am sure *he* has forgotten her completely by now.

Madame Arondel invited only those accessible friends and relatives, a pitifully small group of guests for her daughter's wedding, to be sure, and sad, when you thought of the prewar country weddings – like her own – with festivities that had lasted a week. Lucky nowadays to gather a handful for a wedding luncheon that she would try to make at least suitable.

Aunt Emilie came from Limoges. She was the widow of General Giraud, Madame Arondel's older brother; and she cried a great deal because Chantal's marriage reminded her of that of her own daughter, Suzette, who had died on her wedding eve. The Lavalais family, of the Lavalais flour mills in Saint-Estèphe, was invited. The invitation was only halfhearted, because Madame Lavalais, a childhood friend of Madame Arondel's, plagued her with the recital of constant ailments and illnesses, and the two daughters, long-nosed and big-hipped, were to Chantal the epitome of dowdiness. But Monsieur Lavalais was a jovial, florid man whose cordiality Monsieur Arondel found enjoyable. The Verbois turned down the invitation.

Throughout the banquet, served in the big dining room, on the heavy white damask cloth knotted at the corners to keep it from dragging on the waxed floor, Renaud remained silent, drank a great deal but ate almost nothing, barely touched the roast guinea hens or the *civet de lièvre à la royale*, wild hare simmered in vintage burgundy, chain-smoked, answering the hearty questions in monosyllables, never even smiling at the jokes.

How boring and vulgar they must all seem to him, thought Chantal. They have no idea of his world, Paris, Le Mans, the beautiful sophisticated women in his life! They think that just because he married me, he has become one of them. How glad I am to be getting out of here!

'How about your brother, Count Renaud?' asked Monsieur Lavalais. 'We saw him leave after the church ceremony, and we were surprised. Wasn't he going to attend the *déjeuner*?'

Renaud shrugged one shoulder, squinted against the smoke of his cigarette, answered nothing. Madame Arondel smiled a tight-lipped smile and turned to ask Madame Lavalais about the state of her health. Monsieur Lavalais raised his glass to propose a toast to the newlyweds and their parents. Renaud did not raise his glass. Instead he said coldly, 'It happens that both my parents are dead, dear Monsieur. Would you like to drink a toast to that?'

Nothing could restore congeniality after the embarrassed silence that followed. And as soon as she could, Chantal hastily kissed everyone around the table, said her good-byes to all, took her husband by the hand, and ran out of the house.

Through the wet forestland, along the now muddy paths they had walked during the summer days, Renaud took Chantal to Blazonac.

Thick smoke swirled at them as Renaud and his bride pushed open the door to their room. The window was open, letting in the damp, cold air. The carved white marble fireplace, perhaps because it was filled with green wood, or perhaps because its flue had not been swept in years of its accumulated soot, was spewing out great clouds of acrid wood smoke. Kneeling in front of the open hearth, old Maria was fanning the smoldering fire. That bedroom had long remained unused.

Maria stood, brushed ashes from her skirts, and greeted Chantal. She addressed her, as it was still done then, not as *madame*, but *notre dame*, to affirm unquestioning allegiance. Others were respectfully addressed as *madame* or *monsieur*, but the master and mistress received the old obeisance titles. So naive was Chantal that she did not realize Maria's position at Blazonac was a great deal more secure than hers.

In the church, standing before the high altar decorated by the Arondel maids with autumn foliage and chrysanthemums in shades of gold and red – no white flowers were blooming that late in the fall – Renaud had slipped on Chantal's finger a narrow wedding band. White gold, as the fashion was then. She wore it with the small ring he had given her after Madame Arondel had pointed out that an engagement ring would be expected. It was a tiny ruby, surrounded with pearls, that he had found in a corner of one of his mother's empty jewel boxes. Forgotten there because it wasn't valuable enough to be part of the progressive sale that had swallowed first the jewelry, then the massive dining-room silver, finally most of the paintings, furniture, and valuables from the immense, drafty rooms.

Blazonac castle stood on the very bank of a small lake, called an *étang* in the southwest of France, its east wall rising out of the water. Long green aquatic herbs, *des cheveux de sorcière*, witches' hair, grew out of the mortar and waved slowly in the clear current running to the sluices. The building was heavy, long, and rectangular, with four crenelated towers at the corners. At the end of a long tree-lined drive, the carriage court was entered through a wrought-iron gate, long broken from its hinges and resting askew against the wall. In the courtyard, a fountain fed by a spring still gushed in the center of a circular pond, surrounded by what had been a ring-shaped flower bed. Now the flower bed was overgrown with weeds, and clumps of algae floated in the water. The stone margin was broken.

High steps worn in the center led to the entrance door, guarded by stone lions. A bronze bell hung from a chain on the right for visitors to ring. In better days, the maids also rang the bell to announce meals, or to call the Countess from her promenades in the park or her boat rides on the lake.

The massive carved-panel door opened onto an immense vestibule, furnished with four enormous Henri II cabinets, each flanked by rusty suits of armor. In a corner stood a moldy sedan chair, lined in moth-eaten, musty scarlet velvet, in which some great-great-grandmother must have had herself carried around the house and grounds. Pervading dampness seeped in rivulets from the stone walls, and masonry crumbled into wet sand where it joined the rectangular blocks. A staircase of stone rose to the second floor, dividing at a landing where more suits of armor mounted guard, its branches curving to either side, outlined by their carved banister of darker stone. A smell of mildew pervaded the atmosphere. The room Renaud had chosen for his new wife, because it communicated with his own, was down the west corridor, at the end of a long hall of closed bedroom doors. Chantal wondered whether one of those was Anthenor's.

Maria had done all she could. She had aired the musty room. She had put on the sheets, embroidered with the coronet and lacy initials of some previous countess, the best blankets she could find, and unfolded raveling towels on a rickety stand behind a faded tapestry screen that hid the washstand with its jug and basin. She had taken up a large pot of hot water, lukewarm now. She had brought a load of firewood and lit the smoky fire in the long-unused fireplace to welcome the bride. She had even killed a chicken from the meager flock she fed in the almost empty poultry yard, and she was getting ready to serve the best meal she could muster to Count Renaud and his new wife, and to Renaud's brother, the silent and elusive Anthenor, provided he was around.

Renaud closed the window. The room was warming up a little. He threw his jacket onto a chair. 'Well, I am glad that's done and over with. I'll have some trouble getting used to being treated as a member of your family. What bourgeois! Hopeless . . . The wines were good, though.'

Chantal was ready to apologize abjectly for her relatives. Yes, she could have said, they were not much removed from being rich peasants. They were stolid, with provisions for a year in their pantries, good vintages aging in their cellars, polished floors, solid furniture regularly waxed, and well-ordered accounts. All worthy of scorn – a scorn Chantal was eager to espouse – in the eyes of her slender, aristocratic husband. In past centuries his family had been rich, Chantal's had been poor, or at least close to being poor, and the fact that the situation was now reversed, because of generations of carefree spending on one side, and careful economy on the other, only prompted Renaud to even greater disdain.

His silk shirt was frayed at the cuffs and buttons were missing. Chantal was still wearing the beige suit she had put on that morning for the double ceremony required under French law. Her mother wanted her to get married in a proper wedding dress, but Renaud had greeted the idea with amused contempt.

'A dress made by the village dressmaker, no doubt, like your mother's clothes? And don't forget the orange blossoms . . .'

So, after much argument at home, Chantal had won the concession of a suit, purchased at the best shop in Limoges, since both Angoulême and Bordeaux now lay on the other side of the Demarcation Line. A white suit, said her mother, what would people think otherwise? But the only one they could find in the denuded shops was beige, and Chantal hoped it would meet with the approval of her fiancé. As it turned out, Renaud paid it no attention whatever, observing only that anything was better than a grotesque village bride outfit.

Now he was tired. He had eaten little, but he had drunk too much of the exceptional vintages produced for the occasion. His narrow face was drawn, his aquiline nose more prominent. He ruffled his hair, unbuttoned his shirt, and said with a yawn, 'Let's go to bed.'

The few times they made love before, it had been in the

woods, under the trees, and there was no question of taking off their clothes. Renaud's lovemaking had been quick, no caresses, just enough kissing to melt Chantal's resistance. But now, her heart was pounding. Her imagination could visualize romance, conjure passion, but not the pleasures of sex. Her whole being longed for intimacy, closeness, tenderness, more than for physical pleasure, which she was much too inexperienced even to envision.

'I love you,' she said tentatively to Renaud.

'You what?' asked Renaud. His back to the fireplace, he was undoing his cuff links.

'I love you,' she repeated timidly.

Renaud did not answer. He was frowning at one of the links, caught in the frayed buttonhole.

Chantal gathered up her courage.

'Renaud, do you love me?' she asked, louder than she had intended.

'Look, you needn't shout. I asked you to live with me because I am bored, alone here, with Anthenor gone all the time. Not that I need much company. Most of the time, I prefer being alone too. But this is going to be a long winter with the war lost, and the Occupation, and us cut off from everything. No gas. No cars. Nobody around. I'll have to stay at Blazonac, which I hate in winter. No women in the vicinity – except you, of course. I have come to rather enjoy your company. And anyway, where else would I go for sex? I told you before, I'd have liked just to live with you, but that was out of the question with parents like yours. So, it had to be marriage. But please, don't melodramatize this into some tedious romance. You must learn to behave like one of us, although I rather doubt you can.'

Chantal should have been frozen, crushed, ready to call off the whole marriage and run home to her mother. But she wasn't. Far from it. First of all, she had not been raised to expect outpourings of love in the stern household where scoldings came often and terms of endearment never. Second, she was flattered to appear as a desirable sex object to someone as sophisticated as Renaud, and finally, she could not help but be awed by his world-weary attitude. So she did her best to imitate his nonchalance, sitting across an armchair and raising her legs to pull off her stockings. The sexy (she hoped) intention was lost on Renaud.

'Forget dinner,' he said, tossing back the covers, while she was undoing the hooks and eyes of her skirt.

'Let me tell Maria that we won't be wanting dinner, then.'

'Don't be silly. She's too deaf to hear the bell, so the bellpull by the bed is of no use. Just let her wait. In time, she'll realize we are not coming down.'

At La Prade, servants were always treated with consideration, schedules were adhered to, even if it meant inconvenience. Chantal felt she had moved to another planet, one where none of the old rules applied.

'What about Anthenor, then?'

'I don't know if he'll be around. He can always eat what there is if he turns up. Remember, he left just after church. He didn't even come to the banquet. You know how he is. He doesn't want to be bothered, and I don't blame him.'

Everyone had, it was true, wondered where Anthenor had gone without a word of apology or good-bye. Chantal did have a lot to learn. She joined Renaud in the high, ornately sculpted bed, and they made love, but with no words of passion or tenderness, not even caresses. Renaud seemed almost to avoid touching her body and spoke not a word.

Chantal woke up later in the dark room, lit only by red pinpoints of ash-smothered embers in the fireplace. Something moved outside the window. Was there a hand brushing the glass, fingers splayed against the window-pane? No, it was only the five-lobed leaf of a Virginia creeper, pushed by the wind. She heard a sound like rain, strained her ears. No, it wasn't rain, only the fountain tinkling in the weed-choked pond in the carriage court. A gust of wind rustled the tall trees on the bank of the lake.

An owl hooted, very close by. The entry door slammed heavily, footsteps on the stairs. A door, Anthenor's no doubt, opened and closed. Chantal would have to get used to the sounds of her new home. Most strange, though, was the presence of the aloof man sleeping next to her.

For the first time in her life, she was lying naked and sharing a bed with a man. It felt strange, that body next to hers, skin to skin. Strange, but so good that it must surely be forbidden. The ceremony of that morning seemed distant and unreal. Had she dreamed it all? Would she wake up in her bedroom, the familiar morning sounds of La Prade rising to her open window? Eventually she drifted back to sleep.

It was morning. Renaud woke up, stretched, pushed back his hair, and yawned. 'You'll have to take off that wedding ring at night,' he said. 'When I saw your hand on the sheet just now, my first thought was that I was in bed with a married woman. It makes me nervous. It's all right with married women in the afternoon, but at night, never. That's one of my principles.'

In addition to reminiscences of racing triumphs, Renaud had an immense fund of amorous stories, experiences with worldly women to whom poor Chantal would always compare unfavorably. It took her several months before she realized that these stories, which may or may not have held a grain of truth, existed in fact mostly, if not exclusively, in Renaud's imagination.

He had had the most elegant women in Paris. They wore fur boas, and cloche hats with narrow veils over their straight noses – not ridiculously short like Chantal's – and rings over long black gloves. With them at his side, he had driven in the now defunct Bugatti to the racetrack at Longchamp, or to the automobile races at Montlhéry and Le Mans. They had leaned against the doors of low-slung cabriolets, flat-chested – nothing like Chantal's high, small, and round breasts – smoothly coiffed, holding their long cigarette holders. Chantal visualized them frozen in linear poses, like fashion magazine illustrations.

Renaud only tolerated them, he implied, unless they could distinguish themselves through some extraordinary feature, like the girl who was so beautiful that several *women* had committed suicide after meeting her because they felt their inferiority too hard to bear, and who was so passionately in love with Renaud that she, in turn, attempted suicide (in other versions of the same story, she had succeeded, leaving Renaud shaken by the awareness of the power he had over women). There was also the girl who was so rich, she tried in vain to buy Renaud – not his love, mind you, just his presence – at the price of several racing cars, a yacht, and . . . she would throw handfuls of bills at him, begging and screaming. He, unruffled, would casually take the bill fallen closest to his hand, twist it, and use it to light his cigarette. Not very original? Well, to Chantal, at first, it was the most extraordinary story . . . but only at first. There were also casually mentioned stories of men insanely in love with Renaud, but those Chantal dismissed as having misheard.

But on the whole, Renaud remained cold to these women's (and men's, if that's what he really *did* say) allure, because he was busy elsewhere. He was talking racing performances with other racing drivers. For he was a driver first, a lover only second, and more out of a sense of duty than true desire. Chantal heard the stories of his many near brushes with death, in fiery crashes, of his being nursed back to health by women with enameled faces and long scarlet nails. Of course, it was his duty, as a driving ace – boring, perhaps, but not to be shirked – to sleep with all the women around *and* with their girlfriends. He could not betray the reputation of the daredevils of the *Ecurie* Gordini, Gordini's stable of drivers, whose motto was 'A man has no excuse not to sleep with his mistresses' friends.'

Chantal did not even dare feel any jealousy. In spite of her lack of physical attractions – her dark blond hair always trying to curl and fly away, her small upturned breasts and narrow waist that defied any elegant slouch, the nails she had only recently stopped biting, her inability to smoke a cigarette without a great fit of coughing after the second puff – she was, after all, wasn't she, the one who shared Renaud's bed? She was the Countess, although she heard few people calling her that. So her share was still all out of proportion to her merits, and her humility satisfied Renaud.

'You must be a good wife. Being a good wife is the role for which women have been put on this earth.' She had heard this repeated in many different versions by the nuns and by her mother. And since she lacked authority and was only beginning to develop the imagination that was going to be the curse of her life, she felt that submission was the best way to be a good wife. In rural France of 1940, she was probably right.

As it turned out, no one would ever know just how much of Renaud's past was imagined, but what Chantal did learn seemed to indicate a couple of unsuccessful university years, not much else, before the war began, then Renaud was drafted in September '39. The fall and winter had been spent in training with an engineers' unit, which, sent to the front, had become dispersed without seeing any actual fighting, its scattered remnants making their way south toward home. Renaud had thrown away his gun, his pack, his uniform jacket, and in his shirt sleeves had arrived at night at Blazonac. Any formal mustering process was forgotten, impossible even, in this unprecedented disaster. Thousands of soldiers had been taken prisoner, the rest dispersed, and regiments simply ceased to exist as soldiers discarded their weapons and made for home. Renaud claimed he had been given a citation for bravery, but all the records had vanished, and in any case, the citation was probably just like the models leaning amorously into the door of his racing car, or the fiery crashes, or the specter of death looming over the track: another figment of his imagination.

And yet, Renaud wasn't simply lying. He was the descendant of that long line of knights who embroidered

61

ordinary events into tales of valor. No. That wasn't lying – that was weaving the *merveilleux*, the stuff of which epics and the romances of chivalry are made. Perhaps, through some genetic memory, Renaud was re-enacting, in words, the imaginary deeds of other Renauds of centuries past, those Renauds who had worn the now rusty suits of armor that guarded the great hall. The racer's coverall had been *his* suit of armor, or might have been . . . During those long winter evenings at Blazonac, Renaud was only performing his own modern version of the storytelling ritual of his ancestors, and Chantal, unruly blond hair and admiring blue eyes, was unknowingly doing her best to fill the role of the highborn ladies with flowing hair and tall headdresses who gazed dreamily at their heroes.

On that first morning, Chantal rose, dressed in a tweed skirt and sweater, as she had always learned to do (she had never yet in her life, nor had her mother, owned a dressing robe), and went downstairs.

In the rear of the stairs was the cavernous kitchen, bare stone walls browned by the accumulation of smoky deposits, with dozens of unpolished copper pans, saucepans, cauldrons hanging from hooks suspended from heavy planks on the walls. The fireplace occupied the entire wall opposite the door, large enough to roast an ox and burn an unhewn tree trunk. But who would wrestle a tree trunk into the fireplace now? It was fortunate even to have small logs sometimes to build a puny fire, lost among the pile of unremoved ashes on the gigantic hearth. The fireplace still held the elaborate clockwork system that used to turn the spit, frozen now in rust and soot. The long oaken table was scarred with use, flanked by tall, straight backless benches.

When Chantal came in, Maria was busy feeding into a small black stove, next to the fireplace, pieces of wood haphazardly cut and scattered in a loose pile in, and outside, the wood box. There was eye-stinging smoke in the air, bits of bark and splinters underfoot, every surface was coated with grease and dust.

'Good morning, Maria, I'm starved. What do we have for breakfast?'

Maria's response was her perennial whine – the age-old lament of poor women who must labor under harsh circumstances, bear children, nurse them from drying breasts, work in the fields alongside the men, with babies strapped to their back, and belly heavy with the next one. Maria had given birth to and raised twelve children, and she had, all her life, expected pity from no one except herself, but self-pity flowed as effortlessly as a fountain runs.

'Good morning, our lady. There isn't much. My daughter's cow is drying up, but I was still able to get a panful this morning. It won't last long, though. The milk is getting so thin, it's almost blue. And here's some bread, it is left from the barley loaf I baked last week, it's hard by now, but grilled it will taste better.'

A pan of milk was sitting on a corner of the stove, already gathering a coat of dust. Maria cut a slice from the unappetizing grayish half loaf left among crumbs on the table, speared it at the end of an iron fork, held it a moment to the flames of the fireplace. An acrid smell of burning bread filled the room.

'Ah, when Amelia the cook was here, things were different, believe me, our lady! Every morning, first thing, she baked sweet rolls for breakfast. The Countess also liked a certain kind of coffee she brought from Paris with her, and the kitchen girls fixed her trays with lace doilies and fresh flowers. Even when the Countess was so sick, at the end, she still wanted fresh flowers on her tray each day. I am glad she died when she did – all this would have killed her.'

Not much of an alternative for the Countess, thought Chantal, impishly: dead or killed. But *she* was alive, young, and very hungry. She fixed a tray for Renaud, with thin milk and burned bread, picked one of the last half-frozen chrysanthemums withering outside the kitchen window, placed it on the tray, and went back upstairs.

Renaud was no longer in their bed. He had moved back to his adjoining room. Of course, Chantal knew they would keep separate rooms, since he had told her in no uncertain terms that the idea of a common 'conjugal' bed was distasteful to him.

He lay on tangled sheets, propped on several pillows. On the bed, probably not made up for several days, and all around him on the floor, were dozens of books taken from the library downstairs, carelessly thrown. An overflowing ashtray and several open packs of Gauloise cigarettes were also on the floor.

'I don't want you to bring my breakfast,' said Renaud, without looking up from his book. 'That is maid's work.'

'I don't mind, really, Maria has so much to do, and she is old. You must be hungry.'

'No, I am never hungry. Put it down here. And please, don't disturb me again, I'm reading.'

'When do you want to get up?'

'I don't know if I'll get up at all today. If I do, you'll see. But don't stay around on my account. Go about your own business.'

Her own business? Well, there was certainly plenty to do. She tied a scarf over her hair and descended the majestic stairs where footsteps made imprints in the damp dust. Downstairs, she walked through, surveying her new home.

On the left side of the hall, the grand salon, as large as a ballroom, was now sparsely furnished. All the small, valuable pieces, delicate tables with curving legs, bergères upholstered in pastel satins, vitrines full of porcelain figurines, fans, snuffboxes, were gone. Gone were most of the paintings and the two consoles flanking the mantel that she remembered had held rose Ming vases. The high ornate mirror over the fireplace dripped humidity in rivulets. Plaster had fallen from one corner of the ceiling, breaking the frieze, splintered lath showing through and since more shards kept falling through the open hole, nobody bothered to sweep them out. The red velvet drapes, in the gray morning light, showed bald patches, tears and moth holes.

Did it matter? Was the magic Blazonac had held for her really dead? To be sure, the Countess was gone, but now that she was the Countess, no doubt she would know how to bring it all back. It had spelled gaiety, grandeur, liberty, love. It meant creating the pattern of one's own days, reading novels in bed all day if one wanted to.

Reading novels in bed? She shuddered at the thought of Renaud, who *was* reading novels in bed. No, *that* was not an element of the magical life, after all.

'You have only seen that house in the summer,' her mother had warned her before the wedding – perhaps reading her thoughts, 'when it was full of furniture, with throngs of happy people and guests, cars, music, beautiful meals. It was the gay life then, with money spent faster, much faster than it was coming in. A farm was sold every other year, and still it wasn't enough. But now! The Countess has left her sons nothing but the shell of an estate.'

What did Chantal understand about an estate? And if her mother wanted her to learn, to prepare for the life which would be hers, why did she send her, at twelve, to a convent school, where she saw nothing, learned nothing, experienced nothing, except prayers, Latin, and useless English, along with restlessness and ever-present dreams of escape? Why think wisdom could come so easily? Then how did Chantal's mother acquire her own? She had also spent her adolescence with the nuns – in the same school, in fact. Ah, but she was not cursed with imagination and vague dreams like her daughter . . .

Double doors led to the dining room, almost as large as the drawing room. The table was still there, dulled by moisture, flanked by its twenty-four high-backed chairs. But the blue-and-white-striped silk of the upholstery was tearing and shredding along the edge of the seats, threads hanging along the sides. An immense, ornate carved and curlicued cabinet filled an entire wall and rose almost to the ceiling, its display shelves bare. On the faded silk wall-covering, darker squares marked the places long occupied by still lifes.

When the Countess was alive, meals in the dining room were a festive occasion and sometimes Chantal was invited to stay for lunch or dinner. The four French doors, bare and closed now, with dirty panes, opened out onto the summer garden and the flowered lawn, with curtains billowing in the breeze. The long table was filled with animated guests, and the maids in white lace caps and aprons passed spun-sugar desserts. The still lifes were there then, lush fruit and vegetables, fish and game, a metaphor of plenty. The silk of the chairs didn't shred, this was castle life, brilliant, carefree, mocking, and so desirable. If there were debts and unpaid servants, no one cared. There was witty talk, billiards, croquet, tennis, boating parties on the lake, sports cars in the carriage court.

The library, the billiard room, and the morning room completed the habitable rooms of the ground floor. All were immense, almost empty, except for the library. The books, at least, had not been sold. They stood in ranks on the shelves, bound in red, green, or blue leather, gold shining through the dust, their spines stamped with the Blazonac coat of arms. The massive leather armchairs were cracked, white stuffing pushing through the larger splits. Dust was everywhere, for Maria never bothered.

Poor old Maria! In better days, she had been only a small part of a large staff. There was Amelia, the cook, and the two chambermaids who also served at the table; there was Amelia's husband, Gaston, handyman, yardman, coachman, and chauffeur; there was Justin the gardener, who was said to have worked in Versailles in his younger years, as an apprentice to the great landscapers of the royal park. Justin grew flowers and vegetables in the extensive gardens to the left of the park. He also took care of the grounds, the carriage court hydrangeas, the topiary trees that lined the low wall overlooking the lake, the herbaceous borders, the formal garden that led to the broad avenue of the park.

Justin's wife, Emma, was responsible for the poultry yard. She raised chickens by the hundred, of all breeds, laying hens and roasting poussins, flocks of guinea fowl, with their harsh cry and speckled feathers, gray and white, silly birds that took noisy fright at the slightest disturbance but blessed with tender dark meat that tasted better than pheasant. There was a gaggle of geese, arrogantly lording it over lesser fowl; they would give foie gras and the Christmas roast (and how could one have cassoulet without ample stores of preserved goose?). Ducks waddled through a small hole in the fence, just made to their measure, and single-filed across a path to the duck pond, under the watchful eye of Emma or one of her children, of whom Marcel was the most trustworthy. They would give succulent *canard à l'orange*, or *canard Montmorency*, surrounded by the dark, sweet cherries from the orchard.

But the poultry yard, like the garden, required a great deal of care. It also required a great deal of feed, assorted grains and concoctions, special to each breed of fowl. It now lay empty, except for a few bedraggled hens wandering the deserted enclosure, fed now and then a handful of grain or vegetable peels thrown in by Maria.

She was full of stories of the great old days, of the Countess's likes and dislikes, of the marriage of the Countess with Count Renaud's father, who had died so young and so tragically at twenty-six, his plane shot down during the last war. She spoke of Amelia's cooking as one might speak of legerdemain, as something wonderful to watch but not anything she might attempt to reproduce. She described the fabulous fruit, flowers, and vegetables that Justin would bring to the kitchen in the slanting rays of a summer morning sun, wet with dew, the tall flower stems lying on the oaken table, peaches and tomatoes rolling every which way out of the overfull baskets, crushing petals. Now, her son Paulin came irregularly to scratch uneven furrows among the weeds in the garden and to cut wood for the stove and the fireplace. Many of the fruit trees were dying for lack of pruning and proper care, and the garden was reverting to a tangle of overgrowth.

When Chantal walked back to the kitchen, Maria was sitting at the table sorting dried beans.

'They come from the bottom of the bin,' she said, her voice a lament, 'so there are more pebbles and chaff than beans. I'll put them in for soaking, so they'll be cooked in time for dinner. Ah, Amelia had a way with beans! But it took smoked pork, ham, and two kinds of sausage. Even so, Count Renaud didn't care for them. He would only eat beans in cassoulet, with preserved goose and . . . Well, I'll just boil these with an onion or two. And parsley, if I can find any left in the garden, which I doubt, because the frost last week killed almost all that was left.'

Chantal took a deep breath.

'Maria, I want to start cleaning up here,' she said. 'I'll begin with the pantry. You may come and help me when you are finished, unless you have something else to do.'

Maria's startled eyes wondered clearly what there could possibly be found to clean. But she thought, I have been here more than sixty years, all told, and she less than a day. We'll see who lasts longer. Respect waned for this new Countess who, on the first day, was setting out to do scullery maid's work.

'You will hate that house,' Chantal's mother had repeated, when she was trying, halfheartedly, to talk her out of marrying Renaud. 'It is full of dark corners, with dirt and broken things that have accumulated for years. No one has taken care of it for so long! The Countess's mother-in-law died long ago, and even then . . . After that, the Countess lived in Paris, spending more than she had. She and the boys only came for vacations, nobody looked in corners, the servants were not supervised, they worked only where it showed, they stole and nobody knew, or cared.'

The pantry was the first of those dark, unkempt corners. It was a large room, adjoining the kitchen. Its bare stone walls, as brown with smoke, soot, and dust as the kitchen's, were lined with wooden shelves. On those stood, in a thick layer of solidified dust, hundreds of empty jam jars, crocks, jugs, earthenware pots. Chantal started washing, cleaning, dusting, sorting. Finally, matching pieces were lined together, sparkling clean at last. Broken or cracked pieces she piled on the floor, to sweep away.

On the lower shelves, she found dozens of baskets, some with broken handles and uncoiling wicker, all empty. Some still held a few rotten grapes, or dried leaves. These were Justin's baskets, once filled with the bounties of the earth on a summer day. Other shelves were fitted with bins, which had once held stores of beans, black, red and white, lentils, coffee, pasta, flour, provisions of sugar and salt. All empty now, save for loose grains at the bottom, and a few pounds of wrinkled beans. No provisions, except for some half-empty sacks of germinating potatoes piled in a corner. A smaller sack of onions. A few bunches of carrots with wilted leaves. That was all. And winter was upon them, a wartime winter, with no food to be bought. Well, at least she could clean up and get rid of everything broken and useless.

'Who told you to throw away our things?'

Startled, she turned around. Anthenor was standing in the doorway. She hadn't heard him coming. Tall and lanky, high-cheekboned, he was looking with narrowed eyes at her, at the pile of broken crockery on the floor, at all her handiwork.

'I am only throwing away useless things. And nobody told me, I just thought it had to be done.'

'It will be done when it needs to, and when we have the staff to do it. This is not your work. Where is Renaud? I don't suppose he's getting up today.'

So this was how Renaud spent his days, and how he was going to spend them until things changed – or until *he* changed, or never. He was going to lie in bed, unshaven, smoking, endlessly reading and drinking the acrid red wine of which the cellar still held a dwindling supply. The

Arondels' world of order and neatness which Chantal had scorned was beginning to glow around the edges.

Anthenor stood there, frowning. He did not resemble his brother, his half brother, in fact. The Countess had remarried shortly after the military plane crash that had taken the life of Renaud's father. One day, she had brought home to Blazonac a young husband, who spoke with a foreign accent. His name was strange: Sefar. But Chantal's father, who, as mayor, had access to legal documents, said that it was an abbreviation, his name was really Sepharad, and his family had come from someplace in Asia Minor.

Soon after, the young husband was heard making terrible scenes in their bedroom. Rumor had it he broke things, threatened his wife's life, because, said Monsieur Arondel, in whom the Countess had once confided, he took drugs, morphine and God only knew what else. He had been wounded in the war and had become addicted in the hospital. When they met he was disintoxicated, she thought, but she found out differently, so she was trying to keep him at Blazonac, where he couldn't lay his hands on any drugs, and she hoped that, in time, he would be permanently cured.

Apparently, she was unsuccessful, because one of the Arondels' farm boys, soon after, brought to La Prade several boxes full of strange little syringes that he had found, thrown away in the woods, between La Prade and Blazonac. During the year and a half that the situation lasted, Anthenor was born.

Shortly after the birth, his father had disappeared, and the Countess (who in spite of her remarriage had never ceased being called the Countess) had obtained a divorce. Where was he now? Dead, and buried elsewhere, said some; he certainly could not be placed in the Blazonac tomb, he would have to be buried with his own people, whoever they were. No, said others, he was alive but locked up in an asylum for the insane, driven to mindless violence by the drug.

All who had known him during the brief period of time

agreed that he was tall and blond, and that Anthenor looked like him. Handsome, too, though the boy was skinny and aloof like an untamed feline, with a long-legged gait, accented by the old pair of riding boots he always wore. Straight blond hair fell across his forehead, almost down to his deep-set eyes.

According to the complex inheritance laws, and the terms of her marriage contract, the Countess had inherited half of the Blazonac estate, and Renaud, still a babe in arms, the other half, when the Count had died. When, in turn, the Countess passed away, her sons were to divide her half, which gave Renaud three quarters of the estate, and one quarter to Anthenor. Anthenor was not, of course, a part of the titled family, but the property had never been divided, and of the two brothers, he was the one who showed a passionate interest in running the estate, and in attempting to restore its seemingly hopeless condition. An aristocrat only through his mother, he was as haughty and arrogant as his brother. He probably did not remember his father, but Chantal had heard that he, too, could become violent. All the time she had known him, he did not smile, and spoke little. Monsieur Arondel always said that Anthenor loved Blazonac with a passion, and that it was too bad it would not be all his if he saved it. In any case, he shrugged, the boy certainly was more overbearing than any of the real Blazonacs Monsieur Arondel had known.

Chantal tried to smile up at him. 'Why did you leave right after church yesterday? Your place was set at the wedding banquet, and we missed you.'

'I had things to do.'

'You should have told us you were leaving. My mother insisted on waiting over an hour in case you came back.'

Anthenor scowled. 'You will learn, I hope, if you are capable of learning anything, that I don't need to apologize or to explain. We don't owe anybody anything, except money, and we'll soon pay that back.'

Bewildered – was she supposed to abandon her work? or should she continue? – Chantal took a deep breath.

'Well, since I started this, and since it might be some time before the proper staff is here to do this work, I'll finish it.'

She waited for Anthenor's anger. Silence. After a few seconds, he simply turned on his heels and walked away.

4

WINTER SETTLED IN, cold and damp. Gray day followed gray day, and with each passing hour, Chantal became more deeply immured in despair. It rained a freezing rain most of the time, from which the skeletal trees outside the tall windows barely emerged, lost in icy mist, from the mud underfoot.

She had cleaned all she could clean, swept floors, dusted, polished, sorted. Now there were great empty spaces in drawers and cabinets, where useless clutter had been. Dampness had resisted polishing and streaked the table-tops. All her efforts served only to make the desolation more evident. Dust was already settling again, in a damp, even layer, but Chantal didn't even care anymore. Even the journal she had begun with such high hopes to chron-icle her new life as the Countess lay neglected on her bedside table. So *this* was going to be her life, now and forever. She saw no hope, no escape. This is how hell is won, she thought. You sin once, and this is it. No exit.

Madame Arondel had come twice to visit and perhaps to see how things were going. Chantal received her for-mally, in the frigid drawing room, pretending to ignore the misty puffs of their breaths, one lady entertaining another. But she offered no refreshment, because she had none to offer.

'Renaud is not at home?' asked Madame Arondel with studied casualness.

'No,' lied Chantal. 'He is out with Anthenor. They are both very busy with the care of the estate.'

'Chantal, you look drawn. Is everything all right?'

'Yes, I'm fine, Mother, and all is well. Of course it is.'

She remained closed-faced under her mother's searching

eyes. She would have died before she confessed the truth, that she had been wrong, and that she wished so desperately that it could all be erased and she might return to La Prade. Perhaps, if Chantal had opened her heart and released, sobbing, the floodgates of despair that engulfed her, perhaps her mother would have opened her arms and taken her back. Perhaps . . .

But more likely, Chantal would have heard the accusing 'I told you so' that she feared even more than the cape of leaden sadness that had settled on her shoulders. So, proud – arrogant, even, and she was at a good school for arrogance, at Blazonac! – she casually accepted her mother's gift of eggs, butter, cheese, and half a lamb for roasting, brought in great baskets, covered with starched linen towels, by Pierrot, the farm boy who always accompanied Madame Arondel. We have plenty of provisions, said Chantal's attitude. But since you took the trouble of bringing it here, let's just have Pierrot carry it to the kitchen. Pity you went to all that trouble . . . We'll try to make some use of it, though, since you should not have to lug it all the way back to La Prade.

Anthenor usually left the house at dawn, wandering all day through the rain-drenched woods and farmlands. He had taken the account books back from the steward who had handled the estate business for the Countess. He would do the work himself, he said, and save the ten percent the steward charged. He probably took some meals at the farmhouses – where the fare cannot have been worse than at the château – and he negotiated obscure deals, seldom discussed at home, with lumber merchants, cattle dealers, and moneylenders.

Chantal overheard him, one day, asking Renaud for his signature on a document renegotiating a loan. Need to extend the duration, he said. Renaud signed without looking. Sometimes Anthenor showed up at dinner, most of the time he did not. And when Renaud did not appear at dinner either, then Chantal sat alone at the long table in the freezing dining room, lit by a single dim bulb – all the others having been burned out in the dust-encrusted chandelier and electric bulbs no longer available – and ate watery potato soup, served by Maria, who did not even bother to put on a clean apron for the occasion.

Once or twice Anthenor had come home unexpectedly, in midafternoon, and as Chantal turned from what she was doing, he was there, standing in a doorway, looking at her. Without a flicker of a smile, he would turn and walk away.

Then, one day, he came to the dining-room door, where she was polishing unmatched crystal glasses. He stood there scowling as usual, but Chantal could have sworn she saw a small muscle twitch at the corner of his mouth. He held out a key ring, loaded with heavy keys.

'Do you want to unlock that cabinet over there?'

Chantal remained motionless. Of course she wanted to unlock the cabinet, but admitting it would probably only bring a sneer, and Anthenor would walk away with his keys. So she said nothing.

'Aren't you curious to see what's stored there?'

No answer. But she thought he was smiling at her, and Chantal looked up at his eyes, a dimple quivering on her cheek.

The cabinet revealed treasures. A complete set of hand-painted dishes, green and blue Moustiers faience, at least a century old. Fans, crystal vases, silver snuffboxes, delicate jade and china figurines. Anthenor reached and held out an enchanting enamel bird in a scrolled gilded cage.

'Oh, Anthenor, how lovely!'

'I thought I remembered my mother putting those things away. I am glad I kept these doors locked and the keys in my room. This is why nobody stole it, or took it and sold it.'

Chantal felt as though her fingers were reaching for a small island of the past magic of the château.

A question was on her lips: Who stole? The servants? Renaud? Could Renaud steal something that belonged to him? But she did not ask.

'Would you like to take these dishes out? You can put them on the shelves of the big cabinet, if you think they'll look good. And what about the other things? Would you like to arrange them around the drawing room? It looks a little bare.'

Chantal nodded and looked up gratefully, too overwhelmed for words. Perhaps she wasn't as desperately alone as she had felt all these past weeks – alone even on those infrequent nights when Renaud slipped into her high carved bed and made tight-lipped, remote love to her. She dreaded those, and the unspeakable demands that had left her hurt, humiliated, and sobbing. Did Anthenor want to be a friend? Could there be that much sweetness in the world?

He was holding the caged bird in his hands, frowning. 'It used to play a little tune. I wonder if it's still working. Let's see. Well, it still winds up! I'll put it down on the table.'

The music-box notes tinkled, spaced and crystalline. Slowly, the bird turned on its perch, raised its head. Its beak opened and closed, as a Strauss waltz rang out, clear note after clear note. She looked up. Anthenor's eyes were on her.

'Why are you crying?'

'I am not crying.'

'Would you like the bird for your room? It will be yours.'

Chantal nodded wordlessly, her throat too tight to speak, overwhelmed by a sudden, immense sadness, holding back sobs. In this house, where nothing was hers, where she was a stranger among strangers, Anthenor was making her a gift, a precious object that would belong to her.

She had already understood that Anthenor, and he alone, could dispose of anything in the house. Renaud, heir to the name and title, and who, in fact, owned three quarters of everything, did not feel enough interest even to assert ownership. So, Anthenor's fierce attachment to land and house with all it contained, translated into duty to preserve, and right to give and withhold.

A few days later, Anthenor stopped her in the vestibule.

'I am going to Belmont farm. Do you want to come with me?'

Eagerly she ran to her room, put on her black beret, raincoat, and boots, and caught up with him, already striding down the tree-lined drive, with that long-gaited walk of his.

For a long time, neither spoke, and she had all she could do to keep up with him. One of the farm dogs started to follow them, and Chantal picked up sticks of wood that she threw for him to chase. He would pounce upon them, but refuse to give them back, until she threw another. He then abandoned the first, and ran to chase the next one. A fine cold rain was falling. They walked in silence, Chantal playing with the dog, and running to catch up with Anthenor's long stride.

'Are you glad you married Renaud?' Anthenor said at last, brusquely, not looking at her.

She stopped playing with the dog. She had no answer, none that could be voiced. Surely no one should ever know the truth. It was unspeakable.

'I don't know,' she lied. 'I really don't know . . .'

It would be wrong to speak against her husband. Wives always expressed respect for their husbands, that much she was certain of.

'Come on,' urged Anthenor impatiently. 'Of course you know.'

'Well, I had no idea it would be like this.'

'Why did you marry him then?'

'Because he asked me, and because we were in love . . . I thought,' she added weakly, feeling his eyes hard on her. 'But now I'm not so sure. Is it my fault that he stays away from everything like this? Am I doing anything that displeases him?'

Anthenor gave a short laugh. 'Displeases him? I don't think Renaud cares enough about anything or anybody to be displeased by it, as long as it does not disturb him. And you certainly don't do that.'

A long silence. He was whipping the side of his boot with the riding stick he always carried on his walks.

'No, you don't disturb him, and you don't disturb me. You know, I was against this marriage. Oh, not to you in particular, but against any marriage. Girls are a bother. But I must say that you are different from what I expected . . .'

'Different? How?'

'Oh, you know, not like other girls your age. I thought you'd be prancing around all day, demanding attention, trying to make conversation, fishing for compliments . . . I don't know! Wearing different dresses all the time and pouting if they weren't noticed, and going home to mama to cry. But you are not like that. You don't ask for anything.'

A song was rising in her heart! She had discovered her true calling: She was meant to be a martyr. If Anthenor's words made her so deliriously happy, all despair forgotten, it was because she longed to be admired for the amount of suffering she could bear unflinchingly. Love would come to her out of admiration, gratitude, and the awed realization that she was an exceptional being, quite unlike others, as he had just said. It was the same quality that made Christian martyrs, all martyrs, endure the most awful tortures. For martyrs know, deep in their soul, that they are superior to others, and they are only too glad to be given a chance to show it. Had the good nuns, who praised to the girls the calm resolution of Saint Blandine, thrown to hungry lions, or of Saint Sebastian, pierced with hundreds of arrows, and still proclaiming their faith, had they clearly understood which lesson they were actually teaching their pupils? That such a taste for silent suffering is only the most sublimated form of pride . . . ? An arrogance comparable to none.

Relishing the role she had just found for herself, Chantal said, 'There is nothing to ask for. I want so much to be a good wife! But I am not sure how to go about it. There's so little I can do. So, I am trying to put the house in order, to get some provisions, to make life a little nicer for you and Renaud.'

There. She was no longer forlorn and despairing. She had a role, not forced upon her because of a sin she had committed, but chosen and a noble one. Anthenor was too uncomplicated to understand the profound effect of his clumsy words.

'Life *is* nicer,' he conceded, pushing a branch aside for her, in a caring, uncharacteristic gesture.

Emotion was swirling inside her. Anthenor had said it. She was not like the others . . .

The world had changed; the rain dripping through the barren fronds was no longer freezing, it might as well have been a cool spring drizzle. For a moment, she glimpsed what it was like to be beautiful, and young, and loved. Would Anthenor say more?

No. He had spoken all he had to say. They walked through the winter woods, and she followed him on a long detour that took them to an ugly clearing in the forest, left by lumbering operations.

Many trees had been cut down, sawed into planks, and now all that remained were the raw stumps, wetly red. Sawdust, packed by the rain, was everywhere. Desolation. Anthenor stood silently, counting the stumps with barely moving lips.

'One hundred prime oak trees,' he said, 'cut down three months ago, and at least ten years too soon. Renaud's grandfather planted them, and I have heard he stated they should not be harvested before 1950.' He kicked angrily at a pile of wood chips. 'We needed the money,' he said, teeth clenched. 'My mother had signed some notes, shortly before she died. I obtained an extension on one of them. The oaks paid for half the other.'

He showed Chantal other trees, their trunks marked for the ax with a red stain. 'Two hundred more,' he said. 'To be cut next fall. We sold them to the Blanchard lumber mills. That money went to pay the other half of the note. It will buy us some time.'

At the farm, she met the harried farm wife, not much older than Chantal, but so tired-looking, pregnant, disheveled, and with a small child hiding behind her tattered skirts. She was one of Maria's daughters. She and her husband, woefully shorthanded, worked the Belmont farm.

'This is Countess Chantal, Count Renaud's wife. She is the new Countess now. You will call her "our lady," as you did my mother,' said Anthenor, in his lord-of-the-manor tone. Not a Blazonac, he, but he had learned the manner, and through the Neuvilles on his mother's side, he had inherited enough of the blue to change the tint of the exotic blood that coursed in his veins.

Chantal smiled at the frightened young woman, picked up the child, and pushed the dirty hair out of its eyes. He was scared, too, started to howl, and his mother retrieved him apologetically. Poor girl, thought Chantal, she is impressed by me, she thinks I am somebody important, her mistress the Countess. She doesn't know I am less a mistress in the château than she is in this two-room, earthen-floor cottage. And yet, I am standing next to this tall young man, who wants me along, who thinks I make life nicer, and who says I am different from the others. That I am better, much better. I can suffer proudly, that's why.

They walked back to the château in almost complete silence. Chantal's efforts at conversation met with monosyllabic answers, or none at all. How much money was owed on those notes? Were there other important debts? How much had the sale of the oak trees brought? Anthenor preferred not to tell, grunted, and walked faster. Chantal did not insist. She didn't care that much, anyway, and those matters did not affect her life directly. In any case, she had a mission, and rewards to reap in Anthenor's grudging admiration. With her parents' discreet help, meals became a little better. Chantal discovered sources of supply, and learned to barter with people from the nearby villages. The owner of the grocery wanted to cut firewood in the Blazonac park, and was willing to give a little sugar in exchange, others wanted the right to fish in the upper lake, and traded milk, eggs, and butter. Unconsciously, Chantal was imitating her mother. Her giddy flight from home had foundered close to the nest.

One day, in the almost empty poultry yard, she discovered a hen sitting insistently on the plaster nest egg. A brooding hen! She took the dozen eggs left in a basket in the pantry, and carefully placed them under the warm, soft feathers. The hen settled in, looked at Chantal with satisfaction in her beady eyes, clucked softly, and spread her wings protectively.

'All right,' whispered Chantal to the hen. 'Now don't you let me down. If you do it right, you'll have a dozen chicks by the end of the month.'

Hatching would take twenty-one days, she knew. She marked the date on the calendar in the kitchen, and every day, brought food and water to the hen, who ate and drank without even getting up from the eggs. Twenty-one days later, Chantal ran early to the henhouse, and sure enough: The strongest of the chicks had already broken through its shell, and was standing on unsteady feet, chirping loudly, while its mother was helping others break through. Chantal watched, in fascination, as chick after chick emerged, their down all wet and plastered on skinny little bodies. The mother hen clucked encouragingly, rolled unopened eggs with her beak to help. Only one failed to produce a chick. The hen cracked it open and ate its contents. Then she stood up, staggering on long-unused feet, and rounded up her eleven chicks. Dry by now, they were tiny balls of fluffy yellow down, with black pinpoints for eyes and the loudest chirp. Chantal felt strangely moved.

The hen, walking importantly, and clucking all the time, was scratching the dirt to show her brood where bits of food and gravel could be found. Maria came out of the kitchen, wiping her hands on her old blue apron.

'So that's where you were, our lady,' she exclaimed. 'If

I thought that during my living days I would ever see the Countess kneeling in the poultry yard! Help us all, holy Virgin, Mother of God! It is much too early in the year, and too cold, chicks cannot survive. Mark my word, these will be dead in less than a week. Too cold and damp. Hens should not brood in winter . . .'

But these chicks did survive. When the weather turned bitingly cold again, Chantal rounded them up and herded them into the cavernous kitchen. She fed them dry bread crumbled in milk, and they fought for room around the dish. On a particularly raw day, she found them outside the door almost frozen to death and brought them in. Strong measures were called for. So Chantal warmed some wine in a saucepan, crumbled bread in the warm wine, and put the dish on the floor. The chicks fell all over each other, eating and drinking the heady mixture. Soon, they were staggering drunkenly on the stone floor, and Chantal was laughing so hard that even Maria had to join in. Then, Maria brought out one of Justin's baskets, lined it with an old sack, and put in the drunken chicks, who presently fell asleep, a warm mass of yellow down and pointed beaks. The hen looked disapproving but eventually climbed in and settled on top of them. Sleepy chirps were heard, muffled by maternal feathers.

'They are saved.' Chantal smiled, relieved.

'This is not the way to raise poultry fowl,' grumbled Maria. 'I am sure these chicks will never be roasted. That's not the way Madame Arondel does things at La Prade.'

Maria was right. After that, whenever the weather became cold, or it rained hard, the eleven chicks and their mother would line up at the door, asking and gaining eventual admittance to the kitchen. Hardly a proper barnyard education.

But Chantal had learned something about the secrets of life, and she felt a new power, albeit vague and inchoate, over nature.

Was she learning to be a good wife, a better wife than

others were? A martyr? Would there be gratitude and admiration in people's eyes? In Anthenor's?

No such thing happened. Days evolved into a routine. Renaud was getting up a little more often, though, and sometimes actually talking with her. He discovered that, in school, where she was an excellent student (what else *was* there to do but study, when you were held prisoner in a boarding school?), she had devoured voraciously all the library had to offer and everything that fell under her eyes. In fact, she had already read many of the works he was now plunged in. She could talk about them, even if often to repeat what she had heard in class, where she had been a rapt listener. Renaud would listen to her remarks with a fleeting smile, half amused and half scornful, but the next day she would hear him repeat her exact words, taking full credit for them.

He even attempted to accompany Anthenor and Chantal on visits to the farms and the forest, complaining about the lack of a car, about the hours it took to cover a few miles, and comparing their walking average with his racing performances. After two or three such days, when Renaud announced that he was coming along, Anthenor would somehow disappear and go his own way, and soon Renaud lost interest anyway.

Chantal's efforts, now, were unconsciously meant to please Anthenor, who seemed quite unaware of them. One day, his hand brushed hers, and the slow shiver that ran through her body left her terrified. There she was striving so hard to fulfill her role to perfection, and she thrilled at the touch of her husband's brother! Perhaps, instead of a saint and a martyr, she was meant to be one of those accursed women the nuns had darkly hinted at. They had spoken of adulterous women who loved men other than their husbands. But wasn't this even worse? When was it, and when wasn't it, incest? In any case, thought Chantal, since I am not like the others, perhaps I am one of those who shouldn't have been born, because they brought about

83

scandal, as the Scriptures said. How exciting and frightening . . .

Winter was ending and spring was breaking slowly through the cold. Days were longer now, there was languor and expectation in the air. Some of those early March days were so beautiful, with daffodils and banks of wood violets abloom under the trees in the new soft grass, and a breeze ruffling the surface of the lake. They were days Chantal wanted to hug against her heart.

One evening, Anthenor brought home a large net someone had given him. Chantal recognized it for what it was. Her parents had one just like it that Pierrot spread at night, in the winter and spring, across the inlets of the ponds, to catch pike and perch.

'Let's go out and set the net,' said Anthenor, uncharacteristically eager. 'You know how, Chantal? Come with me.'

Renaud was uninterested, so they went together in the rowboat, as the sun was low. She held the oars to keep the boat in place while he spread the thin net across the mouth of the brook that fed the lake, anchoring it to low branches on the banks. The water was deep and clear, the current steady. There would be fish.

The next morning, they ran downstairs early – was Anthenor waiting behind his door for Chantal's footsteps? – and as they walked across the tall wet grasses, he took her hand playfully and swung it rhythmically. When they leaned side by side to push the boat, he suddenly turned to face her, both of his hands on her waist, and bent his face to hers. Her heart stopped. She waited for his kiss with desperate hunger.

'Chantal,' he stammered, his voice unrecognizable. 'Chantal, I . . .'

The second froze into hours. She remained paralyzed, lips offered, terrified by the intensity of emotion between them. He straightened, ran his hand over his forehead, pushed her away almost roughly.

'Forgive me,' he stammered. 'I don't know what's the matter with me.' A silence. She saw him wet his lips. 'I was afraid you'd fall, that's why I tried to hold you.'

Heart pounding now, flushed, she grabbed at the proffered straw. 'I'm glad you did. It's easy to slip here, especially on the rocks.'

'Let's row to the mouth of the brook,' he muttered, not looking at her. She noticed he was careful to keep his hands far from hers when he passed her the oars.

Lifting the net, he found a half-dozen pike, each maybe ten inches long, all silver and shimmering blue scales, caught by their gills. She saw his hand tremble as he reached for them. She released her emotion with a tentative laugh, and he looked at her gratefully and laughed too.

They proudly brought their catch home and that night, Renaud condescended to come down for dinner, shaved and dressed in a navy blue cashmere sweater mended earlier in the day by Chantal. She'd brushed her hair carefully, put pink lipstick on her lips, rubbed a little on her cheeks, and slipped on the skirt of her wedding suit, with a new natural wool sweater knitted by the girls at La Prade. Anthenor didn't change from his black turtleneck, but Chantal noticed he had scraped the caked mud off his old riding boots.

Two candle stubs were found and lit and the table looked almost festive, set with the Moustiers plates, and a bunch of wood violets and daffodils in a crystal vase. Chantal kept her eyes lowered so she wouldn't meet Anthenor's but thought of nothing but him and his embrace, as Maria served the fish on a great platter, with a sauce Chantal had made with sprouts of herbs just appearing in the garden and a salad of young dandelions, found growing among the weeds.

For music, she'd brought down the bird in its gilded cage, and it turned and sang, its notes scattering a little of the old magic. Does magic die? Or can it just go dormant and wake up again when spring and desire beckon? Was this the old magic, or a new, mysterious one, that strong, invisible current flowing between her and Anthenor?

Renaud was almost enjoying himself, and sneered only a little.

'I always thought a lake was for swimming and boating,' he sneered, 'or for retired railroad employees to sit by on a folding stool with a fishing rod,' he finished lamely.

Nobody listened, Chantal's thoughts full of Anthenor. So Renaud drank several glasses of wine from a barrel Monsieur Arondel had sent earlier, declared it of inferior quality, drank some more, and told his old stories of auto racing and high life in Paris. So carried away was he that he even announced that from now on, he would help with the fishing. He knew better ways to do it. Anthenor said nothing, but he wasn't around the next day, when time came to set the net.

So Chantal looked for Renaud, but he had forgotten his promise and was just settling into the works of Chateaubriand. Not to be disturbed, of course. So she set it alone. The following morning, she went out alone again, listening for Anthenor's footsteps behind her as she walked in the grass by the bank and pushed the boat out as she jumped in. But he didn't come. It was easy to row to the anchored net by herself, but raising it was more difficult. Alone to steady the boat as she lifted the net, she felt the craft tilt dangerously over the mist-strewn water. But she managed it, and again the next day, and often after that.

Sometimes, at night, she'd stand nude before the mirror above the marble fireplace, push her breasts together as in an offering gesture, and repeat to herself, 'Anthenor.' Then, guilt gnawing at her heart, she'd kneel by her bed and recite prayers asking for forgiveness.

It was during that early spring that she began to experience an odd feeling of fatigue. She tried to keep to her routine, but she was constantly overcome by a strange nausea rising in her throat. She became conscious of smells she had never noticed before: the odor of suet in her mother's homemade soap turned her stomach, and she could smell it on her sheets, her towels, everything that had been washed with it. Before, these things had only smelled clean. Now they had to be dealt with cautiously, with pinched nostrils. She could no longer stand the lavender water prepared in La Prade that she used every day after her sponge bath. The sight of the bottle on her toilet stand sufficed to bring on the upset.

Worst of all were Renaud's overflowing ashtrays, and the smell of tobacco wafting through his open door. The tobacco odor settled in his hair, in his clothes, on his skin. It gagged her when he made love to her, so much so that one night, she pushed him away, ran to her basin and vomited. Renaud was disgusted, and stayed away from then on. But the tobacco smell pervaded the house, and she went about breathing carefully through her mouth or holding a handkerchief to her lips.

She finally found that if she went to lie, flat on her back, on the low ivy-covered wall overhanging the lake between the topiary trees now grown shapeless, and breathed slowly, inhaling deeply, trying to think of nothing but the cool clear water flowing just below, the nausea would subside. For the rest of her life, whenever a gagging sensation would come over her, she would just have to think of that low wall, the bitter scent of ivy, the cool water of the lake below, and her throat would loosen, and a great peace overwhelm her.

It was Maria, of course, who guessed first. She questioned 'our lady,' in her respectful but familiar manner, and her diagnosis was clear: The baby would be born in the fall. Chantal did not believe her at first. How could it be? She was only eighteen! How could she have a child? Why, she was as far from having a child as ... And then, the first stirring, an alien, unforgettable feeling. A presence. Another life. She knew.

She said nothing to anyone, but she asked Anthenor if he would, on his next outing, ask Dr Bardon to come by. Dr Bardon was a country doctor, a distant relative of the Arondels. He had attended Madame Arondel at Chantal's birth, and had sat at the bedside of Chantal's grandmother when she died. He was the only physician for miles, still made rounds, riding his bicycle, since his meager allotment of gas had to be saved for emergencies, and she'd be lucky if he would ride the ten miles or so to Blazonac. That evening, she spoke to Renaud and told him how she felt, and what Maria thought.

'So you're going to be sick, and throw up, and complain all the time, is that it?' said Renaud, barely looking up.

Dr Bardon came a few days later, unannounced. Anthenor was out when he arrived, puffing, pushing his bicycle along the drive. But Renaud was home, sitting in the library, surrounded by carelessly piled books. He must have seen the doctor arrive, but he did not come out to greet him. In her high-ceilinged room, lying on her ornate bed, Chantal was examined. Dr Bardon made her remove her underclothes and touched her, to her great embarrassment. Yes, she was pregnant, everything looked normal, she was a healthy girl, though she was much too thin. She should get plenty of rest, drink as much milk as possible. The baby would indeed be born in the fall. Meanwhile, she should see him again about three months hence.

'How's fishing in the lake these days?'

'Well, we have been putting out a net, and we catch pike, small ones, and perch sometimes . . .'

'A net is not the way to get the big ones,' said the doctor, oblivious to Chantal, lying half naked on her bed, trying to cover herself while making casual conversation. 'The big ones are at the bottom, they only come up to feed, it takes a good rod and a lure, with spring flies to get to them. I'll come someday and give it a try, shall I?'

With that, he left the room, went downstairs, where Maria served him a glass of the new homemade quince liqueur in the dining room.

Chantal lay on her bed for a long time, her eyes closed, trying to realize just what the news meant. And then, the stirring came anew, and it was real again, just as it had been a few days earlier, only much stronger now. She

88

folded her arms over her flat stomach – no swelling yet – to enfold the presence living there. She, who was so alone, would now have the full responsibility for another person, a helpless life, whose only hope lay in her care. Was she going to be that wonderful mother her self-image required? Being a great mother, or even just an ordinary one, seemed suddenly so overwhelmingly demanding that she felt panic. I can never do it, she thought. Not me. It's too much.

She waited, but Renaud did not come upstairs. So she went down, and found him still sitting in the library. He did not look up when she came in and spoke. She sat down, forced a smile. She repeated, 'Dr Bardon came.'

'I know,' said Renaud at last, looking up from his book. 'I saw him through the window.'

'You didn't even come out and say hello?'

'No, why should I have? These damn old geezers bore me. I'd have been an hour, getting a report on the health of the whole county, or his fishing prowess.'

'Do you want to know what he said?'

'What he said? About what?'

'About my being pregnant.'

'Oh, that's right. I had forgotten.'

'Well, the baby will be born in the fall.'

'In the fall, then?' said Renaud. 'Well, that gives me plenty of time to move to another room. I'd be disturbed by its crying if I stayed where I am now.'

That was it. Renaud had expressed all his thoughts on the subject. Begging for a display of emotion, love, or concern he did not feel, would get her nothing except, perhaps, if she persisted, some stinging, humiliating retort.

I'll be alone to take care of the baby, thought Chantal without self-pity. Will I know how? Terror swept over her. Please, please, tell me that you'll help me, that someone will help me. All right, not Renaud. Then Providence perhaps? But if Providence heard her silent call, it gave no sign.

Anthenor came home later, and they all three sat down

to dinner. Renaud had brought his book to the table and was reading, ignoring the others. Chantal was timidly trying to stir up some sort of a reassuring celebration, some reaction that would show excitement at her big news, hope . . . love. The meal was a little better than usual, and she had contrived a dessert with eggs, honey, and milk. At the end of the meal, Chantal raised her glass, and said, as lightly and gaily as she could, 'To the blessed event! Anthenor, you will be an uncle in a few months. Isn't that wonderful? Will you help us find a name for a boy, and another one for a girl, just so that we can be prepared?'

Anthenor slowly put down his glass, turned to her. 'You are going to have a child?'

'Yes, it will be born in the fall.'

'Are you happy?'

'I think I am happy, but I'm very frightened too.'

Anthenor looked over to his brother, who was absorbed in his reading. He frowned, then turned back to the trembling girl. 'Don't be frightened, Chantal,' he said slowly, 'I am here.'

5

NAUSEA CEASED AFTER a few months, and for a while Chantal was suffused with a feeling of tired well-being. She could no longer ride her bicycle, and she spent most afternoons sitting in a wicker chair under a linden tree buzzing with bees by the bank of the lake. She worked on a layette, sewing baby clothes cut out of some old-fashioned petticoats she had found folded in a wicker trunk in the linen room. No fabric was to be had in shops, of course, or any ready-made items, or even proper knitting yarn. Her pregnant-woman ration stamps entitled her to a few skeins of ersatz, or 'national' wool, as it was called, brownish and coarse, which she spurned. Instead, she brought out the bulky oversize white sweater she had worn at school after tennis, unraveled it carefully, winding the yarn on a wooden paddle. Washed, dried, and rolled into a huge ball, it gave her the substance for half a dozen baby sweaters. So small . . .

One afternoon, Anthenor brought down from the attic the cradle that had been last used for Renaud and himself. He put it down in the vestibule, a ghostly relic, hung with limp folds of age-grayed lace. But a shaft of sunlight came to rest on it.

Maria scrubbed it and, inspired, produced from somewhere an old, torn lace curtain. Chantal cut out the good parts, made a new cradle skirt, hemmed it, washed and starched it, so that it fell around the wickerwork in ethereal folds. Soon, the old cradle fluttered with hope for a new life. When it had been brought up to her room, set next to her high carved bed, she began thinking of the baby as a person, whose head would lie on the small lacy pillow. And the panic that still rose within her was now mitigated by an anxious desire to feel the tiny body resting in her arms.

Late one afternoon, she heard the clatter of hooves on the drive, and the sound of rolling wheels. A horse and cart turned the gate into the courtyard and stopped smartly at the foot of the stone stairs. She ran outside. Anthenor stepped out and met her. He had found the horse, with its custom-made cart, for sale in the village, and he had acquired it, through some complicated barter that he did not spell out.

'This is for you. We can all use it, of course, but I got it especially for you. This way, you can go into the village for groceries, or visit your mother, even on occasion go to Montbron or La Rochefoucauld, if you leave early enough in the morning. Both are not much more than ten miles away. Do you like it?'

'I have never been so excited. It will change my life. But I've never driven a horse cart.'

'I'll show you how. Here, climb in. Careful, don't hurt yourself. All right? Take the reins, give them a little shake, and say "*Hue.*" That's good.'

'But he's not moving . . .'

'Shake harder, and click your tongue, like this.' Anthenor took the reins, his hands over hers, leaning over her, and the small horse started trotting, at a sedate little trot, with a delicate prancing of the hooves and shaking of the head. The cart was light, a single seat just for two, called a dogcart, with a wraparound backrest, and mounted on two wheels, no larger than a bicycle's. After a brisk trot down the carriage drive, Anthenor showed her how to rein in the horse to a stop, and they returned to the château, Chantal holding the reins, laughing, dimples in both cheeks, and Anthenor almost smiling. Their excited calls failed to bring Renaud down into the court.

After that, Chantal found some reason every day to have Paulin harness the horse, whose name was Bijou, and she would trot off on her errands, beret replaced with a wide straw hat as the weather became warm and sunny.

She learned about horses in general and Bijou in particular. Bijou was skittish. As a matter of fact, Anthenor later found out he came from a circus that was being disbanded, unable to feed its animals, and that he was better schooled in tricks than in regular working habits. Chantal also discovered, on her first trip to La Rochefoucauld, the only nearby town large enough to have store windows, that, terrified by his own image in the glass, he would whinny, rear up, and walk backward. Making him drink was tricky, since he was spooked by his own reflection in the still water of the trough. He would only drink if someone stood by, stirring the water with a stick so no image could form. Anthenor theorized that Bijou must have been attacked during his circus days, by other, larger horses, and that he learned to fear the sight of a horse.

After Chantal had mastered Bijou's equine idiosyncrasies, the horse and cart did change her life. She began to feel a little like a castle lady, sitting on the green leather cushion, the broad-brim straw hat on her head, clattering in and out of the carriage court. Sometimes, on the drive, she would catch up with Anthenor, out on one of his own errands. These cannot all have been very important, because, on occasion, he would climb in and take the reins from her. Then, snapping them smartly, clicking his tongue, he would send the horse into a much brisker trot. They would bring home the few provisions available at the village grocery store, in exchange for food stamps: ersatz coffee, gray macaroni, small cubes of margarine.

One day, the woman who kept the shop, looking left and right to make sure no one was looking, reached under the counter and gave them a packet of chocolate powder. Chantal would remember the cup of hot chocolate they made that afternoon as the most extravagant treat of her life. It had been more than a year since she had tasted chocolate, or candy, or cake. She had almost forgotten the indescribable taste of chocolate, and the first spoonful burst like dark velvet ecstasy. Anthenor drank his own cup with silent concentration, but the shared pleasure brought Chantal to the verge of tears. A cup carried to Renaud, reading in bed in his new room, at the end of the east wing, remained cold and untouched all day. And when Chantal went to collect it, and found cigarette ashes in the saucer, and more floating on the surface of the liquid, she clenched her teeth in frustration.

It was as hard to share the small pleasures of life with Renaud as it was to involve him in its momentous events.

One hot afternoon, a sputtering sound sent chickens from the poultry yard scattering and squawking. Clouds of dust, hiccuping roars announced a car! A car! These had become so rare that the residents of Blazonac seldom saw any, and none pulled into the carriage court. Gas had practically disappeared, and only those who had the foresight to hoard a large quantity might hope to use their car. Even *they* had to obtain a public necessity permit, and to exercise care, for informers were everywhere.

But the car that pulled to a shuddering stop that day wasn't burning gasoline. It was one of the first of the many gazogene-equipped cars that the wartime fuel restrictions were to bring to the landscape of those years.

A huge iron box, like a large trunk pierced with holes, was clamped onto the roof, and filled with layers of wood chips and charcoal. No spur-of-the-moment outings! Several hours before any planned departure, a fire had to be lit in the box. Incomplete combustion of the fuel, fed by a controlled intake of oxygen – limited by the size of the holes in the box and that of the narrow chimney – would produce a combustible gas that large tubes, snaking down and creeping under the hood, fed into the cylinders. In turn, and following subtle adjustments of the ignition system, the engine would eventually cough to life, lurch and rattle, and, after proddings of the choke, would, if all went well, produce speeds of ten to fifteen miles per hour, with acrid smoke streaming out of the holes in the iron box.

Having received the necessary permit, Monsieur Arondel took his Citroën out of its hiding place under the haystack, and, the contraption installed, was soon chugging along the narrow dirt roads, accompanied everywhere by the trusted Pierrot, whose function it was to rattle the car vigorously at intervals, and to restoke the fire from the provision of finely chopped wood that filled the trunk.

Madame Arondel viewed the whole enterprise disapprovingly, and insisted her husband should not drive out on Fridays, because Friday was the day the baker made his rounds to distribute the ever-decreasing ration of bread to the isolated farms in the area. He'd be out with his own gazogene, and *two* cars lumbering on those country roads, now that was courting a collision! Monsieur Arondel manfully pooh-poohed her fears and recklessly set off on a Friday . . .

Sure enough, moments later, the collision did occur, knocking the cumbersome gazogene off the top of the Citroën and sending it rolling into the ditch in a shower of ashes and cinders. Pierrot had jumped off just in time; the car itself wasn't damaged. Monsieur Arondel wasn't hurt, just shaken and humiliated, and the baker escaped unscathed, but Madame Arondel had her moment of triumph!

'I told you so,' she said, a dozen times in so many words, thousands more times by the look in her eyes.

A team of oxen from the farm hauled the disabled Citroën home, and Pierrot secured it again under the haystack, in the big barn.

But on that summer day of 1941, the new contraption was bringing visitors to Blazonac, a rare event. Monsieur André Brousse, florid and fortyish, owner of a large dairy in the area, a longtime friend of the 'old' Countess and a widower, had just remarried, and was bringing his new wife around to meet the local gentry.

Cécile was a small, lithe, exuberant woman, with

delicate features, smartly dressed, with smoothly coiffed dark hair. She jumped out of the car, and opened her arms to Chantal. 'I was told Count Renaud married a beauty, that's why I pestered André until he brought me to Blazonac. I am glad to meet you. You are every bit as pretty as I thought you'd be.'

Chantal was entranced by the rare compliment and she raptly listened to Cécile, who talked animatedly and nonstop. Monsieur Brousse was proud of her and happy to sit and watch the effect she produced. Renaud soon ambled off, without so much as an apology, and Anthenor, who arrived in the midst of the visit, stood awkwardly near the door, unsure whether he should sit or might slip away unseen. Chantal frowned and showed him a chair with a lift of her eyebrows.

'Oh, no,' continued Cécile, after introductions, 'I am not from this area at all. I am from Paris, a true born-and-bred Parisian! I only came to live in the country because of the war. Life in Paris is too hard, now. When I hear people around here complain about food restrictions, I want to laugh! Why, in the country, it's always possible to find something. But in Paris . . .'

More talk of food, thought Chantal, don't people *ever* think of anything else?

Cécile took a sip of the garden-grown chamomile tea Maria had just served. Anthenor was engaged in a discussion with André about the price of cattle and how one could manage to sell a few head outside the watchful eye of the German authorities.

'The city is plunged into total darkness. It is so that enemy planes cannot see enough from above to locate the cities and bomb them. No lights may show from the outside, all windows have been fitted with blackout curtains, thick, dark blue cotton. The few cars in the streets – mostly German army vehicles – have had their headlights painted in the same opaque blue, with only a narrow strip of glass left bare, for the driver to see.'

'I know,' interrupted Chantal timidly. 'I drove a truck

like that once. It was during the last days of June last year when the Germans were advancing.'

Cécile was too taken up with her own story to pay much attention to Chantal's.

'You did? Well, then you know. In the country, I am sure it's easier. The moon gives a little light. But in Paris! With the tall buildings . . . Of course there are no street-lights. It's very difficult to find one's street in the dark, or the entrance to the few métro stations that are still open.'

Chantal refilled the teacups. Cécile pulled a compact from her purse, checked her face, patted her hair.

'And then there is the curfew . . . When I left Paris, it was at nine p.m., but it can be earlier, seven, six even, the Germans decide. If you are still out by then, it is better to spend the night where you are, rather than risk being stopped by a patrol.'

'What do they do to you then?' breathed Chantal.

'I know because it happened to me. Well, they took me to their neighborhood Kommandantur, checked my papers, searched me, and asked a million questions. Then they put me in a room together with the other luckless Parisians they'd arrested that night and gave us work to do. Sometimes, it's boots to shine, I've heard. The night I was picked up, they brought in bags and bags of potatoes that we had to peel, all night, for their canteen, I suppose.

'At five in the morning, when curfew was lifted, an officer walked in, resplendent in uniform and polished leather, and stood there, looking over our miserable group, knee-deep in potato peels. Then his eyes stopped on me. Disheveled as I was, I was still the prettiest of the bunch, so he slowly pulled a bill out of his wallet and threw it disdainfully onto the table in my general direction. "For a fresh manicure, mademoiselle," he said.'

Chantal gasped. So this was another one of the ways you knew you'd lost the war – small, gratuitous humiliations. What would I have done in her place? she wondered. Aloud, she asked, 'Did you take the money? How could you refuse it?'

Cécile's face was very serious. 'Listen,' she said, 'it may be that years from now I'll tell the story differently and claim I threw it in his face. But the fact is that, with all those French people's eyes on me, I reached for the bill and pulled it with my sleeve to the edge of the table as though I'd slip it in my pocket. Then, *after* and only *after* he had left, I pushed it over the edge and ground it into the peels with my heel when I stood up to leave. That's about as heroic as you can afford to be these days . . . at least in the open.'

'And once you were released in the street, were the others proud of you?'

'Some were, but there was one very angry couple who berated me saying I could have caused terrible trouble for all of us and they had a good mind to go into the Kommandantur and report me. I don't suppose they did, but after that, I just didn't have any more heart to stay in Paris.'

'So what did you do?'

'Well, I found a way to cross into the Free Zone at La Rochefoucauld. Then I rented a room in a village. A few days later, I went to look for a job, just something to do until things are normal again. The first place I went to was the Brousse dairy, since I'd heard they needed a secretary. I met André and . . . well, isn't he a dear? We are very happy and guess what? He never did find out I can't type.'

Both girls laughed.

Cécile was in her early thirties, a sometime actress, dancer and singer. She told an admiring Chantal she'd sung in cabarets and on the radio, danced in vaudeville shows, toured the country with a summer stock company. She hinted conspiratorially that she had danced nude in shows racier even than those at the famous Folies-Bergère. She told lighthearted tales of her life as a single, pretty woman in prewar Paris.

Chantal was enraptured. She knew nothing of that world. She had spent her vacations at home at La Prade, sometimes a few weeks in a family resort at the beach of the nearby Atlantic coast. The last few summers before the war had been in another boarding school near Brighton, in England, where her school sent girls who needed to perfect their English to qualify for the all-important – and now so useless to her – *baccalauréat*. She had been through Paris a few times then, in transit to the boat train to England. Oh, she had seen the monuments, even the Bastille Day parade, but she had never, in any way, participated in the city's existence.

Cécile's life was the sort where you slept late, then dressed and made yourself beautiful for your work. The idea of a job that required you to pay attention to your appearance was new to Chantal, and it enchanted her.

'And you know,' Cécile went on, delighted with the total admiration she read in Chantal's intent face, 'so many men! When you are, like me, in the public eye, on display, so to speak, they flock like bees to honey. There was no night that I wasn't taken out to dinner, to some elegant restaurant. Champagne flowed. There was one man in particular, quite a bit older, but so charming! And rich. I was mad about him.'

Cécile's voice trailed off.

'Yes?' said Chantal. 'What became of him? The war?'

'In a way, yes. He was Jewish, you see, so he had to leave. I never heard from him again. The last time I saw him, he said he was going to try and get to America. But I don't know whether he made it or not.'

'I know a young man who wanted to go to America. Perhaps he was Jewish too,' ventured Chantal, the memory of her big adventure stirring again in her mind. But Cécile was so caught up in her own story that Chantal dropped it.

'No, you could not call Nathan young,' Cécile went on. 'But generous, and so kind. Well . . .'

As she went on with her irrepressible chatter, Chantal gathered that Nathan had represented Cécile's main source of income, and that with him gone, leaving her compromised by her association with him, she had found it better to leave Paris and make her way into the Free Zone.

'You know, though' – Cécile sighed – 'in some ways, even with the war and the Occupation and all it brings, Paris can still be fun. Black market is everywhere and if you have money, you don't pay any attention to food stamps. You can get anything you want for a price: lobster, caviar, champagne, clothes, oh! the clothes you can get, because the couturiers still have fabric allotments. Night-clubs are still open, full of German officers, mostly in civilian clothes. They want to have fun, too, they're not any happier about the war than we are.'

'Except that they won it,' interrupted Chantal. 'That makes a difference!'

Cécile shrugged and went on. 'Now, at closing time, since that is long after curfew, the waiters put mattresses right on the dance floor and people sleep there rather than venture out with the German patrols on the streets. You can only guess what goes on. Or so I've heard,' she added quickly, afraid she might shock her naive new friend.

Far from being shocked, Chantal was absorbed in thought: so, you could be found desirable, be chosen, wanted even, not because of anything hard you did, like sacrificing yourself to others, but just because of the way you looked? You could choose the men you liked? Say no? Even say yes, perhaps? Clothes mattered? It wasn't sinful to want to look pretty? It was quite possible to earn a living by singing, playacting, dancing . . . even showing your body, God forbid! The world was opening up.

'There are still cafés, you know, sidewalk cafés just like before the war, even if they haven't got much they can serve openly. People walk in the streets. The city isn't dead during the day.'

'You must be so bored in the country! How do you survive?' asked Chantal politely.

'Well, I am glad I met you. I was tired of seeing only old people. André's mother, his aunts, their friends . . . André told me Renaud had married a very young and lovely girl, so I bothered him until he brought me. He was right. You are very pretty and you know, you could be even prettier . . .' She examined Chantal. 'You could use some of that chamomile tea to lighten your hair, all around your face. It's easy, you'll see. It would set off your blue eyes. You must have been white-blond as a little girl. You could bring it back. By the way, when are you expecting your child?'

Chantal had not thought of much else other than her expected child for several months, but Cécile had now thrown windows open for her.

That night, standing in front of the gilt mirror above the white marble fireplace in her room, she wound up the music box, and as the bird slowly turned and sang its tune, carefully avoiding looking at her swollen waist, she leaned close and examined her face. Yes, she did have bright blue eyes, and a mass of unruly dark blond hair, pushed behind her ears. She fluffed it out around her face, wet her lips. Tomorrow she would wash it in a strong chamomile infusion.

Through Cécile and André, who now came often to call, news of the outside world seeped in. André had acquired one of the illicit shortwave radios, which Cécile had hidden inside the piano. Every evening, they would catch the French-language broadcast of the London BBC. Cécile would sit at the piano, stop playing just long enough to catch a few sentences, play again, stop and listen. This way, anybody watching through the window could see her at the keyboard, peering at her sheet music, with her husband standing by, attentively turning the pages for her. No one could hear the tinny voice speaking of events that were to change the world.

'But it's dangerous to listen to the BBC! If anybody reported you, you'd be in serious trouble,' said Anthenor, interested at last. 'I have been wanting to get a shortwave myself, I know someone who has one to sell, but I'm afraid it's a ploy, and he'll report me if I buy it. What do you think?'

Quite uncharacteristically, fat André Brousse, who had never paid much attention to politics before, had become passionate over the war that was continuing between England and Germany. He was a 'Gaullist,' he said, and that was the first time Chantal heard the word.

'De Gaulle, that colonel who left France and rallied England last year, when Pétain signed the Armistice, is our only hope.'

'Well,' said Anthenor, 'he was condemned to death for treason in absentia. It *is* treachery for an officer to abandon his own army and his country and go over to another, isn't it?' he added hesitantly.

'Not at all,' cried André Brousse, lowering his voice after a warning gesture from his wife, 'not at all. De Gaulle is not the traitor you have heard about. He's our only hope, I tell you.'

'But the German Luftwaffe is bombing England out of existence, isn't it?'

'Yes, the bombings are fierce, but nowhere as terrible as the German press would have it. The destruction hasn't broken the spirit of the English or stopped their war effort. The war is far from over, I tell you, this is only a period, a transition we have to live through. But the final battle, says Churchill, will be fought in Germany by the Americans and the Russians.'

Everyone knew, of course, through the official radio broadcasts and through the German-controlled press, that the German army had invaded Russia and that its advance had been swift and victorious. There were pictures in the paper of hordes of Russian prisoners, hands behind their heads, surrounded by helmeted German soldiers; disabled tanks, stamped with the star of the Red Army, swarming with laughing German soldiers giving victory signs.

'Well,' said André, who now came almost weekly to call, and whose visits seemed expected by Anthenor, 're-member Napoléon? He, too, advanced as far as Moscow, marching all summer, and when he arrived, the terrible Russian winter was already setting in. His troops, camped on a hillside overlooking the city, saw its golden onion domes glistening in the setting sun. They entered it the next day, but then fires broke out everywhere, the entire city went up in flames, they were driven out into the snow, starving troops dying of cold and exposure along the way. It was General Winter who defeated Napoléon, and he is still around to defeat Hitler.'

'Surely, it's different now,' murmured Anthenor. 'Armies are motorized and there's air power, and—'

'A motorized army will be no help in winter when fuel and even oil freeze hard as rock. History will repeat itself . . .'

And there was more, he said. 'The alliance between England and the United States is tightening. Enormous amounts of American matériel are now pouring from transport ships into English harbors.'

'But the United States have not entered the war?'

'Not yet, not yet. But they will. You see' – and André lowered his voice and made sure nobody was within earshot – 'you see, there's going to be a war between the United States and Japan. I have it from persons in very high places.'

Cécile was nodding enthusiastically.

'What does that mean to us?' Anthenor was puzzled, but eager to look farther through that window that was opening onto his narrow world.

'Well, don't you see? Japan will be on the side of Germany, and the United States will line up with England, and probably with Russia. It will be their war too. They'll be sending troops, their air force. Germany will be smashed. At that time, under the leadership of de Gaulle, we will be part of the victorious Allies.'

'Listen, Anthenor,' said André Brousse when the two men were alone, one day. 'There are Resistance groups being formed all over. They're in contact with London and they're just waiting for instructions to start fighting.'

'Who are they?'

'There are all kinds of people in the Resistance. Some

are just patriotic, others are Communists, hunted down by the Nazis, others are Jews who are trying to save their lives, especially since the new laws.'

'What laws?' asked Anthenor, suddenly alert.

'You really *are* cut off from everything, at Blazonac,' exclaimed André. 'You haven't heard that laws have been passed in the Occupied Zone – and I don't doubt for a moment the same will apply in this zone the moment the Germans find it expedient – that discriminate against the Jews? They have to register, and they cannot work or receive ration stamps. Annihilation of the Jews is Hitler's goal.'

Anthenor was silent. André moved closer to him.

'Anthenor, some people here don't even remember that your mother remarried and your name is not Blazonac, like Renaud. I have heard it said your father is – was – Jewish . . .'

'Yes,' said Anthenor, slowly, 'yes. My father is Jewish. His full name is Samuel Sepharad. His people are Sephardic, from Asia Minor, I think, and his father came from Smyrna and settled in Marseilles. My parents were divorced when I was a baby, and I don't usually talk, or even think about it. It means so little to me, and Blazonac means so much. My life is here, now and forever. You will see what I'll do with the estate when—'

André interrupted him. 'You said "is," speaking of your father. He is alive, then?'

'He was before my mother became ill and died. She told me not to repeat it, but now I don't suppose it matters. Anyway, there are enough rumors around, you should know the truth. He is insane. He had a history of violence when they were married, but he grew worse after they separated. His brother had him committed, and as far as I know, he is still there.'

'Do you know where?'

'It's a private hospital near Paris for incurable psychopaths. He was perfectly fine, you know, until he became addicted to morphine after being wounded during the last war,' added Anthenor defensively. 'Hey, don't look at me like that. This is not hereditary madness. My mother told me that when they separated, since she was, at the time, very wealthy, she had settled a large sum on him in order to obtain a swift divorce, and that's the money that keeps him in the hospital. At least it was the case four or five years ago.'

'No chance he might have recovered?'

'I doubt it. My mother said he lived in a padded cell, throwing himself at the walls when the seizures overcame him. He had lost the use of speech, did not recognize anybody. He's probably dead by now.'

'Do you have any feeling for him?'

'Me?' said Anthenor, surprised. 'No. I have nothing to do with him, and I don't even know his people. They broke off with him when he married my mother because she wasn't of their faith.'

'Nevertheless,' said André, gently, 'in the eyes of the Germans, you are fifty percent Jewish, and that makes you a Jew. So you'll be subject to the racial laws when they start to enforce them here. And I doubt it will be long.'

Anthenor was standing there, long-legged, frowning, straight blond hair falling into his eyes. It was true he had never thought much about his birth. He had always lived as a Blazonac, the son of the Countess, who had been born Marie-Esmée de Neuville in another château not far off. His identity was changing in his own mind, in a turmoil of conflicting emotions.

'Then you think,' he said after a while, 'you think I should perhaps be forced, someday, to join those Resistance groups, if only to save my life?'

'No harm in meeting the leaders,' said André. 'Come to Le Maine some evening, late, and I'll introduce you. They'll tell you better than I can just what they are doing. If the time comes, when you feel you want to join other young men in a cause that will help the country and save you at the same time, you'll know where they are.

Meanwhile, you know the woods around here well, you could be of help someday soon.'

André shifted his feet, stood up, walked to the window, looked out into the empty carriage yard, cleared his throat. There was something else he had to tell Anthenor, but that would be difficult to say, unless, of course, it turned out Anthenor already knew.

'I haven't seen your brother in some time.'

Anthenor was lost in his own thoughts.

'I said, I haven't seen your brother in some time. I hope he's all right.'

Anthenor looked up. 'Renaud? He's all right. Of course he is. It's just that he's been going out a lot more these days. Does him good to get out.'

'You know where he goes?'

'No. Walking around, I suppose. He needs to pay more attention to the estate. I hope he's taking an interest and I'll be able to count on him a little someday. After all, three quarters of everything is his.'

A silence. Suddenly, it dawned on Anthenor that André was trying to tell him something and could not bring himself to utter the words.

'Look, André, I'll come clean. I know Renaud has been out pretty late at night. I've been wondering myself where he goes.'

'Does his wife know?'

'Chantal knows nothing. He sleeps at the other end of the château and I don't think she sees him very often. Do *you* know?'

André stood up. 'It's getting late. I'll collect my wife. She and Chantal must have exhausted the subject of babies, clothes, Paris under the Occupation and whatever else it is they talk about all the time. I can't tell you, Anthenor, but keep an eye open, and urge your brother to be very careful. He's playing a dangerous game.'

They went to Chantal's room, and as they opened the door, Cécile was saying excitedly, 'And then the war will be over. We will have won!'

'What will happen, then?'

'*Everything* will happen,' cried Cécile. 'Things will go back to what they were before. Better even! There will be food in the stores, butter, sugar, coffee, chocolate, soap, pastries, candies. There will be perfumed shampoos, remember? There will be stores full of clothes to buy at regular prices, not black market. There will be shiny new cars in showrooms, plenty of gas, everything you could want. There will be dancing and summers at the beach . . .'

All the coast of France was then off-limits to the population. German pillboxes and casemates dotted the flat coast, like gigantic concrete turtles, their swiveling guns trained seaward. Chantal remembered carefree past summers at the beach.

So, she thought, the war will end. So what? What will all that mean to me? It will not change Blazonac much. There will still be those dirty, dark corners, and huge empty shelves and closets, and the damp, and the cold, and dust settling everywhere. Even when the world spills over with things to buy, we won't have money to buy them with. Cars? clothes? travel? when the estate was producing so little and was riddled with debts, inexorably swollen each year by their unpaid interest?

Cécile – with or without André – would probably return to Paris after the war. All right. But me? Don't make me laugh. Armies might come and go, but *she* would remain. She would stay there, ignorant of all but the routine of her impoverished household, living only to the rhythm of the seasons, life passing her by. What could possibly change? Renaud was becoming even more absent, and seldom bothered now to tell her his fantastic tales of automobile racing and fashionable, flat-chested women. Once, hoping to get some conversation going, she asked, 'What color was your Bugatti?'

He did not bother to look up, just shrugged wearily. 'It was any color I want it to be. No color at all, perhaps. That is strictly up to me.'

Was Renaud even giving up his dream world? Did conjuring up the *merveilleux* of his private epic require too much energy? Or was he using his limited reserves elsewhere?

She knew Renaud had started going out often, alone, usually in the late afternoon. When he came home, she did not know. He could come back through the small door in the east tower, and she did not hear. But often now he wasn't in his room at dinnertime. She gave it little thought. He was probably imitating Anthenor, walking through the woods, eating dinner here and there, and more probably, not eating at all.

And where would Anthenor be? Would he stay in Blazonac that he loved with such dark passion, and bring a wife to the château? Everyone recognized him as the real owner. He knew how to talk to farmers, cattle- and lumber dealers, and in spite of his youth and inexperience, he had earned some measure of grudging respect. Yet was it just wishful thinking, or was he becoming more solicitous these days, almost concerned, in his aloof and brusque way, about her welfare and that of her unborn child? So what? What could that change for her?

When they sat down to dinner that night, Renaud wasn't in his room, and Maria said, with pursed lips, that she had seen him leave earlier. Anthenor frowned, looked narrowly at Chantal, said nothing.

After dinner, they sat in the garden, under the linden tree, watching dragonflies buzz the flat leaves of water lilies that grew in the shallow water of the lake, transparent over golden pebbles near the bank. It was still daylight, but the days were getting shorter. On the far side of the lake, where the bank was steep, the tall pine trees reflected in deep dark water. Chantal sat on her usual chair, and Anthenor reclined on the grass nearby, throwing pebbles in the water.

'I have thought of names – one boy's and one girl's – and I will tell you after the child is born,' he said, not looking at her. 'Who will the godmother be?'

'I don't know. I thought Cécile, perhaps.'

'No, Cécile is not one of us. She doesn't belong here. As

soon as things get better, she'll probably go away, or else she will have other things to do. You must pick someone who will always be here.'

'My mother, then. I don't know anybody else. But shouldn't a godmother be younger than the parents, so she'll be there after they die?'

'We all die young in our family,' said Anthenor. 'Madame Arondel will make a good godmother. She is solid, and she will always be here. The child will need someone like that.'

'What about the godfather?' asked Chantal.

'I'd like to be the godfather. I'll look after the child and after you, too. I swear I'll keep Blazonac going, and someday, God help me, I will buy back the lands we sold. I'll reforest the woodlands, restore the château to what it should be.'

'What about Renaud?'

A silence. 'I wish Renaud were dead,' said Anthenor at last, flatly and evenly, taking careful aim at a dragonfly with a pebble.

6

CHANTAL HAD SEWN neat piles of white baby clothes, and she had smoothed the new batiste sheets she had just cut from a long-discarded curtain and sewn for the wicker cradle. She was checking the freshly waxed inlaid parquet floor in her room for traces of dust, when her mother came in from La Prade, bringing in some last-minute supplies for the birth. Madame Arondel laughed. 'The nesting instinct – it means your time is near.' She asked, after a while, 'Where is Renaud?'

But she did not wait for an answer – charitably so. She had long ago discovered the truth about Renaud. Perhaps she had always known it, at least since Chantal's marriage, some of it before. How long could it have taken her to discover what her daughter thought she was so cleverly hiding? Renaud could not always be away on business, or sick with a cold, or busy with the farms. Little by little she understood his unspeakable withdrawal, the helplessness of her daughter's despair. But she never spoke a word of it, and they kept, to each other as well as to everyone else, the proud pretense that all was well. 'Yes, my daughter made a fine marriage to the young Count of Blazonac. They are staying in the country for the duration, and he manages the estate. She is busy running the château . . .'

Her eyes sometimes told Chantal that while self-pity was out of the question, still *she* pitied her, but she respected her daughter's dignity by remaining silent too.

A little later in the morning, sharp new pains. Madame Arondel went downstairs, found Anthenor in the kitchen. He ran out to send for the doctor.

Fortunately for me, thought Chantal, I won't be attended

by old Dr Bardon. He had died a few months earlier and been replaced by a younger man, Dr Vincent.

Dr Vincent was bluff, hearty, a sportsman who played tennis and rugby, and who had come with the reputation of bringing daring new medical techniques. He was in favor of 'painless' childbirth, people said, and he would give chloroform for that newfangled, magical 'twilight sleep' in the last stages of labor.

He arrived, astride his motorcycle, carrying the fishing rods he had inherited from Dr Bardon.

'It's not for a couple of hours yet,' he declared, after a hasty examination. 'I'll be out on the lake. Will you join me, Count Renaud? I'll need somebody to row the boat while I cast.'

Renaud mustered up enough energy to accompany the doctor out on the lake. Anthenor was in his room, door ajar. Chantal's mother stood by her bed, giving her water to drink and counting the time between contractions on the gold watch at the end of a chain around her neck.

After a while, Maria came in, her hair freshly combed, in a clean black dress and white apron, carrying a folded receiving blanket. When Renaud was born, she had received him in this blanket, and Anthenor, too, just a few years later. She had washed it and put it away with her own things all those years, but now the time had come to use it again.

'I am glad you saved this blanket, Maria,' Madame Arondel said. 'You must stay with the Countess, and you will be the one to receive the child when it is born.'

Maria was pleased, but experience had taught her that any expression of happiness or pleasure was liable to bring the jealous anger of Providence to bear on her. So she remained silent, pursed lips betraying no emotion. Something was bothering her, though. Another hour passed.

'The child will not be born,' she told Madame Arondel, 'until all the knots in this house are untied. I have gone through all the rooms untying anything that was tied, but now,' she said severely, 'you must untie your shoelaces.'

'I've heard those old wives' tales before, Maria,' shrugged Madame Arondel. 'Don't be silly.'

Maria had had her twelve children, all without help except for the first, when her mother-in-law had been in attendance. After that one, she told Chantal, she would keep working in the fields alongside her husband until the pains came close after one another. Then, she walked home unattended to give birth. She kept a pair of scissors handy by her bed to cut the umbilical cord. Once, during a heavy harvest season, she had even walked back to the fields afterward to finish the day's work, having swaddled the child and placed it in the wall-hung cradle, safe from dogs and cats. All her deliveries had been easy, because she made sure there were no knots in her house.

She kept muttering to herself and staring at Madame Arondel's shoes. Contractions had been coming very close, but nothing happened.

'Well, if it makes you happier,' conceded Madame Arondel at last, 'I will certainly untie my shoelaces. Here, I'll just tuck them in. Are you satisfied now?'

An instant later, a violent pain tore through Chantal, and she cried out. Was Maria right?

'Go ring the dinner bell, Maria,' ordered Madame Arondel. 'The doctor must come now.'

But the doctor was in the process of reeling in a large pike, and shouted that he'd be in soon.

The pains had become terrible, wrenching. Maria twisted some towels around the bedposts and gave Chantal the ends to hold on to. 'Pull, our lady, pull as hard as you can, then hold on tight as you give a push!'

She knelt by the bed and prayed, 'Holy Mary Mother of God who gave birth to Jesus in a manger . . .'

Chantal pulled and pushed. Holding on to the towels brought a little relief, since they gave some leverage against the immense effort. Another hour passed. Chantal was writhing in pain, bathed in perspiration, but no progress was made.

'The doctor must come now,' urged her mother. 'Right

now. Maria, please go ring the bell again, and call out to him.'

This time, it was Renaud who called back impatiently from the rowboat that they'd be along any time now. 'Just don't make so much noise,' he warned. 'It will scare the fish away.'

More time passed. Chantal had been in labor for hours. Drenched in sweat yet shivering with cold, she was suddenly wrenched by a pain more searing than the rest and she screamed. At that moment, Anthenor's door was pushed violently, slamming against the wall, and he ran downstairs, carrying the hunting rifle he kept hidden in his closet. He ran to the bank of the lake, and taking aim, shot at the water a few feet from the boat.

'You get out here, you son of a bitch,' he shouted at the doctor. 'Next shot, I aim straight at you.'

Renaud, cursing his brother, rowed the boat ashore and the doctor jumped out, raced upstairs, and after a look at Chantal, announced, 'This birth is overdue by hours, now! Why didn't somebody call me? It doesn't look good . . . I'll have to use the forceps. I could give her chloroform but . . . Where the hell? Damn it, I forgot to bring any. No matter. She'll be all right, she's young and strong. There'll be some tearing of tissue, but I'll sew her up as good as new.'

The baby, a seven-pound girl, was born with the red crescent marks of the forceps on her temples.

Chantal lost consciousness during the stitching of the perineal tear. When she came to, her little girl was resting in the lace-skirted cradle by her side. She was dark-haired and so small. Chantal looked at her anxiously, but she could see nothing of Renaud in her liquid bluish eyes. The baby yawned, tiny pink mouth and toothless gums, and she tightly closed her fist on her mother's finger. The bed had been changed, Chantal's hair had been combed. Her own mother's reassuring presence nearby made everything secure. Both she and the baby, exhausted, slept.

Her mother woke her in late evening, helped her sit up

in bed so she could hold her baby and nurse her. Then she left to return to La Prade and her own household. Renaud had gone out earlier, she said to her daughter, urgent business no doubt.

Later, Anthenor pushed the door open silently and walked in.

'I came in earlier while you were asleep,' he said. 'She is beautiful and she doesn't look like Renaud at all.' The child opened her dark blue eyes. 'I think she'll have your eyes. May I hold her?'

He picked up the baby with caution, and held her cradled in his arms, humming to her off-key.

'If you agree,' he told Chantal, 'she will be called Marie-Esmée, like my mother. Do you like that name?'

'I am glad you suggested it. She will be Marie-Esmée, and also Adélaïde, after my own mother.'

A month later, Madame Arondel brought Chantal's own heirloom baptismal dress, all flounces of ecru lace. There were booties and a cap to match. Marie-Esmée would be baptized in style.

The next Sunday, André and Cécile came in their gazogene, the Arondels in theirs. Bijou's harness had been polished, and he pawed the ground in front of the great door while Anthenor handed Chantal up in the cart, holding the sleeping baby, ruffles cascading on her lap. He climbed in next to her, and snapped the reins. The party drove off in the direction of the village church.

There, Madame Arondel and Anthenor held the child over the font, while the priest performed the christening ceremony and baptized her Marie-Esmée Adélaïde de Blazonac, last in the long line of feudal lords who had ruled over this land, been baptized in this church, married there, and brought there for the last earthly rites of the funeral. Their tombs clustered in the small graveyard just outside.

After the service, as the bells pealed in joy for a new soul brought into the fold of the Roman Catholic Church, they stepped outside into a brilliant winter sunshine. Chantal's mother surprised everybody by producing a bag of homemade honey candy to distribute to the waiting village children. Anthenor helped his sister-in-law back into the cart, and Bijou pranced home, trailed by the lumbering cars.

What about Renaud?

Renaud had not been able to get up and dress in time for the ceremony, but he promised he would be ready when they returned. Instead he was engrossed in the sermons of Lamennais, so the baptism banquet of roast goose from the La Prade barnyard and chestnuts from the woods of Blazonac was held off, while he hurriedly shaved and dressed.

Finally, he came down the wide curving staircase, buttoning his jacket, his uncut damp hair curling over his collar. He neglected to greet his guests, or ask to hold his daughter.

'I am out of cigarettes, damn it,' he said to Chantal accusingly. 'Didn't you think of buying some for me in the village?'

The winter of 1941–42 was one of the coldest in remembered times. It is said that winters are always colder when a murderous war is going on. There was no fuel to heat frigid apartments, and in the cities hungry people died everywhere of cold and malnutrition. The German forces were freezing, too, before Moscow, in the annihilating Russian winter, said Cécile, who often came to visit, bringing news of the outside world.

In the Russian cold, as André had predicted, oil froze solid in motor blocks, causing them to split apart, gas turned to chunks of solid ice, sentries became icy statues at their posts. The horrors of Napoléon's retreat were repeated a hundredfold. Hitler refused to winterize his armies, even to issue foul-weather clothing. He told Germany of a pact he made, long ago, with the forces of Ice and Cold and Fog. The German *Volk* was born out of the frozen mists of the north, and the cosmic powers of Eternal Cold would protect the master race they had spawned. Winter would step back before the glorious Nazi. It did not.

At Blazonac, in spite of the bitter cold outside, life flowed quiet and even. Chantal kept a fire burning night and day in the fireplace of her room, and she spent a great deal of her time there or in the adjoining room, formerly Renaud's, now turned into a nursery.

Since Renaud had moved to his new room in the east wing, up a short spiral staircase into the east tower, and down another narrow corridor, she practically never saw him.

Yet, she couldn't have been unaware that his life had changed. He was now going out a great deal. Sometimes, she saw him leave in the afternoon and return late at night. There would be a car waiting for him outside the gate, beyond the first trees, out of sight of the windows of the château. Sometimes, he did not even come home at all, but returned the next morning, head down in his upturned collar, unshaven, to slip into his bed and sleep away the rest of the day. Once, he stayed away for several days. Another time, he came into Chantal's room while Cécile was excitedly telling her the latest news of the BBC, and she suddenly stopped talking, and remained closemouthed as long as he stayed in the room.

Maria began to look at her mistress with pity in her eyes. Anthenor lived with clenched teeth, locked in a cold rage, and Chantal avoided him, because of what she saw in his eyes. Several times, she heard the brothers' voices raised in angry argument. Things were thrown, broken, for Maria and her to pick up later. There was no longer any attempt at a formal dinner, and Chantal ate alone every night.

'Do you know where Renaud is going?' she finally asked Anthenor one day.

He looked at her, with that little muscle jumping at the

side of his jaw. 'Consider yourself lucky you *don't* know. And I hope you don't find out, because it won't make you any happier if you do . . .'

So she nursed and changed her baby, and played with her, anguish gnawing at her soul: What could Renaud be doing that was so terrible? Another woman? She was past jealousy, and anyway, if Renaud was seeing another woman, that wouldn't send Anthenor into those uncontrollable rages. It had to be something worse. But what?

After a few weeks, Renaud was practically no longer living at home. His room was empty for days on end. When he did come home, Chantal would hear the motor on the drive, but it still stopped out of sight. She would hear his voice, and the unfamiliar voice of the driver. Who could possibly be driving a real car these days? It was too cold to step outside, and anyway she wasn't about to humiliate herself by spying, skulking behind pillars. Or perhaps, deep down, she preferred not to find out.

One day, she asked Maria, as casually as she could, 'Do you know who those friends of Count Renaud's are? Who could drive a car like that, at all hours?'

But Maria played deaf. Even if she knew, she wasn't about to answer.

Then, one afternoon, an unfamiliar gazogene pulled, coughing, into the circular carriage court. Two men in dark overcoats stepped out. Chantal recognized Monsieur Routy, a prosperous lumber dealer her father sometimes did business with. She had never seen the other. The men greeted her courteously, and asked if they could see Monsieur Anthenor. Chantal hoped he would be home soon, and asked them to come in and wait in the library. She had a fire built, offered wine, which they refused. So this isn't a cordial visit, she thought, her chest tightening. For a while, they made strained conversation with her. At last, Anthenor came home. His face registered surprise when he saw the men, and he asked Chantal to leave them alone. She walked out gratefully.

She went back upstairs, left doors open so she could

hear, but Anthenor had closed the library door, and all she could discern was the sound of voices. After some moments, the voices rose to the pitch of a furious argument. Finally, she heard the door open and they all stepped into the hall.

'If the restitution is not made within a week, this matter will be brought to the attention of the authorities. We'll press criminal charges, Monsieur Anthenor, sorry as we are to bring your family into this. You know it will mean a jail sentence for your brother, a fine, and still the money will have to be paid back.'

Routy tried to be more conciliatory. 'This is most regrettable. You understand, Monsieur Anthenor, I have attempted to get my partner to consider another course of action, but at this point he just won't listen to me anymore. The most reasonable thing you can do is to raise the money somehow, and the sooner the better.'

Anthenor was silent. Suddenly, he grabbed a walking stick out of an umbrella stand. Chantal saw the men step back a foot, but he only held it in both hands, flexed it and broke it. He threw the pieces viciously against the wall.

'I understand how you feel, Monsieur Anthenor,' said the lumber merchant, 'but you see, my partner tried to speak to your brother, and your brother said we should approach you, it was your business to give us satisfaction.'

'My brother owns three quarters of the property,' stated Anthenor, 'as you certainly know. He signed the bill of sale and you gave him the money. Why should you come here and bother me?'

'I am sorry,' said Routy. 'I had great respect for your grandfather, and your mother – God rest her soul – was a fine lady. But you must understand we have warned your brother, several times we did, and it has been going on for too long.'

'I never heard of this before. My brother never even mentioned it.'

'I am very surprised,' insisted the other man. 'Count

Renaud said you were doing all that's necessary to make matters right.'

'My brother never spoke a word to me. I already told you that.'

'Well, he claimed he had given you the money.'

'No, he did *not*. You know I make all the deals, not him. Why did you negotiate with him? Why not come to me in the first place?'

'Well,' cut in Routy, dropping the conciliatory tone, 'for one, we did not go to him. *He* came to us. He was anxious for a deal, and we gave him the best we could . . .'

Anthenor kicked at one of the suits of armor, which went sprawling in a great clattering of iron.

'Calm down, calm down,' growled Routy. 'All that's neither here nor there. Your brother is the owner, as you said, just as much as and more than you are, so why shouldn't he make deals, too, now and then? The sale is legal after the money has been paid and accepted.'

'Good day, Monsieur Anthenor,' snarled the second man, buttoning his overcoat. 'It's too bad it had to come to this, but we won't wait any longer. The money must be repaid within a week or the authorities will be notified of the embezzlement and we'll start legal proceedings. As much as we hate to do it.'

Anthenor remained standing in the vestibule as they walked out without shaking hands, climbed into their car, and chugged away. He stood there a long time.

Chantal called out to him, 'Anthenor! Please, oh, please, what is going on?'

He hesitated, kicked once more at a piece of the armor, which rebounded clanking against the wall, and slowly walked up the stairs. He came into her room, closed the door behind him, and stood, tall and stooping a little, his back to the fireplace. His jaws were clenched, his cheeks hollow. The little muscle jumped at the corner of his mouth.

'I had no idea. I should have suspected something. But it's just that I never thought Renaud would sink so low.'

'What has Renaud done?'

'You know that stand of oaks near the Belmont farm that we sold last year to the Blanchard mills? Remember, you saw them the first time you walked in the woods with me, when we went to see the farm? Some had already been cut down, milled and removed, and the rest was still standing. Remember? They were marked.'

'I remember the oaks with the red marks.'

'We sold them to repay loans my mother had taken out when she was ill. We received the money last year for the complete stand, and the Blanchard people were going to cut the rest later.'

'So, what did Renaud do?'

'Well, now it seems Renaud went to that other lumber dealer, Routy, and offered to sell him those same trees, and he asked for the money right away. The price was ridiculously low, of course, so Routy jumped at the chance. I don't think for a moment Routy was sincere and honest. I'm sure he knew very well the trees were already sold to someone else, but he probably expected to get in there first, harvest the lumber, and get out. It's such a remote area, he might very well have done it, too. But it didn't work out.'

'What about the other dealer, Blanchard?'

'When Routy went in with his crew and equipment, he found the Blanchard sawmills already set up there. Most of the trees were down and being sawed into planking, with carts pulled up to load. So, he felt he had been had, and he spoke to Renaud. He claims Renaud was rather vague about the whole deal, and told him to speak to me.'

'What about the money?'

'He gave it to Renaud. No doubt about that, he showed me the receipt. Now he wants it back, and Renaud apparently says I am the one who handles the funds, and that I should disburse it. Disburse it indeed! I don't have anything *like* that kind of cash, and there's no way we can raise it at this time.'

'What will happen, then?'

'I don't know for sure, but selling the same thing twice constitutes grand theft. The estate will have to repay, somehow, and there will be legal expenses, and perhaps a fine. Renaud will go to jail, and I might, too, depending on how he testifies.'

'Renaud . . . Perhaps he still has the money?'

'That,' hissed Anthenor through clenched teeth, 'I doubt very much.'

'Why would Renaud do something like that? You always handle business and money matters. Anyway, Renaud is not interested . . .'

'There's a lot about Renaud, these days, that you know nothing about. But it's costing him a lot, and among other things, money he doesn't have. It may end up costing us Blazonac too. He doesn't care, but I do. I care about Blazonac. It is my life, you understand, my life.'

His face was barely recognizable. His eyes seemed sunken and haggard, all color had drained from his hollow cheeks. He slammed his fist on the mantel, swept the mechanical bird to the floor, where it clattered and broke in a sad twinkling of scattered notes. The noise woke the baby in the next room, and she started to cry. Anthenor pushed Chantal out of his way, kicked at the pieces of the gilded cage, and strode out of the room. Chantal stood there trembling, helpless.

Late that night, she heard a car turn into the carriage court and stop in front of the house, directly at the foot of the stone stairs where the lions crouched. It was the first time Renaud's friends had come so close. She ran to the window, hidden by the half-closed shutters. In the brilliant moonlight of the frosty night, Renaud was stepping out of a long, low-slung touring car. He slammed the door and came around to talk to the driver, who rolled down his window.

The driver leaned out. He was a German officer – an SS with a shaved head – in uniform. Chantal saw the twin lightning flashes on his collar and the insignia on his shoulder. Renaud's hand was on the door, the German reached out and caressed his fingers. The two men exchanged a few words in low voices. Then Renaud turned up the collar of his overcoat, and walked, with unsteady steps, up the stone stairs, fumbled with the lock, cursed under his breath. Chantal ran back to her bed, shivering from the cold, and from the scene she had just witnessed, incomprehensible to her and yet heavy with horror. She lay in the dark, moonlight painting a luminescent bar across the room. Her door still stood open.

From deep within the house, she heard Anthenor call out, 'Come here, Renaud. I have to talk to you.'

'Leave me alone, I'm drunk. I don't feel like talking now. I'm going to bed.'

Anthenor was walking down the stairs. He met his brother as he crossed the hall.

'Like hell you're going to bed. You'll go to bed *after* you tell me what you did with the money, you swine.'

'I said, leave me alone. What's the matter with you?'

'What did you do with the money?'

'What money, damn you?'

'The money you got from Routy and his partner when you sold him that stand of oaks, the same ones we had sold six months before to Blanchard.'

'Oh, that! Hell, I'll tell you about it tomorrow . . . Just remind me.'

'You'll tell me right now, you fucking bastard. What did you do with the money?'

'No business of yours.'

'Routy was here today, he said you told him to see me about the money. Is that true?'

'Yeah. That's true. I told him. Aren't Jews supposed to be good at finding money where others don't see any? It's your big chance, man, to show who you *really* are. Hey, calm down, calm down. Look, I'll go to bed and we'll talk about it tomorrow.'

'What did you do with the money?'

'I told you – no business of yours.'

'You're fucking wrong, you miserable degenerate. It *is*

my business. If you don't return it, you go to jail and lose Blazonac.'

'I don't give a damn for Blazonac. Good riddance, if they want to take it. And as far as my going to jail, let me tell you this: I am not going anywhere I don't want to go. I have friends who will see to it. But I can't say the same for you, and it might not be too long either. You losing Blazonac! Ha! That's a good one. You never belonged here, you were just convenient to run errands and do a steward's work . . .'

A crash, a struggle, blows perhaps. Chantal came silently out of her room. She leaned over the railing, but she couldn't see them, under the curve of the stairs.

Renaud spoke in a changed, strained voice. 'All right, Anthenor, take it easy. Come on, man, I was just joking. I told you I was drunk. What do you want me to do? Drop that thing, will you!'

Chantal came down a few steps, just far enough to see that Anthenor had grabbed one of the sabers that hung on the musty wall. Even with its dulled edge, it was still a fearsome weapon. He was holding it threateningly. Chantal called out, 'Renaud! Anthenor! What is going on?'

'Nothing, go back to your room,' answered Anthenor. 'Renaud and I are just having a talk about business, and we are going to go for a little walk. Aren't we, Renaud? You need to clear your head so you can remember what you did with the money, right? You'll feel better in the cold air, it will sober you up.'

Leaning a little farther, she could just glimpse Renaud, now slumped on a banquette, staring vacantly. She went back to her room, cold to the bones and trembling so, she thought she could never stop until convulsive sobs racked her even more. She heard them walk outside, on the lakeside path. Then silence.

Later, Anthenor's door opened and closed. She had no way of knowing whether Renaud had come home or not, but no doubt he had. It was freezing outside, so cold that ice had begun to form in spite of the current, in a thin jagged fringe, along the banks of the lake. This was no night for a leisurely stroll.

Eventually, Chantal must have slept, because a commotion outside wakened her, and she ran barefoot to her window. In the gray light of the early winter morning, she saw men outside, men from the farms calling out in the carriage court. Maria was there, several of her sons and sons-in-law clustered around her. She was crying, wiping her eyes with her apron.

Chantal opened her window. 'Maria! What is going on?'

'Ah, our lady,' cried Maria, 'please, please, don't come downstairs. Stay in, for the love of God! Close that window. Call Monsieur Anthenor, tell him to hurry downstairs. This is terrible, the curse of God is upon us. I knew it, I knew it, no good could come of all this in the end. What are we going to do? Good Lord in Heaven, take pity on us poor sinners. Why do they all have to die so young in that family?'

Anthenor was running downstairs. A moment later the men brought in a form wrapped in a dripping tarpaulin. He directed them to the drawing room, and there, they laid their burden on the parquet floor. He tried to bar the door against Chantal, but she pushed his arm aside, ran, knelt on the floor, pushed the stiff wet tarp aside.

Of course, and just as she knew, Renaud's lifeless eyes were staring at her.

7

HOW THAT DAY passed with Maria keening and the baby crying desperately, somehow sensing the tragedy of the moment, Chantal would never know.

Dr Vincent, blue with cold, came on his motorcycle, and attested that Renaud had died several hours before, hard to tell just when. Drowned, probably, or perhaps a seizure, falling like that in the icy water. In any case, an accident, no doubt, he said, avoiding Chantal's and Anthenor's eyes. No autopsy was called for. He hurriedly signed the death certificate and left, too fast, forgetting even to offer condolences.

The two gendarmes came from the village a little later, very respectful, for this was the château, after all. They entered through the kitchen door, their caps in hand. Embarrassed, not knowing how to state the purpose of their visit, they started out with a few platitudes. They were sorry about the accident that had taken the Count's life, wasn't it a terrible shame, and him with a young wife and child ... Well, that's what we are like, here one day, and gone the next. There had been another drowning in the lake, years ago, wasn't it? Some poacher had taken the shortcut through the woods, where the path divides into two branches, one following close to the steep bank, right under the pines. He must have slipped, because his body was found the next day, caught in the tall reeds, not too far from the sluices. Just about this time of year too.

With much hemming and hawing, the two young gendarmes finally came to the point of their visit; it was their duty to ... well, to generally inquire into what had happened, before the burial permit could be granted. A routine matter, nothing more, as always, in case of an accident. Not that anybody suspected anything else than an accident, God knew.

'Well,' began Anthenor, 'my brother came home late last night, and he'd had a little too much to drink, so we thought we'd go for a walk around the lake before turning in. There was a full moon. I'd seen some otters tunneling under the banks of the lake the other day, I thought they'd be out at night and that would be a good time to spot them and mark the place for the traps. These otters have been killing our fish all winter. Ask the Countess, we were talking to her before we went out.'

'That's true,' Chantal murmured. 'I saw them leave. They told me they were going to walk along the lake.'

'I only had on my sweater and after a while,' continued Anthenor, 'the cold was getting to me, I couldn't feel my hands and my face anymore, so I thought we should turn around and go home. But my brother was wearing his overcoat, he wasn't cold, and he said, no, he wanted to go all around the lake and see if he could find those otters. You knew him, he was stubborn.'

'Just like his grandfather,' put in the shorter of the two gendarmes, born and raised in the village, 'he was a stubborn man too. Heard he wouldn't let kids from the village swim in the lake, summers. Never. Never relented, year after year.'

'Count Renaud liked to have his own way, I'll say that,' added the other gendarme, the son of Justin, the gardener, who had grown up on the estate, and who was just a little older than Renaud.

'He certainly did last night, and we'll mourn that day for a long time,' said Anthenor, his voice lowered. 'He should have known the bank is slippery where it forks under the pines, even more so now the mud is iced over. You know, Marcel, you know the spot. We used to play there, Renaud, you, and I, when we were kids. You almost fell in, one day.'

'Sure, Monsieur Anthenor,' replied Marcel, acutely uncomfortable. He was doing his best to help Anthenor along.

'Sure, I know the spot. It's tricky, out there – mud if it's been raining, slippery pine needles when it's dry, and ice right now. I remember that day. I sure would have fallen in if you hadn't held on to me. I bet that's where the Count slipped and fell. And then, the current carried him off to the sluices where Paulin found him this morning.'

'And if he had been drinking a little too much,' said the other gendarme eagerly, 'he didn't have much of a chance. The water is so cold, these days, we saw sheets of ice forming along the edges this morning when we crossed the causeway. I'll bet he had a seizure the instant he touched water and sank like a rock. Being a good swimmer wouldn't have helped him.'

Marcel next turned to Chantal. He wanted to impress his colleague with a display of courtesy, such as one might have learned living and playing with château people. 'I am sorry, madame la Comtesse, I am real sorry. All this is too hard on you, and you shouldn't be listening to it. It's just too bad it had to happen.'

The other gendarme was painstakingly writing, scribbling notes with a pencil stub on a grimy pad.

'Well, as I said before, this is simply for the record. We feel awful about this, Monsieur Anthenor. First your mother gone so fast, and now the young Count. That's the end of the name. What a shame! An old family like that, why, there've been Blazonacs here longer than anybody even knows. But if it is God's will—' He checked himself. A representative of the Republic had no business bringing God's name into official duty. 'Now we have our report, and there's no need to bother you any longer.'

Anthenor escorted them to the kitchen, where Maria served refreshments all around. Rules of hospitality must be observed even in tragedy.

Immediate practical matters were left in the hands of Maria, who had had much experience with death. During her long life she had buried so many: her parents, her husband, three of her children, relatives and neighbors. She was there, helping when the last Countess had been brought home from Paris to die and be buried in the family plot. Maria knew what must be done.

A bed was carried downstairs and set in the middle of the frigid drawing room. Maria brought down the best sheets, and when she spread them on the deathbed, Chantal saw they were the same ones that had been used on her own bed for her wedding night, richly embroidered by a countess of the last century, with the Blazonac crest in the center, done in cutwork, topped with the earl's coronet. There was a large tear on one side that Chantal had not noticed before.

Renaud was dressed by Maria and Paulin in the gray sharkskin suit he had worn for his marriage. And Chantal took her widow's place, kneeling at the head of the low catafalque. Lying there in state, Renaud had transcended his abortive life, so that now he resembled the recumbent effigies of knights sculpted on tombstones. He should have been wearing a suit of armor, visor raised over the forehead, framing his narrow, aquiline face, with the closed, rounded lids. Instead of a rosary, he would have been holding a sword, hands folded over the pommel.

Chantal could not push from her mind the poignant medieval song they had sung in school, of the death of King Renaud, who comes home to die after a battle, holding his entrails in his hands:

> *Le roi Renaud revint de guerre*
> *Tint ses entrailles dans ses mains . . .*

Renaud, who, said the refrain, would never live to see his twentieth spring and lay dead in the castle keep, while his wife, on her childbirth bed, kept asking why she heard hammering in the courtyard . . .

This Renaud would not see his twenty-fifth spring. His wife, too, had given birth, but she did not wonder what the hammering was about. She knew. Two of Maria's sons were putting together a rough wooden coffin in the carriage barn nearby. Convulsive sobs shook her.

Her mother, kneeling close, took her hand. The Arondels

had arrived as soon as they had received word of the tragedy, bringing kitchen help, provisions, mourning clothes for Chantal, support and authority.

'I know,' Madame Arondel whispered, 'you need to cry, it's good for you. Just don't blame anybody, and don't say anything, no matter what you hear. It's all for the best, you'll see. You have your child. God helps, sometimes, when nobody else can do anything . . .'

All day, and all the next night, and all the next day, and the night after that, the house remained opened to visitors. People came to pay their final respects, kneel a moment by the deathbed, trace a sign of the cross with a bough of boxwood dipped in holy water, over the still form lying there, hands crossed over the chest, fingers entwined with a rosary. At times, during the long wake, Chantal thought she saw, in the flickering light of the candles, a familiar sneer on Renaud's lips.

Food, prepared and brought from La Prade all during the three days, was served in the kitchen for the village and the farm folk, in the dining room for the gentry. Custom forbade that any cooking take place during the wake. All food must be brought from elsewhere, and with the scant stores of Blazonac, this custom wasn't hard to respect.

Anthenor came and went, standing motionless in the doorway for hours, then leaving silently, and returning hours later. Chantal would sometimes look up from under the veil her mother had brought and shown her how to drape over her face, and there he was, hollow cheeks, sunken eyes. Sometimes he knelt briefly next to her, then rose and was gone.

At one point, late during the first night, seeing her doze off, her mother touched her shoulder and guided her upstairs. There, they lay side by side on the carved bed. Her mother took her hand without a word in a rare gesture of affection, and after a while they both slept, a fitful sleep, for a few hours.

This was to be the only rest stolen during those three days and nights. Custom required the widow to sit or kneel by her dead husband. She should not grudge him those few hours, she who was strong and well, and warm, and alive, and he who was going to be taken away from her side, to molder in a cold grave for all eternity.

So, Chantal came downstairs at three o'clock in the morning, having brushed her hair and bathed her eyes in cold water, and replaced the black veil over her face. She talked in whispers with people she could only dimly see through the thin black fabric, she knelt and prayed, with the well-remembered prayers of her school years still so close.

By the second night, she had prayed and cried herself into a trance of wakefulness, and she felt as if she would never need to sleep again. She wasn't tired anymore, she had lost all notion of time, and stared with burning eyes, under her veil. A day, and another night passed.

Suddenly Maria pushed the heavy wooden shutters open to the gray light of yet another early morning, and all heads turned to see the horse-drawn hearse clatter into the carriage court. Several men in black accompanied it. They had come to seal the coffin. The priest arrived, in black vestments, the tall cross carried in front of him by a choirboy – one of Maria's grandsons – while another boy swung a censer. There were no flowers in this harsh February, only the black cover with embroidered silver tears to hide the raw wood of the coffin.

The afternoon before, Anthenor and Monsieur Arondel had stood outside, in full view but out of earshot of the people who came and went, pacing the carriage court, stopping now and then to stand face-to-face in quiet and intense conversation. Finally, Chantal had seen her father reach for Anthenor's hand, the two men quickly embraced, Anthenor resting his head for a second on the broad shoulder of the older man, while Monsieur Arondel patted Anthenor's back reassuringly. And Chantal thought she saw the hollow cheeks relax.

As Monsieur Arondel returned inside the mourning room, he leaned over to Chantal. 'Everything will be all right,' he whispered. 'Anthenor talked to me, and I think that things can be arranged. Especially now . . .' he added with an imperceptible movement of his chin toward the recumbent form. 'Stop crying, you'll make yourself sick. Think of your little one.'

Now the time had come. People were massed outside, all ill at ease and freezing cold in their dark clothes, aired only for marriages and funerals. André and Cécile stepped out from the crowd and hugged Chantal. They had been at the house to spend the second night of the wake, and now they were going to walk with the cortege the two miles to the village.

'Everything will be all right,' whispered Cécile. 'And above all, don't you listen to what anybody might say. Renaud is dead, but you are alive, and so is your daughter, and *that's* all that matters now, don't you forget it.'

Chantal took her place behind the hearse, with Anthenor next to her, her parents behind, friends and relatives after. Then the crowd formed in a loose procession, and the long walk began. In the drive, under the bare trees, now covered with frost, mud had frozen into sharp ridges, and when she stumbled, Anthenor caught her arm.

This was three months to the day after the baptism, and under lowering skies now instead of the brilliant winter sunshine that had greeted them when they stepped out of the little church on that Sunday. Now, Chantal stood in the front pew, grateful for the veil that hid her burning eyes. Anthenor was standing next to her, tall and slim in the black suit and overcoat he had worn at his mother's funeral. (So after all, he was getting more wear out of it than Madame Arondel had expected.) The church was crowded, because, in the country, every family sends a representative to all funerals. This is the way to insure that your own funeral, or that of your kin, will show a respectable turnout that will bring your family honor when the time comes. This one, though, was exceptionally well-attended; the death of young people always causes more of a stir. Especially a sudden death like this one, clothed in mysterious circumstances. As could be expected, the county was buzzing with gossip about the strange ménage at Blazonac, even if Chantal did not begin to suspect it.

'Imagine,' the gossip went, 'first, that high-living, free-spending Countess, all those men guests here every summer, and she dies so young, not even forty, of some mysterious illness . . .'

'She lies here, you know, in this cemetery, next to the Count, who died in the other war. Twenty-five or -six, wasn't he? And what about that second husband with the strange name, what became of him? Some say he's locked up in some crazy house. There are people who remember him. They say that Anthenor is the spitting image of him. Crazy, too, no doubt. Well, *that* marriage is long forgotten, everyone still called her the Countess, it was as though it had never been . . .'

'And now it's the son's turn, and not long after, too. An accident? Well, that's fine for the gendarmes to say. Things were strange, if you ask me, at the château. We saw the young Countess more often with the brother than with her husband, driving around, with that circus horse. Who knows *what* was going on out there, these past months?'

'Is it true what they say about Count Renaud?'

'You mean about him being all the time at that big house near La Rochefoucauld? I certainly heard it too. My husband says the woman who runs the place came from Paris, she was the madam of a brothel there before the war, and she operates the same business right here, with German staff cars coming and going at all hours of the day and night.'

'No doubt, no doubt. And there was gambling, too, with a lot of money changing hands, most of it, unless I am very much mistaken, going to the house, and a lot of black market too! Count Renaud was there all the time, I heard. They say he lost a lot. Wonder where he got it from?'

'Hard to say. Maybe from that bald German he was always riding with, the one with the sports car. I heard they were pretty good friends, if you know what I mean.'

'Do you think his brother killed him?'

'Well, you heard the story, and you read it in the paper. Count Renaud went for a walk in the middle of the night around the lake. He slipped and fell. That's all.'

'You believe it?'

'Do you?'

'Better not to say. There should have been an autopsy. But the last word has not been said, even though the gendarmes gave the burial permit.'

'When they are dealing with people like the Blazonacs, the gendarmes look the other way. Marcel is the son of the old Blazonac gardener, he wouldn't want to embarrass them. Got well paid for it, too, I bet.'

'Are you kidding? The Blazonac people are flat broke. Their mother had borrowed money everywhere, they sold all that could be moved, and I was told they live like paupers in that house. I don't understand how people like the Arondels could have let their daughter marry into that house . . .'

'Pregnant, no doubt.'

'I don't remember the dates, but that would explain it.'

'What do you suppose they are going to do now?'

'What can they do? I suppose Blazonac is going to be sold, sooner or later. Probably can be picked up for next to nothing . . .'

'I meant, do you think there'll be an inquest?'

'There might be. I hope there is. Then we'll all know a little better what we were here for today.'

Now, the church service was ending. The old priest was promising that Renaud's eyes, once washed by the water of his baptism, would reopen to the light of the Last Judgment, when bodies resurrect to eternal life. Then, looking straight at Anthenor, he only said that God gives and God taketh away, and that final judgment belongs to Him only.

Anthenor stared ahead unblinkingly. He hadn't cried once and he hadn't slept, and yet now it seemed as though there was a peace in his face that wasn't there before. But he looked exhausted.

The family plot, in the small churchyard, occupied the place of honor at the right of the church portals. It was surrounded by a rusted wrought-iron fence, whose gate, topped with the Blazonac crest and coronet, like the château's, leaned askew. While the priest was chanting blessings, and the coffin was slowly lowered with ropes into the ground, Chantal looked at the dates on the tombs. 'They all die so young, in that family,' Maria had said. Did anyone remember why and how? Did many of them drown in the lake?

Anthenor and Chantal, with her parents on her left, had to stand once more, this time at the cemetery door, to receive handshakes, hugs, muttered words of sympathy . . . Madame Arondel gave a worried look to Anthenor, who seemed close to fainting. When he staggered and almost fell, she gestured to her husband, who went to stand between his daughter and the tall, exhausted young man, ready to steady him.

Mercifully, André had his gazogene brought around, and, by fits and starts, belching smoke and engine coughing, it took them back to Blazonac. In the drawing room, standing next to the empty deathbed, her mother took Chantal's face in her black-gloved hands.

'I am taking the baby home with us, to La Prade. I'll keep her for the time being. Shh! Don't protest. She'll be fine, the girls in the kitchen will be so happy to have her, and with the new maid, Anna, she'll have an adoring court. Now, I want you to go straight to bed and sleep until you cannot sleep anymore. Then, you'll come to the house, and we'll see what you're going to do.'

Chantal was surprised. 'To do? What is there for me to do? I'll stay here at Blazonac, like before. What else?' It won't make much difference, she was thinking. Renaud had been such a small part of life here, he will hardly be missed. I'll just keep on with my own life, dismal and hopeless. Anthenor will go his own way, as he has done these past few months. I'll grow old . . .

'Staying here is out of the question,' said Madame Arondel severely. 'We'll see where you can go. You could stay with Papa and me, but that's not really good either. Too close. You have to go away.'

'Go away? Why? And where would I go?'

Her mother looked at her pityingly. 'Don't you understand that you *can't* stay here alone with Anthenor? Don't you know what people are saying?'

'What are they saying?'

'Oh, come now, you cannot be *that* naive. They are saying you and Anthenor were lovers, and that's why he killed his brother. Even Cécile came to tell me she had heard it but didn't believe a word of it. For all I know, she might be spreading the story herself.'

'Mother! That's not true, and you know it. It wasn't because of me, it was because of—'

Alarm in her eyes, Madame Arondel raised her hand to cover her daughter's lips.

'Careful, child, careful. Don't say anything. See why you can't stay? One word, one innocent word . . . Don't ever say a word! I know it's not true. Although, God knows your father and I have lain awake in bed night after night, worrying about you. It was a very unhealthy situation, you know, and we didn't see a solution to it, until . . . Well, that part's over now. You must go away, to forget and to give people time to forget.'

'I meant that Anthenor didn't kill Renaud.'

'Well, that we'll never know, and it's just as well. But we can't have you living at Blazonac with Anthenor, to all the world outside like husband and wife. I could think of nothing else when you were standing next to him during the funeral, looking so much like a couple who's burying a distant relative. I kept wanting to pull you over, between your father and me, where you'd be safe, protected from all those dangers you don't even understand. That's why

I had your father move over between you two. I couldn't stand it anymore.'

'What dangers?'

'Well, for one, there's always the chance the authorities in Limoges might decide to start an investigation into Renaud's death.'

'But the gendarmes . . .'

'The gendarmes allowed the funeral to take place, because they reported the death as an accident. But you see, if gossip spreads, there may yet be an inquest. Political feeling is running high, and with Renaud's associations, which you don't know about, he wasn't exactly beloved . . . And Anthenor isn't either.'

'I know about the German officer.'

'You know? All right, you found that out, but do you know about the money Renaud gambled and lost? Do you know he owed a lot more than he had paid when he died? I doubt they'll try to collect now he's no longer here. Also, you know that the night Renaud died, Anthenor had good reason to be in a terrible rage at him.'

'But that was on account of the oaks Renaud had sold a second time.'

'Yes, I know, Anthenor talked to your father, and your father's going to see what he can do. He will advance at least part of the money to repay Routy, and Anthenor can sign a note for the rest. There'll be some legal matters to take care of too. Renaud died without a will, you were married under separation of property, we insisted on that because we wanted to be sure La Prade would be all yours and your children's and nobody else's when the time comes. But at this point, it means you don't inherit anything, the three-quarter share in the Blazonac estate goes to your daughter, who will need a legal guardian until she comes of age. Under the law you can only be one of two guardians looking after her interests.'

'Who will the other be?'

'Your father could be, if the court allows it, if not, we thought we might ask André Brousse. It might even be in the child's interest to renounce her rights to Blazonac. It's so heavily mortgaged, it might demand more than any of us could put in to keep it afloat. Your father was wondering if it would not be better to have her start life free from such a burden. But here again, nothing can be done without court permission.'

Chantal, who a moment earlier had been weighted down by the prospect of continued life in Blazonac, was now terrified at the idea of losing it. Blazonac was her home, after all, her only security. It was her daughter's name, and hers too. She tried to fight to stay and keep her daughter's birthright.

'I'd rather stay.'

But her mother wasn't taking any more nonsense. Chantal's innocence had caused them so much grief already.

'Don't you see, child, how it would all look at an inquest? People would testify. That lumber business, Renaud and the German SS officer, the madam from the brothel, where she keeps boys as well as girls – yes, you might as well grow up. And you were seen everywhere with Anthenor, who's notorious for flying into those terrible rages just like his poor father. It would all come out. That walk, at two in the morning, on a stone-splitting freezing night, do you think it makes much sense? And suppose they decide to exhume the body and they find some indication of violence? If you must know everything, Maria hinted to me she was glad neither the doctor nor the gendarmes looked at the back of Renaud's head, and I didn't dare ask what she meant – just pretended I hadn't heard. A scandal, I tell you, with a trial for Anthenor, prison, dishonor for you, since you'd be mixed up in it, for us, and what about your daughter? If they decided you are an accessory to murder – don't interrupt me, I don't think you are – I don't know what would happen, but imagine your child raised without a mother. And what about us? Remember, we have to live here too. So, you'll leave, go somewhere safe and stay there until tongues stop wagging. Now, go to sleep, and we'll talk tomorrow.'

The next day, her parents had made the decision for her.

'We have written to your Aunt Emilie in Limoges. She lives in town in the rue Pierre-Raymond, such a nice neighborhood. She's alone since her daughter and her husband died. You remember Uncle Gustave? The general? He died five years ago, but you were in school and you didn't go to the funeral. Well, you can go live with her for a while. Marie-Esmée will stay with us at La Prade, and I promise you she'll be very well cared for. You'll come and visit as often as possible – people must not think you ran away. In time, you may even go to Blazonac now and then – not alone, mind you, with us, so people don't talk – but not right away in any case. We'll see.'

The answer from Aunt Emilie came quickly.

'Yes!' she wrote. 'Welcome! Welcome! So glad to have my niece, the young widow. So sad, and so young! I can well understand her wanting to get away for a while. I know, if I were her, I couldn't bear to so much as *look* at that lake. I have already told my friends, all widows like me, and they exclaimed, isn't it strange, another widow come to join us! We'll make room for her in our sewing circle, and she'll be safe. We'll protect her and look after her.'

Another letter from Aunt Emilie was addressed to Chantal and came to Blazonac. The envelope read: 'The Widowed Countess de Blazonac.' Without much of a transition, thought Chantal, I have stepped from the ranks of children to those of the aged and hopeless. This is where dreams of a romantic elsewhere get you. The good sisters were right: Honor thy father and thy mother. Too late now, I am damned. Despair made her shiver again.

And yet. And yet a glimmer of hope: Limoges certainly wasn't such a great city, but it *was* a city. There were people, paved streets, life. She could be away from both her mother's iron will and the gloom of Blazonac. The sewing circle might not be escape-proof. Free for the first time in her short life. Resolutely she pushed aside thoughts of Anthenor.

A week later, Chantal said good-bye to her daughter, in the great, bustling barnyard of La Prade. Anna, the new kitchen maid, carried Marie-Esmée in her arms, while calling chicken, geese, guinea fowl, ducks to the trough filled with food. The baby was laughing, cooing, gurgling, reaching out to the ducklings, and she barely paid attention to her mother. Blinded by tears, Chantal stepped into her father's gazogene, and five hours later, having covered the sixty miles to Limoges, she was effusively greeted by a weeping and laughing Aunt Emilie.

8

AUNT EMILIE LIVED on the rue Pierre-Raymond, a short, tree-lined street close to the center of town. When her house was built some forty years earlier, the town had been much smaller, but it had doubled in size between the two wars, and now, the quiet residential, almost peripheral, street found itself embedded in the fabric of the city.

There was a narrow iron gate, freshly painted in shiny black, with a polished copper plate: *Général G. Giraud*, unchanged since the general's death. In fact, Aunt Emilie always referred to herself now as *Madame Veuve Giraud*, and kept the same calling cards, *Le Général et Madame Giraud*, except that she now crossed out the first three words and inserted *Veuve* after *Madame*. Aunt Emilie saw widowhood as an identity, and just as she had been a general's wife, she was now his widow both socially and professionally, so to speak.

The gate opened onto a miniature walled garden with a doll-sized lawn, surrounded by ten-inch-wide flower beds. The lawn was brown and frozen now, and the rosebushes pruned almost down to the ground – short sticks armed with massive-looking thorns. Winter had reduced the Virginia creeper to a gossamer tracery on the walls, neatly trimmed off along the rectangular stones framing the windows. On the second floor, two shuttered French doors opened onto the balcony.

Steps led to a narrow entrance hall. On the left, in back, was Uncle Gustave's study, now kept unheated and locked, but regularly dusted. In front, in the parlor, Chantal saw the piano in a corner, draped in a cashmere shawl from India – Suzette's piano – a shrine regarded with tearful reverence on past visits. On the right, a small dining room, crowded by its mahogany table and chairs, opened onto the kitchen. Everything smelled of furniture wax, lavender oil, and the faint scent of baking apples. In spite of the fuel shortage, the atmosphere of the small rooms, with their knickknacks and abundance of over-stuffed furniture, was surprisingly warm and cozy.

The stairs were narrow, too, with a polished mahogany banister and a red stair-runner held in place by sparkling copper rods. Chantal recognized with delight the ornament that served as a finial to the newel post, a large, round glass ball, in which extraordinary flowers bloomed, outlined in frosted crystal, changing color, size, and shape according to the angle of vision. She remembered that as a child she had spent hours gazing into the millefiore glass. Her aunt and uncle had bought it, right from the glassblowers on the island of Murano, when they had gone to Venice on their honeymoon. Now, for some mysterious reason, the millefiore seemed to vouchsafe to Chantal that the magical realm of her dreams still existed, had never ceased to exist, in spite of the sinister events she had just endured.

There were three bedrooms upstairs. The smaller, which looked to the back, had its own staircase down to the kitchen, and it was occupied by Léonie. Léonie's husband had been the general's orderly since the time, years ago, when the general was only a major, and now she kept the house shiny and the tiny garden manicured.

The other two rooms opened onto the balcony. One was Aunt Emilie's: more mahogany furniture, a large portrait of a fierce-looking Uncle Gustave with all his decorations gleaming on his black and red uniform of the last war. He was Madame Arondel's older brother, and but for the mustache, Chantal thought they looked pretty much alike.

'As soon as this war is over,' said Aunt Emilie, 'I will have to change the drapes and the bed curtains. That green brocade is faded now and always looks dusty, no matter what. Your uncle was so fond of it, though. He picked the fabric himself when we moved in. But you must be exhausted after your long trip, Chantal my dear. Here is your room.'

The other room had belonged to Chantal's cousin Suzette, the only child of the Giraud, dead in 1918, five years before Chantal was born. But she had heard the story so many times, she knew it as well as if she had lived through every moment of the tragedy herself.

Suzette had been pretty, lively, endowed with such a lovely soprano voice, she was in great demand at the musicales in the military circles of her father's garrisons. There she met one of his subalterns, a graduate of the prestigious Saint-Cyr officers' school, a young man of excellent family and great professional promise, and they fell in love. The date was set and preparations made for an elaborate wedding. Her wedding dress hung waiting in her armoire.

Then, a week before the ceremony, she took to her bed with the flu, sank fast, and although she briefly seemed to rally and sat up asking to hold her bridal veil, she died and was buried on the morning of what would have been her wedding day, one of the legion of victims of the epidemic of Spanish influenza ravaging Europe. Suzette was buried in her wedding dress, and the bouquets that had begun to arrive were piled, instead, around her coffin. The six bridesmaids stood during the church services, in the rose silk dresses Suzette had chosen, while her bridegroom in full dress uniform remained at attention, alone, at the head of the catafalque. He held his sword drawn, the story went, throughout the long funeral mass, just as medieval knights did who drew their swords during the reading of the Gospels to show their readiness to defend God against all enemies. Before the coffin was sealed, he bent to slip a ring on the dead girl's finger and another on his own. A few days later, he had reported back to the front, and was killed there after volunteering for a suicidal mission. He had asked to be buried next to Suzette, and as a child Chantal had been taken each year to bring flowers to the graves, crying each time the story was told, far sadder and more awe-inspiring than the tale of Tristan and Isolde.

She always wondered what it took to inspire a love of such noble intensity, and it wasn't until much later that she would understand that love has less to do with its object than with the nature of the person who loves.

Now, Aunt Emilie opened the shutters wide and quickly closed the windows again.

'Brrr! It's cold, out there. I do wish your father had stayed overnight. We had the couch in the parlor ready for him. But he was anxious to leave. I just hope he won't have trouble on the road with that awful contraption. Frankly, I don't trust that Pierrot of his. There's something shifty and arrogant in his eyes. Now, my love, here is your room. You remember it? You slept here many times when you were little.'

Nothing had changed, and with the shutters kept closed, nothing had even faded. The same cream, rose-sprigged paper on the walls; the same narrow bed with its white organdy canopy starched, draped, and tied back, and the dressing table with the matching skirt. The low chair, with its tapestry seat of cherubs holding a rose wreath, the little fireplace, never used now the house was equipped with central heating, the *bombé* chest with its intricate brass pulls, the closet, small, but still too large for Chantal's scant wardrobe.

Love, peace, and gratitude welled up in her heart.

'I am so glad to be with you, Aunt Emilie,' she sobbed, and she threw herself into the older woman's arms. 'But I already miss my little girl so much!'

'Now, now, you'll make me cry too,' said the aunt, wiping her eyes. 'We'll be very happy, you'll see, and perhaps the baby can come and live here too. Time will heal the sorrow life has brought you. I've had my share, too, and I know one can live and go on after time has done its work.'

She thought her niece was mourning her young husband, but in fact Chantal did not know herself what her heart, so heavy, was really mourning for, unless it was an impossible yearning. She put a picture of Marie-Esmée on the dressing table, next to the silver-framed portrait of Suzette and her fiancé. She had no picture of Renaud.

'Come downstairs for dinner when you are ready,' said Aunt Emilie, 'Léonie will be ready anytime. And you will sleep well, the street is quiet. Most of the other houses were built at the same time and our neighbors are mainly elderly couples or widows like me.' She added, 'And like you, my poor darling.'

Limoges was in the Free Zone. But, of course, there was a German presence, civilians, officers, and soldiers, manning a variety of offices, if no official occupation forces yet. A few months earlier, almost unnoticed by the people of Blazonac, the Japanese had bombed an American base in far-off Hawaii called Pearl Harbor, and that had caused the United States to enter the war. Whatever impact these events had on the course of the World War now spreading to all continents of the Northern Hemisphere, it did not affect daily life in provincial France, except that the already pitifully meager food supplies were reduced week by week. Léonie made miracles with what few stores had been laid by in advance, and with the provisions Madame Arondel managed to send in spite of the difficulty of communications. After a few days, Chantal asked to help and even started to go by herself to do the shopping.

There wasn't much to buy with the paltry three booklets of food stamps obtained after hours of lining up in the cold in front of the City Hall offices of the Kommandantur. The main allowance was now a daily piece of bread about the size of a box of kitchen matches. One day, while Chantal was waiting her turn at the bakery, a stout lady (how could anyone remain stout in those days? wondered Chantal, whose own waist could easily be spanned by her two hands) waddled in, loudly complaining she had found a dead rat in her bread ration. She dangled the evidence by its tail: a small gray body, encrusted with dough. She was angry not so much at the thought that she, or one of her family members, might have bitten into a dead rat, but because she felt cheated of the equal weight of bread. For that she demanded redress.

Everybody in the shop joined in the fray. It was agreed that a dead rat in the bread wasn't all that surprising. Recently, the river had overrun its banks, and the bakery, with its cellar ovens, had no doubt been affected. Lots of rats must have been drowned, and this one may have sought refuge in the vat where the dough was being kneaded. No one found this bizarre or disgusting, and after a moment, hilarity was general, with even the angry lady joining in.

'Eh,' said the baker, who was laughing so hard he had to wipe his eyes on his apron, 'count yourself lucky! Even if you lost a little of your bread ration, you got a whole fat rat, and I didn't even ask for meat stamps!'

Chantal, amused in spite of herself, laughed with everyone else, but from that day on, she and Aunt Emilie were wary of biting into their bread. Instead, they cut it into small bits and examined each one carefully. After Aunt Emilie found a cockroach in hers, it was decided they should change bakers. The next one wasn't much better, though: no cigarette butts, rats, or roaches, but pebbles in every bite!

As in all French provincial cities, the heartbeat of Limoges centered in the old town, where shops clustered on a few steep, cobbled streets. Chantal, who had never before strolled alone and at leisure through a city, soon escaped whenever she could for a walk that brought her invariably to peer in the windows of the rue du Clocher or the avenue Gambetta.

Most goods were sadly lacking, but, of course, Limoges had its world-famous porcelain, made out of the pure white clay, smooth as silk to the touch, mined nearby, called 'kaolin.' Aunt Emilie, delighted in Chantal's interest, explained that, since kaolin wasn't essential to the German war effort, the production of porcelain was allowed to continue when fuel for firing the kilns – mostly wood from the surrounding Limousin forests – was available. A neighbor, Madame Arnoux, whose husband had managed the Haviland factory, obtained permission for a tour, and Chantal could watch the twenty-nine hand operations that produced eggshell translucent vases, bowls, dishes, and cups.

A rolling counter brought the dull, unfired pieces to a station where a girl sat at an ordinary school desk and applied monochromatic brown decals. A precise operation, to be sure, but a far cry from the delicate hand-painting of pastel bouquets Chantal had envisioned! At the next station another pretty girl sat before a revolving potter's wheel and applied, with a thin sable brush, a fine black rim to cups and plates. She smiled up.

'Black and brown?' Chantal raised a bewildered eyebrow. But she envied the girl. Never mind how dull and repetitive it must be, still, it's a job. *She* has a job.

The girl laughed, working with a steady hand. 'Wait till you've seen what happens in the firing.'

Chrysalis-like, when the dull pieces emerged from the kiln, black rim had turned to sparkling gold, and brown blossomed into pastel hues.

Buyers were not lacking, and Chantal averted her eyes from groups of German soldiers rummaging through the wire baskets, in front of china shops, piled with factory seconds sold for a few francs. None of the occupants would have wanted to return home without some Limoges pieces in his pack. A staff car pulled up in front of the best shop, the kind that scorned rejects and specialized, instead, in splendid dining sets with arrays of dishes for every possible occasion. She watched the most exquisite tea set, with its matching gold filigree plates and footed cake stands, being pulled out of the window while an orderly waited at the entrance. She'd heard money wasn't always the preferred currency for such highticket items: Stores of the priceless gasoline, food supplies, and other more mysterious favors apparently predicated better deals.

Enamel, for which the city was just as famous, glittered, jewels in the gray winterscape. Chantal's mother owned an enamel pendant. 'It's an *émail*, an original design. No two like this in the world. Your father bought it for me when we went to Limoges on our honeymoon,' small Chantal was told every time the story of the epoch-making trip was recounted. And now, here were entire windows of the precious ware! When Chantal described with shining eyes the brooches, pendants, and rings she'd admired, Aunt Emilie unlocked the mahogany and glass bookcase and pulled out a faded album, *Les Émaux de Limoges*. Curled up on the horsehair sofa, while Aunt Emilie darned old socks, formerly discarded from the general's drawer and now destined for the poor, Chantal learned that enamel is an ancient art, brought from Byzantium in the currents of trades created on the roads of the Crusades. Another visit was arranged.

'So much to do now that you're here – never thought of going to see those places myself before!' exclaimed Aunt Emilie, adjusting her hat with its small, permanently attached widow's veil draped on the side. In the *émailleur*'s atelier, an old man was mixing ground glass crystals with a solvent and used the mixture to paint a design on a thin heart-shaped piece of silver. When he pulled it from the kiln, the crystals had vitrified into a glasslike shell: on a dark blue background, a Florentine head had emerged, with flowing hair and a little green cap. Chantal gasped.

'Exactly like my mother's pendant! But hers is an original. How could there be more than one?'

The artist smiled. 'I've been reproducing this Giotto for more than thirty years, and I don't expect to stop as long as it's selling so well. Now, if you want to see *really* rare and antique pieces, you must go to the museum . . .' Aunt Emilie couldn't wait to arrange that outing too. But on the way to the museum, tears came to Chantal's eyes when she saw a young mother with a little girl and was reminded of Marie-Esmée.

Yet nothing had prepared her for what she saw, a few

days later, in the elegantly bare window of the Galerie Lejalou. On a velvet pillow lay the most extraordinary jewel, made of large rectangular plates of copper in graduated sizes, gleaming like gold, strung from their narrow end, each encrusted with high, half-melted iridescent crystals over swirls of turquoise, blue, indigo, azure, and violet. More than a necklace, it was an exotic collar – a stomacher almost – fit for an Egyptian queen. Nothing remotely resembling this extravagant ornament had been seen in Limoges before. This Lejalou creation heralded the renaissance of the ancient art of enamel.

When she had feasted her eyes on the Lalique-like opalescence, she saw that the gallery sold art as well. Art galleries flourished in Limoges, since many Paris painters had fled to the Free Zone: the works of Saint-Saëns, Lurçat, Gromaire, Limouze, were seen in windows. The Germans were such greedy buyers of art that even indifferent local painters were cashing in on the bonanza of these newly rich amateurs.

In fact, the large canvas of apple trees in bloom in a crudely green meadow, signed Morné, made Chantal, in her new awareness, wonder how many reproductions of the same scene existed. But as she lowered her glance, her interest in art was lost to a sign posted on the door:

LADY WANTED TO MANAGE GALLERY
SALARY AND COMMISSION
APPLY INSIDE

She started trembling before she knew what she was going to do. Then, she walked home as fast as she could without running to change into her best. Luckily, her aunt was out, attending the sewing circle, so she was spared explanations and argument.

There wasn't much to choose from in her narrow closet: her best had been a pearl-gray gabardine dress with matching Chesterfield coat, the first grown-up outfit made for her during her last school year. It was pretty, with a neat little black velvet collar and pocket flaps. Unfortunately, like the rest of her clothes, like her beige wedding suit, it had been dyed black at the time of her mourning and had shrunk in the vat. No matter, she thought as she shrugged into the coat. I'm so much thinner, I don't even have to tug at the dress. And shorter is in style now. Her black stockings weren't silk, available only on the black market, but a fine prewar lisle. Her flat patent slippers still looked all right. She slipped on the little pearl-and-ruby ring she hadn't worn since her mourning, on the same finger as her thin wedding band, and gave a fleeting thought to her gold chain with the cross. Was Fred of the compelling gray eyes in America now? Alive, or dead somewhere? Had he even really existed? Her hair, washed regularly now with the chamomile infusion Cécile had suggested, shone silvery blond around her face. She applied a little lipstick, wiped it off, but it left a pink tinge that made her eyes bluer. She took, from the back of her drawer, a pair of white kid gloves that had belonged to Suzette, a gift from Aunt Emilie, and, pulling them on, ran rather than walked to the Galerie Lejalou.

Monsieur Lejalou, half artist, half businessman, found himself hard-pressed: The girl who'd managed the gallery was getting married and was only waiting for a replacement so she could leave. Chantal felt strangely serene as she lied about her age, making herself four years older. Otherwise, she told the approximate truth. Her husband had died in an accident. She needed to work, so she'd come to stay with a relative in town. She didn't mention – never even thought of mentioning – she was a countess.

Monsieur Lejalou, mindful perhaps of the elegance the aristocratic *de* of her name would bring to his gallery, impressed perhaps by this young lady's *bon genre* and manners that came straight from the nuns' deportment classes, hired her on the spot. She didn't care if he took advantage of her inexperience and eagerness to offer a ridiculously low salary and commission on the paintings she'd be selling. She was to start the next morning at nine, and the other girl would stay just long enough to show her how accounts were kept, what symbols on the customers' card files told of their credit standing, and above all, to remember to call Monsieur Lejalou when a customer looked as if he was about to make a significant purchase.

Aunt Emilie offered only a token hand-wringing resistance. So soon after the death of your husband? Couldn't Monsieur Lejalou wait a little, a year or so, until you're no longer in mourning? But her niece's excitement was contagious, especially after Chantal took her, arm in arm, that very evening, to walk past the gallery. So impressed was she by the window with its pseudo-Impressionist daub backed by a length of artistically draped fabric, that the term *shopgirl* didn't even come to her mind, and she sat down the same night to write her sister-in-law, describing the 'young widow's' new position in such glowing terms, the Arondels didn't object.

Chantal's new life would have been bliss, except she missed her daughter more and more. She tried to escape thoughts of Marie-Esmée blossoming without her by immersing herself in work. Mornings, she'd open the gallery and was busy all day. Inflation was rampant, since the Germans were freely printing French currency to pay for their requisitions. The price of a pair of shoes she admired in a store window had gone from a hundred to a thousand francs in less than a month. Investing in real estate wasn't wise in wartime, gold had long been hoarded. Buying anything, anything at all – a painting, porcelain, enamel pieces, whatever could be found – was better than holding on to the ever devalued currency. So, business was brisk and the local painters could hardly keep up with the demand for their repetitive views of the old bridge over the Vienne River, red-tile-roofed villages, or meadows in bloom.

Inspired by her glossier surroundings, Chantal was beginning to pay more attention to her appearance. Leaving mourning before a full year was out of the question, but she bought a wide patent belt to cinch her little black dress into her handspan waist. She learned to back-comb her hair and then smooth it away from her temples.

'We have a surprise for you,' announced Madame Lucie, the star of Aunt Emilie's sewing circle. 'You may not know it, but until I retired, I was the best dressmaker in town, quite a trendsetter, believe me. And I'm not so gaga that I don't know what they're wearing today!' She produced a pair of hair combs trimmed with large clusters of black ribbon just like the ones Chantal had admired in milliners' windows. 'Use them to pull your hair back behind your ears. Yes,' approved Madame Lucie, 'yes. Just that way.'

Chantal now applied her pink lipstick every day and Monsieur Lejalou smiled broadly whenever he saw the admiring glances she was receiving from male customers. One day, more fluttery than ever, he suggested, almost shyly, 'I'd like you to wear the necklace in the window. That black dress will set it off and when people comment on it, you'll say I've decided to put it up for sale and you'll get a commission. I'll make more pieces of this type, but there'll never be more than one at a time in the gallery.'

Jewelry? And that showy, gaudy jewelry, when I'm in full mourning, barely two months after I've brought my young husband to his final rest? thought Chantal. I know just how Mother Saint-Ignatius would feel about that, but I don't need her advice. I'm on my own now. Still, of course, she took the necklace off every night before leaving for home.

For some time, Monsieur Lejalou had been expecting an answer to a mysterious request that, if granted, would bring to his gallery a fame all others would envy. Chantal was not privy to this top-secret correspondence, but one day, the mail brought the long-awaited answer. Monsieur Lejalou opened the letter, read it, removed his glasses, wiped them and replaced them on his nose.

'The most wonderful piece of news! Jean-Gabriel Domergue has agreed to my proposal. He will let us hold an exhibit of his latest works, and he will also be available to paint portraits. This is the greatest coup of my career. My mother will be so proud! Jean-Gabriel Domergue at the Lejalou Gallery. Can you imagine! Here, look at the letter yourself and tell me I'm not reading it wrong.'

Unworldly as she was, Chantal could not have been ignorant of the name of the famous Domergue. A distant relative of Toulouse-Lautrec, he had, early in his career, specialized as a painter of women – portraits, busts, nudes. Any woman painted by Domergue, however old or unattractive she might be, became a beauty, while remaining quite recognizable. The beautiful became divine. Some said it was as though he dipped his brush in champagne, or in the pearly, sparkling, insubstantial Paris light. Domergue elongated the neck, lifted the chin. Eyes glanced provocatively under lashes, hair lost its weight and became a luminous, silky halo. His nudes had small, high breasts, a narrow rounded waist, and impossibly long thighs.

He had painted all the celebrities of the twenties, the thirties. He had gone to America to paint the Ford ladies, and the wives and daughters of millionaires, earning a fortune in the process. Domergue was the first, despite the envious barbs of other artists, to 'prostitute' his talent by accepting a commission to paint an advertisement, which became a classic, for the Dubonnet aperitif wine and another for a perfume. Domergue was a legend in his own time – he was to painting what Chanel was to fashion, what Maurice Chevalier was to song, what Diaghilev was to ballet, what Cocteau was to poetry, what Bugatti was to cars.

'We'll remove everything else from the walls,' said Monsieur Lejalou, nervously pacing the gallery. 'Everything. Domergue is sending forty paintings – forty, imagine! It's going to be like fireworks! And anything else will seem dull by comparison.' He continued, 'When you think of the vogue a portrait painter like Van Dongen enjoyed just before the war, and the prices he charged! Why, he makes his subjects look like they had been fished out of a river, after hours in cold water.'

(I know that look, Monsieur Lejalou, but I will not think of it now. You were saying?)

'Not only will we sell every single painting, with so

many people who have money and don't know what to do with it, but they'll want portraits of their wives, their daughters, their mistresses . . . You'll make arrangements for the sittings, Chantal. We'll reserve the best suite at the Grand Hotel, too, for the master to work in, unless he has other wishes.'

The current exhibit, of the local young painter with the unpromising name of Morné – 'stillborn' – who specialized in regional landmarks done in the familiar Impressionist style, was to last until the following week and Chantal was kept busy by constant sales. Buy anything, at any price, was the repeated motto. Inflation ran to three figures. The Germans, mired deeper and deeper in their Russian campaign, spent Vichy-printed French currency with wild abandon. Officers, their pockets full of the freshly issued ten-thousand-franc notes – obtained, no doubt, through illegal means, since their meager army salary could not *begin* to account for such affluence – bought anything the gallery had to offer. Chantal had so much to do, she even took stacks of invitations for the great Domergue show to Aunt Emilie, and the sewing circle calligraphed envelopes, giggling like schoolgirls at the 'naughty' pictures the gallery was going to show.

One afternoon, during a rare moment's respite, Chantal was sitting at her little desk, when a tall figure, long-legged and a little stooped, somehow familiar, walked through the door, stopped and stood there motionless against the light. Anthenor! Her heart missed a beat. She remained still.

He did not greet her. Instead, he frowned at her from a distance.

'What have you done to yourself? You look different. For a moment I wasn't even sure it was you.'

'How did you find me?'

'It wasn't too hard, you know, though, of course, your parents wouldn't tell me. But the mailman knew, and he wanted permission to fish in the upper lake. I had a harder time with your aunt. She wouldn't tell me where to find you, at first. I said I was your brother-in-law, so she started crying, and she said, no, I should not see you. I'd bring back such painful memories. Then she relented. Although you don't look like you are wallowing in tragic memories, I must say.'

'I am working.'

'The Blazonacs don't like their women to work in shops,' stated Anthenor, with the old arrogance. 'Your place is not here.'

(No, I know, Anthenor, my place is in Blazonac, cleaning the dirt of centuries and living in fear, waiting to see if the police are going to charge you with murder and throw me in jail, too, as an accessory . . .)

Chantal had changed, in those few short weeks. For one thing, fear was beginning to desert her, leaving in its place a brand-new and reckless audacity.

'There aren't any more Blazonacs left,' she replied. 'Just Marie-Esmée. And she'll grow away from all that . . . whatever will be left of it,' she added scornfully.

Anthenor was angry now. But he controlled himself.

'I came to bring papers for you to sign, on the subject of the guardianship of your daughter, since your father has been approved by the court,' he said. 'But that's not the real reason I'm here. In fact, I was supposed to mail those papers through the lawyer. But I came . . . I came . . . I really did because I wanted to see you.' She saw his expression soften.

He moved closer to her. Slowly he reached out, put his hand on her shoulder and looked into her eyes. Then something almost resembling a smile came to his face.

'I have been planning this visit for days. Don't say no, now.'

The old emotion, which she had hoped to forget, flooded her again, and made her knees weak. That first walk through the woods to the Belmont farm when despair engulfed her, and then hope, hope to win his admiration through martyrdom. There was the day he'd given her the music box, with the mechanical bird, his offering of his mother's name for her child. He had stood next to her at the baptism and at the funeral. Had she desired him all along? Hadn't she even wondered if the powerful longing she felt wasn't incestuous? Her knees could barely support her now.

'Lock up this place as soon as you can, and come have dinner with me. I told your aunt we were to have dinner at the lawyer's house, and not to expect you home until late. I know a place where we can have a real meal, without food stamps. I've bartered tons of firewood with the owner just for that meal.'

Both his hands were on her shoulders, and his eyes on hers. Chantal could barely stem the delicious fever rising in her veins, coloring her cheeks, drying her throat. She'd go, she'd follow him anywhere.

The restaurant, Le Coq Hardi, was one of the oldest in town, its large dining room decorated with chandeliers, velvet drapes, and an ornate ceiling painted with allegorical figures of abundance. But like all restaurants in wartime it had sadly changed. Most of the tables were empty under the dim light of a few bulbs. No sparkling white napery, but dull checked oilcloth covers with curling edges instead. Only a handful of diners in the great, cavernous room were enjoying the posted menu of the day:

A SOUP OF TURNIP GREENS
(no stamp required)

RICE WITH RUTABAGAS
(1 bread stamp and 1
margarine stamp)

BREAD, SUPPLEMENTARY
(2 extra bread stamps)

DESSERT: AN APPLE
(1 fruit or vegetable stamp)

Chantal knew the food was prepared without salt or butter, the rice gray, broken, and gooey. The sickly-sweet odor of rutabagas pervaded the air.

The owner, bald and portly, was expecting them at the door.

'Good evening, Mr Sefar! This way, please.' The name, so seldom used, surprised Chantal as if she were discovering a new identity for Anthenor. The owner led them across the room as though he was showing them to the cloakroom. In the back hall, he unlocked a door marked PRIVATE and took them through a small office with a door at the back, unlocked that door, too, and showed them up a short flight of stairs. A few steps along a dark corridor, then he pushed open a door and ushered them into the black-market dining room, where no food stamps were required.

It was a much smaller room than the one downstairs, probably a private banquet room in prewar days, its main entrance now barred and accessible only through this secret passage. To the dazzled eyes of Chantal, coming from the dimly lit room downstairs and the dark staircase, it was a glittering treasure cave, with its red flocked wallpaper and red tablecloths. Tall silver candelabras stood on each one of the five or six tables. There were expensively dressed women, in low-cut dresses, their furs thrown over the backs of their chairs, prosperous-looking men in dark suits, German officers in uniform. Anthenor looked out of place, young and shabby with his turtleneck sweater and his worn leather jacket.

But Chantal's fairy-tale necklace glowed, reflected in the mirrors all around the room, the cynosure of all eyes.

She did not recall eating lobster ever before, a whole lobster, with giant claws and feelers served with an unknown sauce, and garnished with sculpted lemon halves and sliced truffles on an immense silver platter. She looked up from the extravagant dish to see Anthenor smiling at her, a radiant smile she had never seen him smile before, showing small, even teeth she did not remember seeing before either. She felt so touched that she reached up impulsively and pushed the lank hair away from his eyes, in a tender gesture that momentarily embarrassed them both. When champagne arrived, Anthenor poured only a few drops in their glasses. They toasted, then he took her glass away.

'I have come to say good-bye, because I will be leaving soon.'

'To say good-bye? But where are you going?'

'I will tell you later. I'll be leaving in a few days, and I don't know when I'll be back.'

Perhaps, thought Chantal, perhaps he just wants to brag and show me that he, too, can escape Blazonac.

'Right now,' said Anthenor, 'I want to enjoy this moment, and I want to see you laugh with that dimple at the corner of your lips. I used to watch for it, you know, but it wasn't there often when you were in Blazonac, though, God knows, I tried to make you smile. I guess I wasn't very good at it.'

He touched her face gently. Chantal laughed, a throaty laugh not of joy, but of a new happiness. He poured just a little more champagne but put the bottle away when she asked for more.

Dessert came, flaming, but its taste was too cloying, too complex with fruit and liqueurs. No longer used to sweets, they could barely touch it.

'More champagne?' asked Chantal.

'No.'

Anthenor turned to face her – with that intent look she knew so well.

'I want you sober for the question I am going to ask you, which is the real reason I came here today. I want to look into your eyes when I ask it, and I want you to look into mine when you answer. I want you, and I have wanted you for so long. Chantal, will you look at me, and tell me you want me too and that you will come to bed with me?'

A stab of pleasure, or its anticipation, pierced her. She felt weak with desire. She closed her eyes and she heard her own voice answer almost shyly, 'Yes, I will come to bed with you.'

He had reserved a room upstairs, probably one of those made available by the establishment for such assignations. She followed him up narrow, winding stairs. Suddenly almost formal, he helped her out of her coat, and when she sat on the edge of the rayon satin-covered bed, he knelt in front of her and put his head in her lap. She caressed his hair slowly, thinking suddenly of the little boy he had been, and that neither he nor she had ever known much tenderness. Tears of self-pity came to her eyes and she raised his face to her lips. His arms went around her, he rolled onto the bed holding her tight, devouring her mouth, holding her face, her hair, in his hands, sliding them down her shoulders, pushing her dress down to her waist.

Her small rounded breasts surged, nipples erect. Anthenor moaned and rubbed his face on them, holding them close to each other in both hands and burying his face in the warm cleft, then caressing the nipples with his lips and biting them gently with those small, even teeth. It was Chantal's turn to moan, in anguish, in demand, in surprise at the unknown surge within her, at the void that suddenly opened deep in her body and demanded filling. She ripped at his clothes, and when they were both naked, he lay on her, wide-shouldered, lean-hipped, and long-legged, his face against her neck, sobbing dry sobs of desire and happiness, reaching for her sex.

She guided him to the warm demanding wetness, but he would not penetrate her right away, in spite of her demand. Instead, he held his own sex hard and quivering just where the lips open and let her agonize with desire for a moment, looking hard into her eyes with taut-cheeked intensity. And then he entered her, creating ring after ring of pleasure, deeper with each stroke, reaching for more and more demanding void to fill, as she strained to meet the hard flesh that wanted hers.

Screams came to her throat, but his mouth was on hers, on her face, his hands holding her to him, raising her hips to his body, moving her so that his sex could satisfy the farthest recesses of her desire.

Suddenly, as if a silent gong were struck somewhere deep in her, wave after wave began to spread in concentric circles, originating from a point at the center of her that released a flow of pleasure with each vibration.

He had drawn back, feeling her climax, and controlling his, almost pulling out, holding his member at the entrance to her vagina and gently rubbing it into the wet, swollen lips. When her pleasure began to subside, he started moving again, harder and harder, and the warmth of his own release flooded her, and she climaxed again, no, not again, but still, as though something had been left unreleased, and one last, overpowering shudder brought a muffled scream.

Anthenor slipped out of her, rolled onto his side, slid down, and took her clitoris between his lips, sucking it gently, while his fingers played with her nipples. The excruciating vibration resumed, but it was different now, the waves of pleasure stronger, and as he felt her clitoral orgasm begin, he slipped on top of her, penetrated her again, and filled her, with the same hardness, and he soon came again, more warm wetness inside her already wet sex.

They lay exhausted, fulfilled, and yet still hungry for each other, tightly intertwined, bodies, hands, faces touching.

A moment later, he lay across the bed with his head resting on Chantal's taut, narrow belly, tracing the line of her waist and hip with the tip of his finger. And then he took her again, slowly and gently this time, talking, almost chanting against her hair:

'I have wanted you so long . . . so long . . . so long . . . I didn't even know I wanted you at first. Or maybe I was afraid of wanting you, I guess. I wanted to be with you, and then I felt I had to stay away, and I would lie in bed at night, and I thought of you, in that room nearby, and Renaud, and I knew what Renaud was like. Toward the end, I would masturbate in my bed, repeating your name, and I had a handkerchief of yours which I kept hidden in my room, and I came in it day after day. And after that, I would avoid you, because I was afraid of you, of myself. Of what could happen.'

His member was caressing her, retreating, pressing, lifting, moving back. Then he reached with his hand, between his body and hers, found the exact pinpoint of her clitoris and held it pressed, while his sex continued its insistent caress. This time, when the vibrations began, Chantal knew what to expect, and she arched her body to meet the ecstasy, all her being concentrated on that single spot, deeper than the root of her clitoris, the fountain from which she knew it was all going to spring forth. Anthenor's climax was coming near, she could feel the vein in his sex throbbing . . .

But he stopped abruptly, and she almost cried out in frustration. His hand had stopped pressing, his sex withdrew. She gasped.

'Let's make it last,' he whispered. 'Try to think of something else for a moment, and relax a little. You'll see, it will be even better.' So she tried to think of . . . what else? The low wall over the lake and the cool clear water, and the bitter scent of ivy. Remember? The waves subsided. The orgasm was not gone, it was there, nearby, quivering, ready to be recaptured at will.

'Start moving again now, slowly, slowly . . .' Anthenor was moving in slow circles inside her, wet fingers pressing on the pinpoint of sensation of her swollen clitoris, in the same circular motion, stopping now and then as she arched gasping, her entire being begging him to continue. He picked up the rhythm, faster . . .

'Now!' he whispered.

Anthenor's hand reached behind her, pressing her buttocks hard against him, and penetrated her rectum with his wet fingers. A sharp pain, lost in the pleasure that came instantly, with the double penetration triggering off a twofold orgasm, and she came in a flood of shudders that wouldn't end, trembling, moaning, convulsed. His own climax broke, too, he too shuddered and sobbed, and fell back, still holding her tight, drenched in perspiration, sperm, vaginal fluid.

A moment passed. Her flesh throbbed, midway between pain and the receding wake of the orgasms.

'I am so thirsty,' she whispered.

'Don't move, I'll get you some water.' Anthenor stood up, found the bathroom but no glass, turned on a faucet, and came back with water cupped in his hands. She drank, spilling water on the bed, laughed, pulled him down. But he remained seated, looking at her.

'Do you know you are still wearing that necklace?' he said suddenly. 'It just reaches your nipples. It is beautiful.'

She smiled. 'Do you always make love like that?' she asked.

'Like what?' Anthenor was genuinely surprised. 'I did not make love to you in any special way. I just did what I felt would be good. It will be different another time depending on how we feel.'

'Do people all make love like this?'

'That, I wouldn't know,' he said seriously. 'I have never watched anyone make love, so I don't know how others do it.'

'Do *you* often make love like this?'

'No,' said Anthenor curtly. 'I don't.'

They had to walk back to Aunt Emilie's house through the silent streets of the sleeping city. He held her hand in the pocket of his big leather jacket to keep it warm and they walked close, feeling each other's hip and leg.

'I'm starved,' said Anthenor suddenly. 'Starved. To think we barely touched that lobster, and even less the dessert!'

'And what about the champagne? We left most of it in the bottle. Your fault. I'd have finished it all if you'd let me.'

'No doubt. But once for a change, I did not want to rape a drunken woman. And if you'd like to know whether that is something I do very often, the answer is yes. All the time. I get them drunk on Moët & Chandon, and I drag them to bed by the hair.'

Chantal laughed so hard, she couldn't stop. Then she realized she was hungry too. No food to be had, of course, in the wartime city, shut down for the night. But she had never been so ravenous.

A smell of baking bread floated in the air as they turned a corner. A bakery was there, closed and shuttered at this hour, but through an open grating in the sidewalk light spilled and voices could be heard. The bakers were already at work in the basement room. Anthenor stopped, squatted on his haunches, and called out, 'Your bread smells good!' This brought a baker, red round face under his tall white hat, peering up through the grating.

'The bakery is closed. We open at seven tomorrow morning.'

'I know you are closed. But we're starving. Didn't have any dinner.'

'Why didn't you have any dinner?'

'Because,' declared Anthenor suddenly, still squatting on his haunches, and to Chantal's astonishment, 'because I was in bed making love to this beautiful woman. Wouldn't you have done the same thing?'

The baker laughed, hands on his hips. 'Come down, then. Careful with your heads, the ceiling is low in the stairs.'

The baking room was a wonderland dusted in flour, with hundreds of cobwebs hanging from the rafters, all powdered in white, a tracery of immense and fragile complexity, arches, lintels, and spires, each minute thread precisely outlined. The ovens were on, great gusts of warm air blew the smell of baking bread into the room.

'That stuff smells good enough when it is baking, but it tastes terrible,' said the baker. 'All sawdust and ground straw, with just a little real flour mixed in . . . Wouldn't touch it myself. Come to the back room.'

The back room, reached through an open stone arch,

was just large enough for racks to cool the oven-fresh loaves, and a table where the baker's two helpers were seated. One got up, pulled up more chairs from a corner for the new arrivals. Everybody shook hands.

'You work at the warehouse, down by the river?' the *mitron*, the helper, asked Anthenor. 'Their night shift finishing just about now, eh?'

'Right,' agreed Anthenor, 'except that tonight, I played hooky.'

Everybody laughed, Chantal blushed and snuggled closer to Anthenor. Was this the arrogant, aloof man she thought she knew? He was positively playful tonight!

'You came right on time,' said the baker. 'Our own loaf just came out of the oven. We have to sift through more than a sackful to get enough white flour for just this one loaf.'

'And what do you do with the residue?' asked Anthenor, with a wink.

'What do you think?' The *mitron* winked back, with a gesture of emptying something into the giant flour bin in the corner. They all laughed.

'Here, help yourselves.' The baker was pushing toward Chantal the large loaf of still-hot white bread. Then a wheel of Fourme cheese, fresh from some farm, yellow with cream, already well cut into. Everybody piled slices of cheese on thick chunks of bread and ate hungrily.

Speaking with his mouth full, Anthenor said, 'Sure could use something wet to wash this down.'

The baker chuckled, reached under the table, and brought out a large jug half full of red wine, handed it to him. Anthenor wiped the mouth of the jug with the palm of his hand, took a long swallow, wiped the mouth of the jug again politely. He heaved a deep sigh of satisfaction, settled back in his chair, stretched out his long legs, hands behind his head.

'No wine for the women,' he declared, playing the heavy. 'Don't know how to drink properly.'

The three bakers thought this was the funniest thing

they'd ever heard, and Chantal laughed to see them all having such a great time.

Satiated, they were soon back in the street, arms tightly linked again, walking to the rue Pierre-Raymond.

'Did you notice,' said Chantal, 'it's not so cold anymore? It's as though spring had suddenly come. There's a softness to the air. Can you feel it? Perhaps winter is finally over.'

The cathedral bells rang four times the quarter-of-the-hour chime and then twelve times. Midnight.

'Today is tomorrow,' said Anthenor. 'When I was small, and I was waiting for the next day for a gift, or for my birthday, I'd always ask, when I woke up: Is today tomorrow? Well, you gave me my gift. Nothing to wait for now.'

They walked a little farther. They had almost reached the sleeping street where Aunt Emilie lived. Then Anthenor stopped, and facing her, put his hands on her shoulders, spoke quietly. 'I cannot put it off any longer, I have to tell you. I am leaving to join a Resistance group. I have been in touch with André Brousse, these past weeks, he is in constant contact with London, and he coordinates the activities of several units. He'll know someone who will know where I am and who can get in touch with me if absolutely necessary, but he will not know my whereabouts himself. You understand, in case he is caught . . .'

Chantal felt cold suddenly again. She had forgotten the war.

'You are going to leave me? Now that we are so happy? How can you?'

'That is why I did not ask you to marry me. If I could stay, I would have asked you to come back to Blazonac and we'd have been married as soon as the legal delays were over. But I can't ask you, because I don't want to involve you.'

'But why do you have to go anywhere? Stay with me!' cried Chantal, suddenly self-pitying.

'I have to leave Blazonac. I've been warned. Renaud's

friends – in particular that SS with the shaved head he was sleeping with – well, it seems they have reported me. I am on a list. My father is – or was – Jewish, that makes me Jewish too, in their eyes. Jews are now being arrested in Paris, and put aboard cattle trains, going east, nobody knows where. The same thing will happen in the Free Zone, as soon as the Germans break the terms of the armistice. Laval is back as prime minister of the Vichy government and he is more of a Nazi than Hitler. I don't want to wait and be arrested some night at home.'

'But what are those Resistance groups?'

'I know some of them. Since you left, the men have been coming to Blazonac, in the dark, when nobody can see them. We sit up late into the night and talk. There are all sorts in those groups, many fugitives from Nazi persecution.'

'Why? Are they Jewish too?'

'Some are. Some are Communists. There are German Jews, who were already refugees in France when the Germans came in and who could not get out in time. There are Freemasons, Hitler is hunting them mercilessly, there are members of the International Brigades who fought for the Liberals in the Spanish Civil War and have no place to go now. I even know one man, in that group, who's a Gypsy. Gypsies are on the extermination list, too.'

'Where will you live?'

'In the woods, in abandoned quarries, in caves in the mountains. I have an idea of where I'll be, at least at first, but I won't tell you, simply so you won't know in case anything happens. There are people who help, some because they understand what is going on, others because they're afraid of the Resistance. Remember how hunting rifles and firearms had to be turned in at the city halls when the Germans first came in? Well, they stayed there, in great piles, and now it's an easy matter for us to break in at night and take what we need. For the time being, the Resistance groups are mostly organizing and learning to survive, but things are getting in gear in London. Soon there are going to be missions to be carried out, and parachute drops . . .

'I have already spent nights with André and the men, hiding everything in Blazonac that can be moved – all the copper utensils in the kitchen, the crystal, the painted dishes you like, whatever is of any value. We dug holes out in the park, we buried everything and scattered moss and leaves on top.'

'Why should you do that?'

'You can be certain the Germans are going to come looking for me and they will search the house. A search always ends in breaking and stealing everything nowadays . . . We'll see if we can save at least what I buried.

'Now, look, it's getting late. Your aunt might still be up, though, watching from behind the shutters, so I will not kiss you. But you know our bodies are one now and our hearts, and nothing will separate us, ever, whatever happens. Look into my eyes. See? Now say to me, "No matter what happens, I am yours forever." Say it, please.'

Her eyes locked to his, she repeated the words: 'No matter what happens, I am yours forever.'

His face intent, Anthenor said, 'And you know that I am yours too. Nothing can change that. Ever. Now, let's walk up to the gate, and we'll shake hands and I'll walk away, and you'll go in without looking back.'

At the gate, as Chantal's hand reached for the lock, Anthenor said, in a fairly loud voice, 'That dinner was endless, but there was no way we could get out earlier. I hope your aunt wasn't worried. Give her my respects, please. I was glad to see that you are well. Good-bye, Chantal.'

They shook hands and he walked away. She opened the gate and went in without turning around.

9

'WEAR SOMETHING SMART for the vernissage,' begged
Monsieur Lejalou. 'Everybody who is anybody will be here,
it will be excitement like Limoges has never seen since
. . . since . . . since the Hundred Years War when the Black
Prince burned the city, but that was a long time ago and I
don't think anybody dressed much for that occasion. You
must look elegant. Oh,' he added hurriedly, mistaking the
panic in Chantal's eyes for hurt, 'not that you don't look
lovely all the time. You do, and you look so . . . *comme il
faut*, you know, good family, and pretty. But do wear
something very chic on Saturday, please.'

Easier said than done. Chantal brought up the matter to
Aunt Emilie, who instantly became as involved as her
niece. The problem was discussed with the widows of the
sewing circle, who all agreed that even if all available
clothing stamps were put together, nothing remotely chic
was to be had in Limoges now.

It was Madame Lucie who had *the* idea, and sent Aunt
Emilie running to the attic and rummaging through wicker
trunks. Old dresses were brought out, unfolded. *Hélas!*
Woolens were moth-eaten, silks torn and broken along
folds. 'Wait a moment, there is still something,' said Aunt
Emilie, 'I'll go back upstairs and unlock your uncle's canteen, it's metal, the moths couldn't have gotten into that.'

The canteen revealed uniforms, tightly woven woolens,
a red jacket splendidly barred with gold braid, the blue
uniform with epaulets. No . . . No . . . Chantal is still in
full mourning. She can't wear those colors. Oh but wait!
Triumphantly, Aunt Emilie brought out Uncle Gustave's
old tuxedo.

'Poor Gustave, he only wore it once. Had it made after

he retired from the army, you know, because he didn't want to wear his uniform when we went to the opening of the Municipal Opera. I remember him that night . . .'

Madame Lucie wasn't listening to her friend's reminiscences. The tuxedo had already been shaken out, examined, found free of moth holes, and the ladies set to work ripping each piece off at the seams. Chantal was measured. A pattern was made to her measurements, the pieces recut, sewn together again. A skirt, short and slim, emerged from the bulky trousers. A jacket, fingertip long, as the new styles demanded, long and narrow lapels, one button at the waist.

'That girl has the most absurdly narrow waist I have ever seen,' complained Madame Lucie, her mouth full of pins, taking in and pinning almost to nothing. Just room for seams and a buttonhole. 'Well, it's just as well, it certainly gives that jacket a line. It might as well have come from Schiaparelli. Emilie, do you still have the shirt that went with that tuxedo?'

The shirt was there, wrapped in folds of black tissue paper, and not even yellowed. It was cut, and cut again, until its pleated bosom fitted smoothly against Chantal's small breasts. Aunt Emilie held out the black tie, and Madame Lucie cut it down on the spot into a narrow bow. The other ladies were transfixed, hands clasped in wonder that such elegance could be produced by their modest group. Until then they had only cut and sewn old, discarded clothes into wearable garments to put in the baskets to distribute to the parish poor. But now, look, will you! Like a fashion magazine.

Two days later, the suit was finished. Chantal only needed appropriate shoes.

Leather had not been available for months, the entire production requisitioned by the Germans for the army. The stores, empty for a while, now offered a variety of ersatz footwear made of woven straw, wood, cork, fabric, and even something that looked like patent but was, in fact, painted and varnished cardboard. Nothing durable, to be sure, but a tribute to the ingenuity and intuitive sense of style of the French.

In the best shop on the rue du Clocher, one pair was displayed in the center of the window on its own circular pedestal that raised it above the others. Chantal had been admiring it for weeks, never thinking once that she might dare to buy it. The shoes were made entirely of a black, velvet-like fabric, built on a high platform, of wood or cork, covered with the same fabric and at least six inches high. The whole effect would have been bulky, except that the platform tapered down, ending in a narrow sole, not much wider than the blades of a pair of skates. The price of these shoes had gone from one hundred francs to one thousand and had now reached two thousand. A fortune . . . Blazonac existed for weeks on much less than that.

But Chantal had just received her first month's salary, and after discussion with Aunt Emilie and much encouragement from Madame Lucie, she went and bought the shoes. They felt heavenly, divine, except that when she tried to walk in them, she stumbled and almost fell, but she quickly caught the knack, and fearlessly stepped out of the shop, braving the cobblestones of the rue du Clocher. Her reflection in the shop windows showed a new Chantal, taller, longer-legged, impossibly slim. Aunt Emilie clasped her hands. 'I haven't seen anybody so beautiful,' she sighed, 'since the days when Suzette came downstairs in a new dress for one of her recitals!'

The blue necklace had long been sold, though Chantal had hated to see it wrapped in tissue paper, placed in an oblong box, disappear into the pocket of a German officer who, blond and long-legged, looked a little like Anthenor. She had thought at the time: Suppose I put my hand on his arm and whisper, 'Wait! I want to tell you something. I wore that jewel only the other day, and I made passionate love wearing nothing but that extravagant ornament, and when I was lying back afterward, it just grazed my erect nipples, and my lover laughed, because I looked like an

Egyptian princess ... Will you still want to buy it for some fat Fräulein?'

The day before the vernissage, with the crates piled in the gallery, in the midst of all the excitement and confusion, Monsieur Lejalou remembered that Chantal must look as splendid as possible and that the well-attended vernissage was another occasion to display the next one of his creations. This time he produced a pair of earrings that sent her into a vertigo of delight. They were his latest design, and the first of what would later be thousands of pairs produced in Limoges by the Lejalou Ateliers. Three short, uneven lengths of narrow black velvet ribbon held three oval dangles of the same hues of blue and indigo enamel, iced over with crystals, like the ones he had used in that first, unforgettable necklace. She tried them on. Sparks of blue jumped from the dancing ovals to her eyes, like lightning. 'Don't forget to say they are for sale, if anybody admires them,' Monsieur Lejalou cautioned her.

The crates were opened and their treasures revealed: ravishing faces, elongated nudes, sensuous busts. The reigning music-hall star Mistinguett, nude with her ostrich fan, Josephine Baker, the dancer, reclining on a striped black-and-white couch, golden bronze body, her face a stylized African mask. A demure black ribbon tied around her slender neck, a well-known starlet glanced with guileless eyes, her innocence belied by her naked breasts. Large canvases, small ones, the walls of the gallery were soon alive.

Monsieur Lejalou chose the most provocative nude for the window – a deeply tanned girl, with short platinum-white hair cut into feathery bangs, standing full face, smiling mysteriously, her feet in the foam of a turquoise-blue Mediterranean or perhaps in the cloudlets of an improbably cerulean sky. Much more than sex, she evoked a world that might exist in a different dimension, a dream beyond dreams, an escape to an absolute elsewhere. Looking at her, one could shut off the wet gray city outside, the winter that lingered on, the war, the dull, sad reality, and indulge in reverie.

Within a few moments, a crowd had gathered. The city newspaper sent its reporter and a photographer who took pictures of the nude in the window. Early the next morning, the paper was out. Chastely cut off at the waist, a nude bust still, it dominated the front page. The story, a biography of Domergue and an enumeration of his triumphs and awards, filled the second page and continued on the third for five columns. The paper sold out that day by eleven a.m.

Later in the afternoon a monsignor, representing the bishop, came to the gallery, white, pudgy hands folded on his violet sash, eyes lowered, and spoke earnestly to Monsieur Lejalou:

'Remove this nude, which is an offense to morals and religion, is likely to send the young to their doom, will break up families, and confound years of virtue with heaven knows what kind of salacious thoughts.'

Had the bishop, incognito, seen the nude, or only heard reports? In any case, he had missed the point entirely, since the painting suggested something far more subtle and exciting than mere salaciousness. But Monsieur Lejalou was overjoyed.

'What will happen if I refuse to remove the offending picture?' he asked, slowly wiping his glasses.

'Well,' murmured the monsignor, eyes still lowered, hands playing with the gold crucifix and chain draped over his purple cummerbund, 'in that case, monsieur, the bishopric will be forced to send a bulletin to all its churches. Priests will be required to warn the faithful in their Sunday sermon, caution them against even walking on this street for fear their eyes might stray. The children of all the catechism groups will be enjoined to stay away from the avenue Gambetta and asked to inform their parents of the danger lurking here. Catholics must avoid this avenue and the Galerie Lejalou under penalty of sin.'

'Yes?' breathed Monsieur Lejalou.

'The weekly newsletter of the diocese will publish a front-page editorial condemning the painter, and yourself, monsieur, as aiders and abettors of Satan. Nuns in convents will be asked to say novenas for the salvation of the souls your rash actions have endangered. Think hard, monsieur, it is not only your eternal soul you are placing in jeopardy, but that of others, innocent ones . . .'

Monsieur Lejalou could barely contain himself. What unhoped-for, marvelous advertising! Thanks to the bishop, he was certain everyone in the city, male, female, young, old, married and unmarried, would make it a point to have seen the nude in the window. By the time the exhibit opened and Domergue arrived, the city would be divided into two camps: those who were against the bishop, and those who were against the painting. Central to the forming of French public opinion is the fact that no group declares *for* any given side of an issue, but that factions can always be found to form *against*. No matter whether they disapproved of the bishop's guidelines on morality, or condemned the painter in the name of whatever ethical or artistic principle came to mind at the time, everyone would have filed past the Galerie Lejalou window. There would be no other topic of conversation, the papers would write of nothing else. It might even displace the war news from the front page and the everlasting vexing problem of victuals from everybody's mind.

Early the next day, and every moment after that, the phone rang ceaselessly. Those who had not received an invitation to the opening begged for one, others demanded, sight unseen, since the gallery was now closed to the public until opening day – to reserve a painting, any painting, large or small, at any price, so long as they could be certain that when they arrived on the day of the vernissage, one piece at least was available with their name written on the blue tag. There were twenty offers to buy the nude in the window, at *any* price. But Monsieur Lejalou put the blue tag on it that meant 'reserved' because it was much too early to sell it.

The day before the vernissage, he did not go to his atelier at all, stayed instead in the gallery watching the animation outside. The usually quiet avenue Gambetta was invaded by crowds unseen before in the neighborhood.

Office girls walked by, arm in arm, giggling and probably comparing their own charms to the elongated limbs in the turquoise haze, mothers with their babies walked slowly by, pushing strollers – the avenue Gambetta was a *long* detour on the way to the park, Limoges babies would have a great outing today – boys and girls detoured from the schools and the lycée. Chantal spotted the girls from Saint-Eustache school, in their dowdy pleated skirts, white blouse, and, yes, blazer with the embroidered emblem snapped on the breast pocket. She watched them, in groups of four or five, strolling on the opposite sidewalk, with only a few boldly darting across the street as if on a bet, tripping on their heavy loafers, then running back to the safety of the group. Middle-aged couples changed the path of their afternoon stroll to pass the gallery, the women scowling, their husbands casting covert glances . . .

On the morning of the Great Day, as Monsieur Lejalou went out to pick up the exhibition catalogs, he forgot to lock the door behind him. A few minutes later, a German officer, booted, carrying a riding stick, walked in, clicked his heels, bowed from the waist.

'*Mes hommages, mademoiselle,*' he said in French, unaware that *hommages* cannot be offered to someone you call *mademoiselle*. 'I want to buy the painting in the window. You will have it delivered at six to my hotel. I am Hauptmann Jaeger, my orderly will be there to receive it. What is the price?' he asked, slipping the riding stick under his arm to reach for his wallet.

Chantal was not intimidated. 'I am sorry,' she said, following orders. 'But this painting is not for sale. There is a tag on it, as you may have seen, that means—'

'I am not interested in tags, mademoiselle, I happen to

like that painting. I wish to own it. Now, please, tell me the price, I am in a hurry.'

'*C'est impossible,*' repeated Chantal, getting nervous but still looking straight at him. 'And anyway, the gallery is closed to the public, you shouldn't be here.'

The German stamped his boot. 'Don't be insolent with me, mademoiselle. You may be beautiful, but aren't you bright enough to know there is a war, and we won that war, and our wishes are commands to you? I repeat, how much is the painting?'

But Chantal could see that at the same time the focus of his interest was shifting from the art to her person. She stepped back a few feet and the Hauptmann followed her, caught up with her, reached out, put his arms around her in a tight vise, and was reaching for her lips as she turned her head away.

'Hello! I am back,' sang out Monsieur Lejalou cheerfully. He had just come in unheard, and could not have missed the scene, but he pretended tactfully to have seen nothing.

'What can I do for Your Excellency?' Good businessman that he was, Monsieur Lejalou had decided, early in the Occupation, that the title 'Excellency' could only flatter German officers, and it saved him having to try to discern rank and other subtleties of uniform and insignia.

The Hauptmann was taken short. He hesitated for a second, while Chantal walked away, pretending disinterest.

'Yes, monsieur, I was telling this young woman that I wish to purchase the painting in the window. Just tell me the price.'

Monsieur Lejalou affected genuine consternation. 'I could not be more distressed, Your Excellency, but this is impossible. I beg to explain . . .'

The German started to speak. Monsieur Lejalou continued, thinking fast. 'We received a call this morning from your government's top level, relayed through the Kommandantur. Someone speaking for a very high-ranking person. *Very* high-ranking, you understand. I am not at liberty to divulge his name. That eminent person wanted the painting, and we obliged, of course. We will ship it at the end of the exhibit. I would not be surprised, not surprised at all, if you saw it soon in Berlin, in some very, very high-placed salon. I am sure Your Excellency understands.'

The Excellency understood very well. Far from being angry, he felt gratified that his artistic flair had been correct and had coincided with that of ... Goebbels? Goering? The fat Luftwaffe Field Marshal was said to be traveling through the region incognito.

Monsieur Lejalou, pressing his advantage, continued, 'As a matter of fact, that eminent person also wished to purchase a landscape by the famous Morné' – the unknown painter whose indifferent works Monsieur Lejalou was trying to promote – 'and we were fortunate to oblige, since, luckily, we had recently obtained two of his rare masterpieces. So, one remains, showing a lovely view of the old city, which I'll be honored to show to you. Madame de Blazonac,' he called out grandly to Chantal, 'would you bring out that splendid Morné we were saving for a real connoisseur?'

Flattered, the Hauptmann adjusted his monocle, examined the daub, discerned in it a light and a sense of color values equal to anything at the Jeu de Paume (perhaps a similarity of names made him confuse Morné with Monet?), and paid the price asked without discussion. As he left, he clicked his heels in the direction of Monsieur Lejalou, ignoring Chantal. As a parting shot, he advised Monsieur Lejalou to get the services of someone more competent 'for the good of this fine gallery.'

After he left, Monsieur Lejalou sat down, mopped the sweat from his brow, counted and recounted the money.

'You see,' he said to Chantal. 'Nothing to it. That's what you should have done in the first place.'

A little later in the day, Pierrot arrived, having driven since early morning from La Prade in the gazogene, with pails filled with flowers Madame Arondel was sending as her contribution to the event. She did not read the bishop's newsletter, and she had only heard Aunt Emilie's gushing about the fabulous job, the famous artist, and how everybody was so proud of Chantal.

In the greenhouses of La Prade, unheated because of fuel economy but exposed to the south and protected by glass, flowers bloomed in extravagant profusion in this early spring. There were orgies of daffodils and jonquils, disheveled Rembrandt tulips, and tall branches of a flowering Japanese tree, with waxy red rose blooms, which grew right from the branch itself without any stem at all, called *vernis du Japon*. Monsieur Lejalou arranged the flowers himself into gigantic bouquets that he stood on high pedestals at the very back of the gallery, against the dark velvet backdrop.

Electricians were installing the last spotlights. Vernissage would begin in two hours. Chantal went home to put on her new tuxedo suit, her six-inch-high shoes, and her dancing earrings.

When she returned, the doors had just been opened, yet a crowd already filled the gallery and she had to push her way through. She returned the timid greeting of the young reporter, adjusted her newly minted professional smile, took her order pad, and was soon besieged with questions about price. In less than two hours, more than half the paintings bore the red tag *Sold*.

'How delightful to see someone so blond in this land of dark-haired women,' said a voice behind her. Startled, she turned around. A shortish man, with graying hair and a neatly trimmed salt-and-pepper Vandyke beard was smiling at her. He has the smile of a faun, thought Chantal. His face looks like it should be completed with little horns showing through a grape-leaf wreath.

'You look exactly like my favorite models! Will you pose for me sometime?'

The master himself! He put his hand under her chin in an almost paternal gesture – looked at her face this way and that.

'Will you have dinner with me tonight so we can discuss your posing at leisure? But please, do something for me now. Take off that bow tie. That's a good girl. Now, open the neck of your shirt. That's it . . . More, another button. Good, you are not wearing a bra, you'll be the perfect model! Undo another button. All right, now, bend your head down, shake your hair, wet your lips. Perfect. Now, lift your chin, and turn your head to the side. Perfect, perfect. That is just the way I am going to paint you . . . Or perhaps a nude bust, with those enchanting earrings and nothing else.'

What would Mother Saint-Ignatius say if she could see me standing here in six-inch heels? thought Chantal, un-buttoned to the waist, hair tousled and face flushed, with heads turning and the master flirting with me? Well then, I'd ask her to stop frowning and to start praying for me. Pray that I'm not dreaming, that it's all real. And if I'm dreaming, then she should ask God that I don't wake up.

Monsieur Lejalou tried hard to be included in the dinner invitation, but Domergue ignored his broadest hints, and suggested instead that the two of them have a business lunch the next day. When the gallery closed, the master took Chantal's arm and led her to the same restaurant where she had dined with Anthenor.

Was she already *blasée*? The decor impressed her a great deal less this time. Respectful whispers greeted their entrance, and the owner hovered while the master gave complicated instructions for a delicate but simple meal. Asparagus, veal with lemon butter, and no dessert. When Chantal's hand went up to button her shirt a little higher, Domergue teasingly took her fingers in his and kissed them. She was already too high to get drunk on the sweet, cool sauternes. Furthermore, she had learned from Anthenor that full awareness is needed to savor special moments.

'Antonielli, the man who worked for me, turned out to be operating on the black market,' Domergue was explain-ing, picking at his asparagus, 'trafficking in gold coins or whatever. Anyway, he was arrested by the police, the French police, but I doubt they'll release him so soon, since I understand the Germans had a bone to pick with him, too, for something like spying for the British, so he might be in for a long time. Anyway, it's not a man like Antonielli that I need. I have decided a woman would be better for the job.'

Chantal was listening intently, searching her mind: did she know anyone who might fill the master's requirements? 'Perhaps Monsieur Lejalou knows someone who could take the job. What qualifications does it require?'

'What about you? Would you like to come and live in Paris and work for me? Mornings, you'll work in the atelier, interview models, make appointments, schedule posing sessions for portraits, get rid of the pests, sort paintings in preparation for the exhibits, work with my secretary in the correspondence with galleries. There are always more requests for exhibits than I can accept, and it takes a certain flair to decide which ones should be accepted, or turned down, or put off.'

'If you think I could learn how to do that . . .'

'I think you can. Then, you'll have to spend a few afternoons at my gallery, on the Champs-Elysées, corner of the rue Quentin-Bauchart. Every other month or so, you'll prepare an exhibit like this one, and you'll go there to make arrangements. We have an exhibit planned in Marseilles already. See to the publicity with the gallery owner, give interviews to the local press and radio. Sometimes, if you tell me the sales and the portrait orders make it worth my time, I'll come, more often I won't. You'll have a salary, and on top of that, a commission when you do a show. And, of course, you'll pose for me now and then. What do you think?'

Chantal was at once thrilled and not a little wary of the master's intentions. 'Would I be able to find a place to live?'

'Officially, there is nothing to be had, because the Germans requisition every apartment the minute it's empty.

But there are ways, if you know people, and my wife and I do. Many have left to wait out the war in the provinces, others have found a way to emigrate to the United States. They all would like their apartments to remain undisturbed, so they like to have friends move in. My wife probably knows something. You don't need much space, just for yourself, do you?'

'I am a widow, and I have a small child. I'd need enough space for a child and a nurse.'

'You, a widow? Even more perversely seductive . . . Have you never been to Paris? Extraordinary.'

By the end of dinner, it was settled. For all his faunlike face and his suggestive remarks, Domergue also had an excellent business sense and a rare instinct for the best ways to market his talent. By the end of next month, he would obtain and send her an *Ausweis*, a permit to cross over into the Occupied Zone, and by then, Madame Domergue, a sculptor in her own right, who seemed older than her husband and played a motherly role in his life, would have found an apartment. 'I am the same age as the Eiffel Tower,' Domergue was fond of saying.

Fifty-three, what an old man, thought Chantal . . .

Aunt Emilie wept. How *could* Chantal dream of leaving? Weren't they so happy together and things working out so well? But Madame Lucie made her wipe her tears, congratulated Chantal, and shamed her friend for putting a damper on such a glorious opportunity.

'But, Emilie, my dear, you can't have imagined that child would spend the rest of her life with us. We've all had full lives, let her have her chance and stop making her feel guilty.'

As for Madame Arondel, she was torn between pride and hesitation: pride because her daughter was making a success of her own enterprise, and in such a short time too. Hesitation because there were sure to be dangers lurking in wait for her foolish, troublesome girl in Paris. But she chose to visualize the Domergues as a fatherly and motherly couple who would watch over her. Chantal wasn't so sure there was anything fatherly in Domergue's interest in her, and she refrained from mentioning she'd be posing – nude or otherwise. Let her mother visualize the job as some sort of glorified secretarial position.

'Mother, I will take Marie-Esméc with me. I have missed her terribly.'

'You know, she is very happy here, and loved and cared for constantly. Why, Anna is with her every minute.'

That was true. In fact, Marie-Esmée had become the complete tyrant, whom Anna carried patiently around all day, with Marie-Esmée pointing an imperious finger at the direction where she wished to go. Anna was round – round face, accented by the little white cap all Arondel servant girls wore, round eyes, round figure – a farm girl who was awed to be allowed to work in 'the big house' and to have been entrusted with the care of 'the little demoiselle,' still enough of a child herself to enjoy another child and yet old enough to have helped raise a brood of siblings.

'You don't even know where you'll live! And you'll need someone to look after her while you are working. Working! As though . . . Well, the less I say, the better, I suppose.'

'Madame Domergue will find a place for me, and . . . yes, you are right, I will need someone to help with the baby.'

Madame Arondel frowned. 'Where are you going to find somebody we can trust enough? Maria has a granddaughter who's looking for a position, but they're all the same in that family – poor housekeepers, and where would they have learned better, I ask you?'

Madame Arondel's maids were strictly trained, closely watched. Once their competence and loyalty to the house had been established, supervision relaxed, and they graduated to the highly desirable rank of almost family members.

She hesitated. 'Well, I could probably spare Anna. She doesn't do much else anyway but look after the baby. She isn't much older than you, but she is a good, sensible girl.

She turned down an unacceptable suitor last month, an out-of-work, lazy, shiftless boy . . .'

Ouch! thought Chantal, but as so often in the past, she simply let her mother talk herself into the perfect solution.

'She could go with you to Paris, and we'll see if it works out. I am sure she'll be happy to go, poor silly girl. And happier to return home, no doubt.'

When she heard the news, Anna would not believe her good luck, then flew into Chantal's arms, wiped her eyes with the corner of her apron, and said she was ready to leave that instant. But it was agreed Chantal would go to Paris first, get settled and organized in her work, then send for her daughter and her nurse as soon as she could obtain an *Ausweis*. Anna beamed at the promotion, from assistant kitchen maid to Paris nursemaid.

As soon as she decently could, Chantal mentioned casually to her mother, 'I think I'll stop at Blazonac, before returning to Limoges.'

'Oh,' exclaimed Madame Arondel, 'I forgot, with all the excitement, I forgot to tell you: Blazonac is closed down. Anthenor has left and Maria went to live with her daughter and son-in-law at the Belmont farm.'

'Anthenor left? Where did he go?'

'Officially, nobody knows, but your father has heard he may not be too far away. Your father thinks Anthenor has joined one of those groups of . . . of . . . terrorists, that's what the paper calls them. You know, those men from God knows where, who have started to hide in the woods, raid city halls for weapons, and, it seems, are in contact with England. Your father says he wouldn't be surprised if André Brousse had something to do with them too. André is under suspicion. The gendarmes have been to his place, several times, too, looking for a shortwave radio and even a transmitter – he's supposed to have one hidden somewhere – but I don't think they found anything. We are avoiding André and Cécile, not because we have anything against them, mind you, just because you cannot be too careful these days, you understand.'

'So what is going to happen to Blazonac, and the farms?'

'Well, the day after Anthenor left, we received a power of attorney and a note from him, asking your father to look after his interests, and since your poor father was already empowered, under the terms of his guardianship of your daughter, to take care of her interests, he is now left holding the bag.' Her mother trotted out her full list of injustices.

'And I don't need to tell you that running Blazonac is no picnic. The situation is disastrous, your father is even talking about lending funds to the estate, out of our own money, you understand, just to keep it operating, and perhaps even get out from under some of the worst obligations. Some burden, and not at all what we needed, with all the work we already have with La Prade.'

Deep sighs, scowls. And yet, deeper even, a profound sense of satisfaction: To all intents and purposes, Blazonac was becoming an extension of La Prade. Why, three quarters belongs to our granddaughter, she thought smugly, and now Anthenor is gone, leaving everything to us. What can we do? Turn our backs? No, no, we'll do our duty; we'll assume responsibilities others are shirking. Her daughter hadn't had to look far for the model of martyrdom.

Chantal smiled inwardly. Blazonac was in good hands, better than it had been for a long time. The insane lumber harvest would stop, Madame Arondel was already talking about plans for reforestation, restocking of the upper lake, to allow the sale of fishing permits. 'Not the lake by the house, of course, you don't want riffraff tramping near the château, no, only the upper one. It's more than three miles away.' The leaks in the roof of the château were being repaired. 'No point in waiting until the whole roof caves in, your father will take care of the bills, accounts can be settled in time . . . when Anthenor comes back, or when your daughter comes of age.' Comes of age? Madame Arondel knew that the care of an estate is planned over long stretches of time.

She'll be too old when my daughter comes of age!

thought Chantal. How old is she anyway? I've always thought of her as old but she is ... let's see. She was twenty-four when I was born. Why, she is forty-four. She was surprised that, for the first time, her mother did not seem so very old after all.

Chantal went back to Limoges to face a distraught Monsieur Lejalou, and to console Aunt Emilie, who was by now blaming herself for that accursed idea she'd had, of cutting down the tuxedo. That suit, especially with its black tie, looked so dignified and ladylike! That's what had impressed Domergue. She was sure of it. She bitterly regretted the one creative flight of her entire unimaginative life.

'Going to live in Paris! So young! At an age where she shouldn't even go *out* unchaperoned! And as the head of a family, with responsibility for a child, and even for Anna, since, after all, that girl will be dependent on Chantal too. And now that France is as good as divided into two countries, I won't be able to go there, see how things are going, or help if need be. I cannot tell you how much I blame myself for anything that happens to that poor girl,' Aunt Emilie whimpered over and over again, wringing her hands, to the ladies of the sewing circle.

But a week later, Chantal stepped off the train at the Gare d'Austerlitz. Invisible wings lifted her off the ground. Wings, yes, she thought to herself wryly, but no halo.

10

CHANTAL NEVER TIRED of walking through the five rooms of the apartment Madame Domergue had found for her. The owner, a lady of Russian origin who had been forced by the Bolshevik Revolution to flee her Saint Petersburg home as a young woman in 1917, had once more gone into exile – this time only a few steps ahead of the invading Nazis.

Madame Lazareff was a commercial artist who painted wallpaper and fabric designs, and she must have used her own apartment as a combined atelier and display room for her collections. Everything in the doll-proportioned residence looked as though it served as a showcase for its owner's talent.

It was located on the rue Pauquet, one of the short, narrow streets, not far from the Place de l'Etoile and the great Arch of Triumph, that cut from one of the major avenues to the next. The rue Pauquet went from the avenue Kléber to the avenue d'Iéna, and later was to become the rue Jean-Giraudoux. The innumerable food stores that must not mar the grandiose majesty of the avenues nearby crowd instead the lower level of the otherwise residential buildings of those small, transversal streets.

In prewar times, the rue Pauquet was, during the morning shopping hours, a riot of colors and fragrances, fruits of the season, meat and game. Now, sadly, many shops were closed and shuttered, and those still open had lines standing in the street. The bakery, with its empty windows, dispensed chunks of a bread even grayer than that in Limoges, and Chantal alternately smiled and became angry when she remembered how the bakers, too, probably sifted out the white flour for their own use, and unrepent-antly threw the residue back in the bins, darkening the already unappetizing mixture.

Directly across from Chantal's balcony, a gourmet shop, which had specialized in exotic fruit, game, rare mush-rooms, caviar of all sorts, truffles black and white, now showed a disconsolate display: two stuffed pheasants, hanging by the feet, as though in a still life, their dusty feathers shedding in a small scatter, and a large color illustrated chart, curling and brown around the edges, showing which mushrooms are edible and which are poisonous. No matter. Chantal did not see the desolation of the hungry, oppressed city. She only saw the tops of the chestnut trees, level with her sixth-floor balcony, their leaves unfolding into a verdant haze.

The apartment, from its small circular entry, its minia-ture hall, living room, and tiny dining room, to the two bedrooms, and even the kitchen, was a wonderland of design and color. There were stripes, patterns, leaves, flowers, bouquets, clusters and sprigs printed on fabric, painted on doors and cabinets. Violet and green, rose and lavender, were the dominant tones.

A double French door, set with beveled glass, opened the living room onto the dining room, and it was easy to see how the space had been conceived for formal living, for some grown-up version of a little girl's tea party.

Chantal's bedroom was a bower of purple and improb-ably pink violets, with purple and pink and green pillows strewn everywhere. The other room, to be shared by Anna and the baby, was abloom with miniature cabbage roses, so tightly massed on the walls that no background was visible. Even the handkerchief-size kitchen had been done in striped green and white, with bouquets of green leaves tied with rose-colored ribbon painted on each of the cabinet doors and garlanding the white tile floor.

The effect was, of course, extravagantly feminine. It was difficult even to imagine a man waking up in the pink and purple bower, a man's hand opening the sprigged cabinet doors, and men's shoes would have been an insult to the pale green carpet that covered the entire floor. Even a visiting man looked out of place, and Domergue, when he saw the place, sneezed elaborately, insisting that his hay fever could not tolerate such an abundance of blooms. Overdecorated? Perhaps, but Chantal loved it – a garden in the spring. It was such a contrast to the gray, war-darkened city, that she saw it as a magic realm, created just to her size.

Madame Domergue thought the motif must have been that of her friend's latest collection, because she remembered having seen the apartment done in white and black geometrics one year, and all in shades of blue another, light in the entrance, and darkening progressively to an all dark-blue bedroom, spangled with silver stars. Chantal, who came from a world where decor *is*, and never changes, imprisoning its inhabitants immutably, tried hard to visualize the black and white apartment and the starry bedroom. She rejoiced that she had happened into the violets and roses period.

After a few days, she went back to the Gare d'Austerlitz, this time to meet Anna and Marie-Esmée, who arrived burdened by bags and food baskets. It took two pedicabs, the only available taxis now in Paris, to take them all back to the rue Pauquet. When she stepped into the flowery apartment, Anna clasped her hands.

'Madame la Comtesse,' she whispered, 'this is as beautiful as a church. Is this yours?'

Chantal laughed. 'First, Anna, you must not call me "madame la Comtesse" anymore. Here I am simply a working woman. And yes, it *is* pretty, even if some people would tell you it's really overdone, but it is just right for us. And last, but not least, it is not mine, I am only renting it, the rent is low, but we must be very careful we keep everything just as we found it, because I want Madame Lazareff to be happy when she returns.'

The baby had no interest in interior decoration. She

186

couldn't quite walk yet, but demanded to be put down. She was pointing insistently to one of Anna's baskets, loosely covered with a folded shawl.

'Hush,' Anna whispered urgently. 'Hush. You mustn't. Wait.'

The baby tried to push the shawl away. Anna took her hand and gently removed it from the basket. Marie-Esmée howled. Then she grabbed the shawl, pulled off one corner.

'A'sen,' she said proudly. 'A'sen.'

The face of a rabbit appeared, a white Angora, pink twitching nose, long, flattened ears, and pink eyes. He looked around warily, one ear went up, then the other. He sniffed the air once or twice and, reassured by his new surroundings, hopped out of the basket and examined the green carpet. Finally, tired by the endless, cramped trip, he stretched along a wall, long hind legs extended, flopped over on his side, and went to sleep.

Chantal was horrified. 'Anna, *what* is that? Are you out of your mind?'

Anna started crying and Marie-Esmée immediately joined in.

'Don't cry, Anna. And you, Marie-Esmée, stop blubbering.'

'A'sen,' repeated the little girl.

Anna sniffled, wiped her eyes.

'It's the baby's pet, madame, she loves him and he is so clean, even Madame Arondel allowed him to stay in the house. Monsieur Arondel liked him too. He named him Arsène Lapin after that famous gentleman thief. But I didn't want to bring it, madame, as God is my witness. I said no, no, we can't, madame will be so angry when she sees it, and I knew there was no food for him in Paris, and no grass to be cut for him in the streets. But the baby carried on so . . .'

'What did Madame Arondel say?'

'She doesn't know,' admitted Anna piteously. 'I just put it in the basket before Pierrot brought the gazogene. Nobody saw him.'

'Didn't the guards at the Demarcation Line search your luggage?'

'Oh, yes, they did. They kept the bottle of cognac Monsieur Arondel had put in the food basket, and also the crock of butter. They said we could have the apples and the eggs.'

Damn generous of them, thought Chantal. Aloud: 'And they let you take that rabbit?'

'Well,' said Anna, 'they were going to take it out, but when the German guard pulled it by the ears, the baby let out such a scream that I started crying too, so the guard looked around, saw that the other Germans weren't looking his way, and he put it back in, covered it, and patted me on the shoulder. He was nice-looking, too. And you know, madame,' she added shyly, 'he winked at me when we passed. Are the Germans all really *so* bad?'

'I don't know.' Chantal shrugged. 'Perhaps individually they are not, but all together, they bring no good.' Now, she thought, I am the head of a household composed of a silly, crying young woman who needs the firm hand of Madame Arondel, a baby who is used to having her own way in everything, and an Angora rabbit who is obviously just as thoroughly spoiled. *What* do I do next?

'All right,' she ordered with new false bravado. 'Get that rabbit situated in the room here, at the end of the hall. Under no circumstances is he to be allowed on the carpet. And you, Marie-Esmée' – she addressed her daughter in tones Madame Arondel would not have disowned – 'you are going to have your dinner, get washed, and go to bed.'

The room at the end of the hall, not much bigger than a large broom closet, was Madame Lazareff's office and studio: a worktable, with hundreds of paintbrushes in jars, boxes of paint tubes, books of fabric samples, stacks of swatches. A plain wooden desk held neatly classified records of her business transactions. Chantal had covered the desk and the table with sheets, so no dust would seep in, and Arsène was moved to that room, with his food and his box, and happily settled under the table. His bathroom manner proved so impeccable that he was, in time, allowed on the carpet and never once forgot himself. After a while, Anna started taking him out on the afternoon outings when she brought Marie-Esmée to the little park at the curve of the avenue below the Palais de Chaillot. There, surrounded by imposing architecture, he would hop out of the stroller and nibble at the grass of the lawn, while Marie-Esmée played imperiously with other Parisian children.

Arsène even served as the introduction to Anna's romance. A municipal guard, splendid in his cape and kepi, approached her one day, saluted, and informed her that *lapins* were not allowed on the grass of the Paris city parks. But, seduced by Anna's round face – her tears, too, perhaps – and guileless smile, he had stayed around to make sure other guards would not disturb Arsène's snack. After that, he was there very often, and from the sketchy stories the baby told, as she was beginning to talk, Chantal could guess that a romance was developing between Charles and Anna.

She had started her work at Domergue's atelier. He lived in the lower part of the avenue d'Iéna, in a town house that had once been the residence of Prince Louis-Napoléon, before he became Emperor Napoléon III. The Domergue apartment was a duplex occupying the second and third floors. From a formal black-and-white-marble lobby, a red velvet-lined private elevator led directly into the grand hall of the master's apartment, which, at first, Chantal mistook for the main reception room: large paintings of the Venetian school in tones of deep garnet and golden light decorated it. Monsieur Domergue's collection of sedan chairs, more than half a dozen of them, lushly gilded and artfully lit from inside, reminded Chantal poignantly of the single moldy one in the hall at Blazonac. A wide double door opened onto the studio. *This* was the main area of the residence, and the interior staircase led to a small, intimate set of rooms on the upper floor, where only close friends were admitted, and where the

Domergues led a secluded private life that contrasted with the animation and constant flow of famous faces that came and went in the great atelier.

There, the master, saturnine with his pointed beard and mischievous eyes – impeccably dressed to his Cartier cuff links, his only concession to work being a corduroy jacket – painted from six in the morning until one in the afternoon. A neat painter, no splashes fell from his palette or from his brush. Mano, his Filipino houseman, prepared and cleaned his brushes, laid out and primed the canvases, placed the appropriate gobs of paint on the palettes, refilled the jars of solvent, and kept stacks of neatly folded white rags ever ready.

Domergue painted fast, with quick, once-over strokes, interrupting his work only to move the model's head this way, turn her bust that way, ask for a spotlight to shine on her hair or on a bare breast, and begging her now and then, as he had Chantal in the gallery, to bend her head down, shake her hair, and then look up smiling with wet lips. He was considerate of his models, but tired quickly of them and needed a constant supply of fresh faces and lithe bodies on the posing dais. After paintings were completed, the girls had all acquired, of course, a certain resemblance, although each one was perfectly recognizable. One of the questions Chantal heard most often, in the galleries, was 'Are they all the same girl?'

To which she answered truthfully, 'No, they are different models, but seen by the same painter.'

She quickly fell into a routine, which left her enough time to spend with her daughter, walking and talking by now, and it was during that period that Chantal, although the French are not overly fond of nicknames, and she had never been given one herself, started calling her daughter Mariès.

Early every morning before six, Chantal would set off for work, incongruously elegant for the early hour, but suitably dressed for her day in the monumental atelier. Also, after the master had washed his hands and shrugged into his suit jacket presented by the Filipino houseman, he would often take her to lunch at Carrère's, one of the places he had patronized before the war, and which continued to serve special clients in a small, cozy black-market room.

She both loved and hated those lunches. Guilt gnawed at her for enjoying *turbot à la crème*, or *asperges sauce mousseline*, while Anna and Mariès were scrimping by on the last of La Prade's potatoes or apples, with turnip greens for a vegetable. But after such a meal, she could go without dinner, conserving the meager supplies at home. And yes, she enjoyed walking into these elegant places in her new Schiaparelli or Maggy Rouff suits, acquired through Domergue's connections – the big hats setting off her lovely face, all eyes turning upon her small waist and ever blonder hair.

'*Petit,*' Domergue would say to the respectful waiter, in his most fatherly tones, 'tell me what you have today.' Then he listened attentively to the recital. Very little red meat was available, but every day some seafood arrival was proposed: lobster, langouste, sole, scallops with their coral, oysters. Often Domergue would say, 'Forget about all this, *petit*. Do you have eggs? Yes? Fresh eggs? Bring them to me with a candle. Lighted, of course.'

The eggs arrived, on a folded linen cloth. Domergue examined them, held to the light of the candle, and declared them fresh enough.

'Do you have butter? Yes? Fresh? Show it to me.'

The butter was sniffed and approved.

'Now, *petit*, you are going to take a small copper pan – not an aluminum one, for God's sake! – and just that much butter. No more. And you are going to cook two eggs just as I will tell you . . .' Detailed instructions followed on how to fry the two eggs. Then, the wine.

'Which red wines do you have?'

A list was recited. Domergue sighed – *not* what he was used to before the war. *Enfin* . . .

191

'Bring me a bottle of that Château Lafite, a pail of hot water, a bath towel, and the small silver tray.'

The first time Chantal heard this, she was puzzled. But the staff at Carrère's knew the master's idiosyncrasies. The wine arrived. Kept in unheated rooms – only the dining room was fairly warm – it was colder than the temperature Domergue preferred. So, while the waiter ceremoniously removed the Cartier cuff links and placed them on the small silver tray, the master let the towel soak in the hot water. Then, he personally wrung it out and wrapped it around the bottle, held it that way for a moment, tasted the wine, and if he found it too cold still, resumed the warm wrap until the temperature was judged just right. Chantal, who at first was terribly embarrassed by the ceremonial, found it watched approvingly by other diners: 'That's Jean-Gabriel Domergue, you know, the painter.' The clear implication was that a man who showed such discrimination over the temperature of his wine surely deserved the artistic esteem he enjoyed.

The contrast between these scenes of opulence and the stark restrictions outside increased as months passed and more and more supplies were diverted to the Russian front. Anna would line up in the early morning for the pint of skim milk Mariès was entitled to, then for the bread, then for whatever scant groceries were available. Electricity was turned on only briefly in the evenings, but during the summer this caused little hardship. In any case, curfew, when everybody must be indoors with no lights showing or be arrested by the German patrol, was at nine p.m. or earlier.

Wartime Paris bore everywhere the mark of its occupiers. At every street intersection stood pyramids of signs, black on white, in German Gothic print. They formed part of the backdrop of the Paris landscape in those years. Little traffic in the streets: the inevitable gazogenes chugged, rare civilian cars, priority vehicles of some service agencies, German trucks painted khaki, troop transports, arrogant command cars with high-ranking officers in the backseat, a few black Mercedes limousines with swastika flags flying on their fenders. Soldiers walked the streets, in their rough ersatz wool uniforms buttoned up to cover the absence of a shirt, or they lined up in front of the *Kinos*, movie houses, that showed German films. At six p.m., large groups poured from the numerous offices, especially in the Etoile neighborhood, where the big hotels and private town houses had been commandeered. The infamous Gestapo had one of its headquarters in the Hôtel Majestic, and people lowered their voice when they spoke of it.

There were also the troops – men and officers alike – apparently sent to Paris as a reward, a sort of rest and relaxation for survivors of the Russian front. They strolled the Champs-Elysées with their Voigtlander cameras, taking pictures of each other in front of the Arch of Triumph. The French population passed them, eyes lowered, walking a little faster. The Germans, too, under strict orders of nonfraternization, looked straight ahead, and never tried to smile, or engage anybody in conversation. Not in the street.

But it was well known that officers were seen in all the night spots and in the most extravagant black-market restaurants. They trafficked heavily, selling either favors available through their offices, or the gold and jewels acquired as bribes, it was said, from people who'd give anything for fear of being routed in the dark hours of the night.

As long as summer lasted, with its long daylight hours and warm weather, life wasn't too difficult. Chantal wrote a note to Martine, who promised to come to Paris soon for a visit. Since her home in Angoulême was in the same Occupied Zone as Paris, she'd have no need for an *Ausweis*. She just had to find room on one of the crowded trains to Paris.

She kept her word and arrived one Sunday morning, after standing all night in the corridor of her train. She would have to leave the same evening in order to return to her job as assistant to her father at the paper mill. The two girls hugged each other ecstatically.

'Chantal! I would never have recognized you! You're so slim, so chic, and so much blonder! What living in Paris can do for you!'

Martine was still plump and sweet-faced, unchanged except for an unfortunate frizzy permanent that ruined her formerly straight, shining chestnut hair.

'You look so good to me, and just the same Martine, who has been my best friend forever. I am so very glad to see you, and we have so much to talk about.'

'Yes we do, and also you must show me Paris. It's my first trip here, you know.'

So, after Martine had freshened up, they went for a long walk, down the Champs-Elysées, across the Place de la Concorde and the bridge, along the quays toward Notre-Dame. Questions and answers tumbled over each other. Chantal told Martine about her short-lived marriage to Count de Blazonac, his tragic death, but neglected to mention Anthenor.

Martine was awed by the castle on the lake, the title, and kept repeating, 'When you wrote me that card at the time of your marriage, all I could think was that you'd be a Countess! And you still are ... Meanwhile, look at me – still not married. Of course, all the eligible men are prisoners of war now.'

'Are you still wearing that pendant Volodia gave you?' Conspiratorially, looking over her shoulder to make sure nobody was watching, Martine undid the first button of her dress and showed Chantal a glimpse of the gold chain, with the strange n-letter pendant.

'I think of Volodia all the time, and I'm sure he thinks of me too. Remember what he said? In my heart, I feel that we are engaged and I know he'll come back for me someday. I heard the Red Cross was trying to help with mail, so I went to ask. They said I could give them a letter, but they wouldn't be able to forward it to America until after the war is over. And then it occurred to me that I didn't even have an address to put on the envelope.'

Chantal shook her head. 'Even with an address, no mail can get through, everybody knows that.'

Martine reflected for a moment, then turned and faced her friend. 'You know, I couldn't believe you'd have forgotten Fred. I thought perhaps your parents had forced you into that marriage. A title! A castle! But now that your husband is dead, do you think of Fred now and then?'

'Not until I saw you today. Would you believe, so much has happened to me, I often wondered if I had not dreamed that whole adventure! But when you showed me Volodia's pendant, I relived it all in a flash.' She hesitated. 'Martine, there is someone else in my life. If you swear you'll never say a word of this to anyone in the whole, entire world . . .'

Martine swore fervently with shining expectant eyes. So Chantal told her about Anthenor, how he was Renaud's half brother, their love, their commitment to each other for life, no matter what happened. When she finished, there were tears in Martine's eyes.

'I understand why you're no longer thinking of Fred. Is Anthenor still in Blazonac, at the château?'

'No. He left to join a unit of the Resistance. I have no idea where he is now.'

'Oh, the Resistance,' cried Martine, 'that's all we hear about at home! You remember my kid brothers, Denis and Georges? They're still in school, but they're crazy about de Gaulle. They listen to his broadcasts on the BBC. They've rigged a small shortwave radio, put it inside the regular radio case in the Ping-Pong room and pretend to play so we can hear at least part of what he says.' She stopped, hand over her mouth. In a lowered voice, she went on. 'Even my father listens with them sometimes, and my mother too. But she's scared we'll be found out. Any one of our employees could be an informer.'

Another hour of playing with Mariès, who passionately hugged the doll Martine had brought that had once been her own, exclaiming over the wonders of the dreamlike little apartment, and it was time to say good-bye, with another night of standing in the crowded train facing Martine. She and Chantal kissed and held each other before she climbed aboard.

A few weeks later, Chantal managed an illegal trip to La Prade to sign the guardianship papers, visit with her parents, bring back much-needed supplies, and, yes, to try to contact Anthenor.

Unable to obtain an *Ausweis*, to go from Paris to La Prade, on the other side of the line, she wasn't deterred. She had simply taken her bicycle with her, bringing it down from the storage room under the eaves of her building, and boarded the train to La Rochefoucauld. There she got off, retrieved her bike from the freight car, rode to a nursery in the outskirts of the little town, bought a bunch of flowers and cycled on to the cemetery. There she dismounted, pushed her bike through the gate, as though she were only going to park it securely inside. She found a tomb near the back wall, placed the flowers on the stone, knelt, crossed herself and prayed, keeping her eyes on the gate.

This elaborate charade was necessary in case the German patrol passed at that time, because La Rochefoucauld was right on the Demarcation Line. Part of the town, and the entrance to the cemetery, were in the Occupied Zone, but the back wall served as a separation between the two zones. Once in the cemetery, it was only a matter of climbing on the tombstone closest to the wall, hauling the bike and dropping it over, then jumping down on the other side. All easy for someone young and light. After that, she'd just pedaled the twelve miles or so to La Prade. On the return, Pierrot accompanied her to the wall, to help lift the bike and hand her over with the food basket.

She'd seen no sign of the dreaded patrol and tended to think of it as an imaginary danger. La Rochefoucauld was such a familiar little market town, how could it hold any danger for people like her?

Still, she'd gone with a beating heart, hoping that somehow she might meet Anthenor, or at least hear from him.

She tried her best to be casual, but Madame Arondel looked at her with narrowed eyes.

'Why should you be so concerned about Anthenor? You're not trying to see him, I hope?'

'Why shouldn't I, if he's nearby?'

'Because things are not nearly as calm as you might think. Since Anthenor disappeared, rumors have been spreading that Blazonac contained some sort of treasure, which Anthenor and his Resistance friends buried by night in the park, behind the château.'

'Mother, that's ridiculous. You know as well as I do how little there was left in Blazonac. A treasure, really! They were forced to sell anything of value long ago.'

'I don't know,' said Madame Arondel. 'Paulin claims he was setting snares in the woods one night and he saw them carrying spades. Some are saying that the German SS officer who was such a good friend of Renaud might have given him something of value. They're whispering it might be grenades, or explosives, or a cache of weapons or gold ingots, or loot the Germans wanted to stash away. Whether it's true or not is hardly the point, these days. Your father is sure Blazonac is watched by the Germans, who are hoping Anthenor and some of his group will show up, to recover whatever they buried, so they can hand them over to the Gestapo. You must promise me, Chantal. Don't go there, *whatever* there was between you and Anthenor. And be sure that you don't go looking for him and make everybody suspicious of you, or us. You understand?'

Chantal understood.

One evening, as summer was drawing to a close, and the leaves of the chestnut trees under the balcony were turning yellow, with patches of brown, there was a knock on Chantal's door. It was late, well after curfew. Cécile stood in the doorway, a scarf tied over her dark hair.

'Cécile! *Quelle surprise!* Come in.'

'Hush, close the door, quick. I don't think I was followed,

but one never knows. I'm so glad to see you! I need to talk to you where no one can overhear us.'

They sat in the violet-sprigged bedroom, doors closed. Even Anna was suspect to Cécile.

'First, I have something for you.'

Chantal's heart pounded in her chest as she tore open the wrinkled envelope. Although he didn't use her name, she recognized Anthenor's uneven script from the account books at Blazonac. The message was short:

I think of you constantly. I want you every minute, the way it was that night, remember? I wake and sleep with that memory. The days we spend here, preparing for battles that will come soon, are made easier, because I know that, after it is all over, we will be together forever. We will lie in each other's arms every night, night after night, into eternity.

No names, no date, the letter ended as it began, without signature or greeting. Chantal folded it and placed it inside her dress, where she could feel the rough edges of the paper against the warmth of her breast. Cécile smiled, an accomplice.

'I have to tell you something of what we are doing, but as little as possible, because the less you know, the better. André is deeply involved with the Resistance, he now serves as liaison with the British. I cannot tell you how I came here, I've been carrying mail and messages from one side to the other of the line, but I am watched now, and I cannot make the trip anymore.

'The Resistance is organizing, and actions are already taking place. You don't hear of them in the press, because the Germans suppress all news of sabotage – the derailing of trains, and the blowing of bridges – but I can tell you the battle has begun. And I came to ask you to do something for us. Listen carefully and tell me if you are willing.'

The corner of the folded letter scratched lightly when she moved. It was as if Anthenor's hand were resting on her breast. Her heart was pounding. She'd do anything.

'There is a young woman, I will call her Françoise, it's not her real name, but that's all you need to know. She has been working with us, but now she must be helped into the Free Zone. When I heard you had come to La Prade without an *Ausweis*, I thought you might help her. Will you?'

'You know I'll try, Cécile. Just tell me what to do.'

'All right, we'll decide which day you can go, and you'll take the train, just the way you did the other times. She will not know your name. She will be on the train, carrying a copy of the *Pariser Zeitung*. Don't sit down, stand at the window, looking at the landscape. Half an hour out of Paris, she'll come walking down the corridor and stand next to you. She'll ask if you've read the *Pariser Zeitung* and you will answer, "I try to read it carefully, but I need a dictionary."'

Chantal repeated the sentence.

'At this point, she will reach into her purse, take out her handkerchief and touch her face. You will do the same. Françoise is Jewish, and she is doubly wanted by the Germans, because she's been involved in an action in Normandy recently, and we have to get her out of there.'

'Of course I'll help,' Chantal assured her, recalling Fred and the truck ride for the first time since Martine's visit. She was proud to be given another part to play in the ongoing war.

It took only two weeks to make preparations for the trip. A long weekend was coming with Domergue away, during which Chantal could take time off to visit La Prade. It seemed only moments until she was standing at the window, in the long corridor, as the train pulled out of Austerlitz station.

She looked at her watch. Exactly half an hour after the train departed, she saw a small, freckled, mousy-looking woman, not much older than herself, with reddish hair pushed under a shapeless felt hat, wearing a rumpled print dress and a nondescript cardigan, come walking casually down the corridor. Hardly Chantal's idea of a Resistance heroine. But, yes, she was carrying a folded copy of the *Pariser Zeitung*. She stopped once or twice, as if to read something of special interest on the first page, folded it again, and came to lean on the brass bar alongside Chantal. Nobody was near, but Chantal felt an instant of panic, thinking, I forgot what Cécile said. Am I supposed to speak to her first?

But the girl asked, in a hesitant, little girl's voice, with an accent Chantal could not identify, 'Have you read the *Pariser Zeitung*?'

Wetting her lips, Chantal replied, 'I try to read it carefully, but I need a dictionary.'

The girl waited a moment, then opened her purse, took out a crumpled handkerchief, touched an imaginary speck from her cheek, and put it back in her purse. Chantal did the same with a neatly folded hankie that, for ten breathless seconds, she feared she had forgotten to bring along. She waited for the girl to speak, but she was silent. After a while, Chantal murmured, 'I hear you are very brave.'

The girl did not answer. A long silence again. Finally, she said in a low voice, 'Oh, no, I am not as brave as you may think. Whatever I did, I did because I had to, but I was scared, and now I'm terrified. So much so that I can't sleep, or else I scream in my sleep. That's why they want to send me to a secure place. I keep thinking people will hear my heart pounding . . .'

Chantal smiled. 'I know that sound. But don't worry. Stay with me and let me do the talking. Wrap this scarf around your throat, button up your sweater. If need be, I'll say you have laryngitis.'

In what seemed no time, they pulled into the little station of La Rochefoucauld, the picture of rural innocence, with green shutters and boxes of cheerful red geraniums in the windows. Retrieve the bike from the freight car. Walk down the side street, avoiding Main Street. Push the bike down to the nursery just outside of town, buy a bunch of pink and orange dahlias . . .

All the time, Chantal could feel tangible waves of panic emanating from the silent girl at her side. Poor thing, she thought, maybe she witnessed atrocities I can't even imagine. She took Françoise's hand, it was icy and trembling. The girl half sobbed. 'I will be caught, I know it, and it will be terrible, like ... like ... I truly wish I was already dead, then at least the fear would be over.'

Chantal squeezed her hand hard. 'Don't say that, please. And don't be afraid. It isn't all that dangerous. You'll see.'

Now take the road to the cemetery gate, pushing the bike. Lean the bike against the wall and open the gate ...

Cadenced boots marked step. The patrol turned the corner and stopped, face-to-face with the girls, less than ten feet away – two helmeted soldiers, rifles slung on the shoulders, led by a young noncom, dagger at the waist. Before the dreaded *'Halt! Papiere!'* could even be spoken, Chantal turned, looked straight into the eyes of the young corporal, smiled, and said provocatively, *'Bonsoir!'*

He was caught short, pleased and surprised this pretty girl could be so friendly. Perhaps he was tired of the hostility, the constant assumption of danger, perhaps he was only a young man, lonely on a balmy late summer evening.

'Bonsoir, mademoiselle,' he answered. Then, searching for a way to allow the conversation to continue, he added, 'Are these flowers for me?'

'Hélas,' said Chantal, lowering her lids. *'Hélas, non*. They are for the tomb of my dear grandmother. Today would have been her birthday.'

'Well,' said the German, 'that's all right. Well ... perhaps you will be in La Rochefoucauld, later tonight, taking a stroll along the river, just under the château. Say, at ... around nine o'clock?'

'Oh,' protested Chantal coyly. 'I couldn't possibly be there ... No.' And then, looking at him flirtatiously, from under her lashes, 'Not at nine, but perhaps, just *perhaps*, you understand, I might be there ... oh ... at around eleven? I'd have to wait until my parents have gone to bed.'

The German corporal was delighted. In his six months of duty in France, he had never attracted the interest of a girl as beautiful as Chantal. He grinned broadly, winked to show he appreciated her coy humor, repeated, 'Eleven,' and barked an order to his men, who had stopped and waited at parade rest. The three were starting to march away. Chantal tried to take Françoise's hand in hers again, but Françoise pulled free.

'*Messieurs!*' she called out. 'We are looking for the church. Can you tell me at what time is the evening mass?'

Chantal almost fainted. There. This was the fulfillment of the death wish. The Germans stopped, stiffened, an order was barked, rifles were unslung. No, they weren't interested in papers. They knew they had something more interesting than some local girls trying to slip across the line to buy a dozen eggs at a farm on the other side.

Mass was only celebrated before noon – never later in the day then. *Everybody* knew that. Asking for an evening mass revealed someone masquerading as a Christian. A Jew, probably.

They were marched into town, taken to a makeshift prison housed in the former parochial school. As they passed the front door, Chantal squeezed Françoise's hand. It was no longer cold and trembling. Françoise tried to smile. 'I'm sorry for what I did, but now I'm not afraid anymore. I knew the worst would happen, and I made it happen. You did what you could for me, but I must not, I should not, get through. I hope they send me to that place of no return where they took my parents and my sisters.'

Chantal shuddered. The horror of the war had reached out and brushed her with bloodstained fingers.

'I will not speak. Tell our people that I swear I will not, no matter what. Anyway, I know no names,' whispered Françoise. 'And don't be afraid. There isn't too much they'll do to you.'

The soldiers separated them brutally when they heard

them speak. Chantal was pushed into a former classroom – a lesson still written in chalk on the board – where five or six people were sitting on child-size benches. Françoise was led to another room down the hall. A door slammed. Poor, poor Françoise, Chantal kept repeating to herself. Isn't there anything I can do for her? She tried the door, found it locked.

No meals were provided in that strange prison, but the nuns who had run the school were now conducting a brisk business selling food to the prisoners. After Chantal had been there for a couple of hours, the door was unlocked by a sentry.

A nun walked in, hands folded in her wide sleeves.

'Good evening, my friends,' she greeted the inmates. 'Would you like some dinner?'

Chantal realized that in spite of the tragedy of the arrest, she was hungry.

'Well, my dear daughter,' said the nun, eyes modestly lowered, 'we could provide you with a plate of good vegetable soup and two boiled potatoes.'

Fine, thought Chantal, surprised that the menu was even announced. 'This will cost you . . .' added the nun, naming a price that wasn't much less than Domergue paid for those lunches at Carrère's, with a bottle of Château Lafite. Now, Chantal understood why, when she'd been searched and most of her money confiscated, several bills had been left in her purse. The nuns had to get their share of the windfall. She was outraged. Outraged, but she paid nonetheless.

The other people in the room had been there for two days, three in the case of an older man with whom Chantal shared her dinner, since he'd run out of money and could no longer order from the nuns. He told her the judge would be there the next day, advised her to lie down on the floor and get some sleep. But sleep wouldn't come on the hard floor with its smell of chalk dust reminiscent of her own school years.

Later during the night, she heard a great commotion

in the next room: Voices shouted angrily, furniture was pushed, the thin partition shook when someone was brutally shoved against it and cried out, in Françoise's thin, quavering voice. Then more shouts, blows, and after a silence, a scream of agony that wouldn't end. Chantal sprang up, banged on the door with all her strength, calling out, 'Françoise, Françoise, I'm here, answer me!' Only silence, and perhaps gasping sobs on the other side. But the door opened, a German reached out to Chantal, shook her roughly, pushed her into a corner, barked threats she didn't understand, but there was no mistaking his menacing gestures.

Later, as dawn was breaking, she heard steps in the hall, saw a bit of paper pushed under the door, imprecations in German, blows. Then doors opened and closed, an engine started, a truck pulled away, then silence again, with crickets trilling in the linden trees of the recreation yard. When she reached for the scrap of paper torn from the *Pariser Zeitung* that Françoise had managed to push under the door, she found it was stained with blood. What horrors had taken place? To what mysterious and terrible destination was Françoise headed? Would she ever know? What is that place of no return?

The old gentleman patted her hand comfortingly. 'The papers keep mentioning that people are being relocated, sent to work camps in the east, where they'll do farm labor until the war is over ... But it doesn't make much sense, does it, not after what we've heard during the night ...' Chantal held tightly on to the bloodstained scrap.

A few hours later, the door was flung open, there were armed guards on either side and the half-dozen prisoners were marched across the small town square to the justice of the peace. They stood endlessly, no chairs provided. Finally, doors were noisily unlocked, and the judge walked in. Why, it's Judge Lampard, thought Chantal, a friend of my grandfather Giraud, before he retired from the bench. She looked to see whether the judge would acknowledge her, but he stared without a flicker of recognition.

He sat at the bench and read, in a monotone, a lengthy series of articles, number this and number that, of the Armistice Code, under which, by authority vested in him by the Forces of Occupation, he was finding each prisoner guilty as charged of attempting to cross illegally into the Free Zone.

Each prisoner, in turn, was asked to step forward to be sentenced. He will recognize me now, thought Chantal, he will give some sign. When her turn came, she looked up and whispered, 'I am the granddaughter of Judge Giraud. Remember? From La Prade? My parents send regards.'

She was interrupted by a burst of anger. 'Silence,' shouted the judge, 'silence. You have compounded your guilt with insolence. You are hereby fined . . . Guard, how much was seized from this woman?'

The sum was named.

'You are fined that amount,' stated the judge, glaring. 'And in addition, your bicycle will be confiscated because it was the instrument of your crime. Next time, I'll sentence you to deportation east.'

Chantal was led to the door, along the corridor and out the front entrance. She expected to see a van pulled up, and to be pushed roughly inside. No. There was no van. Just the dusty little square, with its monument to the dead of the last war, and its tinkling fountain. She was free. Still trying to get some news of Françoise, she walked back to the school, looked up at its newly barred windows, but saw no one, except a German guard who gestured with his rifle that she couldn't stand so near the building.

There was only one thing to do: Without flowers this time, penniless and minus her bike, she looked neither left nor right – what would be, would be. She crossed the cemetery without stopping, climbed over the wall and jumped into the Free Zone. No patrol, not a soul in sight. It took her hours, but she reached La Prade that evening, dirty and very hungry. She recounted her arrest by the German patrol, but didn't mention Françoise and her failed attempt. The Arondels had heard of the prison in La

Rochefoucauld, but what angered Madame Arondel most was not the attitude of the collaborationist judge, nor her daughter's imprisonment, but the prices the nuns dared charge the prisoners for food, and of such low quality at that.

Chantal didn't realize the danger she'd risked. What real harm could happen to her in that little town, so familiar? Only much later did she understand she'd had a narrow escape and could just as easily have been considered an accomplice to Françoise and been shipped as well to wherever they were now sending the unfortunate young woman.

The next morning, she got up early and went downstairs, where she knew she'd find her father, getting ready for his morning round of the estate.

'Papa, may I go with you? I'd like to talk to you.'

Monsieur Arondel was glad of these rare moments he could spend with his daughter, away from his wife's domineering presence. He poured chicory and milk for her. They walked out into the early fall sunshine, cutting through the vineyards where grapes were ripening in a heady scent of fruit and wine.

'Papa, I want to tell you the full story of what happened in La Rochefoucauld,' she confided. And she told him about Françoise.

'I thought perhaps, if I told you, there would be something you could do. Anything. I don't know,' she concluded helplessly.

Monsieur Arondel was thoughtful. 'I doubt I can do much,' he answered at last. 'I'll go to La Rochefoucauld, in any case, and talk to people I know there, see what they know. I'm glad you didn't mention this in front of your mother because she gets so worried. And perhaps I should tell you,' he added, 'that Judge Lampard may not be the all-out collaborationist you saw. He is putting up a good front, but I know that several people were helped by him. So, it's quite possible that, had it not been for him, you'd be much worse off today.'

They continued in companionable silence. After a while, they reached the top of the hill from which La Prade could be seen, with its red tile roofs, the farms, the barns, the master's house nestled among tall evergreens. In the cleft of the hills, the pond shone under the slanting rays of the early sun. Fronds in the distance were turning to red, the vineyards to shades of gold. Chantal slipped her hand inside her father's and he squeezed her fingers. She felt she had learned something important about him and she hesitated. Could she speak to him about Anthenor? But she decided against it, and they talked instead of the coming grape harvest and how hard it would be to find the necessary labor.

11

SHOUTS FROM NEWS vendors on an icy November morning stopped Chantal on her way down to the Domergue gallery, on the corner of the rue Quentin-Bauchart:

'Allied landing in North Africa!
Allied invaders repelled with heavy losses!'

She snatched one of the last papers. Yes, the Allies had tried to land near Algiers. Somebody is thinking of us, she thought hopefully, the world hasn't forgotten us.

'Our own troops firing upon British and American ships!' a distinguished monsieur with a Legion of Honor rosette in his lapel protested indignantly. 'All the doing of that Admiral Darlan, the damned soul of Vichy. But I bet the French soldiers in Algiers have surrendered by now, after a token fight. The Allied Command will soon be established in Algeria.'

He was right, as the German-controlled press was soon forced to acknowledge. But screaming headlines overshadowed that news:

GERMAN REICH ACCEPTS TO EXTEND
ITS PROTECTION TO ENTIRE FRENCH
TERRITORY

Disbelieving groups crowded around the *kiosque*, reading over one another's shoulders the scant, two-page paper.

'Lies, as usual,' shrugged Domergue, when Chantal arrived, breathless, at the atelier. 'Nothing but a pack of lies. What they're really telling us is that they've broken the terms of the armistice and occupied the entire country, because they're afraid of an Allied invasion from the south.'

No more Free and Occupied zones, she thought. No more line to cross. The boot is pressed everywhere. And what about Anthenor? He must be in even greater danger now.

Persecutions against the Jews stepped up. Chantal's concierge, Madame Gilbert, whispered of nighttime raids on neighborhood apartments. Chantal one day noticed a heavy gold bracelet on the wrist of one of the new models, Sibelle, a very young girl with pouting lips.

'Almost a pound of pure gold,' bragged Sibelle, holding up the ungainly piece of jewelry. 'Somebody had it made out of a lot of melted-down gold coins. Ownership of coins is illegal, but jewelry's all right.'

'Where did you get it?'

'Manfred, my boyfriend, gave it to me. It's one of those things he finds in the apartments. Or else the people give them to him, bribes, you know. But who cares? And by the way, I moved yesterday. Take down my new address.'

Chantal only pretended to write the most prestigious location in Paris, at the corner of the Champs-Elysées and the avenue Matignon.

'Twelve rooms,' boasted Sibelle. 'A rotunda balcony and period furniture you wouldn't believe . . .'

From Sibelle's chatter, Chantal gathered her boyfriend was a Gestapo officer in charge of the arrest of Jewish families. He appropriated whatever he liked of their possessions, as well as some empty apartments. Shuddering in helpless disgust, she swore she'd never book Sibelle for another modeling session.

'Good,' agreed Domergue. 'She had a pretty enough face, but I could never get anything beautiful from her, with those mean little eyes.'

Madame Gilbert stopped Chantal as she was picking up her mail. 'You haven't seen the new posters? *La relève*, Operation Relief, it's called. Here, listen, they're talking about it on Radio-Paris right now. Hear that? For every young man who volunteers for farm work in Germany, one prisoner of war will be sent home. My older son's been there since 1940, two years now, his poor wife just can't manage on her pitiful pension, with her little ones. So we've told our younger son, Albert, he should go relieve his brother, help him return to his family. Don't you think it's the right thing?'

Albert was a sleazy youth, who should have been in school, but paraded instead dressed in the latest *zazou* fashion, pegged pants and oversize jacket. He was rumored to traffic in cigarettes, perhaps engage in petty crime, and made lewd remarks under his breath whenever Chantal couldn't manage to avoid him. Yes, it did seem like a good idea to send him wherever they'd put him to work in exchange for his older brother's freedom. Albert left a few days later. Soon, however, Chantal saw hope replaced with bitter disappointment when Madame Gilbert realized that after a few trainloads of gravely ill prisoners had pulled into the Gare de l'Est, no more would be coming.

'Damn Krauts,' cursed the concierge, but sotto voce – informers hid everywhere. 'Now the lying cheats have both my sons.' The crude deception was quickly understood, though, so new posters soon announced the compulsory work service, Service du Travail Obligatoire, STO. No question of volunteering anymore. No mention of relief. The Germans needed labor and they'd get it. All able-bodied men not employed in agriculture or other activities crucial to the war effort were subject to the draft and sent to Germany.

Another of those mysterious visits of Cécile, wearing glasses and a wig that would have made Chantal laugh in other times.

'Men are pouring into Resistance groups. They want to fight for their country's liberation, rather than be pulled out of bed in the dead of night by Militiamen, the new Gamma Force.'

Chantal didn't care to even ask who those Militiamen were. Cécile's visits usually brought news of Anthenor, and her heart was pounding. No letter this time, just a little stick of hazelwood, into which a knife had carved the word *Forever*.

'He is well, his unit is getting larger, and he's rising in the chain of command. Supplies and weapons are parachuted now, at night, from Allied planes. There are coded messages all the time on the BBC announcing the drops.'

'I've heard them,' said Chantal. 'The Domergues have a shortwave radio. *Les carottes sont cuites*, Carrots are cooked, or *L'écureuil grimpe à l'arbre*, The squirrel climbs the tree . . . They're repeated a lot.'

'They bring good news to people like Anthenor. But there's one code we're all waiting for. I know I can trust you: When you hear two lines from a famous poem, you'll know victory is near.'

Soon after Cécile's visit, Chantal encountered one of the dread Militiamen, recruited, it was whispered, with payment of high bonuses. In the hall of her building, she met the son of her downstairs neighbor, a thirty-year-old ne'er-do-well with an aristocratic name, whom she'd glimpsed occasionally, padding around in slippers, unshaven, at all hours of the day. He'd even fleetingly reminded her of Renaud. Now, he stood in the marble entrance, resplendent in his brand-new black uniform, silver gamma signs on the collar. He clicked his German-style boots.

'*Mes respects, madame*,' he greeted her ceremoniously. 'May I call on you one of these days? I'd be honored to escort you to the Ritz, where there's going to be a reception in honor of His Excellency, Herr Doktor Otto Abetz, the diplomat.' He added, 'I hope you wouldn't mind riding in my new car? Yes, it's the Daimler-Benz parked outside.'

Chantal muttered some excuse and decided that only coded knocks at her door would be answered from now on.

The Militiaman's glory was short-lived. Only weeks later, Chantal found a knot of people gathered near her front door. A body on a stretcher was being loaded into an ambulance, German soldiers were rushing into adjacent buildings, shouting guttural orders. 'Shot from the roof-tops,' said somebody. 'They're looking for the sniper.' For days, she averted her eyes from the fading chalk outline and the dark stains on the sidewalk. 'A traitor! Working against his own people! . . . Serves him right. I hope who-ever did it gets plenty more of those Militiamen. And those *sales Boches* too,' whispered a tearful Madame Gil-bert. 'Not only did my older son never come back, but they've got Albert working in a bomb factory in Silesia, not at all the peaceful farm work those damn liars had promised.'

Talk around the atelier revolved now about only one subject: The Americans. 'When the Americans get here . . .' The girls didn't say 'the Allies,' or 'the British.' It was 'When the Americans win the war . . .'

'What can we expect from the British?' retorted Chantal when Domergue pointed out that Americans weren't alone in the fight. 'They're just as badly off as we are, just as exhausted, they need everything just as we do. But Americans! It's a rainbow they're bringing us!

'A rainbow,' she continued, her usual reserve forgotten in her enthusiasm, 'bright colors that mean food, travel, lights, clothes. But the other end of that rainbow reaches the sky and it promises peace, freedom, an open future and the right to pursue happiness.' Domergue applauded her rhapsody, but only half mockingly.

Life went on. People who, like Chantal, had to get up early, dressed in darkness seldom relieved by an hour or two of low-wattage electricity. The gas pressure was too low to heat up a hypothetical cup of coffee. Chantal, like other Parisian girls, painted her legs with a makeup the color of the unobtainable hose, drew a thin line to represent the seam, even a small crosshatch design near the ankle to suggest realistic delicate darning. Then she went out, in her wind-whipped short skirt, bare-legged in the freezing blackness of the unlit streets, face saved, she thought wryly, if such a metaphor could apply to legs.

Evenings were a nightmare: The métro was the only transportation, so the crowds were crushing, many stations closed to save electricity, and the long walks in the blackout thoroughfares where it was difficult to find one's street and one's door, made, by contrast, the freezing, dimly lit apartments seem almost cheerful. Chantal's work continued. There were exhibits now planned in two different cities — one in Rennes, in Brittany, and another in Lille. Domergue was also preparing for a by-invitation-only exhibit that friends from his club had suggested. It would group fifty canvases of what the master considered his most erotic work. All were sold in advance. But Domergue, examining all the canvases normally turned to the wall in his vaultlike storage room, was decidedly unhappy. These were all several years old. He needed something else, something fresh, new, different — something to startle and delight.

One day, he casually mentioned to Chantal, who had already posed for two portraits, a bust, and an almost life-size nude, 'I'd like to do something special for the new show, some studies of two girls.'

Chantal, busy replacing the rejected canvases, paid scant attention.

'Two girls,' he repeated. 'You understand, Chantal, my dear? I want to paint two girls. Would you be one of them? It could be you and Marjo, you know, the tall dark-haired girl who posed last week. You like her, don't you?'

'Yes, I like her. How do you want to paint us?'

'Nude, and making love.'

Chantal was speechless. Make love with another girl? she thought. I wouldn't even know what girls do together. This is ridiculous. I wouldn't even want to try. And yet, a strange, troubling desire stirred in her. Marjo was as slender as she was, and when she had seen her posing nude, she had caught herself wondering how it might feel to touch the brown nipples, so different from her own small pink ones, to reach for—

'Do you agree?' Domergue persisted. 'You wouldn't have

to really make love, you could just pretend. I just need to sketch the line of the bodies, and I'd do the actual painting later. No recognizable faces, of course, that's understood.'

That evening, Chantal lay awake in her rose and violet room, thinking of Marjo's long thighs and her pointed breasts. She was aroused, just as she had been every time she had allowed herself to think of Anthenor, and she caressed herself for the first time. Her orgasm took her by surprise, and she stopped the caress, waited, and when the spasms of pleasure subsided, touched herself again, gently, and the orgasm resumed, as though it was still there, waiting for its release. Thinking alternately of Anthenor inside her, and of Marjo opening her legs to let her see her wet lips, she brought herself to another climax. And that night, she dreamed of unknown pleasures – her lips touching Marjo's breasts, while Anthenor penetrated her with an ever-growing member . . .

The next morning, Domergue continued his campaign. 'I gave Mano the day off, and Marjo said she'd be here later this morning. Are you game to try?'

Despite her studied indifference, Chantal could feel a warmth between her thighs.

When Marjo arrived, in a cloud of Vol de Nuit, the new Guerlain fragrance, icy cold fur coat over silk jersey and warm, fragrant body, she winked at Chantal. 'Feel like faking it?'

She took off her clothes, and went to stand, naked, on the red-draped model's dais, proudly showing herself, hands caressing her own flanks, pressing her breasts seductively. Then she lay on her side, and extended her arms. Domergue was standing at his easel, charcoal in hand, absorbed in sketching.

Chantal hesitated, but Marjo smiled and beckoned to her. She sat on the edge of the stage and Marjo undressed her slowly and caressingly. Then she slid into Marjo's outstretched arms. Marjo pulled her gently, and rubbed her nipples against Chantal's in a purely sensual gesture.

Domergue was sketching, rapidly now, tearing sheets

from his easel block and throwing them in a pile to his right.

'Do what you feel like doing,' he said. 'I'll make many sketches.'

Marjo was still holding Chantal, nipples to nipples, and now she was caressing her body with the palms of her hands, lower, lower, closer. Chantal arched in her direction.

'You do me, now,' whispered Marjo.

Chantal leaned over, and just as in her dream of the night before, she took the brown nipples tasting of orange and sugar in her mouth, and pulled at them gently with her lips, while playing their tips with her tongue. Marjo's hand was reaching down, guiding Chantal's fingers to her sex. Chantal found the wet warm lips, caressed them, desire growing inside her. Marjo reached down too, and caressed Chantal's sex, and both found the exact point of focus of the clitoris, and forgot all, except the pleasure each was receiving and giving and the ecstasy each could feel very near in the other.

Domergue said, 'Don't stop now. It's electric. I am getting it all in my sketches.'

Chantal had learned from Anthenor that orgasm is best if its expectation is prolonged. She stopped, and kissed Marjo gently on the lips. Marjo understood, slipped under Chantal's body and rubbed her sex against Chantal's. Both girls almost cried out in pleasure.

'Now,' said Domergue. 'Stop, I can't stand it. Wait.'

Somehow, he had joined them and was penetrating Marjo from the back, while Marjo had reached for Chantal's sex again, and had taken her clitoris between her lips, titillating its pinpoint with the tip of her tongue, Chantal holding her nipples with her fingers. Both girls climaxed, and Domergue, with a deep sigh, also came and quickly withdrew.

'I don't know how this happened,' he said, ruefully. 'I shouldn't risk these situations too often – with my heart, and all . . . My doctor would be furious. But it is certainly

worth the hazard, and I couldn't have continued working.'
He was already back at the easel.

Chantal knew that what she had just experienced was
not the end, but only the beginning of more pleasures. She
lay on her side, facing Marjo, who smiled at her. They
caressed each other's faces dreamily, while desire flowed
again.

They turned back to each other's body, this time head
to sex, and each took the other's sex in her lips, caressing
the vulva with her tongue, exploring the recesses with
tongue and fingers. Then Chantal reached tentatively behind Marjo. Marjo shivered with expectation and sighed.

Domergue was at his easel, sketching furiously.

Chantal explored the cleft of Marjo's buttocks with
her wet fingers, and gently, very gently, reached for the
opening there. Marjo moaned and offered herself. Chantal
could feel the opening loosen, wanting penetration. Her
fingers slid deeper, deeper, while her tongue imitated the
same movement inside the hot, wet sex. Then, she reached
for the clitoris with her tongue, and as her fingers penetrated deeply into Marjo's rectum, she felt her orgasm on
her lips, and the contractions under her fingers. She held
on, although Marjo was writhing and begging her to stop
. . . but arching her body insistently to the lips and fingers.

Domergue left the studio and returned, holding a dildo.
Chantal had never seen one before, but she lay back,
yearning for her own orgasm, while Marjo's waves of
pleasure receded and she felt their ebb under her hand.

Marjo then took the dildo, and slowly, with a rotating
movement, inserted it into Chantal, who cried out, because it was so big that it hurt. But she could feel her
vagina dilating and growing wet under the demanding
thrust . . . Marjo held it there, moving it gently back and
forth, and bent her head down over Chantal's sex. Chantal
curved her body to meet Marjo's lips.

'That's it, that's it,' cried Domergue. 'I love that arching
body. Keep it up. Just this way.'

Chantal didn't even hear. Filled with the swollen member, larger than any man she could imagine, she tensed to the lips reaching slowly to her. A tongue flicked, just flicked the tip of her erect clitoris. She cried out, 'More, more,' but Marjo made her wait, made her beg for her orgasm, all the time moving the dildo back and forth, gently, pulling it almost entirely out, pressing it on the outer lips near the entrance to the vagina, then pushing it suddenly inside. Another flick of the lips, then wait . . . Wait . . . Chantal was sobbing with desire.

Marjo bent her head, and this time took the swollen clitoris firmly between her lips, while reaching for Chantal's buttocks and penetrating her with two fingers, deep, deep, deeper. All the while her lips fastened onto the bud of the clitoris, and the huge member inside moved back and forth. When orgasm came, it was shattering, and Chantal shivered and gasped, sobbed, wept, before she could lie still, spent.

Spent, yes . . . Yet why was it that Anthenor's face came to her mind, leaning over her intently as he was possessing her? I am not really a lesbian, she thought, reassured a little, it's a man I want.

Marjo was caressing her soothingly, rubbing her shoulders, her back, her feet.

Domergue had left his easel and came back with a bottle of champagne and three glasses.

'Don't move,' he said, 'stay right where you are.' He came to sit on the model's dais between them, and casually touched both their sexes, feeling the warm wetness, played with pink and brown nipples, now relaxed.

'Isn't it too bad that whoever invented lovemaking is already dead?' he asked rhetorically. 'If he were still alive, he might have thought up a few more things like this . . .'

Then he poured champagne, and everybody drank, laughing a little shakily.

Now, Chantal thought, I know why the nuns were always so anxious to separate us, so concerned whenever they saw two girls sitting too close, or walking with arms around each other, in the recreation yard. I know why they

217

worried so, that we would climb into one another's bed, in the big dormitory room after the lights were out. They knew what delights a woman's body could hold for another woman. *We* didn't suspect it, but *they* did. How did they learn? Did they experience it? Did they play with another woman's sex the way we did just now? Did it happen before, or after, they had decided Jesus wanted them for his brides? Or did they only suspect, in a rush of warm desire, and fear to really know? Were their thighs wet under the heavy skirts of their black habits?

That night, alone in her bedroom, she looked long at her body, the small upturned breasts, the flat stomach, in the cheval mirror that framed her image in impossible bouquets. So afraid was she of what she had learned about herself that she promised she would never let another woman touch her. Never. She'd gone mad that day, so long without sex, and now that Anthenor had aroused her, desire was often building within her. That's all it was. She would forget the day, and go to sleep with the image of Anthenor's high cheekbones and intent eyes before her. She kept her promise, but whenever she saw Marjo, for weeks afterward, she couldn't help the troubling images that came to her mind.

That last year of the war brought its violence even closer. These were times of fear and trembling as Resistance actions multiplied. Every day Chantal heard news of some heroic action, commanded from London or Algiers, in which men like Anthenor risked and lost their lives. Locomotives were derailed, bridges blown up as trains loaded with German troops or supplies streamed across them. Trucks carrying ammunition or explosives were ambushed, their drivers killed and their cargo 'liberated' – the new word then – for the benefit of the Maquis, the Resistance.

By now, the occupation forces were no longer attempting to paint an image of a population living in peace and happiness – or at least in submission. Each time a particularly spectacular Resistance operation succeeded, red posters bordered in black appeared overnight on the walls of Paris. Their message was chilling: If the guilty were not found within twenty-four hours, then ten hostages taken at random from the overflowing prisons would be executed. And twenty the day after, and forty after that.

'Lead us to those terrorists,' demanded the posters, 'those murderers who are hiding among you. You can see them now for what they really are, puppets of Communism who don't care if you die, if hundreds of innocents die. Tell us who they are and you will be saving lives, your own and those of your family and neighbors.'

Under such pressure, no wonder division was rampant: There were the collaborators, who wished for a German victory – for political convictions, fear of Communism, or, more often, personal gain. Others supported the Maquis, often for patriotic reasons or sheer hatred of the Nazis. Then, there was all the rest, caught in the middle, simply trying to survive.

The Resistance was divided as well: there was the AS, the Secret Army, composed of former regular army officers, Catholic and fervently patriotic. There were the Communist-leaning FTP, Free-Shooters and Partisans. There were splinter groups, too, their motives and methods all at odds, even if they claimed to fight for the liberation of the motherland. On the shortwave radio, Chantal heard repeated calls to all, AS, FTP, rogue groups, to heed the rallying cry of General de Gaulle and come together into the French Forces of the Interior.

Meanwhile, some of the Parisians turned informers, while others preferred torture and death. And the sound of firing squads was heard over prison walls.

Chantal was standing on her balcony one evening, when she first heard the sirens scream their unearthly wail. Thousands of Allied planes were droning overhead. Ack-ack anti-aircraft batteries sputtered, but the beams of their searchlights fell hopelessly short of the planes flying high, well out of their range. Initial terror, later exasperating orders, disrupted her little household almost every night.

Orders were that the inhabitants had to leave their homes at the first sound of the alarm and run for the shelter posted in the entrance of each building. Anyone found in the streets was suspected of trying to signal the enemy and subject to being shot on sight by the air wardens or the German patrols.

Everybody crowded into the shelters, waiting at first for the bombs exploding closer and closer and for the one, the one you do not hear, until it has buried you alive. But the bombs didn't fall, not then. These raids weren't meant for Paris and the Nazi command knew it. The bombers were on their way, instead, to obliterate the cities of Germany. Yet the psychological ploy – to make the Parisians rage at those English and American pilots, who were at best depriving them of their sleep, at worst taking careful aim to annihilate them – ultimately backfired. After the first alerts were not followed by the sound of explosions, the crowds in the shelters rejoiced that at last *someone* was doing *something* to exact a revenge on those Krauts who'd oppressed them for so long. The planes were on their way to obliterate the Boche cities? Bravo! In the packed shelters, little paths of silence formed around the black uniforms of strolling Militiamen.

The ululating siren sent Chantal down into her designated shelter, the Etoile métro station, carrying a sleepy Mariès in a blanket. Anna followed, hands clapped over her ears. As they searched for a spot where they could sit on the floor and settle the bundled child, Chantal's startled glance met the hunted eyes of a young man cowering in a dark recess. He was trying to cover a bloody gash on the side of his face with his hand. More blood seeped through his torn jacket sleeve, spreading into a large stain. There he was, almost at Chantal's feet, an animal at bay. Seeing her looking at him, he begged, 'Don't say anything, please. Help me. I won't hurt you.'

She wasn't afraid of him. Her first thought was: Here is someone who needs help from me, when I have all I can do already. She sat down on the tile floor, spoke softly over her shoulder. 'I'm not afraid. You're the one who's hurt. What happened to you?'

'I cannot tell you now. But if the Militia find me, I'm a dead man. Please, help me hide.'

Now Chantal was afraid. Not of this hurt, helpless boy, but because she knew that if a Militiaman saw her so much as exchanging words with him, she'd be considered an accomplice to whatever he'd done and would inevitably share his fate. And yet . . . what could she do? She thought of Anthenor – suppose it was him, wounded and needing help? So, she gestured to Anna and they positioned themselves and the bundled child so that he'd be hidden between them and the curving wall, out of sight of anybody walking through the crowd.

When the all clear sounded, he whispered, from the shadows behind her, 'I can't go back to the street. They're looking for me, they'll find me and kill me. I am already condemned to death. You must help me.'

Trying not to think of the repercussions, Chantal took off her trench coat, and the thin, ferret-faced boy shrugged it over his shoulders. Anna gave him her dark scarf to wrap around his neck, at least partially covering the awful cheek wound. He walked out between the two women, pretending he was helping them carry the child up the endless flight of stairs. In the street, Chantal took his good arm, chatting as animatedly as she could, while Anna carried Mariès, still fast asleep. She led him down the avenue, chest tight, heart pounding, thinking, Any moment a hand will slam down on my shoulder, and I will turn and see the silver gamma symbols on a black collar. Her legs were weak, but she reached her front door, and then the sixth floor, and still no hand had grasped her shoulder.

They made the boy sit in the tiny, green-sprigged kitchen while they examined the torn cheek, blood from his arm falling in heavy drops on the garlands painted on the white tile. His name, he told them, was Marcel. He had been a *mécano*, a mechanic's apprentice in the Renault plant in Billancourt. When the call came from STO he fled and joined a Resistance group in the Compiègne forest, north of Paris.

'We've done a few things I won't go into, but you'd know if I told you, because they were in the papers!' he bragged. 'And today, there were four of us, and we were trying to attach explosives under a railroad bridge not far from the La Chapelle junction. Somebody must have informed on us, because all of a sudden, there was a truck. Militiamen with automatics jumped out. They grabbed us, beat us — fists, kicks, and butt of their weapons.' He showed the gash in his cheek. 'But that was just for openers. We were loaded on the truck and they were joking about taking proper care of us so we'd be in shape to talk when we arrived at headquarters.'

He winced as Anna poured iodine into his wounds. Chantal tore one of Madame Lazareff's pillowcases into strips for bandages.

'They were figuring out the bounty they'd get for our capture. I didn't know it, but they get a bonus if they make the prisoners talk. They were making bets on how long any of us would hold out under repeated semidrowning, electric shock to the genitals, pulling off of fingernails. One was playing with a penknife. He pointed it at one of my friends. "Hey," he said to his pals, "I bet that after I take out one of his eyes with this he'll sing like a bird rather than lose the other one." The rest of the Militiamen laughed. "There's nothing to it, the eyeball pops out, just like a grape out of its skin." They all got excited. "Were there ever times one of the bastards let you take out the other eye, too, before talking?" "Yeah," he answered, "a few." And another said, "I guess it doesn't make much difference whether you face the firing squad with one eye, or none . . ." That really broke them up. At that point, the truck sputtered and stopped. The driver yelled something, so the Militiamen jumped out to see what he wanted. Only one stayed behind to guard us, so I shoved him aside and jumped down. He called out to the others, and they all started looking for me, firing at random in the dark. See? It's a bullet wound in my arm, ouch! Careful. The bullet went clear through, I guess. But they couldn't find me. I was lying right there in the gutter next to the truck, though one of them swore he'd seen me run into a side street, and that's where they looked. Finally they gave up and left. As soon as the truck had turned the corner, I ran for shelter down into the subway station, and that's when the sirens sounded, and crowds of people came pouring in, and you found me.'

What am I going to do? thought Chantal. I can't send him out and yet how can I face the dangers he represents? What if there's a knock on the door? And what about Mariès, if they take me away? I don't want my eyes to be . . . What on earth can I do?

Anna, who always cried under the slightest stress, was strangely calm. She is in as much danger as I am, and look at her, Chantal thought. Anna brought food, bread with a scraping of margarine, a little warm skim milk – and she made up a bed on the living-room couch, coolly and efficiently.

'How can we get you to safety? Do you have any idea?' Chantal asked.

'If I could only get across the Seine, near the Bois de Boulogne, there's a safe house in Boulogne-Billancourt where I can stay and they'll help me get back to my group, as soon as my arm's better. But I'm afraid the Militia's looking for me – you know there are checkpoints in the streets all the time – and I'm sure they're setting up extra ones around this neighborhood.'

He stayed in the apartment for two days, and every time footsteps were heard on the landing, he ran to hide under Madame Lazareff's worktable behind piled-up suitcases, nuzzled by a curious Arsène, who took the intrusion as a welcome break in his placid routine. Forty-eight hours were just long enough for Anna to arrange everything. For it was Anna who thought of it. Charles, the *gardien de la paix*, the municipal guard who was by now more or less her fiancé – 'Anna, Cha'l, kiss, kiss,' reported Mariès, making kissing sounds, after her outings in the park – arrived at the door, knocked once, then three times. He had brought an extra uniform under his voluminous cape, and a little later Marcel walked out with him, the wound on his cheek almost invisible under Chantal's leg makeup, two municipal guards casually strolling in cape and kepi. They passed, unchallenged, to the Bois de Boulogne, and walked over to the Seine. There, Charles watched Marcel cross the bridge, and wave from the other side.

Plans for all exhibits in the provinces had long since been canceled. Yet Domergue, in the midst of all the upheaval, still worried about some paintings that had been advance-shipped to the gallery in Lille, whose owner was slow in returning them. Finally, notice came from the station that a small crate of three paintings had arrived and would be available the next morning, as soon as the freight office opened. Chantal volunteered to pick them up.

Securing a pedicab, she arrived at the Gare de l'Est in the gray dawn light and asked the cabman to wait. But as she approached the entrance to the station, a convoy of trucks pulled up. German soldiers jumped out, shouting orders. '*Raus, raus*, out of the way, move back, back. Stand back.'

The crowd of civilians obeyed.

The khaki trucks were entirely closed. A door in the back of the first one opened, and people were pushed out, tumbling over one another – young, old, men, women, children – so many, it seemed impossible the truck could have contained that number. Some were miserably dressed, but there were women in furs and men in comfortable overcoats. The crowd of Parisians, standing transfixed, gasped, because everyone had heard of the nightly raids that roused people from their beds for deportation somewhere east, but few had actually seen it happen. Some maintained it was only a rumor. Now the Germans were no longer attempting to hide their activities. Here they were, at the Gare de l'Est, in broad daylight, all hope of winning over the sympathies of the population abandoned.

The prisoners filed by, an endless gray river of despair. These people went to bed last night, free and reasonably happy, yet afraid of that loud knock on the door, thought Chantal. And then it came – uniforms, boots, guns. They were given ten minutes to gather whatever belongings they could carry in one small bag.

I wonder if Manfred, Sibelle's boyfriend, was one of those barking orders and rifling whatever valuables he could lay his hands on? Everybody is talking of relocation, but here they are, prisoners, and these are cattle cars pulled up on the track, where the passenger trains normally stop. Where are they being taken? East, yes, but not just where these railroads go. Farther east, much farther. But where? Will there be homes for them? And if it's all part of the work program in farms and factories, why are they taking all those old people and small children and . . . What does *relocation* really mean?

As the long procession passed, goaded by Militiamen and German soldiers, Chantal heard a young man cry out, and saw him lunge for the weapon of a Militiaman. There were shouts, he was kicked to the ground and cursed, but Chantal saw a young woman beside him take advantage of the disturbance as though it had been created, reach under her coat, and in a swift gesture hand out a tiny, bundled infant to an old woman standing only a few feet from Chantal. The woman, poorly dressed, reached out, took the child, and covered it with her shawl. It all happened so fast that the guards, their attention focused on the man they were now half dragging, half pushing through the station, saw nothing.

The woman, probably a cleaning lady on her way to

work, waited until the Germans had gone to reach under the shawl and bring out the infant. The crowd of onlookers closed in on her. Chantal came as close as she could. The woman was answering their excited questions.

'Oh, no, I don't know any of these people. I just happened to be standing here. I work in the station, you see – I clean floors – and I was already late for work. But when I saw that woman holding the child out to me, I reached for it, what else was there to do?'

She turned to the well-dressed couple at her elbow. 'It is God, madame, who sends a child like that,' she said.

The woman in the opossum coat, tears streaming down her cheeks, opened her purse and tried to hand folded bills to the charwoman, who refused.

'I have raised five of my own, and now they're grown, and my oldest daughter lives with me – her husband is a prisoner of war in Germany. She'll help me with this little one . . .'

The woman in the fur whispered to her husband, who placed the bills in his hat, and the hat was passed around. Chantal emptied her purse into it. It took some persuading to convince the old cleaning woman that she should accept the money, not for herself but for the child.

'All right,' she said. 'He can use it, poor lamb. I am going to call him *Moïse*, Moses, because he was saved, almost like in the Bible . . .'

12

Les sanglots longs
Des violons . . .
(The endless sobs
Of violins . . .)

JUNE 6, 1944 . . . AT LAST! the moment so long expected had come. Chantal, listening with Domergue to his clandestine radio, jumped for joy.

'This is it, I know, I can't tell you how I know, but when we hear two lines from a famous poem, it will mean victory is at hand!'

Domergue was dubious. 'Pretty melancholy lines to announce something as happy as victory,' he grumbled. 'I wonder who'd pick lines from Verlaine about the sadness of fall to announce a summer victory! No wonder it's taking them so long to win this damn war.'

It wasn't victory yet that the message announced, but the landing of Allied forces on the Channel beaches, an unexpected location when everybody thought it would come on the Mediterranean. The Germans too, apparently, because they were trying frantically to move their troops and equipment through France from the south, to the Normandy front.

At first, the press reported the landings as a failure and another victory for the Reich:

ALLIED FORCES ATTEMPT LANDING ON
NORMANDY COAST

BRITISH COMMANDOS ARE PUSHED BACK TO
SEA

BY OUR MURDEROUS FIRE

This time, the last battle was joined, and although the papers continued for several days to claim victory against the invasion forces, small telling sentences crept into the so-called official communiqués: The Allies, they announced, had been repelled completely, *save for isolated armored elements that have scattered into the countryside.*

'Armored elements,' said the excited gentleman with the rosette, holding forth at the news kiosk, 'that's tanks. They have scattered into the countryside, and then what? Tanks don't simply disappear! They regrouped farther inland, that's what they did. And they'll open the way for the infantry. Where do you suppose they could be, now? Don't you have a map of the Cotentin Peninsula?' he asked the vendor. Eager faces bent over the unfolded map flapping in the unseasonally cold wind.

Finally, the press had to admit the landings had been successful – that troops and equipment continued to pour through the bridgeheads. The fight was now engulfing Normandy, where cows grazed in deeply green pastures separated by ancestral hedges grown tall each spring, pruned each fall, overgrown with creeping vegetation, so thick the tanks couldn't always crush their way through – the murderous hedgerows of Normandy.

Chantal shuddered as front pages showed hundreds of dead Allied soldiers floating facedown in full battle gear, washed by the surf, half buried in sand by the receding tide, or lying in heaps in pastures. Some wore the British helmet, round and flat, others wore an unfamiliar one. American, was it? Not a single dead German was shown. Allied planes spiraled to the ground, trailing thick plumes of fire, but as far as the press and newsreels were concerned, the Luftwaffe remained intact.

Yet, air raids multiplied. Now, the thousands of Allied planes were no longer just droning overhead, on their way to some distant cities. A section of Paris, near the La

Chapelle junction, was bombed; there were dozens of dead. The sound of falling bombs became ominously familiar. Other French cities, used by the Germans as staging areas or communication centers, went up in flames. Even Angoulême had its share – the raids destroyed the station, the railroad junction, but also all the residential district along the avenue de la Gare. Many dead again, friends of the Arondels among them.

Concurrently, the Resistance became bolder. German convoys were attacked everywhere, roads barred and reprisals more ferocious every day, no food to be obtained anywhere. Domergue would no longer paint, barricaded in his atelier, alone, his wife having long ago left Paris for their villa in Cannes.

'I am going to close down the studio and the apartment and join my wife. See how we can weather the rest of the war. Life has become too difficult here. But what about you, my dear? Do you want to stay with my wife and me in Cannes? You are welcome, you know.'

Chantal had already thought about it. 'There's no point in my staying here either. I'm worried about my little girl. No food, the planes flying overhead every night, never knowing when the bombs will fall on Paris again. Thank you for your offer, Maître, but I think I'll try to get back to my parents' farm, down in the southwest. At least there'll be food there, and safety, I hope. It's so far from the front!'

So, Chantal and Anna had packed, only small bags they could easily carry, and yes, of course, Arsène was lodged in the same basket he had come in, covered with the same shawl, under Mariès's close supervision. They boarded a crowded train, after pushing their way through the mobs besieging the Gare d'Austerlitz. Mariès, at first amused by the adventure, got frightened of the jostling crowd and started to cry.

'Hush, darling,' begged Chantal, 'you know you love a train ride! We are going to La Prade, and you will see Grand-père and Grand-mère. Remember Grand-mère?'

Mariès did not remember Grand-mère clearly, but she certainly remembered the barnyard fowl.

'Will feed the chicks?' she asked. 'Will hold the baby ducks?'

'That's right, darling,' Chantal said, hugging her. 'You will, but you must be Mother's good girl and not cry.'

There was no question of sitting down on this train. Compartments that would normally seat eight now held twenty or more. People stood on seats, even dangled their legs from the luggage racks. They pressed in the corridor, where Chantal and Anna took turns holding an exhausted Mariès, who had finally fallen asleep. The only train they had been able to squeeze onto was going to Limoges, which would mean changing trains there and finishing the trip on the local line to La Rochefoucauld. No matter. They were escaping the crazed city, the air raids, the demented sirens, the fear, the random violence.

The trip was endless in the darkened train, crowds of people pushing, jostling, children crying out to parents from whom the crowd had separated them. Twice, the train stopped. Bullhorns ordered the passengers to step out and lie on the ground, away from the track. Chantal lay on the gravel, protecting Mariès's fragile body with her own. Planes were droning overhead, and some had begun to dive. Were they bombers? Reconnaissance planes? After everyone had piled out, and no bombs came, it seemed impossible that all of them could be squeezed back into the compartments. Anna was pulled through the window by unknown hands, then Chantal handed her the baby, who laughed now at the excitement. And finally Chantal climbed in, pushed and pulled through the same window. The bags were lost on the second alert, except for Arsène's basket, which Anna guarded with her life, under the watchful eye of Mariès.

In the Limoges station, pandemonium reigned. A former bicycle factory, now making armaments for Germany, had been bombed the night before and a residential area not far away had been pulverized. Crews were searching the wreckage for dead and survivors. A bridge on the river had been blown up.

The railroad station was in chaos, but as far as anyone could tell, it seemed the line to Angoulême was still open.

'This line goes through Chabanais, and that's Resistance country. Our boys hold that area,' an old man said as they all waited, dead-tired and hungry, sitting on the dirty concrete platform. 'The Germans can't afford enough troops to guard every road, every building, every truck. And around Chabanais, it's wooded terrain, with a lot of forests where the Maquis can hide. It was lucky the train from Paris made it through to here. I wouldn't be surprised if it was the last one. The Resistance cuts the tracks or derails the trains, or just hacks down large trees and fells them across the path of the locomotives.'

Hours late, the train for Angoulême was announced and mobbed. Chantal managed to climb aboard, pulled in Mariès, handed her by Anna, then Anna carrying the precious basket . . .

'A'sen tired,' Mariès kept repeating, yawning.

It took all day – not the usual two hours – to reach the small town of Chabanais. At one point midway, the train was stopped by German soldiers in battle dress. They made everybody get out and the travelers had to walk across an emergency footbridge over a river, holding onto a rope that served as a rail, the water shining dark far below through the rickety planking. On their left, they could see the ruins of a great bridge, its central arch broken in two, the severed sections of track falling into the river in a long V. 'The Gaullist Maquis are everywhere,' somebody whispered, 'and thank God, they are driving out the others, the Communists. But their presence bugs the Germans just as much . . .'

Another train was pulled up on the other side of the bridge, waiting, and Chantal marveled that in the midst of madness someone, probably the Railroad Administration,

231

should care enough about a handful of passengers to try and insure continuation of their journey.

After a while, Mariès yawned. 'I am hungry,' she announced. 'A'sen hungry too.'

All Anna had left was an apple; she cut off a small piece for Arsène and gave the rest to Mariès.

'When we get to Grand-mère's,' Chantal said reassuringly, 'we'll have all *sorts* of wonderful things to eat, Mariès. Remember the jam? and the butter? and the good bread? You can have all you want. And the milk! You'll see how good the milk tastes at La Prade!'

Finally, the train pulled into the Chabanais station, the building a twin to the one in La Rochefoucauld, Chantal thought. Same green shutters, same cheerful red geranium windowboxes. But something was different here. Strange young men were milling on the platform.

'Everybody out. Get out. Get out,' they shouted. What were those uniforms they were wearing? Pieces of uniforms, really. Some wore battle jackets and shorts, workpants, or old French uniforms. Some had helmets on their heads, pushed back, chin straps dangling; others wore civilian caps, one had on the beret of prewar Alpine troops. All wore an armband with the letters *FFI* roughly stenciled in black and carried weapons.

So, this was the Maquis, the men from the Resistance everyone talked about but few had seen. Here in territory they nearly controlled they were out in the open, weapons at the ready, and they had commandeered this country station.

'Everybody out, get out. It's dangerous to stay on,' repeated a young man wearing shorts, a torn shirt, espadrilles, and a garrison cap. He gestured with his tommy gun, but without hostility, almost friendly. His accent identified him as a local boy, who in normal times and at this season would have been perched atop a wagon in the fields, forking up bales of hay. Instead, hay was standing unmowed in the meadows, so heavy with the grain of its tall stems that the weight had crushed it to the ground in large patches. And the men who would have attended to its harvest were here, stopping trains, brandishing American-made submachine guns.

At last, every passenger had disembarked, and now they all stood uncertainly on the platform. The Maquis were gesturing and arguing with the conductor and the engineer.

'Wait until the Colonel arrives,' one of the men shouted, shaking his fist. 'He'll tell you what to do, if you don't believe us.'

The engineer shrugged. He was an older man, he had traveled this line for years, even knew some of these boys since they were knee-high, and he wasn't impressed by the automatic weapons they waved around with inexperienced abandon.

Meanwhile, somebody had unloaded from the baggage car a stack of the German magazine *Signal*, French edition. It was resting on the concrete platform, and two of the young Maquis had spotted it. They were laughing, circling the pile, like two kids planning a prank. One pulled a grenade from his belt. They were going to destroy the Boche magazines.

'Stand back. Live grenade.'

Everybody stood back. A shattering detonation. Pieces of broken concrete flew about. But the magazines in the pile were not destroyed. Instead they were sent shooting in all directions, their pages fluttering, flying, tossing in the currents of air, and finally landing in a wide radius in trees, on roofs, in the fields. Disappointed, the two boys stood back, while one of the older men frowned at the large, jagged hole blown out of the platform.

'The Colonel won't like it.'

Just then, a tall figure appeared in the station doorway, stood there a moment, silhouetted by the evening light. Tall, long-legged, a little stooped, and with that old habit of standing in doorways as if hesitant to cross thresholds. A little older. Authority now where there had formerly been arrogance. Otherwise unchanged, even more than before an untamed panther. Chantal's heart stopped. Anthenor!

'All right, you guys,' the young Maquis with the tommy gun yelled at the engineers, still standing on the locomotive. 'This is Colonel Robert. He'll tell you what to do. And don't forget: We shoot when he tells us to.'

All Maquis leaders had taken *noms de guerre* to protect both their identities and the safety of their families and friends. As for promotions, these were quick, not hindered by red tape, regulations, or any restrictions other than the availability of gold braid that indicated rank in the French army, and which the Allied planes were parachuting in along with other supplies.

Anthenor was indeed wearing the five bars – three, a space, and two – of gold braid of a colonel, crookedly sewn onto the rolled-up sleeve of his dirty shirt. He wore a leather vest, probably hacked out of his old jacket, an ammo belt with hand grenades, camouflage pants, paratroop boots, an automatic weapon slung over his shoulder. He was bareheaded, his straight blond hair falling across his forehead, just as it did the night Chantal had pushed it away, embarrassing them both momentarily in that Limoges restaurant, a century ago. He stood a moment, motionless, squinting in the slanting rays of the sun. His men were grouping around him, agitatedly reporting on events. Anthenor listened, frowned at the broken concrete, the magazines still fluttering in the fields.

'All right, now,' he said, addressing the engineer and the conductor, 'you've heard what my men told you to do. You will uncouple the locomotive so the train stays where it is. Then you will jam the throttle, release the brakes, and jump out. You have three minutes to comply, and my men will help you if necessary. Now,' he addressed the passengers, 'I want everybody here to understand who we are and what we're doing. You are French people and you have a right to know what is going on.

'We are the French Forces of the Interior,' he declared, pointing to the armband. 'We take our orders from de

Gaulle and we receive our supplies from the Allied High Command. Our orders at the moment are to do everything in our power to prevent German troop movement from the south, so the Wehrmacht cannot get its reinforcements to Normandy. This involves blowing bridges, cutting off railroad lines, and other guerrilla operations.

'Now,' he went on, 'the bridge down there' – he pointed to the bridge, which, a quarter of a mile away, straddled the Vienne River – 'has been mined. When I give the signal, the locomotive will steam full speed to that bridge. It will hit a detonator, and the bridge will blow up. One more railway and one more locomotive put out of commission. Is that clear? *Vive la France Libre!*'

The crowd, mesmerized, repeated, '*Vive la France Libre!*' A few added, '*Vive de Gaulle!*' The engineer had finished uncoupling the locomotive, and it stood immobile, steam hissing out of its side vents as the throttle was opened. The conductor jumped out. The engineer adjusted a last handle and jumped out too, just as the engine started to roll, slowly at first, then gathering speed. It reached the curve, banked steeply as it took the turn at full steam and reached the bridge. Nothing happened. It seemed it had already safely crossed, when a silent explosion immobilized it, then lifted it slowly up in the air, along with pieces of concrete, stone, beams. A split second later the detonation thundered, the boom reverberating in rumbling waves through the entire countryside. Debris hung in the air, falling back in slow motion, while dust rose in a cloud that expanded over the ruined bridge. The locomotive fell back and remained frozen above the broken arch, its rear wheels precariously dangling over the void, still spinning.

The crowd watched in silence. All the young Maquis stood silent, too, awed perhaps by the evidence of the power they wielded.

'That's done, then,' said Anthenor, addressing the crowd. 'This mission has been successful. I apologize for the inconvenience, since you must now continue your journey on foot. But remember that by doing this you will, in a small way, help win the victory. And forget you have seen us.' He gave the victory sign, turned on his heels.

Anna nudged Chantal. 'Isn't that Mr Anthenor, from Blazonac -- Count Renaud's brother?'

Chantal nodded impatiently. 'Of course, of course. Be quiet. Wait for me here a minute, and take care of the baby. Why don't you sit on that bench, here? I have to talk to him.'

She ran after him. He was striding through the small station toward a waiting Citroën, sans gazogene. The Maquis had to move fast, and their supply of gas came from all the 'liberated' German trucks found abandoned and empty by the roadside, their drivers shot.

She caught up with Colonel Robert as he was opening his car door.

'Anthenor!'

He whirled around, angry that someone had dared use his real name. He looked at her blankly for an instant, stood there, scowling. Then, slowly, his face relaxed, he reached out and put his hands on her shoulders.

'You! What are you doing here?'

She told him, trembling with insane joy, relief, violent hope. 'Can I see you? Can we be alone for a moment?'

He looked at her intently. 'I'd give my life for an hour with you,' he said. 'My life . . . But we have to move, and I can't let these boys go alone. We have another mission to carry out tonight, not far from here, and this time, it will be dangerous. I'll have to ask some of those poor kids to volunteer for suicidal moves. Some will die. Now, we have been in the open too long. Our orders were to blow up the train on the bridge, period. But I couldn't bear to do it with all those civilians on board, so I defied my orders, did it my own way. And now I find out that *you* were on that train! My God, to think you could have been sent to your death . . .'

'With Anna and Marie-Esmée,' whispered Chantal. 'Do you want to see Marie-Esmée?'

He shook his head. No time. He was thinking. 'Look,

there's no place you can go tonight. So, just walk across the square, there is a little place called Hôtel de la Croix-Blanche. The people who run it are friendly to us. Tell them you are Colonel Robert's wife, they'll find you a place to sleep. You *are* my wife, you know that, it was decided long ago, remember? I never think of you otherwise. If I can, I'll try to come by for you sometime during the night. But I only promise that I'll try.' Without another word, Anthenor turned on his heels, slid into the car, and drove off, tires squealing on the gravel.

The Hôtel de la Croix-Blanche was already overflowing with refugees, more so now with passengers from the train milling in the entrance, but Colonel Robert's name prompted the owner, after some hesitation, to find a space for the Resistance leader's wife and child. It was a servant's room on the second floor, with a single narrow bed, and it opened on the side street near the Vienne River. Exhausted, Chantal and Anna found just enough strength to pull the mattress off onto the floor to make an extra bed for Anna. They nestled Mariès, long fast asleep, on pillows on the floor and covered her with a folded coat. Chantal lay on the box spring, and fell instantly into exhausted sleep.

She dreamed that the locomotive was running down the track, exploded, but why did all the debris drop on her, burning and itching? She scratched her arms, her legs in her sleep. Restlessly, she rubbed her neck, scratched some more, but too many particles were falling from the sky. Finally she woke up. This was not a dream, something *was* biting and burning and crawling all over her body. She turned on the light.

Bedbugs swarmed all over the sheets, teeming flat little carapaces, hundreds feasting on her bare skin. As soon as the light shone on them, they started to retreat, abandoning their meal, creeping back to . . . ? To the wood frame of the old bedstead, which gave them shelter in its dark recesses, until the scent of another warm body brought them out for their nighttime feast. Chantal almost cried out, primeval fear and revulsion swelling in her. But she stifled her scream and examined Anna and the child, undisturbed in their profound sleep.

Not a single bug crawled on them. These lived in the wood cracks and the wormholes of the ancient bedstead, and none had ventured to the other sleepers in the room. Chantal left a small light burning to keep the bedbugs at bay, but there was no going back to sleep on that infested bed. She pulled the single straw chair to the window, sat. Three a.m. It would be daylight soon. She folded her arms on the windowsill, cradling her head, and tried to sleep.

A sound woke her from her fitful doze. No, not a sound. The impression of a sound. A movement that should produce a sound but did not ... She pushed the heavy wooden shutters open just far enough to look outside.

A heavy mist had risen from the river that flowed very near. She could hear it cascading over some rocky rapids. It gave a sense of unreality, softened the outlines of buildings, thick in some places, thinning out in others to immobile gauze scarves. Half obscured by the fog, a spectral pageant was making its way down the deserted street.

Anthenor marched first in the middle of the street, still bareheaded, his weapon reversed, pointing to the ground. Behind him, divided into two single files, came his men – maybe thirty or forty of them – in their ragtag uniforms, all barefoot, all carrying their arms reversed. Between the two files, other men carried stretchers, a still form covered with a dark blanket resting on each. Four stretchers passed. Then they were all gone, without a sound, a ghostly army in a ghostly mist.

Chantal watched and waited, emotions numbed by now – no fear, no pity, no sadness. Only one overwhelming hope: Will I hear Anthenor's steps down the hall, will he open the door and beckon me to follow him? Will I feel his hands on me, his lips on mine? She waited, oblivious of the angry insect bites swelling on her arms and legs. The footsteps didn't come. Anthenor had remained with his men.

It never occurred to her that the word *love* had not been

spoken between them – that no one had ever said to her, 'I love you,' except, oh, but it was so long ago, what was his name? Fred, that's it. Didn't he say those words? Perhaps, but perhaps she had dreamed it all. In any case, the bond between her and Anthenor needed no words. It was as strong as the towers of Blazonac, and when Anthenor said, 'I want you,' love was expressed as fully as any woman could have hoped. Yet now, for some mysterious reason, she was almost glad he hadn't come. It made him stronger, more in possession of himself – and her – because he had forsaken the hours they could have spent together in favor of another duty that had to do with loyalty and heroic death.

In the morning, when she went down, there was a message, delivered by a young Maquis who was waiting for her downstairs.

I know you were near when we passed, taking our men to their final rest. We buried them in the cemetery, and when it's all over, we'll return and give them the heroes' sepulcher they deserve. I know you understand why I did not come to you. Now, we are leaving. More work to do. It won't be long now, the war will be won, and our lives are before us. You'll sleep in my arms tonight like every other night of my life, into eternity.

PS. Please tell your parents I'm doing all I can for them.

The young Maquis gave Chantal Colonel Robert's password and saw to it that breakfast was served to the three women, with milk for Mariès, who never seemed to get her fill. A true farm boy, he smiled when he saw Arsène's twitching nose poke out of the basket, disappeared an instant, and returned with cabbage leaves from the nearest vegetable garden.

The two women walked all day, taking turns carrying Mariès, who was first intrigued by the adventure, and later cranky from fatigue and hunger. They climbed over trees felled across the road, challenged now and then by Maquis sentries, invisible in the thickets by the road until they showed themselves to ask for the password. The closer they came to La Prade, the more familiar the faces became, and Anna recognized several boys from the neighboring farms. Late into the night they finally arrived in the courtyard of La Prade. There were cars parked helter-skelter, curtainless windows were wide open, some with broken panes. Lights burned in the house . . . strange. Knock on the door. A long silence. Then male voices, footsteps. Someone leaned from an upstairs window, the barrel of a submachine gun was picked out by the moonlight.

'Who are you? What do you want?'

Chantal identified herself. Another silence. Deliberation. Finally, 'Go knock on the back door.'

The back door was opened by Madame Arondel, a sweater over her nightdress. She ushered in Chantal and her little group. In the dim light her eyes were haunted. She spoke in a rush of words. 'You, at last! We were so worried, now that all communications from Paris are cut off. How did you manage? You'll tell me tomorrow, the main thing is that you're here. Is the baby all right? And you, Anna? See? It would have been better . . .' Her voice trailed off. No, it might not have been better to stay in La Prade, after all. Much had happened here.

'The house is occupied now by a group of Communist Maquis. They have taken all the rooms, except this old kitchen and the small dining room in the back, that's where your father and I are living. We'll make up beds for you, there's just enough space. I don't need to tell you what they are doing to the furniture in those rooms where they live now. But that's not the worst. The worst, I can't even bear to talk about. I can't speak my mind, you understand, but' – she leaned to whisper into Chantal's ear – 'the Germans were never as bad for us as those . . . those bandits. Now, you three get something to eat and plenty of sleep. We'll talk tomorrow.'

The baby was awake, she ate and drank hungrily. Then she pointed to her pet, who had hopped out of his basket and was sniffing, remembering the familiar scents of the room.

'A'sen come home,' she said.

The next day, Chantal could see what had happened. La Prade was used as headquarters by a group of Communist resistants, those who had no interest in driving the Germans out, or disrupting their lines of supply and communication to the Normandy front. Their concern was twofold – personal and political. First, to settle accounts with collaborators, especially their most immediate enemies, the Militiamen, who were now on the run in that part of France, and other even more personal matters of long-repressed envy and bitterness with anybody whom they knew as prosperous and felt were 'exploiters' of the workers. Second, to create enough disruption, enough anger, to set Frenchman against Frenchman in an atmosphere of terror, so that when the Germans finally left, a civil war could be fomented, that would result in a Communist government filling the vacuum of power left by the departed enemy. These were not the Gaullist FFI, they were instead those who refused allegiance to the General, sang the 'Internationale,' and had taken the law into their own hands.

Their first priority had been to show capitalists like the Arondels just what would happen to people like them when the 'singing tomorrows' promised by Moscow finally arrived. And who had brought this group, composed mainly of industrial Parisian workers, seeking a safe, isolated harbor? Why, Pierrot, the trusted Pierrot, who had worked for the family for so long! He now seemed to hold an important position with the Communist Maquis, came and went in a 'liberated' car, and spat at his feet whenever he saw the Arondels.

First, the house had been ransacked, in a repeated search for an imaginary cache of gasoline. Then, all of Madame Arondel's carefully stocked supplies had been either 'liberated' or wantonly destroyed – jars broken, sacks emptied, bottles smashed with rifle butts. A hand grenade had been thrown into the poultry yard and though by now carcasses had been removed, when Chantal looked for her daughter, she found her running disconsolately from one small heap of feathers to another, looking for chicks to feed and baby ducks to hold. Anna was standing there, weeping, her face in her hands.

In the big courtyard, onto which all the service buildings opened, Madame Arondel's geranium-filled earthenware jars were reduced to shards, spilled earth, and withered plants. The barrels in the winemaking rooms had been shot through with automatic fire, and they had spilled their contents into hundreds of rivulets that ran into each other to form rivers, now dried, smelling of soured wine, slowly obliterated by the dust. Desolation.

'And yet,' whispered Madame Arondel, 'and yet, it could have been worse. You know your father was never a collaborator, heavens! He fought in the last war, four years in the trenches. But just the fact that he is' – she checked herself – '*was* prosperous, is enough to condemn him with these people. Yet someone, we don't know who, someone is protecting us. They had arrested us both, the first day, your father and me, and we thought they were getting ready to shoot us. Then they apparently received orders and released us. We heard them talk among themselves about some Colonel exchanging prisoners he had from their group, in return for our safety.'

'I know,' said Chantal. And she told her mother that someone had told her Anthenor was trying to help them. She did not admit meeting him. Madame Arondel was thoughtful.

'That explains it,' she said after a while, 'that also explains why nobody has touched Blazonac. It is protected.'

But Chantal could see that her mother's gratitude to Anthenor was still tempered by the long-standing disapproval of whatever relationship her daughter might have with him.

Destruction was everywhere. The tall pines along the drive had been felled, some across the roadbed (in prevention of what illusory German traffic? The drive led nowhere but to the house), others had crashed into the meadow, their trunks hacked away. From the pond below the house, gleaming in the morning sun of this June day – four years past those other June days of 1940, which Chantal remembered only vaguely now – rose a putrid stench. Did she recall anything clearly now, other than wartime? Another grenade had been hurled into the water, and the fish were floating, pale bellies up, bloated and rotting in the sunshine, tangled with masses of torn, decaying aquatic vegetation.

War had finally come to La Prade, and from an unexpected direction.

The three or four cars parked in the courtyard were dusty, fenders smashed, parked every which way with open doors revealing savaged interiors. Another car pulled up. Three Maquis jumped out, ignoring Madame Arondel and Chantal. They prodded out a fourth passenger, who stood up uncertainly, staggering a little, hands bound behind his back.

'Oh, my God,' whispered Madame Arondel, 'I can't stand it. You know who this is? It's the mayor, the one who succeeded your father. Why, you know the mayor, he married you to Renaud. I can't bear to see . . .'

'What have they got against him?'

'I don't know. They don't *need* to have anything precise, just a suspicion. They are the law right now, there's nobody to stop them. The gendarmes have long fled to join the Maquis – the other, you know, the Gaullist one . . .'

'Like Anthenor?' said Chantal, just to hear herself pronounce his name.

'Yes, I suppose. André Brousse and Cécile have left their house, too, it seems they are acting as liaison between different Gaullist groups. But it's all so confused. Let's go in, I can't stand to watch this. It's not the first time, you know.'

Blinking in the sun, stunned, perhaps already brutalized, the mayor now realized where his captors had taken him. He had been to La Prade as a guest, a man of moderate opinions, but who leaned toward tolerating the occupiers for fear of the even greater danger as he saw it of the Communists, now winning the war on the eastern front. In the past year, however, he had been heard voicing the opinion that Monsieur Arondel was sympathetic to the Resistance and that he was known to hire young men fleeing the STO, giving them agricultural workers' certificates to help them, so a certain coolness had developed between the mayor and the Arondels. Now, as he recognized Madame Arondel, he tried to greet her with an inclination of his head. She attempted to return his greeting, but she sobbed aloud, put her handkerchief to her mouth, and drew her daughter by the hand inside the house. The three Maquis, red rags around their neck, paid no attention. They waited for their leader to come out of the house.

He appeared at last, *six* rows of gold braid on his sleeve, walked out into the courtyard and intoned, 'We are the Forces of the People at war with the Oppressors, and as such we are empowered to render justice for the people. This prisoner is accused of crimes against the people, of aiding and abetting the Nazis. How do you find him?'

'Guilty,' shouted the troops, the three captors, and four or five others hanging out the windows of the house.

'In that case,' continued the leader, 'carry out the sentence.'

The mayor was led, this time with some solemnity, into the garden, abloom with myriad roses – climbers, bushes, trees, miniature and moss roses – fragrant and alive with bees. His hands were untied.

Chantal had crept out of the house and was watching from around the corner, just as the Maquis handed the mayor a spade that had been left leaning against the wall.

'Dig here!' he commanded, pointing to a spot in Madame Arondel's asparagus garden.

The mayor's eyes met Chantal's. He pointed to himself with a question in his gesture: For me? Chantal shrugged her shoulders in disbelief. Don't be ridiculous, her own gesture said. He dug a shallow trench in the soft earth.

Then before he could even straighten up, without warning, a short burst of automatic fire. He fell, face down, into the trench, arms and legs twitching. The Maquis turned him over with his boot, took careful aim, fired into the side of his head. The corpse jumped under the impact, then lay motionless. The two Maquis lit cigarettes, threw the match into the trench. One put his weapon down on the ground, and, while the other watched, smoking, threw a few spadefuls of earth, just enough barely to cover the body, and went back inside. Neither of them paid any attention to Chantal, who stood, transfixed and powerless.

In whose name had that man died?

Later on, the Arondels gathered from eavesdropping on the Maquis that the mayor was suspected of having harbored a Militiaman they were hunting. In any case, someone had told them he had been *seen* talking to a Militiaman a few days earlier, or at least, to someone who *might* have been one. Robespierre couldn't have done better, in the name of the same people, the same nation. Almost to the day, a century and a half later, Terror had again been made the order of the day.

'They already shot two men the day before yesterday,' sobbed Madame Arondel to Chantal. 'They are all buried in the asparagus patch, where the earth is soft.'

Horror apparently obeys the law of diminishing returns, and too much horror is its own antidote. Madame Arondel's anguish was by now no greater than it would have been in previous months had her asparagus bed simply been trampled, no dead men involved. Today, she had given up on the estate, the waxed floors, the gardens, the wine barrels, the painstakingly amassed provisions. Let's just try to stay alive, said her every glance. Anger and sorrow, despair and revenge, will have to wait until we have strength for them.

She isn't even very angry at them, wondered Chantal. Why, she's almost grateful they let us live. Perhaps she's the wisest: she knows they'll leave someday, but she will remain and rebuild.

Later in the day, as they sat on makeshift beds in the former winter kitchen, Madame Arondel whispered, 'Your friend Martine disappeared just a few days ago. Your father met Monsieur Moreau. Poor man! He and his wife are in a frenzy of worry. Martine had gone to the films, just before they were all closed down . . .'

Martine and Josette, a secretary at the Moreau mills, walked out of the movie theater on the rue Marengo. Josette yawned.

'Not much fun going to a show anymore,' she complained. 'First, there's always those newsreels of the war, and then I didn't care for that German movie about that queen . . . What's her name? Mary, Mary . . .'

'Mary Stuart, I think,' said Martine. 'Zarah Leander was good in the part, but it's just too sad. All those years in prison!'

'Is it a true story?' Josette asked idly. 'Was she really beheaded by that other queen?'

'I wouldn't know. I flunked history.' Martine shrugged. 'They made it up, I bet.'

'Well, I'll say good night,' said Josette. 'If I turn left here, there's a shortcut home. See you at the office in the morning. Hey, Martine, the top of your dress is unbuttoned.'

'I know, I undid it in the theater. So close in there. And almost as hot out here. Good night.'

Martine continued walking in the direction of the Place Saint-Martial. Two young men who'd been walking at a distance behind the girls picked up their pace, caught up with her.

'*Bonsoir*,' they said. 'Mind if we walk with you?'

Martine didn't mind, but she noticed they were unshaven and wore clothes that looked like they'd been slept in repeatedly.

'Do you happen to know if the German checkpoint is still there, just ahead?'

'I don't think so,' replied Martine. 'It wasn't there when I walked up, a couple of hours ago. The soldiers have left for the night, I guess. Who could they expect to arrest, anyway? The streets are practically empty.' They walked on, turned a corner.

'*Halt! Papiere!*' The checkpoint was back in operation: Sawhorses, a van pulled across the street, a group in uniform with automatics.

'Oh, *zut!* 'cried Martine. 'Third time this week I've got to show that damn ID!' But the young men had turned around and started to run. A burst of machine-gun fire stitched a line of ricocheting concrete at their feet. One fell to his knees. The soldiers had already surrounded the three young people.

'What's that all about?' Martine, trembling uncontrollably, still couldn't understand what had happened. 'No need to shoot. I'm local. Here – here's my ID.'

The Germans ignored the proffered papers. They were searching the wounded boy, blood seeping from a leg shot. No papers. No papers either on the other one, but a revolver, holstered against his calf. Under Martine's bewildered eyes, they made the young men open their flies, flashed a light on their penises: '*Juden!*' They'd seen the telltale circumcision. Martine, in her panic, dropped her papers, bent down to retrieve them, and her gold *chai* sign slipped out of the open neck of her dress. The beam picked it out.

'*Was ist das?*' A hand grabbed it. She tried to push the hand away. 'It's a pendant my boyfriend's mother gave me. Her name's Nathalie. See, it's an—'

'Another Jew!' shouted the German. Martine, too, was pushed, screaming, into the van. The door slammed. The barricade had served its purpose. The van pulled away, unseen by all, except a little boy who'd been watching from the half-open window of his bedroom.

'As I said, she didn't come home that night, and no one has seen her since. Her parents are frantic. A little boy says he saw a girl and two men arrested at the checkpoint. But it doesn't make much sense, she'd gone out with Josette, they'd parted less than a minute from the spot where that kid lives. Josette is positive Martine was walking home alone.'

Chantal was aghast. 'Was Martine involved in anything? The Resistance? Helping somebody in the Maquis?'

'They don't think so. Perhaps she talked too much, she was always so friendly! Her mother says Martine mentioned some supposed boyfriend who'd gone to America. But she didn't pay much attention. You know Martine was always a little boy-crazy.'

A silence. 'And that's not all. Now, her two brothers, you remember Denis and Georges? Well, they've gone and joined some Resistance unit, and their parents are out of their heads with worry.'

Chantal couldn't imagine what had happened to Martine. She did recall the long-ago adventure and Volodia's medal, but she could see no connection at all.

Monsieur Arondel had walked into the room. 'All hope isn't lost,' he said reassuringly. 'There's no reason to think it was her the kid saw. I'm sure she'll turn up with a perfectly good explanation,' he finished lamely.

Chantal knew nothing of the night and fog of the extermination camps. But, torn with sorrow, she sensed that something terrible waited at the end of the line for those taken away in the dark of the night. And she saw the same thought in her parents' anguished eyes.

Monsieur Arondel left every morning on disconsolate tours of the idle farms, where hay was drying uncut and wheat was ripening into what would have been a splendid harvest, but there was no hope of bringing the heavy sheaves into the barns. It would all rot with the next rain, lost to all. Why work in the fields, he thought bitterly, when one could take the war into one's own hands, brandish parachuted weapons, lounge around drinking whatever could be stolen and render quick bloody 'justice'?

Anna came running one morning. 'Madame, madame,' she panted, 'you remember Marcel, the boy we found wounded in the métro station and we kept in the apartment? Charles helped him with his spare uniform? Well, I saw him, getting out of a car down in the courtyard. Oh, now we are saved – he'll tell these other men what we did for him . . .'

At last, thought Chantal, at last! Someone will try to help us! When he tells the others how Anna and I saved his life, maybe they'll leave and let us alone.

She almost ran around to the front of the house. Marcel and a group of other young men, all with the red rags around their necks, were lounging around the car that had just brought him. He was unchanged, ferret-faced, only now with a deep scar across his cheek. They had seen Anna, were talking about her, and there was something lewd in their laughter that made Chantal's skin crawl. Still, she walked over to the small group, hand extended. 'Hello, Marcel, remember me?'

Marcel's hand remained in his pocket. 'Sure, baby, sure,' he said. 'How could I forget you?' he leered. 'Still got the hots for me? Want some more? You know you can always count on old Marcel . . .'

Guffaws from the others.

'Did you chase me here, all the way from Paris? Kid, I got to hand it to you, you're hot for it.' He turned to his friends. 'You know that night I blew up the Militia truck in Paris, and killed all six men by myself, and was just walking down the street, as though nothing had happened?'

They knew. They nodded in silent admiration.

'Well,' he continued, 'would you believe this crazy broad here comes along and drags me into her apartment. She couldn't get enough. You can always count on those little blonds, mark my word, although, personally, I prefer them more stacked. But it's war, reduced rations and all!'

This convulsed the others.

Chantal didn't wait to hear more. Chalk off this debt, and let's just hope my mother doesn't hear them. Did it mean you should never try to help anybody? Was this a lesson to live by? She returned to the house, pursued by leers and jokes.

Monsieur Arondel came home from his rounds every noon, sad and angry about the abandoned crops drying in the fields while the country starved. The members of *this* Maquis were not going hungry: cattle, sheep, pigs were 'liberated' from the helpless farmers, shot, butchered, roasted whole, eaten in some orgiastic celebration of power, food, and drink.

News still came on the radio. Paris had not been reconquered, but it was clear the Americans were getting closer. Through the mysterious grapevine of the countryside, Monsieur Arondel had heard that a German car had been ambushed that night near Oradour, by a Maquis group, who had killed the general it carried and his driver, left their mutilated bodies by the roadside, and driven off with the car. Apparently, the car was all they wanted.

'When will they stop?' sighed Monsieur Arondel as the family sat down to a meal of vegetables gathered in the fields. 'Now, I suppose if any Germans are around, they'll take hostages.'

Oradour-sur-Glane was a market center of some six hundred souls, on the way to Limoges. The mayor, a distant relative of the Arondels, operated a garage that sold and repaired cars before the war, and had recently installed gazogenes and repaired farm machinery. His two sons, both in their thirties, were also businessmen in the small community.

The next day, word spread like wildfire from farm to farm and reached La Prade that a German division, which had been trying to travel from the south up to the Normandy front, had left the main road and was heading in the direction of Oradour. People sighed: A German convoy! The Maquis is going to strike at them again, there will be more bloodshed.

Instead, the next morning more urgent rumors flew. 'Something is going on. That German division has stopped at Oradour. The town is surrounded by armored vehicles, there are SS guarding the roads. It's market day, but they are not letting anybody in or out. What are they up to? Are they looking for the ones responsible for the murder of their general? Then they're looking in the wrong place. Those guys aren't in town, they're hiding in the woods.'

The Germans – the SS Das Reich division – wasted no time looking for the guilty parties. They had a more expeditious way of dealing with the matter, since their purpose was no longer punishment, but rather instilling terror into the hearts of the population so they would cease harboring the Resistance and abetting acts of hostility. The SS plan was carried out with lethal efficiency, and everyone in a twenty-mile radius soon knew of the holocaust. The smoke rising black from the village and the strange, sickening odor of burned flesh carried in gusts by the summer breeze brought the terrible news.

The Das Reich SS had indeed formed a cordon of vehicles to seal off the village. An officer had summoned the mayor, who solemnly appeared, sash of office around his waist, flanked by his two sons.

'If it's hostages you want,' he said calmly, 'I am presenting myself and my two sons. Do with us as you wish.'

'No, you don't understand.' The German officer smiled. 'Taking hostages is not our intention at all. All we want to do is verify identities, and make sure no terrorists are hiding among your population. What we really want to do is help protect you from those irresponsible criminals. We only request that you have your constable summon the townspeople. We want all the men to gather. Where is there a building, a barn perhaps, large enough to hold them all?'

The mayor offered his garage, larger than any barn, and right here on the main *place*. That would do, agreed the officer.

Now, in order that women and children not disrupt the verification of identities, the officer also suggested that it would be good to place them in some building where they would be safe. Suppose we rout out some terrorists, there might be shooting, violence. We want to spare the sight of that to innocent little children and sensitive ladies. The church, perhaps? Oradour, like all the villages nearby, possessed its twelfth-century Romanesque church, squat under its low steeple, that rang the Angelus every evening. Whatever qualms the mayor may have had, would never be known. There was no choice.

So, within no more than an hour, the constable, beating his drum and reading the hastily written order, had alerted the people. Men started to stream in the direction of the big garage on the main square. The numbers in the church were swollen by the presence of a group of Paris schoolchildren, sent by their parents to the safety of the small country town, in the care of a charitable organization that housed them in a large, empty house, converted for their use. Did the women and children run in panic to the security of the church? Did they try to escape, but were brutally herded in with rifle butts? Or did everyone simply go in, chatting unconcernedly, and thinking that the noontime meal would have to be delayed?

The men were no sooner assembled in the big, echoing garage, than the doors were pushed shut and barred. Machine guns were set up and firing commenced. All the men inside were killed. Those who perhaps were only wounded died a worse death moments later, when gasoline was poured, and the building went up in flames.

Meanwhile, phosphorous incendiary bombs were thrown into the church and its heavy doors barred from outside. No one knows whether death was swift or slow, for no one escaped, except for one woman who managed to crawl behind the altar in the sacristy, climb through a broken stained-glass window, and fall into tall grass in the priest's garden below. She lay there for several days, until after the SS had left, following an orgy of looting and burning, and she was eventually found by Red Cross rescuers. She could tell little of what had happened inside the church, only stared out of vacant eyes.

The last blow of the war was reserved for Chantal, shortly after the Oradour massacre.

'There was another Maquis operation, last night,' said Monsieur Arondel as the family sat down to its meager meal. 'I was near Le Velzay, you know, at the railroad crossing near Montbron –'

He stopped, watching the reaction of his wife and daughter. He didn't enjoy being the bearer of bad news, but they'd want to know and he had to tell.

'Well,' he continued as he saw them both looking at him intently, 'ah ... it didn't go well. I heard about it this morning in the village.'

He sat, pensive, holding his knife and fork. 'No,' he repeated, 'it didn't go well for those poor kids.'

'Tell us, Jean,' urged Madame Arondel impatiently. (I never heard my mother call him by his first name before, thought Chantal.) It took some time to worm the story out of Monsieur Arondel. How shall I begin? he thought. 'Well, it seems André Brousse went to Montbron ...'

Montbron, another market center that resembled Oradour, was quiet under an afternoon sun when André Brousse drove in at the wheel of a small truck from his dairy, the one with an open bed and removable sides that made the rounds in the early morning to pick up the tall milk cans left at the roadside in front of the farms. He was looking for more recruits to bolster Colonel Robert's unit, as he had done before. Orders from London were multiplying and more volunteers were needed.

At the main corner, in front of the bike shop, several boys, sixteen, seventeen years old, were gathered, lounging on their bikes or sitting on the edge of the shop window. All bored, with nothing to do since school had closed down, discussing that Resistance fighting everyone heard so much about and wondering how *they* could get involved. They watched the truck pull up and recognized André. They knew of his connection with the Maquis.

'*Salut*, boys,' he greeted them. 'How you doing?'

Mario Blanchard, the son of the lumber dealer, shook his head of curly blond hair. 'Nothing much going on here. What's doing out there?'

Before André could answer, tall, gangling Bernard Dumont asked, 'How's Colonel Robert's unit doing? My cousin Eric's with him, but we haven't heard anything.'

André stood in the middle of the group, heavyset among the slender adolescents.

'Well, boys, Colonel Robert's unit is seeing plenty of action, and a lot more's coming now the Allies have landed. As a matter of fact, a strike is planned for tonight and the Colonel could use a bunch of smart guys like you, the kind who can shoot straight – I mean, shoot American automatics. How about it? Want to come along? You can be back before bedtime, and will you have *something* to tell your friends when the war's over! Not a word before, you understand.'

The five boys were excited – now *this* was what they'd been itching for.

'Why, sure, man, I want to go. What kind of a strike is it?' asked Mario eagerly.

'I can't give you details,' replied André Brousse, 'but this much I'm free to tell: You'll be blowing up a train that's bringing German troops to Normandy and you'll take a lot of prisoners.'

'Wait a minute,' protested Bernard, the son of a lawyer. 'You mean you'd take us there, directly into action, without any training? That's crazy! I don't know how to shoot. I'd go, but they'd have to give me at least a couple of days' instruction.'

The others hooted him down.

'Come on, Bernard, what's there to learn? We've all been shooting BB guns since we were twelve!'

'I used to go hunting with my father,' bragged René Brun, whose father owned the bike shop. 'Nothing to it. I'm going if Mario's going.'

'*Allons-y*,' shouted Mario. 'Let's go. What about you, Bernard, you coming, yes or no?'

'All right. But give me a minute to take my bike home and tell my mother I won't be home for dinner.' He pedaled to his house, a short distance away in the bend of the road going up to the church. They saw him talking to his mother through an open window framed by climbing vines, lean his bike against the wall. He rushed back, out of breath.

'I told her we're going to help at the dairy, and she said that's all right. I promised to be home by ten. Let's go.'

The Pelletier twins, dark and big for their sixteen years, had already gone inside to leave their bikes in the custody of the shop. Mario recklessly abandoned his along the sidewalk. The twins had to run to catch up with the truck already rolling. They caught the sides, clung, and pulled themselves up, yelling.

A little way out of town, they made André stop in front of a new brick house and called out to their friend Jean-Paul. André honked his horn. Jean-Paul's younger brother, Michou, came out, curious. He was thirteen and seldom invited to join his older brother's crowd.

'Jean-Paul's not home, he went fishing with Dad. Where you guys going?'

They explained. 'To stop a train, with Colonel Robert's unit. They'll give us American guns. Hey, Michou, want to come along?' offered Mario generously.

Michou couldn't believe his luck. '*Chic alors!* Super! American guns! It sure is swell of you guys to take me along! Wait till Jean-Paul hears about what he missed! Won't he go crazy!'

There were now six laughing boys holding on to the sides of the swaying truck.

'I can't wait to get my hands on one of those guns,' shouted Mario over the din. 'Rat tat tat tat, I'll shoot those Boches like rabbits. Rat tat tat tat,' he went on, spraying the culvert with imaginary automatic fire. 'See? I killed a whole bunch of them already.'

After several miles, the truck lurched from the road onto a deeply rutted track that disappeared into the woods. The boys had all they could do just to hang on. They bumped along, crossed a pasture, wheels sinking in the grass, cut into some woods again, branches whipping.

'I know where we are,' called out René as they all ducked.

'We're not far from Le Velzay crossing. The river's to the left and there's a railroad track down there. See?'

The double line of the rails gleamed in the late afternoon sun, where the tracks emerged from thick woods into a clearing. André stopped the truck, the boys piled out. He gestured to them to be quiet. Then he hooted twice, like an owl. A few seconds later, another hoot coming from the woods below echoed his.

'There's some guys from the unit down there waiting for the new volunteers. That's you, men. Go fight for a Free France and make us proud of you. I'll be here to take you back after you blow up that train. More guys will come later to round up your Kraut prisoners, unless you kill them all.'

He gave a victory sign, visionary eyes focused on the distant track.

'*Vive de Gaulle! Vive la France Libre!*'

Already scampering down the slope, the boys only waved a perfunctory sign in his direction. André sighed. Those kids will be all right, he forced himself to think, though there's been several dead in recent engagements . . . But this one's been well planned. Surprise and immobilize the enemy by blowing up the engine, give them the impression they're surrounded by murderous fire, take them as prisoners after they surrender. Another action just like this one succeeded two weeks ago. Still, who knows? There's always danger.

'This is war,' André said aloud to himself. He lived in constant danger himself, but, fanatically patriotic, he put victory above all other considerations. He backed his truck under low branches that hid it, but from where he commanded a view of the track and the clearing below.

Before the boys emerged into the open, a figure stepped out from the trees, weapon at the ready, bandoleer of ammo, two rows of torn gold braid on the sleeve. Bernard recognized his cousin.

'Eric,' he exclaimed, 'you're a lieutenant now! Guys, this is my cousin, the one I told you about.'

Eric had been a medical student until he joined the Maquis well before the Normandy landings. Now he told Bernard he'd been promoted to second in command to Colonel Robert. With him leading the way, they marched Indian-like in the dappled sunlight shining through green-gold oak leaves.

An abandoned hut stood there, half cayed in by the fall of a dead tree, in a tangle of mossy branches. A young man sitting on a stump stood up, weapon at the ready. Another came out of the hut.

'These are the Moreau brothers, Denis and Georges. They joined up after their sister disappeared, arrested by the Boches, they're sure. It's a personal account they'll be settling today.'

Inside the hut, Denis and Georges pulled aside a khaki tarpaulin to reveal a jumble of machine guns, lying helter-skelter. Their metal glinted ominously in the gloom, a smell of oil and powder filled the room. The boys stood back, awed by the deadly machines.

'Take one each and some ammo,' instructed Eric. 'I'll show you how to use them. Hey, not you, half-pint,' he called out to Michou, who was already struggling to lift one of the heavy weapons. But Michou managed to shoulder it. Now, the boys each pulled one up and they were examining them, silently, taken by surprise at the weight.

'They smell like death,' whispered Bernard to Mario.

'Watch carefully, and I'll show you how to load and to shoot.' They crowded around Eric, who demonstrated the operation. He didn't fire a single shot, though. Security demanded caution, and anyway, wasn't the deadly rattle unthinkable in the deep, waiting woods, alive only with the distant chirping of birds?

Moments passed. The boys tried some halfhearted banter, then silence. Each was shouldering his weapon.

An owl hooted nearby, and Eric responded: '*Whoo, whoo.*' Branches cracked and a tall, slightly stooped figure stepped into view, heavily armed. The boys straightened and Mario saluted, an approximate gesture against his curly hair.

'At ease,' said Colonel Robert with a tired smile that didn't erase a frown. 'Glad you wanted to come and serve your country.' He spotted Michou, struggling manfully to manage the weight of his automatic. 'How old are you? What? Fifteen? You can't be. And no matter, you're too small. You can't come out with us. I want you to go back, wait with André in the truck.'

But Michou begged, 'See, I can hold the gun. I can shoot. I want to serve my country too.'

The train was due in less than a half hour. No time to argue with a recalcitrant kid.

'All right,' conceded the Colonel with a shrug. 'You can come, then, but you'll stay close to me. Now' – he gestured to the rest – 'I'll show you what you're going to do. Eric,' he asked, 'you've secured the explosive charge?'

'Yes, it's clamped to the rail, right where we can see it from ambush. Look.'

They had emerged from the woods. The track was there, very close, and, half hidden among lumps of charcoal and ballast, the black detonator box that would set off the dynamite sticks when the wheels of the locomotive hit it.

'I want each one of you hidden in the cover of a tree or a bush. We won't wait for the locomotive to blow up. I'll shout "Fire!" the moment I see the wheels ready to hit the detonator. You all fire at the same time and keep firing. The Krauts won't know what hit them and with a disabled train, there's no way they can escape. They'll surrender.'

The boys dispersed, crouched behind trunks or in thickets, each listening to the pounding of his heart. Colonel Robert checked them one by one, verified the position of trembling fingers on triggers. Then he disappeared behind a bramble bush thickly hung with vines, with Michou close by his side. Time froze into an eternity of minutes.

A distant whistle announced that the train had passed the Le Velzay crossing. Then chugging was heard. Louder, louder, now the rattle of pistons, the hissing of steam. Louder . . . In a few seconds, the engine would hit the detonator. Fingers tightened on triggers.

But for unknown reasons, the train stopped instead, and firing began from a hundred muzzles pointed out of every window, in an obscene rattle, a barrage of death whistling past the ears of the paralyzed boys, pinging into trees, ricocheting off the ground in small geysers of dirt. Little Michou let out a bloodcurdling scream, escaped from the Colonel's grip, and ran, instantly felled by a volley that slammed him down in a shower of red droplets. In the move the Colonel made to catch him, he was hit, too, at waist level, and fell back into the brambles.

Immobilizing terror gave way to demented panic and all the boys started running, dropping their guns, running toward . . . toward what? The safety of the truck? Or just running away from the unbearable sound of death?

None went more than a few steps. Each was hit, cut grotesquely down in his tracks, body twisting, arms flailing, blood pooling on the layer of dead leaves. Firing went on long after nothing moved any longer, finally died out into isolated shots. Then silence, with only the sound of the gasping train. Mario was moaning softly.

Eric crawled out of his shelter to try and pull him out of the line of fire. A single shot to the side of his head nailed him to the ground.

The Germans waited a moment to ascertain all danger had been annihilated. Then helmeted heads appeared, a group stepped out, covered by muzzles trained out of windows, went to examine the explosives on the track and started to disarm the detonator. Others felt the barrels of their weapons, found them cool enough to grab, and strode purposefully toward the sprawled young bodies. The first one they reached was Mario, and he was still breathing . . .

Monsieur Arondel cleared his throat. The women were listening, transfixed. Chantal covered her face with her hands.

'Well, those poor kids lay there, hidden among the trees, counting on the element of surprise and a disabled train to gain advantage. But the Germans are getting nervous now, with so many ambushes. On every train they have a lookout. This one must have spotted the detonator, he gave a signal, the train stopped, troops firing. And when those kids started to run, why, they were shot like rabbits.'

'My God, the poor parents, and poor Moreaus!' gasped Madame Arondel. 'First their daughter lost the other day and now both their boys! Tell me, did they get the bodies back?'

'Ah . . .' Monsieur Arondel hesitated. 'Yes, at least . . . Well, yes, they did. André Brousse saw what happened from his post on the hill. After the train left, he drove back to Angoulême and he brought back one of the Moreau drivers. It was a Moreau truck that returned all those poor dead kids back home.'

No need to tell them, he thought, what had been done to their faces – how the Nazis had smashed them with boots and rifle stocks, or how André couldn't even at first identify Mario, whose curly blond hair was nothing but a mass of dark dried blood.

No need.

Chantal could no longer contain herself.

'Were they all found?'

'Ah, yes, I think so, more or less, that is.' Monsieur Arondel preferred not to give more details than was absolutely necessary.

'Was that Colonel, Colonel Robert you said, was he there?'

'That's the damnedest thing,' admitted Monsieur Arondel, 'as a matter of fact ... Well, yes, I think he was there, along with those kids. But his body hasn't been found.'

'Perhaps he wasn't killed?' whispered Chantal. 'He might be alive?'

'What could have happened to him? Does André Brousse know?' asked Madame Arondel.

More hesitation. Finally:

'Well, to tell the truth, André confided to somebody that he figured the Germans took the Colonel alive, so they can torture him and get information out of him, about, you know, who is leading them, what their radio code to get their parachute supplies is, who serves as liaison ... André thinks the body will be found along the track, in a couple of days, hundreds of miles from here and ... ah ... no doubt unrecognizable. That has happened before. As a matter of fact, André is so worried about what the Colonel might say under torture ... Hey, Chantal, Chantal, what's the matter? Chantal? Adélaïde' – he turned to Madame Arondel – 'what's the matter with that girl? Did I say something wrong?'

'She just fainted,' snapped Madame Arondel. 'That's all. Anna, Anna, bring some vinegar,' she called out, rubbing her daughter's palms. 'It's just too much for her. She knew all those kids, the Dumont boy, the two Moreaus, Mario. Why, she knew them all from way back. Went to school with their sisters. Don't let her hear those stories from now on, please, Jean. She's anemic, I can tell, she's not that strong and it's more than she can take. Here, Jean, help me stretch her out on this bed. Anna, where is that vinegar? Ah, there you are. Bring me a clean handkerchief, too, silly girl. See? She's coming to. It was nothing. Can you sit up, Chantal?'

Only a few days later, a great commotion was heard at night in the courtyard. Cars were coming and going. A group of men had gathered around a shortwave radio and the Arondels could hear its static and the tinny voice. The next morning, to the astonishment of the beleaguered family, the courtyard was empty and no sound came from the house. The Arondels peered into open windows and saw wreckage strewn everywhere inside. After a few hours, emboldened by the continued silence, they pushed open the entrance door, stepped into the hall. Shards of mirrors, torn curtains, filthied bedding, smashed furniture, broken dishes and glasses, refuse everywhere, but the men were gone. Gone for good?

Hearts in their mouths, they waited, listening all day for the squealing of tires turning again into the courtyard. Nothing. Total silence. Only the bees – undisturbed, millions of them, their hives having escaped the destruction – were all at work, busily gathering pollen for the winter season from the profusion of the blooming garden.

That night was quiet. For the first time in months, Madame Arondel heard birds in the trees in the early hours, just before sunrise.

Had they stopped singing all those past weeks? she thought, surprised. Or did I just not hear them? Another quiet, anxious day of listening, waiting, followed. Still nothing. By the third day, Monsieur Arondel, having consigned the women to the house, behind closed shutters, had enlisted the help of some of his farmers and they dug up the three bodies shot and buried in the garden. They loaded them onto an oxcart, and slowly, bareheaded, at the processional pace of the oxen, drove to the village cemetery, where nobody could be found who would dig a grave for fear of reprisals should the Maquis turn up again. So, Monsieur Arondel doffed his coat, rolled up his sleeves, crossed himself, and with the two other men, dug graves and laid the victims to rest.

Another day of silence passed. Finally, Madame Arondel could stand it no longer, and aided by Anna she started, timidly at first, then with increased vigor, to take inventory of the worst of the wreckage – clean, sort, repair. She was calm, full of energetic efficiency. Still too soon for tears, regrets, rage.

Chantal remained in bed, eyes closed, unable to face the light of day, the conversations she could not have avoided, trying to live with this death which could not even offer the solace of a body to kneel by, a funeral, public tears, sympathy. Nothing. Nothing but images of horror she could not help but conjure. She lay there, while her mother shook her head and tried to make her drink a little milk with an egg yolk beaten in it, a cup of vegetable broth . . .

A few days later, Monsieur Arondel came back from his rounds to the village and around the outlying farms with more news. He spoke to his wife with some hesitation. 'They are saying that . . . ah . . . that Colonel Robert was really . . . ah . . . that he was really Anthenor. Had you heard that?'

Madame Arondel looked up sharply. 'No. How could Anthenor be a colonel?'

'You know how easily rank is gained in the Maquis. Look at the "Chief Colonel" we had here, with his six rows of braid. And, after all, Anthenor had been in the Resistance so long, he joined back in – in early '42, wasn't it? Much ahead of the others who only went in '43 and later. So, he had experience, seniority, he had the manner of a leader, and they say the men liked and respected him. The braid? Well, parachuted braid, they call it.'

'Are you sure?'

'People I spoke with are sure. André Brousse has been around, he's talked. Now, he says, he doesn't have to be afraid anymore, it looks as though, no matter what the Germans did to him, Anthenor didn't talk. Otherwise,

André says, the Boches would have been looking for him well before now.' He shuddered.

Madame Arondel wasn't listening any longer. 'Now I understand everything. Chantal knew it was Anthenor you were talking about when you told us about the ambush at Le Velzay. *That's* why she fainted. I always suspected she was in love with him. So,' she added reflectively, 'sad as it is to say, what happened to him may have been for the best – for us and for her.'

'Poor girl,' said Monsieur Arondel with a deep sigh, and avoiding the issue. 'Poor child! She hasn't had too much luck so far, has she? I hope things get better for her.'

Madame Arondel was divided between sympathy for her daughter's sorrow – a sorrow she could allow herself to acknowledge now it no longer presented any danger – and immediate practical thoughts. As always with her, practical matters came first.

'You have a power of attorney from Anthenor to run Blazonac, and that's good for the time being,' she told her husband thoughtfully. 'But what will happen next?'

He answered only after she had repeated the question. 'I am not sure, but I think that, in the case of a missing person, the civil code prescribes a seven-year delay before the person can be declared legally dead. At that time, ah . . . well . . .'

'At that time,' continued Madame Arondel, 'Marie-Esmée inherits Anthenor's share. Are you sure it would take seven years? Perhaps they'll find his body. Then it could all be settled much sooner. Poor young man, I do feel sorry for him, but he *did* join the Resistance. Nobody forced him. We don't know how many hapless boys he led to their death. And for what?'

'For an idea,' ventured Monsieur Arondel timidly. 'Just an idea, something called patriotism, I guess – the idea that he was helping in the war, fighting for the country, even against terrible odds.'

Madame Arondel was no longer listening. In spite of the deep distrust she had felt for Anthenor since Renaud's

264

death — the fear of what the terrible truth of that death might be, and even worse, of what else that truth might reveal — there was relief that Chantal would no longer be involved with 'those people.' Pity for the wounded girl lying listless, silent tears streaming unchecked down her cheeks, was mounting in her heart. I must do something, she thought.

She went upstairs once more. 'Chantal,' she urged gently. Words of endearment were not part of the vocabulary at La Prade. 'Chantal, listen to me.'

Chantal nodded, imperceptibly. 'I hear you, Mother,' she said quietly.

'Look, your father just came home, he told me, and now we know . . . about that colonel, and the ambush.' She avoided pronouncing Anthenor's name. She sat on the edge of the bed, took her daughter's hand. 'I am sorry, and I understand how you feel.'

Such uncharacteristic sympathy broke the dam of Chantal's anguish, and she sobbed uncontrollably, her head on her mother's lap.

Madame Arondel caressed her daughter's hair in an unusual gesture of tenderness. There were two brothers in that accursed house, she thought, and she has grieved for both of them. Both times we saw her tears, but we never knew their real source. I always think of her as a child, but children's tears are easy to read. Hers, both times, came from a secret that she must keep . . .

She sighed deeply, still stroking her daughter's hair. 'You shouldn't go into real mourning. After all, it wasn't such a close relationship, he was only Renaud's half brother, and you have been widowed for several years now,' she said firmly, still carefully avoiding Anthenor's name. 'But perhaps you wouldn't want to wear colors, at least for a while. You need some summer clothes, you came from Paris without anything, except that pink dress you were wearing. I thought we could have a sheet or two cut, the fine linen sheets from my trousseau, never used yet, you know, they would make good summer dresses for you.'

So for all that last summer of the war, Chantal went about in white linen, her hair tied with a black ribbon. And she alone, with the complicity of her mother, who never mentioned the subject again, knew that she was wearing white mourning for a man she had loved one night and lost before their life had even begun.

Chantal missed the liberation of Paris, the shooting from rooftops, the barricades, the long-awaited arrival of the liberators. Everyone by now, along every road, had waved at Americans, who were driving every possible vehicle in long convoys and incongruous-looking jeeps with incomprehensible names painted under their windshields: *Three Fakes*, or *I Wanna Go Home*, or *Good Guys*, which somehow seemed friendly and unthreatening. A five-pointed white star shone on their hoods. There were laughing GIs, helmets askew, chewing gum, who gave the thumbs-up or the victory sign . . .

But La Prade was too isolated, and Chantal was too listless. She saw none of it.

'"Asthenia," Dr Vincent calls it,' said her mother to those who inquired about Chantal's pallor and the tears that always seemed ready to brim under her lashes. 'Malnutrition, you know, and a delayed reaction to the death of Count Renaud.'

If there were knowing smiles, neither mother nor daughter cared to see them.

And yet, little by little, life was taking over, and Chantal could eventually sleep some nights without the horrible image of torture – of eyes popping like grapes out of their skins . . . Oh, no, no, please, no, not his eyes, please. Eventually, though, she could smile, and even laugh, timidly and guiltily at first, and then one day her mother saw her playing with little Mariès, and the dimples were back. There was her Chantal again. Madame Arondel folded her hands, satisfied: the curse of that awful house of Blazonac was lifted, it was over, never more. Chantal would have a normal life, after all, in a normal world where there was peace and sanity. And feeling better herself than she had in a long time, invigorated perhaps by the challenge of having to re-create her shattered world, she went back to the restoration of her savaged house, with all her maids now returned.

Monsieur Arondel suggested, one day, hoping – who knows? – in his own, hesitant, well-meaning way, to put some balm on the wound he could feel in his daughter's soul, that a plaque should be placed in the cemetery of Blazonac, next to Renaud's tomb. It could say: *In memoriam* . . . since there was, as he put it, 'No . . . ah . . . well, since they didn't find the . . . ah . . . It didn't look as if . . .' But when he saw the stricken look on Chantal's face, he put his arm around her shoulders and said soothingly that there was plenty of time to think about that.

Yet all wounds heal, even though they leave scars on the soul. And Chantal's wound was healing over, a thin scab, to be sure, and she had to take care not to look at penknives, or think of trains, or of the tall figure marching barefoot in the river mist at the head of his men. And she must not, ever, allow herself to think of that night in Limoges. There were so many things she had to be careful not to think about that it reminded her of those months of her pregnancy, when she must breathe only through her mouth for fear of the many odors that provoked nausea. Now, she couldn't even walk in the woods for fear she'd see tree trunks marked for lumbering. She never once went near Blazonac, although her parents hinted that in time she might want to return there to live. One day a leather jacket left hanging in the hall by a visitor gave her a second of heart-pounding, violent, demented hope . . .

Her mother came to her room, one morning, carrying a cup of hot chocolate, a conspirator's smile on her face. 'After all these years! I just got a little packet today from someone who got it from some Americans. Drink this, you'll see how good it is . . .'

Suddenly, Chantal was reliving the day, brisk and cold,

and Bijou's trot on the frozen ground of the long drive, and the chocolate in the kitchen at Blazonac, and Anthenor drinking his cup with concentration. No, Mother, no chocolate, please. I see his eyes, don't you understand, his eyes, and then I think of that knife . . .

But with care, Chantal learned to skirt by the worst moments. And when well-meaning visitors said, 'And isn't it terrible, what happened to Count Renaud's brother? How are you taking it? Of course, you probably never were that close to him, but nevertheless. Did you feel it had to end this way? That there is a curse on that family? Do you think that's why they all die so young?' Madame Arondel frowned protectively and deftly changed the subject.

13

SUMMER WAS TURNING to fall once more when a letter came to La Prade from Domergue. Things were calm in Paris, the war was going on, to be sure, but it was now far away once more, off to the east. The city was alive again, swarming with American troops. The master had many commissions – galleries were clamoring for exhibits. He was ready to reopen his atelier. Would Chantal come back soon?

She wanted to go. In Paris, nobody would speak of Anthenor and nothing would remind her of him. Also, after the initial joy and relief of being 'home' again, secure and looked after, with no worries for Mariès and herself, she was once more stifled by the way Madame Arondel inevitably had of making all decisions and of leaving nobody in 'her' house any privacy whatever. Chantal suspected she had found and read the two short, scribbled notes that were all she had left from Anthenor: The one Cécile had brought her in Paris and the one the young Resistance soldier had handed her that morning in Chabanais. They were unsigned, but Madame Arondel's sixth sense would not have allowed her to remain long in the dark as to their origin. Now, with growing uneasiness, Chantal could remember what she had forgotten so easily during the dismal months in Blazonac: why she had been so eager in the first place to leave the safety of La Prade – for freedom, freedom of any kind.

'I am going back to Paris.'

Madame Arondel wisely accepted her decision. 'It will be good for you. Go alone at first, get organized and see how things work out. Food is still just as scarce there as before and it will be easier for you if you're alone. Leave

Mariès and Anna here, they can join you later, when things are more settled.'

So, Chantal returned to Paris alone, in a city gone insane with joy, drunk with freedom, and alive with tall, smiling young men in olive drab who were winning the war for the world. They walked with a long, loose stride that took up a great deal of space on the sidewalks, and they wanted, more than anything, it seemed, to be seen as friends by everyone.

Chantal's apartment was untouched, and she delighted in walking through the intimate, luxurious rooms. In the middle of all the upheaval – the bombings, the tides of war – the crystal chandelier had lost not one of its pendants, and every slender stemmed glass shone, standing straight upon its own reflection, on the mirrored shelves of the dining-room vitrine. All the fabric blossoms welcomed her, smiling with their pink and rose faces. Now, I am home, she thought. *Forever* spelled the hazelnut branch she'd placed back on her night table. 'He is gone *forever*,' she said aloud to herself.

The next day was Sunday, bathed in a glorious fall sunshine. Chantal had forgotten she owned anything else than the two linen dresses she'd worn all summer and was almost surprised to find all her clothes waiting for her in her armoire. Three years ago, she thought, they'd have been taken to the *teinturier*, to emerge from the dye vat shrunk and ruined. Strange how life erodes you! Anthenor's been dead only three months, and yet I don't have the courage to give up my wardrobe.

For the first time since those dark days of June, she felt the forces of life welling up in her. She'd planned to stay home, but the golden light on her balcony beckoned. I'll just go for a walk, she thought. She put on her Maggy Rouff navy tussah with polka dots, tight bodice flaring into a wide, starched linen collar, knee-skimming full skirt dancing over a frilly petticoat. She didn't expect her step to be so springy when she walked up the avenue Victor-Hugo to the Place de l'Etoile. Dozens of American soldiers lounging in front of the USO smiled at her, called out, begging, 'Mademoiselle, hey, mademoiselle!'

This isn't reality, she thought. Reality is war, passion, terror, death ... the unspeakable death of Anthenor. A phrase of her father's came to mind: 'When American troops arrived in '17, they didn't look like they'd come to fight a war, with those Boy Scout felt hats and rolled-up sleeves. More like schoolboys dressed up for some operetta. Yet, it's because of them the war was won.' That's what it's like now, she thought. A play. Her part in it was to stride, skirt swinging against suntanned legs, ignore those GIs and their friendly foreign voices, but toss her pale blond hair to show her awareness of their desire. Then she was supposed to stop, face one of those eager boys. 'You want me, don't you? Then come with me. I'll take you to my bed and I'll lose myself in your arms. I'm so hungry for the feel of arms around me, for kisses, for tenderness ... Will you give me what I want?'

But she wasn't bold enough to carry out the part that far. Instead, her heart fluttering in her chest like a wounded bird, she walked on demurely, down the Champs-Elysées, the avenue Matignon, the rue Saint-Honoré, where all the boutique windows, as impoverished as before the Liberation, still made a brave effort to offer trifles that would be mailed back to Kansas or Wyoming to spell the stylish gaiety of Paris: silk flowers for the hair, costume jewelry made of wood, painted glass, gilt, Limoges enamel, which she had worn in that other lifetime, perfumes ... In the rue Cambon, the House of Chanel was shuttered and lifeless; Mademoiselle Chanel had openly lived with a German officer and was rumored to have collaborated with the enemy. Arrested, she'd been released thanks to some mysterious, high-placed protection – Churchill's, whispered some. Now, she'd fled to Switzerland. But in the boutique, crowds of GIs fought over bottles of No. 5, just as avidly as the Germans had done.

At the passage of the Ritz, one of those ever-present GIs stepped out of a group, grabbed her to the encouraging

271

shouts of his buddies, swung her around by the waist. 'Hey, baby, *couchez avec moi?*' She pushed him away with mock indignation and walked on, smiling to herself, wishing she could imitate those girls she saw strolling with soldiers who held them tight, arms around their shoulders, in a gesture of protective affection. But she only knew how to remain aloof, pretending to be hurrying on some urgent errand.

Tired of walking, she took the métro in the direction of the Bois de Boulogne. It would be nice to sit there for a while, under the trees with their yellowing leaves, before going home for the rest of the day. The car was almost deserted. When the doors opened, at the Concorde station, a dozen American soldiers crowded in, pushing and laughing. Instinctively, she held her breath: that many soldiers in such proximity would smell, she knew, sour and sweaty, the smell German troops gave off, with their tightly buttoned ersatz wool uniform jackets worn without a shirt, directly over the skin.

After a few seconds, she took a cautious breath: a clean, fresh smell had permeated the whole métro car – chewing gum, spearmint, toothpaste, shaving lotion, clean wool, freshly laundered shirts. The young men were shouting, laughing at jokes Chantal couldn't understand, and they were looking at her, smiling. She smiled back. This prompted one of them, maybe a little older than her, to sit down next to her.

He had pale blue eyes, short blond hair, a totally unlined face. He had slipped his garrison cap under his shoulder tabs.

'Hi,' he beamed. 'My name is Tom. Do you speak English, mademoiselle?'

Chantal remembered all those years of English classes, the summers she had spent in Brighton, and she was surprised to recognize his language as something she understood, very different in accent, but still identifiable. The feeling of unreality came back, it's like a game in which you speak made-up words, she thought. She hesitated only a second. 'How do you do,' she pronounced carefully. 'My name is Chantal. I am glad to meet you. Yes, I speak English a little.'

She had started to extend her hand, but Tom made no gesture to reach for it, and she learned right there that American men do not shake hands with women, as the French do.

Tom and his buddies were overjoyed, there were cries of excitement. Bobs, Dons, Tims, and Jacks, pointing to their chests, introduced themselves. Chantal smiled all around, dimpled, acknowledged all these fresh-faced, enthusiastic boys.

'How do you do, how do you do,' she repeated. But that was not what these laughing American men said. What did they say? It sounded like 'Hi,' although she was sure it couldn't be anything like that, otherwise she would have learned it in English class, wouldn't she?

Tom wasn't wasting any time. He had to make the most of the stroke of good luck which had placed him, on his first free afternoon in Paris, sitting next to a stunning blond who epitomized for him the Paris girls they had all fantasized about so much on the troop transport.

'Look, honey.'

Honey? It must mean something like 'my dear,' thought Chantal.

'We are on our way to a football game, at the stadium in Courbevoie. You know football?'

'Football?' She nodded. 'Yes, I know what football is.'

'Well, this is a big game, two army teams playing. I'd love to take you. It's fun, you know. Please be my date.'

'Your date?'

'Yes, come with me, be my girl. I'll show you a good time, and I'll bring you back home safe after the game. Please say yes.'

The others were laughing, shouting warnings at Chantal. 'He's a wolf, don't listen to him. Come with me instead . . .'

'Are you really a wolf?' She smiled. 'You are not a very dangerous one, are you?'

Wow, thought Tom, this is living! *This* is what a fellow dreamed of during the long, dull months of basic training, the endless weeks on the ship, zigzagging across the ocean dodging submarines, that seasick night on the Channel, the landing in Normandy. Safe enough, and long after the fighting in the area was over, there still were signs of a battle to the death wherever you looked. Now he was in Paris, with his brand-new corporal's stripes, sitting with a genuine Paris girl who asked him with an accent you could eat with a spoon if he was really a wolf. Nothing like *that* had ever happened to him in Hershey, Pennsylvania. He told her so.

'Hershey?' wondered Chantal. 'It is not a large town, is it?'

'Honey bunch, it may not be a big town, but it's a famous one. That's where the Hershey bars come from. And Hershey kisses too.'

A blank. Were there people in this world who had not heard of Hershey bars?

A bar was produced and passed to Chantal. Jokes about Hershey kisses, which Chantal missed completely, brought gales of laughter.

'For you. It's a candy bar, you know, chocolate.'

She shook her head no. 'No, thank you, but I don't eat chocolate.'

She dared not take the risk of chocolate bringing the heartbreaking image of Anthenor, drinking a cup of cocoa, that day in the kitchen at Blazonac.

The boys were surprised. Weren't the French supposed to be inordinately fond of those bars? Chewing gum, then? Life Savers? Spearmint? Jelly candy? Their pockets held a seemingly unlimited supply of things to eat, which all smelled just like them – minty and faintly antiseptic. Cigarettes? Smiling, Chantal shook her head.

Soon, Tom had tightened his arm around her shoulders in that oddly familiar and protective gesture she had envied earlier. She learned that he was twenty-four, a high-school graduate, he told her proudly, who had enlisted in the army in '43. He was born and had always lived in Hershey, Pennsylvania. Chantal thought it strange the way he always added *Pennsylvania* to the name of his hometown, but then he didn't just say Paris either. It was Paris, France.

Hershey, Pennsylvania, was a company town, he explained to her. While she understood the words, she had no idea of their meaning, but apparently that was what was so great about it. Everybody worked for the chocolate company that made those famous bars. Tom's grandfather had come from Germany, a long time ago, and worked there.

'From Germany?' Chantal did not know that all Americans had originally come from somewhere else. Tom explained that to her, more or less.

'But if your family is German, you wouldn't want to fight the Germans, would you?'

'Of course I would. I'm not a German, I'm an American. If you're born in America, you're an American, and nothing else,' he explained proudly and stubbornly. 'Like you are French because you were born in France.'

'Oh, no. I am French because my parents, and their parents, and their parents before them, and many more generations before were born in France. Here, if your grandparents come from another country, you are still thought of as belonging to that country.'

'Okay,' conceded Tom, who didn't really care, 'that's because you live in the *old* country. That's why. And baby,' he whispered, squeezing her shoulder, 'I sure do like what I see right now in that old country. Let me tell you, this is the first time I really understand what we are fighting for,' he added, teasing a smile out of her. 'Tell you what. Let's go see if the Red Cross has some doughnuts and coffee.'

They had arrived at Courbevoie, and he led Chantal away from his group of friends, through crowds in olive drab all walking toward the stadium entrance, holding her possessively with his arm around her waist. Wolf whistles acknowledged her presence, one of the very few women in the crowd of uniforms. She had never heard whistling express anything else than angry disapproval at a show, but it took her no time at all to understand what *these* whistles meant. She laughed, threw back her head in a provocative Domergue pose, shook her hair, and glowed. Tom steered her proudly through the crowds.

'I'll be right back. Wait here, and don't talk to anybody.'

Just time for a few 'Hi's,' and Tom was back, with hot doughnuts held in a square of paper and coffee in cardboard cups. She loved the doughnuts, but could only eat a little of one – too rich and sweet. She found the coffee almost delicious, because for the first time she could recall, it smelled of coffee and not roasted sawdust, even if it was much too watery. She saw everybody drinking coffee, too, and wondered what they would do with these beautiful cardboard cups. Not throw them away, she hoped. But throw them away they did, filling to overflowing immense bins with the cups and paper, the glossy green wrappers of chewing gum, brown and silver sheaths that had held the Hershey bars, the tinfoil and red and white empty cigarette packs, the refuse of a wasteful luxury such as she had never seen. A luxury without aesthetics . . .

The football game did not resemble anything she knew. It wasn't soccer and it wasn't rugby either. The players seemed monstrous, until she realized they wore heavy padding under their jerseys. It was actually quite boring; endless pauses, while players strolled back to their positions, incomprehensible huddles, all those behinds up in the air, leading to a few seconds of frantic, brutal activity, bodies hurled at bodies, leaping, tumbling, rolling, piling on top of one another. Then a whistle and everything stopped again, more strolling back to position, another huddle, another few seconds of violent action punctuated by wild shouts, roars from the crowd, soldiers jumping up and down, others swearing, all yelling, and all the time eating, doughnuts, candy, chocolate bars, chewing gum, drinking coffee or Coca-Cola. Chantal's first impression of that crowd of long-awaited victors was that they smelled so clean, laughed a lot, flirted unabashedly and unthreateningly, and ate, ate all the time, leaving behind enormous amounts of glittering refuse. She loved every minute of her afternoon.

Tom explained that football was played on Saturdays by high-school teams. 'Did your school have a team?' he asked. She laughed at the idea of Mother Saint-Ignatius and her cohorts organizing a game like this one. Tom, although he didn't play (but he was on the swimming team, whatever that was), never missed a game. Students went in groups, each boy had a date, waving the pennant of the school, riding in their cars. Cars? They were in high school and they had cars? Well, some did, and those who didn't borrowed their parents'. A convertible was best. You could ride sitting high in the back, pennants streaming, pompons waving, your arm around your girl. 'Just like this, baby.'

'Why is everybody making so much noise?' she asked as the crowd went wild, screaming, yelling, howling, after one of the players had broken away and run for a few yards carrying the ball, only to be tackled and thrown down brutally, to sprawl headlong on the turf.

'Don't you see?' And Tom explained about yards gained. After the game, Tom hitched a ride on a passing jeep, already carrying three soldiers whom he seemed to know. They hoisted Chantal up, skirt and frilly petticoat flying, to the accompaniment of the good-natured wolf whistles she was already beginning to take for granted. She showed the way to where she lived, and the driver obligingly took her home, careening wildly around corners.

There were crowds of soldiers in the streets on that late Sunday afternoon, more than there ever had been during the days of the Occupation. The German Gothic signs at intersections had been replaced with stenciled American ones that pointed to CONSTABULARY, COMMUNICATION ZONE HEADQUARTERS, this or that ARMY CORPS, such and such REGIMENT or BATTALION, the MILITARY HOSPITAL, the MILITARY POLICE, and the mysterious but ever-present PROPHYLACTIC STATIONS. Jeeps everywhere, command cars, trucks of every description. This was a rich army, with plenty of gasoline, uniforms cut from good fabrics, starched shirts, polished leather, and the exquisite cleanliness that bespeaks luxury. They made the Parisians look shabbily elegant, their shoes revealed for the ersatz leather, wood, and cork they were, their clothes chic and well brushed, but threadbare.

When the jeep pulled up in front of her building, Tom jumped down first, helped Chantal down. He ceremoniously took the key from her hand and opened the front door for her. She hoped the concierge wasn't in her loge watching.

'May I kiss you good night?'

Chantal offered her cheek, but he gently turned her head and kissed her on the lips. It was a chaste kiss, but because it came from so far away, from miles across the ocean, from another world where adolescents rode in convertibles to football games, and because it had taken so much, so many years of turmoil, so much suffering, so many deaths before that young man's lips could press hers, she responded eagerly, and wound her arms around his neck. Tom looked at her intently.

'May I come in for a moment?'

She couldn't bear for the afternoon of carefree playacting to end. She nodded yes. He ran to the jeep, talked to the others, rummaged in the back and came up with a khaki bag, which he slung over his shoulder.

'I'm bringing some food,' he said. 'I'll fix dinner for you.'

Chantal led him up the flight of stairs, and they were laughing, and when they reached her apartment, he took the key from her again and opened the door, standing aside to let her pass. He took in at a glance the circular entry with its miniature velvet banquettes, its striped sateen walls, the pair of urns on pedestals flanking the door to the hallway, and through an open door, the jewel-box decor of the salon,

278

the dining room gleaming with silk and crystal, more doors opening on flowered perspectives, violets here, cabbage roses there. He let out a low whistle.

'Gee! That's pretty swanky. You live here?'

'Yes.'

'You must be rich! Do you live alone? Are you married? Do you have a boyfriend?'

Clearly he was wondering where this girl, about whom he knew nothing, and whose culture was as bewildering to him as his was to her, was leading him. Soldiers had been warned about traps, boyfriends or husbands suddenly springing upon them, threatening, blackmail or worse. They had been told the population was friendly, but there were still collaborators hiding, and the greatest caution had to be exercised. They had been warned about prostitutes, and that so extensively, because it was a subject they all enjoyed dwelling upon, that they hoped the city was nothing but love for sale. And yet ... Caution was a difficult concept to maintain among these young American men, most of them straight from their small towns where only goodwill and friendliness had been the rule. Chantal didn't know any of this, but she sensed his unease. She took his hand again.

'Yes, I live alone, no, I am not married, or rather, I was, but my husband died.'

'In the war?'

'Yes, in the war. He was a Resistance fighter.'

'Gee, I am sorry. And you don't have a boyfriend?'

'Boyfriend? What is a boyfriend?'

'Then,' said Tom, smiling broadly, 'I'll show you what a boyfriend is. I'll be your boyfriend if you let me.'

Chantal's desire welled up, suddenly, for that tall, slight young man who smelled of mint and a spicy shaving lotion, who was at once embarrassingly familiar, calling her baby and honey, holding her waist in public, kissing her right in her doorway, and oddly attentive and courteous in an almost formal way, protecting her from the crowd, inquiring constantly about her needs and desires: Hungry?

Thirsty? Tired? Want to sit down? Too much sun? Too much wind? (He had endearingly taken off his jacket and draped it over her shoulders when a gust of cool wind had swept through the stadium.) She put her arms around his neck again and kissed him, lightly. He responded eagerly, pressing hard but making no effort to open her lips with his own. She was leading him to the pink and violet bedroom, the wounded bird in her heart straining its wings to freedom.

He sat on the bed, pulled her down to him, and kissed her again, hard, on the lips, with that same chaste and dry kiss. He reached to caress her breasts through the silk of her dress, and she sighed in desire. She could feel him hard against her. Still, he made no move to undress her, just that light, furtive caress.

'Don't you want to take off your clothes? And let's get into bed, don't you think?' She must, she must recapture something of the night with Anthenor. It couldn't all be gone forever out of her life.

Tom was clearly bewildered, and said something she didn't understand, about French girls going all the way on the first date. She didn't care, she must have him, have him now. She unbuttoned her dress, and he exclaimed, 'Wow!' when he saw the tight waist-cincher she wore, called a merry widow, black lace, and the slightest boning, flaring lightly over the hips and rising to a half-cup bra that pushed the breasts forward in an offering. She slipped out of the lacy confinement, and offered her pink nipples to his mouth. He kissed them, gently, then harder, but still with that same closed-lip kiss.

He undressed, still wondering whether it was, as he said, 'All right to go all the way.' She caressed him to reassure him, and she saw him take a small packet from his pants pocket. She had never seen a condom before. Considered contraceptives, they were illegal in France, where all the laws before World War II had been geared to forbid contraception, to recoup the terrible losses suffered during the First World War.

'Safer for you, too, baby,' he whispered as he slid under the covers.

She allowed her eyes to rest an instant on the carved hazelwood. The intent face of Anthenor floated into her consciousness.

Tom's lovemaking was artless, none of Anthenor's innate sensuality. But it was sweet and gentle and then he spoke to her, all those unknown words of love: sweetheart . . . honey, baby, I love you, come to me, come to me . . . It must still be unreal. Reality was Anthenor. She strained against him.

He came fast, with a shudder, and then he rolled over, and told her how happy he was, how grateful, how glad that she had let him make love to her. She pressed against him, unsatisfied, sad, yet strangely at peace. Now she knew. It could never be as it had been with Anthenor.

Later, he lit two cigarettes and offered her one, and she was touched again by the caring gesture. They lay on the bed, his arm around her shoulder, making no attempt to caress her, almost brotherly gentle. She put her head on his smooth, hairless chest. His eyes were wandering over the exquisite Venetian dressing table, the pillows strewn everywhere, the drapes theatrically caught up with silken cords and tassels.

'They told us the French would be very poor and starving. But you can't be poor. You must be rich.'

'No,' she protested. 'I am not rich at all. I work for a living.' And to change the subject, 'What sort of work did you do before you joined the army?'

He was surprised anyone would ask.

'I worked for the company, of course. First, I drove a truck, and then I worked in the motor pool as a mechanic, and I would have been promoted to foreman pretty soon.'

'What is a foreman?'

He explained what a foreman did. His father also was a mechanic who had graduated to . . . whatever it was. He was retired now, and all of Tom's three brothers worked for the company. The youngest one was also going to college at night, in order to become an accountant. His sister had married someone 'very smart' who worked in the office, an administrative assistant.

He is a mechanic, thought Chantal, his people are factory workers and yet there is nothing coarse about him, he has those gently protective, courteous manners. Is he special, or is that the way all Americans are?

'Is that you? What does Countess mean?' wondered Tom, holding an envelope he had picked up from the night table. It had held a letter from Aunt Emilie, which Chantal found one day when she needed to jot down an address. It was addressed to the Countess de Blazonac.

'It doesn't mean much today.' She shrugged. 'It's a title.'

'Like royalty? Are you royalty?'

'Oh, no, no. Royalty is something else altogether . . . No, it is just an old title; centuries ago, it used to mean something. Now, it doesn't, although I used to think when I was very young that it did.'

'When you were very young? You're not old now. How old are you?'

'I am twenty-two.'

A silence. Then he sat up.

'Hey,' he said suddenly, 'I promised to fix dinner for you.'

He kissed her again, that strangely innocent kiss. He slipped on his khaki undershirt, pulled on his pants, and went looking for the kitchen. He was awed by the lavish display of luxurious fabrics, the thick pale green carpet underfoot, but the primitive kitchen equipment appalled him.

'A two-burner stove? No fridge? How do you keep your food?'

'There has been practically no food to keep,' sighed Chantal, 'you don't know how little we have need for a refrigerator. As a matter of fact, I don't have much to offer you.'

'Baby,' he said smugly, 'let Uncle Sam treat you. I've got rations here, it's not the greatest food, but it *is* food.'

He upended the bag he had brought up: cans, round and tall, flat, square, tinfoil packets spilled out on the table. There was a small pack of Lucky Strikes holding four cigarettes, a Hershey bar, and a small flat pack of what looked like tightly packed paper. Chantal examined it.

'Toilet paper, baby,' he informed her proudly. 'These are C rations, for war, you know, for survival. Nothing fancy, but everything a guy needs in the field.'

Chantal was impressed by the foresight of the Army of the United States. She doubted the German army, for all its preparedness, had anything like that neatly folded pack of toilet paper 'for survival.'

Tom was examining the cans.

'Okay,' he said, 'first we'll have grapefruit juice for an appetizer.'

One of the packets — wonder of wonders — held a can opener. He punched two triangular holes in each can, handed her one, raised the other to his lips, but she stopped him, and brought out two of the stemmed crystal glasses. He looked surprised, shrugged, and poured the pale gold liquid. It was delicious, tart, sweet, and cool. But Tom made a face.

'Juice should be ice-cold.'

Then a rectangular can revealed a sort of ham, in an unlikely shade of pink. It smelled good, not like ham but like something perfumed to smell like ham.

'Spam,' announced Tom, who was enjoying Chantal's ignorance of those things everyone knew. 'GIs make jokes about it, but it's really not bad. You'll see.'

'Let's get dressed, put on your shirt, and we'll have a feast,' she suggested. 'I'll set the table in the dining room.'

'Aw, why not eat in the kitchen? It's okay,' said Tom.

'Oh, no. I never eat in the kitchen.'

So, they ate in the dining room, off eggshell china plates. Chantal made him take the Spam, in spite of his protests, out of the khaki can, and she placed it in a silver dish. The scrambled eggs with bacon, which came out of the round flat can, were dished out into a small bowl, she arranged the crackers on a lacquer tray. She was apologetic about having no wine to serve.

'That's okay,' repeated Tom. 'I don't touch liquor anyway. My folks don't either. It's against our religion.'

'Wait. Wine is against your religion?'

'It sure is. Drinking is sinful.'

'What religion are you?'

The name of that strange religion which saw a sin in the drinking of a glass of wine included words she didn't understand, but one of them was *Christian*.

'If the water's hot, I've got instant coffee.'

She poured hot water into the Limoges porcelain cups decorated with violets and rosebuds and gold ribbons. Then, he tore open one of the tinfoil packets and shook out a dark powder. Surprise. Instead of floating in dry lumps and spreading into a dusty film on the surface of the liquid, it dissolved instantly and an aroma of coffee arose with the steam.

'You take cream and sugar?'

More packets. Chantal covered her cup with her hand. Cream in after-dinner coffee?

'You drink café au lait after dinner?' she asked, teasing.

Tom didn't know what café au lait was, but he boasted cheerfully that he sure liked a lot of cream and sugar in his coffee.

Before Chantal could even finish her cup, Tom was already washing the dishes, a towel around his waist — scrubbing, rinsing, far more than necessary, flooding the tiny sink, in orgies of cleanliness. All along he whistled, perfectly on key, and sang:

> Just kiss me once, then kiss me twice,
> Then kiss me once again,
> It's been a long, long time.

Then, he asked about a shower. Chantal explained she had no shower. There was a small tub in the all-pink, minute bathroom, but no hot water. She could heat up a pan of water and pour it in. Then, by adding cold water from the tap, he could have a nice, lukewarm bath. That's how she washed herself every day, carefully, not a drop of water wasted. In fact, she had dispensed with the hot water altogether since there had been so little gas to heat it with, and she slipped instead every morning into a cold bath. She had never given it any thought until this moment, but she felt she should not mention it now. All of a sudden, she saw Tom would read that cold bath as some new depth of barbarism.

Tom was more surprised at Chantal's bathroom facilities than he had been by anything the war had showed him. What? he kept repeating, only this dinky little bathroom and in such a 'gorgeous' place, too? Why, his folks' place was nothing like this, just plain comfortable, but there were *two* bathrooms, two and a half, even (a half bathroom? puzzled Chantal who visualized one sawed down the middle: half a tub, half a sink, half a shower . . .), since his mom had a shower built for his kid brother's room. And, baby, let me tell you about the great big hot-water heater in the basement! He had helped his dad install it when he was a senior in high school, because they kept running out of hot water, when all five kids wanted a shower. Now, there was plenty, piping hot. You *can't* wash in cold water!

And then, they had an icebox, see, but his dad got his mom a real fridge, so there was always plenty of ice-cold milk for the boys to drink. (Milk? It was clear he was not talking about baby bottles. He sounded as though he and his brothers, grown boys, always wanted to drink gallons and gallons of ice-cold milk. But then, she thought, I probably don't understand everything he is really saying.) And then, his mom had gone and bought a washing machine, a Bendix, and his dad made payments on it every month. Now, unprompted, he was telling her about home, about what mattered in the world he came from . . .

Chantal listened, unable to understand how plumbing and sundry appliances could prompt such lyrical outpourings.

'There was hot water in the tub before the war' – she shrugged – 'and I suppose there will be again after the war is all over. But it doesn't make all that much difference, does it?'

Oh, but it did! Tom washed and scrubbed, splashed and used up all the towels in the pile on the windowsill, later using the last one to mop every inch of the floor, the walls, wipe the sink and the tub, whistling all along and singing:

> Just kiss me once, then kiss me twice,
> Then kiss me once again,
> It's been a long, long time.
> Haven't felt like this, my dear,
> Since can't remember when . . .

Chantal caught herself humming the catchy tune with him and doing dance steps while she tidied the bedroom.

It was late when he left, worried about missing company curfew. A buddy came by with a jeep to pick him up. Before running downstairs, he held her tight, his short hair still damp, smelling of shampoo and chewing gum, kissed her hard with closed lips, told her he was crazy about her and would call her as soon as he could. He wanted to take her back with him to Hershey, Pennsylvania. Now wouldn't that throw them for a loop? 'Oh, boy, they would all say, always knew old Tom had it in him . . .'

From the balcony, she waved, and watched the jeep careen around the corner, with that odd, top-heavy look of an automobile of an earlier age.

The next day, the concierge called out for Chantal as she was leaving to return to the Domergue atelier. A large cardboard box had just been delivered for her. Chantal opened it and found cans of orange and grapefruit juice, Spam, packets of coffee, sugar, cream, crackers, Oreo cookies, cans of cheese, sardines, cartons of Old Gold cigarettes, bottles of shampoo, cakes of Cashmere Bouquet soap, tubes of Ipana toothpaste, packets of green-wrapped chewing gum, even a bottle of Revson Pink Lightning nail polish. The concierge's eyes opened wide, and she clasped her hands, disapproval forgotten at the sight of such *richesse*. Chantal shared the bounty, bribing her into complicity, she thought, and waited until she was upstairs to read the note written in a careful, round, half-printed hand:

Baby, There was an alert when I got back, and we are on the move this morning. Just had time to round up some stuff for you. Guys from another company will leave it at your house.

We're going to the front, in the direction of some town with a name I can't remember. Anyway, all those French names sound the same. As soon as I can, I'll let you know where I am, and you can bet that I'll see you the minute we park again in old Paree.

Don't forget the guy who's crazy about you, baby, I can't wait to see you again.

Your boyfriend,
Tom

A line of *XXX*'s followed, mysterious hieroglyphics.

It only then occurred to Chantal that she didn't even know his last name. And when the realization came to her, a little later, walking to the Domergue atelier, that she probably wouldn't see him again, she felt suddenly sad, lonely, and strangely deserted, the loss of a friend, maybe, or a brother, if not a lover.

She kept, of her brief adventure with Tom, a longing for the feeling of easygoing security he had given her during those short hours. She couldn't face the idea of solitude *forever* the carved letters on the hazelwood now promised her. She'd emerged alive out of the ashes, and alive she was, hungry for those fresh-faced men, so eagerly available, so unquestioning and innocent. Madame Domergue, with motherly concern, had her invited to join the Franco-American Club, at the Hôtel Crillon, where well-bred young ladies met Americans – presumably recommended by their COs – for Thursday tea dances.

And then in the next year, one late afternoon, as spring was beginning once more to paint the chestnut trees with touches of unfolding green, she was walking home. For the first time of the season, she had gone out without a coat, happy to show off her new pearl-gray spring suit. The close-fitting jacket buttoned tightly, with a deep plunge, and she had dared to wear it without a blouse, so the fabric had rubbed against her skin, and she was conscious of her nipples, pleasantly irritated. She felt lithe, sexy, as she almost danced on her high red fake suede platform shoes, and young, and suddenly impish. She wanted to laugh and play games, games that involved men.

As she turned the corner of the avenue d'Iéna onto the Place de l'Etoile, she almost bumped into a tall American officer who was standing there, raincoat over his arm, looking up at the looming Arch of Triumph. He was holding an open guidebook, and alternately examined the monument and read the text. He apologized profusely for his clumsiness, and she protested that no, it was all her fault. He was handsome, with perfectly even features, and he wore horn-rimmed glasses.

A temptation fluttered into her mind, settled there. She stepped back just a little, looked up at him innocently, wide-eyed. 'Are you Captain Smith, by any chance?'

Surprised, he gulped and straightened his tie.

'No, miss, I am terribly sorry, but I'm not Captain Smith.'

'That's too bad. You see,' she improvised, 'I have a date with Captain Smith, but it is a blind date. Is that what you say? A blind date? I have never met him before, so I thought you might be him.'

'Well, I'm not Captain Smith,' he repeated, shaking his head. 'But I can tell you I *am* sorry about that, miss. I really wish I were,' he added gallantly.

'Me too,' replied Chantal, who could hardly keep a straight face. 'Me too. I wish you were Captain Smith.'

'It's a shame I'm not, isn't it?' said the officer, wondering why this pretty girl was so insistent. Didn't she understand that he wasn't the man she was looking for? But apparently, she did not. He repeated, 'As a matter of fact, I envy Captain Smith, and I do wish I had a date with a lovely lady like you myself. But maybe he lost his way, or he's looking for you somewhere else. Maybe he'll be here soon.'

She pouted as convincingly as she could. 'I don't think so. He was supposed to be here a half hour ago. I have been waiting, looking around for him. He must have been prevented from coming. It's too bad' – she was thinking fast – 'because his best friend is going with my sister, and she said Captain Smith is tall, and handsome, and he wears glasses, and he would carry his raincoat and a guidebook, so I would know him.'

'Ah, but you see,' retorted the officer, 'I couldn't be he; I'm only a first lieutenant!'

Chantal was enjoying herself too much to stop, still hoping he would offer to take the place of that elusive Smith. She insisted. 'Yes, he was going to take me out to dinner, and dancing afterward, or perhaps we would just have stayed in my apartment and talked, depending. Well, now I guess I'll just go home, all by myself,' she said sadly. 'You probably have a dinner date.'

'No,' sighed the lieutenant. 'I wish I had, but it's a lonely man you are talking to. I only arrived in Paris yesterday, and I don't know anybody here yet. So, I thought I would just take in some of the sights, have dinner somewhere, turn in early, and read my guidebook.'

Chantal made a last move. 'Isn't it a shame! You are lonely, and I am lonely! On this beautiful evening in Paris. Don't you have any idea how to fix that?'

The lieutenant, who had been frowning, brightened up suddenly. 'Yes,' he almost cried. 'Yes, I do have an idea. Of course! Why didn't I think of it sooner! You must think I'm awfully slow. It's very simple, and you don't have to have dinner alone . . .'

'Yes?' she said brightly, expectantly.

'If you tell me what unit Captain Smith is in, I'm pretty sure I can help you trace him. Let's find a phone, and I'll make a few calls. I don't suppose you know his serial number, but his division, what outfit he's attached to . . . I *knew* there had to be some way I could help you,' he added, obviously relieved he had found a solution to this beautiful girl's problem. 'It's just that I had to think of a way. Where's my pencil and my notebook? Here. First, give me his first name, and then . . .'

Chantal felt uncontrollable laughter rise in her throat, but she managed to choke it into what sounded, she hoped, like a little cough. She murmured some vague apology about giving up on meeting the captain tonight, and walked away toward the rue Pauquet and the lonely dinner that was the only true element in her story.

She told Domergue about it the next day, laughing merrily. How naive can anyone be! But Domergue stopped her. 'It's not so much naiveté, although I'll grant you this one was pretty thick. But you see, while everybody plays games, they're not always the same, and that's why they won't necessarily recognize your games as such. Just as,' he added, 'you may not recognize theirs, either, so that you may think they are serious when they're not. Just be careful with all games, yours and theirs, my dear . . .'

The advice went in one ear and straight out the other.

A few days later at the atelier, the butler opened the door to an unannounced visitor, and Chantal was already advancing to intercept the intruder, when he rolled past her and fell into the outstretched arms of the master.

Short and round, Colonel Wainwright was from Grosse Pointe, Michigan. He was one of Ford Motor Company's high-ranking executives, and he and Domergue had met several years before the war, when the master had gone to Grosse Pointe to paint portraits of the Ford ladies, mother and daughters. He had invited Domergue to his country club, they had played golf together and become fast friends; the friendship had been renewed and extended whenever he and his wife had come to Paris and Cannes and visited with the Domergues. Now, Colonel Wainwright had just been posted to Paris, at Communication Zone Headquarters, and he was staying at the Royal Monceau Hotel, on the avenue Hoche. Champagne was uncorked, toasts were drunk, even Madame Domergue, who never came down to the atelier, made a brief appearance.

Sitting on the big plush sofa along the wall covered with Domergue's large paintings, the colonel patted the place next to him and asked Chantal to sit beside him. He took her hand in both of his, told her she reminded him of his youngest daughter, who wanted to be an actress, showed her pictures of 'the girls,' who must be his wife and daughters, in front of an immense white house, with horses, with cars, in riding clothes and in evening dress. He asked her to come the following Saturday to a big dance at the Royal Monceau.

'You'll be my guest, not my date, good heavens!' He chuckled. 'I'm old enough to be your father. But you see, all the officers here are looking for dates,' he confided. 'Some of the girls they bring are . . . well, they are just not the right type. We need good-looking young women with class, like you.'

He wrote elaborate instructions for Chantal about the exact time and place for the dinner to be followed by a dance.

'Dinner will be served at six, sharp.'

Chantal paid no attention to the outlandish hour. Yes, she'd be there. She was already making plans: my new dress, the draped gray silk jersey from Grès, will be ready. I'll just need some shoes, something gray, high and dressy enough for a dance. I'll go to that place I know, on the corner of the rue de la Paix and the Place Vendôme, they're sure to have something, or else they'll make me up a pair. And I think I'll wear my hair pulled back, tight, with that huge blond chignon hairpiece Marjo made me buy, pinned low on the neck.

PART TWO

San Sebastián, Spain 1940

14

IN THE MOONLIT June night, Fred, Volodia, Mischa, Herschel, and Isaac had crossed the bridge at Fuenterrabia where Chantal and Martine had left them. They were now in neutral Spain, but kept walking until out of sight and earshot of the Guardia Civil sentries.

'All right,' said Fred. 'I have a little money the girls gave us. I suggest we go to the railroad station, get some sleep in the waiting room and, as soon as the ticket office opens, buy tickets for San Sebastián. It's the next big city, and not too far, so we should have enough. We'll take the first train and I'll tell you what I have in mind.'

The next morning, Martine's thin wad of bills was exchanged for pesetas. After purchasing five tickets, enough remained for a breakfast of *panecillos*, hard rolls, and coffee. After a short train ride, the five young men were sitting on the promenade overlooking the port of San Sebastián. Fred had somehow become the leader of the expedition.

'I have something of value,' he told the others, 'which I managed to hide all this time from the guards. It should help us, but first, I must find a place to sell it. Do you fellows have anything marketable, so we'll have money?'

They all looked at each other.

'You and Volodia have the gold stuff the girls gave you,' said Herschel, hesitantly. 'You could sell that . . . But,' he added quickly, 'I don't think that's a good idea. It might bring us bad luck. Better you keep it.'

'I have a few very rare stamps, the best from my grandfather's collection, which I hid between the soles of my shoes, just when the French police came to get me,' said Volodia. 'Maybe we could sell them. This looks like a big, prosperous city. Look at that huge house, over there! Almost like a palace!'

A palace indeed, Fred told them, the summer residence of the Spanish kings, now used by Franco for his seaside vacations, dominated the bay. San Sebastián in the green northwest of Spain offered a haven against the scorching summers of Madrid and served as the traditional resort of wealthy Spaniards.

'I'll go with you,' said Mischa. 'My mother sewed her pearl necklace into the lining of my jacket and it escaped detection.'

Herschel and Isaac owned nothing of value, but they went along anyway and waited outside while Volodia disposed of the stamps at a fraction of their value. In the best jewelry store in town, Mischa sold his mother's pearls – again at 'refugee' prices. He came out counting pesetas.

'I want you fellows to sit somewhere and wait for me,' instructed Fred. 'I might be a while.'

Alone, he returned to the jewelry store and the eyes of the owner grew large when he saw what the young man had to offer. At that moment, a dizziness overtook Fred.

'May I sit down?' A chair was brought for him and he sank into it. Was it hunger? Lack of sleep? A delayed reaction to his frantic flight from Hitler's murderous arm? Reality dissolved in waves . . . Hitler? When did I hear that name for the first time . . . ?

He was a little boy, nine or ten, and his name was Siegfried, then. His father had brought him to the top floor of the great Mayer Kaufhaus, the block-long department store the family owned in Düsseldorf. Sieg loved those visits: Grandfather Jakob and Uncle Saul would come out of their offices to exclaim over him and he would be escorted to the toy department, where he could pick out anything that caught his fancy.

But today, he was disappointed to find both his grandfather and his uncle looking out the window, too absorbed to fuss over him as usual.

'*Schlamperei!*' Grandfather kept muttering. 'A mess, a complete mess.'

A noisy gang of youths was marching down the normally elegant and sedate Koenigsallee, wearing red armbands, yelling, chanting slogans, singing the 'Internationale.' No police were in sight.

'It's all blowing from Russia like an ill wind,' continued old Jakob. 'It's the Communists who undermined the morale of our troops in 1918, but you'd think it would have been all over, when Liebknecht and that woman . . . what was her name?'

'Luxemburg, Papa, Rosa Luxemburg.'

'Right, right. When they were found floating in the Landswehr Kanal, didn't you think it was the end of that Communist nonsense?'

Floating? thought Sieg. I can float too. Mother taught me how. You just relax and let the water come up all around your face.

'It wasn't the end,' sighed Uncle Saul. 'It just went underground and now, we see it all come out. But there might be some hope. That little Austrian, down in Munich, he seems to be getting more and more people to follow him.'

'I heard, I heard. What's his name again?'

'Hitler, Adolf Hitler. He calls his party National Socialism.'

'Socialism, eh? Doesn't sound that good. Still, anything's better than what happened in Russia in '17. Do you know what that Austrian is all about?'

'Well,' explained Saul, 'as I understand it, he wants Germany to regain the lands it lost, like the Ruhr, you know. The French took it from us because our government was behind in paying war reparations.'

'As far as that's concerned,' Jakob was thinking aloud, 'I see nothing wrong with getting our lands back. The reparations were too harsh and without the Ruhr,

Germany's industry is crippled. Besides, the Ruhr people are Germans!'

'Hitler feels his followers – and there are many, all over the country – can organize and rid us of Communists like these rowdies and whoever's behind them.'

'*Gut, gut.* I couldn't agree more. So, what's wrong with that Austrian?'

'Well, he's saying that the Germans are the master race of the world and that all others are inferior . . .'

'Ah,' replied Jakob, still not understanding the implications. 'Let him say what he wants so long as he gets rid of those troublemakers and their demonstrations. Perhaps he should be given a chance to bring life back to normal.'

'Papa,' said Saul, ignoring the damage, 'there are those who say he is against the Jews and wants to destroy them. Although, personally, I think that's very much exaggerated.'

Jakob was pensive.

'*Ach,*' he sighed after a while, 'there are always some who'll be against us. But, I say, let the politicians talk. We are doing business and prospering, and we want to keep it that way. Perhaps we should get behind that Austrian. What did you say his name was?'

Such forgetfulness was too much for little Sieg.

'Hitler, Grandfather,' he piped up laughing, poking his fingers through the lace curtains. 'His name is Hitler. I won't forget it.'

The three men stood there for a moment. Jakob pulled out his heavy gold pocket watch.

'Five o'clock already. Well, my boys, what do you say we call for the car and take that youngster home? Might as well get there a little earlier for once. Have them close the store, Saul. Not many people will be out shopping, with these rowdies in the streets, looking for purses and wallets to steal. Anyway, this is Friday.'

A moment later, Jakob and his sons were sitting in the back of their Austro-Daimler with Sieg on the jump seat. They passed a group of men dressed in long black coats, black hats pulled over their ears, long hair spilling over their collars, waiting for the Sabbath services to begin. The Mayer men, in their custom-tailored suits, glanced at them.

'*Ach*,' sighed the old man, 'my father never kept the Sabbath and I never did either. You weren't given religious schooling, you were never bar mitzvahed and this boy won't be either. Perhaps you'll blame me someday.'

Sieg was bored by these fleeting regrets that occasionally assailed his grandfather's soul. Learning Hebrew prayers and going to a *shul* was old-fashioned, his mother had told him so, and none of his friends did.

'Please, Papa,' begged Uncle Saul, as he always did at such times. 'You know that old stuff is better left behind. We honor God in other ways; we are good men, we work hard and we serve our country. These people, why, they live here, but they don't want to become part of Germany. They cling to their own language, their own customs, they refuse to send their children to the schools . . .'

Jakob reached for the little box set in the burled wood paneling by his side, raised the silver lid, took out two gum drops, offered one to his grandson and rolled the other one reflectively in his mouth. After a while, he said with some hesitation, 'Perhaps it's those people the Austrian is talking about. If that's the case, well . . . He may have a point. Not that I wish them harm, God forbid! But a little push wouldn't be so bad. Help them join the world – and it doesn't mean they have to stop being good Jews.'

The limousine turned into Mozartstrasse, a wide, tree-shaded residential street, and pulled into the driveway of the imposing Mayer house. Sieg ran into the hall, where his lovely mother, Ilse, swept him into her arms.

The best moment of his day came after dinner. Sieg knew that if he begged enough, he'd be allowed to sit in the library with the grown-ups. That night his mother pulled one of the massive plush photo albums from the shelf and unsnapped the brass lock. Sieg snuggled close to her in a big armchair, secure in the curve of her arm and the warm scent of Arpège, her favorite fragrance, ordered especially for her from Paris, he knew.

'Who's that, Mutti?' he asked, pointing to the picture of two brides and their grooms.

'Why, you naughty boy, you know perfectly well! We've looked at these pictures dozens of times! It's Mutti and Aunt Vera, the day we married your father and your uncle.'

'Which one are you, Mutti? I can't tell.'

'That's me, beside your father. That's him with the glasses and that thick hair with the white streak just like yours, and I'm standing next to him.'

Sieg never tired of his mother's comforting stories.

'And you chose to marry him, because you thought he had such kind eyes behind his glasses. Isn't it so, Mutti?'

Ilse nodded. Did she sigh? Unconcerned, Sieg was already turning the pages.

'And here are all the employees in front of the store, with Grandfather and Uncle Saul in the center. Where is Father?'

Did he hear his mother sigh again?

'Your father must have been ill that day, with one of his headaches, no doubt.'

Sieg knew his father suffered from a strange condition which, for no apparent reason, brought blinding headaches and caused his forehead to swell in angry welts.

'And here's Anton with Papa,' he continued, flipping through the pages. 'But Anton was small then. Tell me, Mutti, is he really my cousin?'

'Not exactly, *mein Süsser*. Anton's father was killed in the war. So, when his mother died in turn, why, your father brought him home and he grew up here. His name is Anton Samelnov.'

Only much later would Sieg understand that Anton's mother, a widow with a young son, had been a valued employee of the store before Heinz married the beautiful gray-eyed Ilse Malinovsky. More pictures diverted him.

'And here is Uncle Saul receiving a medal from the mayor,' said Ilse.

'I see Grandfather next to him. He has a medal too. But why was Father way in the back?'

'Your father was never much interested in business, medals and such,' explained Ilse with a faraway look. 'But you and I must love him, because he is kind and he loves *us* so much.'

Every Sunday morning, Grandfather took Sieg for a walk in the park. Both the old man and the little boy loved the endless retelling of stories of Sieg's childhood.

'Tell me about the day I was born, please.'

'Well' – the grandfather chuckled – 'when your father cried out "It's a boy!" I went to the temple and thanked God. We gave all the employees a day off to celebrate.'

How good it felt to know his arrival had made the family so happy!

'Tell me what you wanted to call me.'

'In our family the first son was always named after some grandparent who'd passed away. So, I thought Isaac would be a good name, after your great-grandfather.'

'But Mother and Aunt Vera would have nothing to do with these old-fashioned names,' interrupted the boy, skipping over pebbles. He knew the story by heart. 'That's why they picked Siegfried. "A fashionable name," says Aunt Vera. And Mother promised she'd take me to the theater to hear the opera . . . She said I was given the name of a legendary German warrior, a real hero born right out of the foam of the Northern Sea.'

Sieg had grown up surrounded by his adoring father and doting mother. A handsome boy, rather small, with his mother's neatly boned features and her large, pale gray eyes, but quiet in contrast to her vivid animation.

'How can you be so secretive with a talkative mother like me?' Ilse always asked him. Sieg just smiled.

He received the best of all possible educations. He learned French and English, and he giggled, strangely titillated, when he overheard his father discuss the choice of a suitable mademoiselle who shouldn't be too pretty since it was too early for his son to fall in love. He attended the most exclusive academy, with the sons of the town's best families.

When he was older, there were long summer afternoons, boating on the park's lake, picnicking, playing games of handball with his mother, Aunt Vera, and Anton. Laughing, shouting, calling out the score in English. Anton, only five years younger than his adoptive father's wife, had grown into a handsome young man – tall, broad-shouldered, with high cheekbones and straight blond hair. At times, though, Sieg was troubled when Anton's eyes would follow Ilse, or when he'd find them off in a corner, absorbed in intimate conversation. His father sitting in the shade, came to drape a sweater over his wife's shoulders, scolded her for giving the boy ice water to drink.

'Ice water will crack his teeth, his beautiful teeth! It will give him a stomachache. Tell me, *mein Junge*, do you have a stomachache? You are not feeling a chill?'

Every winter, Ilse, with Aunt Vera, would take him to Kitzbühel, Austria, for two weeks of skiing and Anton accompanied them. No question of Uncle Saul's leaving the office at that time of year, or of his father's braving the sun-reflected snow that brought on his headaches. Sieg was a proficient skier, but the best were Ilse and Anton, who would leave in the early morning, laughingly ignoring his pleas to come along. Sealskins wrapped around their skis, they'd herringbone slowly up the mountainside and he'd watch them return much later, yodeling and slaloming down the steep slopes.

One night, startled by a sudden thunderstorm, Sieg called out to his mother in the next room. Apparently she didn't hear – she, always so prompt to jump at his slightest stirring. Bewildered, he padded barefoot to the communicating door. It was locked. Frightened now, he rattled the knob, banged on the wood, screaming, 'Mutti, Mutti, where are you? I'm scared. Please, open the door!'

It took a minute or two that seemed like hours to the frightened child. He heard a door open and close, whispers, footsteps in the hall. At last, Ilse opened the door, scooped him up in her arms, carried him back to bed and sat there, warming his hands in hers.

'*Was ist los, mein Süsser?* Mutti is right here. Don't be scared.'

'Mutti, why did you close the door? You never closed it before.'

'*Ach, mein Süsser*, some maid must have made a mistake and locked it when she cleaned the rooms. Hush, now, be quiet and go to sleep. See? The storm is over, no more lightning, no more thunder, it's only a little rain now, go to sleep like a good boy . . .'

During the following days, Sieg stealthily observed his mother and Anton. Two nights running he tested the door between his room and his mother's and found it unlocked. On the third night, though, it was locked again. He padded silently down the hall to Anton's room. A knock brought no answer. Locked. He knew. Something terrible and mysterious was going on between his beautiful mother and Anton. A stab pierced his heart and a taste of ashes rose in his throat. Betrayed! Both he and his father were betrayed! Sieg pretended to be asleep when Ilse came later and sat on his bed.

I hate her, I hate her, he kept repeating to himself. But tears never came to his gray eyes and there was no way he could ever speak a word of his pain to anyone.

15

MEANWHILE, THE RISE of the Nazi Party had been steady, but the fear that its program might translate into persecutions, and persecutions directed against them, never occurred to the Mayers and their friends. Those who had premonitions of things to come were ridiculed. Hitler's accession to power in January 1933 was hailed by all German conservatives, wealthy Jewish merchants among them. Sieg, just fourteen, watched in awe the grandiose ceremonies unfolding in the newsreels and the torch-lit parades snaking through the streets of Düsseldorf, which the whole family went to cheer.

'I have given instructions to our employees,' Uncle Saul announced at the dinner table, 'to answer the phone with "Heil Hitler" and to greet customers the same way. I already fired a couple of Poles who refused to say it. An Austrian, too, who insisted on saying "Grüss Gott." We are good Germans and we want our people to *sound* like good Germans.'

It took no more than two years, though, before the Mayers began to understand that Hitler's anti-Semitism wasn't simply suspicion or hatred of the Jews. It was a view of the world that saw race as the supreme arbiter of history. Pogroms recalled by their Russian and Polish ancestors, they realized in helpless horror, were nothing compared to what the new legislation would bring.

When the Nuremberg Laws burst like a bomb, Sieg was old enough to understand much of what was happening. It was all over the papers and the radio: Jews would be excluded from the German nation. No longer citizens, they were declared 'subjects,' later 'stateless,' until they would, eventually, be removed from membership in the human race, declared nonpersons. Mixed marriages were retroactively forbidden and children of mixed marriages considered Jewish. 'The end has come,' declared Uncle Saul, sitting in despair in the offices of the Mayer Kaufhaus, now identified as 'Jewish-owned' by large signs on the doors.

New laws kept tightening the screws. 'Salami laws,' Grandfather Jakob called them with grim humor, because they came in slices, each one worse than the last. Theft from a Jew would no longer be a theft; crime against a Jew would go unpunished. Grandfather had been ailing throughout the winter and when his children found him dead in his bed one morning, it was mercifully assumed he had died in his sleep.

Anton was the first to take quick action. He had been running the jewelry department at the Kaufhaus and relocation was easiest for him with no property of his own and no family to impede his movements.

Sieg found, lying on a desk, a letter addressed to Anton, from Monsieur Léon Lavine, a Paris wholesaler who supplied jewelry to the store. 'I'll be glad to take you on as a buyer,' answered Lavine.

> You'll be our representative in Australia, where we find our principal source for opals, of the best white, iridescent, black, and fire quality. These are mined mostly in the Coober Pedy region of the South Australia State, some three hundred miles north of the town of Port Augusta.
>
> Local law excludes large mining firms, and grants only small claim to private individuals. You will therefore establish contacts with these miners, visit them at regular intervals, and purchase their rough gems, for which the demand here is growing. Between seasonal trips, you will stay at our Paris offices and be associated with other aspects of the trade.
>
> Although apartments are hard to find, with the sudden influx of refugees from Germany, we have

arranged for you to occupy the flat vacated by one of our employees who has just left for America. It is not large, but convenient to the office.

I'm happy to welcome you, and send greetings to our valued customer, Herr Saul Mayer. We hope your wife will be able to join you soon.

Sieg's father, who saw the letter too, was puzzled. 'Your wife, Anton? Isn't Monsieur Lavine confused? You aren't engaged to be married, are you?'

'No.' Anton shrugged. 'I don't understand why he should say that. I guess he's mixing me up with someone else.'

After Anton's departure, it was Uncle Saul's turn to embark on a series of energetic measures to save what could be saved from the debacle: he bought, in Sweden, the buildings of a bankrupt factory with a modest house nearby and shipped equipment so that production of a line of ready-to-wear work clothes could begin on Swedish soil.

After much wavering, hampered by his wife's lack of interest in the urgency of the situation, Sieg's father gave in to Uncle Saul's urgings. They must sell everything. The store was sold to its erstwhile manager, Herr Wolfgang Gottlieb, an obese, obsequious man. The big house on Mozartstrasse was disposed of through an agency that specialized in the sale of Jewish property. In both cases, the price accepted was far less than the real value. Twenty-five percent was paid outright, the rest supposedly guaranteed by notes deposited in the Düsseldorf Deutsche Bank. It was informally agreed the new owners of the house would gladly return, on demand, whatever furniture and other goods the Mayers couldn't take with them.

'I can't believe this situation will last,' Sieg's father repeated to his son. 'All these people are playing the game of the hour to save themselves trouble, but when these ridiculous laws are repealed – and it can't be long – everything will be returned and life will go back to normal.' Sieg would nod, hoping with all his heart his father was right.

During these final months, he saw a coldness develop between his mother and Aunt Vera. Ilse would whisper to him, 'Your Uncle Saul is taking most of the cash and leaving the notes to your father. Poor man! Your father is happy because the notes are for more, but I'm afraid we'll never see a cent of those.'

Still, on the day of Vera and Saul's departure, as their train was leaving for Keil where they would board the liner *Bremen*, bound for Sweden, they wept.

'You must leave, too, *Liebchen*,' begged Vera. 'You see the swastikas painted every night on the walls of Jewish stores, you hear that awful "Horst Wessel Lied" about Jewish blood gushing under the knife! It can only get worse. Get your son out of here, Heinz will leave if you tell him he must. Don't stay here another week.'

Ilse wiped her reddened eyes, but they held an aloofness that escaped no one except her husband.

Alone now for the first time with his wife and son, Heinz confided in Sieg more and more. 'You'll see, *mein Junge*,' he told him, sitting among crates and boxes, 'you'll see. Now that your uncle is gone, you'll find out what kind of a father you have. I have a surprise for you: We are moving to Switzerland! Yes, Switzerland, which you like so much. I'll open my own business there and you'll see your mother's eyes shine!'

So, the family moved to Luzern. Heinz bought a lovely house with a garden that sloped right down to the lake and a little floating dock from which Sieg and his mother could swim.

'Oh, Papa,' begged Sieg, when he saw the wavelets lapping at the edge of the lawn, 'can I have a little motorboat?'

'No, *mein Sohn*,' said Heinz in horror. 'That's much too dangerous! Suppose you had an accident!'

'Don't be silly, Papa. I can swim. And remember how you used to let me handle the boat on the lake, in Düsseldorf's park? Please . . .'

Heinz gave in, of course, and a small motorboat came to bob at the foot of the short ladder in the clear waters of

Lake Luzern. Sitting at the miniature wheel, Sieg raised his eyes for his mother's admiration, but saw her, instead, gazing far into the distance.

The months that followed saw Heinz happily busy. He leased and decorated a shop in the best Bahnhofstrasse location. MAYER PARIS PELZE spelled the gold lettering above the marquee. The purchase of the splendid selection of gems and all kinds of exquisitely wrought jewelry displayed on opening day, severely depleted his bank account. No matter. Payment on all the notes was due shortly and buyers had seemed unaware of any laws limiting export of funds. 'Laws like that are made to be broken,' Heinz explained to his son. 'People have too much regard for us, the Mayers, to pay attention to those idiotic rules!'

In the euphoria of the elegant crowd pressing into the brand-new salon, intoxicated by the fact that 'Herr Mayer' meant, for the first time, not his father or his brother, but himself, Heinz even overlooked an official-looking envelope delivered by a policeman.

Alas! The triumph was short-lived. Sieg was appalled, returning home from school, to find his father in bed, prey to a terrible headache, and his mother frantic.

'It turns out that cantonal authorities forbid foreigners to own and operate a business on their territory. Apparently your father was warned, but never said a word. He was confident an exception would be made in his case. Poor man! Wrong every time! Now they've closed the shop and confiscated the stock. There'll be legal action, a fine, they've frozen our bank account . . . I don't know what we're going to do.'

It took Heinz several days to recover and for the angry welts on his forehead to subside. Then he resumed his scurrying around, visiting banks and lawyers, hoping against all hope to salvage something from the debacle.

On an early spring afternoon, with the wind blowing brisk, pushing fleecy white clouds whose shadows mottled Lake Luzern in a changing pattern of dark and blue patches, Ilse took her son for a walk.

'*Komm, mein Süsser*, let's go look at the boats on the lake.' Dozens of sailboats were crisscrossing the water, leaning far to port in the stiff breeze. The ferry *to* Vitznau was just about to meet the one *from* Vitznau, sparkling miniature liners, their red flags emblazoned with the white cross of Switzerland taut in the wind of their course. Sieg walked alongside his mother on the wooden jetty running out into the lake.

He loved the way she always showed him off. 'Such a handsome boy!' she'd say, looking fondly at his smooth olive skin and pale eyes, a little sorry the English schoolboy cap covered that white streak everybody was always commenting about. His plus fours tucked into argyle socks marked that period of adolescence when a boy, too old for bare knees, hadn't graduated yet to the long pants of a man. He glanced at her: Ilse, in a small head-hugging cloche, dark suit, and long fur scarf caressed by the wind, was the picture of subdued elegance.

Halfway down the pier, Sieg stopped. 'Haven't we gone far enough?'

'But, my sweet, I thought you'd want to walk to the end, look at the boats. You love boats, don't you?'

'I like boats, but not that kind,' said Sieg. 'I like the ones that take you far away, where you've never been, where nobody knows you.'

'Aren't you afraid of what it might be like there?'

'I want to go,' repeated Sieg, looking into the distance, 'where I can become someone else. Where I won't be Jewish anymore.'

'Hush, my sweet, you can't stop being Jewish, you know that! I understand how you feel, with the insanity going on in Germany right now, but it can't last forever . . . And you know Jews are God's favorite, His chosen people.'

'You don't understand. I don't care whether I'm Jewish or not. I just don't want people to think of me as a Jew. Here, they look at me as Jewish, that's why I want to go far enough away, where I can be somebody else. A Frenchman, or an Englishman, or an American. I haven't decided yet. But it has to be very far from this stupid lake.'

'You can't change what you are,' Ilse insisted. 'You have to remain what you were born to. And aren't you proud of me? Of your grandfather, God rest his soul? Such a good man! You are our flesh and blood, you can never be anything else.'

Sieg dropped the subject. She can't understand what I mean, he thought. Or perhaps she knows only too well, but she's afraid, because she has the same wish herself. Only she's ashamed of admitting it. Well, I'm not.

Ilse remained silent for a moment. 'There is something very important I must tell you, my sweet,' she said. 'It concerns you and me . . . and your father too,' she added hesitantly. 'I'm going to talk to you as I would to a grown man, and you must promise you will tell no one, least of all your father.'

Sieg gave her a probing, scornful look. 'You should know I can keep a secret.'

Ilse lowered her eyes. 'I'm going to do something that will hurt your father. But I have to, both for you and for me. There's no other way.'

Sieg's eyes were following the flight of a seagull swooping down to the water, skimming the surface and lifting up again at a sharp angle. He could feel the waves of the ferries breaking against the old wooden pilings. He held his breath.

'You know,' she continued, 'that your father is mistaken in every single thing he does. He has lost all his money and now he counts on those funds from Germany. He still refuses to understand that *nothing* will be paid. You read the paper, you know what people who have just left Germany are saying: It's a madhouse there, and getting worse all the time. The Nazis are even arresting Jews now, taking them nobody knows where. Some whisper they kill them. But it's too much. That, I don't believe.'

'They wouldn't arrest people like us, or like Dr Rosenthal, the director of the bank on Mannheimerstrasse, or Herr Einhorn who lived next door to us . . . Ghetto Jews, with black coats and long hair, maybe. But that's something else.'

'*Nein*, my sweet, people just like us. All the big houses on Mozartstrasse have been sold, or else the owners forcibly evicted. We were among the lucky ones who got out at a time when there was still the semblance of a sale. Now, no German can legally owe money to a Jew!'

'My father doesn't understand that?'

'No, he's sure that if he goes back, he'll be recognized as Herr Mayer, the former owner of the Mayer Kaufhaus, not just some anonymous Jew. You and I know he's wrong. The truth of the matter is that we're penniless, our account is frozen, we can't meet our bills or the payments due on the house. There's going to be a lawyer to pay, a fine . . .'

'Isn't there some way Papa can find work?'

'What kind of work could he do, poor man? I'm not even sure he could work here legally, under the Swiss laws concerning *Ausländer*, foreigners. And with so many refugees like us here, many looking for a way to make a living . . .'

'So what can we do?'

'All right, my sweet love, I'll tell you what I'm going to do. I'm going to Paris. I can do that, I have my own passport.'

'Why do you say *I*?' asked Sieg, seized with panic. 'You're taking me with you, of course?'

'My love, I *can't* take you. You're on your father's passport now and you'd need his permission. He'll never give it.'

'No,' said Sieg, looking hard at her, gray eyes locked to gray eyes. 'He wouldn't want you to take me to Anton. Because *that's* where you're going, isn't it? You're running away with Anton and leaving me here to rot with my father. You can lie to him all you want, but not to me. I've known for a long time.'

Sieg's heart was pounding in his chest, his eyes blurred. He held on to the shaky railing, the old taste of ashes in his throat and waves of sickness rocking through his

311

stomach with every slap of the water. But Ilse had made up her mind.

'Well, since you know, there's no point pretending any longer. Yes, I'm going with Anton, who's waiting for me in Paris. He loves me, I love him, and we're going to be married as soon as I can be divorced from your father.'

'You? Anton would marry you?' sneered Sieg with the cruelty of youth. 'Why would he? You are old.'

'I'm not old,' snapped Ilse, her small heart-shaped face tight with hurt and anger. 'When you've lived a little longer, you'll understand.'

But frantic, betrayed, abandoned, Sieg understood no emotions other than his own. After a long silence, he went on, 'Aunt Vera and Uncle Saul aren't even answering our letters. They're safe and comfortable in Sweden, why should they bother with us? They must be angry about you and Anton . . .'

'Oh, Sieg, don't be cruel to me,' sobbed Ilse. Then, wiping her tears, defiant again, 'And I don't care what *anybody* thinks, you hear? There's nothing left, country, family, home, money, it's all gone, gone. All I've left in the world is Anton and you.'

'Sure. But you're leaving me behind.'

'*Hör mal zu*, listen to me. I'm not leaving you. It's all arranged with Anton. As soon as I'm in Paris, I'll get in touch with you. You'll take a train, and get off at a village called Vallorcine, right at the French border. A guide will be there, to take you across, through little paths only the locals know, where there are no guards and no passport checks. Then, you'll be in France, and I'll be there to meet you. But we need money to pay the guide and I've none here. The plan is Anton's, and we must do as he says, because he is always right. He did so well during his last trip to Australia that Monsieur Lavine lets him handle important business in the Paris office too. The time has come for both of us to join him. He loves you and he knows *I* can only be happy if you are with us.' Siegfried was listening, half convinced, tempted to believe in his mother's obvious sincerity. She continued, 'So, very soon, we'll be together in Paris. There's a nice apartment for us. You'll go to school. We'll be Monsieur and Madame Antoine, and you'll be called Siegfried Antoine.'

'No,' replied Sieg. 'I know who I want to be. My name will be Fred May. I won't be a German, or a Russian refugee. I'll be a Frenchman or . . . who knows? Fred May, that will be my name.'

He watched his mother hesitate for several days and finally decide she couldn't speak to her husband. Heinz was prey to agonizing headaches again and, half blinded, stumbled through official hearings. But as Anton's calls grew urgent, Ilse, torn with guilt, decided she could no longer put him off. She kissed her unresponsive son a hundred times, swore through her tears that she'd have no rest until her arms closed around him again. Then she called a cab, climbed in with her monogrammed set of alligator luggage, and was gone.

Sieg pressed his fists to his eyes and sat with his chin in his hands, unable to take his eyes off the clock on his desk. When the hands reached 3:45, the departure time of her train, he picked up a book and pretended to read.

Later, he heard his father return.

'*Hallo, hallo*, I'm here! The lawyer wasn't in, although I did have an appointment. I'll just have to return tomorrow. Is your mother home?'

'No, she isn't,' said Sieg.

'Did she tell you what time she'd be back?' insisted his father.

He didn't bother to answer.

Heinz waited, with growing impatience. Finally, dinner-time came and still Ilse hadn't returned. By then, Heinz was pacing the rooms.

'If only we knew where she went! The hairdresser? For a walk? Do you suppose she could have had an accident?

My God, maybe she's in the hospital! Where is the number?'

At last, Sieg closed his book and came downstairs carrying it.

'Mother isn't coming home,' he said very quietly, looking away from his father. 'She's gone for good.'

Heinz didn't understand.

'Of course she's coming home! Don't talk like that, you'll give me an attack.'

'I'm telling you the truth. Look on her dresser.'

Sieg watched his father stumble up the stairs, groping for his glasses as they fell. He'd already seen the note carefully propped against a perfume flask.

Mein lieber Heinz,

Today is the most difficult day of my life. I hate to hurt you, but I cannot go on like this any longer. I must think of myself and my son. Heinz, I am going away. I cannot tell you where, but you will hear from me as soon as I am in a position to talk to you further.

It is my hope that you will understand, when you know the whole truth. Remember, before you blame me too much, that I have been a good wife to you all these years, even when it wasn't easy.

Ilse

But Heinz refused to comprehend. Sieg heard him walk through the upstairs, opening closets, calling, 'Ilse! Where are you? Don't hide! Is it somebody's birthday that you want to surprise me?' But he found only silence and empty rooms. He returned to the dining room, where Sieg was eating alone the meal left for them by the day maid.

'This has gone on long enough,' he shouted, angry. 'Too long. Where is she?'

'Didn't she tell you in her note? All I know is she's gone. She didn't want to stay with you any longer. Or with me,' he added bitterly.

314

'How long will she be gone?' begged Heinz miserably.
'How long? Tell me, please.'

Sieg closed the book he had propped against his glass.
No pity in the large gray eyes. 'She's never coming home.
She's left us forever.'

Under the boy's stare, Heinz's forehead began to swell,
huge welts rising in angry furrows, distorting his features.
His eyes teared behind his thick glasses. He raised his
hand to his face.

'My head, my head,' he moaned. 'I can't see . . . Here,
mein Sohn, come here, give me your hand. Where are you?'

'I'm right here,' said Sieg, not moving.

'Go upstairs, get me my pills, quick, before I pass out.
And bring me a glass of water too. Hurry!'

Sieg went upstairs with deliberate steps, found the pills,
came down, filled a glass with water and put the vial and
glass on the table, within reach of his father, but made no
effort to hand them to him.

Then he stepped back and watched scornfully while his
father dropped half the contents of the vial on the floor
and spilled most of the water. Finally, he saw him lean
back, face grotesquely swollen, eyes closed. He picked up
the book still propped in front of his plate and returned to
his room.

Days passed while Heinz recovered slowly. Sieg went
on silently with his school routine, watching and waiting
anxiously for her phone call. Will she call as she promised?
Or has she already forgotten me?

'I'm sure your mother has returned to Germany,' declared Heinz the first time he felt well enough to share his
son's dinner. 'Where else could she have gone? She never
liked Luzern. Too small-townish she always said. We'll
find her in Düsseldorf.'

We? thought Sieg contemptuously. Let *him* go if he
wants to. I'm staying here and I'll wait for her call.

But Heinz had a plan now. He sold his gold watch, a set
of platinum cuff links that had been a wedding gift from
Ilse, and the massive silver tea set that had graced the

dining room on Mozartstrasse. He showed his son the money.

'There will be plenty for a few days in Düsseldorf. I know your mother. She'll be heartsick when she realizes how worried I was on her account. But I'll forgive her, of course. It's all been too much for her.'

Hiding behind a half-open door, later that night, Sieg watched his father finger a small suede pouch, hesitate, and finally slip it inside his sock. What could that be? he wondered, I never saw it before.

The next day, when he understood his father had irrevocably made up his mind to take him along to Düsseldorf, he was appalled and furious. Appalled enough to break his obstinate silence and yell:

'No, I won't go back to Germany. Never. It's insane. They arrest people without reason and they are never seen again. Papa, you can go if you want, but I won't. I'll stay here and wait for you to return.'

'Stay here all alone? Over my dead body. A boy belongs with his father.' Seeing the rage in his son's eyes, he added quickly, 'Don't believe all those tales. It's perfectly safe. And we're only going for a few days. Just long enough to find your mother and collect some money. Then . . .' He had a sudden inspiration. 'Remember your stamp collection? The people who bought our house never got around to sending it. So, we'll just go over and pick it up.'

The stamp collection, forgotten in the last moments of feverish packing, had been one of Sieg's treasures. Did his father see him vacillate? Encouraged, he went on. 'I'll tell you what I've in mind. After we're together with your mother again, we won't come back here. She never liked Switzerland anyway. So, we'll go . . . we'll go . . . that's it, we'll go to Paris! How would you like that? Fine, then, that's what we'll do.' Heinz was warming to his story, convincing himself, thinking aloud. 'And when we're in Paris, let's see . . . We might decide to go to America!'

This was the end of Sieg's resistance. I have to do as my father says, he thought, there's no choice, but it might not be so bad after all. I'll get my stamp collection back, then we'll simply take the train for Paris. Of course, I'll have to convince my mother to leave Anton, and maybe she will, if I tell her how much I love her. I've never really told her before. Then, we'll be a family again and we'll go to America, where I won't be Jewish anymore. But suppose she won't leave Anton? All right, then, I'll simply stay with them, and my father can do what he wants. He might even go to Sweden and work with Uncle Saul. So long as he does as he's told, he'll be all right.

When Sieg returned from school the next day, his father was waiting for him in exaggeratedly high spirits.

'It's all set, *mein Junge*, all set. Here are our tickets. I made reservations at the Park Hotel. Let's pack just enough for a week or so, then, as soon as your mother is with us again and I've settled my business, off we go to Paris!'

The next morning, they arrived in Düsseldorf. At first, little seemed changed in the two years since they'd left. The railroad station was the same, except for swastika banners flying everywhere above the platform and on the façade. More banners hung from lampposts when the taxi took them to their hotel.

Sieg looked warily at the street scene. A group of boys about his age were marching down the avenue and the cab overtook them. He turned around to look at them, an ache in his heart. They wore the uniform of *Hitlerjugend*, short black pants, light brown shirt with leather shoulder strap, and they carried ten-inch sheathed knives in their belts. Several of Sieg's former friends belonged to groups like those. He had seen the knife unsheathed, proudly displayed by its owner, its blade inscribed *Blut und Ehre*, Blood and Honor. He knew that *he* would never get to wear that coveted uniform and carry that knife.

Pain, anger, and hatred rose in his throat. Not hatred of the monstrous Nazi system that excluded him, not hatred of these arrogant young thugs. No. Sieg wanted more than anything to be with those who were strong, proud, who marched with a group, who belonged. His hate was entirely directed against those weak, those persecuted people who held him down, in bondage to his birth. It is *not* a matter of being Jewish, he kept repeating to himself, it's only a matter of what people *think* you are, since I know we are all alike.

His first encounter with the *Hitlerjugend* had taken place several years before. When students were invited to sign up for membership in the newly formed organization, he lined up with the rest, until a hand roughly pushed him aside, and he heard the word *Jude* uttered sarcastically. He'd have no part in those wonderful weekends of camping, mock war, and sports.

Then, one afternoon, as he was trying out his new bicycle on Mozartstrasse, a group in uniform including some of his classmates jumped him, demanding the bike. Outnumbered and terrified, he gave it up and ran to find his Uncle Saul, who told him no, he could not call the police, but not to worry, they'd soon be leaving this lunatic country and he'd get a new bicycle. Saul either didn't understand that Sieg's tears were not for the bike, but for his loneliness and exclusion, or else he felt it easier to let it go at that.

Sieg watched the *Hitlerjugend* turn a corner, marching and chanting their threatening songs.

Arrival at the hotel was uneventful. Herr Mayer's registration was respectfully recorded, a porter carried their light luggage upstairs to a three-room suite, with a balcony overlooking the *Platz*. More banners fluttered in the early summer breeze. Many uniforms among the crowd, *feldgrau* of the Landwehr and the Wehrmacht, black-shirted SS, even women in uniform. Sieg's eyes searched for the façade of Mayer Kaufhaus, down on the left on Koenigsallee. It was there, unchanged, but the word *Mayer* had been removed, the block-long store was now just *Kaufhaus*, and the giant swastika banners flew from its windows and roof.

He heard his father making calls to those friends who'd certainly have seen Ilse and would know her whereabouts. But either the number rang and rang, or else it was picked up by someone who hung up as soon as Heinz asked, 'Herr Einhorn?' or 'Herr Rosenthal?'

'I bet some of them are having lunch at the Brüderverein, the club we all belonged to.' Insisting that Sieg come along, he walked over, rehearsing a great reunion scene. But the Brüderverein had been turned over to the *Hitlerjugend* as a meeting house. Boys were marching in and out, their leaders wearing swastika armbands over the sleeves of their shirts, and the sound of military drill wafted from an open window. Sieg saw his father panic.

'Are all our friends really gone? Then *how* am I going to find your mother? I know it now: She isn't here and I won't find her because she doesn't want to be found.' Tears filled Heinz's eyes and the blinding headache overcame him.

Sieg felt absolutely no compassion. 'You lied to yourself and you lied to me,' he screamed at his father. 'Everyone we knew is gone. Gone! And look, there are signs on shop windows here, and here, and there, "Forbidden to Jews." You didn't tell me that.'

'Hush,' mumbled Heinz miserably, 'I didn't lie to you. Now let me rest a moment. Why don't you go to the dining room for a nice lunch? I'll call room service as soon as I feel better.'

Later, his headache subsided, Heinz took his son over to the store to call on the new owner, Herr Gottlieb. They were received in what had been Jakob's office, decorated now with Nazi memorabilia, and a large portrait of Herr Gottlieb in uniform, the visor of his swastika-emblazoned cap pulled low over his brow. He received his visitors seated, never offering them a chair.

'Ah . . . ah . . . Herr Gottlieb,' stammered Heinz, 'I came to see you about the notes, the notes on the sale of the store. They are past due, now, as you certainly know . . .'

Silence.

'If perhaps you need more time to acquit the full amount, I'd accept part payment . . .'

Silence. Now there was a frown on Herr Gottlieb's porcine features. Seated behind Jakob's desk, on Jakob's chair, with a tapestry cushion needlepointed, years ago, by Heinz's mother . . .

'So, Herr Gottlieb, I want you to know I'm ready to make any accommodations that are agreeable to you. Only, I need—'

'*You* need?' shouted Gottlieb with sudden brutality. 'I wasn't aware Jews needed anything from decent Germans. I am a patient man, but there are limits. Get out.'

He stood up heavily behind the desk, threatening. Terrified, Heinz staggered out the door with Sieg several steps ahead, walked through the store with every employee's eyes following him. At the door, the doorman – the same Hansi who used to snap to quivering attention whenever the Mayers addressed him with the customary *guten Tag*, and later, in those last years, God help us all! '*Heil Hitler!*' – now, Hansi stood aside and watched them open the door with a sneer of contempt.

An hour later, the police arrived at the hotel: Heinz and his son were escorted to the nearest Gestapo station for an identity check. In a small room smelling of urine and beer, under the pretense of interrogation, Heinz was hit and cursed.

Sieg had been taken away, and what took place behind that other door Heinz could only guess . . . But he heard a boy cry out several times in pain and anguish. When two members of the Gestapo came out, joking that youths that age are softer than girls, Heinz, sitting on the filthy floor, his head in his hands, was still trying to pretend it wasn't his son's voice he'd heard, nor the dull sound of blows resounding on flesh dearer to him than his own.

Early next morning, they were released into the streets without money and papers, as the sweepers were sprinkling water on the cool city's sidewalks, and the first thing they saw was a man pushing a handcart with bunches of pink roses pearly with dew ... They hurt everywhere, clothes torn and filthy, eyes stinging from lack of sleep. Every one of Sieg's steps was a torture.

Heinz tried to hold his hand, but the boy pushed him away with a violence that struck the father perhaps even more painfully than the events of the night.

The doorman at the hotel looked at them but made no move to open the door, and when Heinz reached out, he pushed him away roughly.

'No Jewish pigs in this place. *Raus*. Don't come near this place again!'

In vain, Heinz tried to explain that he had deposited money in the hotel's safe, that he and his son had luggage in their suite, that he only wanted to—

'Raus,' yelled the doorman. '*Raus*, before I call the Polizei.'

The last resort, as Heinz saw it, was to go to the house on Mozartstrasse. It was a long walk to that residential area, formerly covered in the chauffeur-driven Austro-Daimler. Now, exhausted and head aflame, Heinz walked doggedly with the silent boy limping behind him, until they arrived in front of the big house.

Outwardly nothing had changed and polished windows shone. But blond children played with tricycles on the front lawn under the trees. Sieg could hear adolescents shouting on the tennis court. They waited, Sieg remaining a little distance off, until his father gathered his courage, walked up the stairs, and rang the bell. A heavy young woman in a housedress with blond braids wrapped around her head opened the door. When she saw him, she let out a cry of horror and pushed the door closed only to reopen it immediately and, with frantic clucking, gather the children playing on the lawn, leaving an upturned tricycle with spinning wheels. Then she called out to someone in the back of the house. A man came to the door, big and blond, too, shrugging into the jacket of his brown uniform.

'Excuse me, sir,' stammered Heinz. 'I'm Herr Heinz Mayer. My brother and I were the owners of this house. The payments are overdue. And my son left behind his stamp collection, I'd like to—'

'*Raus*,' shouted the man. 'Get away from my doorstep. Don't you dare come close to my wife and children.'

'But I assure you, sir,' said Heinz desperately, 'I will not harm your family. I'll wait outside while you get the stamp collection. It's very important to my boy, here.'

'And take your whelp away too,' yelled the man, gesturing violently at Sieg. 'Don't let him near my children – don't contaminate them with your filth.'

The door slammed. Sieg's eyes were staring, vacant. Heinz remained frozen on the stone steps, until a panful of water thrown at him from an upstairs window woke him from his trance. He tried again to touch his son's hand, but Sieg shook himself free. They walked aimlessly now, and when a passerby approached them, they saw him cross the street rather than brush past them. It was at that moment that Heinz realized his headache was gone and his head clearer than it had been since his wife left him.

'We must eat, *mein kind*,' he said to his son. 'I don't have any money, but perhaps Eber, you know Eber, the maître d' at the Schloss Garten, where we used to go sometimes in the summer . . . I'm sure Eber remembers the good tips we always left.'

The Schloss Garten was flourishing. All the tables in the beer garden were crowded – men in shirt sleeves, uniform jackets slung over the backs of their chairs, and women in light flowered dresses. Waiters hurried from table to table, holding aloft trays laden with overflowing steins of beer, platters of steaming sausage and boiled potatoes. Talking was loud, laughter of women shrill, strains of the 'Horst Wessel Lied.' Siegfried cringed and shrank against the wall. His father stood uncertainly.

'I don't see Eber – so it must be his day off,' he said, trying against all reason to buoy his son's spirits. 'I know what I'll do, though. Wait here for me, I'll be right back.'

He left Sieg hiding in the doorway and made his way to the alley behind.

A moment later, he was back with a crumpled piece of greasy paper holding chunks of cold potatoes and bread.

'Here, *mein Junge*,' he said to the trembling boy, 'we'll go to the park and find ourselves a nice quiet spot where we can eat and rest. Now,' he added with feigned cheerfulness, 'I know where to find all the food we need. And if I go there at night, I'll be able to get even better.'

The gates of the public park bore chilling signs forbidding its entrance to dogs and Jews. So, Heinz led his son along the fence to a spot he remembered having discovered once long ago, as a child, playing with his friends. They came to a remote area where a small green door, half hidden by the overgrowth, stood rustily ajar. Among unclipped hedges, piles of broken pots and half-dead trees still in their transplanting boxes, they found the shelter of a grassy hollow under the low, overhanging branches of a giant pine tree. Father and son climbed down to its safety and hungrily devoured their food.

'Now,' explained Heinz, 'we're going to get some rest and then we'll see about getting to Paris. After that, well, I guess it will be America, here we come!'

Sieg knew his father now carefully avoided mentioning his mother's name. He understood that, after all, other pains were bearable to him, but her loss was the one he couldn't face. His father's forced good cheer was too much for Sieg, though, who finally broke his scornful silence. 'How can we go anywhere? We haven't got a cent.'

'We are still rich, *mein Junge*, because your father is a lot smarter than you think. We have plenty to go wherever we want. You don't believe me? Here, see what the Gestapo missed. I had hidden it in my sock,' he added proudly, 'and when they searched me, they never thought of looking there.'

Sieg continued to stare ahead, but from the corner of his eye he saw the small brown suede pouch he'd glimpsed before leaving Düsseldorf.

'It's something I took out of the safe at the store just before we left. Your Uncle Saul looked and looked for it, but I never let on that I had it. Here, take it. See what's inside.'

Contemptuous silence. Heinz waited and finally reached out gently and placed the pouch on the grass, as close to his son as the boy's recoil would let him.

'I'm going to sleep for a while,' he announced after a long silence. 'I want you to keep this. It's yours. I am giving it to you, my son, because I love you more than anything in the world and so you'll understand we're not desperate after all. We'll just have to figure out a way to get out of here, sell the stuff, and then it will be easy to buy tickets to anywhere in the world you choose, with a lot left over when we get there. Take it, *mein Junge*, and let's go to sleep.'

Sieg remained motionless until he heard his father's regular breathing and knew he had fallen asleep. Overcome by curiosity, he reached out to the brown pouch, looked inside, and slipped it into the cuff of his own argyle knee sock. He squirmed for a long time before he found a position that would allow his torn body to rest.

16

THEY REMAINED IN their shelter for three days. Heinz
found a length of hose lying in the grass, rigged it up to a
rusty faucet, and there was water to drink and to wash,
after a fashion. At night, he went on forays and returned
with table scraps wrapped in newspapers. His search for
food was made easier, he confided happily, by the fact that
all restaurants, to avoid wasting precious food, placed
edible leftovers separate from other waste, in cans marked
Pigs that were emptied by local farmers in the morning.

In spite of pathetic attempts at cleanliness, both of
them looked like vagabonds, disheveled and filthy. Yet,
crouching in the grassy hollow, Heinz knew a peace and
contentment he'd never felt before, able as he was for the
first time to meet his son's needs without help from
anyone. But Sieg wouldn't listen to his father's hopeful
chatter and kept out of arm's reach.

As soon as I can decide what to do, he thought, I will
run away from this stupid, filthy man, and I'll run as far
as the world is wide. His rage and scorn were directed
against his father, not against his tormentors. He wished
instead that he could be with them, strong and triumphant
and wearing a uniform. But he didn't waste any time
hoping for a return to normal times and spurned the
delusion that the laws that had turned his life into a dead
end of pain and terror might ever be repealed. His true
escape would be a flight into another identity. He'd simply
become someone else. Fred May the man was born from
the pain-torn and exhausted body of the boy Siegfried
Mayer.

Little by little, he formulated his plan for escape. He
knew the area fairly well. Anton had taken him hunting

near the Dutch border, not far to the west, and he remembered they had driven through a town called Mönchengladbach, west of Düsseldorf. Once, they had taken a shortcut across some fields and when they'd emerged onto the next road, he'd seen signs in Dutch and they were in Holland.

On the third night, the sound of footsteps cracking dead branches nearby froze them in breathless terror. So, when hours later Heinz left on his nightly scavenging expedition, he admonished his son to lie perfectly still in the hollow's darkest recess.

Later, Heinz was returning, clutching his greasy parcel, almost secure now in his new life. For the first time in his experience, it was a life whose simplified demands he could master. As he hurried along a deserted street, he heard footsteps, too late to duck into a doorway.

A shout: 'Hey, you, over there, where are you going?' Heinz tried to ignore them and continued walking, head down.

'Stop! What are you carrying, you bum? Don't run, or we'll shoot.'

Trembling, Heinz stopped. Three storm troopers crossed the street. Eyes downcast, he only saw the shiny black boots moving closer, converging on him. One of the men grabbed his shoulder, spun him roughly around.

'Let's see what you're carrying there. Stolen goods, no doubt. What's your name?'

'Heinz Mayer,' stammered Heinz, transfixed with terror.

'*Ein Jude!*' exclaimed the man. 'I didn't know there were any left in Düsseldorf. Show me what you've got, you *Hund.*'

Heinz's pathetic parcel fell to the ground.

'Taking food from the pigs, are you? Filthier than the swine, eh?'

The boots were scattering bits of sausage, crusts of bread, mashing potatoes to the sidewalk. Heinz's first reaction was to save his treasure – the food he was proudly carrying back to feed his son. He squatted on the pavement, attempting to gather a few of the pieces. A kick almost sent him sprawling, but he caught himself on all fours. The men were laughing, joking, half drunk, enjoying the unexpected sport.

Another kick to Heinz's face smashed the side of his nose, which began to bleed profusely. Blood fell in heavy drops on the pavement.

'*Judenblut!* We can't have that impure blood dirtying the streets!' shouted one of the Nazi thugs. 'Wash that blood, Jew, wash it up. Clean your filth!'

'That's right,' yelled another. 'Clean it up!'

Heinz tried to ward the blows off his face, but only succeeded in exposing his ribs ... More blood spattered the dark concrete. He tried to rub it off with his sleeve, but only succeeded in spreading the stains. Then a warm shower fell on his neck, trickled down his face, running onto the side of his mouth. The three men pissed on him, laughing uproariously.

'*Gut*, Hermann, *gut!*' shouted one of the men. 'Show that Jew how to wash his filth, show him, Hermann! Show him how we wash Jewish blood from our streets ...'

'Hey,' screamed another, 'he isn't even trying to clean up! He needs to be shown. The Jews will mess up the whole city around them and then they'll leave it that way. Hey, I'll show you ...'

A heavy boot pushed Heinz's head down, crushing it to the concrete.

'Use your tongue, wash your filth,' the Nazi screamed. 'Go on, lick it clean.'

The headlights of a car threw a beam around the corner. The men looked up, but didn't move. They had nothing to fear in this new Reich where they were the masters. The car, a regular police patrol of the Schutzpolizei, the city police, with its distinctive markings, slowed and stopped. A light was flashed on the scene.

'*Was ist los!*' The policeman saw the uniforms. 'You need help, boys?'

'No, it's nothing, *Kumpel*. We're just teaching a lesson to a *Jude* we caught dirtying up the street.'

'*Also*,' said the policeman. 'Still a few of those around. We're always looking for them, but they're harder to trap than rats. You want us to take this one? We've got just the place for him.'

'No,' replied the thug called Hermann. 'No need to take him anywhere. We'll teach him his lesson right here. But first, he has to clean up the mess he made, doesn't he?'

'Right you are,' said the policeman. 'It's a good thing you boys are on the alert. Well, good night and *Heil Hitler!*'

'*Heil Hitler*,' replied the Nazis, giving the stiff-arm salute. The heavy boot hadn't stopped pressing on Heinz's neck. The men returned their attention to him.

'Lick that street clean, you swine!'

Beyond horror, beyond terror, only concerned now to stay alive for the sake of his son, Heinz tried to lick the blood and urine from the pavement. More urine spurted as the three men, jostling each other, tried to aim at the side of his face. He tasted the warm liquid that smelled of beer . . . Finally, the men tired of their sport.

'What do you say we go to bed, fellows? Although I must say I'm glad we took this street. There was good work to be done here tonight.'

'*Jawohl*, there was,' said Hermann. 'But first, let's take care of him, before he fouls this town up anymore.'

This time, the kicks that fell on Heinz were murderous and he was thrown from side to side, kicked again, in the face, the stomach, the kidneys.

'Stand up, you Jew, stand up. I think we'll let you go after all . . .' The men were laughing uproariously. 'Shall we let him go, eh, fellows, *shall* we?'

The kicks stopped. The troopers stepped back a little. Heinz rose in slow agony, looking blindly around him, trying to focus his eyes in the semidarkness, lit only by a dim streetlight. At that time, one of the men took careful aim and the toe of his heavy boot caught Heinz right under the chin, sending him spinning backward. His body crumpled against the wall. One last kick ricocheted him against the masonry once more, and the three thugs started to walk away, hitching their pants and buckling their belts, with the GOTT MIT UNS, God with us, buckle.

Siegfried slept restlessly that night, and woke up very hungry. He sat up, rubbed his eyes, looked to the place over the side, where he expected his father would be watching him, love in his eyes behind his glasses. There would be a package of scraps placed between them on the grass. He would eat without a word, looking straight ahead.

But his father wasn't there. Obviously, he hadn't been back and there was no food. Siegfried's first thought was anger ... Then, perhaps in some mysterious knowledge, the intuition came to his mind of what had happened ... He could not, of course, imagine the scene, but he dimly visualized his father lying dead in the street, and Nazis laughing at the body. For the first time in his spoiled and protected life, he knew guilt, a brief stab that made him close his eyes and bend his head ...

But Sieg also knew that guilt was a luxury not affordable by those who must fight to survive. Terror must guide their steps. He lay in the hollow all day, thinking, mapping his route in his mind. After darkness fell, he crept out of the sleeping city. It took him five nights walking from dark until dawn, getting lost sometimes and having to retrace his steps, hiding during the day in ditches, haystacks, and the small forests left in the Rhineland. Chased, one night, by fiercely barking farm dogs, he ran into a barbed wire fence, but, in his terror, never even felt the deep gashes torn into his arm, until, at the break of dawn, he found himself covered with blood. On the sixth day, and with infection already setting in the wounds, he reached Holland. The authorities of the Dutch town of Roermond saw that he received treatment and notified Monsieur Antoine, 46 rue du Sentier in Paris, that his minor stepson, Fred May, needed to get in touch with him. Ilse and Anton immediately wired the money for a train ticket and, wearing clothes borrowed from the son of the chief of police in Roermond, Fred was soon joyously stepping onto the platform in the Gare du Nord, into the arms of his weeping mother.

'At last, *mein Süsser*, at last! I died a thousand deaths thinking of you out there . . . I couldn't believe it when I called the house in Luzern and there was no answer! So, I phoned the lawyer and was told your father had gone back to Germany to get funds owed him and had taken you along. Why did Heinz go back to that insane country, why? Poor, poor man. Never once in his life did he do the right thing. I wanted so much to get you away from him, but you know, the law was on his side and it took longer than I'd thought to arrange for you to get across the border. But, God be thanked, you're here, safe and sound. Tell me, what did your father say when you left?'

Was his father alive or dead? Fred didn't ever want to talk or even think of those days, and swore to himself he never would . . .

'He didn't say anything. I just ran away.'

'How is he? Is he doing all right? Things are bad, there, aren't they?'

'Not too bad,' said Fred evenly. 'He got some money from people who owed him and he lives in a nice hotel. I think he plans to return to Switzerland. Don't write him, or try to call him, he doesn't want to hear from you. And if he knew where I was, he might send the police after me, or the people from the German consulate. He mustn't think we both deserted him.'

'I won't, my sweet,' promised Ilse, touching her son's smooth cheek. 'I don't want anything like that to happen, now that we're together at last. Life isn't easy here, you know, there are so many refugees from Germany, with more arriving every day. At least, we have an apartment, and Anton and I will be married as soon as the papers can be arranged. You will go to school and if you like, you can help me in the store.'

'What store? *You* work in a store?'

'Yes, I manage the jewelry store for the Lavines. Anton travels a lot, mostly to Australia, and he's going to see if we can all settle there eventually. Meanwhile, you're here, you're safe and that's all that matters. We don't have a great deal of money, but enough to live and with Anton, you know, we'll always make it somehow. Since you have no papers, we must go to the German consulate and get you a passport.'

Fred settled into his new life, surrounded by other German refugees he avoided as much as he could. He hated the sound of the German language, of anything German, and carefully copied the accent of the Parisian boys he met at school, their manners, their clothes, their savoir faire, and tried to erase almost all traces of his past. As for the passport, issued him by the German consulate, stamped with the yellow *J*, he pushed it to the back of a drawer and pretended it didn't exist. The brown suede pouch he hid there, too, but that he never forgot.

He passed the dreaded *baccalauréat* with his class. Thus eligible to register at a university, he chose law and successfully completed his first year. The summer of 1939 he was twenty, and he had just said good-bye to Ilse and Anton leaving for an extended trip to Australia, when, suddenly, fresh rumors of war broke out. But the previous summers had buzzed with the same fears every time Hitler had asserted his 'right' to some neighboring country. Austria and Czechoslovakia had been swallowed amid orgies of patriotic songs and hysterical orations that didn't drown the thunder of marching boots and rolling tanks. So Fred didn't worry too much. He renewed his registration at the Faculté de Droit and wrote reassuring letters to his mother in Port Augusta. The French would never go to war over Poland. Public opinion was too much against it.

The declaration of war took him and most of France by surprise. He had no visa for another country and within hours, the French authorities had taken him into custody as an 'enemy alien,' the bearer of a German passport. He spent the first winter of the war in a camp near Paris and when the camp was moved south to Angoulême, he spoke through the barred gate to two schoolgirls who, inspired by the feats of Deanna Durbin, drove him and four friends to the Spanish border . . .

'Señor,' the jeweler was saying, 'Señor, are you all right? A glass of water, perhaps? No? Well, as I was saying, I'm afraid I don't have enough ready cash, but I'll call a colleague from another store. You must understand, though, that in wartime there are more sellers than buyers for valuables such as these.'

It took some haggling, but eventually a compromise price was reached. A little later Fred joined his friends.

'Let's find somewhere quiet, maybe one of those benches overlooking the harbor, where we'll be safe from people's eyes.'

They sat at the end of the promenade, shielded by greenery. Nobody was near.

'Here's the money I got,' said Volodia. 'My grandfather must be turning over in his grave. He'd have done much better.'

'Here's mine,' said Mischa. 'My poor mother would be disappointed, too, to see how little her treasure was worth . . .'

'I didn't strike such a great bargain either,' added Fred, showing a much thicker bundle of pesetas. 'Let's count it all and we'll divide it five ways. Here. Here's each man's share.'

Five equal wads of bills were quickly pocketed.

'Now,' said Fred, 'we can't stay together. Five is too many, we won't have enough freedom of movement. Let's separate into smaller groups. Volodia, you want to come with me?'

'I'll go on my own,' proposed Mischa. 'I know somebody staying in Madrid. I'll go look for him.'

'All right,' agreed Isaac, who had been a lifelong friend of Herschel, well before the days in camp. 'You're right, Fred. It will be easier that way. Well, fellows, thanks, and when do we meet again?'

'In America. In New York.' Fred answered quickly, as though he had it all thought out before. 'In New York. We'll meet at the Palm Court, in the Plaza Hotel, at noon, one year from today. Check the date. And don't forget. I know it's a good place, because my uncle had lunch there often, when he was in New York. I'll reserve a table for five, and if any one of us cannot be there, he will leave a message with the maître d' for Mr Fred May. Understood? And don't forget the date!'

The others laughed, nodded in agreement. One year from today, at noon, in the Palm Court of the Plaza, in New York, they repeated. Then, they all shook hands and parted.

Two days later, Fred and Volodia arrived in Lisbon intending to procure a visa for the United States. But crowds besieged the US Embassy, blocking the street, pressing at the door to gain entry into the already packed waiting rooms. They had to wait their turn. It wasn't until the next afternoon that they were ushered into the presence of a harassed official. The man wasn't optimistic:

'Do you have any relatives or friends in the United States who can send you an affidavit of support? The US government cannot undertake the responsibility of the support of any more refugees, you understand. Too many have been allowed in already.'

Fred and Volodia looked at each other. No, they didn't know anybody there. Sure, they'd vaguely heard of people who had made their way to the United States earlier, but they had no address, no reference.

'In that case,' said the man, 'I'm afraid all I can do for you is put your names on a waiting list, and we'll contact you when you become eligible for an immigration visa.'

'How long might that be?' asked Volodia, hopefully.

'I couldn't tell you exactly' – the man shrugged – 'two years, perhaps longer. The waiting list is already endless.'

Back in the street. Where to now?

'We might try some other country,' Fred said. 'Wait. Let's go to the harbor and find out if there are any ships leaving soon, and where they are going.'

Down at the harbor, no sailings were scheduled, although several freighters were lying at anchor in the bay.

'The captains are afraid,' said one old salt, drinking beer at the counter next to them in a waterfront café. 'Afraid of the German U-boats. They're saying the Germans will torpedo anything they find on the high seas, regardless of flag, because it might be a British freighter in disguise.'

Fred and Volodia drank their warm beer, bought another for him. Volodia spoke halting Spanish, and the conversation continued in broken Spanish and Portuguese.

'But if you boys were to go to Oporto, now, that's different, over there. I hear there's a ship leaving sometime soon for South America. You might get on that one. It's called the *São Vicente*, and I hope God looks after her, because it's a risky trip, nowadays.'

The next day, they were in Oporto.

'Yes,' said the captain of the SS *São Vicente*. 'I am sailing the day after tomorrow. I'm taking freight to Porto Alegre, Brazil. And picking up whatever the company has for the return trip. It will cost you money, but I think I can take you aboard. I already have a few passengers. But you must have a visa for Brazil, otherwise it's no go.'

To the Brazilian consulate in Oporto.

'Senhores,' declared the bureaucrat behind the desk, 'I am sorry, but we give no visas. No visas. Our waiting list is long, very long. Come back in six months.'

Yet, something in the man's voice left an opening. Fred could sense it.

'Listen,' he said, lowering his voice, 'could we talk to you? Not here, of course,' he added hastily. 'But suppose we meet for lunch at that little place around the corner – O Café Flórida it's called? Right. At what time?'

The man nodded, showed one finger.

'We'll be there waiting for you at one o'clock.'

They waited and waited at the café and when they thought the man wasn't coming, and they were about to leave, there he was, rushing in, glancing furtively left and right.

'I couldn't leave, the chief of the visa division was there, looking over my shoulder all the time, he just went home now. You wanted to talk to me?'

They explained earnestly that they wanted visas right now. Today.

'Well,' said the man, 'perhaps that could be arranged. But I'll have to make gifts to people, you know, so I hope you have money.'

Volodia looked at Fred; they had money to cover their passage, with just enough left over for a meal or two. But Fred whispered to the man, 'I can give you something of great value. Come with me to the window, turn your back to the room so nobody can see what I am showing you.' They walked away and stood near the window, their backs turned to the crowded room.

Volodia remained seated, and when they returned, the Brazilian seemed pleased. 'All right, give me your passports, and the visas will be placed on them. You can pick them up tomorrow at noon.'

As an afterthought, he added, 'You know that you must show certificates of baptism to get into Brazil? No visas should be delivered to non-Catholics. Do you have those?'

Fred and Volodia, in a simultaneous gesture, respectively showed the gold cross and the medal with its low relief of the Virgin Mary. The employee wasn't satisfied. 'That won't be enough. I advise you to find a priest who'll give you the certificates. Otherwise, visa or no visa, they won't let you into the country.'

So they found a small, dilapidated church in a narrow side street, and knocked on the door of the modest house next door. The priest lived there with his sister. They explained to him that they needed baptismal certificates. Of course they were Christians, Fred told him earnestly. 'See, here is my cross, and here is his medal.'

The old priest smiled. 'I want to believe you, *meus filhos*,' he said, 'I do want to believe you. But I cannot issue a certificate of baptism without evidence. So, I propose to baptize you, and I will simply make a mental reservation that the sacrament is valid only in case you were not baptized before. I'll call my sister to serve as your godmother, and the sexton will be your godfather.'

He led them into the sacristy, put on his vestments, pulled the chasuble over his shoulders, and slipped the maniple over his arm.

'What is your Christian name going to be?' he asked Fred.

'Fred.'

'Federico, then. And what about you, *meu filho*?'

'My name is Volodia for Vladimir, Father, Saint Vladimir is a great saint in Russia.'

'Russia is so far away, *meu filho*, we don't know their saints here. And perhaps their saints wouldn't know us, either.'

Volodia nodded. 'Father, what is your own name?'

'It is Rogelio.'

'My Christian name will be Rogelio, then. Roger.'

After the brief ceremony, the old priest took the young men's hands in his. 'This may be God's way to bring more lambs into his flock,' he said, smiling at them. 'Do not forget that if you were not Christians before, now you are. Live in any case according to the Law of God. Farewell, and Godspeed.'

He waved away the few bills held out to him. 'Keep this. You will need it on your journey. And God be with you.'

The next day, the passports were ready, duly stamped and signed. The bearers were entitled to a six-month stay in Brazil.

The trip across the ocean seemed endless, as the *São Vicente* steamed slowly along, carrying a full load of barrels of port and other Portuguese wines to its South American destination. Fred and Volodia sweltered at night in the stuffy, crowded cabins and often preferred to spend the night sleeping on deck instead, with the other half-dozen other refugees making their escape as well. Past the Equator, they watched the Southern Cross rise above the horizon, and three interminable weeks after leaving Oporto, they were in Porto Alegre.

The customs inspector came on board and checked passports. All were in order, but when he looked at Fred's and Volodia's, dismissing with a wave of his hand the proffered baptismal certificates, he frowned, and swore, '*Mãe de Deus!* Now, this is a crude job if I ever saw one! This isn't even the official stamp. Why, it's only a stamp like the ones they put on mail to indicate which day it was received! This isn't the consul's signature, either, and the number of these visas is totally invented! It should be a five-digit and two-letter number, and yours are only four numbers and one letter. Whoever made this up should go to prison . . .'

'What in the world does that mean?' demanded Fred, trying to brazen out of the situation. 'There was a mistake, that's all. We got these visas at the Brazilian consulate, in Oporto. They *have* to be valid. We'll be glad to go to your immigration office and see how to regularize them.'

'No,' shouted the official, angrier now. 'No, you cannot do that, because you cannot get off this ship! Nobody, without a valid visa, can set foot on Brazilian soil.'

Fred and Volodia refused to understand.

'But the ship will leave Porto Alegre tomorrow! We can't stay on board. What are we supposed to do?'

'What you do is no concern of mine. You will return to your port of embarkation, I suppose. And consider yourselves lucky that I am not recommending sanctions against you for attempting to enter our territory fraudulently. *Vão se embora!*'

Volodia looked at Fred significantly, rubbing two fingers together, in the gesture that means 'A bribe, perhaps?' but Fred shook his head, with a gesture that meant 'My pockets are empty.'

The official left, muttering furiously. Fred and Volodia were aghast.

'What are we going to do? Go back to Oporto? It's impossible! We can't return to Europe!'

It was useless to wonder at that point whether the visa was, indeed, a crude fake, or if, perhaps, it was in good order, but the sight of the *J*–stamped passports, probably familiar by now to the official, indicated a desperate owner and had made him count automatically on a substantial bribe.

The captain, in turn, was unhappy to have to keep on board these two passengers who had no money left to pay for the return trip. They offered to work to help defray the fare.

The captain shrugged. 'I have all the help I need on this trip. More, even. With all these unemployed sailors in Lisbon and Oporto, I took on a couple hands more than I needed. Pure charity, mind you. No, you can't work. Just try not to eat too much,' he added as an afterthought. 'It's going to be a long haul. We have several stops to make on the way back. My first freight, now, is to be unloaded in Rio, then I'll stop in Belém to pick up some more, and after that, there will be two or three more ports before I bring you back to Oporto. So, take it easy, and above all, don't try to jump ship when we touch a port, or you'd be in even more serious trouble than you are now.'

More forlorn, endless weeks followed. Two days in the port of Rio de Janeiro, leaning over the railing, looking hopelessly at the tall buildings, hazy in the distance. But soldiers walked back and forth, firearms at the ready, along the dock. Belém was an end-of-the-world harbor, under the stifling heat of the zero latitude, smelling of mildew and rotting fish, the immense estuary of the Amazon rushing past, a threatening fortress on the brow of a hill. There again, soldiers paced the quay.

Another stop, after a few days, this one in the French colony port of Cayenne. There, convicts from the penitentiary worked at loading and unloading ships, bent double by enormous loads, in their tattered striped uniforms, under the eye of watchful guards armed to the teeth . . . Then, long days at sea again.

Finally, one morning, as they woke up in their hammocks, the ship was still. They rushed upstairs and saw land again on the horizon. Another desperate end-of-the-world harbor? Sailors were excitedly milling on the bridge, apparently a liberty had been promised. A tugboat appeared to escort the ship to its mooring. Engines sputtered to life again, land came closer.

'What's the name of this place?' Fred asked a sailor.

'It's called Charleston.'

'Which country is it in?'

'It is,' answered the sailor, scornful of such ignorance, 'in the Estados Unidos de America, of course. Where else?'

Fred and Volodia looked at each other, the same thought in their minds.

'So, we will have come this close to America, so tantalizingly near that we will be looking at its ships, its buildings, its people, breathing its air even. But we are like the damned: they can look at Paradise, and that's what makes Hell even worse for them.'

'Well,' groaned Fred in total exhaustion, sitting on a stanchion, 'I don't think I can take it anymore. What do you say we jump off now and put an end to it all?'

'Not here,' replied Volodia. 'They'd find some way to fish us out. Let's wait until we're back on the high seas. Then, we'll jump, nobody will notice, and even if they do, they surely won't stop the ship for us.'

Fred nodded. It was the only solution, the only possible ending to their torment.

The ship moored. Most of the sailors went ashore, leaving only a token crew on board. It was a hot, humid summer day. Fred and Volodia were left alone, beyond despair, leaning over the railing, still wondering against all hope whether it might be possible to jump and swim for freedom. But there again, guards were pacing the wharfs.

Almost directly below them, a man in a battered straw hat was sitting motionless on a little folding stool, holding a fishing rod to the oil-stained water, fishing quietly, with a pail next to him, unmindful of the rusty hull of the freighter that rose out of the darkly iridescent water directly in front of him.

'Do you think we should try after all?' asked Volodia. 'Jump and let the guards shoot us? It would be faster than drowning on the high seas.'

At that point, the man in the straw hat, who had probably heard some words, but did not get the drift of the conversation, raised his head, squinting in the hot sunshine. 'You are German?' he called out in German too. 'What are you doing on this ship?'

Volodia, always the better one at getting a conversation going, answered, 'You have a Hamburg accent, *Mensch*. Are you from Hamburg?'

'Yes,' replied the man, 'I am. Or rather, I was. I left Germany when all the troubles started, several years ago – now I live in New York City. I'm a lawyer, and I come here on vacation. My name is Goldstein. What are yours?'

The young men introduced themselves, and told of their voyage-of-the-damned odyssey.

'We have decided to jump off the ship as soon as we reach the high seas again,' confessed Volodia. 'Better drown than return to what we left behind. Hitler will soon have conquered all Europe, the madness will be everywhere. There will be no place to hide.'

Goldstein nodded absently. He was thinking. 'Do you have passports?'

'Yes, German passports, with the *J*, you know . . .'

'I know all about those,' interrupted Goldstein. 'Why didn't you get a visa for the US?'

They explained what the embassy in Lisbon had said, the mobs trying to push in, the waiting crowds. He nodded.

'I have a pretty good idea of what it must be like, over there now. And immigration to the US is restricted. No visa, and you cannot land. Listen,' he said suddenly, his mind made up, 'listen, and whatever you do, don't get your hopes up. But there just *might* be a way. I'm not sure, but I have heard that someone did successfully what I am going to try for you. So, throw down your passports, and I'll see if there's anything I can do.'

Could they trust him? In any case, what good were these passports now, to return to a Hitler-dominated Europe? They wrapped the green passports in a handkerchief, tied in a scrap of wood they found on the deck for ballast, and threw them down. The parcel landed almost at Goldstein's feet.

'All right,' he said. 'Now, don't count on anything, boys, because you may yet end up feeding the fish, if my plan doesn't work. I'll be back.'

After he was gone, Fred sighed, looked at Volodia.

'What if we don't see him again? What about our passports?'

Volodia shrugged. 'What good are they?'

Two interminable hours passed. Still standing at the railing, they saw a car stop on the wharf, Goldstein step out, followed by a man in uniform. As the man came closer, they could see *US Immigration* in gold letters on the cap. Their hearts started pounding wildly. Goldstein and the immigration officer climbed the ladder, stepped onto the companionway, were recognized by the sailor on duty, and walked over to where Fred and Volodia stood, unable to walk, their knees suddenly turned to water.

'All right,' called out Goldstein, 'you men have been admitted to the territory of the United States. This official here will check your passports, but it's only a formality, and he will escort you to the immigration office, over there, to sign papers. Everything is in order. Get your things if you have any, and come with us. Let's get off this boat,' he added with a broad grin, 'unless you'd rather stay?'

A half hour later, he was ushering the two trembling, bewildered young men into a seafront coffee shop. He signaled the buxom waitress. 'Three hamburgers, with plenty of fries, and three large Cokes,' he ordered. 'Now that you are free men in America, you'd better start learning the local customs.'

As soon as it got past their lips, no food had ever tasted better to Fred and Volodia.

Satiated, they wanted to know how Goldstein had managed to secure those unobtainable visas.

'Well,' explained Goldstein modestly, finishing the last of his fries, 'I had heard of one case where someone had called the White House and asked Mrs Roosevelt to allow Jewish refugees to land, and she had seen to it personally that permission was granted. So, I simply went to the post office, put in a call to the White House, asked to speak to Mrs Roosevelt. When her secretary came on the line, I said it was a matter of life and death – a humanitarian problem I was sure she'd want to hear about. Next thing I knew, *she* had taken the phone . . . I could hardly believe it, but I explained your situation. She said, with that accent of hers, "Life and death?"'

'That's right.' Fred sighed. 'Death, more likely.'

'She told me her husband was addressing the Congress, but she'd send a messenger to alert him to the action she was taking. Meanwhile, she was going to call the immigration office in Charleston, and she'd tell them she was giving her personal guarantee that the President would allow these two young men to land with immigration visas.'

'Mrs Roosevelt?' Volodia kept repeating dumbly. '*Mrs Roosevelt?*'

'So,' continued Goldstein, 'I hotfooted it over to immigration, and the office chief was on the phone, practically standing at attention, and I handed him the passports. See what he wrote.'

By hand, the chief of the immigration office had written on each passport:

Admitted this day to the territory of the United States, by personal permission of Mrs Eleanor Roosevelt.

'What do you think of that?' asked Goldstein rhetorically, a catch in his throat. The young men couldn't answer. Volodia's curly head was in his hands, and sobs shook his shoulders. Fred stared ahead with his pale gray eyes, tears brimming between the long lashes.

Goldstein waited. After a moment, he asked, 'Well, fellows, what are you going to do, now?'

'If we may impose upon your kindness for just this once more,' said Volodia, blowing his nose, 'we will ask for a stamp, a piece of paper, and an envelope, so we can write Mrs Roosevelt and tell her how she has saved our lives and that we'd like to show our gratitude, somehow. Then, we'll look for a mailbox. After that . . .'

'After that,' continued Fred, a visionary gleam in his pale gray eyes, 'we'll find where the nearest recruiting office is located, we'll go there, and we'll enlist in the Army of the United States.'

The Army of the United States, indifferent to the romantic role it had assumed for the two young refugees, sent them straight to Fort Benning for basic training. Because of his British accent, Fred was nicknamed 'the Englishman' by his unsophisticated barrackmates and alternately, as soon as he had learned to watch his vowels, as 'the Frenchman,' by another group who thought he looked French. Wasn't that what Siegfried had hoped for, on that long jetty, in Luzern . . . ?

Volodia, for his part, loved every moment of the grueling basic training in the humid Georgia summer.

'When I hear these guys bitching about the army, and the drill sergeant, and the food, I wish I could tell them what's going on on the other side!' he assured Fred every time they met.

'Don't even try,' advised Fred. 'Nobody in his right mind could believe what's going on over there.'

Volodia had only one complaint. 'I can speak Russian, and Polish, and German, I manage in French and in Spanish. It's only *English* I can't seem to learn! I understand what they say, but when I speak, it comes out all wrong,' he moaned. Would Volodia's troubles with English plague him for the rest of his life?

At the end of basic training, the army made some routine decisions that were to profoundly influence the lives of its two recruits. Volodia, who had been an engineering student with a specialization in aerodynamics, found himself assigned to the Special Services Division, where he would be attached to a unit making training films for the army.

'Snafu.' He grinned broadly at Fred, when they met to say good-bye. '"Situation normal all fucked up." That much English I know. But God! I am going to *love* that job. Remember that girl, Martine, I think her name was? I told her I'd go to Hollywood and send for her? It might not be so far off. Too bad no mail can get to France now, I'd write and tell her. I'm still wearing her medal, you know.'

In Fred's case, some clerk, recognizing that Fred had started a program in law studies, assigned him to the Judge Advocate General, and from there, upon his application for officer candidate school, he was sent back to Fort Benning, where he graduated six months later as a second lieutenant, commissioned as both an officer and a gentleman.

17

A FEW MORE months passed. Volodia, whose filmmaking unit was now located at one of Hollywood's major studios, called Fred, one day in May 1941.

'Remember the reunion? It's coming close. I'm requesting a leave to go to New York next month, and I think I can get it. What about you?'

'Sure,' said Fred. 'You didn't think I'd forget, did you? I made the reservations weeks ago. There's a lot of talk of war here in Washington, but since we're still at peace so far, I'll see you at the Plaza.'

At five minutes to twelve, heads turned when 2nd Lieutenant Fred May walked into the Palm Court in his impeccably tailored 'officer's pinks,' the regulation beige gabardine pants, which did have, indeed, something of a rose cast, the belted green jacket, with the cutout US brass pins on the collar, and the visored hat jeweled with the emblem *E Pluribus Unum*, which added height to his slight build and romantically shaded the pale gray eyes. He looked extravagantly handsome, and he was well aware of the impression he made.

Volodia stood up from a side table and came toward him, almost unrecognizable with the mass of curly hair now trimmed close, new horn-rimmed glasses, taller, it seemed, in his khaki uniform with the Special Services emblem and chevron braid on the sleeves. When he saw Fred's silver bar, he snapped to attention and saluted. Fred punched him in the ribs and they sat down at the table reserved for five.

'Eh, it's good to see you,' exclaimed Volodia, his accent

still as strong as when they had last seen each other, more than six months ago, 'but are you sure it's okay for a Tech Three to fraternize with an officer?'

'If the Tech Three happens to be an asshole,' said Fred amiably, 'I'd recommend sanctions.'

They ordered drinks. Both kept glancing toward the door.

'Do you suppose anyone will show? I'd better ask the waiter to hold the champagne,' said Fred. 'You look taller,' he remarked, eyeing Volodia critically.

'I am not taller,' answered Volodia. He added, with a reflexive look, 'I just stand straighter, I guess.'

They watched the entrance. Who would come? Which of the five who had parted on that warm afternoon, exactly a year ago, on the promenade overlooking the port of San Sebastián, which ones would be here today? They remained silent as minutes passed.

A commotion at a table near the entrance. A tall girl, probably a model, with carefully coiffed platinum hair, sitting with an older woman, was pushing her chair back and getting up in the flutter of her chiffon dress, arms extended, to embrace the man who had just walked in, small, dapper in a light summer suit.

'Mike! How lovely to see you! I thought you never ate lunch!'

'This is an exception, honey lamb. It's when I work that I never have lunch.'

Mischa! Fred and Volodia stood up, grinning. So, Mischa had made it too! He sat down, begged for an immediate drink. His story was long and involved, but it boiled down to this: From San Sebastián he had made his way to Madrid, where he'd found the friend he knew was there, David Epstein from Berlin. David was waiting for an affidavit that an uncle of his, a garment manufacturer in New York, was sending. A telegram to New York, and Uncle Samuel sent *two* affidavits. When they had obtained their visas, David and Mischa made their way to Morocco. From there, a plane took them to the Bahamas and from the Bahamas,

346

there was no problem reaching New York. Mischa, now Mike, was working for Juliet's, Mr Epstein's wholesale dress firm. As for Dave, he had shown no interest in business and was studying English literature at Columbia University. Mischa was responsible for the ads that appeared in the trade journals and in the wholesaler's cataloges. The girl at the table over there was a model with whom he worked occasionally. No, he hadn't heard anything from Isaac and Herschel. Nobody had, apparently. It was getting late, would they show?

Fred gestured for the champagne. They reminisced happily, their eyes still fixed on the entrance. No sign of Isaac and Herschel.

Just as the champagne arrived, wheeled in, in its silver bucket on a stand, a maître d' approached the table.

'Mr May?' he asked tentatively, looking at Mischa, the only one of the group in civilian clothes.

'I'm May,' said Fred.

The maître d' proffered a silver tray, on which rested a battered yellowish card, written in smudged pencil, with the address:

Mr Fred May
Palm Court, Hotel Plaza
New York, Amerika

(A scribbled mention, in the corner, asked to hold the card for this date.)

Lieber Fred, Volodia and Mischa,

Shalom! We write this from Cyprus, where the British are holding us for the moment, but someday we will be in Palestine. Then, we will have come home.

We wish you health and happiness. *Mazel tov!*

Next year in Jerusalem.

Isaac and Herschel

347

The three men remained silent. The past, so close, and yet so far removed, already dimming in their memories, was here, tangible, in the grimy postcard.

'So,' said Fred, breaking the silence, and propping the card against two champagne glasses, 'so, we *are* all here today after all!'

Volodia removed his glasses, and blew his nose. Mischa smoothed his already thinning hair, and, to break the tension, suggested that they invite Millie, the model at the nearby table, whose companion was leaving. She came over and sat down, in a cloud of warm, floral perfume that Fred recognized instantly in quick, heart-wrenching nostalgia. Ilse never used anything else.

'You are wearing Arpège, aren't you?'

Millie was pleasantly surprised that these guys in uniform should know a French Lanrin perfume! She smiled, and then shook her head, ruefully.

'I'm at the end of my last bottle, I'm afraid. You can't get it from France anymore . . . Don't they have a war, or something, over there?'

A few weeks after the Palm Court reunion, sitting at his desk in Washington, Fred was reading a letter from his mother. He had, of course, been in touch with her since his arrival in the United States, and he knew that she was happy in Australia.

Ilse wrote, in her neat, Gothic-inspired script:

My sweet,

Anton is no longer working for Monsieur Lavine, who seems to have closed down his Paris business and, as far as we know, may even have disappeared. We fear the worst, with the Nazis occupying Paris, but there are no communications at all with Europe anymore, so we are in the dark about what might have happened to him and his family. How sad! The madness is everywhere now in these poor countries . . .

But here, at least, things are quiet. Anton was able to transfer from Lavine's to an American company from New York, Mandel Gems and Jewelry Co., and he continues doing the same work as a buyer, just as he was doing for Monsieur Lavine. So we are relatively secure for the moment.

We have acquired a big station wagon, camping equipment, and we travel, sometimes for ten days, two weeks at a time. I always go with Anton, because it was so long until I could be with him that we wouldn't be parted for a moment now. We drive out in the country. Much of it is just barren expanse, the Outback, parched beyond belief. It is so hot and dusty that most of the inhabitants of the small mining towns live in dugout houses. The only tree we've seen in Coober Pedy had been built out of welded iron bars for children to play in!

We camp out at night in the desert, we build a fire, and there is nothing but a great silence and the night and the starry sky around us, except that we can hear wild dingoes, sometimes very close, only the fire keeps them away. Anyway, Anton, you know him, always has a gun at hand. We eat, and then we go to sleep under all those stars, in our big sleeping bag. My sweet, if I dared be happy, after all that has happened and is still happening now, I would say that I am happier than I have ever been in my life before. Could you understand that? Perhaps not, until the day you love someone the way I love Anton . . .

We have met several people from Germany, even some from Düsseldorf, but nobody has heard from your father. Do you have any news? I know he doesn't want to hear from me, but still, I feel so guilty that sometimes at night I cannot sleep, and I wonder if he is all right. I do hope he went back to Switzerland!

Anton is going to Canberra sometime soon to arrange

our visas for America. Since he works now for an American firm, he thinks visas can be arranged without too much delay.

I am so proud of you, my sweet! Your picture, with that uniform and the hat that makes you look so divinely handsome, is always with me. You are my other love.

Mutti

The postal mark, from Port Augusta, was three weeks old. Fred left the letter on his desk when he went out to lunch. He had been back only a couple of hours when a call came to his desk. 'Lieutenant May? Sir, could you please come to the commanding officer's office ASAP, on the double? There's a transatlantic call for you, from Australia, military priority.'

Fred smiled; Anton is good at arranging things. He must have gained access to a military phone, and he is calling to announce he has the visas, but really to be able to tell Ilse that he heard my voice. He was grinning as he stepped into the CO's office.

The connection was poor, static grinding through the words, and something that sounded like great winds sweeping through. He could not distinguish any words. So he said, then shouted, 'Hello? Hello? This is Fred. Anton, is that you? Anton, can you hear me? This is Fred. Anton?'

A silence. Howls of the winds.

'Hello, this is Fred. Is this Anton?'

A voice finally came through, but it wasn't Anton's. It was Ilse's, but so distorted that at first he wasn't sure. 'Mother? Mutti? Is that you? This is Fred. Yes. Fred here. Can you hear me?'

Was it sobs he heard over the cosmic winds?

'My sweet, my sweet, this is so terrible, I cannot tell you . . . It is too terrible, too awful, I can't, I can't . . .'

Silence again. This time, he was certain he heard agonized sobs.

'Mother? Mother? Listen to me. Where are you? Are you calling from a military phone? Mother, I understand. Don't try to speak. Listen – if there is someone there with you, ask that person to take the phone. You hear me, Mother? I don't want you to try to talk.'

A second or two passed. Another voice came on, a clipped Australian accent.

'Hullo? Leftenant Morris, here.'

'Leftenant Morris, this is Lieutenant May. My mother seems unable to speak. Could you please tell me what's the matter?'

Lieutenant Morris cleared his throat.

'Well, ah . . . I say, this is most distressing, most distressing indeed, but I am afraid there has been an accident.'

'What sort of an accident?'

'An accident, I fear, that involved a light lorry-type vehicle, also, most unfortunately, the lives of three members of our military personnel and one civilian . . . unauthorized civilian, I daresay . . .'

One civilian? Anton then, no doubt. What in the world had happened?

'A slightly irregular situation, you understand, but in view of the fact . . . Ah . . . No charges will be pressed, indeed. Most distressing.'

'I appreciate your cooperation, Leftenant,' said Fred as patiently as he could, 'but could you be a little more precise? Was the civilian in question my mother's husband?'

'It would appear,' stammered the lieutenant nervously, 'that this is the case. I will try to give you what information we have, according to the report we have just obtained. If I may say, I am frightfully sorry, mate.'

According to the report the Australian Military authorities had received, Anton and three Aussie officers had taken the 'light lorry-type vehicle' out on an unauthorized hunting trip, near Mount Arden, in the foothills of the North Flinders Range.

Somewhere – Fred was totally unfamiliar with the

geography of that area and the place names he heard meant nothing to him – the car seemed to have missed a curve, and driven off the road into a ravine, rolled over and burned. This was an untraveled region, and it took some time before the vehicle was listed as missing. Coincidentally, Mrs Anton Samelnov appeared at the military post, concerned because she had heard no news from her her husband. A search party was sent, and the car was found, after much backtracking, since it wasn't visible from the road, and only on the third day after it had disappeared.

'There were no survivors, of course,' said Fred, his throat tight.

'None, unfortunately. As a matter of fact, you understand, Leftenant, ah, I don't know how to put this but . . . The fire was quite destructive, of course, and then wild animals had been there. So the . . . ah . . . remains were found scattered over a fairly wide area, but there is little doubt as to the identity. I say, Leftenant, I am frightfully sorry,' repeated the Aussie officer.

'I see,' said Fred. 'My mother and I are grateful for your sympathy, as well as for your help. May I speak to her now?'

'I think she has composed herself somewhat,' said the Australian, relieved to end the difficult conversation. 'I'll hand her the telephone.'

Ilse's voice came on, firmer. No more sobs. Only so strained that Fred could barely recognize it.

'It was God's way,' she said, 'to punish me for what I have done. Now, I understand why it happened. My crime in leaving your father and you was so great that it called for the worst punishment. So, God gave me Anton, and he gave me happiness, and then he took Anton away. Now, it is not only the burden of what I did to your father that I will have to bear, but it is Anton's death.' Her voice strangled. A silence, then firm and strong again. 'You see, I am as guilty of Anton's death as if I had killed him myself. Now, I must atone, so that God doesn't take you too.'

Silence. The cosmic winds howled.

'Mutti, Mutti,' cried Fred. 'Listen to me. Don't be foolish. You are not guilty of anything. Listen to me. Are you there? Are you there? Answer me.'

But the line had gone dead. Call back? The duty officer shook his head; there was no record of the origin of the call. Fred ran to the post office, sent telegram after telegram to his mother's address in Port Augusta. But no answer came. He called Mandel Gems and Jewelry in New York. Mr Mandel hadn't even heard of Anton's death; he was appalled, but knew nothing and could do nothing, except repeatedly express his sympathy to Fred, with offers to help his mother in any way he could. Military priority calls to authorities in the Port Augusta area brought little result, the accident had been recorded, but no additional information had been received after the report transmitted on the phone by Lieutenant Morris.

Fred lived days of anguish.

Finally, a small package came in the mail, with an illegible postmark and an Australian stamp. The address was in Ilse's hand. The package contained a few papers, photos, her wedding ring, and a few small pieces of jewelry. The note enclosed said:

Mein Süsser,

God's hand has shown me the way. I know in my heart and I think I have known all along that your father is dead. God took him to punish me for what I did. But that wasn't enough. Only, He wanted me to taste happiness for a while, so the punishment would be greater, before he took Anton too. So now, Anton is gone, and I must bear the guilt for that, as well.

Only you remain, *mein Süsser.* I am going to atone to God and pray that, if I give Him my life in repentance, He will let you live. Heinz and Anton were innocent, just as you are. Only *I* am guilty.

I love you, *mein Süsser,* and I always will. Never

think of me with sadness; I will be in a place where guilt lets you rest.

Mutti

Two days later, an official letter came from the police division in Port Augusta informing Lieutenant May that the body of Mrs Anton Samelnov, nee Ilse Malinovsky, had been found, dead of a single gunshot wound. Near her hand was the revolver with which she had shot herself, and a note simply indicating that Lieutenant Fred May, with full address in the US Army, was her next of kin.

Fred's despair was second only to his anger ... Why couldn't he have been there, talked to her, why couldn't she have waited to see him? Had he done all he could? And why did she have to bear the burden of that immense, all-encompassing guilt? Of course she wasn't guilty, any woman would have done what she did. She deserved love and happiness, just as much as anybody else. Why, oh, why didn't he even try to go to her in Australia, after he learned of Anton's death? Perhaps he could have obtained a compassionate leave, if he had thought of trying and tried enough. Why, she was as innocent as ...

As me? thought Fred with lightning clarity. Remember, Siegfried Mayer, that night in Luzern after she left when your father was in such pain? Remember those days in the park in Düsseldorf? You weren't weighing two loves against each other then, Siegfried Mayer, or rather, yes, you were; but self-love weighed infinitely heavier than any other kind. You rejected your father, and that love of his, so touching, so helpless, those eyes of his behind his glasses. And those parcels of food he brought at night that you ate so disdainfully. You hated him because he was wrong all the time, he wasn't strong, he was ineffectual, life was too much for him, and yet he loved you more than himself. And then, that night he disappeared ... *that*, I can't bear to think about.

But tears and their relief wouldn't come to the burning gray eyes of Lieutenant May. Only rage and as he lay on his cot in the bachelor officers' quarters, wide-awake through night after night, devouring guilt.

I am the one God should have taken . . . But Fred was young, hungry for life, and life was surging all around him.

The sky had exploded over Pearl Harbor, and the United States had just plunged into the war, a war that now engulfed the hemisphere, with its demands, and yes, the urgency of a great adventure in which Fred would no longer be a hunted fugitive, but a full-share participant. After a while, he began to be able to sleep once again, removed from the horrors of the past, and even the tragedy of recent days, so that, eventually, although he did not forget, he continued living, and in time, could even look at Ilse's photograph without wanting to die.

Since no orders for his transfer had come, he registered at Georgetown University Law School, crammed several courses, and with the help of a dean rendered understanding by the unusual circumstances, he was able to pass the bar. He received his promotion to first lieutenant, only days before his orders finally came. He was first posted to Algiers, where American forces had already been established for over two years. One formality remained: he was to be naturalized as a US citizen. No military personnel could be sent overseas without US citizenship, because foreigners in American uniform and bearing arms would not fall under the Geneva Convention, the rules of war would not apply, and they could be shot on sight or executed upon surrender rather than taken prisoners.

The ceremony was short, hundreds of men in uniform, from a dozen countries, swore their allegiance to the United States of America and received their naturalization papers. The name Fred May became legally confirmed. Fred had reached that long-dreamed-of goal; he was at last an American in America. Better yet, he was also an officer and a lawyer.

After three months in Algiers, he was transferred again,

still to the Judge Advocate General, but in London, this time. He spent several months there, caught up in the fever of the last battle being fought on the Continent. From London he eagerly followed every minute of the liberation of Paris in August of '44. Finally, a few months later, new orders came. This time, he was assigned, still with the Judge Advocate section at headquarters of the Communication Zone, COM Z in military parlance, to Paris, France. His billet would be at the Royal Monceau Hotel, avenue Hoche, an area he remembered well from his youthful years in Paris. Lieutenant May's gray eyes lit up when, just as he was to ship to France, his promotion to captain arrived.

PART THREE

Paris, 1945

18

CAPTAIN MAY LANDED early on a sunny winter afternoon at Orly Field and found the ride through Paris, which he saw as little changed in spite of all intervening events, intoxicating in itself. Now, as he surveyed his billet, he had to admit that the Royal Monceau lived up to his expectations. True, as a mere captain, he didn't rate a suite. Those were reserved for generals and some of the bird colonels.

But his third-floor room looked directly down on the majestic avenue Hoche. When he stepped out onto the balcony, and leaned on the wrought-iron railing, he was surprised to find the Arch of Triumph so close to the left, a looming presence, much larger and more imposing than he had remembered.

The decor of the room was European palace hotel style, of an approximate Louis XV persuasion: caned curved headboard, inlaid rosewood commode under a large rococo mirror, a pair of matching bergères lined up along the edge of the Savonnerie carpet. Such as it was, it quite satisfied his idea of what Paris should hold in store for him this time around.

Ever since landing, Fred's memories had been of those other encounters he had had with the fickle city. I first came here as a hunted refugee of the Nazis, he reminisced, wearing another boy's clothes, charitably donated. Later, I left as a prisoner of the government of the Third French Republic, an enemy alien under armed guard. And now ... Well, look at me now, will you! I've returned once more, this time a victor in a victorious army, having survived the fall of the Third Republic. Paris, you cannot keep me away, it seems. Fortunes of war indeed! I wonder what guise I'll assume next? Soldier, beggar, or king? It would have to be as a king, since I've been here, let's say, as a virtual beggar, and have come back this time as a soldier.

Fred unpacked with care, undressed, and took a long, luxurious bath in the marble tub, noticing, for the first time in months, the gold cross he always wore but tended to forget. Now he saw it shining through the rich lather on his tan chest. He shaved, splashed on just a hint of cologne, smoothed the waves from his black hair. He dressed slowly, enjoying the fresh shirt, knotted his tie, put on his pressed officer's pinks and his new short Eisenhower jacket. His image, reflected in the baroque mirror, convinced him the Eisenhower wasn't dressy enough for a night at the Royal Monceau, so he replaced it with his best belted green jacket. Much more suitable, said the mirror.

On the desk, next to a bronze inkwell stabbed with a fountain pen disguised as a quill, his hat was resting where he had thrown it. Too bad he couldn't wear it indoors, it added to his height and shaded his pale eyes in a way women found irresistibly romantic. But tonight, he would stay right here at the hotel, where the gala Saturday dinner would be followed by a dance, a visiting stateside big band providing the music. Later, he might take some of his colleagues from the Judge Advocate General for a night on the town. He knew his way around Paris in general, and Montmartre in particular, his French was flawless, so they could have no better guide to the more exotic entertainment the city had to offer.

He walked leisurely down the wide, curving stairs, his footsteps cushioned by the thick red carpet. A crowd in uniform was milling in the vast mirrored lobby. In the dining room, tables were already filling. An abundance of brass, of course. A few women, WACs, WAVES, in uniform, most of them eagerly escorted. A few French girls too. Most of them are not worth a second look, thought Fred disdainfully. Frowzy, frumpy broads, the kind these officers wouldn't even glance at, back home. But here, starved for female companionship, anything seemed more tempting to them than another evening spent in the exclusive company of men. Personally, Fred preferred, at least tonight, not to spoil the splendor of the evening, of the grand hotel, and – all right, he'd admit it – his own immaculate person, by associating with girls who didn't belong in a place like this, with their vulgar voices, their flawed teeth, their too short skirts with uneven hemlines.

Still, there were a few who weren't too bad. The tall brunette with long hair in a black suit, standing near the dining-room door in the midst of an admiring group, for instance. Too tall, not his type, but good-looking and with style. How he admired those waists you could encircle with your hands! French girls had always had small waists, but never as narrow as he saw them now. Nothing to it, he thought, they just starved for four years . . .

Another girl was walking in, dark, too, perched on those high platforms that ought to have looked clunky but instead put a lithe, dancing grace in her step. She smiled at him flirtatiously over the head of her approaching date. Ah, thought Fred, Paris is still Paris, and a damn better Paris than last time, even. It's good to be alive and to have won the war.

All the chandeliers were blazing in the vast dining room, gleaming on the white napery, just as they'd shone a few months earlier on the assemblage of German officers. The tables reserved for members of the Judge Advocate General were already filled when Fred arrived and took the last place. He knew most of the other officers, whom he'd met in Washington, London, or Algiers, and he shook hands all around. Hopefully, he surveyed the table for signs of gourmet French food. *Hélas!* There were relishes composed of carrot sticks, celery, and large canned olives resting in glass dishes filled with crushed ice. Stewards were serving plates of Virginia ham, sweet potatoes, canned green beans, and a square of red Jell-O, its edges melting into the gravy. No wine, these were army premises and only coffee was served with the food. Sliced white bread and pats of butter completed the imported fare. Fred frowned – the three-star dinner he had been looking forward to would have to wait for another night, if it was available at all in a city famished for several years.

He ate little, listening absently to his colleagues who were discussing a proposed modification of the court-martial procedure, in which he felt not the slightest interest at the moment. His mood was dreamy. Was there truly something ineffable about Paris? Was it electric? Magnetic? What was it they said about those telluric currents that crisscross the earth with beneficial effects, long understood by primitive men, and which influenced early settlement in some privileged places of which Paris is claimed as the prime example? He was filled with an inexplicable expectancy. It is, he thought, as though I were poised at the very edge of the world, looking over. He was acutely conscious of his own smooth good looks in the impeccable uniform, and he had a sudden premonition that something, just as perfect as himself, would come his way, out of the golden glow that bathed the room, dispensed by rows of endlessly reflected lights.

The meal was over. More coffee was being poured. A hum of voices filled the air, strains of music were beginning to waft into the room from the ballroom on the other side of the great hall. America has done well for me, Fred thought, but tonight, it is surpassing itself, throwing in Paris to top off its gift package. He leaned back in his chair, smoothed his glossy hair with the palm of his hand, lit a cigarette, exhaled blue smoke . . .

Major Steve Jarvis, sitting on his right, touched his arm. 'Look at that blond over there, sitting next to the fat bird colonel. Now, that one is really something, don't you think?'

Back in the States and in civilian life, Stephen Baylor Jarvis II was a socialite, from an old family listed in the Social Register as 'from New York City and Newport, Rhode Island,' and his tastes were the kind Fred usually embraced as his own. Now as he leaned behind Jarvis to see the girl, he was forced to admit that, once again, the major had demonstrated his unerring good judgment.

On the other side of the vast room, at a table also occupied by two colonels and a two-star general, Fred discovered a delicate profile, with a slightly turned-up nose, sweetly rounded brow accented by pale blond hair tightly pulled back into an enormous, smooth chignon, low on the nape of the neck. The girl wore a silver-colored dress, of some silky fabric, artfully draped around slender bare shoulders. She was listening to the fat colonel, whose guest she seemed to be, her head turned up, attentive, smiling, a hint of a dimple at the corner of her lips. Fred gazed at her in rapt concentration. Here at last was a woman to match the perfection of his world tonight. Smooth pale gold hair, pale silvery dress, she made the other women in the room look disheveled and unkempt. Was *she*, perhaps, what was going to happen to him?

I can't keep staring like this, thought Fred. I just have to be watchful and figure out some way to talk to her later. Let's see. If I move my chair a little, can I see her without craning my neck? A little more. Now, I have her in my field of vision.

The girl was leaning over now, her attention turned to the general opposite her, whose face Fred couldn't clearly see. She is better than beautiful, he decided, she is exquisite. But . . . why do I feel I've seen her before? Ridiculous. If I'd met a girl who looked like that, I would surely remember her.

He saw her laugh, throwing her head back just enough to show the taut line of her throat. I'm sure I've seen her before, but where? The movies? No. Then where? The feeling was exasperating, as if he were trying to reach an object on a shelf, but no matter how he stretched, it still remained just out of reach.

'I'm certain I've seen that woman before,' he whispered to Jarvis. 'I know her from somewhere, "long ago and far away," as the song says, but I can't place her now. I'll find out tonight, though, I swear.'

'Think hard,' advised Jarvis. 'Was it when you spent your summers in France?'

Fred had never told his colleagues about his real past. Instead, faithful to the promise made to himself long ago, Fred May had killed and buried Siegfried Mayer, and created a vaguely defined but aristocratic American past for himself, one that featured adolescent school years in an exclusive prep school in Switzerland and summers of travel in France to explain his fluency in French and German.

'She must have hair way down past her waist,' sighed Jarvis. 'I was always a sucker for long hair.' For all his sophistication, Major Jarvis was innocent of the wiles of French fashion that year. 'It must be something when she unpins that hair,' he continued. 'That's a sight I'd give a lot to see . . .' Then he realized Fred wasn't even listening, all interest focused across the room. Stephen Jarvis II was nothing if not a gentleman. 'But if you think you know her . . . well, it's only fair. I won't cramp your style. Good luck, Fred. I hope you can get near her, but it won't be easy, with that wall of brass.'

A group of unescorted WACs walked in, and although no whistles would shrill from this gentlemanly crowd, Fred could feel interest perk up. Several of his colleagues stood up casually and strolled over, adjusting their ties, to where the women stood, trying to beat out the others already converging with the same studied indifference. Jarvis joined them, turning his head to wink at Fred before crossing into the hall.

Fred lit another cigarette and watched the general at the girl's table get up, imitated by the colonels, and the minor scramble to help the blond girl with her chair. He made a wager with himself. If she's too tall for me, I'll drop it. She stood up.

No, she wasn't too tall. Just right, and probably even smaller than she looked, perched on those precarious platforms. She had that breathtaking waist, of course, but also breasts that could make a man's throat go dry. The general, big-bellied and balding, was holding her elbow, and the two colonels followed, practically wagging their tails like eager puppies, thought Fred disdainfully. As she passed his table, their eyes met. Was she wondering, too, whether they had met before? But she turned to listen to some remark from the general, who wanted to make sure every man in the room saw the spectacular woman hanging on his every word. The group was walking in the direction of the ballroom. Fred made up his mind. He'd give them some time to get settled, and for a couple of dances, too, since she'd have to dance at least with the general and with the fat colonel. Then he'd make his move. He mustn't wait too long, though, otherwise she would be on the dance floor and he could never get close to her.

Twelve minutes went by. Long enough? No, another five. He checked his watch. Now! Fred stood up, adjusted his tie, touched his hair, strolled toward the ballroom and stood at the entrance, watching.

The general was telling jokes, at which the colonels were laughing appreciatively, and the young woman – did she understand any of them? – was listening politely, smiling, laughing even, in a well-bred show of restrained gaiety. Colonel Wainwright was making the most of his discovery – the epitome of the sort of date an officer and a gentleman should aspire to in Gay Paree. A real officer, of course, one with breeding and manners, membership in the right country club, preferably a couple of Lincolns in his garage back home. Now, those thirty-day wonders crowding around these days, well – officers, maybe, this was wartime, after all – but gentlemen? Don't make me laugh. Those were something else. Wops, wogs, hebes, and God only knew what else the war had dredged up. Let *them* get by with whatever they found in the streets. But you, brother officers and country-club members, eat your heart out – just look what Daddy Wainwright has found.

The orchestra played 'Kiss Me Once, and Kiss Me Twice'

and Fred guessed she was humming the song to herself, softly. An untouched glass of Coke was in front of her. He took a deep breath. Now. He moved forward.

'I beg your pardon, sir.'

Colonel Wainwright frowned at the intrusion. A handsome, dark-haired young captain was standing respectfully beside his chair, in a version of relaxed attention. Not a bad-looking boy, good manners, thought Wainwright, his scowl softening a little.

'Sir, ah . . . I am Captain Fred May. I was wondering, sir, would you think me out of line if I asked for the honor of being . . . ah . . . introduced to this lady?'

Fred had put on the hint of an earnest stammer. His gray eyes were lowered, avoiding the girl, but she had heard his name. She remained very still.

'Well, my boy,' growled Colonel Wainwright, 'this is a brash move, I must say . . . Still, we don't want to discourage initiative on the part of our junior officers, now, do we?' he added in the direction of the general.

'Besides,' chuckled the general, 'the lady might enjoy the company of someone younger and better-looking than you, eh, Wainwright? Pull up a chair, my boy.'

But Fred couldn't sit yet, because, with a flourish, and eager to display the full effect of her title, Colonel Wainwright was saying, as loudly as he decently could, hoping to be heard at the neighboring tables, 'Countess de Blazonac, may I present to you Captain Fred May, of the Army of the United States?'

Playing her musical-comedy countess role to the hilt, Chantal graciously extended her hand, raised high, bent at the wrist. Fred bent low over it, not quite touching his lips to her fingers. Approval shone on the faces of the brass. The boy had manners. On the suspiciously swarthy side, but still a gentleman, apparently.

'Sit down, sit down,' growled Wainwright, pleased after all with the way things were turning out. 'I see you're with the Judge Advocate General. Are you a lawyer in civilian life?'

'I am, sir,' replied Fred, still as close to attention as one can be when seated. 'Graduated from Georgetown.'

'Where are you from, Captain?' asked the general.

A split-second pause. Where am I from? Düsseldorf, Germany, *that's* where I'm from, but it would hardly do in this place and in this company. Then he remembered how Jarvis answered the same question: 'From New York City and Newport, Rhode Island, sir,' murmured Fred smoothly. Perfect, mused the brass. Perfect. Breeding. Society. Money, too, no doubt. Still, I can't quite place his looks: Italian? Greek? No, he wouldn't have those manners. Irish? That's it, could be a black Irishman, there's some that are okay, down east . . .

A moment of silence, while the brass speculated on the ethnic origins of Captain May.

And during that moment, Chantal turned to face him. 'We have met before, Captain May, and I am disappointed that you do not remember me. Perhaps I have changed more than you have. Do you recall a town named Angoulême, in the southwest of France?'

Yes, of course, he remembered now! This was the schoolgirl who, with that other, the plump one – what were their names? Chantal and Martine, that's it – had spoken to his friends and him through the barred gate of the detention camp, who had driven them, grinding gears all the way, in that purloined truck to the Spanish border, who had given him the cross he still wore today under his khaki shirt as a badge of his new identity . . .

With total recall, he relived in less than a second that frantic summer night, in June 1940, just hours ahead of the invading Nazis. At the same time, panic gripped him: she's going to tell how we met – the camp, the guards – how she took us to the border, saved us! It will make her the heroine of one hell of an adventure, and expose me as a fraud and a liar. Me, Fred May from New York City and Newport, rescued by her from a French detention camp for German citizens. What do I do now? Run from disgrace? Mutter some excuse and slink away? They are all asking

367

her: 'When? Where? It must be quite a story! And what about you, May, you dog, how could you forget a woman like that?' Do I step outside and throw myself under a passing truck?

But wait. Easily, effortlessly, Chantal was lying. Not lying, exactly, but at the very least not telling the precise truth. Had she instinctively guessed the complexities of American society, of which she knew nothing, and couldn't possibly understand? In any case, she had allied herself with him, against all others.

'Oh, I am afraid it isn't much of a story . . . That was . . . Let me see . . . That was years ago, wasn't it, Captain? I was still in school and you . . . You were with some friends. I don't think we saw each other again, it was just that once.'

She turned to the brass, with an airy gesture of her hand. 'I must have been wearing my school uniform, and I don't think he paid any attention to me. I was too much of a child for him, then. Of course, I'll confess that I wasn't quite as blond as I am now.'

The brass chuckled appreciatively. All right, all right, thought Wainwright, smugly pleased with his unerring intuition. Traveled in Europe, associated with the gentry there. Good boy.

'I bet you parlay French pretty well, don't you, May?' brayed the general.

'I do, sir,' admitted Fred modestly, still weak-kneed, but the panic slowly ebbing. 'And German, too. Learned both in school in Switzerland.'

'Well,' continued the general, anxious to contribute to the camaraderie of the moment, 'write down the name of your CO, and I'll make it a point of calling to tell him he's got himself a damn good man in his section . . .'

An angel passed. Chantal sipped her Coke daintily. The band struck up a slow number:

> Long ago and far away,
> I dreamed a dream one day . . .

Fred's circular bow included all the officers at the table. 'Don't you agree, ah ... sir, don't you agree that there'd be no excuse if I didn't ask the Countess to dance this number with me?'

'Go right ahead,' chuckled the general. 'Go right ahead. You won't find a more appropriate one.'

Fred stood up and bowed ceremoniously in front of Chantal, escorted her to the dance floor, put his arm around that tiny waist. 'There are so many things to tell you,' he whispered against her hair, 'that I don't know how to begin. I'm trying to decide which is the most important so I can tell you that first. I know: I'm still wearing your cross. Always have, since the night you gave it to me.'

'I am glad, and I'm sure it protected you. So you *did* make it to America, after all. And you fought in the war? And now you are back? There were many times when I thought that all that happened that night almost five years ago had only been a figment of my imagination. Can it all be true?'

'I'm not sure either. Tonight, it all seems like an illusion, something done with mirrors.'

A warm scent rose from the cleft of her breasts, the tuberose and jasmine overtones of Guerlain's L'Heure Bleue. He tightened his arm around her waist. So many questions crowding to be asked, they both thought.

'What became of Martine?'

'It is terrible and a mystery. She disappeared, and no one knows what happened to her. Her parents keep hoping that she was deported, through some terrible error, and that she'll return when the war is over ...'

'These five years must have been hell,' whispered Fred. 'I know anything one might say tonight would sound like clichés, but I, for one, can understand what it must have been like over here.'

'Yes, many awful things have happened, and many people are dead. What about your friends? Volodia?'

'Volodia is now Roger Volod. He's doing fine, making films for the army at a studio in Hollywood. He spoke of

Martine, and we would have written except, as you know, all communication with occupied countries was cut off. He wrote me a few months ago that he planned to stay in California after the war and work in the movie industry. It seems he's a very talented director. Remember, he *said* he was going to go to Hollywood? Well, he made it.'

'And Mischa? Has he lost all his hair?'

'Mischa became Mike with very thin hair, yes, and he was in New York, working in the garment industry. Then, he was drafted and fought with the infantry at the landing in Normandy. He was killed last June, near Sainte-Mère-Eglise, in the Cotentin Peninsula on D day plus nine.'

'So sad, so sad. Poor Mischa! Another dead . . . And what about Herschel and Isaac?'

'They must be in Palestine by now. Last time I heard from them, they were in Cyprus on their way. There's talk of a Jewish state being formed someday soon, in spite of British opposition. And you? You tell me about you.'

Chantal told him that she had married a man who owned an estate near her parents and that was how she had acquired that ridiculous title which impressed Colonel Wainwright so much. She had a little girl named Mariès, who was three, pretty, imperious, and dark-haired. There had been a great deal of Resistance fighting in her area. Her husband had died. She had come to live in Paris, and she worked for a famous painter.

The way she told the story, deftly telescoping details, he might have understood that her husband had died fighting in the Resistance. She did not say so, specifically, but her story subconsciously blended Renaud and Anthenor into one. I'll elaborate later if I have to, she thought, but right now I don't want to . . .

> Long the skies were overcast,
> But now the clouds have passed:
> You're here at last!

sang the vocalist. Fred held her close, smooth blond hair fragrant near his face.

'All evening, I knew there was something special in the air. An expectancy. Something extraordinary was going to happen. And it has. When I saw you across the room, and I knew I'd met you before, but I couldn't remember where, because you look so stunningly different, I was sure that what was going to happen was *you*.'

She looked up; his gray eyes were tender. Fred could do great things with his eyes when he wanted to, and tonight, he wanted to very much.

He saw no need to tell her of his desperate odyssey, which had ended so miraculously. Perhaps, later, he would, but the less said the better. He enjoyed his new persona too much to tarnish it with other, less glamorous images.

Tonight, he was Captain Fred May, dancing with a Parisian countess under the ornate ceiling of the grand ballroom at the Royal Monceau. Male eyes at every table reflected envy. Whatever war was still going on now, at the receding front, in the distant Ardennes forests, mattered little to him now. Fred had won his own personal war, and he had won it gloriously. They danced as many dances as possible with the brass cutting in good-naturedly now and then. But none of Fred's colleagues was bold enough to cut in, and Jarvis, sitting at a large table across the dance floor, with several other officers and WACs, gave him a discreet victory sign over Chantal's shoulder.

They danced to 'Did You Ever See a Dream Walking?' and to 'I'll Walk Alone,' and to 'Smoke Gets in Your Eyes,' and 'Lullaby of Broadway.' Chantal was moving as in a dream. All ballroom dancing had been strictly forbidden throughout the Occupation, as the Germans saw danger in groups of young people, especially the young men, gathering without their supervision, under the dangerous influence of music and wine. It was only in the years before the war, when she was a teenager, that Chantal had danced a few times at private parties and at the summer gatherings the old Countess organized at Blazonac. The thought of Blazonac and Anthenor surged into her memory, bittersweet and tragic, but she refused to let it claim her.

By the time the evening was over, she found it hard to emerge from the trance of the insidious rhythms, Fred's arms and his melting gaze.

The traditional 'Goodnight, Sweetheart' was ending. Fred escorted her back to her table, bowed and said an overly formal good-bye. He murmured again what a pleasure it had been to renew this old acquaintance, and even begged for the honor of calling on her at some later date. But of course, while dancing, they had already made a date for the next night, and he knew he would see her the night after that, and the night after. Fred had already made up his mind.

Colonel Wainwright and the general took her home, in the general's car, with the starred flags streaming on the fenders. And during the ride, the general, who had spoken of his lovely wife all evening with tears of emotion gleaming in his eyes, kept brushing her breast and squeezing her knee every time the car took a turn and gave him an excuse to press against her.

19

To call Fred May's courtship of Chantal overdone, overpowering, overostentatious, overenthusiastic – *overanything* – would not begin to do it justice. It was also overkill.

It might seem Fred had inherited from poor Heinz a lack of common sense where matters of measure were concerned. As soon as he had decided that he would marry Chantal – that she was the perfect match to forever erase the stigma of a past he wanted to put behind him and help perfect the new image he had so carefully constructed – he threw himself into the conquest with wild abandon and a great deal more energy than necessary. Indeed, Chantal was all too ready to be enchanted by this handsome, impeccably groomed, sexy man, his charms enhanced by the aura of his uniform. Yet she soon found herself to be in turn dizzy, dazzled, grateful, amused, bewildered, and even a little worried by his excess.

Gifts arrived several times a day: flowers in great bouquets, perfume from Guerlain, anything scented with L'Heure Bleue, the only perfume she ever wore – cologne, toilet water, lotion, bath salts, powders. The PX was combed for anything that might remotely tempt her, all carried upstairs by an impressed concierge, herself surfeited with cartons of Phillip Morris or Old Gold cigarettes and bottles of whiskey from the PX.

Then, there was Fred himself, in love. No, not in love. That would do insufficient justice to the feelings he was striving to project. Possessed, agonizing, dying over an overwhelming passion, would be closer. He did not promise his love just 'forever.' It was 'forever and ever and ever after.' When he called her 'my love' he would add, 'my life, my everything.'

She was a goddess, the embodiment of his mortal dreams. Chantal was flattered, of course – what woman wouldn't be? – but her common sense told her it was altogether too much. He couldn't possibly feel as much emotion as he expressed. Nobody could. And there were odd moments when the gray eyes seemed to forget their part in the play and remained strangely cold and detached, almost calculating, in spite of the passionate words spoken by the lips.

He wants me, no doubt about that, she thought, but he doesn't have to go through this elaborate display for my benefit! He is a very attractive man, by far the most desirable one I know. Those incredible eyes, that skin, smooth, dark, and creamy, those even features, why, I'd go to bed with him in a minute! But he doesn't even ask, and he ignores all my hints and suggestions. Instead, he produces this elaborate minuet of romance, orchestrated entirely for my benefit. It is nice, I can't deny it, and extremely flattering, but there's something wrong somewhere. What is it?

She consulted with Marjo, who had remained her best friend. Marjo was deeply in love with her colonel from Texas, and they were making plans to marry as soon as, the war over, the interdict on fraternization would be lifted and members of the US forces would have permission to marry 'aliens.' The word amused Chantal and Marjo no end, because in French *aliéné* meant 'insane' and they felt it must represent fairly well the idea American officialdom had of young women such as they were – starved to near perfection of body, perched on unstable pedestals of wood or cork, dressed in extravagant fashions with padded shoulders and cinched waists, adorned with false and misleading hairpieces, barely able to communicate with the men they captivated. Yet, they seemed to hold an appeal that couldn't be matched by the stateside girls in their neat skirts and sweater sets, sensible shoes, short hair parted with a barrette, whose pictures the men carried and produced on every occasion.

'No mystery. They are over there, and we are over here.' Chantal laughed.

Marjo was now working exclusively as a high-fashion model, showing the collections of Raphaël and the new couturier who was the new rage, Jacques Fath. Since she and Chantal were about the same size, all Chantal had to do was stop at the models' dressing room at Fath or Raphaël, and borrow for the evening whichever of the outfits from the current collection caught her fancy, even shoes, hats, and bags to complete the effect. So, at no expense she was dressed by the two reigning couturiers in Paris. None of this elegance was wasted on Fred, who commented delightedly on every new dress, suit, coat, or accessory.

Neither Marjo nor Chantal ever gave a thought to that passionate scene in Domergue's atelier, on that winter day when war was at its darkest. It was part of a bygone era, dark ages of the mind, of the war, of the years without men.

Marjo had come up with a theory concerning Fred's tenacious chastity. 'Don't worry, *chérie*,' she told her, 'I knew a man like that once who was insane over me. Yet, it took three months – three whole months – before I got him into bed, and believe me, all kinds of thoughts crossed my mind during that time. I even thought he was impotent, maybe. Well, I was wrong, it was nothing like that. When I finally got him into my bed, he was a tiger, I tell you, a tiger! Never had a better lover, until . . . And you know what the matter was, all that time?'

'*Aucune idée*. What?'

'Well, he finally confessed he'd been recovering from a venereal disease, and the doctor had told him to abstain for a while, or there would be danger of contagion. So it was for *me*, really, that he acted that way and three months beyond the doctor's limit for extra safety! Such heroic restraint, don't you think? Well, perhaps Fred is getting over something like that. Could you sort of ask him, tactfully?'

'I could never bring up such a subject . . . *Non, certainement pas*. You see, we are on such passionate terms, but at the same time, we are not very close. There is something . . . I don't know, something formal, almost distant, literary – as though he was quoting from a text when he tells me how he feels about me.'

'Perhaps it's because you don't understand him very well.'

'No, I don't think so. We speak French most of the time, anyway.'

'Well, perhaps then it is just because he wants to marry you, and that's the way they behave in America when they are serious and want to marry a woman.'.

'Did your colonel behave that way with you?'

'No, I dragged him to bed right away, but afterward, he seemed to feel terrible about it, for reasons I can't understand. Guilt of some sort. He is getting over it now, but for a few days, you'd have thought that the sight of a bed stirred up all sorts of dark thoughts in his mind . . .'

'Strange . . . There's a lot to learn about men from other countries,' mused Chantal. 'Now, if Fred were to ask me to marry him, I wouldn't say no. I might say perhaps, I might say yes, but I can tell you that I would not hesitate for one second to jump into bed with him. Those eyes! That skin! I am dying to feel that skin against me.'

'*Tais-toi*' – Marjo shrugged – '*tais-toi*, you make me want to try for a shot myself at your handsome Captain May. Intimacy with him must be delicious!'

Indeed, a few nights later, as they were walking along the Seine, in the twilight of that spring of 1945, just a few days after victory in Europe, VE day, had sent Paris, and the world, into another frenzy of joy and hope, Fred asked her to marry him.

'Please, marry me. Be my wife, and you will be the most adored, the most cherished woman who ever lived,' he whispered. Chantal, for all of her look of elegance and sophistication, had little experience with the expression of love and passion. Certainly neither Renaud's nonchalant courtship, nor the months of her brief, strange marriage to him could have taught her much. Anthenor, ardent and intense, had been a skillful lover on that one night – not even a night, just a few stolen hours – of which the memory still haunted her when she lay awake in her bed. But while Anthenor had expressed urgent and demanding desire and eternal commitment, she could recall no words of love, or even tenderness. There had been no need left unfulfilled, though, and words of love would have been superfluous to the extraordinary chemistry between them.

Now, love, in all its most precious forms – devotion, protection, passion – was lavishly offered. And perhaps a memory of long ago came to her then, a memory of that magic, elusive kingdom to which she had aspired as a child. Under the teachings of the good sisters, she had seen it for a time as the kingdom of Heaven, attained through martyrdom, and later she had aspired to the kingdom of perfection, the lofty, lonely peak earned by the faithful wife, the ideal mother. She had reached none, but had learned simply to survive and make a life for herself. Not so easy, she thought, not so easy at all in the troubled times through which she'd lived.

Blazonac had not been that kingdom. Would she find it in the even more nebulous and impossible-to-envision world where she would begin anew as Mrs Fred May? As Chantal May? Was there a rainbow arched over a new horizon? Was that where *Life* waited for her with open wings?

Fred's gray eyes were earnest, his words irresistible. 'Marry me, say that you will be my wife, and you will make me the happiest of men, the most fortunate of mortals . . . You will be my adored wife, cared for like no other.'

Wow . . .

Overwhelmed by the passion of the man who loved her so and wanted her with such burning purity – tempted

377

also by the adventure, by the unknown life he was offering her – Chantal accepted without further reflection. And why reflect? She would ultimately say yes, whether it was today or next week.

'Yes, I will marry you.'

How different this was from Renaud's casual proposal . . . Renaud? How many light-years ago had she known Renaud, anyway? The calendar said five years, but that meant nothing. Was she even the same person, or was it some distant acquaintance of hers who had stood next to him in front of the high altar of the village church?

Now that they were engaged, she thought Fred could drop his reserve, and she tried to indicate to him that it would be all right to do so. 'Do you want to come to my apartment? Perhaps stay the night?'

But Fred rejected the offer. She was his adored, his worshiped goddess, the one woman in the world who would soon be his wife. He respected her too much to diminish, to spoil in any way, the totality and the fullness of his love by . . . with . . .

Chantal, puzzled, thought perhaps Marjo was right, but she couldn't muster the courage to question him and resigned herself to sleeping alone one more night. Fred held her tight, kissed her smooth blond hair, her cheeks, her eyes, lightly touching his own soft yet firm lips to hers. She pressed against him, making him feel her breasts against his chest, and played the tip of her tongue against his mouth, trying to part his lips.

But he laughed nervously, strangely aloof, almost annoyed. 'It tickles,' he said. Then, he caught himself and added tenderly, 'Don't do that. You don't know how hard it is for me to control myself.'

But Chantal knew he was lying, and wondered if, in some way, and in spite of his extravagant protestation of love, he didn't find her repulsive. She brushed the thought aside, as his arms tightened around her again and he whispered still more endearments.

Then, he reminded her of a dinner party the next night, at Maxim's on the rue Royale, which would be attended by members of his office.

'Please, wear the white Raphaël dress, you know, the one with all the black embroidery and the tassels on the shoulders. And, please, do your hair with your big chignon hairpiece. Steve Jarvis will be there, and he keeps raving about how long your hair must be . . .'

'Didn't you tell him that it is fake? It's the Raphaël look this year, that's how they are showing the collection, because it balances well with the wide shoulder line. All the models wear hairpieces like that, it's no secret, nobody could possibly think it is real. It's just something you wear, almost like a hat. I'll tell him!'

'No, my sweetest love, don't tell him. Let him think your blond hair falls way down below your waist, in thick, heavy tresses. I like that. We talk about it a lot.'

Chantal laughed and shook her head, striking a Domergue pose, as she did every time she found herself at a loss. For she felt a tiny gnawing of unease, as though, under Fred's so easily controllable passion, she had perceived an ominous hint of voyeurism.

His courtship continued unabated in the weeks that followed. Caught up in the whirlwind, Chantal still wasn't quite free from all concern. First, there were her parents, who would have to be informed and whose consent and blessings, for good form and the sake of future relations, had to be sought and obtained. Then, there was Mariès, whom she wanted to bring back to Paris. Fred was enthusiastic about Mariès, spoke of winning her over and making himself worthy of her love, just as though she were a miniature Chantal.

Yet, all through those idyllic days, something was clearly bothering Fred. At first, Chantal thought it was only a matter of finding what he considered a suitable engagement ring. But he was now becoming single-minded over the matter.

'I don't *need* an engagement ring.' Chantal laughed.

'Please, don't worry about it. I am perfectly happy without it.'

But Fred was not. He described in detail the twin engagement rings his father and his uncle had presented to their future brides. No ring for his own marriage would be, in his eyes, a step backward – one totally inconsistent with what he saw as his steady social ascent, soon to be crowned by his marriage to a countess. (She chided herself, 'Didn't I feel the very same way about marrying a count myself?') There had to be a ring, a suitable one. And anyway . . .

'Anyway, what, *mon chéri*?'

'Nothing, darling, nothing. Don't trouble yourself about it. Please don't.'

But there was an unspoken question in his silences, so she forced the issue.

'Fred, you are becoming obsessive about the ring, and I can sense there's something you're aching to ask me. What *is* it?'

'All right,' he said, taking her hand in both of his over the dinner table, his gray eyes melting. 'All right, my adored love. Do you remember that night when you drove us to the Spanish border?'

'Of course. I remember very well. How could I possibly forget?'

'When we parted, you gave me your cross.'

'I did, and I'm so very glad you never took it off. It was as though we were meant to meet again, wasn't it?'

'And I, in turn, I gave you something too. Do you remember?'

'You gave me something? No, I don't recall. What was it?'

'Think hard. I took something out of a pouch, and I put it in your hand and told you not to lose it.'

'I don't . . . Wait a minute. I remember now! After Martine and I were back in our room, she was showing me the gold letter Volodia had given her, and she wanted to see what you had given me. I reached into the pocket of my school blazer. It was . . . Oh, I remember now!

Martine thought it was a pretty piece of glass, maybe a small crystal from a chandelier.'

Fred was shaking his head, face drawn, gray eyes darkened with something that might have been anger.

Chantal felt a twinge of fear. 'What was it, then? Was it really something else? Tell me.'

'My sweet, adored love, it wasn't a piece of glass. It was a nine-carat diamond, a pear-shaped, flawless, nine-carat diamond. I have been hoping you would wear it now as my engagement ring.' Anger was gone from his eyes. It had been only a fleeting shadow.

But now it was Chantal's turn to blanch. 'What in the world could I have done with it? I am sure it is long lost. Oh, Fred, you should have *told* me what it was. What could I know of diamonds? How could you give me something of such value and not explain?'

'I told you not to lose it. I wanted to give you something and that's all I had.'

He explained how his father had managed to smuggle some unset diamonds past the Nazis when they left Düsseldorf.

'They were part of the jewelry department's stock, in the store my family owned. My father took them out of the safe when we had to leave and he finally gave them to me to help my escape in case the situation worsened. Remember how I told you I was going to America? I knew they'd pay for my passage.'

Chantal was transfixed. Another revelation of Fred's past! How tame her war seemed compared to his! How generous of him! They were his lifeline and yet he gave me one. And *I* had to lose it! It didn't occur to her to wonder what had become of his father.

'As things turned out,' continued Fred, 'every time I thought of it later, I was glad I'd given it to you. It made all the difference in the long run.'

'You're not saying that to make me feel better?'

'No. I sold all but one of the stones to pay for my passage. I gave away the last one to obtain a visa to Uruguay, which turned out to be counterfeit. When they wouldn't let me land in Montevideo, if I'd still had one, I'd have used it to bribe the immigration official into allowing me into Uruguay. So, today, I'd be rotting away in some mildewed jungle at the end of the world. I'd never have seen you again. Instead, I *did* go to America and tonight, I'm here with you. We're in that fairyland of the 1900s, the Grande Cascade, under the trees of the Bois de Boulogne . . . If this isn't Paradise, then, my love, tell me what it is.' He kissed her palm, gazed tenderly into her eyes. 'And don't worry another minute about that stone.'

But Chantal was reacting to the lost gem in characteristic Arondel fashion. She was appalled. 'I have no idea what I did with it . . . Oh, Fred, I feel terrible. It's lost, and it's all my fault. Forgive me.'

She was thinking aloud, 'How could I possibly trace it? Wait. What did I do after I showed it to Martine? I must have put it back in the pocket of my blazer. But what became of that blazer? I'm pretty sure my mother had it washed, and then she put it away with the rest of my school uniform. She told me not too long ago that, when the time came, my complete Saint-André uniform was in La Prade, ready and waiting for my daughter. But, of course, the diamond would have fallen out in the wash . . . It had to.'

'Could it still be at the bottom of that pocket?' Fred insisted. 'It's worth looking!'

Chantal was pessimistic, but because she felt so guilty and to please Fred, she told him she'd go to La Prade the following weekend. Travel was easy again. The trains were running almost normally, temporary trestles crossing rivers where bridges had been blown up. She would take the gold cross with her, carefully hidden in a knotted handkerchief. She'd tell her mother she had suddenly remembered, after all these years, how she might have left her cross in the pocket of her school blazer. It would give her the excuse to look for the garment, search the pockets, and either come up triumphantly with the gold cross if she found the diamond, or if she didn't, to ask a million questions about who had washed the blazer, where, and try to trace the fate of the priceless stone.

Taking advantage of the same trip, she thought privately, she would tactfully inform her parents that she had met an American officer, a lawyer in civilian life, that . . . well, a certain feeling had developed between them, and he had expressed the desire to meet her parents and her daughter. Could she bring him to visit someday soon? And at that time she would also take Mariès back with her to Paris.

The following Saturday, Chantal arrived at Angoulême. The railroad station, destroyed by the Allied bombings a year earlier, had been replaced with temporary plywood shacks and a path in the center of the avenue de la Gare had been cleared of the rubble of its bombed-out houses.

Madame Arondel met her, wearing a dark silk print, indistinguishable from the ones she'd worn for years, accompanied by a new, trusted young driver named Loulou, and a newly acquired but prewar Citroën, identical to the ill-fated one the Maquis had destroyed. New cars would not be available for some time to come.

At La Prade, everything was back to normal, better tended even than before. Geraniums bloomed in scarlet profusion in new terra-cotta urns. The burned-out spot where the charred carcass of the car had stood for so long was obliterated by new grass. Inside the house, pristine order reigned again. Scarred walls had been repainted, woodwork and floors waxed to ultimate gloss, chairs reupholstered, new mirrors fitted into the frames, fresh curtains hung at the windows.

Mariès, who had been allowed to stay up to greet her mother, embraced her with an affection tempered only by the eagerness to show how big Arsène had grown, and how many, many baby ducks and baby rabbits there were now in the barnyard and in the hutches.

Anna cried, wiping her eyes on the corner of her apron, and gave Chantal the latest news of Charles. He was still in Paris, still working as a municipal guard, but as soon as he had completed the seven years of seniority which would guarantee him a small pension for his old age, he would resign his position. There was only a year and a half to go. Then, they would be married, and they would take over one of the Blazonac farms, Hautevallée, the one bordering on the upper lake and which had been abandoned for years. The buildings were being restored, and Monsieur Arondel would lend them the basic livestock and equipment to get started. Another red-tiled roof repaired, another piece of Blazonac returned to productive life.

Chantal found her father aged and tired-looking. He had lost weight and complained of vague but persistent pains, Madame Arondel confided.

'Overwork,' she scolded, 'no doubt. You have no idea of the amount of time, effort, and money we are pouring into Blazonac! As for your cross, it couldn't possibly be there,' she maintained. 'I examined that blazer, and everything else, when I put your school things away, and I can tell you, it's gone. The pockets are clean and empty, trust me.'

But Chantal insisted.

'Very well' – her mother shrugged – 'suit yourself, look and see if I am not right. The box is on the top shelf of the big armoire, in the linen room at the end of the hall. Here's the key. Take a footstool, and don't upset the piles of sheets under the box. But I promise you, those pockets are empty.'

Chantal ran upstairs, found the armoire, unlocked the door, dragged a footstool from a corner, climbed on it, and pulled out the big white cardboard box. It nearly tipped over, spilling its contents, but she managed to bring it down, holding it in precarious balance.

Wrapped in tissue paper were starched white cotton blouses, knee socks for summer, black wool stockings for winter. Two pleated skirts, one in blue flannel, the other in a lighter plaid. Several sets of cotton underwear. But *where* was the blazer? It wasn't in the box. Anguish gripped her.

She was about to put everything back and replace the box, when she noticed that more tissue paper at the bottom was actually wrapped around something. She tore at it – the blazer – washed, pressed, neatly folded, the Saint-André emblem firmly snapped into place, and even basted in long white stitches to keep it perfectly flat. With trembling hands, she unfolded the garment and reached inside the left pocket. She was left-handed, so that was the more likely resting place for any object forgotten there. Her fingers searched frantically. Nothing. Nothing at all. Not even a speck of lint.

Nothing in the right pocket, either . . . Her throat was dry and her hands trembled uncontrollably. She was much more upset on Fred's account than on her own. He'd become so single-minded about that stone, how could she face him?

Reluctant to put the blazer away yet, she slipped it on to see if it would still fit, and to give herself time to regain her composure. It did fit, much more loosely now than five years ago, and the once familiar feel of the navy blue fabric brought back a host of memories.

She brushed the creases with the palms of her hands, smoothing the lapels and the front. The lapels lay flat, but the bottom, the left bottom seam, puckered a little at the edge, so she grabbed it in both hands to pull it down. As she did, she felt something under her fingers, like a small pebble lodged in the bottom seam. Her heart stopped. She felt more carefully. Yes. There *was* something there.

Take off the blazer, and break the thread hemming the lining, pull the lining, reach in where the fabric folds at the bottom. A lot of navy blue and whitish lint had accumulated there, and yes, yes, yes! Lodged in all that lint, something's shining. Pull it out. It *is* the diamond, pear-shaped indeed, and incredibly large, now that I know what it is. I have it, I have it! How happy Fred is going to be!

Now, undo the knot in the corner of my handkerchief

as soon as my hands stop trembling. No, I can't do it . . . Sit down on the footstool. Wait a second.

'Chantal! Did you find anything? I'd be astonished if you did!' Madame Arondel called from the bottom of the stairs.

'Just a moment, Maman. I'm still looking.'

Still need a minute to make the substitution. All right now. Undo the knot, take out the gold cross, put the diamond in its place and knot the corner again. Put the hankie in the pocket of your suit, and don't forget it's there, this time, please! Now!

'Maman, Maman, I found the cross. I found it! Come upstairs. Look, here it is. There was a tiny rip at the bottom of the pocket, see? It must have slipped through right here, and fell to the bottom inside the lining. Oh, I am so glad, so very glad!'

Madame Arondel was happy too. One more small object had been returned to the patrimony. She examined the gold cross, found it as shiny as if it had been worn all along, but then gold doesn't tarnish, does it? She insisted Chantal put it around her neck and never take it off again.

As soon as she could safely go back to her room, Chantal transferred the fabulous diamond from her pocket to a zippered compartment in her purse. She would wait to really look at it until she was back in Paris.

The atmosphere at dinner was festive. The finding of the cross – lost, everyone remembered, on the very day the Germans occupied Angoulême, and found now, just after the war had ended – was viewed by all as a happy omen. Chantal felt the moment right to mention Captain May, and she saw her mother's eyes narrow. But for once, Monsieur Arondel spoke up, and said that both he and his wife would be glad to meet the American captain. Everybody spoke so much of those Americans, it would be interesting to meet one in the flesh. But stern warning was quick to come from her mother: 'Meet him, you understand, and that's all. I hope, Chantal, you are not getting into anything foolish and premature that you would regret . . . again.'

It was agreed the American captain could come to visit a month from now, and Chantal would come too. But they were not to travel together, God forbid, what would people think? Then, Anna and Mariès could return to Paris with her.

Later, during the meal, Madame Arondel said, with studied casualness, 'Do you remember Monsieur Alphonse Lavalais, the owner of the flour mills of Saint-Estèphe? He was a guest at your wedding with his wife and their daughters. Well, he was here a few weeks ago to see your father on business, and I asked him to stay for dinner. He is renovating his mills, enlarging the buildings and adding new machinery. Within a few years it will be a very large operation. We had heard that his wife passed away last year, and at dinner he told us he is lonely, now that both his daughters are married. Still quite a good-looking man, you know – couldn't be much over fifty. He asked about you, and said he'd like to have us all visit Saint-Estèphe the next time you come to La Prade. He showed great fondness for Mariès, too. I am sure he is interested in you, and if you ask me, you could do a lot worse. Why don't you give it some thought? You'd have security, a good home, a solid, respected businessman for a husband. What more does a widow want?'

What more indeed?

But Chantal was deaf to the interest of widowers who *couldn't* be much over fifty, with daughters almost her own age, blind to the path pointed to by practical good sense, and forever cursed with the desire to chase rainbows. The widower from Saint-Estèphe would have to find himself another bride.

A month from now, wearing the nine-carat diamond set by Cartier, she would present both Captain May and her decision for her parents' approval. And if they didn't approve, it would make very little difference to her.

She smiled at the thought of her mother's face if she had

known that the gold cross had traveled the world, while the diamond she would soon see had been resting all the time, on the top shelf of the big armoire upstairs.

20

'I AM NOT SO sure,' Madame Arondel muttered in the general direction of her husband. 'I wonder if that girl is not getting herself into a peculiar situation . . . again. The fact is, we know nothing about that young man.'

'Well,' ventured Monsieur Arondel, occasionally bolder than he had been in the past, 'well, we knew a great deal about her first husband, and yet . . .'

'You understand perfectly *well* what I mean,' retorted his wife. 'Don't pretend you don't.'

Madame Arondel was sitting at her writing table, in the big sunny room that opened onto the garden, the rose arbor and the shade of the linden tree. Around her were piles of wedding announcements and envelopes, which she was addressing in her firm, slightly slanted hand. She examined once more the engraved announcement. French style, it opened to a double page. On the left was the bride's announcement:

Monsieur and Madame Jean Arondel have the honor of announcing the marriage of their daughter, Chantal, Comtesse de Blazonac, to Captain Fred May, of the Army of the United States.
The religious ceremony will be celebrated at Saint Pierre de Chaillot Church, Paris, on July twentieth, nineteen hundred and forty-five. The pleasure of your presence is requested.

Domain of La Prade   16 rue Pauquet
                                        Paris, XVIth

The right-hand page was the groom's announcement.
Since Captain May had informed the Arondels that both
his parents had died tragically in a car accident, some years
before, he was announcing his own wedding:

*Captain Fred May, of the Army of the United States, has
the honor of announcing his marriage to the Countess of
Blazonac, née Chantal Arondel.*

New York City, New York   APO 476
Newport, Rhode Island

Madame Arondel sighed impatiently. Of course, he was
very handsome, his manners impeccable. '*Too* impeccable
for the country,' she had remarked to her husband in her
usual elliptical style. 'Whoever heard of bringing those
armloads of flowers to a place like La Prade, where anything that will grow blooms in profusion? Still, the gesture
was nice. But don't tell me he can keep up all that formality
all the time! Then what? What do we *know* about him?
Nothing, except that he produced that incredible ring, so
he must have a family fortune somewhere. And, somehow,
he doesn't *look* American to me,' she added with an authority undiminished by the fact that she had never seen
an inhabitant of the United States before. 'Aren't they
supposed to be tall, and blond?'

'Americans all come from somewhere else, except for
the Indians, and these are hardly blond,' answered
Monsieur Arondel, with a reckless tinge of irony. 'So, there
must be all kinds of types. But as I was looking at him, I
kept wondering who he reminded me of – and it's just
come to me. Do you recall that Polish tailor I used to go
to, before the war, in Angoulême? Jewish, they said he
was. Well, he had a son, handsome young man, who looked
just like Captain May – same big gray eyes, same dark
good looks.'

His wife shrugged. Wasn't it just like her husband to get

lost in irrelevant musings? A few things bothered her about this marriage to a man of unknown background. Still, the captain was a lawyer, and then, of course, there was that ring. Sent from home, he said, where it had been kept in a bank vault with the rest of his family valuables. At least he must come from moneyed people, and Chantal wouldn't be marrying into poverty like the first time. Yet, there was something vaguely disquieting about that young man, something she couldn't define. As though he was playing a role, trying to appear as someone he was not. She had so far given little thought to the fact that her daughter and granddaughter would go live in a faraway country, separated by an ocean. Her own world was so limited that distances meant little to her. As to whether that young man looked, or didn't look, like the son of a Polish Jew who used to tailor in Angoulême, why, that was typical of those absurd wanderings of which her husband had begun to make a specialty.

'Don't be ridiculous, Jean,' she said. She noticed that he stooped a little more recently. 'Stand straighter, please, don't stoop like that. And don't forget your hat, the sun is quite hot today.'

Monsieur Arondel straightened his shoulders, took his Panama from the rack in the hall and stepped outside. She watched him cross the courtyard and saw his shoulders sag again. He is tired, she thought, perhaps it's a delayed reaction to all those troubles of the war, and all the extra work with Blazonac.

She returned to the task at hand, and continued to address envelopes. Her neatly written, alphabetized list was long, but she wanted to finish it today, and she'd give the stack to Loulou this afternoon when he went to the post office.

A bee buzzed, dancing in and out of a slanting sun ray that bisected the room with its bar of floating motes. Blue pigeons cooed on a low roof, chests puffed, courting the females. Their attentions rejected, they'd fly away in a whirring of wings, only to return and land hopefully a few feet away. Her pen scratched the creamy vellum of the envelopes:

Monsieur et Madame André Brousse . . .

She was writing steadily, absorbed in the task at hand, as she always was. She paused briefly when she reached the L's on her list, rested her chin on her hand for a moment, pensively, and then wrote resolutely:

Monsieur Alphonse Lavalais . . .

Mariès had been entranced by the handsome man who had arrived in a car loaded with expensive toys, had kissed her hand, called her a little doll and a princess, had oohed and aahed over anything feathered or furred that she had shown him in the barnyard, and had solemnly promised that Arsène could come with them to America, where he would be treated as befitted his looks and his personality, as a king among rabbits.

And the way he looked at Chantal! No doubt the girl looked good – she was actually turning out to be a beauty, much more beautiful than her mother had ever expected – but the adoration and devotion in his eyes, in his words and in his every gesture, was something the undemonstrative Arondels had simply never encountered.

Fred had assured Madame Arondel over and over again that her daughter would be the most adored, the best cared-for wife, and that he was honored to become a member of the Arondel family. Quite a change from Renaud, there, she thought, assailed by bitter memories.

Also, if nothing else, he would remove Chantal from what her mother privately still thought of as the curse of Blazonac. She suspected Chantal had forgotten little, and still carried an unextinguished torch for Anthenor. She had seen her shudder when her father had innocently suggested a ride to Blazonac to show Fred the château which belonged to Mariès, or would, as soon as the legal delay necessary to establish the death of her uncle had passed. In that way, at least, the marriage would be a good thing. Distance would help her forget and finish healing the wounds.

Dogs barked in the courtyard, the mailman on his bike turned in under the arched gateway. He dismounted, propping his cycle against the stone wall of the well, mopped his brow, adjusted his cap, walked to the door, and pulled the bell chain. Madame Arondel heard Anna's steps, the greetings and the brief conversation about hay-making time being near. She saw the postman climb on his bike again, and disappear through the gateway.

Anna came into the room with the mail on a tray.

'Thank you, Anna. Just put it down here, on my table. I'll look at it later.'

Idly, she glanced at the few pieces of mail: the postwar newspaper, *La Charente Libre*, folded under a white band, printed with the address; an official-looking letter for Monsieur Arondel from the Agricultural Services in Angoulême; another, a long envelope, unfamiliar shape, addressed to her. No stamp, but what looked like a foreign postmark. 'APO' read the circled mark, and a number. What was that? She turned it in her hand suspiciously. Where had she seen this handwriting before? She reached for her letter opener, slit the letter open. It contained another, this one addressed to Chantal de Blazonac.

Who could be writing to Chantal in her care? And from that mysterious APO place, which seemed also to be part of the address of Captain May? Dark forebodings assailed her. She reflected no longer than a second before she decisively slit the second envelope open and extracted two sheets of paper, folded in thirds. She turned the pages covered with tightly packed, untidy writing, lines scrawled crosswise, until she could find the signature. The name she saw there made her blanch.

The Blazonac curse had not been lifted after all.

The letter was dated some six weeks earlier, from what seemed to be a military hospital in a place called Houston, Texas, in the United States.

It was signed by Anthenor.

Anthenor was alive after all.

In his uneven scrawl, impatiently written and barely legible in parts, the story intended for Chantal unfolded to Madame Arondel's widening eyes. When his Resistance group had stopped the German train and his men were being massacred, he was hit, too, with a bullet in his stomach that, it was discovered later, had lodged in his spine and paralyzed his legs. Still, he had been lucky enough to fall into a dense thicket where he had lost consciousness and escaped detection. When he came to, several hours later, it was dark, and he had managed to crawl to the roadside, where passing farm people had spotted him the next morning, picked him up and taken him in. They had cared for him as best as they could, keeping him hidden under a haystack.

A few days later, they had flagged down the first American convoy passing on the road from Angoulême to Limoges, and somehow explained that they were harboring a high-ranking Resistance fighter, badly wounded in a fight against the Germans. American soldiers jumped from their vehicles, ran to the haystack, saw the stripes of rank on his shirt sleeve, and without further question, loaded him onto one of their trucks and took him to their base near Poitiers. After first aid, he was transferred to a US Army hospital unit.

There, his wounds were given a complete examination, and he was declared to be in need of extensive surgery, much more extensive than could be performed in the field hospitals. So, along with a number of wounded American soldiers, he was flown to a staging medical unit in England, where initial surgery was performed, the bullet removed, and he was placed in traction to immobilize his mangled spine. After a few days in the British hospital in Dorset, he had been assigned to a hospital ship filled with other serious cases such as his, and after days at sea, had been taken by military ambulance to this hospital in Texas, where the heat and humidity had made him believe at first that he was in the tropics.

Several more surgical interventions had been performed,

over the past year, and at first, the doctors didn't think he would ever walk again. He was in such agony all that time that painkillers had fused time and place in a vague, timeless haze in which he had lost track of all reality.

But six months ago, a young doctor had taken over his case and decided to try an innovative technique on him. Final surgery had been attempted, which, among other processes he didn't understand, involved the welding of several vertebrae. He had remained in traction again for weeks, but then the worst of the pain was miraculously gone, leaving only a soreness. And finally, under the triumphant eye of the young surgeon, he had been assisted to his feet, managed to stand, and even to place one foot in front of the other before he had to be helped back to his bed. He *would* walk again! Recovery and rehabilitation would be long, the doctor feared he'd retain a limp all his life, but in six months' time, he would be able to go home. To Chantal.

Home to Chantal. The lines that followed made Madame Arondel blush, a blush quickly replaced by anger. The graphic terms in which Anthenor described the carnal happiness he envisioned with her daughter added the fuel of fury to her embarrassment.

He wrote bluntly of his overwhelming desire for Chantal. He reminded her of their moments of passion, and promised nights without end after they were both safely at Blazonac. They'd be married as soon as he returned and all would be well. Please write me soon, he asked urgently, as soon as they forward this letter to you. He lived only for the moment when he could see her handwriting, and read her words, telling him that she was his woman, his wife, and then it would all have been worth it – all the horror, and the ordeal of fire and pain.

Anthenor was coming back! In spite of her inexhaustible ability to invent subjects of worry, this was the one eventuality Madame Arondel had never considered. She closed her eyes to get used to the image of Anthenor alive. All right. It had to be accepted, since it couldn't be helped. Mariès would no longer be sole owner of the estate, but she would still be represented, for her three-fourths ownership, by her tutor and grandfather. Accounts were in order, and perhaps there would be some way, now that the property was no longer as debt-burdened, some way the Arondels could recoup the investment they had lavished on Blazonac. A great deal of thought and care would be required to handle this situation. Bad, indeed. But that part wasn't the worst. There was the immediate problem of Chantal.

Let Chantal hear that Anthenor was alive, and let her feel the fevered desire steaming through the cramped lines of his writing. Then, almost certainly, she would break her engagement, cast away the nine-carat solitaire, causing no end of embarrassment to her parents, and fly back into the arms of her former brother-in-law. A fine scandal! How all the gossipmongers would be vindicated! The elapsed time, the slow healing process – all would have been for nothing. And the looming questions about Renaud's death, never quite put to rest, would be reopened. Suspicions, whispers, would be fed by the sight of the happy couple. An inquest, perhaps? And with what result? Feeling was still running high between former Resistants and collaborators. Families whose sons had died on the missions of Colonel Robert's group would not greet his return without mixed emotions either.

Meanwhile, she, Madame Arondel, would lie awake at night, listening to the pounding of her own heart. And her beautiful daughter, who had shown herself competent and successful in her own enterprises, she thought proudly, why, she would return to the stark poverty of desolate Blazonac, where everything decayed, to waste away her youth. As for Anthenor – his first passion spent – he would return to his old self, aloof and surly, roaming the woodlands in disreputable clothes. Except that now, she thought bitterly, that long, bold stride had become a limp, and God only knew how long it would be until, aggravated by the damp winters, his injuries kicked up, and he was immobilized again, unable to walk, and this time forever.

She gazed out the open window, where bees buzzed on the climbing roses massed along the arbor, thought for a while. Then, she took a sheet of stationery, and she wrote, without hesitation or crossed-out words:

Dear Anthenor,

My daughter shared parts of your letter with us, and after all these months, during which, I'll confess, we feared the worst, it was indeed a deep happiness for all of us to hear that you are alive, soon to be well and return home.

Chantal asked me to write you on her behalf, as she is at present extremely busy with the preparations for her forthcoming marriage to Captain Fred May. She also asked me to send you her wedding announcement, which you will find enclosed.

She wants me to tell you how glad she is to have heard from you, and how reassured she feels now on your account. She knows that, as her deceased husband's brother, you will join in her happiness, and she looks forward to the pleasure of having you meet her husband. This, however, will be for the future, as she and Captain May will make their home in the United States, leaving in a few months, surely, *hélas*, before you can return.

We are all extremely fond of Captain May, a lawyer in civilian life, and I must say that the affection he shows for your little niece, Marie-Esmée, deeply touches my heart.

My husband and I rejoice to see you soon, and I trust that you will find my husband's stewardship of the estate has brought many beneficial results. He expects you will be pleased when you review the books with him. Even so, much remains to be done to bring the estate to any degree of profitability.

My dear Anthenor, in the expectation of the day when we can welcome you at La Prade, both my husband and myself, as well as our daughter, send you our most affectionate greetings.

Adélaïde Arondel

She reread the letter and could find nothing to change. If Anthenor attempted to contact Chantal after that, there would still be time to take other measures. But she very much doubted he would. True to his violent character, it was far more likely he would fly into a rage when he read of Chantal's callous betrayal and would never speak her name again.

Madame Arondel smiled to herself at the image of her letter hastily read, then torn into bits, crumpled, and thrown across a hospital room.

PART FOUR

Texas, 1945

21

THE LETTER FLEW across the hospital room. Huge fans hummed incessantly on the ceiling of the vast orthopedic ward of the 36th Division Military Hospital near Houston. Outside, the Texas summer simmered in a vapor of moist heat.

Anthenor didn't even finish reading the letter the mail-cart volunteer had just delivered, the first ever addressed to him in all the months he had been lying on this hospital bed, where the traction apparatus still dangled over his head. Anger blazed up, as he tore open the creamy envelope that had been enclosed in the letter, and glanced at the printed announcement it contained.

His face now livid with rage, he raised his arm and threw the crumpled paper as hard as he could across the room, the effort bringing a sharp stab to his spine. As he lay back, gasping with the sudden pain, he saw, forgotten in the folds of his sheet, the envelope bearing a French stamp and his address, in a firm, slightly slanted hand. With a vicious swipe of his hand, he sent it, too, fluttering to the floor.

The patient in the next bed, his left leg immobilized in an ankle-to-hip cast held up by traction straps, turned his head and smiled wryly. 'Good news from home, eh, buddy?'

Anthenor gave no sign he had even heard the remark. He continued staring at the ceiling, teeth clenched, a small muscle twitching on the side of his jaw. The soldier in the cast shook his head. 'Not too many guys in ortho that don't get a Dear John sooner or later, boy,' he sympathized. 'Welcome to the club.' He added, 'Dames don't care for gimps, I guess.'

Anthenor did not understand much of what the GI said. He knew little English, and during his months in the hospital, he had learned to understand only the most often repeated phrases, like: 'Does it hurt?' and 'Take this, you'll feel better.' One of the first words he had learned was *walk*. 'I doubt he'll ever *walk*,' the old doctor had said, shaking his head with a defeated look. Later, the young surgeon had ventured, hesitantly, 'Let's try fusion and see if he'll *walk*.' Finally, after the last operation, the surgeon had squeezed Anthenor's shoulder one morning, after examining the latest X rays, and said, very quietly and smiling, 'I think you'll *walk*.' This, Anthenor had understood clearly, and closed his eyes in unspeakable gratitude.

'Your girl's getting married, is that it? And she's got the goddamn nerve to send you an announcement? Right? Well, boy, you did the right thing to throw the fucking letter away. Now say, "Goddamn women!" Say it, it'll make you feel better, you'll see. Say it, "Goddamn women!"'

Anthenor turned his head and stared at him.

'Say it after me, "Goddamn women!" Go ahead, say it.'

Anthenor's face almost relaxed. 'Goddamn women,' he said at last, slowly and carefully.

'Right, buddy, that's goddamn right. Say it again, man.'

This time, Anthenor practically smiled. 'Goddamn women,' he said louder, 'goddamn women.'

After that initial effort, his English made swift progress under the tutelage of PFC Billy Powers, from Mobile, Alabama. And onto Anthenor's accent became superimposed the incongruous cadence of the deep South.

His pain, and his anger at the callousness of Chantal's betrayal, did not subside, but it did help a little whenever the black rage welled in his heart and gripped his chest, to repeat endlessly, 'Goddamn women.'

Now that his deepest reason to want to go home had evaporated, it seemed to him the days dragged on, all monotonously alike. Reeducation therapy in the mornings

402

was followed by exercises in the swimming pool. Then standing on the treadmill for stationary walking exercises. Then back to the ward for rest. After lunch, walking down the hall, at first with a walker, in slow, painful, measured steps. Later, with two canes. And now, six weeks later, he was on one cane only, assisted by a gray-haired, motherly-looking nurse, who called him 'sonny.'

The humid heat continued, seeping into the rooms, in spite of the perpetual whirring of the great ceiling fans. One afternoon, Anthenor was dozing after lunch, straight blond hair wet across his brow, taut cheeks, long legs now free from casts and traction restraints. High heels beat a staccato in the hall, stopped at the open door nearest his bed.

'Hello, boys, how are y'all? I'm your new volunteer, my name is Bunny. What's your name, sweetheart?'

Anthenor opened his eyes. The girl was pretty, in a breezy way, in her pink-striped volunteer uniform. Bright chestnut hair, a sprinkling of freckles across a blunt nose, lots of white teeth. Smiling, vivacious, engaging, talkative. 'What's your name, sweetheart?' she repeated, looking at the chart she carried. 'You tell me, honey, 'cause for the life of me I can't pronounce it. Okay?'

Anthenor stared at her, unsmiling. He hated, with all the force of his old arrogance, that overwhelming friendliness which he considered undue familiarity.

'Anthenor,' he said between clenched teeth.

'Well, honey, I'll call you Tony, okay? Call me Bunny. We'll get along just fine, you'll see. Now, sweetie, if you'll just try to get up, I'm supposed to take y'all for a little old walk. Here, let me help you.'

She chattered away animatedly while she helped him to his feet with gentle care. He stood up, leaning on her shoulder. She smelled of cologne and shampoo, clean and fresh. From the flood of words she spoke, he vaguely understood that his former nurse had been assigned to other patients, now that he was recovering, and that Bunny would come every day to help him learn how to walk

403

again. She was a newcomer to the hospital, having just joined its group of volunteers.

Leaning on his cane and on her shoulder, he walked in careful steps, slowly, pain throbbing at first, then lessening a little as he found the right angle, favoring his right side, letting his weight rest on his left leg and his other leg drag a little.

'Where're y'all from, honey?' asked Bunny.

He explained, in his sketchy English, that he was from France, had been fighting in the Resistance when he was wounded. France? Bunny's interest was sparked.

'You're French?' she said. 'Parlay voo Françay? I am afraid that's all I know. I took Spanish in school, see. My daddy said sure, it's not as smart as French, but here, in Texas, it's a heck of a lot more useful. Although I didn't learn an awful lot of that, either. Always wanted to meet a real Frenchman, though. They're supposed to be so romantic.' She looked up at him leaning on her shoulder, tall, aloof. 'And you know what? You're pretty romantic-looking yourself, honey, with those cheekbones and that cowlick. And you'll be even better-looking after you put some flesh on those bones. Careful, now, lean on me a little harder, will you? We're supposed to try taking a hundred steps today. Think you can do it? Let's count. One, two, three, four . . . I'm right proud of you. Eleven, twelve, thirteen, fourteen, fifteen. Wow, a real pro. Great. You're doing swell, honey. Soon, you'll be good as new.'

Encouraged by Bunny's resolute cheerfulness, and the lessening in the intensity of the pain, Anthenor was beginning to feel better than he had since he could remember. He was walking now, unsteadily, dragging one leg, but walking all the same. He leaned less and less on her.

'Here,' she said, patting his hand, which rested on her shoulder. 'Don't be afraid, honeybunch. Lean hard. I'm strong.'

He walked twice the hundred steps required by the therapist that day, and only stopped because Bunny was afraid he'd overexert himself. She helped him return to bed, smoothed his sheet, and seeing his hair wet with perspiration stuck to his forehead, she reached out, and brushed it back.

The gesture made him relive, with bitter intensity, that night in Limoges, in the black-market restaurant with red flocked walls, where Chantal had pushed his hair back with infinite tenderness. He closed his eyes and pretended he had fallen asleep. Bunny patted his cheek and walked out on tiptoe.

After that, every afternoon, he found himself listening for her decisive steps, anticipating her breezy arrival. They went for longer and longer walks, and she took him, via the elevator, down into the hospital garden, where, in spite of the stifling heat, he felt almost intoxicated by a feeling of freedom. Confined for so long, he gulped deep breaths of the humid air.

'What business were you in, back home, honeybunch?' asked Bunny one day.

Anthenor explained haltingly that he owned farms, supervised their operation.

'Well,' she enthused, 'now, isn't *that* a coincidence! My daddy owns a big ranch too – the Hollis Diamond Bar Ranch – it's famous all over Texas, best longhorn cattle you ever did see. We've got I don't know *how* many head. We live in a ranch house, real large and comfortable. You've got a ranch house too?'

He told her about Blazonac as well as he could. It wasn't a ranch house, he said. It was a castle, very old, built centuries ago on a lake with woods all around.

Bunny was dazzled. Her Frenchman owned a castle! She'd heard of castles and seen pictures of the ones in the Loire Valley. She visualized Blazonac as something between Versailles and Chambord.

'A real castle? With towers?'

'Yes, there are four towers.'

'Honey,' she breathed, 'you've got horses? I love to ride.'

'Horses?' said Anthenor. Stretching the truth a little, 'I've got a horse. His name is Bijou . . .' Then the pain again, and that taste of ashes – Bijou and the dogcart, Chantal laughing, dimpled, under her wide-brimmed straw hat.

From the rest of the conversation, Anthenor learned that Bunny's mother had divorced her father years ago, remarried, and moved to Florida, where she had died not too long ago. 'But I didn't mourn her, honey, not serious like,' confessed Bunny. 'I hardly knew her.'

He also learned that the Hollis Ranch, as well as other lands her daddy had acquired over the years, contained numerous oil wells. 'Like my daddy always says, ranching is fun, but oil sure is good for cash.'

Anthenor understood little of what constituted the wealth of Texas, but the thought of vast expanses of land a man could pace to his heart's content stirred his soul.

A week later, sitting under a tree heavy with clusters of feathery lavender blossoms, which she called a crepe myrtle, Bunny asked quietly, 'Tony, honey, tell me something. Do you have a girl, back home?'

Anthenor stared straight ahead, cheeks taut. 'Yes.' He nodded. 'Yes, I do. I have a girl.'

Then, he turned to face her. With his hands, he showed the gesture of tearing a letter to pieces, crumpling it, and throwing it far away. He was surprised when the gesture didn't hurt. Then, he made as if to wipe his hands against each other, and said, 'Goddamn women.'

Bunny laughed, a short, pleased little laugh that attempted sympathy. 'Sweetie,' she said, 'this is hardly proper language for a lady's ears, but I see what you mean. Tell you what, if she didn't feel she could wait for you till you got better,' Bunny went on sententiously, 'then she was the wrong girl for you, that's all. And in that case, it's better it ended now rather than cause more unhappiness to you both. I'm sure y'all will find the right girl soon,' she added demurely. 'You're a real good-looking boy, you know.'

Anthenor was ignorant of American codes and clichés – the right girl, the wrong girl, it meant little to him. And even if he had understood, he probably would have had to admit that Chantal, whom he still wanted so passionately, was, in Bunny's code, the wrong girl, and not just because she had betrayed him. Suppose he'd said, 'Yes, the girl I love was my brother's wife, and I wanted her all the time she was married to my brother. Then he died, drowned on a cold night in the lake by the castle, and to this day many people think I killed him. Of course, there's nobody, but I, to know whether I did or not.' Yes, choosing Chantal was a far cry from choosing 'the right girl' for the Senior Prom.

Bunny waited. Silence. She went on, 'Don't you want to know if I have a beau? A beau, you know, a boyfriend?'

Anthenor said nothing. She sighed. 'I'm just like you, see, Tony honey, I put my trust in the wrong man. And he broke my heart. So, I know how you feel, and I can understand what you're going through.' She sighed again, deeply, looked at Anthenor soulfully. He was listening attentively, understanding only part of what she was saying. She mistook his attention for deep interest.

'Well, if you *must* know, I did have this beau, see. Real tall, big and handsome. His name is James Spigner, but everybody calls him Spike. Played a lot of football. Spike and I used to go steady in high school, and then I went away to college and he pinned me in my junior year.'

Pinned in her junior year? Is 'junior year' a time or a place? In either case, strange way to be pinned, whatever that means. His eyes remained unblinking.

Bunny continued pouring out her heart. 'After that, I thought, and my daddy thought, and Spike's folks thought, too, that it was just a matter of naming the day. And when he was sent overseas, why, he gave me the sweetest ole ring before leaving. We were supposed to get married as soon as he came back. Well, he went overseas, and at first, he wrote me all the time, but then he stopped writing regular letters, just a note now and then to say he was fine and he hoped I was too. Then, nothing, for the longest time. Nothing. Not a word.

407

'I kept writing, asking him please, tell me, what's the matter, did I say anything to make you mad? Like when I told you I'd gone to the country club and danced all the dances with Bobby Joe who used to be your roommate at college? And then, last month, just last month, this letter arrived. It seems he's met this girl in London. He writes he fell in love with her, and he wants to be released from any promise between us. I cried and carried on for days, so much so, my poor daddy thought I'd make myself sick. That's when he suggested I come to the hospital and join the volunteers. Do me good, he thought.'

Anthenor nodded. He understood the general idea. He sought a phrase that would express sympathy. 'Goddamn men,' he said forcefully.

Bunny couldn't help laughing. 'Hush, you naughty boy.' She giggled. 'I told you that's no language for a lady's ears, even if you're right. But *some* men are okay, honey. As my daddy says, it's only a matter of meeting the right one. You see, Spike must have been wrong for me. That's all there is to it.'

Anthenor nodded. It was not in Bunny's nature to remain melancholy for very long. 'Tell me about your castle,' she asked. 'Do you live there with your folks?'

'No, I live alone. My mother is dead. My father . . . my father too,' he concluded to simplify things and because he did not know the words, or whether in fact his father was still alive or dead.

'You must have lots of servants to take care of a whole castle.'

Anthenor thought of old Maria. 'Not many,' he conceded. 'Not enough. I need more.' He thought for a second. The word he was looking for was one he heard constantly since he had come to America. 'I don't have much money,' he explained.

'Why,' cried Bunny, 'you're land-poor, honey. But don't worry. We can fix that. I want my daddy to meet you. You come on out to the ranch on Sunday. I'll pick you up with my car. My daddy's throwin' a barbecue, and y'all will have a real good time.'

In a flash, and completely unknown to Anthenor, Bunny had just decided she was going to marry him. Now *that* would erase the stigma of Spike's defection. And it would set him back on his heels, now, wouldn't it, when he heard Bunny had married even before him, and to a glamorous Frenchman, a Resistance fighter, real tall and romantic-looking, honey, with a castle in France.

Everybody would know what stuff little ole Bunny was made of, and at the same time, she would become the mistress of an honest-to-God castle, in Blazonac, France.

Anthenor was looking forward to Sunday, in spite of himself, and was surprised to find himself enjoying the preparations for the outing. For the first time in months, he would be out of the hospital pajamas and robe. He was issued the uniform the US forces provided soldiers from other countries who had joined in their fight, with the name of their homeland on a sleeve patch.

He studied himself in the long bathroom mirror: a fresh haircut had trimmed the straight blond hair baring his forehead, to just above the eyebrows; clean-shaven, high cheekbones; fresh pressed khaki pants and shirt with *France* embroidered in red on his sleeve patch. He cinched the webbed belt to his narrow hips. Bunny was right, he *was* too skinny. Pale, too, with his tan long faded.

It felt good, though, to stand, walk, granted with a cane, but free from restraints and almost from pain. His leg still dragged, but he had learned to hold himself straighter, and the limp was already less noticeable than it had been a few weeks before.

He had just made his slow, careful way along the graveled drive to the gate, when Bunny pulled up, laughing, honking festively. He climbed in next to her, smelled the fresh lemon shampoo in her windblown hair. He admired the big maroon Oldsmobile convertible.

'It's a '41, honey,' explained Bunny. 'There were no cars built for civilian use here after that. All the industries went into the war effort. Rough on people like my daddy who change their cars every year. But we hear they've begun to design new models, and now the war's over, they'll come out with some real beauties. My daddy says Studebaker is planning to surprise everybody!'

Anthenor had never sat in a convertible before, and he enjoyed the feeling of open air and the speed that sliced through the sultry heat.

Bunny was driving with the authority of someone who considered a car as an extension of her person. She looked particularly pretty, in a white dress, high-heeled sandals, and a necklace of pink beads. She saw him examining her, smiled at him. 'Look, no shift.' She showed him. 'It's automatic. You can drive it if you like, on the way back.'

The immensity of the flat Texas plain astonished him, accustomed to the limited horizons of the hilly country of his birth. Flat and empty. There were a few houses, gas pumps, general stores here and there along the highway, then miles of empty, dusty land. How could a man ever pace this land, stretched flat to an invisible horizon, swathed in golden dust?

'How far is the ranch?'

'Not that far, honey, just about fifty miles more. We'll be there soon.'

'You drove more than fifty miles every day to come to the hospital?'

'Sure did, sweetie,' said Bunny cheerfully. 'And aren't you glad I did?'

He had to admit he was. The wind, the fresh lemon smell, the cheerful, talkative girl, filled the painful void in his soul. If he had known how to express it, he'd have had to admit he was almost happy at the moment.

Suddenly, a sign by the roadside: HOLLIS DIAMOND BAR RANCH. Bunny turned onto a narrower unpaved road branching off the highway. A cloud of dust followed the car in a lengthening plume. Enormous herds of cattle raised their heads, bearing sets of long, fearsome horns. Here and there, men sat on horseback, while others dismounted to open gates, and to herd cattle into large pens. More cattle gathered around vast feed bins or long drinking troughs. Anthenor had never even suspected that such immensity of land could exist, even less belong to one man, or such masses of cattle be gathered in one place. When he said so to Bunny, she laughed.

'Cattle ranching is my daddy's *second* hobby, to tell you the truth, Tony. Some years it's profitable, others it costs him money, he says. But the oil keeps pumping, year in year out, and that's where *real* money comes from. Oil flow's good for cash flow. My daddy first made his money in oil.'

He said nothing. 'Real' money, as opposed to any other kind, had little meaning to him.

The barbecue was in full swing when Bunny playfully brought her Oldsmobile to a stop right in the middle of a vast lawn that was the only green spot around, scattering guests who pantomimed panic. A crowd immediately gathered around them, engulfing Anthenor, who stood, bewildered, soon leaning on his cane more heavily than he had earlier in the day. Bunny introduced him around. He understood no names, only saw smiles, a sea of faces. Finally she took him by the hand and led him to a group of men standing near the long buffet tables, glasses in hand.

'Daddy, I want you to meet that young man I told you about. His name is Tony Sefar.'

Brad Hollis extended his hand. He was older than Anthenor had imagined him, sixty, perhaps, ruddy-faced, stocky, a mane of white hair visible under the broad-brimmed Stetson. His handshake was crushing.

'Proud to meet you, my boy. You're a real war hero, Bunny tells me. Always glad to welcome those boys who were fighting for freedom. I want you to meet our good friend, Tom Carruth, our state senator, a real bright young man, too.'

Tom Carruth was surprisingly young to have attained such a high elected office. He stood almost as tall as Anthenor, but much broader shouldered, his forehead perspiring under the pushed-back Stetson. He had boyish features, a firm handshake. 'Proud to meet you, sir,' he told Anthenor, 'and glad the state of Texas could make its own small contribution in bringing back to health one of those brave French Freedom Fighters.'

Anthenor bowed, not trusting his English to respond to such florid language. He was introduced to another man, slight, balding, with searching eyes behind rimless glasses.

'Dave McCullough, editor of the *Texas Sun*. Brad here told me about you, and I've been anxious to meet you. We'd like to run a story on you.'

Soon Anthenor was feeling almost at ease in that group of men, open, friendly, ready to take him in unquestioningly, only curious to know more about him and a war that had been fought so far away.

He told them haltingly how he had joined a Resistance unit early in the Occupation, become in time its leader, and had directed a number of operations against German forces. His group had blown up bridges, destroyed troop transport trains, ambushed trucks and convoys. Yes, he had lost many men. He had been wounded in one of the last engagements of the war, after the Normandy landings. All his men had been killed, he alone had survived against all odds, paralyzed from the waist down, and he lived and walked, he acknowledged thankfully, only because American forces had taken him in charge.

'Did y'all have any sort of rank, in the Underground?' inquired McCullough.

'I hesitate to mention,' said Anthenor, 'but I was a colonel. There was no existing . . . ah . . . structure, right? So the firstcomers were in line for high rank. I was one of those.'

'Real proud, real proud.' Brad Hollis beamed. 'So we're privileged to welcome here a high-ranking Resistance fighter.' And changing the subject, 'Bunny tells me you are a rancher, too, back in France?'

Anthenor explained that, in terms of what Texans seemed to call ranching, he was hardly a rancher, but he did own extensive woodland and several farms.

'How do y'all work those farms?' inquired Hollis.

Anthenor explained the *métayage* system, under which the tenant pays no rent but shares in the product of his work with the landlord.

Hollis shook his head. 'Just like sharecropping, boy. Poor system, not productive enough. Cuts up the land. Can't mechanize enough. I say inject capital, mechanize, and supervise the exploitation with a competent foreman. Bunny tells me you own a castle too?'

'Yes,' said Anthenor. 'I do. Or rather, I own a share of it, and the same for the land. I had a brother who died, and his little daughter inherited his share. But yes, it is a castle, a very old one.'

'How old?'

'Nobody knows, since the original fortified castle has long been destroyed and rebuilt several times over the centuries. Except for the towers, which date back to the medieval structure, and the vaulted cellar rooms, the present château was built in the fifteen hundreds.'

The men whistled. Now, that *was* old! Bunny was right. This young man had potential. Spike would have been my first choice, thought Brad Hollis. But since that bastard has seen fit to jilt my little girl, break her heart, and take up with some foreign floozy, why, this Tony Sefar might just be okay. It'd be fun, after the situation in Europe settles down, to take a trip over to France. Never been back there since that one time, during my honeymoon with Bunny's mother. Just might sail over, take a look at the situation of my . . . all right, my son-in-law's estate, see how the potential of that land could be developed with judicious injection of capital. My son-in-law? Well, sure looks like *Bunny's* made up her mind.

He clamped his hand on Anthenor's shoulder and steered

413

him to the food. Sides of beef were slowly turning on spits, enormous vats of chili simmered wafting spicy aromas, strings of sausage were broiling, fat hissing on grills.

Brad pointed to the sausage. 'Deer meat,' he said. 'Do you shoot, Tony?'

Anthenor allowed himself a rare levity. 'Only US-made automatic weapons.'

Brad laughed heartily.

Tables were loaded with bowls of salads, beans, potatoes, huge baskets of tortillas, and a fiery salsa. A bar dispensed Jack Daniel's and keg beer. Anthenor barely tasted the food, daunted by the sight and smell of the overabundance, and accepted a beer.

Bunny detached herself from a group, and came to take him by the hand. 'At last,' she pouted, 'Daddy'll let me introduce you to my friends. Whatever on earth did you two have to talk about for so long?'

Anthenor was quickly surrounded: Misty Carruth was the younger sister of the senator, Sally McCullough, the daughter of the newspaper editor, and Larry, his son, a 4–F who wore thick glasses. Bobby Joe was ... Names, faces pressed around him. Bunny held his hand, later slipped hers possessively under his arm, told everybody how she had nursed him back to health, how she drove every day to the hospital to help him learn how to walk again, how glad she was to have met him, and how meeting him was 'just one of those things' ... Soon, all the guests understood that Tony was 'Bunny's young man' or 'Bunny's beau' as she steered him happily around the grounds, taking him into the house to show him the comfortable, cluttered rooms, the vast kitchen, gleaming with all its stainless steel appliances, the adjoining cold room, where sides of meat aged and dozens of cases of beer and Jack Daniel's were kept cool.

There were the spacious stables, with quarter horses for the use of Mr Hollis, Bunny, and their guests. There were the garages, with Cadillacs and Lincolns lined up just like the horses in their stalls. Farther back, behind a row of tall, dusty trees, the ranch buildings clustered, with special stables for the workhorses, the kitchen and the bunkhouse where the ranch hands lived. Mexican men, dozing against a wall in the hot afternoon sun, stood up, tipped their sombreros. 'Buenas tardes, señorita.'

'Buenas tardes, Paco. Buenas tardes, José y Ramiro.'

Trucks were parked nearby, *Hollis Ranch* painted on their side, with the diamond bar, the same cabalistic sign he'd seen on the panel marking the turnoff road.

Bunny pointed to the horizon, where tall metallic towers drew geometric patterns. 'Oil derricks. Only a few are visible from here. There's more farther on, and a lot more still on lands Daddy bought or leased, when the war brought up the price of crude. He says prices will stay up. So now, he's formed a syndicate that leases a lot more land everywhere in the South, mostly in Texas, Louisiana, and Oklahoma. It's called the Hollis Oil Company, it finances oil exploration and leases. Daddy's just an old wildcatter at heart. That's how he got started in life – drilling lots of dry holes, and a few that turned out gushers, he always says.'

Anthenor was limping more obviously by now, and his back ached. He was looking forward to his quiet hospital bed. He felt intoxicated and dizzy, not from the single beer he had left almost untouched, but from too much distance and speed in an open car, after all the sedentary months, too much sight and smell of rich foods after years of rationing, too many people, too much prosperity . . . too much open land, too big a horizon. He needed to close his eyes and rest.

When he limped back into the ortho ward, leaning on Bunny's shoulder, PFC Powers winked at him.

Bunny helped him undress, tucked him tenderly into bed, then leaned over and kissed his lips. Anthenor smiled and returned her kiss, lightly caressing her face before closing his eyes.

After Bunny had left, Powers whistled to attract his

attention. 'Got yourself another girl pretty damn quick, buddy boy.' He leered.

Anthenor realized he had actually forgotten Chantal – not thought of her once all day. The remark brought her image back, clear and painful.

'Goddamn women,' he said tiredly.

Shortly thereafter, Brad Hollis announced the wedding of his daughter, Beatrice, to Mr Anthenor Sefar, a colonel in the French Resistance, a rancher and castle owner from Blazonac, France, now recovering from wounds sustained in heroic action. They were married in a simple ceremony at home, as circumstances required. There were no more than five hundred guests, meat turned on spits for days, and truckloads of cases of Jack Daniel's were consumed. Bunny wore a lovely white lace dress from Neiman-Marcus in Dallas and Anthenor a lightweight gabardine suit made by Brad's tailor.

The day before the wedding, in the middle of the rehearsal dinner, an unexpected guest had appeared, greeted by initial cries of surprise and welcome, followed by an embarrassed silence. Spike was home! Spike had received an early discharge on account of a lingering pneumonia he had contracted in the London fog. No sooner had he arrived home and found that the entire Spigner clan was attending Bunny's wedding rehearsal, than he had jumped into the only car left in the garage, and here he was, still in his uniform, a bear of a man, cordial, eager, he said, to add his congratulations to everyone else's. No mention was made of his English love interest, apparently forgotten with his first breath of the humid Texas air. Instead he was making effusive plans for returning to work on the Spigner Ranch, just like he'd never been away, he said.

Bunny greeted him with cold restraint, and to her father's suggestion she said no, no, it would not be at all proper to add Spike to the number of the ushers who were to escort guests to their places the next day. Anthenor felt acutely ill at ease, in spite of everybody's efforts to be cordial and warm. Spike, in an attempt at congeniality, took him aside after dinner, clamped his hand on Anthenor's shoulder.

'You're getting yourself the best little woman in Texas,' he affirmed, 'and that's a tall order. I was a jerk, a bastard, and an asshole to let her go, and I'll have a long time to be sorry about it. But . . .' He extended his hand, and shook Anthenor's firmly. 'It sure looks like the best man won. Congratulations and all good wishes.'

By the evening of his wedding day, Anthenor, tired and his back hurting, had been shown off, paraded, commented on, explained, as Bunny's beau, Bunny's man, Bunny's groom, Bunny's husband, so much that, with darkening heart and narrowing eyes, he was beginning to think of himself as Bunny's trained poodle.

That night, in the bridal suite of the best Houston hotel, decorated with tall sprays of white orchid, baby's breath, and lilies, Bunny emerged from the bathroom in a night-gown and negligee ensemble of creamy lace and chiffon, expecting words of love and tender caresses. She had naively hoped all along that Anthenor's silences covered a shy and reserved nature, and that torrents of warmth, love, and appreciation would pour out, as soon as he felt secure in his position and reassured by her commitment.

There were no words of tenderness. At first, a forced smile and grudgingly extended arm when she snuggled against him. And then rising desire, silent, hard-eyed desire. His lovemaking seemed to her demanding and dirty, and she told him in tears that she would never, never, tolerate those filthy things he wanted to do to her. She'd rather die by her own hand, she added dramatically. Uncomprehending and unrepentant, Anthenor went to lie down, in a black rage, on the couch in the living room of the suite.

The marriage lasted exactly three months and ten days. There were no quarrels, only tears and supplications from Bunny, who refused at first to believe that her husband could be unhappy in her company, embarrassed by her father's generosity, unwilling to adapt to his new surroundings and his new life, arrogant and resentful rather than grateful. Attempts to make him jealous over Spike's frequent visits came to nothing. He would just stalk out, return late at night when he hoped everyone was asleep, and say not a word, even in answer to his wife's anguished demands for an explanation. Some nights, in the closeness of their bed, he took her, hard and fast, but never attempted again those erotic acts she had objected to on their wedding night.

Then one day, Anthenor simply disappeared, leaving behind the well-provisioned checkbook Brad Hollis had given him as a wedding present, and the clothes Bunny had bought him. He only took his GI-issued uniform, and left a note explaining succinctly that he was returning home, and would send back the amount of money he was borrowing to finance his trip as far as New York. He did that indeed, a few weeks later. The French consulate in New York provided him with the necessary papers and a return ticket.

He was back shortly at Blazonac, where he resumed his pacing of the estate, stopping only when the pain in his leg and back forced him to rest.

He dealt with Monsieur Arondel in the management of the properties. Never once did he ask about Chantal or mention her name. He avoided her mother, and remained uncommunicative when he was forced to see her. Silent, aloof, living alone, with only Maria's daughter from the neighboring farm to cook his meals.

Blazonac became more desolate every day, most of the rooms closed off, and never even aired. Many people thought Anthenor was brooding over the dead men and boys he had commanded. And there was so little jealousy over his way of life, that rumors about Renaud's possible murder eventually went almost unvoiced too.

A few days after Anthenor's departure, Bunny, more relieved, in spite of herself, than heartbroken over the abrupt ending of her impulsive marriage, discovered she was pregnant. She told no one but her father, and, after a quickie Mexican divorce, accepted Spike's humble, repentant, and passionate proposal. Their son was born prematurely and named Bradley Hollis Spigner. If Spike suspected anything, he never said a word.

The boy grew up tall and darkly blond, and everyone agreed that he had something of his mother's vivid coloring, and that his brown eyes were much like Spike's. Few people remembered Bunny's abortive marriage to that strange, silent Frenchman, whose name had never been quite understood and was never pronounced again.

However, when Brad H. Spigner reached the age of nine, he was assigned to a French-language class in his private academy, and immediately developed a passion for the language and all things French. As he progressed in his studies, it became evident he was not interested in business, nor in ranching, like his father and both his grandfathers, nor in oil, like his grandfather Hollis. He cared only for French studies, especially literature, history, art . . . Bradley Hollis shook his head and refrained from comment. The boy might have been a disappointment, yet how could anyone be disappointed in someone so entirely attractive? And whenever old Brad Hollis allowed himself to think of it, he had to admit his grandson had the warmth and charm of his mother and the lean elegance of his real father, far removed from the rough stockiness of Spike. That boy would never need to earn a living, his grandfather thought fondly, so he might as well enjoy himself and spend his youth doing just what he wanted to.

So, the doting grandfather financed summers of travel in France, a Junior Year at the Sorbonne, and a bachelor's degree at Yale. When the boy announced his intention to continue his studies with a master's degree and a doctorate in French literature and civilization, his grandfather had only one question: Which university are you planning to apply to?

PART FIVE

California, 1967

22

'THIS IS CRAP to beat all crap,' complained Pinky May-pole, one of the writers.

Channing sighed, pushed a strand of blond hair out of her eyes, and her nine-carat pear-shaped diamond, her trademark, flashed in the rays shining through the hermetically sealed windows of the Tri-Zone Network conference room. Air-conditioning kept the temperature at low cool in spite of the fearsomely hot winter sun, glaring in the western sky, and absorbed the smoke rising from cigarettes in overflowing ashtrays.

Sitting next to her, Pinky, who had pink skin, and a pink scalp showing through his sparse albino hair, fished a small enamel box out of the pocket of his rumpled white linen jacket and placed it on the table in front of him. Next he tore a blank page from his notebook, folded it in two, creasing a careful edge so the paper would lie absolutely flat. He reached into his pants pocket, extracted a money clip from which he pulled out a bill, which he placed on the table, next to the box and the folded paper. From the box, he shook out a little white powder onto the paper, unsnapped the gold razor blade that hung from a chain around his neck, and methodically cut a line. Then, he rolled the bill into a thin tube, fitted one end to his nostril and sniffed deeply . . .

He shook his head, took a few slow breaths, and replaced the paraphernalia: the box went back into the inner pocket of his jacket, the bill was returned to the money clip, and he snapped the razor blade back onto the chain dangling on his hairless chest. A feeling of deep well-being seemed to suffuse the pink face, and the pinkish eyes blinked behind clear-rimmed glasses.

'They keep that up,' sighed Pinky, 'and they'll drive me to *drink*.' Everybody nodded sympathetically.

'Now,' he added, brightening visibly, 'let's have that cast for the season special again.'

'You heard me the first time,' said Matt Bullock, the producer. 'We are fortunate to have signed up the Boston Celtics and Louis Armstrong as guest stars, and also Lori Lamont, the Playmate of the Year. Now, it's just up to you guys to write them into the first episode. That ought to start off *Just Deserts* with a bang. Ratings are in your hands, boys and girl,' added Matt, with a circular glance that took in the four members of the writing team.

'Who's the director?' asked Channing, diamond flashing again as she crossed her arms. 'And why isn't he here?'

'He's got a weak stomach, sweetheart,' muttered Pinky. 'Can't take it.'

Paying no attention, the producer answered Channing. 'We're fortunate as well,' he intoned in his pompous style, 'in that we could get Peter Baldwin. He was signed up yesterday. But he couldn't be here today, he's shooting on location in Colorado.'

'You're going to *need* him on this one,' interrupted Dusty Shapiro, the oldest member of the writing team, who had recently started to let his hair grow long over his collar, apparently to compensate for his balding crown. 'Peter's the only director who can turn crap like this into Nielsen ratings. Has he seen the casting?'

Before Matt could answer, Kevin Taylor, last member of the writing team, observed acidly, 'Peter directs the series, it's only fair he doesn't unload the special on some poor slob who needs work . . .'

'All right, boys and girl,' concluded the producer soothingly, addressing the four-writer team again, 'you've got your work cut out for you. Let's meet again next week same time and place, see what you've come up with. And remember, if you feel you can't do it, there are plenty of others who can.'

Chairs were pushed back, papers gathered. Channing

snapped shut her Italian leather script case stamped *Channing May* in gold, and walked out with Pinky, Kevin, and Dusty.

'Hi, Miz May,' said Ramon, the sloe-eyed parking attendant who had a crush on her. 'You sure look good in those pink suede pants. Real sexy, like always. How did it go today?'

'Great, Ramon, just great. TZN is in for one hell of a 1968 season. Ratings will shoot down so low, so fast, they'll break the bottom of the charts, if they're planning a lot more junk like the special of *Just Deserts*.'

Just Deserts was a TV series, already in its third season, and Channing was one of the writers. The preposterous premise of the show involved the geriatric comedian Bud Stockfield, and a cast of regular, lesser stars, marooned, through some long-forgotten set of circumstances, in the Sahara desert. There, they had managed, thanks to an ingenious studio prop department, to re-create a vaguely Arabic microcosm of their Beverly Hills neighborhood. The weekly suspense was provided by a guest star, usually a bosomy starlet who somehow appeared in the Timbuktu-like setting and seduced the aging comic.

Two problems arose regularly with the writing of each episode: First, the logistics of getting the girl there. Anybody in his right mind could wonder, if the regular cast couldn't get out, how could the guest star get in? But sitcoms operate on their own suspension of disbelief . . .

Channing, who had the knack of sitting silently through three quarters of the story conference, and then, quietly, coming up with just the right line, or the funniest resolution to the thorniest situation, had also contributed several of the more unlikely entrances: Once, Suzy Saint-Clair had been a photographer, illustrating a story on the desert Tuareg tribes, and her runaway camel had galloped over dunes, range after range, only to collapse at the feet of the comic and his cohorts, who happened to be gathering dates in a palm grove reminiscent of the Palm Springs landscape. Another time, Cindy Asher, a former Miss

California, had been kidnapped by tribesmen, and she had escaped, crossing a thousand miles of desert on foot, without ruining her hairstyle or so much as dislodging her false eyelashes, to stagger sexily within sight of the marooned group. The following week it was Kim Livingston who had accidentally fallen off a light plane in which she was practicing stunts – or bailed out, prior to crashing, or whatever ... Didn't Sandy Curtis materialize out of thin air once as the result of a scientific experiment gone wrong, and couldn't she come out of a bottle next? thought Channing. No, the genie bit had been done before, and her sympathies went out to that other team ...

The other problem was caused by the comic star himself. As soon as the name of the guest was announced, he'd go into a frenzy, begging the producer to reconsider.

'My public will never go for that,' he'd moan. 'How could I fall for an old broad like that? Twenty-eight, if she's a day!'

Bud Stockfield would never see sixty-five again. And the network rules were definite on the subject: Seduction of nymphets by old men was not appropriate prime-time fare.

The team of writers kept alive the hope that, someday, perhaps in the last season, when it had been determined the series would be canceled, they could write in a she-camel as guest star, with torrid seduction scenes between her and the old goat.

Or a female goat, fantasized Channing. A good-looking goat, of course, Bud's got his image to consider, after all. Wouldn't do anything to hurt it, God forbid. A sexy goat.

Bud-the-old-goat wooing a sexy she-goat, at least nobody could raise the cry of bestiality. But would it pass in prime time?

Channing sat in her black Corvette. She seldom used the snap-on top, and drove her car open year-round, in the mild southern California climate. Now she tucked her flyaway blond hair under a visor cap, adjusted sunglasses, and pulled on her driving gloves, with cutoff fingers. She turned on the ignition.

She snapped on the radio. Last year's platinum hit wailed at her:

> Strangers in the night
> Exchanging glances
> Wondering in the night
> What are the chances . . .

For some reason she preferred not to analyze, the words had always made her uneasy. Something personal and unpleasant lurked behind those strangers in the night. She turned to KMPC, the news station. 'February 26, 1967, dateline Vietnam. The US Army announces it has started its biggest offensive to date in the Vietnam War. On the Cambodian border . . .' She sighed, turned the knob, settled on Jefferson Airplane, followed by a Jimi Hendrix single.

I'll stop by to see Leigh before going home, she thought, it's still early. She turned onto Wilshire Boulevard and made a right on Rodeo Drive. Through incredible good luck a parking space opened just in front of Delven's green-and-white-striped awning. Leigh was inside, helping her salesgirls return dresses to the racks. She pretended to frown when she saw Channing walk in.

'If you're looking for more suede pants, you're in the wrong place, lady,' she said mock severely. 'But there's a western shop down the street that carries them.' Then she smiled. 'Hello, Channing, it's good to see you. Let's sit down. It's been a busy afternoon here. Are you coming from the studio?'

'Straight from. It's been quite a day there, too. I'll spare you the highlights of the new season, but let's just say it's got to be meant for an audience with an IQ lower than its body temperature.

Leigh laughed her rich contralto laugh.

'What else is new? Have some coffee.' A salesgirl brought coffee, in white porcelain cups with the green Leigh Delven logo, to the couch, strewn with fashion magazines, where they sat. Leigh was happy with her full-page ad in *Vogue* and commented on the cover, featuring Mariès, Channing's lovely daughter. 'Best face they've had in months!' Channing's eyes lit up with pride. Then, both women leaned over the blueprints for the addition to be built onto Leigh's boutique, growing success demanding more space. As she was slipping the rolled plans back into their cardboard tube, Leigh asked casually, 'Have you seen Roger Volod lately?'

Over the years, Roger had remained a close friend of the Mays, and Leigh had met him at their home. He'd invite her occasionally to dinner or escort her to a premiere, and Channing kept hoping something would develop between him and her dearest friend, but Roger hung tenaciously on to bachelorhood. As for Leigh, sorely tried by life, she was a scalded cat who kept clear of any involvement. Still, could Channing hear a hint of interest in her voice?

'Spoke to him once or twice on the phone. He's been absorbed by his new film, and I'm sure he'll tell you all about it. Mariès claims he's let his hair grow into an explosion of gray curls . . .'

'Everybody's using barbering – or the lack of it – as a political statement nowadays.' Leigh shrugged. 'At least, I hope he isn't sporting a beard.'

'An unkempt frizzy mane,' mused Channing, 'that was Roger, almost thirty years ago. It all started with a truck ride. He was Volodia, then, and there was no way any one of us on that night could have known where it would take us. Except Volodia, who somehow seemed to know. A long ride from home . . . And I have a feeling it's not quite over yet and that I should keep my safety belt fastened.'

'Wasn't it Roger who first brought you to the studios?'

'Yes, it was, and I'll be forever grateful to him for that. Just a fluke, or else a part of that ride I was talking about, however you want to look at it. After we came to California, I needed a job, and found there weren't many art galleries in Los Angeles at the time. Roger was directing TV shows for TZN then, and he offered me a position on his staff. Created it for me, probably, though he never said so. I was listed as "production assistant," but I did a bit of everything and wasn't at all above going for coffee on occasion.'

'Had you ever done any writing before?'

'Never, unless you'd count a few sporadic attempts at keeping a diary – each mercifully short-lived. But part of my job at TZN involved dealing with the scripts, making sure there were enough copies, that every page was there and in the proper order. After months of flipping through those thousands of pages, I eventually got curious and started reading them. I'd expected to be awed by the skill and talent. Instead, I found dialogue that didn't ring true, missed opportunities for a laugh. I began to think that I could dream up wackier situations, stronger exit lines . . . I kept quiet at first, but when I'd gathered my nerve, I confided in Roger over one of my coq-au-vin dinners. When he didn't immediately respond, I felt foolish, pretentious, and hurried to change the subject. Then, a couple of weeks later, out of the blue, he asked me to sit in on a story conference and afterward kept asking me for opinions and ideas. God, I don't want to bore you with a blow-by-blow account, but when one of the writers quit, I was offered the job. One thing led to another, so that now, I've risen so high in the profession that, at this very moment, I've been entrusted, along with three other geniuses, with the lofty task of figuring out a way to get the Boston Celtics stranded somewhere in mid-Sahara. And if I maintain my meteoric ascent, I might, I just *might* someday get to write dialogue for King Kong or Bozo.' Channing stopped, smiled. 'Seriously, now, I kid about the job,' she went on, dropping the flippant tone, 'because it's comedy writing, after all, and I'd be as good as dead if I took it – or myself – too seriously. But I'm the first to admit there's only one thing worse than having *to* work, and that's having *no* work. To tell the truth, the job is great. It's fun more often than not, the money's good, and I'm damn lucky Roger was here to give me my chance. By the way, Leigh, how did *you* learn how to run a boutique?'

'I'm like you, I guess. Idiot savant. Never trained, really. Just went ahead and did it. With reasonable success, if I may say so myself. Until ten years ago, my only experience was *buying* clothes, but I've done all right at selling them too. Still, buy or sell, *I* never had to switch languages. How did you learn English so well and so fast?'

'Much of the credit goes to the good nuns in Angoulême. They did one hell of a job! I can still see Mother Saint-Ignatius clapping her hands and stamping her foot to mark the five tonic accents of the English pentameter:

> I wandered lonely as a cloud
> That floats on high o'er vales and hills,
> When all at once I saw a crowd,
> A host, of golden daffodils . . .

'A strange way to do justice to William Wordsworth's lilting lines . . .'

'But an effective one to teach proper accentuation of the language. And then we had to write three different paraphrases of pieces like Milton's sonnet "On His Blindness" just so we'd learn about synonyms and nuance. For an encore, we'd be assigned ten pages of George Eliot's *Scenes of Clerical Life* to turn into narration in the indirect discourse, with proper sequence of tenses – after we'd dutifully corrected the word *wife* to *sister* every time the minister's wife was mentioned. A printer's error, said Mother, how could a cleric possibly have a wife? Still, how many native speakers receive this kind of grounding? And in the summers we were sent on holiday to England. Then, after I came here to live, I was fascinated by the newness, the vitality of American English, the words, shiny like Christmas tree ornaments, those priceless idioms! The first time I heard someone say, "I must look like something the cat dragged in," I thought, How colorful, what does a cat drag in, and how does it look? A "cliff-hanger" made me visualize myself hanging from a cliff, the chalk grating my fingernails . . .'

'Is it by speaking English that Chantal became Channing?'

'Of course, and by eating hamburgers, drinking Coca-Cola, dressing differently. God, I remember the day I arrived with Mariès at Union Station, in Los Angeles. It was October, I'd dressed her in a miniature travel outfit, and I, of course, was wearing proper attire for the season, a tweed suit and black velvet pillbox with pheasant feathers. The temperature was simmering at a hundred and three and everyone was running around in shorts and halter tops! Anyway, how long could you remain Chantal from La Prade, driving a car with California license plates?'

Leigh nodded. 'Time does its inevitable work, too, as well as geography. Only my mother back in Indiana still calls me Leah.'

Channing hugged her friend, then glanced at her watch and jumped up.

'I must run along before I get caught in heavy traffic on Pacific Coast Highway. Let's have lunch soon. I'll call you.'

Then, they both guiltily remembered the one person whose name hadn't been mentioned and should have been.

'How's Fred, by the way?' inquired Leigh lightly. 'I meant to ask you ever since you came in.'

'Fred's fine, just fine. Busier even than usual. He's working on a big case with the Securities and Exchange Commission. Financial fraud or something. The case has been dragging on for years, but it's finally coming to trial, and he's knee-deep in briefs and depositions. So I hardly see him. But he's great.' Channing's tone was as light as Leigh's. 'I'll tell him you asked. And I know Mariès will be reassured you liked her *Vogue* cover. She hated those earrings the stylist insisted on.'

Leigh, her dark hair falling smoothly over her cheek, watched her friend pull away from the curb and waved.

The Corvette shot down Wilshire Boulevard, turned onto San Vicente, where miles of coral trees already in bloom bore enormous pods of crimson, butterfly-shaped flowers. No leaves yet, this was still winter, a California winter. Joggers puffed on the central grassy strip, others had collapsed at the foot of the gnarled trunks. I do love this country, thought Channing, so why am I always dreaming of leaving to go elsewhere? Without even being sure of where I'd want to go. Home? Where's home for me by now? I've lived here longer than anywhere else. No reason to feel like an exile. And yet I do.

She turned into Fourth Street, down to Santa Monica Canyon, a brief, ramshackle neighborhood, opening to the Pacific Coast Highway.

Traffic was still light, the sky over Point Fuma tinting to an improbable mauve that dissolved into orange and purple strata. Old wooden beach houses blocked the view of the sea for several miles, and once more Channing wondered how a large city like Los Angeles could be so heedless of its approaches. The seaside cliffs were not granite, but a crumbly shale that disintegrated constantly into clumps of dirt and loose rocks, rolling onto the blacktop. Then, there was the tangle of wires overhead, festooned from wooden poles, providing telephone and electricity to the beachfront shacks. Built in the early days of beach living, and not much more than cabins, they commanded frightful rents in spite of their unkempt surroundings. And why can't they put utilities underground? wondered Channing for the thousandth time.

The small bridge over Las Flores Creek, a dry gully for the most part of the year, a raging torrent during the rainy season, marked the boundary of Malibu, where real estate prices shot up tenfold. At the Sea Lion Café, live sea lions splashed in a tank by the roadside. Malibu is – all outsiders will agree, who do not live there, their back to the land and facing nothing but expanses of Pacific Ocean all the way to China – Malibu is more a construct of the mind than a reality. Only the residents know better.

Five miles of highway, an underdeveloped shopping

center, dominated by the rustic barn of the Malibu Inn papered with glossy, signed photographs of stars. Then the Colony, off to the left, isolated on its spit of land inhabited by motion picture and television people, and in the foreground, the Malibu Pharmacy and Coffee Shop's circular building, a tribute to architectural aberrations of the early fifties, the Dark Ages as far as southern California is concerned, where everyone lives in the here and next. To the right, vast expanses of geranium fields, and blue mountains behind.

Again, emptiness, the highway veering to the brow of the unstable cliff, away from the ocean. A flash of sparkling sea, when she reached the top of the rise, with Point Fuma stretched out over the setting sun and its horizontal bands of crimson and violet. Finally the sharp left turn onto Paradise Shores, an exclusive stretch of beachside properties with a guarded entrance, houses pressed against one another, keeping the ocean out of sight.

Twenty miles from the studio, almost as much from Fred's office in Century City. A long drive. Was it worth it? Why not live in town? Channing pulled up to her house, the exclusive low numbers indicating a private colony: 35 Paradise Shores, when the county map would have given her house a number in the thirty thousands.

Channing pressed the clicker in the side pocket of her car and the electric garage door rose. She drove in, parked the Corvette, clicked the garage door shut, picked up her scriptcase, crossed the patio abloom with lush multicolored impatiens, and knew once more when the fresh scent of salt and wet seaweeds assailed her why one lived in Malibu, rather than on some safe and convenient street in Beverly Hills.

Yes, the long drive had its rewards. As she walked into the vast, cathedral-ceilinged living room, nothing of the world was visible, except the sea, and the low sun that was painting a fantastic universe of red, pink, and dark blue zones, with a pewter-colored beach on which wavelets embroidered changing borders of silver. Tonight the rising tide would bring waves crashing under the house built on pilings, and spotlights would go on all along the outer edge of the deck, to turn the cresting masses of water to green opalescence. Living in Malibu, one forgot the land and its bondage. Only the sea was in sight.

The dog, Fortune, (Champion Sir Harris of Fortune Bay, according to his pedigree), came bounding. Channing greeted him, went into her bedroom to change her clothes, stepped out of the new pink suede pants and into another pair, suede, too, but black and battered, pulled from a row of other suede pants in her closet, replaced her mauve silk shirt with a ragged black turtleneck sweater. The Newfoundland who could go run on the beach anytime he wanted to, but didn't, was quivering with impatience for the daily evening ritual of his walk.

Following him, she ran barefoot down the stairs that joined the house to the beach. Walking on the edge of the surf, she had to roll her pants up to her knees. The dog was already gamboling in and out of the waves, scattering hundreds of sandpipers and sea gulls and sending them flying into swift circular patterns. Channing walked and ran, preceding the dog or chasing him, throwing bits of driftwood for him to fetch. At the Point, she stood, feet on a patch of sand surrounded by tidal pools, with crabs scurrying and starfish clinging to crags in the rocks. Then, she turned around, and blinking in the setting sun, walked back in the descending tide that was abandoning clumps of seaweed on the satiny sand.

Over twenty years since Chantal had married Fred May. Almost as many since she had become Channing. To simplify things, at first, because everybody wanted to abbreviate Chantal into Chan, Channy, and then people supposed that the real name behind the nickname must be Channing. Finally, she had even begun to think of herself as Channing, since there was no common measure between Chantal from La Prade, or Blazonac, or Paris, and the woman California had made of her. Had she really become Channing, now, or was the chic, throwaway name

434

only a glossy, easily scratched varnish that went with the certificate of US citizenship and the green passport of which she was so proud?

Twenty years, and after all, they had gone very fast. Although in the first panic after her marriage, she thought life had stopped and would never move, leaving her mired in its quicksands. Fred's passionate courtship had begun to cool soon after the wedding ceremony was performed. Without words, he made it clear he had reached his goal to marry a woman who would help erase forever the stigma of a past he wanted to bury and that was it. The wedding night came and the glorious sex she had imagined, in the arms of her new husband, with smooth golden skin, never happened. Fred made love distantly, almost politely, as something he had to do but didn't enjoy, leaving her alone with her desire. Other nights had been the same, and had remained the same over the years. Caresses annoyed him, he disliked being touched, he said angrily once. A *wife* could provide no erotic fulfilment to him. That's the way it was and he didn't want to talk about it.

In time, Channing learned to live with a situation she couldn't change, and it never occurred to her to seek a divorce. In the world she came from, divorces were rare, frowned upon, and wasn't this already a second marriage? She reasoned that the few hours of total bliss she's known with Anthenor must have been the entire share of ecstasy allotted to her by destiny. No more to be expected. And her few brief experiments with men chosen for their sex appeal confirmed that conviction in spite of their passionate performance during the afternoon engagements on the couches of their bachelor apartments. Fred was absent many nights, spending late hours in his office, she presumed, but no questions were asked and no explanations given. Otherwise, their life was reasonably happy, and the sore subject being tacitly ignored by mutual consent, harmony reigned. They talked about the house, the beach, work the dog. Themselves never, and Mariès seldom.

Early, Mariès had shown an unerring sense in identifying

the core of problems, an eye for the hidden painful spot, and an instinct for judging people at their true value, unwilling ever to be thrown off by pretense. She saw straight through Fred and judged both him and her mother severely, with the clear eyes of adolescence, unclouded by the ambiguities of experience.

The sound of Mariès's sports car brought Channing running up the stairs from the beach, brushing wet sand from her legs and feet.

The red MG was pulling up. Channing watched her daughter stop the car, turn off the ignition, and, without bothering to open the low door, jump out, long legs in tight jeans, lithe and agile. Who did I see before jump out of a sports car without bothering to open the door?

Out of a dimly remembered past, suddenly vivid, Channing (or wasn't this Chantal?) saw the courtyard of La Prade, a low, cigar-shaped Salmson cabriolet, and the Countess pulling up, turning off the ignition, and jumping out. The resemblance between Mariès and her grandmother, whom Channing barely remembered except at moments like this, and whom Mariès had never known, was striking: tall, slender, dark hair, oval face with small features, imperious manner. And the same gestures. Identical, a third of a century and half a world away . . .

'Hello, Mother, what are you looking so preoccupied about? More crap at the studio? I'll never understand why you don't dump the whole job. All your brain-racking is making absolutely no contribution to the world. Someday, you'll have to raise your consciousness, and the sooner the better.' Raising one's consciousness was one of the concerns of the year 1967.

No point in arguing that payments on the elegant Malibu beachfront house were high, or mentioning the upkeep of three cars, or the expensively slouchy clothes. Even less in hinting at the frequent cries for financial help from Mariès, whose quest for identity had led to a sometime modeling career, an oft-interrupted BA at Barnard, and small parts in movies directed by Roger Volod, such a longtime friend, he was fond of saying, that he was the first old man to cast a lecherous eye on her, when she was playing naked on the beach at the age of six. Fred's partnership in a Century City law firm brought in a nice income, but Channing paid for many of the necessary luxuries.

Instinctively sensing she was on shaky ground, Mariès changed the subject. 'Is Fred coming home for dinner?'

'I don't know,' said Channing. 'Just came home myself. Only took the dog for his walk. The beach is beautiful tonight and the water is almost warm.'

Just then, the phone rang. It was Fred. Hesitantly, he explained to Mariès that he was not coming home for dinner. He was attending a lecture, a group meeting of some kind. Mariès didn't sneer. Obviously, this time she believed his story.

'I'll buy you dinner at the Pharmacy,' she proposed generously to her mother, 'provided you take your Diners Club card along.'

In the car, she said, musing, 'Fred's not the same, these days . . .'

'Oh' – Channing dismissed the matter – 'we see him so little. He has his private life . . .'

'No, no, it's not just his "private life" now, as you so diplomatically put it. Something is going on with him. He's different, more thoughtful. There's something else happening beyond his, if you'll excuse the euphemism, "private life."'

'What could be happening to him?'

'Soul-searching, if you want my opinion. He's reading, all of a sudden, a man who never read before. You see all these brochures and magazines he gets from Brandeis University? *Judaism, Zionism, Israel Today, The Chosen People* . . . And he's gotten into a regular correspondence with that old friend of his, Herschel, in Tel Aviv, who's in the Knesset. And that other Israeli friend, Isaac Greenberg or something who's a lawyer like Fred. And God knows what else he gets at the office. What *is* he up to?

Hey, it looks like everybody's here, tonight,' she concluded in one of her characteristic non sequiturs.

They parked in front of the circular window of the Pharmacy. The usual crowd, in scruffy, ragged clothes, sat at the small tables and at the circular counter. Yet, a second look revealed famous faces: John Huston, the director, looking like some ancient biblical patriarch, was there; Burgess Meredith, the actor, with a jaunty wool cap; and Leon Breu, the novelist, handsome, bluff and gruff and sunburned from a day on his yacht at sea; many lesser stage and screen personalities, as the gossip writers would put it. Channing, of modest fame, through her writing credits seen on every TV screen at prime time, blended in perfectly: torn black sweater, tousled blond hair, and the diamond she never took off, in spite of endless entreaties by her daughter who found it not only vulgar but dated. As for Mariès, she had earned her personal standing by being seen on many magazine covers and in a few forgettable movies. More, her casual aristocratic look was instinctively recognized by the California crowd, although they could not label it. 'Class,' they called it, for lack of a better expression. Mariès scorned jewelry, her looks somehow conveying that she had plenty of it carelessly left around somewhere. Mariès intimidated many, her mother occasionally.

'What will you have, Mother? The steak strips with onion on sourdough? What else would anybody come to the Pharmacy for?'

Burgess Meredith, 'Buzz' to his friends and neighbors, stopped by their table. His hair under the peaked cap had been dyed a bright red, with matching eyebrows. He caught Mariès's eye. 'Television,' he said mock ruefully, waggling a red eyebrow. 'Better than starving!' Burgess, the best character actor in the business, was in no immediate, or even long-range, danger of starvation.

The last Olympics decathlon champion walked in, the blond on his arm with tangled pale hair, barefoot in army fatigues, recognized by all as a famous young actress.

438

Leon Breu was walking out. He patted Channing's shoulder. 'Don't tell me you two broads are mother and daughter, 'cause I wouldn't believe it,' he said gallantly. 'Sisters, maybe. *That* I might believe.'

'You'd be wrong, Lee darling,' answered Mariès pleasantly. 'I'm much too old to be her sister. I'm the mother.'

Breu surrendered and ambled over to his Jaguar with European license plates.

Back-to-back to Mariès, in the adjoining booth, sat Howie Stein, a character actor with a bald head, who kept up a running feud with her since she had haughtily spurned his groping advances in the Motion Picture Academy parking lot. He turned around, pretending he had just seen her.

'Hi, sweetheart,' he asked bitchily. 'I'd like to know what you put on your nose to make it shine. It works so well!'

Mariès was quicker than a cobra. 'Same thing you put on your head, hockey puck,' she purred, 'only less of it.'

They ought to know better than to tangle with Mariès, thought Chantal. Aloud, 'You ordering dessert? You know what they have.'

'I think I'll have the chocolate cream pie. You won't break down and join me? For once?'

'You know I can't have anything with chocolate. It's not a matter of diet, it's just . . . oh, the past . . .'

'Someday,' put in Mariès without much interest, 'you'll have to tell me about it, so it can be exorcised.'

'No exorcism needed. It's only a matter of . . . memories, both bitter and sweet perhaps. The taste of chocolate brings me back to Blazonac during the war. One day after we had not tasted any for so long, we were given a packet of chocolate powder and I drank a cup in the big kitchen. Anthenor was there too. I saw him drink his with so much concentration. And later, when we heard the Germans had tortured and killed him, the taste of chocolate brought back that time and I could only remember his face at that moment.'

'Where was Renaud, during that charming little domestic scene?' asked Mariès, who had no direct memories of Blazonac other than those acquired on two brief trips to her grandmother's in recent years.

'Renaud was in his bed, reading, as usual. That's how he spent most of his days. I brought him a cup, but he didn't touch it.'

'So, that cup of chocolate you shared with Anthenor was such a highly charged sensual experience. Were you in love with him, then? And was he with you?'

Channing was tired, pleasantly so. It had been a long day. The insanity at the studio was temporarily forgotten. Her daughter's sudden interest intoxicated her, and she felt like confiding, fear of Mariès's black-and-white judgments forgotten in the warmth of the moment.

'Yes, I was in love with him, though I did not know it then. And he was in love with me. I didn't think in those terms at the time, though. Remember, I was just about eighteen, straight out of convent school, and I wanted so much to do my duty, be a loyal wife, and later a good mother. I was frightened when I found myself attracted to him.'

'Did you sleep with him?' asked Mariès, looking straight ahead.

Channing didn't answer.

'So, you slept with Anthenor,' continued Mariès, still looking away. 'Tell me about it.'

'I'll tell you. I slept with him once, and only once, but that was after Renaud had died and I was in Limoges. We spent a few hours together. It is the most exciting and perfect memory of my life. I have never known anything like that again. But it was just that once.'

'Why?'

'He had come to say good-bye. He was forced to leave Blazonac, because of the Occupation. As you know, he is half Jewish, and he was joining the Resistance. I heard from him after that, but I didn't see him. Except once . . .'

'Tell me about that too.' For once Channing had her daughter's total attention.

'That's when I was trying to leave Paris, with you and Anna . . .'

'And Arsène in his basket. You told me about that awful trip,' interrupted Mariès. 'I remember Arsène very well and I still miss him. But I don't remember anything else of those days. Tell me. How did you see him?'

'The French Forces of the Interior stopped the train, made everybody get out at a small railroad station. People were standing there, bewildered, and the young Maquis – you know, that's what we called the members of the Resistance – were milling around, waiting for their colonel to give instructions about blowing up the train. The colonel arrived, Colonel Robert, they called him, and it was Anthenor. So tall, and lean and heartbreakingly handsome. My heart stopped. I talked to him, and he said he would come to me during the night if he could, but he wasn't able to promise because they had an operation planned for that evening.'

'Those were exciting days,' conceded Mariès. 'Did he come to you?'

'No. But I saw him. You and Anna were asleep. I couldn't sleep, because there were bugs in my bedstead, so I went to sit at the window. Then, I heard something like a muffled sound, and walking through a low ground-fog, came this silent procession, with Anthenor leading his men, all barefoot, their weapons reversed, bearing their dead on stretchers. That's the last time I saw him.'

'He didn't see you?'

'No, but he knew I was there, and he knew I understood why he didn't come to me that night. He was staying with his men.'

'So much heroism,' interrupted Mariès, ruefully, 'and all for so little! The Resistance didn't accomplish much the Allies might not have done easier and with much less bloodshed. But it satisfies some need the French have to fight only after the real fight is over. Not during. *After*. A national flaw, I guess.'

Oh, for the twenty-twenty vision of youth, Channing thought. 'At the time,' she said patiently, 'we saw it as patriotism. And it still would be. Anyway, it's the last time I saw Anthenor.'

'Are you still in love with him?'

'Perhaps you can't understand that, but the girl I once was, and still am, is still in love with the boy he was and must still be. Apparently, *he* isn't in love with me anymore, though! He refuses to read my letters, never mentions my name. You know that.'

'Yes. When I went to visit him in Blazonac, he'd walk out of the room if I even spoke your name. But if you ask me, I think it means he still loves you although he's angry at you. Probably because you married Fred.'

'Then why didn't he let me know he was alive? When we heard that all his men had been killed and his body couldn't be found, we were sure he had been taken by the Germans, tortured for information, and killed. You know, darling, that summer in La Prade, I had no clothes because my suitcase had been lost, so Grand-mère had dresses made for me out of linen sheets, and I thought of it as white mourning for the man I loved. That's when I found I couldn't bear to eat chocolate. And I kept having visions of him being tortured. I don't want to think about those days.' She shuddered.

'And then Anthenor came back?'

Mariès's interest could be seduced by stories of the past, that romantic past she didn't remember but sometimes thought she did, through her mother's often-tapped memories. The war, the Occupation, the Resistance, there was danger, glamor, excitement . . . Blazonac, seen close up, unheated on freezing rainy winter days, as on her last visit, depressed her and made her angry, and she had stayed there as little as possible, rebuffed by a surly, uncommunicative Anthenor. But with distance, it recaptured its appeal.

'Yes, he came back, and you know the story. But by the

442

time he returned to Blazonac from that military hospital, I was already married to Fred and living in California. So I never saw him again.'

'Why didn't he write you? Let you know he was alive?' repeated Mariès.

'That's what I never understood. After I heard he had come back, I wrote him several times, but my letters were returned unopened.'

A silence.

'Mother,' asked Mariès quietly, 'did Anthenor kill my father? You were there, you must know. Grand-mère won't even talk about it.'

'I have always refused to wonder,' said Channing slowly. 'Perhaps I was afraid of what I'd think. You were just a few months old. They had that terrible fight, and they went for a walk, late at night, around the lake. A freezing winter night. I heard Anthenor come back, but Renaud had moved to a room at the other end of the château, because he was afraid your crying would disturb him, so I couldn't hear whether he'd returned or not. And the next morning, they brought him back from the lake, wrapped in a wet tarpaulin. I pushed the canvas aside, and there were his dead eyes, wide-open . . .'

Channing put her face in her hands. Mariès wasn't moved. She had never felt anything but scorn and resentment of her father.

'A great father Renaud must have been, and some husband! How come you couldn't get a decent one, at least once, Mother? You don't know how to pick your men!'

'Fred is a good husband,' protested Channing defensively. 'He has his quirks and I accept him as he is. Otherwise—'

'Otherwise,' cut in Mariès, 'you'd have to admit you struck out again, Channing May. And this is Mariès May speaking, knowing what she's talking about.'

'Yes' – Channing smiled – 'this is indeed Mariès May. Marie-Esmée de Blazonac would know better. She would

443

have spent her growing-up years at Saint-André, and she would have learned to settle for something else in life than happiness – like martyrdom. Mother Saint-Ignatius would have seen to it!'

'Never. Less is not enough.' Then, suddenly nostalgic at the sound of her true name: 'Mother, what will become of Blazonac? Will it go to complete ruin?'

'Probably. Since Grand-père died, there's no one but Anthenor to run it, and he just doesn't have the necessary capital to restore the château and install running water and a full electrical system, reorganize the farms and equip them. Since the war, plowing, for instance, is no longer done with a team of oxen, tractors have to be bought, and I don't know what other farm machinery. I only know it's expensive. The truth is that with the new economy, estates like Blazonac can no longer pay, no matter what. They can only be owned by people who have large incomes elsewhere and don't care how much they sink into properties of that kind, just so they can have the pride of ownership and enjoyment of a splendid historic castle by a lake, with woodlands. A place like Blazonac is either priceless or worthless, depending on who owns it. I am afraid that, for you, it is worthless.'

'How I wish it could be returned to what it once was! To what it was in the time of . . . of my grandmother. Tell me about it.'

And Channing, sitting in the car parked in the dark, cool night with the rhythmic roar of the ocean a few feet away, told Mariès of Blazonac in the time of the old Countess, the rowboat parties on the lake, dancing in the grand salon, the dining room with the twenty-four striped satin chairs, the maids in white caps serving spun-sugar desserts, lace curtains billowing in the evening breeze, of the weeping willows sweeping low over the water, the stone staircases winding up in the towers and down to the vaulted cellars and the magic. She told her of Bijou and the dogcart, and she told her of the day she, Mariès, was born, and Dr Vincent, who had forgotten to bring his chloroform. She

444

told her of her baptism, when she wore the Arondel lace dress . . . Mariès, sophisticated and brittle as she tried so hard to be, never tired of the Blazonac lore.

'Sometimes, you look so much like your grandmother, it catches my throat. Like tonight, when you jumped out of your car without bothering to open the door. She did that too. As a matter of fact, in those days, her sports car probably didn't *have* any doors.'

Mariès smiled, entranced. The coffee shop where they had sat moments ago with its tawdry plastic booths, and the scruffy crowd of merchants of illusion, all illusion dispensed with in their off-hours, was forgotten. Reality was there, in the cool California night; it was there, palpable, in the thick stone walls, the heavy towers of Blazonac, the lake, its water flowing toward the sluices. The church in a village of which she bore the name. The tombs, all with the same name engraved in stone.

Mariès had never changed her name officially. Her sundry university registrations, her screen and modeling credits listed her as Mariès May, a name she read as a pun on her real name: Marie-Esmée. And at times like this, she saw herself, nostalgically, in her true persona as the last link in the long line of noble ancestors who had borne the same name.

The waves broke, a few scattered lights shone on the horizon – tankers leaving the port of El Segundo, steaming north along the coast to other coastal ports. Unwilling to end the moment of closeness, mother and daughter sat in the car. For once, Mariès was listening, asking questions, and not dismissing her mother with one of her merciless one-liners.

Channing asked, hesitantly, 'Tell me, Mariès, what do you think is happening to Fred?'

'You'd know better than I would. I'm not close to him, nobody is. And I'd say that whatever is bothering him is coming at him from way back. His family was Jewish, from Germany, and he suffered from the persecutions under Hitler. Didn't he tell us that he wanted to break away completely from his background, become someone else?'

'Yes. You know how I met him. I told you before, although I don't like to talk about it, even to you, since it's something that makes him uncomfortable. He wants it forgotten. It never occurred to me, young and ignorant as I was, to think he was Jewish. He said he was a political refugee.'

'Well,' said Mariès, 'he was, if anybody was, and being Jewish must have been a terrible thing then. Now, Anton was only his stepfather. Do you know how his real father died?'

'It was in Germany, I think. He never talks about it and he said something once about his father having disappeared. But I have the feeling something horrible happened. Perhaps Fred knows about it, perhaps he doesn't even know for sure . . . But there's something which has begun to obsess him. I've heard him talking on the phone to that new friend of his, the rabbi, Irv Mandelbaum.'

'No doubt Fred *is* haunted now. And I'd like to know by what ghosts,' said Mariès pensively. Then, the spell broken, 'Come on, let's go in. Check with the answering service, see if the world has forgotten us.'

The world had forgotten nothing, and the answering service had a list of messages. One was from Roger Volod, who had been calling Mariès unsuccessfully for two days. This time she felt obliged to return the call. 'Hello, Rog. What's happening?'

'Darling, I am glad to hear your voice. We just finished shooting *A Sign That Means Life*, and if editing goes well, we're in for an Academy nomination for sure, perhaps even an Oscar.'

'I know you were working on that picture. Didn't you tell me it was based on some real-life incident?'

'Not just some real-life incident, sweetheart. A major event in my own life. It's about a girl I met, a friend of your mother's, back in France, and if you want the whole story, ask Channing, she'll tell you. Anyway, that girl was

446

called Martine, she gave me her baptismal medal, and I gave her a gold chain, with a *chai* sign, you know, the Hebrew letter that means *life*, that my mother had given me before we were separated, forever, as it turned out.'

Roger Volod paused. Old memories get sharper and more cruel as I get older, he thought. First, they soften with time, but later in life they surge up again and eat at your heart. He continued, 'Well, Martine wore that pendant throughout the war, and never showed it to anybody. She was waiting for me to come back to her, and you know, I thought of her, too, and would have come back, except that . . .'

Mariès waited. She remembered having heard the story from her mother, but she didn't want to spoil the bittersweet pleasure Roger took in telling her of that poignant memory of his youth.

'Except that, not long before the end of the Occupation in France, she was stopped at a street check by Germans who were looking for members of the Resistance, they searched her, found that medal, and assumed she was a Jew, hiding by not wearing the yellow star. She was taken away that night, and nobody knew what had happened to her, until a year after the war was all over. Then, a Polish woman, Janka, who'd been a barracks-mate of Martine's at Belsen, managed to contact her parents. She told them of the starvation, the disease, how Martine had lost all her hair from typhoid fever, still she never complained, remained cheerful throughout, even when the bombers came. Until, in the last weeks before VE day, an Allied raid hit the ammunition factory where they worked. There were tremendous explosions, fires. But Martine was in a part that didn't burn, instead she and the other prisoners there were buried alive. Janka worked in another area of the plant that wasn't destroyed. She said they could hear survivors crying for help for days, under the rubble. But the German guards forbade anybody from trying to help, or even approaching. Eventually, there was silence . . .'

Roger's voice faltered. A pause. She knew he was removing

his glasses and blowing his nose. 'Meanwhile,' he continued, 'her two brothers had joined the Resistance to avenge her and been killed.'

Mariès sighed. I was alive during those years, she thought, but too young to remember anything. My first memories don't go back further than the first grade in Malibu, with the exception of Arsène, my Angora rabbit. Yet all that horror happened in my lifetime, and I am only twenty-five.

'So' – Roger was absorbed in his past and in his film – 'the movie tells the story just as it happened. Except that I sublimated the guilt I feel over Martine's fate – and her brothers' – by having the character who represents me commit suicide when he learns of the three deaths he is responsible for.'

Mariès was touched. 'You're not guilty of anything, Rog, you never intended to hurt anyone,' she murmured soothingly. Then, 'It does sound like a great film, and I'm sure you do deserve an Oscar. Let's wait for the nominations. Now, darling, I must get off the phone, I think my mother has calls to make. See you sometime soon.'

Channing was waiting for the line to return Peter Baldwin's call, in Vail, Colorado.

'Hello.' A bright, cheerful voice. It was Terry, Peter's wife, whom everybody adored. 'I understand the cat's out of the bag for *Just Deserts*. Pinky called earlier, and Dusty, and Kevin. Everybody was wailing.'

Peter came on the line. 'Hi.' He chuckled. 'I know all about the special. Calm down, they could have signed up Godzilla, too. Always think it could be worse, in this business. Like the series being canceled, for instance.'

Later, as Channing was sitting up in bed, with reading glasses, her hair pulled back by a white bandeau, jotting down ideas for the script, Mariès came in, padding barefoot on the thick white carpet, in her pink terry minirobe, her smooth dark hair brushed back, hanging long and straight over her shoulders. In spite of her twenty-five years, she could have been sixteen with her freshly washed face. She sat on the edge of her mother's bed, gently removed the glasses and put them on the night table. Then she took the pen and papers and laid them down with the glasses.

'I've decided to go back to school,' she told her mother. 'I'll enroll at UCLA for the master's program in French. Show business is all right, but it's not enough for me. Let's face it, bit parts will never make a great actress out of me, and as far as modeling is concerned, I'll be damned if I ever go for a look-see to hear that they were looking for a younger type. Besides, I'm getting hungry in the mind.'

Channing reflected that it would be difficult to find a younger type, and yet she knew exactly what her daughter meant. Hollywood time was accelerated. That moment would come, inexorably. Both she and Mariès knew it.

'UCLA? Weren't you happy at Barnard? You said they had such a great Romance language program there.'

'Undergraduate, yes, but for graduate work, I think I'd like to try UCLA. Also, I wouldn't want to break all my ties with the studios here, just in case. I think I'll look for a new agent too. I'm sure Roger can direct me to a more aggressive one. But meanwhile, I'll go tomorrow and register for the spring quarter. It will be fun to be exercising my mind again.'

Channing could only approve – nothing else than approval was expected of her.

23

UCLA BASKED IN a glorious spring sunshine, lawns verdant, hibiscus bushes starred with saucer-size blooms after the rains.

Students crowded the walks of the campus on this first day of the spring quarter, as the noontime carillon scattered notes from a musical comedy song, a different tune every day. Today it was 'Stranger in Paradise,' an extravagant promise to newly registered students.

The enormous amphitheaters were drawing streams of undergraduates to required courses, aspiring them through their portals. Mobs besieged the windowless Graduate Business Administration Building. A more modest affluence made its way to the Ralph Bunche Building for Social Sciences, better known as the Waffle, for its flat, geometrically patterned façade, and famous even more for its inadequate elevator system than for the distinguished teaching that was offered there.

Central campus, the Quadrangle, formed of the four original brick Romanesque buildings, dated from the twenties, and formed the nucleus of the now gigantic UCLA, sprawling, spectacularly landscaped campus. Royce Hall, the theme building, was an exact replica of the many-gabled basilica of Sant' Ambrogio in Milan – only larger, of course; this was California, after all, not *just* medieval Italy. The library opposite, with the carillon in its towers, had already been demoted to Undergraduate Library, superseded by the enormous new Research Library.

Next to Royce Hall, seedy Haines Hall housed two of the lesser departments: anthropology upstairs, its gruesome collections relegated to the basement, some of the more appealing artifacts displayed in glass cases near the entrance – arrows, quivers, and shields from the Amazon, beaded moccasins and woven baskets from western Indian tribes. Oddly enough, this definitely non-European *étalage* heralded the approaches of the small, but august, department of French, housed on the ground floor.

Mariès had parked in one of the distant structures, cursing under her breath because she could not find in her bag the quarters necessary for the automatic gates, and had to try parking lot after parking lot until she found a kiosk where the attendant would accept her bill. Later today, she'd remind herself to buy a parking permit that ought to guarantee her parking no farther than a mile or so from Haines Hall, where her classes would be. Now, she hurried across campus, long black hair flying, slim and tanned in her pastel blue Courrèges sleeveless minidress, books and notepad in hand. She was climbing the stairs that led to the entrance of Haines, when the electric bell trilled.

That's all right, she thought, unworried, nobody is on time the first day.

The glass cases filled with rotting shreds of pre-Columbian textiles, child-size Peruvian mummy cases, and an enthusiastically endowed fertility figure carved out of obsidian, gave her a start. She checked her catalogue of classes. This was Haines, wasn't it? To make sure, she walked down the hall, to where she could see the open door of a departmental office.

'Hello! Excuse me. This is the department of French, isn't it?' she asked the two surly secretaries, who did not even bother to look up.

She repeated her question patiently. Nothing. She waited, inwardly seething. Finally, one of the women looked up coldly from her desk and let drop from pinched lips in the general direction of Mariès: 'What else do you think it could be?'

Mariès controlled an urge to indicate what else she thought. As she passed the glass partition, she could not help notice that both women were leafing through fashion magazines.

Checking numbers on doors, she finally found Room 196, indicated in her schedule of classes as the temple of FRENCH 615: POSTWAR DIRECTIONS IN FRENCH THOUGHT, Course required for MA and Ph.D candidates. Instructor: Mr Lefort (on leave 1966–67). Visiting Professor: Mr Apollaud (Spring Term). M, W, 12:00–1:40.

Less than a dozen students were already sitting scattered in the room, most of them having modestly chosen seats as far as possible from the instructor's podium, still vacant. A far cry from the crowds assaulting business, math, computer science, and engineering courses. Only a dilettante or a very serious student would register in 'postwar directions.' In addition, the requirement for a fluent knowledge of French, all lecturing, reading, and writing of papers being in French, whittled enrollment down even further. Mariès sat near the window, looking at the yews and cypresses just outside, with the gables of Royce Hall in the near background. For some reason, the view made her think briefly of Mallarmé's *Afternoon of a Faun*. Italy? No, the Faun was in Sicily. Students were talking among themselves in low voices, most of them already acquainted from their previous courses. Mariès, who had done her undergraduate work at Barnard, over the course of five and a half years, with interruptions every time a more fascinating alternative hove into sight, didn't know anybody here yet.

Her watch showed 12:30. Shouldn't the instructor be here soon?

The door opened once more. Not the instructor yet. A male student, who stood on the threshold, looking the room over, hesitant.

'This is French 615?' he asked. 'The secretaries refused to tell me how to find the room.'

'French 615, yes, of course. Come in, come in.' This from a matronly, middle-aged woman, the only one sitting at the foot of the podium, a recycler obviously returning to university life after many years devoted to other pursuits.

Or to no pursuits at all, thought Mariès, always charitable. Pursuits had never been lacking in her own young life.

The young man was still standing in the open door, unhurriedly wondering now where he wanted to sit. Mariès gave him a second glance. He was tall, probably six two or three, long-legged, lean-hipped, with dark blond hair pushed across his brow, high cheekbones, and freckles on a short nose. She took in the Patek-Philippe watch, the worn denim work shirt, white Levi's, woven rope belt, and Gucci loafers, their trademark stirrups cut off, but Mariès knew Gucci loafers with or without.

Not bad at all, she thought. He makes me feel overdressed. Did an unconscious approving nod of her head perhaps imply the chair next to hers? He gave an imperceptible smile, moved slowly, threading his way through the scattered chairs, followed by several pairs of hopeful eyes, and came to take the place next to Mariès.

She ignored him studiously, checking her notepad, testing her pen. He pushed his chair back just a bit, to where he could observe her without her seeing him. She immediately guessed the maneuver and countered it by moving her own chair back, too, which brought her level with him. As she turned her head slightly, she met his eyes on her.

'Hi.' He smiled. '*Ça va?*'

Before Mariès could answer, the door opened authoritatively and the instructor walked in.

Professor Christian Apollaud, visiting from Yale University, was the drawing star of the department that term. American-born, he was one of those men who sense early in life that some flaw in appearance or character limits their chances within the culture to the lower spheres of success, so they decide to desert their own world and embrace another. Christos Apollonides, born of immigrant Greek parents, had, twenty-five years earlier, decided success would sooner be found as a Frenchman in America and he was right. He had learned to speak French in a manner that dazzled his naive students unaware of its limitations. Sandy-haired and slight, he dressed, he hoped, the way a Frenchman would, and resolutely refused to speak English unless forced to. Then, it was with an indefinable, faintly British accent that attempted to hint of Mayfair rather than Chicago, his hometown.

Mariès, who'd had plenty of experience on the subject, instantly sensed another self-inventor.

Just like home – someone else trying to be what he wasn't born to. Let's see how *he* handles it, she thought, mildly interested.

Professor Apollaud made his way to the podium, stopped to remove the light overcoat he wore, in spite of the warmth of the day, over his gray suit, and laid it over the back of a chair, near the matronly student who officiously fussed to straighten a fold.

The ten or so students waited, in total rapture. Obviously, they see it as a spiritual experience about to begin, Mariès thought to herself ironically.

Apollaud climbed the one step to the chair, sat down, unbuttoned his jacket's single button, took a pack of Gauloises out of his pocket, and produced a box of *Régie française* matches.

French matches, observed Mariès, impressed. I can see this is *graduate* school!

He struck the match, lit the cigarette, and rolled the end between his lips, curiously formed into a perfectly circular pucker.

Gay, thought Mariès. It makes sense.

He exhaled, closed his eyes for a second, a performer concentrating before his stage entrance. Tension in the room was audible, pens poised over notepads. Apollaud spoke. 'It would be a grievous error, even in a sub-absolute context, to confuse the *in se* and the *per se* . . .'

Everybody wrote:

and waited. He inhaled, exhaled.

'The *in se* and the *per se* of existential consciousness cannot be compared to either the antithetical relationship explored in the un-definition of the *I* and the *me* or . . .'

Everybody wrote:

I   me

and looked up. Apollaud was warming to his subject.

'Under a deceptive clarity, the concept of being versus nothingness hides a complexity of thought that must be subjected to exegetical analysis in order to . . . in order that . . . inasmuch as the concept of essence versus existence determines the de-clarification of . . .'

Mariès wrote: *Existentialism is simple, but it can be made to seem complicated.*

Crush the half-smoked cigarette in an ashtray. A half smile, condescending, to his audience.

'In the realm of definition, praxis – and I give the term its full ontological meaning, of course – implies an *in situ* dialectical commitment. You are surely aware of its mediatic implications in terms of externalization . . .'

Apollaud was lighting yet another cigarette. A small movement on her right attracted Mariès's eye. The young man sitting next to her had written on his notepad:

¿

and was holding it out to her. On her own pad, she wrote:

!

and showed it to him. He smiled, and wrote:

Does this emperor have any clothes?

She wrote:

He is mother naked.

He wrote:

> *My name is Brad H. Spigner. Glad to meet you.*

She wrote:

> *Mariès May. Me too.*

He wrote:

> *Want a cup of coffee when this is over?*

Ten cigarettes later – Apollaud only took a few puffs, and lit the follow-up with the half-smoked stub – and about three hundred involved, incomprehensible sentences further along the line of the same indecipherable thought (If thought indeed there was, observed Mariès), the electric bell announced the end of the class.

Mariès looked at the other students' pads. They had all jotted down a few words, then given up. The lack of content added to the obscurity of expression made the taking of notes a vain undertaking. Yet, shining eyes expressed admiration, with the conviction that some deep, important revelation was hiding under the harshly accented abstract words, a meaning accessible to only a chosen few initiates. In more practical terms, those who believed would, in time, obtain the coveted degree. Others would sit in vain, deaf to the arcane wisdom, untouched by grace. Degreeless.

Brad was waiting outside the room when Mariès came out the door. They walked together silently for a while, flowing with the stream of students.

Inside the Student Union, Brad brought two cups of coffee from the urn at the counter, and sat facing her at a table near the enormous tapestry motif that formed a background to the room.

'Want to ask questions, or should I start?'

She smiled, enchantingly – in her imperious oval face, smiles of pleasure came rarely – and shook her long, straight, shining hair.

456

'I'll ask. Whatever is a nice boy like you doing in a class like that?'

'Same as you, I guess. Taking required courses, so I can get into the ones I'd really enjoy afterward ... Poetry, especially the Symbolists, and Baudelaire, Rimbaud, Mallarmé, Valéry, and civilization if they'll let me put that in my program. I want to take courses in French history, history of art and architecture, even if they don't count toward the degree. In fact, I don't care all that much about the degree. It's just that I have to have an officially announced goal to convince my family, especially my grandfather, who finances it, that I have a good reason to be in school.'

'Wait a minute' – Mariès laughed – 'you're answering all the questions before I even ask them. Now it's my turn.'

Two hours and missed classes later, they were still sitting in front of their cold cups of coffee, oblivious to all the comings and goings, absorbed in each other.

They talked about themselves; Brad was the son of ranching people from Texas. His father's family, the Spigners, operated a large cattle ranch, as did his mother's father, Bradley Hollis, after whom he was named and who saw him more as son than grandson. Brad Hollis also had some oil interests.

'Hollis Oil?' asked Mariès, expecting a laughing denial. 'That's right,' he said curtly.

He had learned French, he told her, because he felt a strange attraction to that language and to France, ever since he had taken his first French class as a boy. Nobody at home could understand this obsession, and he couldn't explain it himself.

'A French ancestor, perhaps?' suggested Mariès.

'Not that I know of, and I doubt that anybody in my family, for several generations, came from anywhere but Texas ...'

'Maybe you're a changeling?' She grinned that irresistible Vogue grin.

457

'Hard to believe, too. I look a lot like my mother, people say.'

Mariès told him in turn that she had been born in France. Her father had died when she was a baby, and her mother had later remarried. *May* was her stepfather's name, but her real name was Marie-Esmée de Blazonac. Brad repeated the name delightedly, savoring the syllables: Marie-Esmée de Blazonac. How beautiful! It sounded just the way she looked: elegant and aristocratic. She told him of her first years, of which she remembered so little, and the château by the lake, that belonged jointly to her and her uncle, a reclusive bachelor who had always lived there.

Brad was entranced. 'Tell me more,' he insisted.

So, she told him about the long, tree-lined drive, the majestic gated entrance, the carriage courtyard with the fountain in the center. She described the wide, worn stone steps guarded by lions *couchant*, the heavy wrought-iron gate, with the Blazonac coat of arms and motto above, *Lo Faraï*; 'I will do it,' in the Limousin dialect, the language of the troubadours . . .

Brad's Texas eyes were wide – the language of the troubadours! 'More,' they entreated.

So, she told him about the tall evergreens reflected in the deep water on the far bank of the lake, and the park, with chestnut trees and oaks, statues standing at the *rond-points*, walks with their thick carpet of cutout leaves, soft underfoot during the fall season. There was the vegetable garden, once designed on a pattern, intricate as a tapestry, so the colors of the vegetables, the red of the beet leaves, the lacy plumes of the carrots, and the celadon of the lettuce heads would illustrate the geometrically planned beds. There were rose trees standing at the corners of every bed, in the medieval tradition, to represent the prayers of the gardener rising to God . . .

'And now,' she continued, 'sit back and brace yourself, if you like my dream castle, because now, I'm going to tell you the truth.'

The century-old elms along the avenue were dead, or

dying, she said cruelly, victims of a blight that had devastated all those in the area, skeletons in need of being removed and replaced. The avenue had never been paved, and deep mud made it impassable in winter, a hazard in summer when the mud hardened into sharp ridges. The majestic gate? It had long ago fallen off its hinges. What was left was rusted and broken, leaning askew against the wall. The wall that enclosed the park with the noble trees and the statues? In disrepair, too, crumbling in places, covered with rank masses of ivy elsewhere. The statues had vanished from their pedestals – only pieces of broken marble could sometimes be found, when your foot dug through layer after layer of rotten leaves. The fountain in the carriage court was no more than a trickle, feeding clumps of slimy brown algae in a basin with a cracked margin . . . 'I won't tell you about the tapestried vegetable garden, I'll let you guess.'

His eyes were still dark with fascination.

'You want to know more?' Sadness and anger were in her voice. 'I'll tell you more. The inside of my fairyland castle? It's so damp in winter that rivulets of moisture trickle down the stone walls. On the other hand, there's no running water, and just one electric line. Do you have any idea of the cost of installing water pipes and electrical conduits in stone walls that are six feet thick? And bathrooms? And a regular kitchen? The kitchen now is a dark cavern, with an antiquated black stove in a corner and a fireplace large enough for tree trunks. And while there *are* plenty of dead tree trunks around, there's no one to cut and carry them. So, the hearth's always cold now. The woman who cooks for my uncle just lights the stove. More? The twenty-four authentic Louis XIII high-backed chairs in the dining room have all lost some legs and part of their backs, they stand askew, hung all over with shreds of what used to be the striped satin of their seats. And there are bright squares on the faded silk walls, where six still lifes used to hang . . .'

But, strangely, the wonder still hadn't dimmed in Brad's eyes. 'Why, it's just a matter of upkeep – replanting, plumbing, remodeling, refurnishing, stuff like that.' He shrugged. 'It's done all the time. What's the problem?'

'The problem is simple,' said Mariès bitterly. 'The problem is money. It would cost a great deal, and neither my uncle nor myself have any. I even hate to go there now, because it depresses me to see the desolation and to be so helpless. My mother works as a writer for TZN, my stepfather's a lawyer in Century City. It means a comfortable life, but no capital to invest in something as impractical as Blazonac, from which no return can be expected anyway. Only more expenses all the time.'

Brad shook his head, unconvinced. Mariès had no notion of the enormous Hollis oil fortune, or the way Brad had been raised in which money was never an issue. It was simply there – unlimited – and it was there to serve, to make life more pleasant and productive for those who controlled it. Since Brad's birth, twenty-one years ago, his grandfather's oil leases and exploration had grown into a vast empire, of which the old man had retained a majority interest. He was now over eighty, and both capital and continued revenues had steadily accumulated. Brad could draw any allowance he wanted, although – unlike those of the playboy he so easily could have become – his needs were modest.

Brad also knew that, someday, according to his grandfather's will, he would inherit most of the oil interests, while his mother, Bunny Spigner, would receive as her share the entire ranch, operated, since her marriage, by her husband, Spike, who ran it along with the Spigner holdings. Brad had never thought that control of the immense fortune would make much difference to him or to the way he wanted to live. He'd continue to travel, study, immerse himself in his studies as long as he felt like it. After that? Brad hadn't yet considered the time beyond.

He said to Mariès, for lack of better words, 'How you love it! Is it beautiful?'

'Yes. There are three lakes, each feeding into the other. The castle is built so that in calm weather its towers reflect in the water like in a mirror. It's so ancient, stately, that it breaks my heart. I used to dream of seeing it restored someday, just the way it used to be, in the time of my profligate grandmother after whom I was named, who burned the candle at both ends and died before she was forty. My mother says it's unnerving how much I look like her.'

Were there tears in her eyes? Brad wondered. The castle's reflection in the still waters of the lake shimmered in his own mind's eye.

'Oops,' cried Mariès, looking at her watch, 'too late to go get my parking permit today. Damn, I'll have to hunt for parking on Wednesday again!'

'Where do you live?'

'In Malibu.'

'My apartment's in Santa Monica. You could leave your car in the garage of my building, and we could drive to campus together, if you like. I hope you don't mind, but I only own a beat-up Volkswagen. It would save you a lot of parking problems and hiking to classes. I happen to have received a permit for lot five, right by central campus. Somebody made a mistake, I guess. Might as well take advantage of it.'

Brad would have died rather than reveal to Mariès what he had just recently learned himself. Grandfather Hollis had donated a million dollars to the Regents of the University of California, ostensibly for endowment of geology research into oil-bearing shales – and if anything useful came out of it, so much the better. At worst the little investment might smooth corners for Brad at UCLA. University authorities saw it the same way, and student Bradley H. Spigner received a preferential parking permit. Also best seat tickets to all the sporting events, for which Brad couldn't have cared less, arrived in his mailbox with regularity. He probably could have asked for a great deal more, but would never have dreamed of it.

He did not mention, either, that what Mariès assumed would be a modest student pad, was in fact the penthouse on the roof of the Black Gold Towers, the fabulous residential building on Ocean Avenue, with a panoramic view of the Pacific, private elevator, and his own personal gym. The Black Gold Towers was only one of the many Hollis Oil real estate investments.

There, Brad lived without furniture, simply because he hadn't yet felt the need for any. His foam rubber mattress lay on the thick carpet that had come with the penthouse. His books were arranged in neat piles all along the walls, and on the simple, unfinished wood desk where he studied. Only a few objects revealed that the occupant wasn't an ordinary impoverished grad: a Romanesque Virgin, sculpted in wood, simple and touching, which he'd found and bought in an antique shop in Chartres, for a sum on which many students would survive for a year. An Aubusson tapestry, a seventeenth-century *verdure* he had admired while visiting a castle in the Auvergne, and found to be available at a price, was the only ornament on the vast living-room wall. A broken stone capital, from a ruined twelfth-century chapel, rested near Brad's bed on the floor. It showed the Three Wise Men asleep, lying like cord wood, in the naive medieval perspective, under the symmetrical folds of a blanket – the angel of the Lord touching his finger to theirs, while pointing with the other hand to the star they were to follow. These ancient objects, worn and priceless, deeply moved his heart, and he never tired of examining them, touching their surfaces, worked, so long ago, by other hands.

That night, Mariès drove to Malibu in a daze, and when she arrived home went straight to her mother's bedroom, where she found Channing in a thick white turtleneck sweater over flannel pajamas, sitting at her typewriter. She put her hand on her mother's shoulder. Without turning around, Channing rolled the paper down to blank space and typed in capitals:

462

Looking over her mother's shoulder, Mariès read above:

JUST DESERTS SPECIAL

STATE DEPARTMENT HAS DECIDED TO ORGANIZE A
GOODWILL TOUR TO SAMOA. WILL SEND THE BOSTON
CELTICS ON EXHIBITION GAMES SO THEY CAN HELP
SAMOAN BASKETBALL TEAMS SHARPEN THEIR SKILLS.
LOUIS ARMSTRONG IS MANAGER OF THE TEAM.

SOMEHOW, DIRECTIVES GET MIXED UP. BRIEFING TEAM,
WITH TYPICAL STATE DEPARTMENT EFFICIENCY, READS
THEM AS SAHARA INSTEAD OF SAMOA. FLIGHT PLAN
COORDINATES ARE PREPARED AND GIVEN TO NAVI-
GATOR.

EVENTUALLY, NAVIGATOR REALIZES HE IS NOT OVER
SAMOA, BUT IN MIDDLE OF NOWHERE IN SAHARA DE-
SERT. PLANE IS LOW ON GAS. GAGS WITH PILOT. PLANE
MUST LAND. SEES LIGHT WHICH IS CAMPFIRE BUILT BY
THE BUD STOCKFIELD GROUP.

PLANE LANDS, SURPRISE BOTH SIDES. CELTICS FILE OUT,
GAGLINE FOR EACH CELTIC. LOUIS COMES OUT LAST.
GAGLINE FOR LOUIS.

STEWARDESS ON FLIGHT IS LORI LAMONT. SHE STEPS
OUT AFTER PAUSE. GAGLINE FOR BUD.

Mariès reached over and turned off the typewriter. Then
she sat at the foot of the low, wide bed, crossed her long,
tanned legs, and smiled.

'I take it you had an interesting day?' asked Channing,
turning her chair to face her.

'I was going to regale you with an account of Professor
Apollaud's lecture, but something much more exciting
happened. I met a man I could love.'

'Not many of those around,' observed Channing equably.
'What's he like?'

Mariès described Brad, then shook her head. 'And would
you believe it, he's *younger* than me! About five years, I

guess, from what he said about his life. A child, except he doesn't look like a child, but very much like a man who happens to be young. Can you imagine? I've always fallen for men old enough to be my father. Can you understand what happened to me?'

'I think I do,' mused Channing. 'I suppose you're going to see Brad again?'

'Of course. I'll park my car in his garage and drive to campus with him.'

The phone rang. Mariès jumped. It was Brad. 'Mother,' she whispered, her hand on the receiver. 'I'll take it in my room. Please hang up this extension.'

An hour later, when Channing wanted to use the phone to check a point with Kevin Taylor, the line was still busy. Fred had left a message that he wouldn't be home till late and could be reached at Irv Mandelbaum's office number. Channing padded to the kitchen, the marble floor cold under her bare feet. She opened the brushed stainless steel refrigerator, took out the milk, and poured some in the dog's dish. Then she filled a glass for herself, took a sip, went over to the bar, and tipped in a few drops of brandy. She tasted it, made a face, and added in a generous helping. As she passed Mariès's closed door on the way back to her room, she could hear her daughter laughing delightedly. Still on the phone.

Channing put the glass on her desk, and sat at her typewriter. She took a fresh sheet of paper, adjusted her reading glasses, and continued with the *Sahara* follies until her stamina failed and then she typed a line of twelve stars:

*   *   *   *   *   *   *   *

her private code that meant: That's all, folks. Nothing would get more inanities out of me tonight. Then, she thought of Buzz's waggling red eyebrow.

'Better than starving.' She laughed to herself, and drained her glass.

464

24

'PASSOVER? ASKED CHANNING in vague answer to something Fred had just said. 'When is Passover?'

'Next Friday is the day of the first Seder,' said Fred. 'A night different from all others.'

She was bringing breakfast to the deck over the ocean, on a sun-drenched Sunday morning. The tide was low, leaving a two-hundred-foot-wide expanse of flawless beige sand, already stippled by the minute feet of thousands of sandpipers. 'Roller bearings,' Channing called them, for the funny mechanical way they walked – no, ran, no, glided in unison – all the way to the edge of the water, following the receding wave, to peck at microscopic sea life on the very edge of the surf. Then, as the next wave advanced, the whole group would turn together, quickstep out of reach of the water, and stop just an inch ahead of its advance without ever having to look back or wet their feet.

Each house had its flock of sea gulls too. The ones that had attached themselves to the May house were floating among the kelp, keeping a watchful eye on activities on the deck. When Channing appeared with her tray, one of the gulls saw her first and rose, soon followed by the rest of the flock. They all started gliding, swooping in narrowing curves over the deck, swan-white bellies and black-tipped underwings, feet pulled flat along their bodies, necks extended, a picture of grace, a far cry from the ungainly, squawking birds that landed on the sand to squabble noisily over morsels of food.

Fred was already sitting, in his terry robe, casually leafing through the Sunday papers, rolled-up sleeve revealing the long scar on his arm, now a dented white furrow on the tanned skin. Channing in white shorts and turquoise sleeveless sweater, her hair pulled back with the belt of the sweater, was setting coffee and rolls on the table between them.

The sea gulls narrowed their curves, and began a crescendo of demanding squawks. The dog lying flat on the deck pretended to ignore them. One gull landed on the railing, beak wide open. Channing handed him a bit of bread, which was inhaled. The boldness of their colleague encouraged a dozen other birds to perch on the railing, too, lined up, demanding. Channing laughed, gave them the rest of her roll, then walked back inside the house and returned with a bag of the kibbles she always tried in vain to get the dog interested in. She handed some to the birds on the rail, who pecked them out of her hand, and threw handfuls to those who had continued their curves and swoops. The birds caught bits of food like acrobats, doing extraordinary twists and turns and midair recoveries of incredible grace. Fred had looked up from the paper and was watching them. Some had pale gray wings the color of his eyes.

'Only sea gulls on the Pacific don't know the taste of seafood,' he said.

On the balcony of the next house, a hundred feet away, their neighbor had appeared, in his robe, too, also carrying a bag of dog food. His personal flock lifted off from the kelp beds. He was throwing handfuls, caught by the flying acrobats.

'Hi!' he called out to Fred and Channing. 'I feel like the government, feeding everybody. Don't you?'

The dog was lying motionless, nose flat to the deck, dark eyes swiveling, hoping that one bird, just one, would miss in its flight recovery and would land in front of him with a thud. It had happened once before, and he had pounced, but the bird had quickly regained its balance, and stood him off with a vicious beak, until it could fly away. Still, he thought, things could always happen differently someday. Let's just be patient and watch. He

466

scorned the bits of kibbles that landed near his nose, waiting instead for the unwary bird that would venture within reach.

None did.

'What were you saying about Passover?' asked Channing again. 'Isn't it the Jewish equivalent of Easter? Tell me about it.'

Fred explained curtly, and with a tinge of annoyance, about the Jews in Egypt. They had marked the lintel of the door with the blood of the sacrificial lamb, so the Angel of Death would pass over their house and spare their firstborn. The Seder was the meal, with sweet wine, bitter herbs, a roasted egg, a bone, all ritual foods that symbolize ... 'Oh, well ...' his voice trailed off.

'Did your family have a Seder, when you were growing up?' Channing was eager for interest, exchange, conversation. Anything but the absence and silences growing more obvious in recent months.

'Oh, no, my family wasn't religious at all. You see, in the Germany of those days, there were few Conservative or Reformed Jews like there are here now. You were Orthodox, with strict beliefs and observance, or else you simply broke away and secularized to live like other Germans.'

'Did you ever want to study Judaism then?'

'No, I wanted no part of it. I desperately wanted to be someone else. When we were in Switzerland, after we had to leave Germany because of the persecutions, I had already thought of my new name, and I looked at myself in mirrors and shop windows thinking, This is Fred May.'

'You were baptized in Spain?'

'No, in Portugal, in Oporto. It was a condition of getting a visa to Brazil. But I was happy about it, I felt baptism erased the stain of being Jewish. I have nightmares about feeling that way, now. A stain! Can you imagine! Hitler's worst crime wasn't the sufferings he inflicted on us – it was that he made some of us ashamed to be what we were. And I was one of those. I'll never live long enough to atone.'

467

Channing held her breath. There was a visionary look in the gray eyes. Fred had never, in all their years of married life, communicated as much, and on such a personal level. Should she ask questions? Probe? Or just let him reveal himself? He leaned back in his chair, rubbed his forehead, smoothing his hair back in a familiar gesture. Channing saw the white streak was now almost entirely engulfed in a much wider area of gray that had not been there recently.

Satiated now, with no more food being proffered, the gulls were standing on the beach, balanced on one foot, motionless, like wooden decoys.

Channing sat straight on her chair, facing Fred, the sun in her eyes.

'I've joined the temple,' Fred said finally, as if it was an effort to pronounce the words. 'It was Irv's advice and he's giving me instruction. I want to erase the Christian baptism and everything else.'

Fred's confidence made Channing so happy, in spite of the alienation it implied, that she wanted to open her arms and hug the world. What could she do to show him she was his wife, stood with him, would follow him wherever he wanted to lead?

'I'd like to learn about Judaism, too,' she said eagerly. 'I lost all interest long ago in the Catholic religion, and I'm interested in what Judaism offers. Could I take instruction with you? Then I could even convert. I've often thought that . . .' she added, a little desperately.

Fred interrupted, 'Oh, no, no, don't you understand? *You* are part of what I want to get away from. Just as you were part of what I once thought I wanted to be. You were a Catholic, raised by nuns, you wore a cross around your neck, and later, you had that name, with that medieval title of aristocracy . . . *That* was as far from being Jewish as one could get! I wanted it desperately. But now that I've begun to see a light, there's a road I must travel to get to it. And I can't travel it with you. It is a long, lonely journey of the soul.'

Silence. Channing was blinking back tears. It's the sun,

she thought. It's too strong, I need my sunglasses . . .

Fred continued, 'I was with my father when he disappeared and probably died,' he said slowly. 'I have never told anyone what happened. We were hunted, hiding under a tree in an abandoned corner of a city park. He would venture out at night to get food scraps out of garbage cans. I felt nothing but scorn for him and anger . . . And then, one night, he just didn't come back . . .'

'Did you ever know what happened to him? Did he have any papers, any ID?'

Fred shook his head in misery. 'No. His papers and his money had been taken from him by the Gestapo a few days earlier. I am haunted now, don't you see, by what could have happened to him. Did he survive? Was he taken to a camp? What happened to him then? I know, years have passed, yet he might still be alive somewhere, old and alone. I feel I must go to Germany and try to find some lead as to what might have happened to him. There might be records of a body being picked up, or of someone who took in a hurt and confused man. I have to go or I'll lose my mind.'

'I'd like to go with you,' offered Channing, although she knew there was no ticket for her on this journey of the soul. 'Do you want me with you?'

Fred shook his head. 'No. No. I must travel that road alone. I told you.'

Mariès emerged from the house onto the balcony, sleekly stunning in a white tennis dress, exquisite flower face, black hair cut square, hanging to the middle of her back. In the weeks since she'd known Brad, their romance had flourished, blossomed, whatever it is a romance does when two people are head over heels in love, happy, and together all the time, Channing thought fondly, with both tears and a smile in her eyes.

'Hi, old folks,' she greeted them breezily. 'I'll let you sun those weary bones at home! Brad's picking me up in a minute. We've got a set of singles at the tennis club and later, we'll have lunch at Trancas. We're going to a party

469

tonight, so I'll just take some clothes along and change at Brad's. I'll see you either late, or in the morning. *Ciao!'*

The bell rang, the dog sprang up, barking uncontrollably. Brad came in, tanned too, even more handsome than Channing remembered him since the last time she'd seen him, dark blond hair barring his forehead, high cheekbones, and that smile that lit up the room.

What's the matter with me? wondered Channing. The other day, I looked at Mariès and saw her grandmother. Now, I look at Brad and I see Anthenor – a livelier, more vivid version, of course, an Anthenor who'd have blossomed out instead of closing himself off. Exuberant instead of withdrawn. Now, why do I have to think of Anthenor? Is Mariès right? Could this be old age already? That time when the present loses its immediacy and memories of long ago come floating to the surface unbidden. That's what's happening to Fred too.

Brad was greeting her effusively, came to the deck, shook hands with Fred, threw bits of food to the gulls. A few of the birds found the energy to rise and swoop for it. The sea shimmered, each wave bringing it closer now. Channing, leaning on the railing, murmured, as if to herself:

> *Midi le juste y compose de feux* . .
> (Noontime above, there composes with fires . . .)

Brad looked at her gratefully and finished the quote:

> *La mer, la mer toujours recommencée.*
> *(The sea, the sea, forever recommenced.)*

'Such simple words, and so perfect! There's a mathematical purity to Valéry's poetry . . . Something like the prisms of a crystal, or the facets of a diamond,' he added, catching the flash of Channing's.

'*Midi le juste* will be upon us if we don't get out of here fast,' urged Mariès, racket and bag in hand. They left, the dog disappointed to see the excitement subside, but beginning now to watch for signs of his afternoon walk.

'As I was saying,' continued Fred after a long silence, 'I

want to go back to Germany. Irv will come with me for a while. We're planning to leave soon after the Passover holidays.'

'Let's be realistic about it,' said Channing gently, sitting on the foot of his chaise. 'Chances are you won't find anything about your father. It's more than twenty-five years ago. So, let's assume you don't. What will you do then?'

'I'll have to atone, somehow,' murmured Fred.

In spite of the tragedy of Fred's sorrow, Channing felt that for the first time in their years together, they had broken through a barrier.

'Darling,' she said, taking his hands in hers, 'I understand. But don't you see? You're full of remorse. Remorse is repentance, and if you repent, you shall be forgiven. That's what I've always learned. You need do no more than sincerely regret, with all your heart, whatever it is you've done against God's Law, and He will forgive you.'

Fred stood up. Just to get away from me, she thought sadly. He looked down at her.

'You speak this way because you were raised a Christian. Sure, it's easy for Christians! They believe Jesus came to earth to offer his sufferings in exchange for God's forgiveness. Your church has her *Agnus Dei qui tollit peccata mundi*, the Lamb of God who erases the sins of the world. So, because of Jesus' sacrifice, just say you're sorry and all is well. But you see, we Jews don't have it so easy. No free lunch where I come from. We're still waiting for our Messiah, nobody's come yet to take our sins upon his own shoulders! Repentance means nothing. You can't assuage guilt so easily! Sacrifice still must be made.'

'What must you do, then?'

The sun was behind Fred. Backlighted, his face showed deep lines of sorrow.

'I'll tell you,' he said. 'I'll let you know when I know myself. But it's not going to be easy, either for me or for you. Even the innocents have to pay.'

Channing was still attempting to reason. 'Darling, you

are building what happened to your father into more of a responsibility than it really is for you. You were a boy, scared and just trying to live. That's all!'

'Oh, no, that's not all. That's only part of it. I denied him because I wanted to become someone else, and I did! And it was all for nothing, nothing at all! The new name, the new identity, May, Mayer, it mattered then, but who cares in the *real* world? Look at Rabbi Mandelbaum, he's my age, he was born in Germany too, he survived the same times I did without selling his soul! Roger was baptized with me, yes, but it meant nothing to him, he's been a member of the temple all those years, he makes no secret of his birth! Mischa, remember Mischa? He rests under a Star of David in that military cemetery near Arromanches! And Isaac, Herschel, they fought to form the state of Israel, they're devoting their lives to it! None denied his father, his people! Just me. And now, I don't know who I really am, and I can't go on like that. I am a man with an empty core.'

'You are my husband,' she said gently.

Fred shrugged. 'And not much of that, either. It hasn't been fair to you, and I know it. Now I'm seeking the truth that will make me whole.' A silence. He continued, looking away in the distance.

'I've made all the necessary arrangements at the office. My cases will be taken over by Steve Albright. He's a go-getter, very smart. Everything will be fine there. I'll give you a power of attorney for our personal affairs, and I'll sign the house over to you.'

'No need to do that for a short trip! How long are you planning to be away?'

'I have no idea. No idea at all.'

'Are you thinking of a couple of weeks? A month, maybe? Longer?'

'I told you. No idea.'

A sudden thought, like a cold blade in the pit of her stomach, and chills ran through her in spite of the hot sunshine.

'You plan not to come back, is that it?'

Fred fixed his gray eyes on her. He looked suddenly exhausted. 'I'm not certain yet, but you could be right. I'm probably not coming back. I'll let you know when my mind is made up.'

That taste of ashes she thought she'd forgotten now that she'd learned to live a placid life, that taste was in her mouth again, and the cold, and the emptiness, and the terror. Suddenly, Fred's presence, under any terms, any restrictions, so long as he was here, so long as she kept her identity as his wife, became the center of her reality. *Don't leave me alone, I can't survive without you. I have never been alone in this country! I don't even know how to go about getting the income tax returns done . . . Please, please, stay.*

'Fred,' she murmured, 'remember Paris? The Royal Monceau? And when you told me about the diamond? And how I found it? And the day you came to La Prade? Weren't we happy then?'

Fred shook his head. 'I don't know,' he said sadly. 'I was lying. I always lied in those days – to you, to myself. Now, I'm looking for truth and peace, rest from guilt. My mother knew and she was right. Guilt won't let you rest.'

Two joggers came running along the surf's fringe, their dogs galloping ahead and charging the sea gulls. A gay couple who lived down the beach, Channing knew them by sight but had never learned their names.

'Hi,' shouted one of the men as they passed below the deck. 'If you two aren't the picture of the perfect couple! Looks like you're posing for a poster: "We found Paradise on Paradise Shores."'

Fred leaned on the railing, waved in greeting. 'I wasn't aware it showed that much,' he called back.

Channing was crying quietly. Tears had never moved Fred much before, but now, he was so much a prisoner of his own torment, he didn't even see them. She asked, 'You're not going to Germany to stay, of course. Where are you planning to go afterward?'

473

'Well . . . Isaac Greenberg, who was in camp with me, you know he's a lawyer in Tel Aviv. They need an extra man in his office, someone who would work for a minimum salary to help with immigration cases, land contracts for new settlements, someone to devote his life to Zionism and Israel. So, I might . . . But I don't want to talk about it anymore.' In an unexpected gesture of affection that stilled her heart with hope, he put both his hands on her shoulders. 'You deserved better. It wasn't your fault I was born in such troubled times that bred troubled beings like me, and tore them body and soul, in ways I wouldn't even want you to know about.'

Looking past her, 'Want to go for a game of tennis?'

So, Channing washed her face, exchanged her turquoise sweater for a white Lacoste, and they drove down the coast to the tennis club. There, Mariès and Brad, engaged in an athletic singles match two courts over, waved, and pantomimed humorous admiration for their more sedate moves.

Channing and Fred played their last game that day.

Their last game.

After that day, Fred spoke very little, barely came home, and left one day without saying good-bye. Channing found his closet empty when she returned from the studio, but he'd been living so little in the house that his departure had left no other physical empty space. He called that night from the airport, to say it was better to avoid a farewell scene and he would call her again from Europe. He didn't – wrote a long letter from Germany instead, filled with instructions about insurance policies, the accountant, the sale of his car, et cetera. Nothing about them. A postscript added that no trace of his father had been found yet.

Three months later, Channing received a last letter from him, postmarked Israel, advising her to seek a divorce on grounds of desertion, and telling her which of his colleagues at the office should handle it. He hated to treat her like this, and he hoped she'd rebuild a happier life for herself.

The letter was signed *Fred*, but the return address, chillingly, indicated *Heinz Mayer*, care of the Isaac Greenberg law offices in Tel Aviv. Channing shuddered when she remembered that Heinz had been his father's name. So, Fred had now become his father by way of atonement.

Solitude? Yes. For months, there wasn't a night that she didn't think how easy it would be to simply cease to exist. She felt suspended in midair, with no place to land. And yet, little by little, the taste of ashes faded from her mouth, she could smell the aroma of coffee again, and the salty tang of the sea. She could sometimes laugh at the studio without effort, timidly enjoyed her visits and lunches with Leigh, who sensitively avoided the subject of Fred. She learned about servicing the car and renewing the insurance policies, how to file receipts and canceled checks, and the way to the accountant's office.

All along, she sat every night and wrote pointless, inane plots, but none more absurd than the plot of her own life. She had long removed her nine-carat diamond, because in the days that followed Fred's departure, its flash had come to hurt, physically hurt, her eyes. But sitting pensive at her silent typewriter, a vivid thought occurred to her. That stone obviously no longer belonged to her, it must be returned to Fred. She placed the Cartier box in a larger one, carefully stuffed tissue all around, wrapped and addressed the package to Heinz Mayer. *The* rightful original owner, panged her heart. Then she wrote an accompanying note:

My dear Fred,

She rolled out the paper, crumpled it, rolled in a new sheet:

My dear Heinz,

Your father gave you this diamond to help you to safety and it should help you today to complete the long voyage. Make the best use of it for the good of the causes you are working for.

The mark it has left on my finger is still there and nothing can erase the memories that brought it to me in the first place. I can't help but think of myself as your wife still, and I'd be glad if you'd ask me to join you in Tel Aviv, to come to know Judaism and work alongside you.

Perhaps we have learned enough about ourselves and each other so that we could find the closeness that eluded us all those years. Think of it, my dear Heinz, and please get in touch with me, if only to tell me the package arrived safely.

She hesitated: Shall I write 'With all my love?' No. What she felt for Fred wasn't love, it was – and hadn't she known it all along? – the need for an anchor, an identity. So she wrote simply:

As always,
C

If she thought hard about it, that's the way it had always been between them: He'd promised to care for her, cherish her, smooth the road of life for her. He meant to. He hadn't succeeded, but then, neither had she. He'd hoped to find happiness with her and didn't. Not our fault, she thought sadly, it's just that the past wouldn't let him. Or me, perhaps, either. Haven't I kept Anthenor's hazelnut wood stick with the word *Forever* hidden all these years in the secret compartment of my jewel box?

Mariès had moved in with Brad and they came to visit Channing every week, breathless, youthful, exuberantly happy. Channing always hurried to arrange her face into a mask of insouciant gaiety when she saw their car pull up, and greeted them with eyes that reflected theirs, at least as well as she could.

'Mrs May,' asked Brad one day, 'this is formal, so I'm not calling you Channing. I would like to ask you for the hand of your daughter Marie-Esmée de Blazonac. She says that I'm too young to get married, but perhaps, if I have your express blessing, it will be another argument in my favor.'

'My blessing is yours, my son.' Channing smiled, playing the game. 'And tell my hussy of a daughter that she'd better make an honest man out of you.'

Mariès pretended to be angry, but there was a softness in her eyes and a new gentleness that wasn't there before. I'm not even intimidated by her anymore, thought Channing, but then, there isn't much that I'm afraid of now.

25

'PLEASE, DARLING, SAY yes,' repeated Brad, sitting on a chaise lounge. 'I said, "Let's get married." That's what we both want, isn't it? Why wait?'

Mariès didn't answer, her back to him as she stood looking out. But as she turned her head a little, he could see a smile creasing the side of her cheek outlined by the light.

The view from the terrace of his penthouse stretched all along the curve of Santa Monica Bay. A necklace of lights outlined the shore, otherwise indistinguishable from the sea. To the left, the dark mass of the Palos Verdes hills, against the lighter sky, dotted with sparkles, and then the bay cities, Hermosa Beach, El Segundo, Redondo Beach, Venice, Ocean Park, all fused now into a seaside metropolis invisible in the dark, present only through their string of shimmering lights reflected in the water. The curve continued to the right. Less population, fewer lights there, leading to the far reach of Point Fuma, beyond Malibu. Somewhere out there, in the midst of this cosmic landscape and seascape of lights and dark water, thought Mariès, one of those pinpoints is perhaps Channing's, trying at this very moment to figure out a way to get Lulu Lambert within the sweaty embrace of Bud Stockfield.

Brad pulled Mariès to his side and they lay silent side by side in the balmy night. Then she reached over, unzipped his jeans, and found his sex in its nest of dark blond curls. It surged immediately to full hardness and she sighed as she ran her fingers along the shaft, then leaned over, engulfing Brad in the silky tide of her dark hair. She teased the tip with her tongue, sucked delicately each one of his balls into her mouth. Then, as Brad was already straining, she straightened up, let go of him and remained a few moments, her hand poised over his sex. He arched toward her, his body begging. Instead, her hand made slow, magnetic circular motions above him, until it descended, very slowly, and with the tip of one fingernail, just touched one of his balls. Brad was writhing in desire. So, finally, she began the rhythmic motion with her tongue and lips while her hand rubbed the base of his hard member.

'Wait. Slow down. I want to do you, too,' whispered Brad.

He sought the point of her clitoris and rubbed it gently, insistently, while she sighed and moved a little to place herself under the very tip of his fingers. Their pleasure rose to throbbing orgasms and when their lips met, she tasted her juices and he found the salty musk of his own. They let the wave recede slowly.

'A few more times like that,' gasped Brad, 'and the building will need earthquake reinforcement. That was good for openers. Now, suppose we go inside and really make love?'

An hour later, as Mariès, standing nude, was pouring glasses of orange juice, Brad came to sit on the low kitchen bar.

'As I was saying before you so rudely interrupted me,' he insisted, 'let's get married. I know you were only trying to take my mind off the subject . . .'

Mariès laughed. 'It *did* work for a while, didn't it? Should I try again?'

'I'm serious. You do want to marry me, don't you?' asked Brad intensely.

She faced him, her face grave this time.

'I've told you before, but if that isn't enough, I'll tell you now. I do love you, Brad, and I do want to marry you, sometime in the future. Now, let's not talk about it anymore until we're ready to do something about it.'

Brad sprang to his feet. 'Hurrah,' he shouted, 'I'm ready now! Ready enough for two! Let's do it tonight. No time like the present, to coin a phrase. Let's do it before you change your mind.

'Pack a small bag. We're flying to Las Vegas. Whatever you need, anyway, we can find there. I am going to do something I don't like to do because it's ostentatious, but this is no ordinary occasion. I'll get the company plane based out here to fly us out.'

He started to dial numbers, while Mariès, laughing and complaining of a worsening case of dizziness, slipped into the bedroom to pack a few toilet articles. To these, she added, as an afterthought, the only white outfit she could find in her closet – a white silk knit sweater bought in Saint-Tropez the year before, forgetting the green frog embroidered on the back with the inscription around it: *Il faut embrasser bien des crapauds avant de ...* 'You must kiss a lot of frogs before ...' and a short white pleated skirt. She slipped into a red jersey minisheath with a wide patent belt on the hips and flat red shoes, and came out to find Brad hanging up the phone. Eyes shining, excited, he was ready to go as he was, in jeans and shirt sleeves, only grabbing his beat-up Hermès windbreaker as he escorted her out.

'Come on. The plane will be waiting at Van Nuys airport in fifteen minutes.' He drove in a way never intended for his low-powered little car.

The dented Volkswagen pulled into the airport parking lot just as the Hollis pilot was stepping out of his own Jaguar. Brad hailed him, but the pilot hesitated for a second to identify Mr Hollis's grandson, the company's scion and heir, in the tall young man stepping out of such a disreputable car. Squinting, he finally stepped forward. 'Good evening, Mr Spigner. Good evening, miss.'

'Hi, Stan. I want you to meet my fiancée, Miss Mariès May. We are flying to Las Vegas to get married.'

'It's an honor, and please accept my congratulations,' said Stanley Billings ceremoniously. He added, 'I enjoyed seeing you in *The Great California Earthquake*, Miss May.'

'Thank you,' replied Mariès. 'It's a good thing you didn't sneeze or blink, otherwise you would have missed my entire sequence. And we appreciate your congratulations – you're the very first person to know.'

Brad and Mariès settled into the facing banquettes in the cabin. A large map of the world, on the bulkhead, showed red dots for every Hollis branch office, explained Brad. Brochures about oil exploration, financial reports, letterhead notepads filled the leather pockets by the seats. Ashtrays and matches bore the Diamond Bar company logo.

'Want a drink?' Brad was pointing to the bar. Mariès, dry throat and pounding heart, shook her head no.

Stan came running.

'Flight plan's filed. Let's go.'

'Make a few calls during the flight,' asked Brad. 'You know: the Dunes, flowers, whatever.'

'Righto,' acquiesced Stan.

The plane took off in a wide arc, overflying the ocean, veering to the checkerboard of the Los Angeles lights, lighted swimming pools glowing cool phosphorescent turquoise. It skimmed over the first mountain ranges, emerged out of the fog to the black desert, and very soon, the lights of Las Vegas were under the wings, clustered in the middle of nowhere, with the improbable blaze of the Strip a separate glittering entity. A limousine was waiting at the airport.

At the Dunes Hotel, Joey Costello, the PR man, was waiting by the entrance, anxious to escort Mr Spigner and Miss May to the Hollis suite.

'Time was so short, you understand, Mr Spigner, we just couldn't do much by way of preparations. We hope you'll make allowances, and please, do call for anything you might want.'

On the top floor of the Dunes, the Hollis executive suite bore the stamp of the best Houston decorator: an impersonal subdued but opulent style, with indirect lighting, walls of tobacco-brown suede, massive square glass tables and steel sculptures. Hotel employees were already swarming into the suite. Some were arranging enormous bouquets of white flowers, others were wheeling in a champagne bucket, and a service table with frosted crushed-ice bowls of caviar and silver trays of smoked salmon. The management had 'personally,' said the card, sent a gigantic basket of hopelessly unripe fruit, swathed in bows and cellophane. The man from the jewelry store downstairs was getting off the elevator carrying a case, containing a choice of wedding rings.

Mariès, dazed, sat cross-legged on one of the deep suede couches. On the wall facing her, a large portrait showed an older man, ruddy-faced with a shock of white hair and creased, humorous eyes. *Bradley Hollis* said the brass plate, *Founder and President of the Hollis Oil Company*. To the right, the smaller portrait of an adolescent with straight blond hair across his forehead: *Bradley Hollis Spigner* said the plate. The cheeks were rounder, but yes, this was Brad, five or six years earlier. More than the penthouse, more than the corporate plane, more than the executive suite, the two portraits, for some reason, suddenly brought to Mariès the awareness of an empire that stretched to the far reaches of the planet, behind the handsome, unassuming youth she had fallen in love with and would marry within minutes, unless this was all a dream and she woke up before . . . or changed her mind.

Brad was on the phone, making arrangements. She called out to him, 'Darling, I'm getting panicked. All this makes me feel like a fortune hunter. I knew your family had money, but I had no idea what that much money meant. Let's not get married yet. Let's take a little time to get used to the idea, okay? We can stay here tonight if you like, go down to the casino, catch a show, whatever. Then we'll go back home tomorrow and think some more before doing anything reckless. Agreed?'

Brad nodded his head in agreement, came over, took her in his arms.

482

'I'm so glad you suggested a little judicious mulling over. Let's do just that, but quick – we have five minutes to decide whether we want to be married here in the suite, or in a wedding chapel.'

Mariès laughed, returned his kiss, and accepted a drink. 'Here,' she whispered.

By the time the minister arrived, hastily decked out in vaguely ecclesiastical robes and carrying a Bible, Mariès had dreamily relinquished control to Brad. She had changed into her white dress, frog and all. Since her shoes had begun to hurt, she had kicked them off. So, a few minutes later she stood, long tanned legs and bare narrow feet, her shining black hair loose over her shoulders, next to Brad in his white shirt sleeves. Just before the minister intoned the words of the service, she reached out to the nearest bouquet, pulled off a single white daisy, which she held in both hands, with stiff Pre-Raphaelite grace, throughout the ceremony. Stan the pilot, and Joey the hotel PR man, served as witnesses. Brad placed on Mariès's slim finger the ring she had chosen – the narrowest, simplest one from the selection eagerly proffered. She had refused an engagement ring, because the engagement had been so short.

When Brad bent down to kiss his bride, he felt her face bathed in tears.

'This is the first time I've cried since . . . since Arsène died, long ago,' she whispered in his ear.

The hotel rep uncorked champagne. The local Hollis Oil director and his wife, rousted by Stan – and to Brad's surprise – had rushed from a family party to arrive just as glasses were passed around for the toasts. Stan made a little speech, wishing happiness to two great people. He was answered by the Hollis Oil man, who in turn expressed the certainty that the marriage of Mr and Mrs Spigner would meet with as much success as the company enjoyed. Mariès urged everyone to the food, and Brad made them swear secrecy until he had time to inform his family. They all agreed that the young couple should be the first ones to break the news to Mr Hollis and their parents. Finally, everyone left and they were alone.

It was already early morning.

'Being happy always made me hungry,' said Brad. 'But now, I am positively starved. Starved beyond anything caviar and salmon can do for me.'

'Me too,' cried Mariès, springing from the depth of the suede couch. 'Tell you what. Forget limousines and all that jazz. Let's go downstairs, walk along the Strip till we find a breakfast joint where they'll make us a serious breakfast with eggs and steak . . .'

'And pancakes, and ham, bacon, sausage, and about a ton of hash browns,' shouted Brad. 'Race you to the elevator.'

They ran out, Mariès still barefoot. Waiting for the elevator, Brad reached for her hand with the brand-new ring and kissed it, looking into her eyes.

'You'll make my heart explode with happiness,' sighed Mariès.

It was well past noon the next day when they called Channing. Mariès announced herself as Mrs Spigner from Las Vegas.

They heard Channing gasp. A silence.

'Mrs Spigner from Las Vegas,' Channing finally said. 'It's a good thing your mother has a strong heart. Still, I need to catch my breath. I should have known something like this would happen, because it would be too much to expect anything resembling ordinary behavior from you.' Her throat caught. A split second and she went on, 'Darling, I am so happy *for* you, and *with* you. Tell Brad I welcome him to my heart and family with open arms. But,' she went on, 'I had a call just a moment ago from Brad's service. They have been trying to locate him for the last couple of hours. He should call his grandfather's home in Houston. They said it was urgent.'

Brad's face tightened when he heard Channing's

484

message. He dialed his grandfather's number at the ranch near Houston, where the old man still lived, with a staff headed by Mrs McPhee, his longtime housekeeper.

Mr Hollis had been rushed to the hospital earlier in the day, the victim of a minor heart attack. He was now resting comfortably, said Mrs McPhee, and the doctor didn't think he was in any immediate danger. He should stay in the hospital, nice and quiet, for a few days. But Mr Hollis had insisted that he wanted his grandson to be notified. Could Brad come and see him in the hospital? 'Let's go,' said Brad to Mariès. 'I'll call Stan, he's staying in the hotel. I'll tell him to be ready to fly us out to Texas in twenty minutes.'

But Mariès shook her head. 'You go without me. This is not the time to shock your grandfather with an unannounced bride. Can you imagine what it might do to his heart? Besides, there should only be familiar faces around him at this moment. Are your parents there?'

'No. Mrs McPhee says they left a few days ago for a Caribbean and South American cruise. They have been contacted by ship-to-shore phone, and I'll talk to them before leaving.'

Brad called the ship and reached Bunny and Spike just about to go ashore in Trinidad.

'I'm on my way to Houston,' he told them. 'I've got the West Coast company plane, and I'll be there in a couple of hours. From what Mrs McPhee says, there's no immediate concern; we know he's had those minor heart attacks before, and everything's under control. Better not get him scared by all rushing to his bedside, so I suggest you both stay with the ship, call the hospital tonight and I'll keep you posted. Dad, please, don't let Mom get hysterical. I'm sure Grandfather will be fine, and in any case, I'll be in touch with you tonight.'

Brad and Mariès parted at the airport, in spite of Brad's renewed entreaties that she accompany him to Houston. But she was inflexible. This was neither the time nor the place to announce this sudden wedding. As soon as his grandfather had recovered, then they would break their news and she would meet his family. She watched the Hollis turboprop, with the company logo on its side, taxi off, Brad sitting in the cockpit next to Stan, waving at her until the plane veered out of sight. Then she turned back, and the limousine drove her to the suite, still abloom with its bridal bouquets.

Then, stretched on the wide bed, in the dove-gray bedroom, Mariès called her mother in Malibu. She told her about old Mr Hollis's heart attack and Brad's hurried trip to Houston. There was no reason to worry too much, the housekeeper had assured Brad, his grandfather was resting comfortably in a suite of the Bradley Hollis Wing at the Methodist Hospital in Houston.

'And what about you, Mother?' asked Mariès. 'How are you? So much has happened to Brad and me in the past twenty-four hours, that I haven't even asked.'

'I'm fine,' Channing replied, 'just beginning to control the pounding of my heart through careful breathing. The only thing wrong with me, as you would undoubtedly see it, is my being at work on ideas for the 1969 season. If the series survived the last one, there's no reason we can't brazen out the next.'

'Any great thoughts?'

'Lots, although you might not call them great. How about having Tamara Morgan turned into a mermaid, swimming up the Niger and washing up at Bud's feet? I'll just have to figure out how Tamara grew her fishtail and what Bud's doing, wading knee-deep in crocodiles . . .'

'Scaring them to death by clicking his false teeth at them,' suggested Mariès, always helpful. 'But I didn't call you to discuss the higher forms of art. Outside of the news from Brad's grandfather, I wanted to tell you I'd like to stay with you while Brad's away. May I come home?'

'Nothing I'd like better, and nothing makes me happier than hearing you call the house *home*. It's been a long time since we had dinner at the Pharmacy.'

'It's a date for tonight, then. I'll pick up Brad's car at Van Nuys airport and I'll be over by six. Tell the guard at the gate of the Shores to let me in. He might not, when he sees Brad's conveyance.'

Channing turned off her typewriter, went to the bathroom to freshen her makeup, saw her blue eyes in her tanned face, almost unlined, almost unchanged, yes. And yet, different, different in mysterious ways, from the portrait on her bedroom wall, the one Domergue had painted of her when she was twenty-two. Her forty-fourth birthday had just passed, unnoticed by all but herself.

'I remember when my mother was forty-four, and I thought she was old! Yet I feel just the same as I did when I was twenty – the only difference is that now, I try not to let it show.'

She went to Mariès's room, removed a pile of scripts that had accumulated on the bed, smoothed down the spread, opened the window for fresh air.

It was late when Channing and Mariès finally made it to the promised dinner at the Pharmacy, because they had sat together for hours on the big bed in Channing's room, talking about the sudden marriage. Mariès's happiness was both tempered by the awesomeness of what the Hollis fortune meant, and enhanced by the dawning of an awareness of the potential it brought to her life and Brad's.

'It's a good thing Brad is so totally grounded in reality, and that he knows what really matters in life,' sighed Mariès. 'Me, I'm afraid my first reaction would be to become very stingy for fear of showing off . . .'

'He's used to all that money, and it doesn't intimidate him. Just let him *show* you how to live with it,' advised Channing.

They talked about Brad's affection for his grandfather.

'How old is he?' asked Channing.

'He'll be eighty-two in a couple of months. Brad's mother, Bunny, is about your age, so he was already getting on when she was born. But Brad says he's in good all-round health and should live for a long time yet. I think Brad is closer to his grandfather than to his father and mother. I know that he talks about him more often, and seems to have more childhood memories that involve the old man, than Spike and Bunny.'

'Are Spike and Bunny at the hospital too?'

'No. They'd left a few days ago for a cruise. They've been reached by ship-to-shore, but Brad thinks there's no point in bringing them back in a panic just to find the old man up and about ... or else frighten him by converging on him like that. He says his mother tends to get hysterical. Gee,' continued Mariès after a silence. 'This is just like old times, with you. How do you manage? You never change. I was afraid you'd be depressed and lonely after Fred left. Many women in your place would have felt deserted, they'd have come apart, with tears and recriminations. They'd have blamed the man. Then they'd have blamed themselves. But you didn't. Not for a minute. Of course, he wasn't really the center of your life. Still, you took it like a trooper. It's probably just that you didn't care all that much.'

Mariès the universal expert, as usual.

Channing started to speak, checked herself. Why tarnish her image of stoic fortitude? 'You're probably right.' She nodded in agreement.

The few days Mariès spent with her mother at Paradise Shores recalled the placid times of 'before,' the days of the old equilibrium so painstakingly achieved by Channing and suddenly pulled like a rug from under her feet by Fred's departure. Early each morning, they ran on the beach together, hair streaming, feet splashing in the surf, the dog circling madly, barking in ecstasy. They fed the sea gulls at breakfast on the deck. Days, Channing drove to the studio for the usual rounds of story conferences and Mariès went to UCLA to finish the term and the three courses she was still enrolled in.

'If I didn't know better, I would think Christ Apollo has a crush on me. He seems to direct every pretentious pronouncement in my direction. Maybe he thinks he's intellectualized Brad out of the picture and kept me for himself, a prisoner of existential hogwash.'

Brad had decided some weeks ago that he couldn't take any more of Apollaud's brand of hot air. He had dropped the course, forfeiting the degree, and he reveled instead in courses in the history of medieval art, Renaissance architecture, history of the Crusades, and auditing any French-related courses available. Mariès had decided to stick it out, perhaps because of something she'd seen in Channing's expression when she had tentatively mused that she might drop out too.

'Brad can afford to do just as he pleases in life. Can you, too, Mariès May, and should you?' was what she had read. Anyway, she thought, it was just a matter of a few weeks, a small price for a clear conscience and approval in her mother's eyes. And now, although married, she intended to complete her courses.

Evenings, mother and daughter would eat steak strips at the Pharmacy or chili at the Malibu Inn, or seafood at Trancas, further north on Pacific Coast Highway, the latter a 'real' restaurant, lit up with fairy lights and so dressy that you had to wear shoes. Later, Brad would call, for endless conversations that Mariès took in her room, sharing the news with Channing afterward.

'The doctors are unhappy,' confided Brad, 'because the old man isn't bouncing back the way he did the other times. His blood pressure fluctuates wildly. They want to keep him in the hospital, as long as they read signs that mean danger of another attack. For the first time today, as I held his hand, I realized he's an old man. And when Dad called, I told him he and Mom should come back. I don't know why. I guess it was something I saw in my grandfather's eyes. Something like fear . . .' Brad's voice was strained.

Late the next night the phone rang again and there was Brad's anguished voice. His grandfather had another, massive heart attack and had just died, in spite of all the doctors' efforts. There were tears in Brad's voice.

'Mom and Dad had arrived just a couple of hours before, and we were all three sitting by his bed, ready to leave

489

him for the night. He seemed fine and in better spirits than when I called you yesterday. His doctors had said he could go home soon. As I bent over to kiss him good night, he took my hand and he whispered, "There is something you'll have to know, but you must be careful that nobody is hurt." Then, his face contorted, he reached his hands to his chest. Dad rang, the nurse ran in, unhooked the respirator over the bed and placed it over his face, doctors rushed in with their machines, and we were all ushered out. We waited in the hall for an hour, and then his doctor, who's an old friend, came out, took Mom's hands, and, of course, we knew. Oh, darling, he went so fast, so fast . . . He was just talking to me. Saying there's something I should know. Now, I'll never . . .'

Brad had never faced death in his young life, or even deep sorrow of any kind. His grief had all the sharp edge of the first-time experience. Mariès knew better than to try soothing words or consoling clichés. Later, maybe. Now she kept repeating, 'My poor, poor darling. I understand, my love, I understand.' She was in tears, too, when she put down the phone.

Early the next morning, Brad called again. It had been a sleepless night, but his mother had surprised them. She, who could get hysterical over a missed hair appointment, had shown great fortitude, and his dad was handling everything with Brad's help. Brad also had other news.

'I've just told Dad about you and about our marriage. He was genuinely happy, and we went to Mom and told her too. Now, she tells me she is crying both for sorrow and for joy. Please, darling, come, and be with us, with the family for the funeral. You're my wife and this is your place. Stan is flying back to pick you up. Mom has seen your picture in magazines, she thinks Mariès May is the most beautiful girl alive . . .' So Channing drove Mariès to Van Nuys, where the plane arrived shortly afterward, and she returned alone to Paradise Shores.

* * *

When Mariès landed at the ranch, Bunny hugged her and they cried together. Spike put his arm around her shoulders and called her babe and honeybunch. She stood with Brad and his parents at the Methodist Church services and at the graveside.

Two days after the funeral, Hal Stemmon, Bradley Hollis's personal lawyer, and a longtime friend, called Brad into his office.

'You understand, Mr Spigner . . . ah . . . may I call you Brad? We haven't met for a long time, but I used to see you at the ranch when you were, oh, maybe ten years old. Last time I saw you, you were having a fine time with your first horse. You know, your grandfather adored you.

'Now, Brad, I didn't ask you to come alone to my office today on account of the will. Your grandfather's testament will be opened tomorrow, in the presence of your parents, too, and, as you probably know, there's no secret to the Hollis will: all the ranching interests go to your mother, together with twenty percent of the oil company revenues. You are to inherit eighty percent of those revenues, no strings attached. Your grandfather's philanthropies are all set up as foundations and will continue to function as before. Bradley, several years ago, reorganized the company under independent management, so you'll have no responsibilities except for a few ceremonial appearances as titular chairman of the board. It's difficult to calculate the income that will accrue to you, Brad, all I can say is that it will be very, very high. I do hope you will manage it wisely and should you need advice, you know you can always call on me.'

Brad inclined his head. His grandfather had always wanted him to be free to follow his own course.

'As I said, all this will be detailed tomorrow, when you're all gathered here. But I have instructions from your grandfather to speak to you alone and to hand you some documents. You are to examine them here, in my office, and I am to make myself available to you for any advice, counseling, or help you might feel you need after you have reviewed the contents of this envelope.'

He handed Brad a manila envelope worn around the edges. Brad, nonplussed, opened it, and shook out a few yellowed photographs. The first showed his mother, much younger, slimmer, in a white lace wedding dress, holding the arm of a tall, slender man, leaning on a cane, who looked, unsmiling, into the camera. In front of them a table, loaded with flowers, a wedding cake, champagne glasses. The other pictures showed the same couple, Bunny smiling, kissing guests, her tall companion standing aloof, straight hair, like Brad's, barring his brow, darkly handsome, showing a forced smile in only one of the pictures, but almost scowling in the others.

Bunny and who?

Then, a short letter, on his grandfather's personal stationery:

Dear Brad,

I have a difficult thing to tell you, that should have been told long ago. Never should have been hidden, in fact. But neither your mother nor I said anything at first, and then, as time went on, it became more and more difficult to speak. But you must know . . .

The letter told him of Bunny's brief marriage to the French Resistance fighter, Tony Sefar, said his grandfather, who was Brad's biological father. Spike had never known the truth, but the old man thought he might have suspected it. The important thing now was that Bunny should not be hurt, nor Spike, who had been to the boy everything a father should be. Hal Stemmon would help Brad decide the best course of action.

Brad put the manila envelope and its contents back on the desk. He shook his head.

'I don't know what to say,' he began. 'This comes as a shock, to say the least. Does anybody know what became of . . . of . . . Mr Sefar?'

'I think there is one more document left in the envelope,' said Stemmon.

It was a marriage certificate. The marriage of Beatrice Hollis and Anthenor Sefar from Blazonac, France.

Brad's eyes grew wide in disbelief – Mariès's uncle was named Anthenor, too, and how many Blazonacs could there be? But this is beyond ridiculous, she says her uncle never left the château, always lived there as a sort of recluse, never married. How could he have come to Texas and met my mother? Impossible. Still . . .

'Shock is no longer the word for it. I am totally confused,' he said to the lawyer, 'and I must think. You see, this may be a lot more complicated than it seems.'

And he explained.

It took a conference with Mariès, who said yes, she had vaguely heard that Anthenor had been treated for his wounds by the US Army. She never knew it had been in Texas, he never talked about it anyway. She recognized him in the photographs and, bewildered, they had to admit the evidence that Brad and Mariès – with one chance in billions – had met, fallen in love, and married. They were cousins. No, half cousins, since Anthenor was only a half brother to Renaud, Mariès's father. They looked at each other in disbelief and then fell into each other's arms.

'Darling,' Brad said to Mariès, 'let me call Dad right away and ask him to come here, to Mr Stemmon's office. He can handle any situation. He'll know just what to think and what to do.'

So, Spike arrived, big, bearish and kind as always, with his slow drawl and his reassuring manner. Well, he admitted, of course, at the time, he had suspected, now that it was mentioned, that maybe Brad wasn't born prematurely, but since Bunny hadn't seen fit to tell him differently, he'd been happy for her to give him that wonderful son. Anyway, everything that had happened was all his fault, and no one else's. He and Bunny had been in love since high school and they were to be married as soon as he returned home from the war. Then, because of some damn fool overseas infatuation, he'd jilted her, then he'd returned to claim her, only to find her on the eve of her marriage to that strange, silent Frenchman who had never felt at home in the US. He didn't blame Bunny, the poor girl was hurt and on the rebound. All his fault, as he said before. Well, he confessed how happy he'd been when Bunny was deserted, got a divorce, and he could finally ask her to marry him. 'All my fault,' he repeated, 'and gee, son, I hope nothing's changed as far as you and your mother and I are concerned. I can tell you nothing will be changed from our end. And you, honeybunch,' he said, turning to Mariès, and engulfing her in his bear hug, 'why, all that only makes you even closer to us.

'Just you let me talk to Bunny,' drawled Spike. 'No point getting her all riled up. There's no problem that I can see, nothing is really changed, now is it?'

He thought for a while, patting Mariès's hand.

'If you kids feel you should go sometime and visit Mariès's uncle, well, now, wouldn't that just be grand? The poor guy sounds kind of lonely from what Mariès said, and seeing his niece so happy, and meeting Brad and all, why, it might make him feel real good.'

Mariès threw herself into the burly man's arms. 'Your heart is as big as your land, Spike,' she said through tears of joy, relief, and happiness.

'Well, hon,' murmured Spike, caressing her hair, 'well, it's not too hard to find room in one's heart for people you already love . . .'

Two days later, thanks to Spike, everything was arranged. Bunny had, he thought, been secretly relieved to see her twenty-year-old secret revealed with so little suffering all around. Surrounded by her ever-adoring husband, her son who lavished attention on her, and that beautiful girl, whom she already regarded as a daughter, she still happily reigned over all she surveyed, her kingdom only enlarged and strengthened.

* * *

When Channing heard the news, she was dumbstruck at first. Then a turmoil of emotions began to swirl in her mind: Brad was Anthenor's son! No wonder he'd reminded her so much of him! And the thought brought back vividly the never forgotten, never dimmed image of the man she'd loved so long ago and who wouldn't even hear her name today. You were never good at keeping your men, Channing, she said ruefully to herself.

'There's no use indulging in clichés, like how small the world is,' she confided to Leigh, a few days later, as they were sunning companionably alongside each other on the beach. 'The fact is, instead, I feel there's a circle of destiny closing in. But I have no idea what's next. Do you?'

Leigh shook her head, rolled over on her stomach to tan her back. She had no idea either. Channing went on, struck by a thought. 'If such a thing had been discovered in the world where I grew up, why, it would have been considered a tragedy! It would have passed into the folklore – a blot on the family's honor, casting shame onto the second generation. Pretending all those years a child is your husband's, when it isn't, that would have brought a woman disgrace, retreat to a convent for the rest of her days, I don't know! Instead, they all take it in stride, Spike's only concern is that Bunny's feelings shouldn't be hurt. The kids . . . Well, wouldn't you know, far from being shattered by the revelation, they're delighted! Say they knew all along there was something special between them.'

'Who's right and who's wrong, what do you think?' asked Leigh, reaching for the tube of Bain de Soleil cream.

'Your question reminds me of something a GI named Tom said to me one sunny day in the métro when I couldn't understand the world he came from: "That's because you're from the old country, baby." If you ask me, there's a great deal to be said for that new country. They sure know how to make loving easy, baby! I wish Anthenor had learned something from them!'

A pause, while Leigh traced her neck and chin with the sun lotion. Her mind was on another aspect of the extraordinary news. She'd often heard her friend's stories of the stern do-as-I-say Madame Arondel. She smiled a conspirator's smile. 'Who's going to break it all to your mother?'

Channing gasped, then she laughed wholeheartedly. 'It's not going to be me, so I don't care. But I must say, I'd give anything to watch Mariès handle it!'

When Brad and Mariès left for Blazonac, Bunny and Spike were already making plans to meet them there a few months later, if Anthenor would welcome them too. Mariès was the only one to secretly wonder whether Anthenor's arms were ready to open as wide as all those Texas hearts had been.

In the plane, sleep wouldn't come to them.

'It's because we haven't made love as we do every night. I want you too much to rest,' whispered Brad. 'We'll have to make do. Put your hands on the blanket, here, close to mine. We're going to make love without touching.'

And he whispered the words that arouse desire, his and hers. He told her of his hard member penetrating her, swelling inside her. He described his pleasure and told her just how she felt.

'I'm moving slowly, gently, just a circular motion. I caress the lips with my tip each time that I withdraw. Slowly, slowly ... Now I am thrusting and you want me deeper, bigger, until I distend you. I won't stop now, no matter what. I'm taking you because you're mine, and I will come deep within you. I feel you vibrate, that's good, let go, you're going to come hard, very hard, all over me. *Now*!' This was the ultimate orgasm, the kind the brain distills; the brain, the most erotic organ of all.

Brad murmured fervently, 'Our marriage has been consummated in every possible way.'

Later, after their breaths had become even again, he laughed. 'I'd hate to think what my pants will look like in the morning, unless I go change in the bathroom.'

When he returned, Mariès suddenly remembered reality. 'Darling, in all the excitement I completely forgot about Apollaud's course, and those others. There were still three weeks to go. What should I do?'

'Forget it,' suggested Brad, stretching his long legs, yawning. 'I have a feeling you'll have plenty to occupy you where we're going. How about restoring Blazonac to full splendor? Isn't that what you've always wanted?'

26

'STOP WAILING, CHANNING,' admonished Leigh severely. 'Wailing never cured anything. And anyway, I don't even understand what you're wailing about.'

'It's my hair,' moaned Channing, enjoying the relief of pushing back her real problems and the luxury of placing the minor ones in someone else's more competent hands. 'It's my hair. It won't do anything, except fly about. It's neither long, nor short, nor anything. Why can't it be like yours, always chic and right? What should I do?'

Leigh's hair, in all circumstances, fell perfectly shaped, over her right eyebrow, black and satiny. It never flew about.

'It's just because you never made a decision about it, that's all. You let it have its own nothing way when you need to be firm with it. Short and smooth, I always say, short and smooth. Why don't you go to Michel's of Brentwood? He's been doing my hair for years, he'll know what to do for you. Your color's fine, don't do anything about it. You're lucky to live at the beach, it gives you blond streaks without bleach. But you need styling.' Leigh had an infinite fund of patience when it came to her best friend. 'And remember, short and smooth!'

Channing duly noted Michel's number. 'Leigh, that's not all. I have to go to the Emmys next week. *Just Deserts* has been nominated. I'll be at a table with the Baldwins, Peter and Terry, and you know Terry will look stunning. There's also going to be Pinky, and Kevin, and Dusty, the other writers. With their wives . . .'

'Pinky's *wife*?' said Leigh, incredulous.

'Yes. I understand they'll both dress alike in rose-colored tuxedos with matching Indian beaded cummerbunds. And my date will be ... oh, you don't know him, he's one of the cameramen, very young, and tall, and shy, and he asked me and ... well, his name is Blake, Blake Simmons.'

Leigh's interest was aroused. 'Very young? How young is that? And how shy can he be if he asked you to the Emmys?'

'He's not exactly a child,' conceded Channing, 'but he must be at least ten years younger than me. And he may not be shy really – more like reserved, come to think of it.'

'Why would he ask you and not one of the barely nubile beauties who turn up every week on your show?'

'I guess he likes me,' Channing said reflectively, 'although I never thought much about it before. He pays those little attentions to me at the studio, like going out to put up the top on my car when rain is predicted. I often see him looking at me with that gentle, concerned look of his. And to tell the truth, I feel good when he's around. There's a quiet strength about him. Don't look at me that way, Leigh, you're being ridiculous and you'll make me blush. Love is the farthest thing—'

'I'll be tough on you, Channing, because I'm your friend,' said Leigh. 'The fact is, you've never had a true relationship with a man in your life. Tell me, have you ever felt secure with a man? In love, happily in love?'

'No,' replied Channing without hesitation. 'No. I've been disappointed. I've been frightfully unhappy. I've learned to accept and pretend. I have also loved passionately, a man who was far away. But I see you wouldn't call that kind of love a relationship. The man I loved that way was ... is ... I don't want to talk about it.'

Leigh read pain in her friend's eyes and returned to those problems that could be solved.

'All right,' she said. 'So you need something to wear. Have you looked in your closets? Surely you can find something there.'

'I looked and that's why I'm so depressed. All I see is

suede pants. Suede pants in all colors. Legions of them. How *do* all those suede pants get into my closet?'

'They get into your closet,' replied Leigh, an edge of annoyance now sharpening her contralto, 'because you buy them. Because no matter what you set out to get, you never bring back anything *but* suede pants. That's why you can't find anything else in your closet. Come by the shop tomorrow, I'm sure we can find something. And it won't be suede pants.'

Channing was enjoying the conversation enormously. She had managed to place both her immediate problems in Leigh's capable hands. She was now tempted to a little healthy self-indulgence. 'Seriously, I am lonely, Leigh, so desperately lonely . . .'

Leigh had a remarkable gift for eluding impossible subjects. 'What do you hear from Mariès?' she asked, a magic question. 'Tell me about her.'

Channing's loneliness receded a little. There was so much to tell about Mariès.

'She and Brad are busy restoring Blazonac. Mariès's uncle welcomed them with open arms . . .'

Well, maybe Anthenor didn't open those arms *that* wide, at first. Mariès, who called practically every day, on a field telephone the company had loaned Blazonac, until permanent lines could be installed, had told her mother of a very restrained greeting, followed by days of absences, during which Anthenor disappeared every morning to reappear only late at night when he was sure everyone would have retired.

And then Mariès, her voice, well, glowing, thought Chantal, announced, 'I must tell you what happened yesterday.'

She had gone to the old rose garden, by the lake, to find the best spot for a boathouse Brad had bought at an estate sale. 'It's all latticed and curlicued wood. I'll have it refinished in white, to match the new garden furniture, and that's where we'll keep the motorboat for skiing on the lake.' There, among the reeds, where the lily pads grew in shallow water, she'd found an old rowboat, rotted, half submerged, with shreds of some kind of fishnet stuck to its boards. Why did Channing's chest hurt suddenly?

Mariès continued. 'Suddenly, I felt a presence behind me and there was Uncle Anthenor, standing there. He was looking at the boat, too, and I swear, Mother, there were tears in his eyes. No? You don't believe me? He bent down, pulled a piece of the net. Then, without looking at me, he said, "Your mother and I used to go and set that net during the war. She was the most beautiful girl in the world and I was . . . I was . . ." There was a sob in Anthenor's voice. So, I asked him, "Tell me about you and my mother in those days." But all he said was "No, I don't want to hear her name again. Ever. You hear me?" He tried to walk away but I put my arms around his neck and said, "Someday, when you're ready, you'll tell me why. I know I don't look much like her, but I'm exactly like your mother, my grandmother, in that big portrait I took down from the attic. Look at me! Don't you see?" He just stood there, with that little muscle jumping at the side of his mouth. So I asked him, "Uncle Anthenor, won't you love us and be happy with us, please? Life could be so good if you could only stop being angry. You're my godfather, too, remember?" But he just walked away, and his shoulders sagged, and it was so sad . . .'

Mariès paused, recapturing the poignant moment. Then, her voice brighter again, 'That evening, Brad and I were just sitting down to dinner, with Anthenor's place empty like every night, when he appeared and smiled a smile so much like Brad's it nearly broke my heart.' Anthenor had simply walked over to her chair, bent over, and kissed the top of her head. Then, he put his hand on Brad's shoulder.

Happiness was palpable in the air, and Anthenor was practically animated throughout the meal, even noticed the menu prepared by Raymond, the new chef Mariès had hired from Le Coq Hardi, the finest restaurant in Limoges.

'I went there, Mother, to talk to Raymond because I'd heard he was the best chef around. It's an old place, first opened in 1895! With allegorical figures painted on the ceiling that they're just restoring now. Raymond told me that, during the war, they had a black-market restaurant hidden on the second floor, but, of course, Raymond wasn't there then. He heard they took people upstairs through a room with a secret door that looked like a closet. Can you imagine?'

Chantal could, vividly. They also had rooms upstairs, she remembered and wondered if Anthenor did too.

The next day, Anthenor had asked Brad to accompany him to the farms, and they had come back at lunchtime, excitedly making plans, eating quickly, and were out again until dark. Now, they were out together almost every day. Anthenor knew exactly what was needed to modernize the operations, and within a few weeks, workmen were hired to remodel and enlarge the farm buildings, machinery had arrived, brightly colored tractors were plowing new fields, breeding cattle were lowing in rebuilt barns with red tile roofs. Now, both men were inseparable, and seen from a distance, Mariès could barely tell them apart, so tall and lanky, except that, at times, Anthenor's leg would drag a little. But just a little and not often.

The next news was that Anna and Charles had agreed to be replaced at Hautevallée farm. Anthenor and Brad had suggested they move to the long-abandoned estate steward's house near the entrance to the park. The house had been restored to their specifications, and Anna appointed to supervise the household staff, still incomplete, but being recruited. Charles would oversee the personnel who'd work in the grounds and gardens, to landscape and maintain the approaches to the château, who would see that supplies of fresh cut flowers and vegetables were brought daily to the kitchens.

Mariès herself was supervising the restoration of the house. First electricity was brought to all the rooms, and running water, and central heating, with enormous oil tanks in the cellars, and bathrooms were being installed, ten of them. 'It took teams of stonecutters from Italy six months to dig channels in the stone walls so all the pipes could be concealed. And now, there's light everywhere, artfully hidden sources of soft light, or massive iron fixtures, or graceful chandeliers in the bedrooms. Brad brought the lighting expert from La Scala in Milan to design the lighting. In fact, I love what he did – theatrical, yes, but then the château *is* like an opera setting, isn't it?'

Yes. An opera. With death by drowning at the end of the first act. Smile into the phone, Channing, and ask more questions, for this is the fifth act: Transfiguration, now.

Mariès said one day, 'I'm no longer calling you from the field phone the company loaned us, but from one of the sixteen extensions.'

'Sixteen?' asked Channing. 'Where, in heaven's name?'

'Well, we needed one for each of the bedrooms, and Brad and Anthenor's office and the kitchen, and . . . oh, and, of course, we also have an intercom. That's how I communicate with Anna when I can't be downstairs . . .'

The drive had been paved, she reported, with a lovely gravely sand-color surface that felt smooth and elastic underfoot. The dead trees had been replaced with new ones, elms, too, but of a blight-proof strain, that would grow to enormous size. They were already so big they had been brought on truck beds, in gigantic tubs. Expensive? Well, shrugged Mariès, I wouldn't know. Brad said he didn't want to wait for years to see the drive fully shaded.

The gate? Oh, yes, the gate was taken to an artisan shop, near Bordeaux, and since it was too far gone to be repaired, a replica had been handwrought, using ancestral techniques. It was in place now, between the repaired stone pillars, whose broken finials had been located, hidden in overgrowth nearby. The Blazonac coat of arms, gilded in greenish, rubbed-off gold, crowned it as it had for centuries before.

The carriage courtyard? Well, the spring was no longer flowing on account of cracked pipes. New pipes and the services of a specialist from Paris, and the water now rose ten feet in the air, in a straight and slender jet. No, Mariès didn't want an elaborate fountain with sculpted figures. Just the jet, the way it used to be. Flowers, of course, banks of them.

The massive entry door had been taken down, sanded down to the bare wood, and they had found traces of a lovely celadon green paint in the cracks of the wood sculpture, so a celadon rub had enriched the pale oak color, exactly the way it was when the door was first installed in 1585, according to the date restorers had found chiseled in the upper inside corner. On all the outside walls, and in the great entrance hall, the stones had been cleaned back to their original tone.

Inside the house? Well, there was just too much to tell. It had to be seen. But no invitation followed. Channing's throat was tight. Brad had enticed a decorator named Alain Wertz away from his job at the Versailles restoration, continued Mariès after an awkward split second's pause, and Alain had moved to Blazonac, where he would spend a year, two years, whatever, until everything was perfect. Alain had sent word to a number of antique dealers, who had started to channel the best pieces they could procure for Brad and Mariès's approval.

One day, the dining room was finished.

'Oh, Mother, it's like magic,' cried Mariès. 'Alain found the same exact silk for the walls that was there before. All the chairs have been repaired, and, oh, Mother, it is so perfect, the light blue striped walls and the striped chairs . . .

'I shouldn't say this,' she whispered conspiratorially, 'because private persons ought not to bid against institutions, but Brad did bid anonymously against a national museum for a set of still lifes we'd been told about – fruit, fish, flowers, game, you know. Well, when they arrived, Anthenor stared at them and he looked like he was going to cry. He recognized them! Can you believe it? They were the very ones that had been sold from the dining-room walls when my grandmother was sick. Now, he looks at them like a hungry man contemplating a feast.

'For the longest time, Alain couldn't find a chandelier we liked. All too formal. I wanted to keep the country-house feeling in the dining room. So, finally, Alain had one made, by the glassblowers in Biot, and it's immense, and simple, with candles in dozens of little cups of bubbly glass. It takes a maid all morning to clean it and refill the candle cups, but it's well worth it at dinnertime!

'The curtains were hung last week, white lace, so full, trailing and billowy, when we open the French doors to the terrace over the lake . . .

'Our porcelain arrived from Limoges. Haviland made it, and since we expect to entertain a lot, we ordered a full set for forty – white with a thin gold-and-blue band. We also got ten dozen plates in *bleu de four*, that dark blue porcelain Haviland makes, you know it? We'll mix and match,' said Mariès happily, reverting briefly in her excitement to California idiom.

'The tracing of the tapestried vegetable garden has been found under weeds two feet thick, would you believe it? Some of the box edges weren't quite dead, still trying to push pale little shoots smothered by all that rotting vegetation! Now we have a permanent team of gardeners, hired away from Villandry castle in the Loire Valley, the one with the famous Renaissance gardens? Oh, yes, one hundred specimen tree roses have arrived from the Delbard nurseries, they are being planted at the corners of the beds. Prayers rising, remember?

'What? You want to know about your old room, Mother? You mean the one in the west wing, the room with the carved marble fireplace?

'Oh, I don't know. Yes, yes, of course, that's the room where I was born . . . What color do you see it in? Sort of a rose? Yes, that would be perfect, and I could use that marvelous rose Aubusson carpet Alain just found, and the Boulle commode from Sotheby.'

Anything, anything at all, thought Channing, heart pounding. Oh, please, please . . .

'Do you think Bunny would like it?' continued Mariès

brusquely with what Channing recognized as the I-don't-want-to-hurt-you-more-than-I-have-to tone her daughter used whenever she felt compelled to reveal a painful fact of life to her naive mother. 'Bunny and Spike will be visiting soon, and at first I was worried about Anthenor's reaction, but he's glowing with such an intensity of excitement these days, I doubt anything can spoil it. Anyway, you know how cordial and bighearted Spike always is, so I wouldn't be surprised if the three men became as thick as thieves in no time . . .'

All right, Channing, don't let your heart bleed all over the white carpet. Close your eyes tight, now open them and put a smile in your voice to ask about more of the wonders.

'Grand-mère comes almost every day from La Prade, in her new Citroën DS, that car with a front like the business end of a vacuum cleaner, and she goes straight to the kitchen, scowls at the maids, and takes Anna aside to scold her, just like when she was young, and Anna loves it.

'Mother, you'd told me so much about the spun-sugar desserts in my grandmother's time that I sent to the Danieli in Venice for their famous spun-sugar recipes. And we had a small dinner party last night to try one of them. Anthenor had just returned from a trip to Paris, he came down to the salon in such a smart navy blazer and gray flannels, looking so handsome that I gasped. We had the Brousses for dinner, remember them? André and his wife, Cécile? André was involved in the Resistance with Anthenor, I think . . .'

'The Brousses! Mariès, tell me, did they ask about me? Did you all talk about me? Did you tell them—'

'Mother,' interrupted Mariès, her voice even tighter than before, 'I am not going to tell you anything you don't know. Yes. Cécile asked about you, and when she did, Anthenor got up and left the room. I've tried, believe me, I *have* tried, but it doesn't matter what's said, he simply walks out.

'The other night I even brought down an old album I'd found, and there were pictures of you, and you looked so young then! Like a schoolgirl. I tried to show them to Anthenor, because he was there with you, and me as a baby, and Renaud, I think it was, but . . . Mother, Mother, don't cry like that, please, you break my heart and there's nothing I can do, believe me. Somehow, you've hurt Anthenor terribly, and I don't know how. Maybe someday, I can find out. But please, please, don't cry . . .'

'I wasn't really crying, just some sort of a cold I'm getting over, darling. And in any case, it's not sadness, you know. Just . . . oh, emotion, perhaps, because you are talking about things I used to know so well. And, anyway, I'm so happy for you. Tell me about the spun sugar dessert.'

'It was a huge success. Juliette brought it in proudly, holding the dish in both hands, and it looked like a pink cloud and all the candles in the chandelier twinkled and the curtains billowed in the breeze . . .'

But Mariès's heart was in her throat, too, and more news had to wait for the following week.

'Now, the staff is complete. It's a good thing we have Anna and Charles to supervise everybody. Charles walks through the grounds with his hands behind his back, just as he lorded it over the Paris parks as a municipal guard. Anna scolds the young maids and sounds more like Grand-mère every day.'

It had been over a year, now, since Brad and Mariès had moved to Blazonac. Meanwhile, Channing went through the motions of living and waited for the news that came regularly on the phone. One day, the mail brought an envelope, heavy cream vellum, simply embossed *Blazonac* on the back. Channing's address was in Mariès's seldom-seen handwriting.

'How do you like this?' she asked rhetorically. 'The French Nobility Association has acceded to my request to allow Brad to pick up the title of the Blazonacs, since I was the only heir to it, could not use it myself as a woman, according to custom, and needed permission to transmit it to my husband. So, we are happy to inform you that we are now the Count and Countess of Blazonac, as so many of my ancestors have been over the centuries,' wrote Mariès.

Oh, how hard it is to unravel the sweet from the bitter in the tangled yarn of memory, thought Channing. But how bitter the bitter is. All along one question was on her lips, one question she never asked anymore:

What have I done to become the outcast of this blissful family, left stranded on this faraway shore so ineptly named Paradise? Chased rainbows and found ... oh, no, no pot of gold. Only loneliness and memories getting sadder every day.

Instead, she asked about the new tennis court, the swimming pool, and the way the great kitchen had been completely restored. Tree trunks burned again in the cavernous hearth. 'The copper utensils Anthenor buried during the war – I'm sure you know the story, Mother? When he dug them up, they were so tarnished, it looked like they could never be polished. Well, you should see them now! Shining like the sun! And the pantry, so big, so desolate, when we saw it first, there were still rows of glass and pottery jars, empty bins, and lots of broken baskets. You probably don't remember it ... Well, now it's become a cold room, and we added a new pantry between the kitchen and the morning room. The cellars? Their floor has been spread with sand, wine racks were installed, a cellar master came from Château Haut-Brion, near Bordeaux, to advise Brad and Anthenor about the proper way to start a wine cellar. I think they've already laid in five hundred bottles of great vintages, which will get better with the years. Anthenor says a wine cellar is something he's always wished he could have and take care of.'

And Channing thought, I might as well be dead. No, everyone speaks respectfully of the dead, because they might hear. For me it's as if I had never been born – as though I *had* no existence. My daughter calls me, probably from rooms where no one can overhear our conversation. Oh, Brad does come on the line now and then, very hearty, very affectionate, to say hello . . . But I know the harmony of this grandiose household is so fragile it can be destroyed by the sound of my name . . .

'Are you dreaming, Channing?' asked Leigh. 'You were telling me about Mariès and Brad restoring the château . . .'

'Oh, yes, yes, of course. I guess my thoughts wandered. It all sounds quite splendid, and Anthenor is even thinking of starting a Thoroughbred farm. They are very happy, and so am I,' she finished lamely.

'Don't forget to come by the shop tomorrow,' reminded Leigh sternly. 'I'm sure I have just the right thing for you, somewhere. And please, don't sound so . . . melancholy. You do have to learn to live alone. We all do, sooner or later.'

The next day, Channing spent three hours at Michel's, and came out shaking her short, smooth blond hair. So becoming was the new style that looking in the mirror of her car visor, she saw, for the first time in months, that the dimple near the corner of her mouth was still there.

At the boutique, Leigh greeted her warmly, and produced armfuls of potential outfits for the Emmys. Flowered crepe dresses, silk suits with no back, long skirts with beaded tops. 'No. No. Not me, not me at all. It's beautiful, but it's not for me . . .'

And then, while Leigh's back was turned, she saw it. There it was. Right on the end of the rack.

Suede pants? Of course not. These were *antelope*, not suede at all. Narrow black antelope pants with lace inserts on the sides, and a top made of alternated bands of antelope and black lace with almost no back. Size six. The fit was perfect. Leigh sighed, shrugged her shoulders and had a salesgirl place the outfit in a green-and-white-striped Devlen box.

She and Leigh went for lunch to La Scala's Boutique, where crowds were pressing, but Leigh's quiet authority obtained the best table by the window instantly. Over their spinach salad, they talked about the shop, Channing's job, parties at the beach, people they knew, and laughed a lot. Both knew their gaiety could be maintained as long as they avoided the subjects that really filled their minds, threatening at every moment to spill, like tears that can no longer be contained.

Ten years earlier, Leigh had lived through a murderous divorce, so she could marry the man she had fallen in love with. Nothing had been spared her then; in the legal coast-to-coast battle she had even been sued by her lover's wife for alienation of affections, and had lost. But then, ultimately it had all been worth it, a thousand times yes, said Leigh without ever faltering, because she and John had married and they had the most heavenly, wonderful four years together. Four years worth an eternity. She didn't regret anything, said Leigh firmly, no tremor in her contralto. Four years and no longer because she had had to watch the man she loved, and younger than she, suffer unspeakably and die of an unforgiving illness.

And Channing, too, alone, abandoned, excluded, unspoken of, laughed prettily, shaking her now short smooth hairdo in a Domergue pose.

'Dessert?' she said hopefully. 'We deserve it.'

'No,' replied Leigh. 'Two black coffees. Don't look for rewards. Next you're going to start thinking you're making a sacrifice of your happiness so your daughter can have hers, and that would be really low because it's not true at all. You are not sacrificing anything at all. Let the kid live her life, will you, and don't make her feel guilty, whatever else you do. Now, drink your coffee, with saccharin if you must, and tell me about the nominations *Just Deserts* won in the face of its lamentable competition . . .'

* * *

On the night of the Emmy awards, Channing was still sitting at her dressing table, brushing iridescent turquoise and violet shadows to her eyelids, when Blake arrived, heralded by the noise of barking. He parked his obviously rented Cadillac and when she opened the door, the dog rushed and the barking became a frenzy of greetings. 'I like dogs,' said Blake quietly.

'Sure,' he confessed when she asked. 'I rented this car. I drive an old Ford, but I didn't think that was good enough for you.'

Channing, who had never seen him away from the studio, and usually behind his camera, peering into the lens through his steel-framed glasses, was surprised to find him looking almost elegant in his tuxedo. 'An Oscar de la Rental,' he joked, with unexpected humor. She was touched to see that he had exchanged his old-fashioned glasses for smart horn-rims.

He must have prepared for this day, she thought. Perhaps he sees it as a romantic date! Why, this is ridiculous. I'm hardly the woman for him.

Blake was attentive and gentle as he steered her proudly to the table of the *Just Deserts* team, and instead of gawky, he suddenly looked lean and scholarly, so she allowed herself the small luxury of leaning on his arm more than necessary.

All eyes were on their table. Was it because of Channing's smooth hairdo, her pale hair pulled back with a huge jet barrette and her sleek black lace and antelope outfit? Was it because of Pinky and his 'wife' in their matching tuxes? Was it, more likely, because, as Peter Baldwin breathlessly announced when he arrived minutes later, with Terry, slender in white sequins, because the rumor flying from table to table was that *Just Deserts* was predicted to win the award for best direction and best writing?

Blake's arm was resting casually on the back of Channing's chair when she leaned back. She smiled up at him and met his eyes. He was smiling at her too.

After the endless series of minor awards, Channing was already getting sleepy from the drinks and all the champagne and the noise, when she heard the name of her show, and in quick succession Pinky's, Kevin's, Dusty's, and hers. *Just Deserts* had won the best writing award, and the four writers jumped to their feet. Kevin and Dusty embraced their wives, Pinky's lips brushed the balding forehead of the bearded man in the pink tuxedo. Blake stood up and chastely kissed Channing on the cheek. They accepted their statuettes with words of thanks. When Channing's turn came, she could only say that she concurred with her colleagues and had nothing to add. Then she saw Blake's earnest face, and his eyes behind the brand-new glasses, so she said, because she felt this was the truth, 'I do have something to add, after all. I want to thank the camera teams who provided such beautiful pictures that they made our words sound better than they are . . .'

Applause came from all the cameramen in the big room.

After Peter had collected the Emmy for best director and mentioned Matt Bullock's name with gratitude, Matt nearly choked with emotion and had to be given a glass of water.

'Loosen your corset, sweetheart,' whispered Pinky bitchily. But excitement was running so high that nobody paid attention, even when he pulled out his paraphernalia and cut himself a line.

Yet, in the midst of happy congratulatory shouts and popping corks, Channing felt suddenly tired and sad, and empty, and depressed beyond words, in spite of her statuette holding a globe with uplifted arms, among the clutter of half-empty glasses. Tired, sad, with a dark void instead of a soul: all this is meaningless, the show is awful, the writing semiliterate at best, this is all pretend, there's no substance to *any* of it, no reality . . . So, she begged off the party at the fabulous Sunset Boulevard home of the Bullocks, and asked Blake to take her home.

In the car, she laid her head back, closed her eyes, and

she wasn't even aware that tears were running down her cheeks until Blake wordlessly handed her his big folded handkerchief. He asked no questions, drove silently all the way to Malibu and turned onto Paradise Shores. When he unlocked her door and handed her back the key, he held her hand and asked quietly, 'May I call you someday soon?'

She shook her head. 'No, oh, no. Don't call me, please don't. Love and romance are so far from my mind. I'm just too tired, sad and tired unto death . . .'

In the house, she put her Emmy on the kitchen floor to refill the dog's water dish, and left it there. She threw herself across her bed and sobbed into an uneasy sleep, from which she awoke at five in the morning, still in her rumpled antelope and lace costume, cold and hurting all over.

27

THE RAINY SEASON that yearly drenches southern California under a relentless deluge, from late January to early March, failed to come that year. The skies remained cerulean, the sea gentle as a lamb, the beach smooth as satin. Mornings, Channing woke up in her bedroom suspended over the water, the center of a cosmic sapphire of sky and ocean.

Now, she left earlier for the studio, still driving her trusty black Corvette (five years old, but why change it?), because the success of *Just Deserts* had spawned another comedy series, based on an idea suggested by Channing herself: *Life in the Fast Lane*.

It dealt with a family of ordinary people, whose humdrum lives were made exciting by the wildly extravagant view they took of themselves and the simplest events. A greeting became an invitation to romance, a misplaced key suggested an international spy ring in constant surveillance, a chance remark became heavy with implications, all to be embroidered into a wild pattern of imaginary intrigue and adventure. Blake and his crew started each half hour with a split-screen technique that showed simultaneously the real event as it took place, and the way the protagonist saw it. From there, the adventure took off, and, through unexpected twists, became real or not, leaving it to the audience to unravel myth from reality. The cast was fresh, young, and talented. The new writing team, two other women in addition to Channing, was companionable, not bitchy like Pinky or bored and cynical like Kevin and Dusty. The witty, antic ideas Sophie and Delillah contributed made Channing wonder, sometimes, if she was good enough for the other two.

Meanwhile, *Just Deserts* continued with renewed vigor. Bud Stockfield had acquired a new set of dentures that outshone the California sun and his stylists had discarded toupees in favor of the new weaving technique that blended thick curls into Bud's thinning hair. An endless supply of starlets, playmates, and beauty queens was dredged up and improbably dropped, dragged, catapulted, or materialized onto the desert-cum-Beverly-Hills-Palm-Drive set. One parachuted right into a date palm, another girl's inflatable raft was pierced by the horn of a charging rhinoceros ('A *rhino*, Pinky? In the water? Wasn't it rather a hippo?' 'Never mind, sweetie, hippos have no horns. I said a rhino—') as she was solo sailing the course of the Niger in search of a long-lost but unforgettable lover, who turned out to be none other than Bud Stockfield. Imagine how surprised she was to find him there, even if the audience was not. But then the Nielsen box doesn't record groans . . .

Evenings, Channing sat at her typewriter and worked late into the night on one or the other of her shows. Whenever the phone rang, she tried to suppress the wild hope that the voice would be Mariès's, and picked it up only on the third ring. She knew that with the nine-hour difference between France and the West Coast, her evening hours were Mariès's early afternoon, and the time she usually called. Indeed, almost once a week, it was Mariès's increasingly authoritative voice that answered her carefully composed 'Hello?'

'Mother,' asked Mariès one evening in early summer, shortly before the yearly television hiatus that separates the end of the season from the beginning of the new one. 'Mother, has Grand-mère said anything to you about her health?'

'No, she hasn't mentioned anything at all. She always writes me once a month, if only to scold me because I haven't answered her last letter yet. But she's never said a word about being ill. What's the matter?'

'We don't know exactly, and she'd die – literally –

before telling us that anything is wrong, you know how independent she is. But Loulou told Anna she's been having fainting spells recently. Once, she nearly fell as she was getting out of the car, and the same thing happened another time as she was walking out of the house at La Prade. Also, I'd already suspected something was wrong with her, because she doesn't come to Blazonac nearly as often as she did before, and she seems almost absent-minded when she does. I went over to La Prade yesterday, and found her, at four in the afternoon, sitting in her bedroom slippers, just staring vacantly out the window. You know that's not at all like her. She asked twice if I'd heard from you or talked to you, and I swear there were tears in her eyes.' A short silence. Then, 'Of course, she's old,' Mariès added blithely. 'Close to seventy, I think . . .'

Seventy, thought Channing, but that's not so old . . . Then she caught herself and remembered that, when her mother was forty-four and she twenty, she had thought her old.

'You can only judge age on the basis of your own experience,' she said gently. 'To me, seventy doesn't seem all that old. What do you suppose could be the matter with Grand-mère?'

'I don't know. I wanted to take her to Paris to see someone really good, but she refuses. She will only see Dr Vincent, and he's getting on, too. So in desperation, I asked him to go over to La Prade tomorrow and examine her. If he thinks anything is seriously wrong, he'll try to convince her to see a specialist, and we can bring one here from anywhere. In any case, I'll let you know soon.'

Channing had trouble visualizing her vigorous, fearsome mother diminished in any way, and pity flooded her heart for the aging woman, proudly concealing an illness that might be mortal.

'I . . . I think I should come to La Prade and be with her,' she said, anxious to hear her offer accepted. 'I could be there in just a few days . . .'

But Mariès was quick to dissuade her. 'Oh, no, no.

There's no need at all for you to come. I'll visit her every day and I'll see to everything. Anyway, it's probably nothing. A virus, maybe. I'll keep you informed.'

She is afraid of Anthenor's unpredictable (or all too predictable?) reaction, if I come to La Prade. There's no way she could avoid asking me to Blazonac, and then, what would Anthenor do if I passed the door, or even set foot on the estate? Smash the hundred-candle chandelier to bits? Break up all the *bleu de four* porcelain? Set fire to the château? Perhaps he would throw somebody in the lake?

'Mother? Mother?' asked Mariès. 'Why did you gasp? What's the matter? I told you not to worry about Grandmère. I'll take care of her and call you every day, until we're sure she's in no danger.'

'I know you'll do the best there is, darling,' said Channing. Then, smoothing concern out of her voice, tuning in eagerness instead, 'Tell me about the last of the guest rooms. Are they all finished now?'

She knew Mariès was happily inexhaustible on the subject of the renovation of her château. Talking about it was a good way to keep her there on the line, with her crisp voice so close, and sometimes even muffled sounds of life at Blazonac in the background: a door opening and closing, Mariès turning away from the phone to give instructions to a chambermaid, voices out in the hall, the village chimes, the whir of Brad's helicopter, the distant whinny of a horse. Channing knew the Thoroughbred farm had become Anthenor's special project, that his best two-year-old had just won some cup or other at the Deauville racetrack and was favored to win at Longchamp a little later in the season.

'Oh, yes, the rooms are all done at last. Now we can entertain in style! Alain had linens made by Porthault, to match the decor of each room and bath. You'd love the lilac room, with sprigs of lilac of the palest mauve on the moiré walls, the lily of the valley room, all white on white, and the hyacinth room, for which Alain found the most

517

exquisite antique painted paper, dull gold and blue . . .'

'Have you done my old room in rose, as you planned it?' asked Channing as offhandedly as she could. 'I was just wondering how it came out.'

But Mariès was no dupe. 'It breaks my heart, too, Mother,' she whispered, her throat tight. 'I wish more than anything that you were here with us, sharing in all the excitement and happiness, and all the things there are to do. But it's impossible, we both know it and it's no help torturing yourself about it, or me, although I know you don't mean to. Anthenor is at home here, after all, and we can't drive him away, even if we wished. You can't imagine the anger in his face, with those tight cheeks of his, if he so much as sees a letter from you on the hall table! His resentment even seems to extend to Grand-mère. I told you already that he's barely polite to her when she comes to Blazonac. I had hoped time would ease up whatever resentment it is that's eating at him, but on the contrary, I swear it's getting worse . . .'

'Don't feel bad about it, darling, because it doesn't matter at all, really.' Channing spoke as cheerfully as she could in order to restore the eggshell veneer of pretense. 'I'm very happy here, and who wouldn't be? I have a lot of work, the shows are successful and will probably run for a couple more years, and then, there'll be new ones. You know how I always loved the beach, anyway, and it's been such a glorious winter. No storms, no rain.'

'Oh, something I nearly forgot,' continued Mariès, relieved to be on safe ground. 'Your good weather reminded me. Brad would like you to go to the Rolls-Royce dealership in Beverly Hills and look at their new model, the Corniche. It's a convertible, and if you like it, please order one in the color of your choice. I just got one in dark green and I love it. The leather on the seats is so supple, it's hard to believe it can be as resistant as it is! I take my two borzoi hounds everywhere I go, so that's important to me. You can have your dog in yours, too, and never see a scratch on the leather. By the way, how is old Fortune?'

Channing was still trying to keep things light. 'Oh, fine, fine . . .'

'Still terrorizing the sandpipers and sea gulls on the beach? Waiting for a gull to crash-land on the deck?'

'Still waiting. You know him.'

'Wonderful companion, isn't he?'

'The best,' said Channing, her voice steady. Just a month before, the Newfoundland had died, of a new intestinal disease, parvovirus, that had appeared out of nowhere, said the vet, and was turning into a raging epidemic. Labs were already at work trying to develop a vaccine, but nothing could save poor Fortune. He died in terrible convulsions followed by shock. Channing had never told Mariès, simply because she didn't want the precious conversations with her daughter to degenerate into a recital of sadness, loss, and loneliness. So, she chatted on heroically for a few more moments, inventing fun the dog had on the beach the other day, when the low tides uncovered rocks, and left pools teeming with sea life . . . She laughingly said that she didn't need a new car, but yes, indeed, she'd drop in at Rolls and look at the Corniche. It might be fun to drive such a splendid vehicle after all (even if, she thought privately, it would make her feel like England's Queen Mother). 'And please, tell Brad he's a dear, and you, too, darling, and I love you both.'

After hanging up the phone, she sat for a long time, her fingers pressed over her eyes. Then she shook her head, smoothed her eyelids toward the temples, turned back to her desk, and reread the inane lines that were to be her contribution to the next episode of *Just Deserts*. A paradigm of my life. Nothingness and emptiness with just a little glitter on top. And not even much of that . . .

Unable to write another word, she turned off her typewriter, flicked off her desk light, and stood up. After the thick white carpet, the marble floor of the foyer was cold under her bare feet. In the kitchen, she did not turn on the light and avoided looking at the corner where the dog's water dish had stood. The empty place there brought tears to her eyes every time, so she was learning to avert her eyes. She filled her nightly glass of milk, feeling the eerie reflection of the refrigerator light on her face, walked over to the bar, poured in her usual dose of brandy, and returned to her room. The spotlights on the deck played on the calm, slowly rising tide. Tonight, it would not quite come under the house. Freighter lights in the distance showed where dark water met black sky. Shouts close to shore: the Lester boys from up the beach were sailing their brand-new red-and-white-hulled catamaran parallel to the waves, sails billowing, and the spotlights of her deck picked it out briefly. Then it was gone, the happy cries of the teenagers fading in the distance. She put the glass of milk down on the wide, low glass table that stood by her bed, in front of the clock radio, and next to the prescription bottle of fifty sleeping pills . . . Tonight? Why wait? What was the point of stringing on pointless day after pointless day?

The same reason that had stayed her hand all those other nights stayed it again tonight. No indeed, it wasn't fear of falling into the sleep from which one doesn't awaken, or of the anguished death that comes only after hours of convulsed nausea and vomiting, promised, she had read somewhere, to those who err in the exact dosage of the pills. No. There was no fear, except one, left for Channing: the dread of one more day of this absolute exile.

Yet, she didn't pour out the forty remaining capsules into her hand when she drank the ice-cold milk, pungent with the jigger of brandy. She placed only one pill on her tongue, just enough to guarantee her a night of sleep without dreams. For Channing knew she couldn't afford the luxury of ending her life because of the guilt her daughter couldn't fail to experience. It would be a terrible legacy – one she couldn't be selfish enough to bestow. Imagine Mariès learning that I have died this way! She'd blame herself, blameless as she is, endlessly, and poison her own life. Whatever has happened to me is of my own doing, and nobody else's, even if I don't quite understand what I did to deserve it. Fred was right: Troubled times breed troubled people, but the sins of the mothers must not be visited ... Channing's last thought, before the barbiturates took over her consciousness, was that she had to find some other way: make it look like an accident ...

She slept, and woke up to another brilliant day.

At the studio, Blake, who was again wearing his old steel frames ('More comfortable,' he just said when she asked why he had abandoned his smart horn-rims), was waiting for her and mentioned casually that he knew a kennel that had a litter of Newfoundland puppies. Would she like to go see them? 'Get one puppy, or two?' he asked, gently concerned about something he saw in her eyes. Blake was the only person to whom she had confided the death of her old friend. But she shook her head. 'No, thanks, Blake, not yet.'

She could not bear to think of another pair of anxious eyes waiting for her return, another water dish in the kitchen, another love to despair over, another tear at the thin, oh-so-thin skin that refused to grow thicker over the deep painful scars on her soul.

A week and a few more days passed. Mariès called several times. Dr Vincent could find nothing to explain Grand-mère's obvious fatigue and listlessness, but he suspected central nerve damage. So, Brad had flown in a professor of neurology from the Pasteur Institute in Paris. The great doctor examined Grand-mère, but reserved his diagnosis and requested that she come to Paris for a series of tests. Grand-mère's stubbornness in refusing to go consumed a few more days, but she had finally given in and agreed, at last, to go next week. No sooner. Meanwhile, said Mariès, almost amused, 'Grand-mère has left La Prade so seldom in her life that going to Paris seems to her like an expedition! She asked to speak privately to each one of us. She gave me a box of jewelry and told me I must make sure you got it if anything happened to her. To Brad, she gave endless recommendations about her will and different matters concerning the estate: La Prade will be yours, of course, when she dies, and she thinks that, if you agree, we should simply annex the lands to Blazonac and give you suitable compensation.'

I see, thought Channing. Pay the wayward daughter off. Aloud, 'Does she seem very ill?'

'As a matter of fact, she seems a great deal better now. That old do-as-I-say look is back in her eyes. So, I feel she'll be with us for a long time, and there's no need to even think about all those estate matters now.'

Channing listened. Did Grand-mère know more about her condition than she let on? Was she, in fact, leaving her last instructions in case she never returned to La Prade?

'The strangest thing of all,' continued Mariès, 'and I could hardly believe my ears, so I made her repeat twice to be sure I had heard correctly, is that she also wants to see Anthenor. As a matter of fact, that's how I finally understood why she kept postponing going to Paris: Anthenor is away with the horses and the trainers, his colors are racing at Enghien and Longchamp this week and he's only due back in a couple of days. She refuses to go until she's spoken with him.'

'Couldn't he come back sooner, if he knew Grand-mère wants to see him?'

'I doubt he would. He knows, of course, that she's ill, but he is so deeply angry at her, for reasons I cannot for the life of me even begin to guess, that he might even stay away longer. You knew Anthenor, once, and he hasn't changed.'

(Yes, darling, I did know Anthenor once . . .)

Aloud, 'But will he even consent to go to La Prade when he comes back?'

'Well, Brad promised Grand-mère that he'd bring Anthenor to her and he will, one way or another, even if he has to trick him into going. *Chose promise, chose due*, what's promised is owed. We think Grand-mère simply wants to make her peace with Anthenor, and I suspect she has a notion of why he's so resentful of her. Cécile and André Brousse are convinced it must be some ancient story, possibly dating back to the war. They say, and it's true, that he has a memory like an elephant. He forgets nothing, and doesn't forgive much, either. So, he's living with some old demons we know nothing about.'

The next day, the calm weather that had lasted for months gave way to one of those terrible ocean storms, spawned by typhoons, that come all the way from the Philippines to batter the coast of southern California.

The evening news announced its approach, and Channing heard the first crashing waves just a little later. So, she took no sleeping pill that night in order to remain awake and aware in her glassed-in bedroom, suspended on wooden pilings at the very edge of the furious ocean, and she felt the first onslaught rushing like crashing trains under the trembling house. All night the assault continued, worse than any Channing had ever known in all her years in Malibu. Lumber, washed away from a construction site up-current, floated like jetsam in the swirling tide, and was thrown to bang rhythmically with each advancing wave against one piling after another. Six front pilings, six echoing blows, until the current had carried the plank away . . . Bigger beams came later, battering rams that shook the flimsy structure with such force that cabinet doors slammed open and shut, dishes rattled, and the chandelier hanging on its twenty-foot chain from the cathedral ceiling of the living room swung and tinkled endlessly, an eerie counterpoint to all the booming and crashing.

The next morning, her clock radio went on at its usual hour, and news of the storm, with the story of the damage it was causing, was all over the early broadcasts. Several houses on Seal Beach had been washed away. Residents of threatened areas were warned to stand ready to abandon their houses. Paradise Shores was named among the endangered beachfront colonies.

The storm had brought Channing the undreamed-of

opportunity she had been trying to conjure up throughout those past weeks. Die a seemingly accidental death. How easy it would be to simply let herself slip into the raging waters, the innocent victim of an unquestionable accident! But Channing did not take advantage of the chance to end it all. In fact, human nature being what it is, faced with real physical danger, the instinct to live took over, and she only fleetingly wished to die during the fearsome storm.

When she ventured out on the road, in the gray morning light, opaque with thick water mist, she saw that two houses had lost some of their front pilings and were hanging askew, wrought-iron railing from their decks flailing about like broken wire. Police cars with bullhorns arrived, driving slowly along the private road, warning residents to stay in, not to try to leave and go to work, but to stand ready to evacuate on short notice, carrying whatever valuables they wanted to take along.

What valuables? Channing tried to remember where she had left the deed to her house and the insurance policies, but she couldn't find them and was unable to remember whether they were here – and if so, where? – or in the safe-deposit box at the bank. Oh, well, surely the county and the companies would have records. She first took Anthenor's hazelwood stick from its secret compartment, put it with her few pieces of good jewelry in a handkerchief that she tied in a knot and threw into a blue TZN tote bag. She was reaching for the dog's leash when she checked herself and, at a loss to find more valuables worthy of saving, put in the bag a half-empty jar of instant coffee, added an old sweater she saw hanging on a hook in the back porch . . . That was about all she could think of.

Then, the phone began to ring ceaselessly. First, Roger Volod, just back from a year's work in Europe, where he had seen Mariès and Brad, 'the Count and Countess of blazing Blazonac,' he said fondly. Roger offered Channing the hospitality of his Valley ranch. Next, Peter Baldwin, speaking for everybody on the *Just Deserts* team, to express concern and offer any help. Sophie, then Delillah.

'Want to come and stay with us? Get out of Hell's Shores! Plenty of room here for you . . .'

Blake's call followed. He'd been trying to get her for hours, but found her line busy. He too wanted to come and get her, or else remain, and join in the sandbagging that had already started all along the coast. Channing, strangely exhilarated, thanked everybody, but said no, I'll stay, that's the police advice for the time being. The next tide, it was announced, would be even higher than the last, and it had already begun to rise. The phone silent at last, she drank her coffee, pulled on rubber boots, and went out into the road to see what the neighbors were doing.

Small groups, dressed in a motley assortment of rain gear, bathing trunks, and pajamas, stood disconsolately. No question of driving out. The street was deeply flooded. The giant breakers of the night had arched over the seawall, tearing it from its concrete moorings like a child's sand castle, broken and carried off entire sections of the black-top of the street, leaving in their place deep holes filled with muddy water. Enormous clumps of trailing seaweed, torn from the ocean floor, stuck to parked cars like slimy alien creatures.

She saw TV and news teams arrive on foot, since all cars had to be abandoned at the Pacific Coast Highway turnoff, and walk along the exclusive private road with hand-held Minicams and mikes, begging the assembled residents for interviews. A young actress Channing knew by sight obliged by giving a heartrending, sobbing account of her night of terror, and a few other neighbors joined in to lament melodramatically on cue, to the delight of the newsmen.

The tide was now rushing in again, more enraged than the last one, and the residents huddled in garage doorways seeking shelter from the torrents poured over the roofs by breakers. The sound of cracking pilings was heard over the din. These were the concrete ones, under the newer houses, those same pilings that had, when they were first built, made the older, wooden ones seem frail and almost

525

ridiculous. Now, under the furious onslaught of the storm, wood pilings quaked and bent but did not break. Concrete snapped. So much for the state of the art. Rumor was that yet another house was leaning into the sea . . . 'Whose?' All were equally concerned. Solidarity in the face of disaster had once more arisen with the new storm in the usually clannish colony where groups were constantly at each other's throats over encroachment of view or offending architecture.

As soon as the tide had reached its highest point and begun to recede, a human chain was formed to pass hastily filled sandbags to men who stood, in the breeches of the seawall, waist-deep in swirling water, building ineffectual ramparts against the next surge of the ocean. Channing, still in her rubber boots and now wearing an old yellow slicker borrowed from a policeman, stood in the chain. When a newsman from her network recognized her, he stuck his microphone in her face. 'This is Channing May, ladies and gentlemen, a writer on two of TZN's most popular comedies. Miss May, may we please have your reactions to this storm?'

Channing straightened her aching body, pushed a strand of hair away from her face, leaving a streak of mud and sand on her cheek, looked straight into the camera and intoned, in her best imitation of a glib commercial: 'Welcome to the Paradise Shores block party, ladies and gentlemen. Come and share with us the joy and the fun of our lovely Pacific beaches. Meet your neighbors and participate in their meaningful activities. Leave your boring, your safe houses in the flatlands, dear friends, and move this instant to Malibu – or should I say Malibubu? – to learn all about life, *Life in the Fast Lane!*'

Her interview was played on the nine o'clock news, repeated at eleven, her muddy, impish face smiling under the yellow oilcloth hood, with a half-demolished house assaulted by giant waves in the background. A vice-president of CBN and the producer of the show called to congratulate her for her presence of mind in associating their show to the event, and since storms were very much in the news right now, why not concoct right away an episode involving a tempest, a hurricane, a cyclone, or a tornado? It could even replace one of the already-scheduled programs.

Her house was holding on. Fissures had appeared in the walls, and the pilings had shifted but were still there. The coming tide would be the maximum one, but after that, the charts promised lower levels tomorrow and an abatement of the storm. Just hang on tonight.

Exhausted, after hours on the sandbag chain, but unwilling to leave for safe ground and a friend's house, the formal order to evacuate delayed until the coastal engineers could calculate what danger the next high tide would bring, Channing huddled on her bed. In dull fascination, she watched immense waves, taller than any yet, rising as high as her house, still lit by the spotlights on the deck to glassy transparency. An awesome, splendid sight. Fish and seaweed rose, caught motionless in the surging water. Then each wave crashed down on the deck, water seeping onto the already soaked white carpet on which great circles edged in yellow brown showed the worst leaks. Silvery fish thrashed on the planks, slid back into the water. The thick sliding glass doors that formed the entire front of the house shivered, rattled, but had held fast so far. Another and another wave came, with rhythmic regularity. Suddenly a crack appeared on the glass, lengthened, abruptly turned to the side. Still, the glass held.

Then, it was as though the Pacific had gathered its strength, and, this time in horror, she watched as in an almost slow motion, the next wave rose and rose, higher than any other yet, and when it came into the glare of the spotlights, it was lifting, in the midst of its transparent green water, the catamaran it must have washed from the side of the Lester house farther up the beach. She saw the red-and-white double hull, numbers clearly visible, mast in place and sails stretched into floating shrouds, carried in the wall of water. She saw it rise and rise, level with her eyes, higher and higher, rise above the house, where she heard it crash on the roof above her head, along with torrents from the wave that had carried it. A breathless second, during which she expected the splintering crash of the roof and the wreckage of the boat falling through over her head. Another second . . . How long would the roof hold? She heard fearsome cracking sounds, and cascades poured down along the glass, less than two feet from the edge of her bed . . . How much time did she have? Should she get out now, run in the street, lit by police searchlights? Give up at last on Paradise Shores?

That's when the phone rang. It had rung several times earlier, but she hadn't answered. Everybody she knew had already called, asked the same questions, made the same offer.

'Is it as bad as it looks on the news? Are you in any kind of danger? Why refuse to leave for safe ground? There's nothing you can change by staying there. Don't be so stubborn, Channing. Come over to my place, there's a cozy room waiting for you – people who are your friends, who care about you. Please, darling, let me pick you up at the Pacific Coast Highway turnoff in an hour. Let me help you.'

Channing was tired of explaining that she preferred to stay, of arguing against common sense, so she'd decided to let the phone go unanswered tonight. She knew Blake had been turned back earlier as he tried to make his way on foot past the entrance now guarded by sheriff's deputies and firemen instead of the usual private guard. She was weary of repeating, 'I want to stay, but I can't say why.' How could she admit that a part of her longed for an end to loneliness?

It kept ringing. Surely, she thought ironically, anybody *this* persistent wants to experience vicariously the terror and thrill of living in a glass cage, held by toothpicks, on the edge of a raging abyss. Someone, perhaps, who hopes that in the midst of our conversation, I'll cry out in horror as the roof collapses over my head, the pilings break, the floor tilts, and my bed slips into the boiling sea. What a story to tell!

'You won't believe this. I was just talking to her and she told me how a catamaran had crashed on her roof only minutes before. Then I heard another crash, she cried out, and then nothing but the sounds of the storm. No, they haven't found her body yet. Awful. Her fault, too. Why on earth did she insist on staying there, alone, with houses collapsing all around? It was inevitable. Who do you suppose will replace her on the show? Writers are a dime a dozen, a new one will be easy enough to find and she wasn't all *that* talented. Always suspected she owed her first job to her friendship with Roger Volod. Oh, well, a new writer might manage to administer CPR to that terminally boring *Just Deserts*. I hate to pun, but Channing May did get her just deserts. Imagine the sheer stubbornness . . .'

The phone was still ringing. Whoever was calling wasn't going to give up. Matt Bullock, trying in the midst of it all to reschedule a story conference? 'I'll just take it off the hook.'

Another huge wave was approaching. It rolled close, closer, smashed violently at the house, slapping a mass of dark seaweed and driftwood against the plate-glass window. She heard a sharp crack. A zigzag line now bisected the entire length of the glass, and she saw it quiver as tree trunks hit the pilings.

Still, she lifted the receiver, was going to rest it on the night table. Instead, through long force of habit, she raised it to her ear. She heard the signal that announced an overseas call. But it wasn't Mariès, it was a man's voice, indistinct, muffled by the storm. Calling her name.

'Is that you? Channing?'

Or was it *Chantal* the voice said? She couldn't be sure.

'It's me. Listen to me . . . I have just . . . Can you hear me?'

But Channing heard nothing more, because half of the heavy plate glass had come crashing in, jagged edges slicing deeply into her brow, her right eyelid, her cheek and shoulder. The other half followed, striking her head, and before she lost consciousness, as blood poured from severed veins, she thought, So this is how it all ends . . . The phone fell to the floor, she could no longer hear the voice saying over and over, 'Can you hear me? It's all so clear now! I will—'

But the roar of the next wave rolling into the room silenced the faraway voice as all the lights in the house went out.

28

AT THE SHERIFF'S command post, the order to evacuate had finally been given. Most residents were already out of their houses anyway, huddled in what was normally the guard's two-room cabin. Deputy Keith Logan picked up his bullhorn, signaled his partner.

'Anybody you know left in the houses?' Neighbors named a few people they hadn't seen since the sandbag chain was stopped by the mounting tide. The Stoddards, in one of the less exposed houses near the point and . . . 'Channing May, at number thirty-five. She must still be inside.'

The bullhorn brought out the last die-hards. The Stoddards, protesting, because they didn't feel in immediate danger, he carrying a sleeping child, she dragging a terrified dog on a leash. At number 35, the deputy called out, 'Mrs May? Can you hear? Evacuate immediately, Mrs May. Now.'

Silence. All the lights were out in the May house. Strange . . .

'You don't suppose she could be asleep?' asked Ron, the younger deputy.

'I doubt it, if you see what I see,' answered Logan, his flashlight beam picking out the catamaran sprawled on the flat roof. 'If nothing else, *that* would have made her wake up. Go get one of the firemen and have him bring his ax.'

The fireman arrived. Sure he knew the orders. Still, he was dubious. 'She won't like it if we break her doors down and she's just fine.'

'Something tells me she isn't,' replied Logan.

The bleached-oak patio door splintered. Inside, deep

water swirled where the decking had been washed away, garden chairs crazily colliding in the eddies.

Another blow broke through the beveled glass door.

'Shit,' muttered the fireman when he felt the rush of wind howling off the ocean into the house. 'Something did happen.' They tried to snap on the lights. Nothing.

'Water shorted the circuit box.' The cones of light from their torches revealed the living room with its wildly swinging chandelier, objects fallen from their shelves, pictures dancing askew on the walls. In the kitchen, the refrigerator had crept to the center of the room, its door wide open, amidst a litter of broken dishes.

'Mrs May? Are you there?'

The three men crossed the hall to the master bedroom, shone their flashlights on the bed. The young deputy averted his eyes.

Half fallen out of bed, Channing lay in a red pool that had soaked a wide stain on the sheets and was dripping from her neck and shoulder onto the carpet. Her face was covered with blood that ran into her fanned-out hair. Shards of glass littered everything, the seawater inundating the floor was pink.

'Holy Mary, Mother of God!' swore Logan under his breath. 'It's a dead woman we've got there. Nobody could lose that much blood and still be alive. We've got to get her out of here, though. Nick, the phone?' he asked his partner.

'Off the hook and out. I'll run down the street and get the ambulance. It's been parked on the highway since the evacuation order came. Maybe they can make it down here if I lead the way.' He dashed out, grateful to leave the chilling scene.

'Poor girl,' said the fireman. 'I don't think running will help her a lot. I can't find a pulse and . . . it's hard to tell, with all that blood, but I think she may have lost an eye. Probably doesn't matter, anyway.'

The ambulance arrived. The two paramedics raised

Channing's left eyelid, the good one, shook their heads. The stethoscope.

'I'm not even sure I'm getting a heartbeat, the house is rattling so. We're getting drenched. Better get her out of here fast.'

They wheeled her out on the stretcher, loaded her into the ambulance. Working efficiently, they started a saline IV in her arm, placed her face under the respirator that pumped oxygen into her lungs.

'Another DOA?' asked the driver. Neither of the paramedics answered, busy trying to get vital signs stabilized.

'Pressure bandages for the wounds, although it looks like she's stopped bleeding. Not a good sign.'

They'd just brought her into Saint John's Hospital in Santa Monica when Dr Bach, the internist, arrived, roused from his bed at this late hour, yet impeccable, not a hair out of place, shrugging into his white starched coat. Unsmiling, concern clear in his eyes.

'She's in shock, pulse racing, temperature plummeting,' reported the intern.

Warm blankets were rushed in. Wounds examined, better bandages applied. The IV continued dripping, saline solution now replaced with plasma. Whole blood was prepared. Dr Bach frowned as he examined the deep bruise on the side of her head.

'Keep her on oxygen. I'm most concerned about that head wound. It's more than just a laceration. There's a distinct swelling of the optic disks, looks like pressure is building up on the brain. I want cranial X rays immediately. And,' he asked the intern standing by deferentially, 'call UCLA Hospital. They've just received one of those new experimental CAT scanners, I'll want them to stand by with it and a tech just in case we need it.' He added, 'Call the staff neurosurgeon on duty, too. I'll want his opinion on the X rays, and he may have to operate immediately.'

A young nurse who'd been adjusting the flow of the IV

shook her head sadly. 'Poor woman, if she lives, she's going to be disfigured. It's terrible! Looks like she had a pretty face,' she whispered.

Silly girl, thought Bach. We're trying to save a life and she worries about a face.

The intern saw it the same way. 'With a closed casket, it won't matter anyway,' he joked with hard-won cynicism.

'Any ID? Any next of kin?' asked Dr Bach. 'All we know about her is that she didn't have enough sense to get out of Paradise when all hell broke loose . . .' The sheriffs had brought Channing's purse. The nurse opened it: Channing May, her age, born in France, divorced, writer, employed by TZN. The nurse recognized the name from the credits of that funny show *Life in the Fast Lane*. Placed in evidence next to the driver's license, a neatly typed card:

> In case of an accident or an emergency,
> please contact my friend Leigh Delven.
> She will in turn notify my daughter
> who resides in Europe.
>
> If Mrs Delven is unavailable, contact
> Mr Blake Simmons.

Addresses and phone numbers followed. Leigh was at home and, in spite of the late hour, she answered her phone on the first ring. She'd been urgently trying to contact Channing without success.

'You understand, Mrs Delven, she's in a coma, which might be irreversible for all I know. But we're doing all that can be done,' Dr Bach assured. 'Yes, you certainly can come, but no, you cannot see her now.'

The X rays revealed a large subdural hematoma, a clot caused by blood seeping from inside the skull, exerting pressure on the meninges. Dr Levine, the neurosurgeon, was already scrubbing. Bach looked at Channing's still form, remembered the savaged face, the split eyelid, the glimpse of white cheekbone through the deep cut. He remained pensive a moment. Then he called the nurse.

'Get in touch with Dr Harmony, the plastic surgeon. Might as well use the best man.'

To Harmony, awakened by his wife:

'Look, she's in a coma, and I'd say chances aren't great that she'll pull out. Levine is going to operate, but as you know, it's touch and go. No, we didn't need the CAT scan, the clinical picture and X-ray findings clearly established the diagnosis. Now, I'll let you be the judge. Her face is pretty badly damaged. Think you want to try and put it back together, just in case she makes it?'

Dr Harmony was thinking fast. 'If we're going to do it at all, the sooner the better. You're aware of how fast the healing process starts on facial tissue. By tomorrow, the results wouldn't be as good. By the way, how old is she?'

Dr Bach told him, and her name, and what she did.

'Why, I remember seeing her on the news. She won an Emmy this year, I think. Very attractive woman. Let's do it, there's nothing to lose.'

Before hanging up, Bach explained that an eye seemed damaged, might even have to be removed. But he'd hold off calling the ophthalmologist until they'd had a better look. Harmony arrived, boyish good looks belying his formidable reputation, as Channing was being prepped. He assisted while Levine drilled the burr holes, drained what looked like an incredible amount of clotted blood, closed the holes. Then he took over. His deft hands examined first the mangled eyelid. Levine leaned over. Under the crusting blood, the cornea was revealed intact. The doctors' glances met, relief visible over the masks. But each eye was red and swollen and was treated by irrigation and antibiotic ointment, patches were applied. Then, Dr Harmony closed the gaping cuts with the microfine sutures that had contributed to his fame. When he was finished, the torn face was whole again, only a thin red line visible between the fine knots.

'Blood pressure's up, still well below normal, though. If we can only keep her pulse stabilized . . .' The anesthesiol-

535

ogist's eyes never left his instruments. Finally, he hung up another unit of whole blood.

Leigh was waiting when Channing was wheeled back into the ICU and ran to the gurney, but all she could see of her friend were bandages swathing head and face, leaving only the nose and mouth exposed. A tube ran from the nose. A red IV bottle swung above.

'Sorry, Mrs Delven,' said Dr Bach, severe face and kind voice. 'You can't come in. She's alive, but she's comatose. Now, if the hematoma we just removed was the only cause, she ought to recover, unless . . .' He thought, unless cranial bleeding resumes, or else there's some deeper trauma to the brain that we can't see. No need to explain. 'In any case, all we can do is wait. Why don't you go home and get some rest?'

The first thing to do, of course, for Leigh, was to call Mariès. But when the operator finally connected her with Blazonac, a maid informed her, as well as she could understand, that both the Count and Countess were away, attending a house party in Scotland. They'd be hard to reach, but she'd make every effort. Should she inform Madame Arondel, who happened to be staying at the château for a visit?

Then someone came on the line and Leigh spoke and cried, listened and spoke reassuringly again.

In spite of the surgery, Channing remained in a coma. Dr Levine, when he examined her the next morning, saw all the symptoms of a cerebral edema, swelling of the brain. How long before it subsided? Would it leave that portion of the brain affected? Did the operation help? In any case, no sign of improvement, yet. She breathed unassisted, but remained under oxygen. He walked out of the ICU shaking his head.

Overseas calls to Leigh's house were frequent and long. Between those calls, she rushed to the hospital and was allowed to stand by the bed in the ICU, lost in a sense of

536

helplessness. She couldn't even hold her friend's hand. Blake was there, too, eyes red behind the wire rims, but he could only pace the waiting room anxiously.

'What?' a frantic Mariès cried when she was finally reached in Scotland, back from an excursion to the Isle of Skye. 'I'll jump on the first plane from London. Meet the BOAC flight at LAX tonight.'

Leigh returned once more to the hospital. In the hall, she met Dr Bach, frown erased, practically smiling.

'She's regaining consciousness. She spoke a moment ago, a few words we couldn't understand. She's trying hard to say something, maybe you'll know what it is.'

Channing was still in the intensive care unit, but the oxygen had been removed, as well as the tube in her nose. Only the IV still dripped into her arm. Leigh came close, took the other hand.

'Channing, it's me, Leigh. Can you hear me?'

The bandages nodded imperceptibly.

'Leigh,' she whispered.

'Darling, you are going to be fine. Mariès is on her way, Blake is here . . .'

'The storm . . .' she guessed Channing tried to say.

'The storm is all over. Your windows are being repaired. The house weathered it all. Now it's up to you to do the same. You just have to rest. Promise me you won't worry.'

Channing shook her head weakly, but insistently. 'Leigh, the phone . . . I think Fred called me . . . Now, I can atone with him.'

That was almost more than Leigh could take . . . 'What in the world would you have to atone for? What you need now is to get strong. Everything will be all right, Channing, I swear to you it will.'

Channing squeezed her hand. 'Let her rest now,' urged the nurse. 'The doctor says that if she continues to make such marked progress, we can move her out of the ICU tonight.'

Leigh had just enough time to speed to the airport to meet the overseas flight.

By next morning, Channing had been moved to a sunny room, abloom with baskets sent by the studio, Roger, Sophie, Delilah, all her friends who called anxiously every day but hadn't been allowed to see her. Only Blake was ushered in, stood by her bed, shuddered at the bandaged head and face.

'It's me, Blake. I'm so happy you're going to be all right.'

'Blake,' whispered Channing, 'I cannot see you, but it feels good you're here. You've always been special to me.'

Dr Harmony held a conference with Dr Bach, and it was decided the bandages could come off that very afternoon. Leigh wanted to be there, so did Blake, but only one person could be present. They both happily deferred to the doctors' wishes.

'I'm feeling much stronger.' Channing spoke in a clear voice when Dr Harmony announced his presence. 'I'm ready for . . . whatever there is to be ready for,' she added, remembering the broken glass, the deep cut, her eye, the blood gushing.

With a nurse assisting, Dr Harmony swiftly removed the bandages. Only pads over the eyes remained. She reached tentatively for her face, expecting mangled flesh. She found smooth skin instead.

'Now,' said Harmony, helping her sit up in bed, 'the nurse is going to hold up a mirror and you can look for yourself. I must caution you, don't expect raving beauty. There's still swelling of the tissues. But I think you'll be happy with what you see.'

He lifted the gauze pads. For several seconds, her eyes, held so long closed under pressure, couldn't focus. Finally, the room floated dimly into view. But close up, she saw her face: her face, almost unmarked except for a barely perceptible pink line.

And in the doorway behind her . . . standing there with that way he had of hesitating on thresholds . . . reflected in the mirror – Anthenor! She closed her eyes. When she reopened them, he was sitting on the edge of her bed, covering her hands with kisses.

538

'Chantal, my Chantal,' he kept repeating.

Neither the doctor nor the nurse could usher him out until she was quite sure it wasn't another drug-induced dream.

She was doing so well that night that she could sit up by herself. Leigh combed out her matted hair and dry-shampooed it, then pulled it back under a pink bandeau. But Channing breathed only for the moment Anthenor was allowed in.

Anthenor, unchanged, as lanky as a youth, but even more handsome now with his deep ruddy tan, crinkles at the corners of his eyes, silver glints in the straight blond hair still barring his forehead. But most of all, a tenderness she'd never seen . . .

'When your mother thought she was going to die and finally told me what had happened, how she'd destroyed my letter to you from that hospital, I first thought I'd strangle her. And then I saw tears running down her face, and for the first time in my life, I cried too.

'You know, I was in such rage and despair at what I thought was your betrayal . . . I was so closed up on my own pain, I hurt so, I never said a word to anyone. I couldn't even stand to hear your name after that time – it brought a taste, a taste of ashes to my mouth . . .

'Will you ever forgive me? There's so much time to make up for! I called you that very night, but you couldn't hear me, and then your line went dead. Mariès was away. I tried all the numbers she had for you in her book, but no one answered. So, when Leigh finally called Blazonac and I spoke to her, I was beside myself, so I begged Mariès to let me come here instead of her. It took some argument, but at last, she said she understood. She's going to call you tonight.'

* * *

Sitting in bed, the scar less visible by the hour, a touch of pink on her lips, Chantal felt like a glowing convalescent, ready to go home. Dr Bach ruled, 'Two more days.'

'How does *he* look?' asked Mariès in one of her delirious phone conversations. No calls, the doctors had said, but as usual *she* had no trouble intimidating the desk.

'How does he look? I can't even begin to tell you, darling. Am I happy? Now, let me think . . . Except that I'm afraid I stopped thinking the minute I saw him. When he called me during the storm? I didn't know, wasn't sure it was him, didn't want to allow myself to believe it was, I guess. So, I tried to think it was perhaps Fred who wanted me in Israel with him, another sort of exile . . . but it was the end of exile instead!'

The next day, it was Leigh, all business.

'Here's a dress for you to leave the hospital in. The doctor says you'll be discharged tomorrow. Yes, I know, Anthenor told me too, he doesn't want to be married in France, where it would take weeks of delay with all the papers. Where? Anthenor has a suite at the Bel Air Hotel, so I suggested the garden there, by the Swan Lake. Does that sound good to you?'

'It sounds divine. Do you suppose I can get married in my suede pants? The best pair, of course, unless they're all ruined by seawater. But that's all I have, really.'

'Do you think I've been totally idle? Anthenor gave me his Carte Blanche – literally. I pillaged the shop. I ransacked Rodeo Drive. There's a whole *wardrobe* waiting for you at the Bel Air. I know your taste, your size, you'll like everything. And you'll adore your wedding dress. Hush, not a word out of you. I know you can get clothes in Paris, but you won't have a minute to yourself for the first couple of weeks, I'm sure, so you must bring at least a few things. You might as well know, all hell is going to break loose with festivities the moment you get to Blazonac. Mariès is talking *fireworks*!'

And Mariès, breathless, a little later on the phone: 'You understand, Mother, why I didn't come? I was in a frenzy with worry, but I knew it would be important for you to see Anthenor and see *him* first, have a chance to become reacquainted with the wonderful man he has become. Then, he made it clear he wanted to marry you right away – deep down, he's probably terrified of losing you again if he waits! And then it dawned on me he wants to bring you home *himself*. No one else. Just you and him.

'So now,' she concluded, 'I'm no longer worried, but I'm going out of my mind making preparations for your return.' A chuckle in her voice. 'Grand-mère pretends to be quite calm, but she went to the beauty parlor for the first time in her life and came back with waves and a rinse!'

A limousine, constantly cautioned by Anthenor to drive carefully, brought her to the Bel Air, but she felt wonderfully exhilarated and refused to lie down until she'd touched all the clothes picked for her by Leigh, hanging in the closet: Two Chanel suits, a draped jersey dress, a black satin tuxedo suit, Saint Laurent casual dresses, a half-dozen pairs of shoes and bags from Gucci. A set of Hermès luggage, monogrammed CAS, Chantal Arondel Sefar, with a card from Anthenor, 'To my wife.'

That night, Anthenor insisted they have dinner in the suite – although she felt well enough to go out and dance until all hours – and tucked her chastely into bed.

'Tomorrow,' he said, 'we're getting married at five in the afternoon by Judge Campbell, a superior-court judge, a friend of the Hollises. Brad contacted him.'

'But darling, I'm not ready! My hair . . .'

'I understand it's all arranged. You know Leigh.'

He gently kissed her lips. 'Tomorrow,' whispered Anthenor, 'and not a minute too soon.' And he went to sleep in the other room.

*　*　*

She awoke to bright sunshine, the incessant ringing of the doorbell as more flowers arrived: daisies 'For Luck' from Mariès and Brad, a crystal jar of white violets. 'These are from me,' admitted Anthenor. 'Remember the wood violets under the trees by the lake in Blazonac?' Wild flowers from Sophie and Delillah, and roses from Blake with a card:

I've accepted a job to replace, on an emergency basis, the head cameraman for a major feature production being filmed in Indonesia. I'll have left by the time you get married, but I'll think of you on the plane and always. Remember me as your friend. I wish you all happiness with Anthenor.

Breakfast was wheeled in, and Anthenor, in his dark silk paisley pajamas, folded his long legs to fit under the silly table. Then unfolded them as more flowers arrived, this time a giant white orchid arrangement from Hollis Enterprises which barely made it through the door. 'No more floral deliveries,' he requested.

It wasn't long until Michel of Brentwood arrived, curly and cherubic, to do her hair and makeup.

'Your hair is a little longer, I won't cut it, just give it a lovely sweep. There. Now, under a light base, your scar doesn't show at all! I bet that in a month you won't be able to find it yourself. You've lost a few pounds, it gives your face an ethereal quality.'

Before finishing, Michel had to see the dress.

'Can you believe I haven't looked at it myself? It arrived this morning with strict instructions from Leigh not to open it until the last moment.'

'The time is now, then,' urged Michel.

The striped green-and-white Delven box revealed a dream of a dress: long torso embroidered, no, encrusted, with a thick design of crystal and pearls, with a flowing ankle-length skirt, yards and yards of apricot silk voile, just the color of her tanned skin. It slipped on like a glove.

Michel was rummaging through the mounds of tissue

paper. He held up a matching beaded Juliet cap. 'Let me adjust it, and I'll finish your hair around it.' In a minute, it was perfect.

'You are a dear, Michel, but now you must run out and put on your own tie and jacket. I want you at my wedding too.'

She was still contemplating her reflection in the mirror when Anthenor appeared, smiling, behind her.

'It's getting to be a habit.' She smiled back. 'But please, darling, keep appearing in mirrors, so I'll just have to turn around to find you there.' Anthenor, elegant in a dark suit, Hermès tie, and gold cuff links. Fondly, she remembered the battered leather jacket.

'Now,' he said, his arms around her, 'remember that night in Limoges? I had a question to ask you and you answered it. Today, I'm going to say something I've never said before in my life. I love you. I love you so,' he added fiercely, 'I love you so, I died for years, and I love you so, I'm alive now.' Channing – no, it was Chantal – made herself small against him. She could hear his heart pounding, saw his eyes clouding.

A knock on the door announced the judge had arrived.

Anthenor shook his head, looked at her attentively: 'You look delicious. Better than ever before, even though I didn't think it was possible.' He took her arm. They stepped outside under the arched passageway, emerged into the sunshine of the luxuriant garden. An orchestra began to play. The swans floated on their own reflections . . . Through a mist glazing her eyes, she saw the gazebo dripping with blooms, a crowd gathered on the lawn. Leigh stepped out, stunning in an extravagant green taffeta coat over a strapless dress, and came to stand next to Chantal. Peter Baldwin came forward, shook hands with Anthenor and walked to his side.

'Hey, Anthenor, you have about one minute to change your mind,' piped up a voice. Why, it was Pinky, who else, good old bitchy Pinky, standing at the edge of the group with his 'wife,' matching gold razor blades gleaming in

543

open shirts. 'Girls don't have anything that—' An indignant hush from the crowd silenced him.

Together now in front of Judge Campbell, Anthenor intent, his profile taut. When he reached for her hand, he kissed it and slipped on her finger a circlet of diamonds. 'It's called an eternity ring,' he whispered.

As she repeated the vows, 'until death us do part,' it suddenly seemed like such a short time! Couldn't the State of California – or God, who must hold even more power – make it a little longer, like forever, considering they'd wasted so much time at the beginning?

But there was no time to argue, because when the judge declared, 'I now pronounce you man and wife,' Anthenor took her in his arms, looked into her eyes, and kissed her long and deep. The judge presented 'Monsieur and Madame Sefar' to the assembly and tactfully made only the briefest of speeches, allowing there was no point in letting the champagne get warm.

'Throw the bouquet,' somebody called. But Chantal carried no bouquet. So she took off her little Juliet cap and threw it in Leigh's direction, shaking her hair loose. Leigh's attention was elsewhere, instead Roger Volod reached up, caught it with his long arm, Roger who looked so handsome since his now close-cropped curly hair had turned almost all white.

'Eh, it looks like I'll be the next one down,' he exclaimed, his accent no better than twenty years ago. 'About time, too, if some good woman will have me.' Wasn't he standing awfully close to Leigh, who looked up at him, under the fall of her smooth black hair, with a secret smile Chantal had never seen?

There was barely time to kiss everyone and wipe tears of joy from old friends' eyes, for Anthenor was growing anxious. He'd sacrificed to Chantal's past and he wanted her to himself now.

'Just an hour to pack and get ready to leave,' she gasped back in the suite.

'Wrong.' Anthenor grinned with a wicked leer, loosening

his tie. '*Half* an hour. Because first, I want to exercise those rights I have just acquired.' Oh, the sweet urgency, the lovemaking half dressed in a crush of voile and starched linen, hard and fast and as shatteringly fulfilling as she remembered, his lips caressing the new eternity ring. Then rushing, laughing, to pack everything, the limo ride to the airport, the plane.

A bottle of Roederer Cristal was reverently brought to their seat after dinner, with a card, handwritten by Mariès. How does she arrange those things? wondered Chantal.

She snuggled as close to him as possible. 'Air France first-class seats recline almost like beds.'

'Almost, but not quite,' groaned Anthenor. 'There's a wedding night still owed us. Good night, my wife, my only love. I'll watch you sleep.'

EPILOGUE

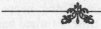

THE AIR, GETTING off the plane, the air, softly moist and cool, so gentle after the dry California heat. Hello, France, I'm back, open your arms to me! And the Loire Valley welcomes her with an honor guard of tall hollyhocks that grow wild on the sandy levees of the river, offerings of summer roses spilled over garden walls and fairy-tale castles glimpsed through towering fronds.

A table awaits for them at Roc-en-Val, the little inn in Montlouis, near Vouvray, under sweeping branches. No need to order, the chef has prepared the menu requested from the Château of Blazonac: a light tartare of Loire salmon, veal and truffles in a champagne glaze, and for dessert, *fraises des bois*, the tiny wild strawberries, with an earthenware jug of clotted cream.

Anthenor's eyes, his eyes of love, are on her. 'Sleepy after the sweet Vouvray wine? I'm sure there's a room for us if you like.' French doors open on the river, chintz curtains surround the bed, cool sheets. And Anthenor's body against hers, lean, long muscles . . .

'Just a preview of much better to come,' he whispers afterward. 'I love you. Sleep.'

Is this the same person, the erstwhile Channing, the one who couldn't fall asleep without pills? What? Five o'clock already? With the sun still so high?

'Don't you remember summer days are longer here than in California? But there's no need to hurry,' assures Anthenor, stretching. 'Mariès isn't expecting us until nightfall. Plenty of time to get there.'

In the car – Mariès's personal Rolls sent to Paris for them – Anthenor is thoughtful for a while. Then:

'I wanted to speak to you about this before we were

married. But it all went too fast . . .'

She waits, holding his right hand tight.

'It's about Renaud and the way he died. I wanted to tell you myself I didn't kill him. Things happened just the way I described them at the time: I turned back after a while, but he kept walking, and the last time I saw him, he was taking the path that goes right along the bank, under the pines, hunched in his overcoat. He must have slipped and fallen into the water. That's all I ever knew.'

'Why didn't you explain? Make people listen to you?'

'How could I? No one accused me to my face, it was only rumors, and I could never even pin down their exact source. And then, I was advised to keep quiet.'

'Don't tell me. By my mother, of course. She was afraid that if your innocence was certain, she couldn't have kept me away from you and Blazonac.'

'Yes.' He sighs. 'I guess that was it. If it all happened now, I would know what to do. But I was so young then and scared . . . So much time wasted! But,' he adds, brightening up, 'it was perhaps for the best. If your name had been linked to mine during those Resistance days, you'd have been arrested . . . God knows what else. All that matters is that now, we're here, together. Did you look in the zipper compartment of your purse?'

Astonished, she pulls out the hazelnut wood where the etched word *Forever* still stands out, white on the brown bark.

'I found it in the bag you'd prepared, apparently, for evacuation, when I went to your house with Leigh, to order the repairs and put things back in place. When I saw it, I had to turn my face away. By the way, Leigh will handle everything, even sell the house if you want to.'

The car rolls between a double row of oaks and chestnut trees. Blazonac isn't far now, red-roofed farmhouses cluster around *logis*, master's houses, just like the ones of Chantal's childhood. A little town, as the road bends.

'Why, it's Chabanais, Anthenor! Remember Chabanais, darling?' The Hôtel de la Croix-Blanche, torched by the Germans a few days after the locomotive was blown up – and all the bedbugs incinerated, she hopes! – has been rebuilt, much bigger, and now boasts an 'American Snak Bar.' They cross the bridge over the Vienne River and the place where she saw him with his men in that ghostly procession.

'Now, we're on the road I walked with Anna and Mariès, so tired and hungry, climbing over tree trunks felled to stop German convoys ... This is where a young Maquis appeared out of the woods and I gave him your password. I never forgot it. It was *Lo Faraï*, the Blazonac motto.'

'You're the only one who remembers all about those times everyone has almost forgotten,' says Anthenor, thinks aloud. 'Except me. *I* haven't forgotten anything.'

And at last, in the distance, etched in gold over the night sky, crenellated towers.

'See? The towers of Blazonac. Mariès had trees cut back and a special lighting system installed, just so you could see them from afar when you arrive. You are home, Chantal. Home.'

Entering the long, tree-lined drive with its elms so evenly tall, gravel crunches under the wheels of the Rolls. This is where I played with the farm dog and ran to keep up with Anthenor ... This is where I stumbled in the deep frozen ruts and he caught my arm when ... when ... Will there be ghosts waiting for me?

The gate is here, much more monumental than the old one, its coat of arms gleaming gold. It opens majestically in front of the car, welcoming them to the carriage court as she has never seen it, bathed in the glow of imposing bronze lampstands. And on the stone steps, Mariès with her flower face, her mother smartly coiffed, and Brad with that smile of his. No ghosts at all. Just love.

Anthenor tightens his arm around her shoulders. 'Look.' On the lake, in myriad sparks, swirls of light reflected on the water, rocketing over the towers, fireworks are starting. Three words light up, in a shower of cascading fire:

LIFE AT LAST